DEATH ON THE
INSTALLMENT PLAN

ALSO BY CÉLINE

Guignol's Band

Journey to the End of the Night

ABOUT CÉLINE

Louis-Ferdinand Céline; a critical biography
by Merlin Thomas

Published by New Directions

DEATH ON THE INSTALLMENT PLAN

BY

LOUIS-FERDINAND CÉLINE

Translated from the French by
RALPH MANHEIM

A NEW DIRECTIONS BOOK

First published as ND Paperbook 330 in 1971
Published simultaneously in Canada by
Penguin Books Canada Limited
Manufactured in the United States of America
New Directions Books are printed on acid-free paper

New Directions Books are published for James Laughlin
by New Directions Publishing Corporation,
80 Eighth Avenue, New York 10011

SIXTEENTH PRINTING

Preface

In an article on *Journey to the End of the Night,* Céline's first novel, a French critic—Robert Faurisson—puts forward a humanistic definition of great literature: It "should appeal not only to man's heart, intelligence, love of truth, but to the whole man; however pessimistic, it should help him to acquire an acceptance of life. A work excellent in other respects but inculcating a disgust with life is not great literature." Faurisson goes on to ask how it comes about that for all its horror, bitterness, hatred, and general blackness *Journey to the End of the Night* is still, thirty years after its original publication, widely regarded as one of this century's greatest novels. The question applies equally to Céline's second novel, *Death on the Installment Plan.*

The intense blackness in Céline's work converges from several sources. As a physician Dr. Destouches (his mother's first name was Louise-Céline, hence the pseudonym) was obsessed by death and human suffering. A wound received in the First World War left him with insomnia, headaches, and a continual roaring in his ears. His childhood in the world of small Paris shopkeepers may have been less sordid than the picture painted in *Death on the Installment Plan:* unlike Ferdinand, he was a studious child with an aim in life—his medical vocation came to him at an early age; a friend from his medical-school days goes so far as to say that his parents lived in perfect harmony; and a number of Céline's own utterances show that he felt a good deal more affection for his parents than one would gather from *Death on the Installment Plan.* Be that as it may, he was profoundly affected by the mentality of the *petits bourgeois* and *lumpenprole-*

tariat among whom he grew up, by their cynicism, their deep distrust of their fellowmen, their persecution mania. On leaving elementary school he began to earn his living at odd jobs, and his experience of "business" and bosses in the "good old days" before the First World War never left him. He often came back to it in letters and interviews. In *Death on the Installment Plan* he writes: "If you haven't been through that you'll never know what obsessive hatred really smells like . . . the hatred that goes through your guts, all the way to your heart." And "my main pleasure in life is being quicker than the boss when it comes to getting fired . . . I can see that kidney punch coming . . . Bosses are all stinkers, all they think about is giving you the gate . . ." And he generalized his experience; he saw no reason to suppose that anyone would be better than the people he had known. On the point of setting out for England, he wonders "if the English weren't going to be meaner and crummier, a damn sight worse than the people around here."

The blackness is further intensified by his literary attitudes and by the literary personality he composed for himself. He believed that literature had sidestepped man's baseness as he knew it, that writers had resolutely embellished man, that *his* experience was the truth, which it was his mission to tell. His purpose in writing, he once said, was to blacken himself and others; we should all be freer if the whole truth about human "crumminess" were finally told.

He succeeded quite well in his mission and yet—to go back to Faurisson—he does not, at least in his early books and specifically in *Death on the Installment Plan,* disgust us with life. Far from it. Perhaps, indeed, we do feel freer.

Even in Céline's explicit statements there are certain exceptions to his overall view of humanity: he makes no secret of his tenderness toward children and whores as well as animals. But although this might suffice to redeem Céline the sinner, it would hardly lead us either to accept life or to accept Céline as a great writer.

The explanation seems obvious today: the vision set forth in the first novels is not such as to destroy the world under our feet. This was much less evident in the thirties, when the books first appeared. At that time many readers and critics, even among those whose opinion was generally favorable, were too shocked by the nightmare, by Céline's directness of expression and his revolution in style, to notice anything else. Since then, however, a great deal has happened—both in history and literature. We are no longer shocked; we can see more clearly. And there is hardly a page of *Death on the Installment Plan* that does not reveal Céline's deep attachment not only to the world— to places, colors, clothes, furniture, boats and barges, lights in the distance—but to people as well. "A man's real mistress," he had said in *Journey to the End of the Night,* "is life." His feeling for his mistress is expressed with the utmost diffidence and suspicion. He distrusts her as Ferdinand distrusts Nora in the second book. He vilifies and derides her. She is futile, a brief quiver in anticipation of death, insidious in her blandishments, always on the lookout for new ways to take us in. But he is always awake to her beauties, and the vigor of the disgust or derision with which he reacts to her ugliness only underscores his passion.

This seems a rather tall order, but here is an example from *Death on the Installment Plan.* A cluster of suburban villas in the early morning: "All kinds . . . rocky, flattened, arrogant, bandy-legged . . . pale, half-finished ones, skinny, emaciated . . . staggering . . . reeling on their frames . . . A massacre in yellow, brick-red, and semi-piss color . . . Not a one that can stand up right . . . A collection of toys plunked down in the shit!"

One critic calls Céline's world a river of muck with a luminous surface. True, the grime and the glow are both present, but especially in *Death on the Installment Plan,* one is inclined to ask, Which is the body of the stream and which the surface?

For all his insistence on truth Céline was not a realist. André Gide once said that he wrote not of reality but of the hallucinations provoked by reality. Céline himself spoke of transposition "to the plane of delirium," of a method of capturing emotions, not objects. He never describes, never relates "objectively" what happened. Things and events become inseparable from the emotions they arouse—hate, disgust, suspicion, wonderment, naïve enthusiasm, tenderness, nostalgia, even love—and laughter, a great deal of laughter, intermingled with everything else, enhancing, tempering, or calling into question. Céline spoke of his manner as "comic lyricism," and this lyrical attitude toward fact is characteristic of him. Once when questioned about the details of his early life, he said: "That's of no importance. Anyway you can find it all in *Journey* and in *Death on the Installment Plan.*" But in *Journey* Bardamu-Céline makes the trip from Africa to New York in chains, aboard a galley! In *Death on the Installment Plan,* to cite only one example, Ferdinand refuses with striking success to learn English during his stay in England, whereas young Destouches, who also spent some months in England, learned the language very well. Almost all Céline's books are, in form at least, "autobiographical"; his biography remains obscure except for the barest framework.

In the opening pages of *Death on the Installment Plan* Céline states his intentions by introducing the narrator, the "I," who will be telling the story of Ferdinand's childhood and early adolescence. This "I" appears to be Céline's literary personality or pose, a prolongation of the Bardamu of *Journey to the End of the Night.* He is gloomy, downtrodden, disabused, a doctor but also a poet, a latter-day François Villon. Unlike Dr. Destouches, who by all accounts was devoted to medicine and his patients, the narrator looks on medicine as a fascinating nightmare at best, and regards his patients as "pests." Ferdinand is this man as a child—though one wonders in view of his recalcitrance and bewilderment how he ever got through medical school.

A head wound incurred in the war has left the narrator with a tendency to delirium, reflected in such hallucinations as the orgiastic stampede from the Bois to the Place de la Concorde and the sea voyage over the rooftops of Paris. Further on, Ferdinand has similar delirious visions, so similar that one wonders whose delirium it is—whether it is brought on by Ferdinand's fever or by the narrator's wound. But the narrator's delirium is programmatic; its function goes far beyond Ferdinand's explicit fevers. It is a manifesto for Céline's "comic lyricism," his method of transposing "to the plane of delirium."

The narrator is a storyteller. He entertains Madame Vitruve and her niece Mireille with his stories, and he is at work on a book, *The Legend of King Krogold,* a mock medieval romance. It too, with its delirious pageantry, its lyricism, its mixture of persiflage and monumental horror, is a statement of the author's intention. The narrator— and the boy Ferdinand, who inherits the *Legend* from his adult self—escapes into it from the meanness and boredom of daily life. In Céline, however, legend is far more than an escape; it engulfs all life, the daily as well as the exceptional. "There is no softness or gentleness in this world," says Death to Prince Gwendor. "All kingdoms end in a dream."

Another programmatic trait in the narrator is his persecution mania. He suspects all manner of plots against him at home, in the neighborhood, at the clinic where he works. Ferdinand in turn is a victim. If we take his story of his childhood—it is "his" story because by a magical effect of style the narrator *becomes* Ferdinand—at its face value, he never did anything wrong. Others, the crumminess of people, are responsible for all his troubles. Yet he feels guilty. He knows—though he never stops projecting his guilt outward—that his laziness and mulishness have something to do with it. He makes fun of his father, who blames everything on the Jews, the Freemasons, and the Japanese, but his own outlook, the suspicion and distrust that make him so unyielding, is not very different.

Death on the Installment Plan—this lyrical autobiography in which impressions and emotions overshadow fact and in which the distortions of memory, far from being corrected, are jealously preserved, witness the mounds of artichokes in the food shops of Rochester, England—is the story of a boy who grew up with this century of progress. Department stores, motorcars, and airplanes are coming in. Fine craftsmanship, small shops, and spherical balloons are going out. The boy is avid for freedom, a notion there is very little place for in his home or in the shops where he tries to earn his keep. His struggle with his parents and his bosses ends in disaster. He is temporarily saved by his encounter with a different kind of boss—a bohemian, an editor, a universal inventor—who opens up the heavens and the secrets of science to him, though in his character and way of life he is no better than anybody else. But progress is inexorable; forces real and occult carry the universal genius to his doom.

Céline often said that he regarded himself primarily as a stylist. He wrote with great care and the apparent disorder of his style is a well-laid trap. He held that the French literary language was stiff and spent with age, that classicism and academicism had emasculated the language of Villon and Rabelais, and that in our age emotion could be captured only in the spoken tongue. He regarded his use of popular French as his chief contribution to letters. In *Journey to the End of the Night* the style—sentence structure, vocabulary—is still relatively literary, though there too a strong popular admixture lends a tone that had never before been heard in French prose. In *Death on the Installment Plan* this spoken style is perfected. It is also in this book that the three dots, which so infuriated academic critics at the time, appear in force; they mark the incompleteness, the abruptness, the sudden shifts of direction characteristic of everyday speech, and signify a declaration of war on the flowing prose period.

English-language readers who are bored with this brand of punctuation, which has unpleasant associations especially in American letters, will observe that in Céline its use is not a sign of vagueness or sloppiness, but rather reflects the agitation, the fast-flying emotion he wished to convey.

Céline was in love with argot—underworld slang—which in French is extraordinarily rich and hermetic, a complete language; he called it the language of hatred. But Céline's language is not argot; if it were, only the underworld would be able to read it. It is the language of the common people of the Paris region, a language that continuously absorbs words and phrases of argot, usually after they have been discarded by the underworld. In his use of this medium he is faithful to its spirit, but by no means realistic. He embroiders, transposes, invents new words and corrupts old ones for his own purposes. He employs this richly imaged, down-to-earth, lowdown language in incongruous upper realms, in scientific and philosophical disquisitions; and

he mixes it with noble discourse in parodies of noble discourse or for other purposes.

A more detailed discussion of Céline's style would have
to deal with technical matters of French morphology and
syntax, which would be of little interest to English-language
readers, or with problems of translation, which would
interest only translators. Still, there is one question that
may call for an answer: Why a new translation?

I have said that people thirty years ago were shocked by
Céline's subject matter and style. The previous translator
was an able craftsman, but he too seems to have been
shocked, at least by the style, which he evidently regarded
either as a mistake or as conceivable only in French. The
three dots and what they stand for are largely eliminated;
the swift abrupt ejaculations are transformed into the flowing periods that Céline had rejected; and the language is to
a considerable extent ennobled. I have tried to give an idea
of Céline's style.

R.M.

DEATH ON THE
INSTALLMENT PLAN

Here we are, alone again. It's all so slow, so heavy, so sad . . . I'll be old soon. Then at last it will be over. So many people have come into my room. They've talked. They haven't said much. They've gone away. They've grown old, wretched, sluggish, each in some corner of the world.

Yesterday, at eight o'clock, Madame Bérenge, the concierge, died. A great storm blew up during the night. Way up here where we are, the whole house is shaking. She was a good friend, gentle and faithful. Tomorrow they're going to bury her in the cemetery on the rue des Saules. She was really old, at the very end of old age. The first day she coughed I said to her: "Whatever you do, don't stretch out. Sit up in bed." I was worried. Well, now it's happened . . . anyway, it couldn't be helped . . .

I haven't always been a doctor . . . crummy trade. I'll write the people who've known her, who've known me, and tell them that Madame Bérenge is dead. Where are they?

I wish the storm would make even more of a clatter, I wish the roofs would cave in, that spring would never come again, that the house would blow down.

Madame Bérenge knew that grief always comes in the mail. I don't know whom to write to anymore . . . Those people are all so far away . . . They've changed their souls, that's a way to be disloyal, to forget, to keep talking about something else.

Poor old Madame Bérenge; they'll come and take her cross-eyed dog away.

For almost twenty years all the sadness that comes by mail passed through her hands. It lingers on in the smell of her death, in that awful sour taste. It has burst out . . . it's here . . . it's skulking through the passageway. It knows us and now we know it. It will never go away. Someone will have to put out the fire in the lodge. Whom will I write to? I've nobody left. No one to receive the friendly spirits of the dead . . . and let me speak more softly to the world . . . I'll have to bear it all alone.

Toward the end the old lady was unable to speak. She was suffocating. She clung to my hand . . . The postman came in. He saw her die. A little hiccup. That's all. In the old days lots of people used to knock on her door and ask for me. Now they're gone, far away into forgetfulness, trying to find souls for themselves. The postman took off his cap. I know I could talk about my hatred. I'll do that later on if they don't come back. I'd rather tell stories. I'll tell stories that will make them come back, to kill me, from the ends of the world. Then it will be over and that will be all right with me.

At the clinic where I work, the Linuty Foundation, I've had a lot of complaints about the stories I tell . . . My cousin Gustin Sabayot makes no bones about it, he says I should change my style. He's a doctor too, but he works across the Seine, at La Chapelle-Jonction. I didn't have time to go see him yesterday. The fact is I wanted to talk to him about Madame Bérenge. I got started too late. Seeing patients is a rough job. At the end of the day we're both pooped. Most of the patients ask such tedious questions. It's no use trying to hurry, you've got to explain everything in the prescription twenty times over. They get a kick out of making you talk, wearing you down . . . They're not going to make any use of the wonderful advice you give them. But they're afraid you won't take trouble enough, and they keep at you to make sure; they want suction cups, X rays, blood tests . . . they want you to feel them from top to toe . . . to measure everything, to take their blood pressure, the whole damn works. Gustin has been at it for thirty years. One of these days I'm going to send those pests of mine to the slaughterhouse at La Villette for a good drink of warm blood, first thing in the morning. That ought to knock them out for the day. I can't think of any other way to discourage them . . .

The day before yesterday I finally decided to go and see Gustin at home. The suburb where he lives is a twenty-

minute walk from my place once you've crossed the Seine.
The weather wasn't so good but I started out just the same.
I thought I'd take the bus. I hurry through my consultation. I'm slipping out past the accident ward when an old
bag spots me and latches on to me. She drags out her words,
like me. That comes of fatigue. She has a voice like a
grater. That's from liquor. She starts whining and whimpering, she wants me to go home with her. "Oh, Doctor,
please come, I beg of you! . . . My little girl, my Alice!
. . . it's on the rue Rancienne, just around the corner . . ."
I didn't have to go. My office hours were over, supposedly.
She insists . . . By that time we're outside . . . I'm fed
up with sick people; I've been patching up those pests all
day, thirty of them . . . I was all in. Let them cough.
Let them spit. Let their bones fall apart . . . Let them
bugger each other. Let them fly away with forty different
gases in their guts . . . To hell with them . . . But this
sniveling bitch holds me tight, falls on my neck, and blows
her despair in my face. Her despair reeks of red wine . . .
I haven't the strength to resist. Anyway, nothing would
have made her let go. I thought maybe when we got to the
rue des Casses, which is a long street without a single
lamp, I'd give her a good kick in the ass . . . So for the
hundredth time I weaken . . . And the record starts up
again. "My little girl! . . . Please, Doctor, please! My
little Alice . . . You know her?" The rue Rancienne
wasn't around the corner . . . It was completely out of my
way . . . I knew exactly where it was. It's after the cable
factory . . . She's still talking, and I listen through my
private haze . . . "Eighty-two francs a week . . . that's
all we've got to live on . . . with two children. And my
husband is such a brute. It's shameful, Doctor."

I knew it was all a lot of hokum. Her whole story stank
of booze and sour stomach.

By that time we'd got to their hangout. I climb the
stairs. At last I could sit down . . . The kid wore glasses.
I sit down beside her bed. She's sick all right, but even so
she was playing with her doll, kind of. I thought I'd cheer
her up. I'm always good for a laugh when I put my mind
to it . . . She's not dying, but she does have trouble
breathing . . . She's certainly got an inflammation . . .
I make her laugh. She gags. I tell her mother there's nothing

to worry about. The bitch! Now she's got me cornered, she decides she can use a doctor too. It's her legs, all covered with black-and-blue marks where she's been beaten. She hikes up her skirts. Enormous bruises and deep burns. Her unemployed husband did that with the poker. That's the way he is. I tell her what she can put on them . . . I take a piece of string and make a kind of swing for the miserable doll. Up and down she goes, from the bed to the doorknob and back. It was very funny . . . that was better than talking.

I apply the stethoscope. She's wheezing pretty bad, but it's nothing dangerous. I tell the mother there's nothing to worry about . . . exactly the same words as before. That's what gets you down. The kid begins to laugh. She gags again. I have to stop. Her face is all blue . . . Mightn't she have a little diphtheria? I'll have to see . . . Take a specimen? . . . Tomorrow.

The father comes in. With his eighty-two francs they can't afford wine, all they've got to drink is cider. "I drink it out of a bowl," he says right off the bat. "It makes you piss." And he takes a swig from the bottle to show me. . . . We all say how lucky it is that the little angel isn't too sick. What interested me most was the doll . . . I was too tired to bother about grown-ups and diagnoses. Grown-ups are a pain in the ass. I was determined not to treat a single one until next day.

I guess they think I don't take my work seriously. To hell with what they think. I drink their health again. The consultation is absolutely free, gratis, for nothing. The mother brings up her legs again. I give her a last piece of advice. Then I go down the stairs. On the sidewalk there's a little dog with a limp. He follows me without a moment's hesitation. Everything attaches itself to me today. It's a little fox terrier, black and white. Seems to be lost. Those unemployed punks upstairs, what ingratitude! They don't even see me to the door. I bet they're fighting again. I can hear them yelling. He can stick the whole poker up her ass for all I care. That'll teach her to waylay me at closing time.

I turned off to the left, toward Colombes. The little dog was still following me . . . After Asnières comes La Jonction, and then it's not far to my cousin's. I couldn't

stand seeing him drag along like that. Maybe I'd better go
home after all. We turned back by way of the Pont Bineau,
skirting the row of factories. The dispensary was shut up
tight when we got there . . . "We'll feed the little mutt,"
I said to Madame Hortense. "Somebody'll have to get some
meat . . . We'll call up first thing in the morning. The
S.P.C.A. will send a car for him. We'd better lock him up
for tonight." Then I went out again, easy in my mind. But
that dog was too scared. He'd been beaten too much. Life
is hard on the streets. When we opened the window next
day, he wouldn't wait, he jumped out, he was even afraid
of us. He thought we'd locked him up to punish him. He
couldn't understand. He didn't trust anybody anymore.
It's bad when that happens.

Gustin knows me well. When he's sober, he has good
ideas. He has a sense of style. His judgments are reliable.
There's no jealousy in him. He doesn't ask much of this
world. He's got an old sorrow . . . disappointment in
love. He doesn't want to forget it. He seldom talks about
it. She was a floozie. Gustin is good as gold. He'll never
change till his dying day.

Meanwhile he drinks, kind of.

My trouble is insomnia. If I had always slept properly,
I'd never have written a line.

"You could talk about something pleasant now and
then." That was Gustin's opinion. "Life isn't always disgusting." In a way he's right. With me it's kind of a mania,
a bias. The fact is that in the days when I had that buzzing in both ears, even worse than now, and attacks of
fever all day long, I wasn't half so gloomy . . . I had
lovely dreams . . . Madame Vitruve, my secretary, was
talking about it only the other day. She knew how I tormented myself. When a man's so generous, he squanders
his treasures, loses sight of them. I said to myself: "That
damn Vitruve, she's hidden them some place . . ." Real
marvels they were . . . bits of Legend, pure delight . . .
That's the kind of stuff I'm going to write from now on
. . . To make sure they're as good as I think, I rummage
through my papers. I can't find a thing . . . I call Delu-
melle, my agent; I want to make him hate me . . . to
make him groan under my insults. But he's not so easily

fazed. It's all one to him, he's loaded. All he says is that I need a vacation . . . Finally Vitruve comes in. I don't trust her. I have my reasons. I light into her, point blank: where did you put my masterpiece? I had several hundred reasons for suspecting her . . .

The Linuty Foundation was across the way from the bronze balloon at the Porte Péreire. Almost every day when I'd finished with my patients, she'd come up to deliver my typescripts. A little temporary structure that's been torn down since. I wasn't happy there. The hours were too regular. Linuty, who had founded it, was a big millionaire, he wanted everybody to have medical treatment and feel better without money. Philanthropists are a pain in the ass. I'd have preferred some municipal dispensary . . . a little vaccinating on the side . . . a modest racket in certificates of good or bad health .·. . or maybe I could have supervised a public bath . . . in other words, something soft. Well, so be it. I'm not a Yid * or a foreigner or a Freemason, or a graduate of the École Normale; I don't know how to make friends and influence people, I fuck around too much, my reputation's bad. For fifteen years now they've seen me struggling along out here in the Zone; * the dregs of the dregs take liberties with me, show me every sign of contempt. I'm lucky they haven't fired me. Writing picks me up. I'm not so badly off. Vitruve types my manuscripts. She's attached to me. "Listen," I say, "listen, old girl, this is the last time I'm going to give you hell . . . If you don't find my Legend, it's the parting of the ways, it's the end of our friendship. No more intimate collaboration . . No more grub and bub, no more dough."

She bursts into lamentations. She's a monster in every way, her looks are awful and her work is awful. She's an obligation. I've had her on my neck since I was in England. She's the fruit of a promise. Our acquaintance goes way back. It was her daughter Angèle in London who made me swear to look after her forever. I've looked after her all right. That was my vow to Angèle. It dates back to the war. Besides, come to think of it, she knows what she knows. Okay. Supposedly she's tight-lipped, but she remembers . . . Angèle, her daughter, was quite a number.

* See Glossary.

It's amazing how ugly a mother can get. Angèle came to
a bad end. I'll explain if I'm forced to. Angèle had a sister,
Sophie, a big tall screwball, she's settled in London. And
Mireille, the little niece, is over here. She has the combined
vices of the whole family, she's a real bitch . . . a syn-
thesis.

When I moved from Rancy to Porte Péreire, they both
tagged along. Rancy has changed, there's hardly anything
left of the walls or the Bastion. Big black scarred stones;
they rip them out of the soft ground like decayed teeth.
It will all go . . . the city swallows its old gums. The bus
—the P.Q. *bis* they call it now—dashes through the ruins
like a bat out of hell. Soon there won't be anything but
sawed-off dung-colored skyscrapers. We'll see. Vitruve
and I used to argue about our troubles. She always claimed
she'd been through more than I had. That isn't possible.
Wrinkles, yes, she's got more. There's no limit to the
amount of wrinkles people can get: the loathsome traces
that the good years dig in their flesh. "Mireille must have
put your papers away."

I leave with her and escort her out to the rue des
Minimes. They live together, near the Bitrounelle chocolate factory, in a joint that calls itself the Hôtel Méridien.

Their room is an inconceivable mess, a junk shop full
of miscellaneous articles, mostly underwear, all very
flimsy and cheap.

Madame Vitruve and her niece both do it. They have
three douche bags fully equipped and a rubber bidet. They
keep it all between the beds; there's also an enormous
atomizer that they've never succeeded in getting to work.
I wouldn't want to be too hard on Vitruve. Maybe she
has had more trouble than I have. That's what makes me
control myself. Otherwise, if I were sure, I'd lick the hell
out of her. She used to keep the Remington in the fireplace; she hadn't finished paying for it. So she said. I don't
pay her too much for my typing, I've got to admit that
. . . sixty-five centimes a page, but it mounts up in the
end . . . especially with big fat books.

When it comes to squinting, though, I never saw the like
of Vitruve. It was painful to look at her.

That ferocious squint gave her an air when she laid out
the cards . . . tarots. She sold the little ladies silk stock-

ings . . . and the future too, on credit. When she puzzled and pondered behind her glasses, she had the wandering gaze of a lobster.

Her fortune-telling gave her a certain influence in the neighborhood. She knew all the cuckolds. She pointed them out to me from the window, and even the three murderers—"I have proof." I'd also given her an old blood-pressure contraption and taught her a little massage for varicose veins. That added to her income. Her ambition was to do abortions or to get involved in a bloody revolution, so everybody would talk about her and the newspapers would be full of it.

I'll never be able to say how she nauseated me as I watched her rummaging through that junk pile of hers. All over the world there are trucks that run over nice people at the rate of one a minute . . . Vitruve gave off a pungent smell. Redheads often do. It seems to me that there's an animal quality in redheads; it's their destiny: something brutal and tragic; they've got it in their skin. I could have laid her out cold when she went on about her memories in that loud voice of hers . . . She had hot pants, and it was hard for her to do much about it. Unless a man was drunk and it was very dark, she didn't have a chance. On that point I was sorry for her. I myself had done better in the way of amorous harmonies. That, too, struck her as unjust. When the time came, I'd have almost enough put by to settle my accounts with death . . . I had my esthetic savings. What marvelous ass I'd enjoyed, I've got to admit it, as luminous as light. I had tasted of the Infinite.

She had no savings, that goes without saying. To earn her keep and get a little enjoyment on the side, she had to take a customer by surprise or corner him when he was too tired to resist. It was hell.

By seven o'clock the good little workers have gone home. The women are doing the dishes, the males are tied up in radio waves. That's when Vitruve abandons my beautiful book and goes out in pursuit of her livelihood. She pads from landing to landing with her slightly damaged stockings and her crummy lingerie. Before the crash she managed to get along, what with credit and the way she terrified her customers, but today the identical crap is given away at street fairs to stop the gripes of losers at the shell game.

That's unfair competition. I tried to tell her it was all the fault of the Japanese. She didn't believe me. I accused her of doing away with my wonderful Legend on purpose, even of throwing it in the garbage . . .

"It's a masterpiece," I added. "We've got to find it."

That handed her a laugh. We rummaged through the pile of merchandise.

Finally her niece came in. She was very late. Christ Almighty, what a rear end. That ass of hers was a public scandal. Her pleated skirt helped to bring it out . . . A rounded accordion. The unemployed are desperate, sex-starved; no dough to take a girl out with . . . They were good and mad. "What about giving me some of that ass!" they'd shout at her. Square in her face as she comes through the hall. It's rough always getting a hard-on for nothing. The youngsters with finer features than the rest feel entitled to it, they expect life to coddle them. It wasn't until later that she began to go down and hustle . . . after no end of calamities . . . For the present she was just having fun.

She didn't find my beautiful Legend either. She didn't give a damn about "King Krogold" . . . the only one who cared was myself. Her school of life was the Petit Panier, a dance hall near the Porte Brancion, just before the railroad.

They didn't take their eyes off me when I got mad. In their opinion I was a champion creep. A stick-in-the-mud, jerk-off intellectual, and so on. But now, surprisingly enough, they were scared I'd clear out. If I had, I wonder what they'd have done. I have no doubt that the aunt thought about it plenty. Lord, the winning smiles they treated me to when I began to talk about a change of air . . .

In addition to her amazing ass, Mireille had romantic eyes and a bewitching look, but a hefty nose . . . a beezer. That was her cross. When I wanted to humiliate her a bit, I'd say: "No kidding, Mireille, you've got a nose like a man . . ." But she was good at telling yarns, like a sailor. She made up all sorts of things, at first to amuse me, later to make trouble for me. I like to hear a good story. That's my weakness. She went too far, that's all. I got violent in the end, but she certainly deserved the thrashings I gave

her, and if I'd killed her, she'd have deserved that too.
She finally admitted it. The fact is I was pretty generous
. . . I socked her for good reason. Everybody said so
. . . at least the ones who were in the know.

I'm not being unfair to Gustin Sabayot when I say that
he didn't knock himself out with his diagnoses. He got his
ideas from the clouds.

The first thing he did when he stepped out of his house
in the morning was to look up at the sky. "Ferdinand,"
he'd say, "today it's going to be rheumatism, one case
after another. You want to bet?" He read that in the
heavens. He was never very far off, because he had a
thorough knowledge of the climate and the human temperament.

"Aha! a bit of hot weather after a cold spell. That
calls for calomel, take my word for it. There's jaundice in
the air. The wind has changed . . . From north to west.
From cold to rain . . . That means two weeks of bronchitis . . . There's no point in their even getting up. If
I were in charge, I'd make out my prescriptions in bed
. . . After all, Ferdinand, when they come to see us, all
they do is gab . . . For doctors who get paid by the call
there's some point in it . . . but for us? . . . on a
monthly salary . . . what's the use? . . . I could treat
them without stepping out of the house. Damn pests. I
don't have to see them. They wouldn't wheeze any more
or less. They wouldn't vomit any more, they wouldn't
be any yellower or redder, or paler, or less idiotic . . .
That's the way it is and nobody's going to change it!"
That's how Gustin felt about it, and he was damn right.

"Do you think they're sick? . . . They moan . . . they
belch . . . they stagger . . . they fester . . . You want
to clear them out of your waiting room? On the double?
Even the ones who damn near suffocate every time they
cough? . . . Offer them a free pass to the movies . . .
or a free drink across the street . . . you'll see how
many you've got left . . . If they come around and
bother you, it's mostly because they're bored. On the day
before a holiday you never see a soul . . . Mark my
words, the trouble with those poor bastards isn't their
health, what they need is something to do with themselves

. . . they want you to entertain them, cheer them up, fascinate them with their belches . . . their farts . . . their aches and pains . . . they want you to find explanations . . . fevers . . . rumblings . . . new and intriguing ailments . . . They want you to get interested, to expatiate . . . that's what you've got your diplomas for . . . Ah, getting a kick out of his death while he's busy manufacturing it: that's Man for you, Ferdinand! They cling to their clap, their syphilis, their T.B. They need them. And their oozing bladders, the fire in their rectums. They don't give a damn. But if you knock yourself out, if you know how to keep them interested, they won't die until you get there. That's your reward. They'll come around to the bitter end." When the rain slanted down between the chimneys of the power plant, he'd say: "Ferdinand, this is sciatica day . . . If I don't get ten cases today I'll send my parchment back to the dean!" But when the soot came back at us from the east, which is the driest quarter, over the Bitrounelle chocolate factory, he'd crush a smudge against his nose and say: "I'll be buggered if the lungers don't start bringing up clots before the night is out. Damn it all, they'll wake me up a dozen times . . ."

Sometimes in the late afternoon he'd make things easier for himself. He'd climb up the ladder to the enormous cabinet where the samples were kept. And he'd start distributing medicines directly, free of charge, and absolutely without formality. "Hey you, Stringbean, you got palpitations?" he'd say to some sloven. "No." "Haven't you got a sour stomach? . . . A discharge? . . . Sure you have. Just a little? Well then, take some of this, you know where, in two quarts of water . . . it'll do you a world of good! . . . How about your joints? Don't they ache? . . . No hemorrhoids? And how about your bowels? . . . Here are some Pepet suppositories. Worms too? You think so? Well, here are some wonder drops . . . Take them before you go to bed."

He suggested something from every shelf . . . There was something for every disorder, every symptom, every obsession . . . Patients are amazingly greedy. As long as they've got some slop to put in their mouths, they're satisfied, they're glad to get out. They're afraid you might call them back.

With his Santa Claus act I've seen Gustin reduce to
ten minutes a consultation that would have taken hours if
handled conscientiously. But I myself had nothing to learn
in that line. I had my own system.

I wanted to talk to him about my Legend. We'd found
the first part under Mireille's bed. I was badly disappointed
when I reread it. The passage of time hadn't helped my
romance any. After years of oblivion a child of fancy can
look pretty tawdry . . . Well, with Gustin I could always
count on a frank, sincere opinion. I tried to put him in the
right frame of mind.

"Gustin," I said. "You haven't always been the mug
you are today, bogged down by circumstances, work, and
thirst, the most disastrous of servitudes . . . Do you
think that, just for a moment, you can revive the poetry in
you? . . . are your heart and cock still capable of leaping to the words of an epic, sad to be sure, but noble . . .
resplendent? You feel up to it?"

Gustin stayed where he was, half dozing on his stepladder, in front of his samples and the wide-open medicine
cabinet. Not a word out of him, he didn't want to interrupt
me.

"It's the story," I informed him, "of Gwendor the
Magnificent, Prince of Christiania . . . Here we are . . .
He is breathing his last . . . as I stand here talking to
you . . . his blood is pouring from a dozen wounds . . .
Gwendor's army has just suffered a terrible defeat . . .
King Krogold himself caught sight of him in the thick of
the fray . . . and clove him in twain . . . Krogold is no
do-nothing king . . . He metes out his own justice . . .
Gwendor had betrayed him . . . Death comes to Gwen-
dor and is about to finish his job . . . Get a load of this:

"The tumult of battle dies down with the last glow of
daylight . . . The last of King Krogold's guards vanish
in the distance. The death rattles of a vast army rise up in
the shadows. Victors and vanquished give up their souls
as best they can . . . The silence stifles their cries and
moans, which become gradually weaker and less fre-
quent . . .

"Crushed beneath a heap of his followers, Gwendor the
Magnificent is still losing blood. At dawn Death stands
before him.

" 'Hast thou understood, Gwendor?'

" 'I have understood, O Death. I have understood since the beginning of this day . . . I have felt in my heart, in my arm as well, in my friends' eyes, even in the step of my charger, a slow, sad spell akin to sleep . . . My star was failing in thine icy grip . . . Everything began to leave me! O Death! Great is my remorse! Endless my shame . . . Behold these poor corpses! . . . An eternity of silence will not soften my lot . . .'

" 'There is no softness or gentleness in this world, Gwendor, but only myth! All kingdoms end in a dream . . .'

" 'O Death, give me a little time . . . a day or two. I must find out who betrayed me . . .'

" 'Everything betrays, Gwendor . . . The passions belong to no one, even love is only the flower of life in the garden of youth.'

"And very gently Death gathers up the prince . . . He has ceased to resist . . . His weight has left him . . . And then a beautiful dream takes possession of his soul . . . The dream that often came to him when he was little, in his fur cradle, in the Chamber of the Heirs, close to his Moravian nurse in the castle of King René . . ."

Gustin's arms dangled between his legs.

"Well, how do you like it?" I asked him.

He was on his guard. He wasn't too eager to be rejuvenated. He resisted. He wanted me to explain the whole thing to him, the whys and wherefores. That's not so easy. Such things are as frail as butterflies. A touch and they fall to pieces in your hands and you feel soiled. What's the use? I didn't press the matter.

In going on with my Legend I might have consulted some sensitive soul . . . well versed in fine feelings . . . in all the innumerable shadings of love . . .

I prefer to manage on my own.

Sensitive souls are often impotent. They need to be whipped. There's no getting away from it. Anyway, let me describe King Krogold's castle:

". . . A great monster cowering in the heart of the forest, vast crushing hulk, hewn out of the rock . . . kneaded from bilging foulness, credences edged with

friezes and redans . . . dungeons upon dungeons . . .
from the distant seashore the crests of the forest ride in to
break like waves against the outer walls . . .

"The lookout, wide-eyed for fear of being hanged . . .
Higher . . . still higher . . . On the summit of More-
hande, on the tower of the Treasure House, the banner
flaps in the gale . . . It bears the royal arms. A snake
beheaded, bleeding at the neck. Traitors, beware! Gwendor
has paid for his crime. . . ."

Gustin was done in. He was dozing. In fact, he was
sound asleep. I locked up his medicine cabinet. "Let's get
out of here," I said to him. "We'll take a walk by the
Seine. It'll do you good." He didn't want to move. I kept
at him and he finally agreed. I suggested a little café on
the other side of the Île aux Chiens. When we got there,
he fell asleep again in spite of the coffee. Not a bad idea,
I admit. It feels pretty good in those bistros around four
o'clock . . . Three artificial flowers in a tin vase. The
riverfront is deserted. Even the old soak at the bar is beginning to accept the idea that the *patronne* won't listen
to him any more. I leave Gustin alone. The next tugboat
is sure to wake him. The cat jumps off the old woman's lap
and comes over to sharpen his claws.

The way Gustin turns up his hands when he sleeps, it's
easy to read his future. A man's whole life is in his palms.
With Gustin it's the life line that's prominent. With me it's
luck, the fate line. My chances of long life don't look too
good. I wonder when it will be. I've got a furrow at the
base of my thumb . . . Will it be an arteriole bursting
in my encephalon? Or in the central gyrus? . . . Or in that
little convolution of the third ventricle? . . . Metitpois
often used to point out that spot in the morgue . . . A
stroke is a tiny little thing . . . A little break in the gray
mass, no bigger than a pinprick . . . But the soul has
passed through, carbolic acid and all . . . Unfortunately
it might turn out to be a neoplasm of the rectum . . . I'd
give a lot for the arteriole . . . Your health! . . .
Metitpois was a real master. We used to spend whole
Sundays poking around in the grooves . . . investigating
the different ways of dying . . . That fascinated the old
man . . . He wanted to get an idea of how it would be.
He personally hoped for a nice cozy flooding of both

heart ventricles at once when his time came . . . He was
laden with honors! . . .

"The most exquisite deaths, remember that, Ferdinand,
are those that attack us in our most sensitive tissues . . ."
He had a precious, elaborate, subtle way of talking, like
the men of Charcot's day. His prospecting of the Rolandic,
the third ventricle, and the gray nucleus didn't do him
much good . . . in the end he died of a heart attack,
under circumstances that were anything but cozy. An attack
of angina pectoris that lasted twenty minutes. He held out
for a hundred and twenty seconds with his classical
memories, his resolutions, the example of Caesar . . .
But for eighteen minutes he screamed like a stuck pig
. . . his diaphragm was being ripped out, his living guts
. . . a thousand open razors had been plunged into his
aorta . . . He tried to vomit them out at us . . . I'm not
exaggerating. He crawled out into the living room . . . He
damn near hammered his chest in . . . He bellowed into
the carpet . . . in spite of the morphine . . . You could
hear him all over the house and out in the street . . . He
ended up under the piano. When the cardiac arterioles
burst one by one, it's quite a harp . . . it's too bad nobody ever comes back from angina pectoris. There'd be
wisdom and genius to spare.

We'd done enough meditating, it would soon be time for
the venereal patients. That was at La Pourneuve, out past
La Garenne. We worked together there. Just as I had
foreseen, a tugboat whistle blew. It was time for us to be
going. The venereal clinic was quite a place. While waiting
for their injections, the clappers and syphilitics got acquainted. There was embarrassment at first, then they got
to enjoy it. As soon as it was dark in the winter, they'd
rush out to meet near the slaughterhouse down the street.
Those people are always in a terrible hurry. They're afraid
that sweet little erection won't come back. Mother Vitruve
had figured it all out on her way to see me . . . The
youngsters with their first dose . . . it makes them melancholy, it really gets them down . . . She used to wait for
them at the exit . . . Motherly tenderness was her act
. . . touching sympathy . . . "It burns pretty bad, doesn't
it, boy? I know how it is . . . I've nursed them . . .
I've got an amazing kind of herb tea . . . Why don't you

come home with me, I'll make you some . . ." Two or
three cups of coffee and the kid would come across. One
night there was a terrible shambles down by the wall, an
Algerian with a hard-on like a horse was buggering a little
baker's boy for the hell of it, right near the night watchman's cabin. The watchman, who was an old hand at
watching, took it all in . . . first the kid sighed, then he
whimpered, and then he began to howl. He writhed and
struggled, there were four of them holding him . . . Even
so he got away and ran into the old man's cabin for protection. And the watchman locked the door.

"He got himself finished off. Believe it or not," said
Vitruve. "I could see the watchman through the blinds.
The two of them were at it. Birds of a feather if you ask
me."

She didn't believe in sentiments. She took the lowest
view and she was right. To get to La Pourneuve you had to
take the bus. "You can spare five minutes," Gustin said.
He wasn't in any hurry. We sat down in the bus shelter,
the one before the bridge.

It was right there on the riverfront, at Number 18, that
my parents went broke in the winter of '92. That was a
long time ago. Their business was "Notions, Flowers,
Feathers." There was only one shop window and all they
had in it was three hats. The Seine froze over that year.
I was born in May. The springtime—that's me. I suppose
it's our fate, but you get sick of growing old, of seeing
everything around you change, the houses, the numbers,
the streetcars, the hairdos. Short dresses, creased hats—
who cares?—the horseless carriage, the future belongs to
aviation—it's all the same! It's all a drain on your attention. I don't feel like changing anymore. There are plenty
of things I could complain about, but I'm stuck with
them. I'm a mess, but I adore myself as much as the
Seine stinks. The day they remove the hook-shaped lamp
post from the corner by Number 12, I'll be very sad. Man
is temporary, I know that, but we've already temporized
enough for my money.

There come the barges . . . Nowadays each one has a
heart of its own. It thuds loud and sullen in the echoing
darkness of the arches. Enough of that. I'm falling apart.
I'll stop complaining. But don't let them pile on any more.

Things seem pretty crummy, but if they could carry us away with them, we'd die of poetry. In a way that wouldn't be bad. Gustin agreed with me about all those endearing little things, except that he looked to the bottle for forgetfulness. Why not? . . . There was always a little beer and nostalgia in his Gallic moustache.

At the venereal clinic we used to mark vertical bars on a big sheet of paper as we went along . . . That was all there was to it. A red stroke: Salvarsan. Green: mercury. And so on. The rest was routine . . . All we had to do was pump the juice into their buttocks or the bend of their arms . . . It was like larding a roast. Green! . . . Arm! Yellow . . . get those pants down! . . . Red! . . . Both buttocks . . . Another one in the ass! . . . Ditto! Bismuth! Blue! Dripping vein! Swine! Get those pants on! . . . Swab that arm! . . . The rhythm was merciless. Batches and batches of them . . . Endless lines . . . Limp cocks . . . pricks . . . dripping peckers . . . oozing. Festering . . . Starched sheets, as stiff as cardboard! Clap! . . . Queen of the world! The ass is its throne! Heated summer and winter! . . .

Sometimes the poor bastards are good and worried . . . but after a while they start passing each other sucker's remedies and screwing harder than ever . . . as long as Julienne doesn't notice . . . They'll never come back . . . lying to us . . . howling for joy . . . urethra full of razor blades! Prick split in two! Cock in mouth. Get that crack ready!

Here's case history Number 34, timid little white-collar worker with dark glasses, wise guy. Every six months he goes to the Cour d'Amsterdam and gets a dose on purpose, so as to expiate by the rod . . . he pisses his razor blades into the little halfwits he meets through the ads . . . It's his way of saying his prayers, as he puts it. Number 34 is nothing but one big microbe. Here's what he wrote in our toilet: "I'm the terror of all cunts . . . I've buggered my big sister . . . I've had it twelve times." He's a punctual customer, quiet, well behaved, and always glad to be back.

That's our bread and butter. It's not as bad as working on the railroad.

When we got to La Pourneuve, Gustin said: "Say, Ferdinand, just now . . . while I was dozing, don't try to tell me different, you read the lines of my hand . . . Well, what did you see?"

I knew what was worrying him: his liver. It had been sensitive around the edges for a long time, and lately he'd been having awful nightmares . . . He was building up to a cirrhosis. In the morning I heard him throwing up in the sink . . . I told him it was nothing, why upset him? The damage was done. The main thing was that he should keep his jobs.

At La Jonction he'd landed his job in the welfare bureau soon after taking his degree. Thanks to a little abortion, that's the long and the short of it . . . the girl friend of a city councillor who was very conservative at the time . . . Gustin had just set himself up next door, he was poor as a churchmouse. It had come off smoothly, his hand hadn't begun to shake. The next time it was the mayor's wife. Another triumph! . . . Out of gratitude they had appointed him charity doctor.

In the beginning everybody had liked him in his new job. And then all of a sudden they didn't like him . . . they were sick of his mug and everything about him . . . they couldn't stand him. So they did everything in their power to make life miserable for him. They ran him down, accusing him of everything imaginable, of having dirty hands, of getting his doses wrong, of not knowing which drugs were poisonous . . . of bad breath . . . of wearing buttoned shoes . . . When they'd tormented him so much he was ashamed to be seen in the street and after threatening a thousand times to fire him like a fart, they changed their minds and began to tolerate him for no good reason, except that they were sick of regarding him as a punk. . . .

All the filth, the envy, the vexation of the district had put its mark on his map. He'd suffered all the gall and rancor of the pen-pushers in his clinic. The hangovers of the 14,000 alcoholics of the district, the gastric catarrhs, the excruciating stoppages of the 6,422 cases of clap that he wasn't able to cure, the ovarian pangs of the 4,376 menopause cases, the querulous anxiety of 2,266 sufferers from high blood pressure, the irreconcilable contempt of 722 bilious headaches, the persecution mania of 47 tapeworm owners, plus the 352 mothers of children with worms, and the nondescript mob, the vast horde of masochists with manias of every kind, the eczema patients, the albuminous, the diabetic, the fetid, the palsied, the vaginous, the useless, the "too muches," the "not enoughs," the constipated, the repentant queers, whole shipments of murderers had been flowing over his face, cascading under his glasses morning and afternoon for thirty years.

At La Jonction he lived right in the middle of the shithouse, directly over the X-ray room. He had his three-room apartment, and it was a good solid stone building, not a plywood box like nowadays. But to hold your own against life you need dikes ten times higher than in Panama and little invisible sluices. He'd been living there since the Exposition, the big one, since the happy days of Argenteuil.

Now there were big *"buildings"* all around the place.

Occasionally Gustin would still attempt a little distraction . . . He'd bring in a little cutie, but that didn't happen too often. His great sorrow came back to him as soon as any sentiment started up . . . after the third meeting. He preferred to drink . . . There was a bistro across the street with a green front and a banjo player on Sundays. It was handy for the French fries, the girl really knew how to make them. The rotgut burned his innards . . . For my part, I haven't even tried to drink since I've had that buzzing in my ears day and night. It knocks me out, it makes me look like I had cholera. Gustin auscultates me now and then. He doesn't tell me what he thinks either. That's the one thing we're discreet about. I've got my troubles too, I have to admit it. He knows my case, he tries to cheer me up: "Go on, Ferdinand, go ahead and read, I'll listen to the damn thing. Not too fast, though. And cut out the gestures. It wears you out and it makes me dizzy."

"After the battle King Krogold, his knights, his pages, his brother the archbishop, the clerics of his camp, the whole court, went to the great tent in the middle of the bivouac and dropped with weariness. The heavy gold crescent, a gift from the caliph, was nowhere to be found . . . Ordinarily it surmounted the royal dais. The captain entrusted with its safekeeping was beaten to a pulp. The king lies down, tries to sleep . . . He is still suffering from his wounds. He wakes. Sleep refuses to come . . .

He reviles the snorers. He rises. He steps over sleepers, crushing a hand here and there, leaves the tent . . . Outside he is transfixed with the cold. He limps, but still he makes his way. A long file of wagons rings the camp. The sentries have fallen asleep. Krogold moves along the deep trenches that defend the camp . . . He talks to himself, he stumbles, recovers his balance just in time. Something is glistening at the bottom of the ditch, an enormous blade. It trembles . . . A man is there, holding the glittering object in his arms. Krogold leaps, overturns him, pins him down, it's a common soldier, and slits his throat like a pig with his short sword. 'Glug, glug!' the thief gurgles through the hole. He drops everything. It's all over. The king bends down, picks up the caliph's crescent. He climbs out of the ditch. He falls asleep in the mist . . . The thief has had his just deserts."

About that time the crash came and I almost got fired from the clinic. Gossip again.

I heard about it from Lucie Keriben, who had a dress shop on Maidenform Boulevard. Lots of people came to her shop and they gossiped a good deal. She let me in on some pretty rotten rumors. So vicious in fact that it couldn't have been anybody but Mireille . . . I wasn't mistaken. Pure calumny of course. She was spreading it around that I had been organizing orgies with some of my female patients in the neighborhood. Really lousy stuff . . . Secretly Lucie Keriben was kind of glad to see me having a little trouble . . . She was jealous.

So I wait for Mireille to come home, I hide in the Impasse Viviane, where I knew she'd have to come by. I wasn't making enough money yet to go off and write full time . . . I was still good for another hitch of bad luck. I was in a foul humor. I see her coming . . . she passes in front of me. I give her a kick in the seat that sends her sailing off the sidewalk. She gets my meaning, but she won't talk. She wanted to see her aunt first. The little bitch wouldn't come clean. I couldn't get a word out of her.

She'd spread all that gossip to get me worried . . . then I'd hurry up and give them what they were after. Violence was no use. Especially with Mireille, it only made her more spiteful than ever. She wanted to get married.

To me or somebody else. She was fed up with factories. At sixteen she'd already worked in seven of them in the western suburbs.

"No more job," she'd announce. At the Goody Gumdrops English candy factory she'd caught the director getting sucked off by an apprentice. What a place! For six months she tossed dead rats into the big sugar vat. At Saint-Ouen she'd been snagged by a forelady, who'd taken to swotting her in the washroom. They had walked off the job together.

Mireille knew all about capitalism before she even began to menstruate. At the free camp in Marty-sur-Oise there had been fingerplay, fresh air, and rousing speeches. She had developed nicely. On Federates' Day,* she was an honor to the settlement house, it was she who brandished Lenin on a pole from La Courtine to Père-Lachaise. The way she came swaggering down the street . . . the cops were flabbergasted. And with those luscious legs she had the whole boulevard horning out the *International.*

The little pimps at the dance hall where she hung out didn't realize what a number they had on their hands. She was still a minor and scared of the vice squad. For a while she tagged along with Robert, Gégène, and Gaston. But they were building up to a mess of trouble . . . She would be their downfall.

I could expect just about anything from Vitruve and her niece, especially Vitruve; she knew too much about me not to make use of it some day.

I appeased them with money, but the kid wanted more, she wanted the whole works. When I tried to get around her with affection, it looked mighty suspicious to her. I'll take her out to the Bois, I said to myself. She's got a grudge against me. I've got to do something to catch her interest. I had my plans for the Bois, I'd tell her a nice story, I'd flatter her vanity.

"Ask your aunt," I say. "You'll be home before midnight . . . Wait for me at the Café Byzance."

So there we go.

After the Porte Dauphine she was already in a better humor. She liked the swanky neighborhoods. At the Hôtel Méridien it was the bedbugs that got her down. When she

* See Glossary.

picked up a little boyfriend and had to take her slip off, the marks made her feel ashamed. They all knew it was bedbug bites . . . They were all familiar with the liquids and the stuff you burn . . . Mireille's dream was a room without bugs . . . If she had cleared out then, her aunt would have had her brought back. She relied on her for the dough she brought in, but there was also a little pimp, Bébert from Val-du-Grâce, who had the same ideas. He ended up on snow. He'd been reading the *Journey* . . .

As we were approaching the Cascade, I began to get confidential . . .

"I know you've got a boyfriend in the post office who gets a kick out of letting you whip him . . ."

She was too happy to put on airs or beat about the bush. She told me all about it. But when we got to the Pré Catalan, she was afraid to go on, the darkness frightened her. She thought I was taking her into the woods to beat her up. She felt in my pockets to see if I had a rod. I didn't have a thing. She felt my pecker. On account of the passing cars, I suggested we go over to the island where we could talk more at our ease. She was a slut, she had a hard time coming and danger appealed to her. The youngsters rowing on the lake lost control, got tangled in the branches, cursed, tipped, and ruined their little lanterns.

"Listen to the ducks gagging in the diluted urine!"

"Mireille," I say, once we were settled. "I know you're a champion liar . . . one thing you don't trouble your head about is the truth . . ."

"Go on," she says. "If I were to repeat a tenth of what I heard . . ."

"Okay," I say, "you can turn that off . . . I'm full of indulgence for you . . . I'd even call it weakness. Not on account of your body . . . or your face or your nose . . . What attracts me is your imagination . . . I'm a voyeur. You tell me dirty stories . . . And I'll tell you a beautiful legend . . . Is it a bargain? . . . fifty-fifty . . . you'll be getting the best of it . . ."

That appealed to her. She liked talking business . . . I filled her in . . . I guaranteed there'd be plenty of princesses, yards and yards of genuine velvet, brocade to the very linings, furs and jewels . . . beyond imagining . . . we were in perfect agreement about the setting and

even the costumes. And then at last our story started
in:

"We are in Bredonnes in Vendée . . . The city is making ready for a tournament . . .

"Here come the courtiers in fine array . . . naked
wrestlers . . . mountebanks . . . their coach rides by
. . . plowing through the crowd . . . Pancakes frying
. . . three knights in damascened armor . . . they have
come from far away, . . . from the South . . . from
the North . . . their bold challenges ring out . . .

"Here comes Thibaud the Wicked, a troubadour . . .
at daybreak he reaches the city gate along the towpath. He
is weary and footsore . . . He has come to Bredonnes in
quest of haven and shelter . . . and to seek out Joad the
Dissembler, the sheriff's son, to remind him of a sinister
affair, the murder of an archer in Paris, near the Pont
aux Changes, in their student days . . .

"Thibaud enters the city . . . At Sainte-Geneviève
ferry he flatly refuses to pay the fee . . . he comes to
blows with the ferryman . . . The archers appear . . .
they overpower him and drag him away . . . Here he is,
bound hand and foot, foaming at the mouth, in tatters,
dragged before the sheriff. He struggles furiously, and
flings the ugly story in his face . . ."

The tone appealed to Mireille, she wanted more. We
hadn't got along so well in a long time. Finally it was time
to go home.

There were only a few couples left on the paths. Mireille
was all cheered up. She wanted to catch them in the act.
We abandoned my beautiful Legend for a furious discussion about whether what women really wanted was to
shack up with each other . . . Mireille, for instance,
wouldn't she like to lay her girl friends a little? . . .
goose them maybe? . . . especially the dainty little ones,
the gazelles . . . what with those athletic haunches of
hers . . . that sumptuous ass . . .

"What about dildoes?" she remarked. "Sure, that's why
we watch. Why we look so hard when girls are having fun.
To see if they won't grow one . . . So they can tear each
other to pieces, the bitches. So they can rip each other's
guts out. And bleed all over the place. So all their rottenness
can come pouring out of them! . . ."

My sweet little Mireille was well informed. She followed
my little show perfectly . . . I thought I'd better warn
her: "If you repeat one word of this in Rancy, I'll make you
eat your shoes!" And I grabbed hold of her under the gas
lamp. I could already see the triumphant look on her face.
I could feel it in my bones that she was going to tell the
whole world that I had behaved like a beast . . . in the
Bois de Boulogne! I began to see red . . . To think that
she'd taken me for a ride again. I give her a good smack.
She grins. Defiantly.

From the thickets and copses, from all sides, people
run out to watch us, by twos and fours, in droves. All
brandishing their cocks. The ladies have their skirts hiked
up front and back. The brazen, the loose, and the cautious . . .

"Attaboy, Ferdinand!" the whole lot of them shout.
What a noise! It rose up out of the woods. "Give her the
works. Clout her! Sock her!" Naturally all that encouragement made me rough.

Mireille begins to shriek and run. I run after her. I
knock myself out. I give her some wicked kicks in the rear
end. They land with a dull thud. Hundreds of Ranelagh sex-
fiends come running up, they collect by the prickloads in
front of us, they pull up from behind . . .

The grass is full of them, thousands are pouring down
the drive. More and more of them come stepping out of
the darkness . . . The women's dresses are in tatters,
tits torn and dangling . . . little boys without pants . . .
they knock each other down, trample each other, toss each
other up in the air . . . some are left dangling from the
trees . . . along with smashed-up chairs . . . An old
bag, English, comes along in a little car and sticks her head
out the window so far it almost falls off . . . she was
beginning to get in my way. Never had I seen eyes so full
of happiness. "Hurray! Hurray!" she shouts without even
stopping her car. "Great stuff! You'll crack her ass open.
You'll send her sky-high. You'll knock the eternity out
of her. Hurray for Christian Science!"

I ran still faster. I ran faster than her car. I gave it
everything I had, I was dripping with sweat. As I charged,
I thought of my job . . . I'd be sure to lose it. That
gave me the chills: "Mireille! Have pity! I adore you!

Will you wait for me, you damn slut! Will you listen to me?"

When we got to the Arc de Triomphe, the whole crowd began to whirl like a merry-go-round. The whole mob was chasing Mireille. The square was littered with corpses. The living were tearing off each other's pricks. The English-woman was toting her car over her head at arm's length. Hurray, hurray! She knocks over a bus with it. The traffic is blocked by three files of Mobile Guards with shouldered rifles. All for our benefit. Mireille's dress flies away. The Englishwoman flings herself on the kid, claws at her breasts . . . trickling, pouring, red all over. We fall, we writhe all together, we strangle each other. Pure bedlam.

The flame under the Arc de Triomphe rises, rises higher, breaks, scatters through the sky . . . The whole place smells of smoked ham . . . Then Mireille whisper-ing in my ear, speaking to me at last: "Ferdinand, my darling, I love you! . . . I admit it, you have wonderful ideas!" The flames rain down on us, everyone picks up a big chunk . . . We stuff them sizzling and whirling into our flies. The ladies put on bouquets of fire . . . We fall asleep inside each other.

Twenty-five thousand policemen clear the Place de la Concorde. It was too much for us inside each other. It was too hot. There was smoke coming out. It was hell.

My mother and Vitruve in the next room were worried, they kept coming and going, waiting for my fever to go down. An ambulance had brought me home. I had col-lapsed on top of a sewer grating on the Avenue Mac-Mahon. The bicycle cops had found me.

Fever or not, I always have such a buzzing in both ears that it can't get much worse. I've had it since the war. Madness has been hot on my trail . . . no exaggeration . . . for twenty-two years. That's quite a package. She's tried a million different noises, a tremendous hullabaloo, but I raved faster than she could, I screwed her, I beat her to the tape. That's how I do it. I shoot the shit, I charm her, I force her to forget me. My great rival is music, it sticks in the bottom of my ear and rots . . . it never stops scolding . . . it dazes me with blasts of the trombone, it keeps on day and night. I've got every noise in nature, from the flute to Niagara Falls . . . Wherever I go, I've got drums with me and an avalanche of trombones . . . for weeks on end I play the triangle . . . On the bugle I can't be beat. I still have my own private birdhouse complete with three thousand five hundred and twenty-seven birds that will never calm down . . . I am the organs of the Universe . . . I provide everything, the ham, the spirit, and the breath . . . Often I seem to be worn out. My thoughts stagger and sprawl . . . I'm not very good to them. I'm working up the opera of the deluge. As the curtain falls, the midnight train pulls into the station . . . The glass dome shatters and collapses . . . The steam escapes through two dozen valves . . . The couplings bounce sky-high . . . In wide-open carriages three hundred musicians soused to the gills rend the air, playing forty-five bars at once . . .

For twenty-two years she's been trying to carry me off . . . at exactly midnight . . . But I can fight back . . . with twelve pure symphonies of cymbals, two cataracts of nightingales . . . a whole troupe of seals being roasted over a slow fire . . . It's bachelor's work . . . that's for sure. It's my second life. Anyway it's *my* business.

If I mention it now, it's to explain that I had a little attack in the Bois de Boulogne. I often make a lot of noise when I talk. I talk too loud. People make signs at me to lower my voice. I drool a little, I can't help it . . . It's very hard for me to take an interest in my friends. I tend to forget their existence. I'm preoccupied. Sometimes I puke in the street. Then it stops. It's almost quiet. But the walls begin to shake and the cars go into reverse. The whole earth trembles and me with it. I don't speak . . . Life begins again. When I get to see God in his place, I'll blast his ear, the inner ear, I've studied those things. I wonder how he'll like that. I'm the Devil's stationmaster. The day I go, wait and see how the train jumps the track. Monsieur Bizonde, the trussmaker, whom I do little jobs for, will find me paler than ever. He'll get used to it.

I was thinking about all that in my room while my mother and Vitruve were padding about next door.

The gate of hell in your ear is a little atom of nothing. Move it a quarter of a hair's breadth . . . a micron . . .

and look through. You're done for! That's all. You're
damned forever. You ready? No? Do you think you can
make it? Kicking in isn't free of charge. A beautiful shroud
embroidered with tales—that's what the Pale Lady wants.
The last gasp is very demanding. It's the last movie and
nothing more to come. A lot of people don't know. You've
got to knock yourself out. I'll be up to it soon . . . I'll
hear my ticker give its last slobbery *pfutt* . . . and then
plop! It'll wobble in its aorta . . . like an old broom
handle . . . It'll be all over. They'll open it up to check
. . . on that sloping table . . . They won't see my beautiful legend, nor my music either. The Pale Lady will have
taken it all . . . Here I am, madame, I'll say to her,
you're the greatest connoisseur of all . . .

I was dead to the world, but even so I couldn't get
Mireille off my mind.

I had no doubt about her spilling the dirt all over the
place.

"My oh my!" they'd be saying at the clinic . . . "Ferdinand's been overdoing it. He goes out to the Bois to get laid
. . . (the way they always exaggerate). With Mireille of
all people . . . debauching all our young women . . .
They're putting in a complaint . . . He's a disgrace to his
profession! A rapist and an anarchist . . ."

No less! It made my blood boil in my bed to think about
those fairy tales, I was oozing all over like a toad . . . I
was suffocating . . . I wriggled and thrashed . . . I
threw off all the covers . . . Suddenly I felt strong as an
ox. But it's perfectly true that those devils were following
us! That charred smell all over. An enormous shadow shuts
off my view . . . It's Léonce's hat . . . An agitator's
hat . . . with a brim as wide as a race track . . . He
must have put out the fire . . . It's Léonce Poitrat! I'm
positive. He's always been shadowing me . . . He's out
to get me. He hangs around the Préfecture a damn sight
more than legitimate business warrants . . . After six
o'clock . . . He's all over the place, always active, organizing the apprentices, doing abortions . . . He doesn't
like me . . . I give him the creeps. He's out to get me.
He admits it.

He's the bookkeeper at the clinic. He wears a flowing

bow tie. That hat blocks off part of my sleep . . . My
temperature must be rising . . . I'm going to explode . . .
At meetings he's the life of the party, you should see him
. . . He can shout for two hours on end at those trade-
union blackmail sessions. No one can make Léonce shut
up . . . if anybody tries to change a single word in one
of his motions, he blows his top. He can shout louder
than a colonel. He's built like a brick shithouse. He can't
be beat for hot air and his cock has no equal either, comes
up harder than thirty-six biceps. Cast iron. That's him.
He's secretary of the Bricklayers and Roofers' Union of
Vanves La Révolte. Elected no less. His buddies are proud
of Léonce, the lazy pugnacious bastard. For pimping on
the labor movement he hasn't his equal.

With all that he wasn't satisfied, he was jealous of me,
my ideas, my spiritual treasures, my looks, the way people
call me "Doctor." There he was with the ladies, waiting
. . . for me to make up my mind, for me to kick in . . .
Nothing doing. Just to burn him up . . . I'd stay right
on the ground where I was . . . It would be a miracle
. . . I'd even kiss him in the hope of killing him . . . by
contagion!

What's that noise upstairs . . . various noises . . .
It's the pianist giving lessons . . . No, practicing . . .
He's nervous. He must be alone . . . C . . . C . . . C!
Not so hot. B . . . B . . . Come, come. Try again . . .
E . . . E . . . D . . . It'll come out all right in the
end! an arpeggio with the left hand . . . and now the
right hand's perking up . . . B-sharp! Christ almighty!

Through my window I can see Paris . . . spread out
below me . . . And then it begins to climb . . . toward
us . . . toward Montmartre . . . One roof pushes the
next, sharp, cutting, bleeding in the light, streets blue, red,
and yellow . . . Lower down, the Seine, pale mists, a
tugboat buffeting the current . . . with a tired wail. Still
farther off, the hills . . . Everything looks alike . . . The
night will take us in. Is that my concierge banging on the
wall?

I must be in pretty bad shape for her to come up . . .
Mother Bérenge is too old for all those stairs . . . Where
can she be coming from? . . . She crosses my room ever
so softly . . . She doesn't touch the floor. She doesn't

even look to right or left . . . She leaves by the window,
out into the void . . . There she is, off in the darkness
above the houses . . . there she is, over there . . .

D . . F . . . G-sharp . . . E . . . Shit! Isn't he
ever going to stop? That must be his pupil starting in . . .
When fever spreads through you, life gets as flabby as a
barkeeper's belly . . . You sink into a muddle of entrails.
I hear my mother rubbing it in . . . She's telling Madame
Vitruve the story of her life . . . Over and over again,
to make it clear what a time she's had with me. Extravagant . . . irresponsible . . . lazy . . . nothing like his
father . . . he so conscientious . . . so hardworking . . .
so deserving . . . so unlucky . . . who passed on last
winter . . . Sure . . . she doesn't tell her about the
dishes he broke on her bean . . . Oh no! D . . . C . . .
E . . . D-flat! That's his pupil, in trouble again . . .
skipping sixteenths . . . he's tangled up in the teacher's
fingers . . . He's skidding . . . he can't straighten out
. . . his nails are full of sharps . . . "Watch that beat!"
I roar.
My mother doesn't say a word about how he used to
drag her through the back room by the hair. The place
was really too small to argue in . . .
Not one word about all that . . . nothing but poetry
. . . Yes, we lived in cramped quarters, but we loved each
other so. That's what she was saying. Papa was fond of
me, he was so sensitive about every little thing that my
behavior . . . so much to worry about . . . my alarming
propensities, the terrible trouble I gave him . . . hastened
his death . . . all that grief and anguish affected his heart.
Plop! The fairy tales people tell each other . . . they make
a certain amount of sense, but they're a pack of filthy stinking lies . . . The stinking bitches get so het up filling each
other full of bullshit that they drown out the piano . . .
I can puke in peace.
Vitruve is no slouch at telling whoppers either . . .
she lists her sacrifices . . . Mireille is her whole life . . .
I can't catch it all . . . I'd better go to the can to vomit
. . . probably a touch of malaria too . . . brought it
back from the Congo . . . I'm pretty far gone in all
directions . . .

By the time I get back to bed, my mother is in the middle of her courtship . . . the days when Auguste rode a
bike . . . not to be outdone, the other one goes on
shamelessly . . . about her desperate efforts to save my
reputation . . . at Linuty's . . . Oh no! I can't stand it!
I sit up . . . I'm at the end of my rope . . . I can't move
. . . I just lean over and vomit on the other side of the
doss. If I've got to be delirious, I'd rather wallow in stories
of my own . . . I see Thibaud the Troubadour . . . He's
always in need of money . . . He's going to kill Joad's
father . . . Well, at least that will be one father less in
the world . . . I see splendid tournaments on the ceiling
. . . I see lancers impaling each other . . . I see King
Krogold himself . . . He has come from the north . . .
He had been invited to Bredonnes with his whole court
. . . I see his daughter Wanda, the Blonde, the Radiant
. . . I wouldn't mind jerking off, but I'm too sticky . . .
Joad is horny in love . . . Oh well, why not . . . I've
got to get back . . . A sudden surge of bile . . . The
effort makes me bellow . . . This time my old bitches
can't help hearing . . . They come in and patch me up.
I throw them out . . . in the hallway they start shooting
the shit again. After the way they'd been running me down,
the tide changes . . . they discover my good points . . .
they're dependent on me for a good many things . . .
Better be realistic . . . they'd been overdoing it . . .
After all, who brings home the bacon? . . . My mother
wasn't making much, working for Monsieur Bizonde, the
famous trussmaker . . . Not enough to get by on . . .
It's hard at her age to make ends meet on a commission
basis. And who keeps Madame Vitruve and her niece
going with his clever ideas? . . . Suddenly a new wave of
suspicion. They begin to hedge . . .
    "He's a scatterbrained brute . . . but good-hearted
. . ." You've got to admit that. Yes, of course. There's
the rent and groceries to think about . . . Mustn't exaggerate. They hasten to put each other's minds at rest.
My mother is no workingwoman . . . She says that over
and over again, it's her litany . . . She's a small business-
woman . . . Our family ran itself ragged for the glory of
small business . . . We're no drunken workers, up to our
ears in debt . . . Oh no! Certainly not . . . There's a

big difference and don't forget it . . . Three lives, mine, hers, and most of all my father's were ground down by sacrifice . . . Nobody even knows what became of them . . . they paid our debts . . .

And now my mother knocks herself out trying to recapture those lives of ours . . . she's reduced to her imagination . . . they've disappeared . . . our pasts as well. Whenever she has a free moment, she tries to put things back on their feet . . . but inevitably they collapse again . . .

She flies into terrible rages if I even begin to cough, because my father had a chest like a bull, good strong lungs . . . I can't stand the sight of her anymore, she gives me the creeps. She wants me to share in her fantasies . . . I'm not in the mood. One of these days I'm going to do something bad! I want to have my own fantasies . . . C! E! A! the pupil is gone. The pianist is relaxing . . . Doing a *berceuse* . . . I wish Emilie would come up . . . She comes every evening to straighten out . . . She hardly says anything . . . I forget she's there . . . Ah, here she is! She wants me to take some rum . . . The drunks next door are bawling again . . .

"He has a high fever . . . I'm terribly worried," my mother repeats for the hundredth time.

"He's so kind to his patients," yacks Vitruve.

At that point I was so hot I dragged myself to the window.

On a long tack across the Étoile my gallant ship glides through the dusk . . . under full sail . . . she is heading straight for the Hôtel-Dieu . . . The whole town is on deck, still and calm. All those dead—I know them all . . . I even know the helmsman . . . He's my buddy . . . The pianist has caught on . . . He's playing the tune we need: "Black Joe" . . . for a cruise . . . to catch the wind and weather . . . and the lies . . . If I open the window, it will be cold . . . Tomorrow I'm going to kill Monsieur Bizonde, who keeps us going . . . the trussmaker, in his shop . . . I want him to travel . . . he never goes out . . . My vessel groans and pitches over the Parc Monceau . . . She's slower than last night . . . She's going to hit the statues . . . Two ghosts go ashore at the Comédie Française . . . Three enormous waves carry off the arcades of the rue de Rivoli. The siren screams against my windowpanes . . . I close my door . . . A roar of wind . . . My mother appears with her eyes popping out . . . She scolds me. Misbehaving as usual. Vitruve comes running . . . More good advice. I rebel . . . I give them hell . . . My fair ship is limping. Those females can wreck the infinite . . . She's off course, it's shameful . . . Nevertheless she heels over to port . . . there's no more graceful craft afloat . . . My heart follows her . . . Those bitches would do better to run after the rats that are fouling the rigging . . . She'll never make that tack with her ropes so taut . . . got to slacken them . . . let out three turns before the Samaritaine! I shout all that out over the rooftops . . . My room is going to sink. I've paid for it, haven't I? Every last cent. With my lousy rotten existence . . . I shit in my pajamas . . . What a mess! Things are bad. I'm going to founder at the Bastille. "Ah, if only your father were here" . . . I hear those words. I explode. It's her again. I turn around. My father, I say, was a skunk! I yell my lungs out . . . "There was no lousier bastard in the whole universe! from the Galeries-Lafayette to Capricorne . . ." At first she was stupefied. Transfixed . . . Then she gets hold of herself. She calls me the lowest of the low. I don't know which way to look. She bursts into tears. She rolls on the carpet in anguish. She rises to her knees. She stands up. She comes at me with the umbrella.

She hauls off and gives me a couple of cracks full in the face. The handle breaks in her hands. She bursts into tears. Vitruve throws herself between us. She never wants to see me again. That's what she thinks of me. She sobs so hard the whole place shakes . . . All my father left behind him was his memory and carloads of trouble. Memory is an obsession with her. The deader he is the more she loves him. Like a she-dog that can't get enough . . . But I won't put up with it . . . I'll protest if it kills me. I repeat that he was a sneak, brute, hypocrite, and yellow in every way. She starts up again. She's ready to die for her Auguste. I'll smash her face. Hell! I haven't got malaria for nothing. She upbraids me, she lets herself go, she has no consideration for the state I'm in. I'm in a blind rage. I bend over and lift up her skirt. I see her calf as skinny as a poker, without any flesh on it, her stocking all sagging, it's foul . . . I've seen it all my life . . . I puke on it, the works . . .

"Ferdinand, you're out of your mind!" She backs away, gives a start and runs for it. "You're out of your mind!" she cries again from the stairs.

I stagger and fall flat. I hear her limp all the way down. The window is still wide open . . . I think of Auguste, he liked boats too . . . He was an artist at heart . . . He had no luck . . . he drew storms now and then on my blackboard . . .

The maid is still there beside my bed. "Lie down here in your clothes," I say. "We're cruising . . . My ship has lost all her lights over the Gare de Lyon . . . I'll give the captain a receipt, so he'll come to the Quai d'Arago when they set up the guillotines . . . the quay of morning . . ."

Emilie laughs . . . she doesn't get it . . . "Tomorrow," she says. "Tomorrow . . ." And she goes back to her kid.

Then I was really alone!

Then I saw the thousands and thousands of little skiffs returning high above the Left Bank . . . Each one had a shriveled little corpse under its sail . . . and his story . . . his little lies to catch the wind with.

The last century—I can talk about it, I saw it end . . . It pulled out by the road past Orly . . . Choisy-le-Roy . . . Rungis, where my aunt Armide lived, the eldest of the family . . .

She talked about all sorts of things that nobody remembered. The day we picked for our visit was a Sunday in the fall, before the hardest months. We wouldn't be back until spring for the surprise of finding her still alive . . .

Old memories stay with you . . . but they're delicate, fragile . . . I'm sure we took the horsecar in front of the Châtelet . . . We and our cousins would climb up to the top deck. My father stayed home. My cousins would joke; we'd never find Aunt Armide in Rungis, they said. All alone in the house without a maid, she was sure to have been murdered, and what with the floods we probably wouldn't be notified until it was too late.

So we'd jog along to Choisy along the river. It took hours. That gave me a little fresh air. We'd be taking the train back.

When we got to the end of the line, we'd have to hurry. Over the big cobblestones . . . my mother would tug at my arm to make me keep up . . . We'd meet other relatives, also on their way to visit the old lady. My mother would have trouble with her bun, her veil, her straw hat, and her hairpins and hatpins . . . When her veil was wet, she'd chew at it in irritation. The avenues on the way to my aunt's were full of chestnuts. I couldn't pick any up, we hadn't a moment to lose . . . Beyond the road there were trees, fields, an embankment, clods of earth, and then the country . . . farther still, countries unknown . . . China . . . and after that nothing at all.

We were in such a hurry to get there that I made in my pants . . . To tell the truth I was in such a hurry all through my childhood that I had shit on my ass until I was drafted . . . We were all wringing wet by the time we got to the first houses. It was a sweet little village, I realize that now; with quiet little nooks, winding lanes, moss, all picturesque as hell. The fun was over when we reached her gate. It squeaked. My aunt had sold "ready to wear" at the Carreau du Temple for close on fifty years . . . All her savings had gone into her cottage in Rungis.

She lived at the back of one room, beside the fireplace, always in her armchair, waiting for people to come to see her. She kept the blinds drawn on account of her eyes.

Her cottage was in the Swiss style; that was all the rage in those days. Out in front there were some fish pickling in a smelly pool. A little more walking and you'd be at the door. Then darkness swallowed you up. You touched something soft. "Come closer. Don't be afraid, little Ferdinand . . ." That meant smooching. I couldn't get out of it. It was cold and prickly and then kind of warm at the corner of her mouth; the taste was awful. Somebody lighted a candle. The relations huddled together and began to gossip. It gave them a kick to see the relic kiss me . . . I was sick to my stomach from just that one kiss . . . and from walking too fast. But when she began to talk, they all had to shut up. They didn't know how to answer her. My aunt conversed only in the imperfect subjunctive. Old-fashioned. It cramped everybody's style. It was time for her to be moving along.

There had never been a fire in that fireplace behind her. "The draft was never quite sufficient . . ." The real reason was economy.

Before we left, Armide offered little cakes. Dry-as-dust cookies taken from a tightly covered receptacle that was opened twice a year. Everyone declined of course . . . they weren't children anymore . . . The cookies were for me, Ferdinand! . . . To show my pleasure and appreciation I had to jump up and down for joy . . . My mother pinched me, that was my signal to perform . . . I ran out into the garden, always the little imp, and spat it all out to the fish.

Everything that's washed up was there in the darkness, behind my aunt, behind her armchair. There was my grandfather Léopold, who never came back from India, there was the Virgin Mary, Cyrano de Bergerac, Félix Faure, Lustucru,* and the imperfect subjunctive. That's how it was.

I let the relic kiss me once again before leaving . . . And then hurried departure; out through the garden at breakneck speed. In front of the church we ditched some cousins, the ones who were going to Juvisy. In kissing me they gave off every known smell, rancid breath between beard and shirt front. My mother's limp was worse from sitting still a whole hour, her leg had gone to sleep.

When we came to the cemetery at Thiais, we'd dash in for a minute. There were two more of our dead at the end of one of the lanes. We scarcely looked at their tombs and lit out like thieves. We'd catch up with Clotilde, Gustave, and Gaston after the crossroads at Belle-Épine. My mother was dragging her bad leg and bumping into things. She even sprained her ankle once trying to carry me just before the grade crossing.

In the darkness our only thought was to reach the big apothecary jar at the pharmacy. That was on the main street, it meant we were saved . . . Against a background of raw gaslight gusts of music flew from the clattering doors

* See Glossary.

of the wineshops. We felt threatened and quickly crossed
the street. My mother was afraid of drunks.

The inside of the station was like a box, the waiting
room was full of smoke, with a rickety oil lamp dangling
from the ceiling. Huddled together around the little stove,
the travelers hawked and coughed and sizzled in their heat.
There's the humming of the train, it crashes in like thunder,
you'd think it was tearing the whole place apart. The
travelers shake themselves, break into a run, and storm the
carriages like a hurricane. We're the last two. I get a good
clout to teach me not to play with the door handle.

At Ivry we have to get out; we take advantage of our
day out to drop in on Madame Héronde, the seamstress.
She mends all our lace, especially the old things that are
so fragile and hard to dye.

She lived in a shack at the far end of Ivry, on the rue
des Palisses, in the middle of the fields. This was a good
chance to stir her up a little. Her work was never ready on
time. The customers were ferocious; nowadays nobody
would dare to gripe the way they did then. I used to see
my mother in tears almost every night over the seamstress
and the lace that never came back. If our customer got
peeved about her torn Valenciennes, she wouldn't be back
for a whole year.

The plain beyond Ivry was even more dangerous than
the way to Aunt Armide's. No comparison. Sometimes
there were toughs. They'd insult my mother. If I turned
around, I'd get a smack. When the mud got so soft and
mushy that your shoes came off in it, it meant we hadn't
far to go. Madame Héronde's shack was in the middle of
an empty lot. Her mutt heard us and began to bark like
mad. We caught sight of the window.

Our visit always came as a great surprise to Madame
Héronde; she couldn't get over it. My mother upbraided
her, unloaded her grievances. Finally both of them burst
into tears. There was nothing for me to do but wait and
look out . . . as far as possible . . . across the plain,
heavy with darkness, that stretched out as far as the banks
of the Seine and ended in a long cluttered line of housing
lots.

Our seamstress did her mending by the light of an oil
lamp. The smoke choked her and the light was ruining her

eyes. My mother kept after her to have gas put in. "It's really indispensable," she said again as we were leaving.

Mending tiny little insets, pieces as delicate as spider webs, she was certainly ruining her eyes. It wasn't only self-interest that made my mother say these things, but friendship as well. I never visited Madame Héronde's shack when it wasn't dark.

"They're installing it in September," she said every time. It was a lie to make my mother leave her alone . . . my mother thought well of her for all her faults.

My mother was in mortal terror of thieving seamstresses. Madame Héronde had no equal for honesty. She never did us out of a single penny. And yet she was poor as a church-mouse and we entrusted her with treasures! Whole chasubles of Venetian lace, such as you wouldn't even see in a museum nowadays. When my mother spoke of her later on in the family circle, it was with enthusiasm. It brought tears to her eyes. "She was a real fairy, I've got to admit. It's too bad she couldn't keep her word. She never delivered anything on time, never once . . ." The fairy died before the gas was installed, of fatigue, carried off by the flu, and also no doubt by the sorrow of having a skirt chaser for a husband . . . She died in childbirth . . . I remember her funeral well. It was at Le Petit Ivry. There were only the three of us, me and my parents, her husband hadn't bothered! He was a handsome man, he drank up every cent he ever owned. He spent whole years at the bar on the corner of the rue Gaillon. We saw him there for at least another ten years every time we passed. And then he disappeared.

When we left Madame Héronde's, it wasn't the end of our visits. At Austerlitz we had another gallop and then a bus ride to the Bastille. The Wurzems had their workshop near the Cirque d'Hiver. They were Alsatians, cabinet-makers, a whole family of them. It was Wurzem who antiqued all our small pieces of furniture, the kidney-shaped tables, consoles, and so on. For the last twenty years he'd done nothing else, first for Grandma, then for other people. Marquetry doesn't last, it's a perpetual head-ache. Wurzem was an artist, an excellent craftsman. They all of them lived in the shavings, his wife, his aunt, a brother-in-law, two female cousins, and four children. He was never on time either. His vice was fishing. He'd often spend a whole week by the Canal Saint-Martin instead of filling his orders. My mother would shout herself blue in the face. He always had some insolent comeback. Then he'd apologize. The whole family would burst into tears; there'd be nine of them crying and we were only two. They were a shiftless lot. They never paid their rent. In the end they were thrown out and had to take refuge in the "jungle" off the rue Caulaincourt.

Their shack was down at the bottom of a pit, you had to walk over planks to get to it. We'd start shouting from far off and head for their lantern. What tempted me at their place was to upset the glue pot that was always teetering on top of the stove. One day I made up my mind. When my father heard about it, he told my mother that I'd strangle her one day, it was my nature. He could see it all.

The nice thing about the Wurzems was that they never bore a grudge. After the worst bawlings out, as soon as you'd give them a little money, they'd be singing again. Nothing ever got them down. Shiftless, never a look ahead. That's the working class for you. No sense of responsibility like us. My mother always seized on these incidents as object lessons to show me how not to live. I thought they were very nice. I went to sleep in their shavings. My mother had to shake me when it was time to race down to the boulevard and jump into the Halle-aux-Vins bus. I loved the inside of it, because of the big crystal eye that lit up the faces all along the benches. Pure magic.

The horses gallop down the rue des Martyrs, the people move aside to let us pass. Even so we're very late in getting back to the shop.

Grandma is griping in her corner, Auguste, my father, pulls his cap way down over his eyes. He's pacing about like a lion on the bridge of a ship. My mother collapses on the stool. She's in the wrong, there's no use explaining. Nothing we had done that day appeals to them. Finally we close the shop . . . We say good-bye politely. The three of us set out for home and bed. It's still an awful hike. We lived on the other side of the Bon Marché.

My father wasn't an easy man to get along with. When he wasn't in his office he always wore a cap, the nautical kind. It had always been his dream to be the captain of an ocean liner. That dream made him mighty bitter.

Our apartment on the rue de Babylone looked out on the Mission. The priests sang a good deal, even at night they'd get up to sing a few more hymns. We couldn't see them on account of the wall that was right against our window. That made it kind of dark.

My father didn't make much at the Coccinelle Fire Insurance Company.

When we got to the Tuileries, he often had to carry me. The cops all had big bellies in those days. They hung around under the lamps.

The Seine is surprising to a kid, the way the wind ruffles the reflections, and the black emptiness below, shifting and grumbling. We turned down the rue Vaneau, and then we were home. There was always a to-do about lighting the hanging lamp. My mother didn't know how. My father Auguste fumbled, cursed, swore, and kept upsetting the holder and the mantle.

My father was a stout, blond man who'd fly into a rage over nothing, with a chubby round nose like a baby's over an enormous moustache. He rolled his eyes ferociously when he was angry. He never remembered anything but troubles. He'd had plenty. He made a hundred and ten francs a month at the insurance company.

With his yen to serve in the navy, he had pulled seven years in the artillery. He would have liked to be imposing, well-off, and respected. At the Coccinelle office they treated him like dirt. His pride tormented him and he couldn't stand the monotony. He had nothing in his favor but his school diploma, his moustache, and his lofty principles. To make things worse I got born. We were on the downgrade.

We still hadn't eaten. My mother was pottering about with pots and pans. She had stripped to her petticoat for fear of grease spots. She kept muttering that her Auguste didn't appreciate her good intentions and the difficulties of the business . . . He sat with his elbows on one corner of the oilcloth table cover, mulling over his troubles . . . From time to time he put on a scowl to show that he couldn't hold himself in much longer . . . Still she kept trying to mollify him. But when she tried to pull down the

beautiful yellow globe of the hanging lamp, he really flew
off the handle. "Clémence! Stop that! Christ almighty!
You're going to start a fire. Haven't I told you to use both
hands?" He began to bellow something awful, he was so
mad I thought he was going to bite his tongue off. In his
bad spells he used to turn purple and swell up all over, he
rolled his eyes like a dragon. It was horrible to look at.
My mother and I were scared stiff. Then he broke a dish
and went to bed.

"Turn toward the wall, you little pig! Don't turn around."
I had no desire to . . . I knew . . . I was ashamed . . .
it was my mother's legs, the skinny one and the fat one
. . . She continued to limp about from one room to the
next . . . He was trying to pick a fight . . . she insisted
on finishing the dishes . . . She tried to clear the air with
a little tune . . .

> And through the holes in the roof
> The sun shone down upon us . . .

Auguste, my father, read *La Patrie*. He sat down beside
my crib. She came over and kissed him. His storm was
subsiding . . . He stood up and went to the window. He
pretended to be looking for something down in the court.
He let a resounding fart. The tension was down.

She let a little fart in sympathy and fled kittenishly into
the kitchen.

Later they closed their door . . . the door to their
bedroom . . . I slept in the dining room. The mission-
aries' hymn came in over the walls . . . And in the whole
rue Babylone there was only a walking horse . . . clop
clop . . . that late cab . . .

To raise me my father was always taking on extra jobs.
Lempreinte, his boss, humiliated him in every possible
way. I knew Lempreinte, he was a redhead who had gone
pale, with long golden hairs, just a few of them, instead of
a beard. My father had style, elegance came natural to
him. That vexed Lempreinte. He avenged himself for
thirty years. He made him do nearly all his letters over
again.

When I was still smaller, at Puteaux where they'd put me
out to nurse, my parents used to come and see me on

Sunday. There was plenty of fresh air. They always paid in advance. Never a cent owing. Not even when things were at their worst. But in Courbevoie, what with worrying and doing without all sorts of things, my mother began to cough. After that she never stopped. It was slug syrup and later on the Raspail method * that saved her.

On account of my father's style Monsieur Lempreinte suspected him of fancy ambitions.

From the garden of the nurse's place in Puteaux you could look down over the whole of Paris. When Papa came to see me, the wind ruffled his moustache. That's my earliest memory.

After the fashion shop in Courbevoie went bankrupt, my parents had to work twice as hard, they really ran themselves ragged, she as my grandmother's saleswoman, he doing all the overtime he could at La Coccinelle. But the more he exhibited his high-class style, the more Lempreinte detested him. To keep from getting bitter, he took up watercolors. He used to paint at night after supper. They brought me back to Paris. I'd see him in the evening drawing, mostly boats, ships at sea, three-masters in a heavy breeze, black and white or in color. He had it in his blood . . . later on, memories of his days in the artillery, batteries galloping into position . . . or he'd do bishops . . . at the request of his customers . . . because of the bright robes . . . And dancing girls with hefty legs . . . My mother would offer a selection of his watercolors to the peddlers at lunch hour . . . She did all she could to keep me alive, I just shouldn't have been born.

At Grandma's on the rue Montorgueil she sometimes spat blood in the morning while arranging the sidewalk display. She'd hide her handkerchiefs. Grandma came out . . . "Wipe your eyes, Clémence. Crying won't help matters . . ." To get there early enough, we'd get up at daybreak and cross the Tuileries as soon as the housework was done; Papa would turn the mattresses.

The days were no joke. It was exceptional if I didn't cry a good part of the afternoon. In that shop I came in for more slaps than smiles. I apologized for everything I did, I was always apologizing.

We had to be on the lookout for theft and breakage.

* See Glossary.

Junk is fragile. I ruined tons of the stuff, never on purpose. The thought of antiques still makes me sick, but that was our bread and butter. The scrapings of time are sad . . . lousy, sickening. We sold the stuff over the customer's dead body. We'd wear him down. We'd drown his wits in floods of hokum . . . incredible bargains . . . we were merciless . . . He couldn't win . . . If he had any wits to begin with, we demolished them . . . He'd walk out stunned with the Louis XIII cup in his pocket, the openwork fan with cat and shepherdess wrapped in tissue paper. You can't imagine how they revolted me, grown-ups taking such crap home with them.

During working hours Grandma Caroline ensconced herself behind the Prodigal Son, an enormous tapestried screen. Caroline had an eye for light fingers. Customers are low characters, especially the women. The fancier they dress, the worse crooks they are. A little piece of Chantilly slips like a breeze into a practiced muff.

The shop was hardly a blaze of light . . . And in the winter it's especially treacherous on account of the ruffles . . . velvet, furs, canopies big enough to enfold three bosoms . . . not to mention the long-range boas of all kinds starting from the shoulders, the waves of diaphanous chiffon . . . Birds of overwhelming sorrow . . . The lady struts, plowing through piles of bric-a-brac, clucks, retraces her steps . . . scatters things all over the place . . . pecking, cackling . . . finding fault for the hell of it. We were goggle-eyed trying to find something that would appeal to her, there was plenty to choose from . . . Grandma was always out rustling . . . looking for white elephants at the auction rooms . . . she brought back everything, oil paintings, amethysts, whole forests of candelabras, cascades of embroidered tulle, cabochons, pyxes, stuffed animals, armor, parasols, gilded monstrosities from Japan, alabaster bowls and worse, gimcracks without a name, and objects nobody ever heard of.

The lady gushes and burbles in this treasure-house of shards. The heap settles back into place behind her. She overturns, she jingles, she twists and turns. She's just come in to look. It's raining, she's come in out of the rain. When she's had enough, she leaves, promising to come again. Then we have to gather up the rubbish in a hurry.

We crawl around on our knees, scraping under the furniture. If nothing's missing, if every handkerchief, knickknack, piece of cut glass, every gewgaw is accounted for,
we heave a great sigh of relief.

Mother slumps down, massaging her leg cramped from
standing, speechless with exhaustion. And then just before
closing time, the furtive customer steps in out of the darkness. He slips in softly, explains his business in a whisper,
he has a small object to sell, a family keepsake, he undoes
the newspaper wrapping. We don't think much of it. We'll
wash his treasure in the kitchen sink, we'll pay him in the
morning. He leaves with a mumbled good-bye . . . The
Panthéon-Courcelles bus races past, almost grazing the
shop.

My father comes in from his office. He keeps looking at
his watch. He's on edge. We've got to make it fast.

He puts down his hat. He takes his cap from the nail.
We still have to eat our noodles and make our deliveries.

We'd put the light out in the shop. My mother was no
cook, but she managed to work up some sort of mess.
When it wasn't egg soup it was sure to be macaroni. No
mercy. After the noodles we sat still for a moment, a little
meditation is good for the stomach. My mother tried to
entertain us, to dilute our embarrassment. If I didn't answer her questions, she'd keep on trying. "There's butter
in them, you know," she would say gently. The light came
from a naked gas jet behind the screen. The plates were
in darkness. Stoically my mother helped herself to some
more noodles to encourage us . . . It took a good swig of
red wine to keep them down.

The alcove where we ate was also used for the washing
and for storing the junk . . . There were heaps of it,
mounds . . . The stuff that couldn't be patched up, that
couldn't be sold, that wasn't fit to be shown, the worst
monstrosities. From the transom draperies hung down into
the soup. There was also, for some reason or other, a big
coal range with an enormous hood that took up half the
room. In the end we'd turn over our plates for a smidgin
of jam.

It was like living in a filthy museum.

After we moved away from Courbevoie, Grandma and

my father stopped talking to each other. Mama kept talking the whole time to keep them from throwing things at
each other. Once we had downed our noodles and enjoyed
our sampling of jam, we hit the road. The sold article
would be wrapped in a big canvas. Usually it was some
piece of drawing-room furniture, a "kidney," or occasionally a *poudreuse*. Papa hoisted it up on his shoulders and
we'd start for the Place de la Concorde. After the Splashing Fountains I'd be kind of scared. As we headed up the
Champs-Élysées, the darkness was immense. He sped along
like a thief. I had trouble keeping up. It seemed like he
was trying to ditch me.

I'd have liked him to talk to me, all he did was grunt
insults at strangers. By the time we reached the Étoile, he
was in a sweat. We took a little rest. When we got to the
customer's house, we had to look for the service entrance.

When we delivered in Auteuil, my father was in a
better humor. He didn't take out his watch so often. I'd
climb up on the parapet and he'd tell me all about tugboats . . . the green lights, the whistle signals between
the strings of barges. "She'll be down at the Point-du-Jour
in no time." We'd admire the wheezing old tub and wish
her a happy journey . . .

It was when we were going to the Ternes section that he
really got into a foul mood, especially if it was a dame
. . . He couldn't stand them. He'd be in a temper before
we even got started. I remember one time we were going
to the rue Demours. Outside the church he gives me a
clout and a vicious kick to make me shake a leg crossing
the street. When we got to the customer's house, I couldn't
keep from crying. "You little bastard," he shouts at me,
"I'll give you something to cry about! . . ." He climbed
up the stairs behind me with his little tea table on his neck.
We rang at the wrong door. All the maids looked out. I was
squealing like a stuck pig . . . On purpose . . . to get
his goat! What a ruckus! At last we find the right bell. The
maid lets us in. She sympathizes with me. The lady of the
house swishes in. "My, what a naughty little boy! He's
made his papa angry." He didn't know which way to look.
He would have liked to crawl into a drawer. The lady tries
to comfort me. She pours my father a glass of cognac.
Then she says: "Polish it up, my good man. I fear the

rain will leave spots. . . ." The maid gives him a rag. He
gets to work. The lady gives me a piece of candy. I follow
her into the bedroom. The maid comes in too. The lady lies
down in a mess of lace. All of a sudden she hikes up her
dressing gown and shows me her fat legs, her behind,
and her clump of hair. Whew! She goes poking around inside with her fingers . . .

"Come, little darling! . . . Come, little love! . . .
Come, suck me in there! . . ." Her voice was ever so soft
and tender, no one had ever spoken to me like that before.
She opens it out. Oozing.

The maid was doubled up with laughter. That's what
held me back. I ran off to the kitchen. I wasn't crying
anymore. They gave my father a tip. He didn't dare to put
it in his pocket, he just looked at it. The maid was laughing again. "I guess you don't want it," she asked him. He
ran out to the stairs. He forgot all about me, I had to race
after him in the street. I called him all the way down the
avenue. "Papa! Papa!" I caught up with him on the Place
des Ternes. We sat down. It wasn't very often that he
kissed me. He squeezed my hand.

"Yes, my boy! . . . Yes, my boy!" he kept repeating
as if to himself, looking off into space . . . He had feelings deep down. I had feelings too. Life has nothing to do
with feelings. We went straight back to the rue de Babylone.

My father distrusted his imagination. He talked to himself in corners. He was afraid of being carried away . . .
He must have been steaming inside . . .

He was born in Le Havre. He knew all about boats. A
name that kept coming back to him was that of Captain
Dirouane, who had been in command of the *City of Troy.*
He'd seen his boat putting out to sea, moving out of the
basin. She never came back. She had been lost with all
on board off the coast of Florida. "A fine three-mast bark!"

Another, the *Gondriolan,* a Norwegian, overloaded, had
crashed into the locks . . . Bad handling. He told me all
about it. Twenty years later the incident still filled him
with horror and indignation . . . And then he'd go back
into his corner. And mull things over some more.

His brother Antoine was something else again. With
real heroism he had crushed every impulse to wander. He

too had been born right near the Great Semaphore . . .
When their father died . . . he taught French at the lycée
. . . he'd gone straight into the Bureau of Weights and
Measures, a steady job. To play it absolutely safe he'd
married a young lady in the Statistics Division. But a
yearning for far-off places kept plaguing him . . . He
still had adventure in his bones, he never felt buried enough,
he kept digging in deeper and deeper.

He and his wife would come to see us on New Year's
Day. They were so thrifty, they ate so miserably and never
spoke to a soul, that the day they conked out nobody in
the neighborhood remembered them. Everybody was surprised. They died in secret, he of cancer, she of abstinence.
They found Blanche, his wife, on the Buttes-Chaumont.

That was where they used to spend their vacations.
Just the same, it took them forty years, always together, to
commit suicide.

My father's sister, Hélène, was a different story. She had
wind in her sails. She ended up in Russia. She got to be a
whore in St. Petersburg. For a while she had everything, a
carriage, three sleighs, a village all her own, with her name
on them. She came to see us at the Passage twice in a row,
done up like a princess, stunning and happy and all. She
came to a tragic end, shot by an officer. She had no will-
power. She was all flesh, desire, music. It made my father
puke just to think of her. When she heard of her death,
my mother said: "What a terrible end! But it's a fit end
for an egotist."

Then there was Uncle Arthur. He was no model either.
The flesh was too much for him too. My father had a
certain liking for him, a kind of weakness. He lived like a
regular bohemian, on the fringe of society, in a shanty,
shacked up with a housemaid. She worked at the restau-
rant outside the École Militaire. Thanks to her, there's no
denying it, he managed to eat very well. He was a dandy,
with a goatee, corduroy pants, pointed shoes, and a long
slender pipe. Nothing ever got him down. Making women
was his main occupation. He was sick a good deal, seriously
so when the rent came due. He'd stay in bed for a week
or more at some girl friend's house. When we went to see
him on Sundays, he didn't behave very well, especially with
my mother. He'd take little liberties with her. That made

my old man see red. When we left, he'd swear by eighty thousand devils that we'd never go back.

"Really, that brother of mine! His manners are disgusting! . . ." But we'd go back all the same.

He would draw boats on his big drawing board, under the skylight; yachts cutting through the foam, that was his style, with gulls all around . . . Now and then he'd do some work for a catalog, but he had so many debts he always felt discouraged. He was cheerful when doing nothing.

From the cavalry barracks next door you could hear all the bugle calls. Arthur knew all the words that went with them by heart. He'd start in again at every refrain. He made up some smutty ones. My mother and the housemaid went: "Oh! Oh!" Papa was furious because of my tender years.

But the screwiest member of the family was certainly Uncle Rodolphe, he was really off his rocker. He would titter quietly when you spoke to him. He only answered his own questions. That could go on for hours. He insisted on living in the open air. He never consented to have anything to do with a store or an office, not even as a watchman, not even at night. He preferred to take his meals out-of-doors, on a bench. He distrusted the insides of houses. When he was really too hungry, he'd come to see us. He'd turn up in the evening. That meant things were pretty rough.

He made his living carrying baggage in the railroad stations. It was a job that took stamina and he kept at it for more than twenty years. He had an in with the "Urban Express." He ran like a rabbit after cabs and baggage as long as he was able to. His high season was when people were coming back from vacation. His job made him hungry, and always thirsty. The coachmen liked him. He was screwy at the table. He'd stand up with glass in hand, clink it all around, and strike up a song . . . He'd stop in the middle and burst out laughing without rhyme or reason . . . and drool all over his napkin.

We'd take him home. He'd still be laughing. He lived on the rue Lepic at the Rendez-vous du Puy de Dôme, a shack on the court. He kept his belongings on the floor, there wasn't a single chair or a table. At the time of the

Exposition he became a "troubadour." He'd stand outside the papier-mâché grottoes along the Seine, drumming up trade for "Old Paris." His coat was a patchwork of rags of every color. He'd keep warm by bellowing and stamping his feet. In the evening, when he came to dinner in his carnival rig, my mother made him a hot-water bottle. His feet were always cold. To make matters worse, he took up with the "wench." She was a spieler too. She stood in a painted cardboard grotto at the other entrance. Poor thing, she'd already begun to cough her lungs out. She didn't last three months. She died right there in his room at the Rendez-vous. He didn't want them to take her away. He bolted his door. He came home every night and lay down beside her. It was the smell that put them wise. Then he went raving mad. He didn't understand that things die. They buried her by force. He wanted to carry her all the way to Pantin himself, on a hod.

Finally he went back to work by the Esplanade. My mother was horrified. "Dressed like a scarecrow, in this cold. It's a crime." What upset her most was that he wouldn't wear his overcoat. He had one of Papa's. They sent me to have a look. I was underage, so I could get through the gate without paying.

He was there behind the fence, dressed like a troubadour. All smiles again. "Hello," he said. "Hello, son . . . D'you see her? D'you see my Rosine? . . ." He pointed a finger across the Seine . . . the plain, a point in the mist . . . "You see her?" I said yes. I never crossed him. I told my parents he was all right. Pure spirit, that was Rodolphe!

Late in 1913 he went away with a circus. We could never find out what had become of him. We never saw him again.

We left the rue de Babylone to open another shop, to try our luck again. This time it was in the Passage des Bérésinas, between the Stock Exchange and the Boulevards. Our living quarters were over the shop, three rooms connected by a spiral staircase. My mother was always limping up and down those stairs. Tip-tap-plunk, tip-tap-plunk. She'd hold on to the banister. The sound gave my father the creeps. He was always in a temper anyway, because the time wouldn't pass. He kept looking at his watch. With Mama and her leg in addition, it didn't take much to start him off.

Our top room was above the glass roof of the Passage; the windows looked out on an open space, so they had bars to keep out burglars and cats. That was my room, and it was also the place where my father could draw and paint when he came home after his deliveries. He'd fuss over his watercolors, and when he was finished, he'd often make as if to come down and catch me playing with myself. He'd lurk in wait on the stairs. I was quicker than he was. He only caught me once. But he'd always find some excuse for giving me a licking. It was a battle between us. In the end I'd always apologize for my insolence . . . It was an act, I hadn't done anything.

He'd ask me questions and answer them for me. When he was through licking me, he'd stay there behind the bars, looking out at the stars, the atmosphere, the moon, the night high above us. That was his quarterdeck. I knew that. He'd be commanding the Atlantic.

If my mother interrupted him, if she called him to come down, he'd start griping again. They'd collide in the darkness, in the narrow cage between the second and third floors. She'd be in for a good smack and a volley of insults. Tip . . . tap . . . plunk! Tip . . . tap . . . plunk! Whimpering under the onslaught, she'd run down to the basement and count her wares. "Why can't you leave me alone! Godammit to hell! What have I done to deserve this? . . ." His bellowing shook the whole house. In the narrow kitchen he'd pour himself a glass of red wine. Nobody let out a peep. That was how he wanted it.

In the daytime I had Grandma, she taught me to read a little. She herself wasn't very good at it, she had learned late, after her children were born. I can't say she was tender or affectionate, but she didn't talk much, which is a good deal, and she never hit me . . . She hated my father's guts. She couldn't abide him with his education, his high principles, his idiotic rages, and his catalog of complaints. For her money her daughter was an ass to have married such a prick . . . making seventy francs a month in an insurance company. As for me, the kid, she hadn't quite made up her mind what to think of me, she was keeping me under observation. She was a woman of character.

At the Passage she helped us as long as she could with what junk she still had left from her stock. We only lighted one window, that was as much as we could fill . . . It was a discouraging lot of bric-a-brac, decrepit with age, gray elephants, crap; if that was all we had to sell, we were sunk. We only kept going by scrimping . . . always noodles and pawning Mama's earrings at the end of every month . . . It was a wonder we had anything to eat at all.

We took in a little money doing repair jobs. We did them a lot cheaper than anybody else, we'd take them at any price. And we delivered day and night. For a profit of two francs we'd hike out to the Parc Saint-Maur and back.

"It's never too late for the brave," said my mother cheerfully. Her specialty was optimism. But Madame Héronde was always holding things up, she went too far. Every time she kept us waiting there was a crisis, the whole lot of us damn near starved. By five in the afternoon my father would be back from the office, trembling with anxiety, looking at his watch the whole time.

"Clémence, I repeat for the hundredth time, if that woman gets robbed, what's going to become of us? . . . Her husband will sell it all! . . . He spends all his time in the whorehouse, I know it for a fact! . . . Everybody knows . . ."

He dashed up to the top floor, bellowing the whole time. Then back down to the shop. Our house was like an accordion. The amplification was terrific.

I'd go scouting for Madame Héronde as far as the rue des Pyramides. If I didn't see her coming with her bundle bigger than she was, I'd run back empty-handed. Then I'd go look again. Finally, when all hope was gone, when it was plain that she had been lost with all on board, I'd sight her off the rue Thérèse, gasping in an eddy of the crowd, listing under her bundle. I'd tow her to the Passage. In the shop she'd collapse. My mother gave thanks to heaven. My father couldn't bear to witness these scenes. He'd climb up to his attic, looking at his watch at every step, refurbishing his obsession. He was building up to the

next outburst, the Deluge that wouldn't be long in coming
. . . Getting into trim . . .

The Pinaises screwed us. My mother and I go traipsing
over to show them our selection of lace. For a wedding
present.

They lived in a palace across from the Pont Solférino.
I remember what struck me first . . . the vases, some were
so big and fat you could have hidden inside. They'd stuck
them all over the place. Those people were very rich. We
were shown into the salon. The beautiful Madame Pinaise
and her husband were there . . . they were expecting us.
They give us a friendly reception. My mother spreads her
stuff out in front of them . . . on the carpet. She gets
down on her knees, it's handier. She talks herself blue in
the face, she really knocks herself out. They stall, they
can't make up their minds, they simper, they put on the
dog.

Madame Pinaise reclines on the sofa in a dressing gown
with a lot of ribbons. He takes me around in back, gives
me a few friendly little pats, cuddles me a little . . . My
mother on the floor is doing her damnedest, plowing
through the pile, brandishing the merchandise . . . Her
bun comes undone, her face is dripping wet. She's awful to
look at. She gasps for breath, she loses her head, she
clutches at her stockings, her bun topples, falls in her eyes.

Madame Pinaise comes over to me. They both start
tickling me. My mother is still at it. Her spiel isn't getting
her anywhere. I'm about to come in my pants . . . A
flash! I see her . . . Madame Pinaise . . . She's swiped
a handkerchief. It's disappeared between her tits. "My
compliments, madame. You have such a nice little boy!
. . ." That was to throw the dust in her eyes. They'd seen
all they wanted. We quickly did up our bundles. My mother
was sweating big drops but smiling just the same. She
didn't wish to offend anyone . . . "Another time perhaps," she excused herself ever so politely. "I'm so sorry I
couldn't tempt you . . ."

In the street, outside the doorway, she asked me in a
whisper if I hadn't seen her slip the handkerchief into her
corset. I said no.

"Your father will be sick. We had that handkerchief on

consignment. Valenciennes openwork. It belonged to the
Gréguès. It wasn't ours. But imagine! If I had taken it
away from her, we'd have lost her as a customer . . . and
all her friends too . . . there would have been a scandal!"
   "Clémence, look at your hair. It's undone. It's all over
your eyes. You're green around the gills, poor thing.
You're falling apart. You're running yourself ragged . . ."
Those were his first words when we came home.
   So as not to lose sight of his watch, he hung it up in
the kitchen above the noodles. He gave my mother another
look. "You're positively green, Clémence." The watch
was so's we'd get through with the eggs, the stew, the
noodles . . . with our tiredness and the future. He was
fed up.
   "I'll go get dinner," she suggested. He didn't want her
to touch anything . . . He couldn't stand the thought of
her handling the food . . . "Your hands are dirty! Hell,
you're played out!" She went to set the table. She dropped
a plate. Infuriated, he rushed to help her. The place was
so small we were always bumping into things. There was
never room enough for a wild man like him. The table
rocked, the chairs began to waltz. It was a terrible mess.
They collided. They got up full of black-and-blue marks.
We went back to our leek salad. It was confession time . . .
   "So you didn't sell anything? . . . All your trouble was
for beans? . . . You poor dear . . ."
   He began to sigh something awful. He was feeling sorry
for her. He envisaged a future full of shit, we'd never get
out of it.
   Then she gave it to him straight . . . a handkerchief
had been stolen . . . and the circumstances . . .
   "What's that?" He couldn't take it in. "You didn't say
anything? You let them get away with it? The fruits of
our toil!" He was in such a rage that he cracked at the
seams. His jacket burst. "It's abominable!" he roared.
In spite of the uproar my mother kept yelping some kind
of excuses . . . He had stopped listening. He seized his
knife and brought it down in the middle of his plate . . .
it split, the noodle juice ran all over the place. "No, no!
I can't stand it." He rushed around, waving his arms. He
took hold of the little sideboard, the Henri III. He shook
it like a plum tree. There was an avalanche of dishes.

Madame Méhon, the corsetmaker who had the shop across from us, came to the window to enjoy the fun. She was an indefatigable enemy, she had detested us from the start. The Pérouquières, who had a bookstore two shops further down, make no bones about opening their window. Why should they stand on ceremony? They prop their elbows on the windowsill . . . My mother's going to catch it, that's a safe bet. As far as I'm concerned, I have no preferences. For yelling and boneheadedness, there's nothing to choose between them . . . She doesn't hit so hard, but more often. Which of the two I'd rather somebody killed? Well, all in all, my father, I guess.

They don't want me to see. "Get up to your room, you little pig . . . Go to bed! Say your prayers . . ."

He bellows, he rushes, he explodes, he bombards the kitchen. There's nothing left on the nails . . . Pots, pans, dishes, crash, bang, everything goes . . . My mother on her knees implores heaven for mercy . . . He overturns the table with one big kick . . . It lands on top of her . . .

"Run, Ferdinand," she still has time to shout. I run, passing through an avalanche of glass and debris . . . He charges into the piano that a customer had left us as security . . . he's beside himself. He bashes his heel into it, the keyboard clangs . . . Then it's my mother's turn, now she's getting hers . . . From my room I can hear her howling . . .

"Auguste! Auguste! Stop!" And then short stifled gasps . . .

I come part of the way down to look . . . He's dragging her along the banister. She hangs on. She clutches his neck. That's what saves her. It's he who pulls loose . . . He pushes her over. She somersaults . . . She bounces down the stairs . . . I can hear the dull thuds . . . At the bottom she picks herself up . . . Then he takes a powder . . . He leaves through the shop . . . He goes out in the street. She struggles to her feet . . . She goes back up to the kitchen. She has blood in her hair. She washes at the sink . . . She's sobbing . . . She gags . . . She sweeps up the breakage . . . He comes home very late on these occasions . . . Everything is very quiet again.

Grandma realized that I needed a little fun, that it wasn't good for me to be in the shop all the time. It made me sick to my stomach to listen to my lunatic father shouting his inanities. She bought a little dog for me to play with while waiting for the customers. I wanted to treat him like my father treated me. When we were alone, I'd give him wicked kicks. He'd slink away to whimper under the furniture. He'd lie down to beg pardon. He acted exactly like me.

It didn't give me any pleasure to beat him, I'd much rather have kissed him. In the end I'd fondle him and he'd get a hard-on. He went everywhere with us, even to the movies, to the Thursday matinee at the Robert Houdin.* Grandma treated me to that too. We'd sit through all three shows. It was the same price, all the seats were one franc, one hundred percent silent, without words, without music, without titles, just the purring of the machine. People will come back to that, you get sick of everything except sleeping and daydreaming. The *Trip to the Moon* * will be back again . . . I still know it by heart.

Sometimes in the summer there were only the two of us, Caroline and myself, in the big hall up one flight of stairs. In the end the usher would motion us to leave. I'd have to wake up Grandma and the dog. Then we'd hurry through the crowd and the bustle of the Boulevards. We were always late in getting home. We'd come in panting.

"Did you like it?" Caroline would ask me. I didn't say anything. I didn't like personal questions. "The child is secretive . . ." That's what the neighbors said.

On the way home she'd stop at the corner of our Passage and buy me a copy of *Illustrated Adventure Stories* from the newspaper woman with the charcoal footwarmer. She'd hide it for me in her panties, under her three thick petticoats. My father didn't like me to read such hogwash. He claimed it corrupted you, that it didn't prepare you for life, that I'd do better to learn the alphabet out of something serious.

I was going on seven, I'd soon be going to school, I shouldn't be given any wrong ideas . . . the other shopkeepers' children would also be going to school soon. The time for tomfoolery was past. On our way home from

* See Glossary.

deliveries he'd make me little sermons about the seriousness of existence.

Whacks alone won't do it.

Foreseeing that I'd be a thief, my father blared like a trombone. One afternoon Tom and I had emptied the sugar bowl. It was never forgotten. But that wasn't my only fault. In addition my behind was always dirty, I didn't wipe myself, I didn't have time, that was my justification, we were always in too much of a hurry . . . I never wiped myself properly, I always had a sock coming to me . . . and hurried to avoid it . . . I left the can door open so as to hear them coming . . . I shat like a bird between two storms . . .

I bounded upstairs and they couldn't find me . . . I'd go around for weeks with shit on my ass. I was conscious of the smell, I'd be careful not to get too close to people.

"He's as filthy as thirty-six pigs! He has no self-respect! He'll never make a living. Every boss in the world will fire him! . . ." He saw a shitty future in store for me.

"He stinks! . . . We'll always have him on our hands . . ."

My father looked far ahead and all he saw was gloom. He put it in Latin for emphasis: *"Sana . . . corpore sano."* My mother didn't know what to say.

A little further down the Passage there was a family of bookbinders. Their children never went out.

The mother was a baroness. De Caravals was her name. She didn't want her children to learn bad language at any cost.

They played together all year long behind the windowpanes, putting their noses in each other's mouths and both hands at the same time. Their complexions were like celery.

Once a year Madame de Caravals took a vacation all by herself. She'd go visiting her cousins in Périgord. She told everybody how her cousins came to meet her at the station in their "break" drawn by four prize-winning horses. They would drive together through endless estates . . . The peasants would troop out to kneel on the castle drive as they passed . . . that was the kind of stuff she dished out.

One year she took the two kids with her. She came back alone in the wintertime, much later than usual. She had on deep mourning. You couldn't see her face behind all the veils. She offered no explanation. She went straight up to bed. She never spoke to anybody after that.

The change had been too much for those children who never went out. The fresh air had killed them . . . That disaster gave everyone pause. From the rue Thérèse to the Place Gaillon all you heard about was oxygen . . . for more than a month.

As for us, we often had the chance to go to the country. Uncle Édouard, my mother's brother, was only too delighted when he could do something for us. He'd suggest excursions. My father never accepted. He always found some pretext for getting out of them. He didn't want to be beholden to anybody, that was his motto.

Uncle Édouard was up-to-date, he had a way with machinery. He was mighty clever with his hands. He wasn't extravagant, he wasn't the kind to involve us in a spending spree, but even so the slightest outing is bound to be rather costly . . . "A hundred francs," my mother would say, "don't last long when you go out."

Nevertheless the sad story of the Caravals had got the whole Passage so upset that something had to be done. It was suddenly discovered that everybody looked "peaked." Advice was passed from shop to shop. No one could think of anything but microbes and the perils of infection. The kids came in for a wave of parental solicitude. They were made to take whole jugfuls, whole barrelfuls of cod-liver oil, reinforced, in double doses. Frankly, it didn't do much good . . . it made them belch. It made them greener than ever; they could hardly stand up to begin with, now the oil killed their appetite.

I have to admit that the Passage was an unbelievable pesthole. It was made to kill you off, slowly but surely, what with the little mongrels' urine, the shit, the sputum, the leaky gas pipes. The stink was worse than the inside of a prison. Down under the glass roof the sun is so dim you can eclipse it with a candle. Everybody began to gasp for breath. The Passage took cognizance of its asphyxiating stench . . . We talked of nothing but the country, hills and valleys, the wonders of nature . . .

Édouard offered once more to take us out one Sunday, all the way to Fontainebleau. Papa finally gave in. He got our clothes ready and the provisions.

Édouard's first three-wheeler was a one-cylinder job, as massive as a field howitzer, with half a coachman's seat in front.

We got up that Sunday much earlier than usual. My ass was given a thorough wiping. We waited a whole hour at the meeting place on the rue Gaillon before the contraption got there. Our departure was something. It had taken at least six men to push the thing from the Pont Bineau. The tanks were filled. The carburetor spewed in all directions, the steering wheel quaked . . . There was a series of terrible explosions. They tried it with the crank, they tried it with a strap . . . They harnessed themselves to it by three and sixes . . . Finally a tremendous explosion . . . the engine began to turn. Twice fire broke out . . . and was quickly extinguished. My uncle said: "Pile in, ladies and gentlemen, I think she's warm now. Now we can get started . . ." It took nerve to stay put. The crowd pressed in on us. Caroline, my mother, and I wedged ourselves in. We were tied so tightly to the seat, so squeezed in among the clothes and gear that only my tongue protruded. But I came in for a good little whack before we moved off, just to keep me from getting any ideas.

The three-wheeler bucked and settled back . . . It gave two, three big jolts . . . A terrible crashing and belching were heard . . . The crowd shrank back in terror . . . They thought we were goners . . . But the monster was climbing the rue Réaumur in frantic fits and starts . . . My father had rented a bike . . . Since he couldn't pedal up the hill, he pushed us from behind . . . The slightest stop would have been the end . . . he had to push with all his might . . . At the Square du Temple we stopped a while. We started off again with a crash. In full flight my uncle poured grease, straight out of the bottle, into the connecting rods, the chain, and the whole works. It always had to be swimming in grease, like the

engine of an ocean liner. There's trouble in the front seat.
My mother has a bellyache. If she takes time out, if we
stop, the engine is perfectly capable of conking out . . .
if it stalls, our goose is cooked . . . My mother bears up
heroically. My uncle, perched on his infernal machine,
looking like a shaggy deep-sea diver surrounded by a
thousand tongues of flame, adjures us over the handlebars
to hold tight . . . My father is tagging after us. He pedals
to the rescue. He picks up the parts as they fall off, pieces
of levers and pedals, nuts, cotter pins—and some bigger
things. We hear him cursing and swearing louder than
the clatter of the machine.

The cobblestones were the cause of our disaster . . . At
Clignancourt they snapped all three chains . . . At the
Vanves tollgate they demolished the front springs . . .
We lost all our lamps and the big horn shaped like a
dragon's maw in the rills where the road was being repaired at La Villette . . . Near Picpus and on the highway we lost so much stuff that my father missed some of
it . . .

I could hear him cursing behind us: that it was the end
of the world and night would catch us on the road.

Tom ambled along ahead of our expedition, we took
our bearings by his asshole. He had time to piss wherever
he pleased. Uncle Édouard was more than clever, he had
real genius for repairs of all sorts. Toward the end of our
outings he had everything in his hands, his fingers were
doing all the work, between jolts he juggled with splinters
and wrist pins, he played the leaks and pistons like a
trumpet. His acrobatics were marvelous to watch. But at
a certain moment everything came tumbling out on the
road all the same . . . We'd go into a drift, the steering
gear would founder, we'd run plunk into the ditch. Crashing, gushing, snorting, the thing would run us all into the
mud.

My father came up bellowing . . . The tin can let out
one last BWAAH . . . And that was all. The bastard
passed out on us.

We stank up the countryside with crankcase oil. We dis-
entangled ourselves from the catafalque . . . and then we
pushed the whole thing back to Asnières. That's where the
garage was. My father was magnificent in action, his calves

bulged in his ribbed woolen stockings . . . The ladies
along the road couldn't take their eyes off him. My mama
was proud of him . . . The engine had to be cooled off,
we had a small collapsible canvas bucket for the purpose.
We'd take water from fountains. Our three-wheeler looked
like a factory mounted on a pushcart. There were so many
hooks and pointed gadgets sticking out on all sides that we
ripped our clothes to tatters pushing . . .

At the tollgate my uncle and Papa went into a bar for
a beer. The ladies and myself collapsed wheezing and panting on a bench outside and waited for our pop. Everybody
was in a foul temper. In the end I was the victim. Storm-
clouds hung over the family. Auguste was aching for a
tantrum. He was just looking for a pretext. He was pooped,
he was sniffing like a bulldog. No one but me would do, the
others would have told him where to get off . . . He took
a stiff drink of pernod. He wasn't used to it, it was a dumb
thing to do . . . On the grounds that I'd torn my pants
he gave me a royal thrashing. My uncle stuck up for me,
kind of. That only added to his fury.

It was on the way back from the country that I got my
worst lickings. There are always crowds of people at the
city gates. I screeched as loud as I could just to get his
goat. I stirred up mob sentiment, I rolled under the café
tables. I heaped mountains of shame on him. He blushed
from head to foot. He hated attracting attention. I hoped
it would make him bust. We started off again with our
tails between our legs, our backs bent over the infernal
machine.

There were always such scenes on the way back from
our trips that my uncle gave up the whole idea.

"Of course the air is good for the little fellow," they
said, "but the automobile gets him upset . . ."

Mademoiselle Méhon had the shop straight across from
us. You can't imagine what a dog she was. She was always
trying to pick a fight with us, she never stopped plotting,
she was jealous. And yet she was doing all right with her
corsets. She was an old woman and she still had her faithful clientele, handed down from mother to daughter for
the last forty years. Women that wouldn't have let just
anybody see their bosoms.

Things came to a head over Tom, who'd got into the
habit of pissing against the shopwindows. Still, he wasn't
the only one. Every mutt in the neighborhood did worse.
The Passage was their promenade.

The Méhon woman crossed the street for no other purpose than to provoke my mother, to make a scene. It was
scandalous, she bellowed, the way our mangy cur befouled
her window . . . Her words resounded on both sides of
the shop and up to the glass roof. The passersby took sides.
It was a bitter brawl. Grandma, ordinarily so careful about
her language, gave her a good tongue-lashing.

When Papa came home from the office and heard about
it, he flew into such a temper you couldn't bear to look
at him. He rolled his eyes so wildly in the direction of the
old bag's shop window we were afraid he was going to
strangle her. We did our best to stop him, we clung to his
overcoat . . . He had developed the strength of a legion-
naire. He dragged us into the shop . . . He bellowed loud
enough to be heard on the fourth floor that he was going
to make hash out of that damn corsetmaker . . . "I
shouldn't have told you about it," my mother wailed. The
harm was done.

In the weeks that followed my life was a little more
peaceful. My father was absorbed. Whenever he had a
moment's free time, he'd glare at the corset shop. She did
the same. They'd spy on each other from behind the
curtains, floor by floor. The moment he got home from the
office, he'd begin to wonder what she might be up to. It
was directly across the street . . . When she was in her
kitchen on the second floor, he'd be standing in the corner
of ours, muttering ferocious threats . . .

"Will you look at the rotten old bag! Isn't she ever
going to poison herself? . . . Couldn't she take some
mushrooms? Couldn't she swallow her false teeth? Hell!
She even examines her food for ground glass . . ." He
couldn't stop staring at her. He had no time for my propensities . . . It was better in a way.

The neighbors were afraid to commit themselves. Dogs
urinated all over the place, on their windows too, not just
on hers. It was no use sprinkling sulphur, the fact is that
the Passage des Bérésinas was a kind of sewer. Piss brings

company. Anybody who felt like it pissed on us, even grown-ups, especially if it was raining out in the street. They came in just for that. People even crapped in the little side alley, the Allée Primorgueil. What call had we to complain? Often a pisser, with or without a dog, gets to be a customer.

After a while my father wasn't satisfied with bristling at the corsetmaker, he'd work himself up against Grandma. "The dirty old bag—huh!—with her stinking mutt, you want me to tell you what she's been doing? . . . You don't know? . . . She's sly . . . she's underhanded! She's an accomplice. Well, there you have it. They're in it together, cooking up some lousy trick . . . and it's nothing new! Ah, those two bitches! . . . What for? You really want to know? To drive me raving mad. That's all. That's the long and the short of it."

"Come, come, Auguste. I assure you . . . You're imagining things. You make a mountain out of the least word . . ."

"I'm imagining things? Why don't you come right out and say I'm nuts! Go ahead! Imagining things! Ah, Clémence, you're incorrigible. Life goes on and you don't learn a thing . . . We're being persecuted, that's what! Stepped on! Ridiculed! They're dishonoring me. And what have you to say? That I'm imagining things! No! Oh, it's too much!"

And damned if he didn't burst into tears. It was his turn.

We weren't the only ones in the Passage with stands, kidney-shaped tables, little chairs, and fluted Louis XVI pieces. Our competitors, the junk dealers, sided with Méhon. That was to be expected. My father couldn't sleep anymore. His nightmare was cleaning the sidewalk outside our shop. He'd wash down the flags every morning before going to work.

He'd come out with his pail, his broom, his rag, and the little trowel he'd slip under the turds, to pick them up and throw them in the sawdust. What a humiliation for a man with his education! The turds increased in number and there were many more in front of our shop, lengthwise and crosswise, than anywhere else. Obviously a plot.

Mademoiselle Méhon was at her second-floor window grinning from ear to ear as she watched my father battling the shit. It gave her a kick that lasted all day. The neighbors collected to count the turds.

Bets were laid that he wouldn't be able to clean it all up.

He'd make it fast, then he'd rush in to put on his collar and tie. He had to be at La Coccinelle before anyone else to open the mail.

Baron Méfaise, the director, counted on him implicitly.

This was when tragedy hit the Cortilènes. A drama of passion at Number 147 in the Passage. It was in the papers; for a whole week there was a dense crowd parading, grunting, pondering, and spitting outside their shop.

I'd seen Madame Cortilène lots of times, my mother made her blouses of fine Irish linen with lace insets. I remember well her long eyelashes, her eyes full of gentleness, and the looks she gave even a kid like me. I'd often jerk off thinking of her.

During fittings you get to see shoulders, skin . . . The moment she left, it never failed, I'd run up to the can on the fourth floor and masturbate strenuously. I'd come down with big rings under my eyes.

Those people had scenes too, but they were over jealousy. Her husband didn't want her to go out. He did the going out. He was a former officer, small and dark-haired, with a terrible temper. They sold rubber goods at 147, drainage tubes, instruments, and "articles" . . .

Everyone in the Passage said she was too pretty to keep that kind of shop . . .

One day her jealous husband came home unexpectedly. He found her upstairs starting up with two men; it gave him such a shock that he pulled out his revolver and shot her first and then himself, straight in the mouth. They died in each other's arms.

He hadn't been out more than fifteen minutes.

My father's revolver was a military model, he hid it in the bedside table. The caliber was something enormous. He had brought it home from the army.

The Cortilène tragedy might have given my father

grounds for the worst tantrums, something to yell about. Actually it made him clam up. He hardly spoke at all.

There was no lack of turds on the sidewalk outside our door. With all the people who passed, there was so much spit it made the pavement sticky. He cleaned it all up. And not a peep out of him. That was such a revolution in his habits that my mother began to watch him when he locked himself up in his room. He'd stay there for hours. He neglected his deliveries, he gave up drawing. She'd look in through the keyhole. He'd pick up his gat, he'd turn the cylinder. You'd hear "click, click" . . . He seemed to be practicing up.

One day he went out alone and came back with cartridges, a whole box of them. He opened them up in front of us, to make sure we'd got a good look. He didn't say a word, he just put the box down on the table beside the noodles. My mother was scared stiff; she flung herself on the floor, she clasped his knees and implored him to throw it all in the garbage. It was no use. He was as stubborn as a mule. He didn't even answer. He shook her off roughly and swilled a quart of the red stuff all by himself. He refused to eat. When my mother kept after him, he pushed her against the cupboard. Then he beat it down to the cellar and closed the trap over his head.

We heard him shooting: Ping! Ping! Ping! . . . He took his time, the shot rang out, followed by a tremendous echo. He must have been shooting at the empty barrels. My mother called down to him, screaming through the cracks . . .

"Auguste! Auguste! I implore you! Think of the child! Think of me! Call your father, Ferdinand!"

"Papa! Papa!" I bellowed . . .

I wondered whom he was going to kill. Mademoiselle Méhon? Grandma Caroline? Both of them like at the Cortilènes? He'd have to find them together.

Ping! Ping! Ping! . . . He went right on shooting. The neighbors came running. A bloodbath, they thought . . .

He ran out of ammunition. In the end he came upstairs . . . When he raised the trap, he was as pale as a corpse. We clustered around him, we held him up, we settled him in the Louis XIV armchair in the middle of the store. We spoke to him ever so gently. His revolver, still smoking, dangled from his wrist.

When she heard the shooting, Madame Méhon shat in her skirts . . . She came over to see what was going on. Then right in front of all the people my mother told her good and loud what she thought of her. And my mother wasn't the bold kind.

"Come right in! Take a good look! Look at the state you've driven him to. A good man! A family man! Aren't you ashamed of yourself? Oh! You're a wicked woman!"

Madame Méhon hadn't much to say for herself. She went back home in a hurry. The neighbors gave her hard looks. They comforted my father. "My conscience is clear," he kept mumbling under his breath. M. Visios, the pipe dealer who had been in the navy for five years, tried to placate him.

My mother wrapped the weapon in several layers of newspaper and then in a cashmere shawl.

My father went up to bed. She cupped him. He went on trembling for a couple of hours at least.

"Come, child . . . come!" she said when we were alone.

It was late. We ran down to Pont Royal by way of the rue des Pyramides . . . We kept looking to left and right to see if anybody was coming. We threw the package in the drink.

We returned home even faster than we'd come. We told my father we'd been taking Caroline home.

The next day he had terrible aches and pains . . . it killed him to stand up. For the next week at least, it was Mama that had to scrub the sidewalk.

Grandma had her doubts about the forthcoming Exposition. The last one in '82 hadn't done anything but screw up small business by making a lot of damn fools spend their money in the wrong way. After all that ballyhoo, all that fuss and bother, there was nothing left but two or three empty lots and a pile of rubbish so disgusting looking that even twenty years later nobody was willing to take it away . . . not to mention the two epidemics that the Iroquois, the blue, the yellow, and the brown savages had brought over.

The new exposition was bound to be even worse. There was sure to be cholera. Grandma was positive.

The customers were already beginning to save up, they were putting pocket money aside, finding a thousand pretexts for not buying anything . . . they were waiting for the "opening." A rotten bunch of griping blackguards. My mama's earrings never left the pawnshop.

"If the idea was to get the peasants to come in from the country, why couldn't they arrange dances for them at the Trocadéro? . . . It's big enough for everybody. They didn't have to rip the whole city open and plug up the Seine . . . Should we throw money out the window because we've forgotten how to have fun by ourselves? No!"

That was how my Grandmother Caroline saw it. The moment she left, my father began racking his brains, trying to figure out what she had meant by her bitter words . . .

He discovered a hidden meaning . . . personal insinuations . . . threats . . . He was on his guard.

"At least I forbid you to discuss my private affairs with her! . . . Exposition hell! You want me to tell you, Clémence? It's a pretext. What she's getting at? You want to know? Well, I had a hunch the moment she opened her mouth. Divorce! . . . That's what she wants!"

Then he pointed across the room at me in my corner. Ungrateful wretch! Sneaky little profiteer . . . getting fat on other people's sacrifices . . . Me . . . with my shitass . . . my boils . . . my insatiable consumption of shoes . . . There I was! All this was about me, the scapegoat for all their misfortunes . . .

"Oh! Godammit! Godammit to hell! If it weren't for him! Oh! What's that? I'd clear out so fast. Bah! I can promise you that. I'd have done it long ago . . . long ago. Not tomorrow, see! This minute! Godammit! If we didn't have this little hunk of shit on our hands! She wouldn't keep harping, believe you me. Divorce! Oh! DIVORCE! . . ."

He was all shriveled, shaken with spasms. He was like the villain in the movies, only worse because he swore out loud . . .

"Oh! By all the whorehouses in hell! Freedom! Bah! Self-abnegation? Yes. Sacrifice? Yes. Privation? Yes. The whole shooting match and then some. And all for this perverted little shitass! Oh! Oh! Freedom! Freedom! . . ." He disappeared into the wings. On his way upstairs he belabored his chest with great dull blows.

The mere mention of "divorce" threw my mother into convulsions . . .

"Why, Auguste, I do everything I can! You know that! I work my fingers to the bone. I do the work of ten, you can see that for yourself. Things will get better! I promise you! I implore you! One day we'll be happy, all three of us! . . ."

"What about me?" he shouted down from upstairs, "I suppose I don't do my best. And a lot of good it does . . ."

She surrendered to her sorrows. The floodgates burst.

"We'll bring him up properly, you'll see, I swear it, Auguste! Don't work yourself up! . . . He'll do his best too . . . He'll be like us! He'll be like you! You'll see! He'll be like us. Won't you, child?"

We started delivering again. We saw the big monumental gate going up at the corner of the Place de la Concorde. It was so delicate, so fancy, so full of frills and gingerbread from top to bottom, it made you think of a mountain in bridal dress. Every time we passed by, we saw something new being done to it.

Finally they took the scaffolding away. Everything was in readiness for the public . . . At first my father pooh-poohed the whole thing, and then he went after all, all alone one Saturday afternoon. To everybody's surprise he was delighted . . . Pleased, happy, like a kid who's been to fairyland . . .

All our neighbors, except Madame Méhon of course, came running over to hear him tell about it. At ten that night he still had them spellbound. In less than an hour on the grounds, he had seen everything, been everywhere, understood it all and a lot more, from the Pavilion of Black Snakes to the Gallery of Machines, and from the North Pole to the Cannibals . . .

Visios, the sailor who had been all over the world, said the whole thing was marvelous. He'd never have believed it . . . and he knew a thing or two. My uncle Rodolphe, who had been working in the sideshow done up as a troubadour ever since the Exposition opened, was non-existent as a storyteller. He was there in the shop with the rest of them. Draped in his finery, he'd grin for no reason, he'd make paper birds and wait for supper to be served.

Madame Méhon was at her window, worried sick to see all the neighbors coming over our way. For her money, it was sure to end in some plot. Grandma stayed away a whole week. Papa's bumptiousness gave her a pain. And every night he started his lecture all over again, adding new touches. Rodolphe got hold of some free tickets. So one Sunday the three of us dove into the crowd.

At the Place de la Concorde the mob got hold of us and really pumped us in. We came to, breathless and half unconscious, in the Gallery of Machines. It was terrifying! Hanging in midair in a transparent cathedral with little panes of glass that went way up to the sky. The racket was so awful we couldn't hear my father, and he was shouting his lungs out. Steam gushed and spurted on all sides. There were giant kettles as big as three houses, gleaming pistons that came charging at us out of the bottom of hell . . . In the end we couldn't stand it, we were scared, we beat it . . . We passed the Ferris wheel . . . but what we liked best was the bank of the Seine.

It was weird the way they had rigged up the Esplanade . . . terrific . . . Two rows of enormous cakes, fantastic cream puffs, full of balconies crammed with gypsies swathed in flags, music, and millions of little light bulbs that were lit in broad daylight. That was wasteful. Grandma was right. We moved on, crushed worse and worse. I was right near all the feet, the dust was so thick I couldn't see where I was going. I swallowed whole mouthfuls and spat cement . . . Finally we got to the North Pole . . . An explorer, real friendly, was explaining the show, but so confidentially, so softly, all wrapped up in his furs, you could hardly hear a thing. My father told us what was what. Then the seals came out for their dinner. They bellowed so loud there was nothing else in the world. So we beat it.

In the big Refreshment Palace lovely orangeade was being dished out in a long line at a little moving counter absolutely free of charge . . . Between us and it a riot

was going on . . . A seething mob struggling to get at
the glasses. Thirst has no mercy. If we'd attempted it,
there wouldn't have been anything left of us. We fled
through another door . . . We went to see the na-
tives . . .

We only saw one, behind a fence, he was boiling himself
an egg. He wasn't looking at us, he had his back turned.
It was quiet there, so my father started gabbing again with
lots of animation, trying to enlighten us about the curious
customs of tropical countries. He wasn't able to finish, the
nigger was fed up too. He spat in our direction and disappeared into his cabin . . . I couldn't see straight or open
my mouth. I had breathed in so much dust all my passages
were blocked. From one eddy to the next we made it to the
exit. Even after we'd passed the Invalides I was still being
jostled and trampled. We were so shaken, so shattered
by fatigue and excitement we hardly recognized each other.
We took the shortest way home . . . by way of the
Marché Saint-Honoré. Then we went straight upstairs
and drank all the water in the kitchen.

Our neighbors, with Visios, our sailor, in the lead, the
perfume dealer from Number 27, Madame Gratat from
the glove shop, Dorival the pastrycook, and Monsieur
Pérouquière, popped right over to hear about it. They
wanted us to tell them all about it and then some . . .
Had we been to see all the exhibits? . . . Hadn't they
lost me? . . . How much had we spent? . . . What! At
every turnstile? . . .

Papa told them the whole story with thousands of
details . . . some of them true and others not so accurate
. . . My mother was happy, it had been worth it . . . for
once Auguste was being really appreciated . . . She was
mighty proud for his sake . . . He puffed himself up . . .
he laid it on thick . . . She knew he was telling fairy tales
. . . but that's what it is to be an educated man . . . she
hadn't suffered for nothing . . . the man she had given
herself to was somebody . . . a thinker . . . there was
no denying it. All those poor bastards sat there with their
tongues hanging out . . . Pure admiration!

Papa made it all up as he went along, without the slightest effort . . . There was magic in our shop . . . with
the gas turned off. All by himself he put on a show a

hundred times more amazing than four dozen Expositions
. . . But he didn't want the gas . . . Just candles. Our
shopkeeper friends brought their own glims, dug out of
their storerooms. They came back night after night to
listen to Papa and kept asking for more . . .

His prestige was enormous . . . They could think of
nothing better. In the end, I guess, Madame Méhon must
have taken sick over there in her hovel, haunted by bitter
thoughts . . . They'd told her everything, down to the
last syllable . . .

About two weeks later she couldn't stand it anymore
. . . One night she came down all alone and crossed the
Passage . . . She looked like a ghost . . . She was in
her nightgown. She banged on our window. We all turned
around. She didn't breathe a word. She stuck a piece of
paper on the glass. The inscription was brief, in big
capital letters: LIAR . . .

Everybody burst out laughing. The charm was broken.
They all went home . . . Papa had nothing more to
say . . .

The pride of our shop was the coffee table in the middle,
Louis XV, the only piece we were really sure about.
People were always making us offers. We didn't try very
hard to sell it. We couldn't have replaced it.

The Brétontés, our fancy customers from the Faubourg
Saint-Germain, had noticed it a long time ago . . . They
asked us to lend it to them for a play they were putting
on, a comedy, with some other society people in their
private house. The Pinaises were in it, and the Cour-
manches, the Doranges whose daughters were so cross-
eyed, and a lot of others who were customers more or less.
The Girondets, the Camadours, the De Lambistes, who
were related to the ambassadors . . . The cream of the
cream! . . . It was going to be put on one Sunday afternoon. Madame Brétonté was sure their play would be a
howling success.

She came back more than ten times, always to pester us
about that table. We couldn't refuse, it was for charity.

To make sure nothing would happen to it, we took a
cab and delivered it ourselves in the morning, wrapped
in three blankets. Then in the afternoon we came back

just in time to take our seats, three stools near the door. The curtain hadn't gone up yet, but already it was marvelous. The ladies, dressed fit to kill, all burbling and sashaying. They smelled so good you almost fainted . . . Looking around, my mother recognized all the best pieces from her shop. Her boleros, her neckbands, her Chantilly lace. She even remembered the prices. And hadn't they had them made up nicely! Lace could be so lovely . . . And wasn't it becoming to them! . . . She was in seventh heaven.

Before we left the shop, I had been warned that if I gave off any smells, I'd be thrown out one-two-three. I had given myself such a wiping the toilet was all stuffed up. Even my feet were clean in my dress shoes . . .

Finally the people took their seats. Somebody called for silence. The curtain rolled up . . . Our coffee table appeared . . . plunk in the middle of the stage . . . same as in our shop . . . That set our minds at rest . . . A few bars on the piano and the actors were saying their lines . . . Oh, how beautifully they spoke . . . all the characters coming and going and posturing in the bright light . . . They were marvelous . . . They started bickering and arguing . . . they were getting madder and madder . . . but it made them more charming than ever . . . I was carried away . . . I wanted them to start all over again. I didn't quite get it all . . . But I was captivated, body and soul . . . Everything they touched . . . their slightest gestures . . . the most commonplace words were enchanted . . . The people around us applauded, my parents and I didn't dare. . . .

On the stage I recognize Madame Pinaise, she's absolutely divine . . . There were her legs again and those throbbing tits . . . She's lying on a deep silk divan . . . sheathed in an airy négligé . . . She's desperate, she's sobbing . . . All on account of Dorange, another of our customers . . . He's bawling the hell out of her, she has no one to turn to . . . The heartless blackguard slips around behind her and takes advantage . . . she's bent over our coffee table, bawling . . . he steals a kiss . . . and starts to bill and coo . . . It was nothing like home . . . Finally her resistance breaks down . . . She sinks back gracefully on the couch . . . He gives her another

buss, square on the lips . . . She swoons, she passes out
. . . Whew! . . . and him waggling his ass . . .
    I really caught on . . . the polite passion . . . the
deep luscious melody . . . All those visions to jerk off
on . . .
    Our coffee table, I've got to admit, looked mighty good
there. The hands, the elbows, the bellies of the plot all
rubbed against it . . . La Pinaise clutched it so hard you
could hear it crack all the way across the room, but the
worst was when handsome young Dorange, in a very tragic
moment, made as if to sit down on it . . . Mama's heart
jumped in her throat . . . Luckily he bounced up again
. . . almost instantly . . . During the intermission she
kept worrying . . . what if he did it again? . . . My
father understood the whole play . . . But he was too
far gone to talk about it just then.
    It did something to me too. I didn't touch the soft
drinks or even the cookies that the society people passed
around . . . Those socialites are used to mixing grub
with magical emotions . . . They're pigs. It's all one to
them as long as they're chewing. They gulp it all down at
one sitting, the rose and the crap it grows in . . .
    We went back to our seats . . . The second act passed
like a dream . . . Then the miracle was over . . . We
were back again among plain ordinary things and people.
    We waited, all three of us on our stools, we didn't dare
let out a peep . . . We waited patiently for the crowd to
drift out, so we could take our table . . . Then a lady
came in and asked us to wait just a little while . . . We
agreed . . . The curtain went up again. We saw all the
actors, all the people in the play. They were all sitting
around our table . . . all playing cards together. The
Pinaises, the Coulomanches, the Brétontés, the Doranges,
and Kroing, the old banker . . . They all sat there
facing each other . . .
    Kroing was a funny little old man, he often came to my
grandmother's shop on the rue Montorgueil, always very
friendly and polite and completely shriveled up. He used
violet perfume, it stank up the whole shop. He collected
only one thing, it was his only interest in life: Empire bell-
pulls.
    The game on our table started quite amicably. They gave

each other cards as politely as can be. Then things went kind of sour, they began to speak sharply, not at all like in the play . . . They weren't talking for the fun of it anymore. They shouted numbers at each other. The trumps resounded like somebody getting a licking. Behind their father the Dorange girls were squinting something awful. The mothers and wives were left strictly to themselves, sitting with their chairs against the wall, all tensed up and scared to breathe. A command rang out. The players exchanged places. On the table the dough was piling up . . . Heaps and mounds of it . . . Old man Kroing was pounding the tabletop with both hands . . . In front of the Pinaises the pile kept growing and swelling . . . like an animal . . . They were red in the face with excitement . . . With the Brétontés it was the exact opposite . . . They were losing their pazazz . . . They were as pale as ghosts . . . They didn't have a cent left in front of them . . . My father went pale too. I wondered what he was going to do. We'd been waiting at least two hours for the game to end . . . They'd forgotten us . . .

Suddenly the Brétontés stood up . . . They offered to stake . . . their castle in Normandy! They announced it solemnly . . . on three cards! . . . And little Kroing won . . . He didn't seem happy about it . . . Brétonté stood up again . . . "I'm staking the house," he muttered. "The house we live in!"

My mother was thunderstruck . . . She jumped up like a spring. My father couldn't hold her back . . .

She climbed up on the stage with her limp . . . in a voice still shaken with emotion she addressed those big gamblers: "Ladies and gentlemen, we've got to take our little boy home . . . he ought to have been in bed long ago . . . We're going to take our table . . ." Nobody raised any objection. They all acted as if they'd been hit on the head . . . They were staring into the void . . . We picked up our table and whisked it out fast . . . We were afraid they'd call us back . . .

When we got to the Pont Solférino, we stopped a moment for breath . . .

Years later my father was still telling that story . . . with priceless gestures . . . My mother didn't care for it . . . It stirred up too much emotion in her . . . He always pointed out the exact place in the middle of the table where we plain people had seen millions and millions vanish in a few minutes, and all a family's honor and all its castles go up in smoke.

I didn't learn very quickly with Grandma Caroline. Even so, the day came when I could count up to a hundred and read better than she could. I was ready to take up addition. It was time for me to go to school.

They chose the grade school on the rue des Jeûneurs, right near the shop, the dark door on the other side of the Carrefour des Francs-Bourgeois.

You went down a long corridor and there was the class-room. It looked out on a little court, and on the other side there was a wall so high that the blue sky was blotted out. To keep us from looking up, there was also the big tin shed that covered part of the yard. We were expected to concentrate on our lessons and not to bother the teacher. I hardly got to know him, all I remember is his spectacles, his big stick, and his cuffs on the desk.

It was Grandma who took me to school for eight days, on the ninth I fell sick. In the middle of the afternoon the matron brought me home . . .

Once I got to the shop, I couldn't stop puking. Waves of fever ran through me . . . a heat so dense that I thought I had turned into somebody else. It was kind of fun if I only hadn't had to throw up so much. My mother was suspicious at first, she thought I had eaten too much nougat . . . It wasn't my way . . . She begged me to control myself, to make an effort not to vomit so much. The shop was full of people. When she took me to the can, she was afraid somebody'd swipe her lace. I was feeling worse than ever. I threw up a whole basinful. My head began to boil. I couldn't hide my joy . . . All sorts of funny things were going on in my head.

I'd always had a big head, a good deal bigger than other children. I could never wear their berets. Suddenly, as I was puking, my mother remembered this monstrous de-formity of mine . . . She was worried sick.

"Auguste, do you suppose he's coming down with meningitis on us? That would be just our luck . . . it's all we needed . . . That would really be the end! . . ."

I finally stopped vomiting . . . I was baked in heat . . .
I was terribly interested . . . I'd never suspected so much
stuff could fit inside my noodle . . . fantasies . . . weird
sensations. At first everything looked red . . . Like a
cloud all swollen with blood . . . right in the middle of
the sky . . . Then it disintegrated . . . and took the
form of a Lady Customer . . . enormous . . . gigantic
. . . She began to order us about . . . up there in the
sky . . . She was waiting for us . . . hanging in midair
. . . She commanded us to get busy . . . she made signs
. . . to get a move on, the whole lot of us! . . . to clear
out of the Passage p.d.q. . . . Every last one of us . . .
There wasn't a moment to lose!

And then she came down, she came toward us under the
glass roof . . . She filled the whole Passage . . . an
enormous strutting figure . . . She didn't want a single
shopkeeper left in his shop . . . not one of our neighbors
was allowed to stay put . . . Even Madame Méhon came
along. She had grown three hands and four gloves . . . I
could see we were going out for a good time. Words danced
around us like around actors . . . Impassioned cadences,
surprise effects . . . magnificent, irresistible inflections
. . .

The gigantic Lady Customer had stuffed her sleeves full
of our lace . . . She cleared out the showcase . . . right
out in the open . . . She wrapped herself in point lace,
whole mantillas, enough chasubles to cover twenty priests
. . . And amid the frills and finery she grew and
grew . . .

All the little good-for-nothings in the Passage . . . the
umbrella vendors . . . Visios of the tobacco pouches
. . . the girls from the pastry shop . . . they were waiting . . . The tragic and glamorous Madame Cortilène
was there beside us . . . her revolver slung on a strap
. . . It was full of perfume and she was spraying the whole
place . . . Madame Gounouyou with the veils, the one
who'd been shut up indoors for years on account of her
runny eyes, and the caretaker in his cocked hat . . . they
were all in a huddle as though getting ready for some
shindig, all in their Sunday best, and even little Gaston, one
of the bookbinder's kids that had died, he had come back
for the occasion . . . his mother was just nursing him.

He was sitting on her lap good as gold, waiting to be taken for a walk. She was holding his hoop for him.

Old Aunt Armide drove in from the cemetery in Thiais; she drew up in a brougham at the end of the Passage. She had just come for the drive . . . She had grown so old since the previous winter that she had no face at all, only a lump of soft dough in its place . . . I recognized her anyway by the smell . . . She gave my mama her arm. My father Auguste was all ready, slightly ahead of time as usual. His watch hung from his neck, as big as an alarm clock. His rig was something very special, morning coat, straw hat, hard rubber bicycle, cock in evidence, stockings molded by his calves. All spiffed up like that, with a flower in his buttonhole, he got on my nerves worse than ever. My poor mother, overcome with embarrassment, returned his compliments . . . Madame Méhon, the old battle-ax, was carrying Tom balanced on her hat in among the feathers . . . She made him bite everybody who came by.

As we trooped along behind the enormous Customer, there got to be more and more of us. We pushed and jostled in her wake . . . And the Lady kept growing . . . If she hadn't bent down, she'd have gone through the glass roof . . . As we were passing by, the printer . . . death notices and visiting cards . . . popped out of his cellar, pushing a baby carriage with his two brats in it . . . there wasn't much life in them either . . . All bundled up in paper money . . . Nothing but hundred-franc notes . . . all counterfeit . . . so that was his racket . . . The music dealer from 34, who owned a phonograph, six mandolins, three sets of bagpipes, and a piano, refused to leave anything behind . . . He wanted us to take the whole lot with us . . . We harnessed ourselves to his showcase, and the whole thing collapsed under the strain. There was a terrible crash.

An orchestra of brilliant soloists pours from the stage door of the Plush Barn, the café-concert across from 96 . . . They get together a long way from the giantess . . . they blare out three terrific chords . . . violins, bagpipes, and harps . . . the trombones and double basses blow and scrape so loud and lovely that we all howl with delight . . .

Slender, trim usherettes with fragile little caps are

bouncing all around us . . . They fly through the air and
land in the tangerines . . . At 48 the three elderly sisters,
who hadn't set foot outside their shop in fifty-two years,
who are always so courteous, so patient with their customers, suddenly start driving out the clientele with big
sticks . . . Two old bags conk out on their sidewalk,
disembowelled . . . The three old ladies tie footwarmers
on their asses to make them run faster . . . Objects rain
in all directions from the gigantic Customer . . . stolen
knickknacks. They drip from every fold in her clothing
. . . Her accessories keep falling off and she keeps picking them up . . . Outside César's jewelry shop she repairs
her dress and wraps herself in chains and pearls, all phony
. . . Everybody laughs . . . She takes a whole salad
bowl full of amethysts and throws them by the fistful
through the skylight . . . We all turn violet. She bombards the glass roof with topazes from the next tray . . .
We all turn yellow . . . We were almost at the end of the
Passage. There's an enormous crowd ahead of our procession and a howling mob behind us . . . The woman from
the stationery store at 86—I had swiped some pencils
from her—fastened on to my pants . . . And the widow
with the antique cupboards went for my dick . . . It was
no fun . . . It was the umbrella man that saved me, he
hid me under his parasol.

If Aunt Armide had found me again, I'd have had to
kiss her right in the headcheese . . .

This time Uncle Édouard and his three-wheeler were
chasing my father . . . he had his nose so close to the
road that it almost bent his bicycle. A big pebble lodged
in one of his nostrils. The engine cooed as softly as a
lovesick pigeon, but Uncle Édouard had his eyes attached
to two strings and was dragging them smack over the
road for fear of missing something . . . On the front
seat Aunt Armide, wedged in among the cushions, was
passing the time of day with a gentleman all in black.
He was hugging a thermometer three times as big as
me . . . That was the doctor from the Hespérides, who
had come for a consultation . . . He was filled with con-
sternation . . . Thousands of luminous particles darted
from his face . . . At the sight the neighbors took off
their hats and bowed down to the ground. And then they

showed their backsides . . . He spat on them. He didn't
have time to stop. We stormed the entrance all together
. . . We invaded the Boulevards . . .

As we were crossing the Place Vendôme, a fierce gust
of wind inflated the Customer. At the Opéra she swelled
up twice as big . . . a hundred times! . . . All the
neighbors scurried under her skirts like mice . . . No
sooner were they settled than they dashed out again in a
panic . . . then they rushed back again to hide in the
caverns . . . The confusion was awful.

The little dogs from the Passage ran squirting in all
directions, doing their business, going for people's asses,
nipping ferociously. Madame Juvienne, Number 72,
toiletries, expired before our eyes, under a mountain
of mauve flowers, jasmine . . . from suffocation . . .
Three passing elephants trampled her slowly to death, a
thousand little rivulets of perfume came pouring out . . .

Four little baker's apprentices who worked for Largen-
teuil, the pastrycook, came running up . . . carrying the
enormous pipe from the Mohammed Tobacco advertise-
ment that lit up at six o'clock . . . They smashed the
bowl against the Marché Saint-Honoré, trying to move the
buildings out of the way . . . First they bashed in the
one on the right—POULTRY—and then the one on the
left—FISH.

But we had to keep going—especially the giantess. Our
giantess . . . with two planets for tits . . . I was being
knocked around pretty bad . . . my father tried to hold
me up but it was no use . . . He got caught in the spokes
of his bike . . . He bit Tom's tail. He trotted along ahead
of us barking, but no sound came out . . .

The caretaker put me back on my feet, all he had on
was the top of his uniform . . . The lower end of him
was thin air . . . We got a good laugh out of him with
his long pole for lighting the gas with . . . He stuck it
up his nose, every inch of it.

As we were crossing the rue de Rivoli, the Customer
missed her step, she tripped over a bus stop shelter and
smashed a building . . . the elevator squirted out and
gored her eye . . . We passed over the ruins. On the rue
des Jeûneurs, my little friend Émile Sarsaparilla, popped
out of my school . . . a hunchback . . . that's how I'd

always known him . . . and green around the gills, with
a big wine-colored smudge running out of his ears . . .
Now he didn't look bad at all. He was handsome, pink,
and natty . . . I was glad for his sake.

Now all those people we had known were running in
the caverns underneath the Lady, in her drawers, through
whole streets and neighborhoods, compressed inside her
petticoats . . . They went where she chose. We were
squeezed tighter than ever. My mother held me by the
hand . . . Faster and faster . . . At the Place de la
Concorde I realized she was taking us to the Exposition
. . . It was mighty kind of her . . . She wanted us to
have fun . . .

The Lady, our Customer, had all the money, all the
shopkeepers' cash, stashed away on her . . . She was
going to treat us . . . It was getting hotter and hotter, and
we were still wedged against the Lady . . . In among the
drapery, next to the lining, I saw thousands of things hanging. All the stolen goods in the world . . . As we galloped, the little "Byzantine" looking-glass, the one we'd
been looking for for months on the rue de Montorgueil,
fell on my head . . . it left a bump . . . If I'd been able
to, I'd have sung out that it was found, but we were already so penned in I'd never have been able to pick it
up . . .

The time had come, we all realized, to squeeze a little
tighter. We were shoved into the gate, the monumental
gate, the arrogant gate, that rose into the sky like the bun
on a lady's hair . . . Going in like that without paying,
we were all scared shitless . . . Luckily we were swept
in by the swish of petticoats . . . We were crushed, suffocating, crawling on our bellies . . . Up above, our
Customer bent down when it came time to go through.
Was it all over? Were we under the Seine? Would the
sharks be coming to ask us for a penny? What do you
think? When do you ever get admitted to anything for
free? . . . it just doesn't happen . . . I let out a yell
so sharp, so piercing that the giantess lost her head. All
of a sudden she picked up her skirts, every single frill and
ruffle . . . and her drawers . . . and lifted them sky-
high, way over her head . . . A tempest rushed in, a wind
so glacial we screamed for pain . . . There we were on

the quai, frozen stiff, abandoned, shivering, helpless. Down below, between the embankment and the three barges, the Customer had flown away! . . . Our neighbors from the Passage turned so white I couldn't recognize a single one of them . . . The giantess had fooled us all with her magnificent thefts . . . There wasn't any more Exposition . . . it had been over long ago . . . Already we could hear the howling of the wolves on the Cours de la Reine . . .

It was time to get going . . . But we couldn't run right . . . A lot of feet were missing . . . Small as I was, I ran Madame Méhon over . . .

My mother lifted her skirts . . . But she ran more and more slowly . . . on account of her calves . . . suddenly they were as thin as wire . . . and so hairy they got tangled up in each other like spiders . . . The people up ahead wound her into a ball . . . and let her roll . . . But the buses were coming . . . at fiendish speed . . . They thundered down the rue Royale . . . blue ones, green ones, lemon-colored ones . . . The shafts broke, the harnesses gushed out across the Esplanade and fell against the trees in the Tuileries. I sized the situation up at a glance . . . I harangued . . . I exhorted . . . I rallied my troops . . . I laid down my plan of attack . . . We try to back up on the sidewalk outside the Orangerie . . . But it's hopeless. Almost instantly poor Uncle Édouard and his motorcar are run over at the foot of the statue of Bordeaux * . . . A few minutes later he comes out of the Solférino métro station with his three-wheeled tub welded on to his rear end like a snail . . . We lead him away . . . He has to hurry, to crawl faster and faster on account of the hundreds of motorcars . . . Reine-Serpollets from the automobile show. They bombard the Arc de Triomphe. Hell-bent for the cemetery, they descend on our routed army. . . .

For a split second I caught sight of Rodolphe, leaning against the pedestal of the statue of Joan of Arc, smiling happily . . . He's auctioning off his troubadour costume . . . He wants to be a general . . . This is no time to disturb him . . . The asphalt is all ripped up . . . A chasm opens . . . Everything falls in . . . I skirt the

* See Glossary.

precipice . . . I catch Armide's pocketbook just as it's
about to disappear . . . There's an inscription on it in
beads: "In fond remembrance" . . . Her glass eye is inside . . . We're so surprised we all laugh like hell . . .
But the avalanche of punks is coming on from all sides
. . . This time there are so many of them the rue Thérèse
is full up to the fourth floor . . . a hill of packed meat
. . . we start climbing . . . It buzzes like a manure pile
all the way up to the stars . . .

But to get back home we have to bend back four thoroughly padlocked iron gates . . . We push by the hundreds and thousands . . . We try to get in through the
transom . . . Nothing doing . . . the bars bend but
jump right back into place, they snap in our faces like rubber bands . . . A ghost has hidden our key . . . He
wants a prick and won't settle for anything else . . . We
tell him to go to hell. "Fuck you," he says. We call him
back. There are ten thousand of us trying to argue with
him.

Echoing down the rue Gomboust, a hundred thousand
cries of disaster come to us in bursts . . . That's the
crowds that are being massacred off the Place Gaillon
. . . the buses are still raging . . . the apocalypse goes
on . . . the Clichy-Odéon plows through the desperate
mob . . . the Panthéon-Courcelles storms in from the
rear, sending the pieces sky-high . . . they rain down on
our shopwindow. My father beside me moans: "If only
I had a trumpet!" . . . In despair he sheds his clothes,
in a second he's mother-naked, climbing up the Bank
of France . . . he's perched on top of the clock . . . He
rips off the minute hand and brings it down with him . . .
he dandles it on his knees . . . It fascinates him . . . it
gives him a kick . . . we're all feeling pretty gay . . .
But a detachment of Guards bursts in through the rue
Méhul . . . the Madeleine-Bastille goes into a spin, tips,
and crashes into our gate . . . Luckily the whole thing
collapses. The axle catches fire, the van bursts into crackling flames . . . The conductor is whipping the driver
. . . They're coming faster and faster . . . They take the
rue des Moulins, they climb the grade, they take the fire
with them . . . a hurricane . . . The cyclone strikes,
weakens, rises up again, and breaks against the Comédie

Française . . . The whole building bursts into flame . . .
the roof comes loose, rises, flies away in flames . . . In
her dressing room La Screwball, the beautiful actress, is
frantically poring over her lines . . . Her soul has to be
saturated with poetry before she can appear on the stage.
She gargles her crack so hard that she stumbles . . . she
falls plunk into the fire . . . She lets out a terrible scream
. . . The volcano has swallowed up everything . . .
    Nothing is left in the world but our fire . . . we're all
cooking in it . . . A ghastly redness rumbles through my
brain with a crowbar that dislodges everything . . . blinding me with terror . . . It gobbles up the inside of my
bean like fiery soup . . . using the bar for a spoon . . .
It will never go away . . .

    It took me a long time to recover. My convalescence
dragged on for another two months. I had been very
sick . . . it ended with a rash . . . The doctor came
often. In the end he insisted they send me to the country
. . . That was easy to say, but we hadn't the cash . . .
They took me out in the fresh air whenever possible.
    When the January quarter came due, Grandma Caroline
went out to Asnières to collect the rent. She took me with
her. She owned two brick and stucco houses out there on
the rue de Plaisance, a little one and a medium-size one,
she rented them out to working-class people. They were
her property, her income, her savings.
    We started off. We had to go slow on my account.
I was weak for a long time, I'd get nosebleeds for no reason at all, and I peeled all over. After the station it's
straight ahead . . . Avenue Faidherbe . . . Place Car-
not . . . At the Town Hall you turn left and then you
cross the park.
    At the bowling alley between the fence and the water-
fall, there's always a crowd of funny old codgers . . .
lively old grampas full of spunk, always good for a joke,
and some that grouse the whole time, retired shopkeepers
. . . Every time they knocked the ninepins over, the jokes
flew thick and fast . . . I understood all their gags . . .
better and better as time went on . . . The funniest thing
was when they had to pee . . . they'd trot behind a tree,
one at a time . . . They had an awful hard time of it

. . . "Hey, Toto, watch out you don't lose it . . ." That's
the kind of thing they said. The others took up the refrain.
To me they were irresistible. I laughed so loud my grandmother was embarrassed . . . Standing around in that
wintry blast listening to their cracks . . . it was a good
way to catch your death . . .

Grandma didn't laugh much but she wanted me to enjoy
myself . . . It was no joke at home . . . she realized
that . . . and this was cheap entertainment . . . We
stayed a little while longer . . . When the game was over
and we finally left the little old-timers, it was almost
dark . . .

Caroline's houses were beyond Les Bourguignons . . .
after the Market Gardens, which in those days extended
all the way to the dikes at Achères.

So as not to sink into the muck and manure, we had to
walk single file on a line of planks . . . You had to be
careful not to bump into the frames . . . whole rows of
them full of seedlings . . . I went behind her, still laughing but careful to keep my balance, remembering all those
cracks . . . "Did you enjoy it all that much?" she asked.
"Tell me, Ferdinand. Did you really?"

I didn't care for questions. I shut up like a clam . . .
To own up brings bad luck.

We got to the rue de la Plaisance. That's where the
work began. Collecting the rent was a headache . . . the
tenants were in full revolt. They fought every inch of the
way and they never paid in full . . . never . . . they
tried every slimy trick . . . The pump was always out
of order. The discussions were interminable . . . They
started griping about everything under the sun before
Grandma even opened her mouth . . . The shithouse
was stuffed up . . . They were very dissatisfied . . .
they shouted their complaints from every window in the
place . . . they wanted it fixed . . . and right away!
. . . They were afraid we'd put one over on them . . .
They hollered to prevent us from mentioning the rent
. . . They wouldn't even look at the bills . . . Their
shithouse was really stopped up, it was overflowing into
the street . . . In winter it froze and the bowl cracked
under the slightest pressure . . . Every time it cost eighty
francs . . . The bastards wrecked everything in sight

. . . That was the tenants' way of getting even . . . And making children . . . Every time we came back there were new ones . . . with less and less clothes on . . . Some of them were stark-naked . . . Lying in the bottom of a cupboard . . .

The worst drunks and slovens treated us like dirt . . . They watched every move we made as we unplugged the drain. They followed us to the cellar when we went down for the bamboo pole to clean out the siphon . . . Grandma pinned up her skirts with safety pins and stripped to her shift on top. Then we went to work . . . We needed lots of hot water. We had to get it from the shoemaker across the street and bring it over in a pitcher. The tenants wouldn't give us a drop. Then Caroline started poking down into the drain. She worked her pole back and forth and dislodged the muck. The pole alone wouldn't do it. She plunged in with both arms, the tenants all came out with their brats to watch us cleaning out their shit . . . and the papers . . . and the rags . . . They'd wad them up on purpose . . . Caroline was undaunted . . . what a woman! Nothing could get her down . . .

She fought her way through. The tenants saw the drain was working again. They couldn't help admiring her energy . . . not to be outdone, they began to help us . . . They brought out wine . . . Grandma clinked glasses with them . . . she wasn't one to bear grudges . . . We wished each other Happy New Year . . . it was all very cordial and friendly . . . That didn't bring in any money . . . They were unscrupulous . . . If she'd given them notice, they'd have had time for vengeance before moving out . . . They'd have wrecked the whole joint . . . Both houses were full of holes . . . Every time we went out there we tried to fill them in . . . it was a waste of time . . . they kept making more . . . We took putty with us . . . Pipes, attics, walls, and floors were all shreds and patches . . . But what they attacked most viciously was the toilet bowl . . . The whole thing was full of cracks . . . It made Grandma cry to look at it . . . Same with the garden gate . . . They'd bent it double . . . it looked like licorice . . . For a while we'd given them a concierge, a friendly, obliging old woman . . . she hadn't lasted a week . . . She was so horrified she cleared out.

In less than a week two of the tenants had gone up to strangle her . . . in her bed . . . some nonsense about doormats.

Those houses are still there. Only the name of the street has changed . . . from "Plaisance" to "Marne" . . . That was the fashion for a while . . .

Lots of tenants have come and gone, bachelors and spinsters, whole families, generations . . . They've gone on making holes, and so have the rats, the little mice, the crickets and woodlice . . . No one has plugged them in ages . . . Uncle Édouard inherited the houses. They've taken so much punishment they've got to be regular sieves . . . no one paid his rent anymore . . . the tenants had grown old, they were tired of arguing . . . so was my uncle . . . they were even sick of fighting about the shithouse . . . there was nothing more to wreck, there was nothing left. They turned them into storerooms. They put in their wheelbarrows, their watering cans and coal . . . At the moment we don't even know exactly who's living there . . . they've been condemned to widen the street . . . they're going to be torn down . . . As far as we know, there are four families . . . Portuguese, so they say.

Nobody's bothered to try to keep them up . . . Grandma knocked herself out, it didn't do her any good . . . when you come right down to it, that's what killed her . . . messing around that day in January even later than usual, first in cold water, then in boiling water . . . always in the draft, putting oakum in the pump and thawing out the faucets.

The tenants came out with their candles to needle us and see if the work was getting ahead. The rent? Well, they wanted a little more time. We should come around next week . . . We started back to the station.

At the ticket window Grandma Caroline had a dizzy spell. She clutched the railing . . . it wasn't like her . . . She had chills all over . . . We went back across the square to a café . . . While we were waiting for the train, the two of us shared a grog . . . When we got to Gare Saint-Lazare, she went straight home to bed . . . she was all in . . . she came down with a high fever, same as I'd had in the Passage, but hers was grippe and it turned to

pneumonia . . . The doctor came morning and evening
. . . She was so sick that we in the Passage didn't know
what to tell the neighbors when they asked.

Uncle Édouard shuttled back and forth between her
place and the shop . . . She was worse than ever . . .
She was sick of having her temperature taken, she didn't
even want us to know what it was . . . She still had all
her wits about her. Tom hid under the furniture. He didn't
budge, he hardly ate . . . My uncle came to the shop.
He had a great big balloon full of oxygen.

One night my mother didn't even come home for supper . . . Next morning it was still dark when Uncle
Édouard shook me in my bed and told me to get dressed
quick. To go and kiss Grandma, he explained . . . I
didn't know exactly what he meant . . . I was still half
asleep . . . We walked fast . . . It was on the rue du
Rocher . . . second floor . . . The concierge hadn't
been to bed . . . She came out with a lamp to light the
hallway . . . We went upstairs. Mama was in the first
room crying, . . . down on her knees, slumped against a
chair. She was moaning softly, mumbling in her grief . . .
Papa was standing . . . he didn't say a word . . . He went
out to the landing . . . then he came back again . . .
He looked at his watch . . . He tugged at his moustache
. . . Then I caught a glimpse of Grandma in her bed in
the next room . . . She was breathing hard, gasping, suffocating, making a disgusting racket . . . The doctor was
just leaving . . . He shook hands with everybody . . .
Then they led me in. I could see she was fighting for breath.
She was all yellow and red, her face was covered with
sweat, like a wax mask beginning to melt . . . Grandma
stared at me, but her look was still friendly . . . They
had told me to kiss her . . . I was already leaning against
the bed. She motioned me not to . . . She smiled a little
. . . She wanted to tell me something . . . There was
a rasping sound in her throat . . . it wouldn't come out
. . . in the end she made it . . . she spoke as softly as
she could . . . "Work hard, my dear little Ferdinand,"
she whispered . . . I wasn't afraid of her. We understood
each other deep down . . . The fact is that I have worked
hard, all in all . . . That's nobody's business . . .

She wanted to say something to my mother too. "Clé-

mence, my little girl . . . take care . . . don't let yourself go . . . please, for my sake . . ." That was all she
could manage. She couldn't breathe at all . . . She motioned us to leave . . . to go into the other room . . .
We obeyed . . . We could hear her . . . The whole
apartment was full of it . . . We stayed there at least an
hour, stunned and silent. My uncle went to the door. He
wanted to see her, but he didn't dare disobey. He only
pushed open one of the double doors, that way we could
hear her more distinctly . . . There was a kind of hiccup
. . . My mother jumped up . . . She went *eek,* as if her
throat were being cut. She crumpled up in a heap on the
carpet between her chair and my uncle . . . Her hand
was clenched so tight over her mouth that we couldn't take
it away . . .

When she came to, she screamed: "Mama's dead" . . .
over and over . . . she didn't know where she was . . .
My uncle stayed on to keep watch . . . We went back to
the Passage in a cab . . .

We closed the shop. We rolled down all the blinds . . .
We felt kind of ashamed . . . kind of guilty . . . We
didn't dare to move . . . for fear of spoiling our grief
. . . Mama and all of us cried with our heads on the
table . . . We weren't hungry . . . We didn't want anything . . . We didn't take up much room, but we'd have
liked to make ourselves even smaller . . . to apologize
to somebody, to everybody . . . We forgave each other
. . . We begged and promised to love each other . . .
We were afraid of losing each other . . . forever . . .
like Caroline.

Then came the funeral . . . Uncle Édouard attended
to everything all by himself . . . he had made all the
arrangements . . . He had his grief too . . . He didn't
show it . . . He wasn't demonstrative . . . He called
for us at the Passage just as they were taking away the
body . . .

Everybody . . . neighbors . . . and people with nothing else to do . . . came over and said: "Be brave." We
stopped on the rue Deaudeville to pick up our flowers . . .
We took the best . . . Nothing but roses . . . They
were her favorite flower . . .

We couldn't get used to her absence. Even my father was shattered . . . There was nobody but me to have scenes with . . . I was getting better but I was still so weak it was no fun to pick on me. Seeing me so wobbly, he hesitated to bellow at me . . .

I dragged myself from one chair to another . . . I had lost six pounds in two months . . . I was wasting away. I puked up all the cod-liver oil . . .

My mother couldn't think of anything but her grief. The shop was sinking beyond rescue . . . Even at rock-bottom prices we couldn't sell our trinkets . . . The customers were all stone broke . . . they were making up for their wild extravagance at the Exposition . . . They had as little mending done as possible. They thought twice before spending five francs . . .

My mother would sit there for hours without moving, on her bad leg, in an impossible position, benumbed . . . When she got up, it hurt so bad that she'd limp the whole time . . . My father would pace about upstairs in the opposite direction. The sound of her limp drove him nuts . . .

I'd pretend I had to do something. I'd go to the can and play with myself . . . I'd give it a tug or two . . . I couldn't get it up . . .

Aside from the two houses that had gone to Uncle Édouard, there were three thousand francs left from Grandma's estate . . . But that money was sacred . . . Mama said so right away . . . We must never part with it . . . We unloaded the earrings, they went for loans, one in Clichy, the other in Asnières . . . And yet our stock was getting sleazier and skimpier . . . enough to break your heart . . . it was hardly fit to show . . .

Grandma at least had been enterprising, she'd bring us stuff to sell on consignment . . . white elephants that other dealers were willing to lend her . . . But with us it wasn't the same . . . They were suspicious . . . no get-up-and-go, that's what they thought of us . . . We were going to the dogs . . .

When my father came home from the office, he'd dream up solutions . . . some pretty grim ones . . . it was he who cooked our bread soup . . . Mama wasn't up to it . . . he'd be stringing the beans . . . why wouldn't we turn on the gas and all commit suicide? . . . My mother just sat there . . . He blamed it all on the Freemasons . . . and Dreyfus! . . . and all the other criminals who were out to get us.

My mother was off her rocker . . . even her movements were weird . . . She'd always been clumsy, now she dropped everything. She'd break three dishes a day . . . She never came out of her daze . . . She was like a sleepwalker . . . If she went into the shop she'd be afraid . . . She didn't want to move, she'd stay upstairs the whole time . . .

One night when we were going to bed and not expecting anybody anymore, Madame Héronde turned up. She began to hammer at the shop door and sing out . . . We'd forgotten all about her. I went to open. My mother didn't want to be bothered, she even refused to see her . . . She just went hobbling around the kitchen. So then my father spoke up:

"How about it, Clémence? Make up your mind. If you leave it to me, I'll just send her home, you know that." She thought it over a minute, then she went down. She tried to count the pieces Madame Héronde had brought back . . . She couldn't count right . . . She was all muddled with grief . . . ideas, figures, it was all a fog . . . Papa and I helped her . . .

Then she went up to bed . . . Later she got up and came down again . . . She spent the whole night straightening out the shop, furiously, obstinately putting the stuff away.

In the morning everything was in perfect order . . . She was a different woman . . . You wouldn't have recognized her . . . All of a sudden she felt ashamed . . .

What a terrible humiliation to have let Madame Héronde see her so frazzled!

"When I think of my poor Caroline! . . . of the energy she had up to the last minute. Ah, what if she'd seen me like that!"

Suddenly she bucked up. During the night she had even made all sorts of plans . . . "Well, Ferdinand, son, if the customers won't come to us anymore, we'll go find them! . . . spring is coming, we'll close the shop for a while . . . We'll do all the markets in the suburbs . . . Chatou! . . . Le Vésinet! . . . Bougival! . . . where they're putting up all those fine villas . . . where all the fancy people live . . . That will be better than stewing in our own juice . . . than hanging around here waiting for nothing! . . . Besides you'll get some fresh air!"

The idea of doing the markets didn't appeal to my father one bit! . . . A risky business . . . It panicked him to think about it . . . He foresaw the worst complications . . . We were sure to get our last remnant of merchandise stolen! . . . We'd be stoned by the local shopkeepers . . . Mama let him talk . . . She'd made up her mind.

Anyway, we had no choice. We were skipping every other meal . . . We'd taken to lighting the stove with tapers instead of matches.

One morning the time came and we raced off to the station. My father carried the big bundle, an enormous piece of canvas stuffed with merchandise . . . Everything we had left that wasn't too disgusting . . . Mama and I lugged the cartons . . . On the platform at Saint-Lazare he ran through the list of his fears again. Then he beat it to the office.

In those days Chatou was quite a trip. We were there at the crack of dawn . . . We bribed the local cop . . . he rolled out the red carpet and found us a place . . . We found a stand for our stuff . . . We had a pretty good spot . . . between a butcher and a man selling little birds. But they didn't want us there . . . that was plain from the start.

The butter-and-egg man behind us kept griping the whole time. For his money we were screwballs with piles of rubbish. He made some very crummy remarks!

The alley we were in wasn't the best place, but it was near the park . . . in the shade of magnificent linden trees . . . About noontime the ladies appeared . . . simpering and my-dearing . . . If a wind started up, we were lost. At the first breeze all our stuff blows away, all the bonnets and hankies and ribbons . . . Those things are just waiting to take off, they're as light as clouds . . . We fastened them with mountains of clasps and clothespins. Our stand looked like a hedgehog . . . The

ladies strolled by . . . capricious creatures . . . butterflies followed by one or two cooks . . . then they'd turn
and come back . . . my mother tried to catch them with
her spiel . . . to draw their attention to her embroideries
. . . to the boleros she was taking orders for . . . to her
"Brussels type" lace . . . or Madame Héronde's gossamer
marvels . . .

"Isn't it amusing to meet you here! . . . In this drafty
market! . . . Oh, you have a shop? . . . Do give me
your card! . . . Of course we'll come to see you!"

They went on to gush somewhere else, we didn't sell
them much . . . Well, it was publicity . . .

Now and then a tornado would pick up our doodads
and drop them on the veal cutlets next door . . . The
butcher gave us a piece of his mind . . .

We'd have made out better if we'd brought along our
handsome dressmaker's dummy with the firm bust . . .
that would have brought out our exquisite treasures . . .
the muslin and satin frills, the creations of Madame
Héronde's fairy wand . . . To maintain a Louis XV
flavor, an atmosphere of refinement, amid the tripe and
vegetables, we'd haul out a real museum piece, a dimin-
utive masterpiece, the rosewood doll's cupboard . . . We
kept our sandwiches in it.

Our dread, maybe even worse than the wind, was
showers . . . All our finery turned to pancakes . . . The
ochre ran out in rivers . . . the sidewalk was all sticky
with it . . . The stuff felt like a lot of sponges . . . The
trip home was awful. We never complained in my father's
hearing.

The following week it was Enghien and certain Thurs-
days Clignancourt . . . the Porte . . . We were right
next to the Flea Market . . . I liked the markets all
right . . . they made me miss school. The fresh air pepped
me up . . . When we saw my father in the evening, he
gave me a pain in the neck . . . He was never satisfied
. . . He met us at the station . . . I felt like dropping the
little cupboard on his dogs to make him jump.

At Clignancourt it was an entirely different clientele
. . . We'd only lay out our junk, our worst crap, the
stuff that had been in the cellar for years. We let it go for
beans . . .

It was at the Flea Market that I met little Paulo. He worked for a woman two rows behind us. He sold buttons up and down the avenue, near the Porte, or he'd stroll around the market with his tray on his belly, held up by a string around his neck. "Thirteen for two sous, ladies . . ." He was younger than me but awfully smart . . . We made friends right away . . . What I admired about Popaul was that he didn't wear shoes, just boards tied on with tapes . . . They didn't hurt his feet . . . So I took off mine too when we went out on expeditions together on the fortifications.

He sold his buttons quick, in baker's dozens, bone and mother-of-pearl, you didn't have time to look . . . After that we were free.

In addition he had a little racket. "It's easy," he explained as soon as we had no secrets from each other. In Bastion 18 or in the streetcar shelters near La Villette, he'd make little dates with soldiers and butchers and soften them up. He asked me to come and meet them. I couldn't, because it was too late when he did those things . . . You could make five francs, sometimes more.

Behind the weighing house he showed me, I didn't ask him to, the way grown-ups sucked him off. Popaul was lucky, he had juice, I didn't have any yet. One time he made fifteen francs in a single evening.

I had to lie to get away, I said I was going for French fries. My mother knew Popaul well, she couldn't abide him even at a distance and she forbade me to go with him. We went just the same, we'd go wandering around as far as Gonesse. I found him irresistible . . . Every time he got a little scared, he had a tick, he'd suck in his tongue, and suck and suck, it made him look awful. In the end, from seeing so much of him, I began to do it too.

Popaul's boss, the one that sold the drygoods, had a funny little jacket she put on him; it was very special, like a blazer, all covered with buttons, big ones and little ones, thousands of them, in front, in back, a whole sample case, mother-of-pearl, steel, and bone . . .

Popaul's idea of heaven was absinthe; his boss poured him a little aperitif whenever he came back sold out. It made him spunky. He smoked army tobacco, we made

our own cigarettes out of newspaper . . . he didn't mind
sucking people, he had a dirty mind. Every man we passed,
we'd bet how big it was. My mother couldn't leave her
stand, especially in that kind of neighborhood. I'd slip
away more and more . . . And then here's what happened:

I'd thought Popaul was a regular guy, loyal and faithful.
I was mistaken. He behaved like a queer. Why not face it?
He was always talking about an arquebus. I didn't know
exactly what he meant. So one day he brings it over. It
was a big rubber band on a forked stick, a kind of slingshot, for shooting sparrows. "Let's practice," he says.
"Then we'll smash a window! . . . There's an easy one
on the avenue . . . After that we'll try a cop! . . ." OK,
it seemed like a good idea. We go off by the school . . .
"We'll start here," he says. School was just out and it was
handy for a getaway. He passes me his beanshooter . . .
I put in a big stone. I pull it way back . . . as far as the
rubber will go . . . "Take a gander up there!" I say to
Popaul. And ping! . . . crash! . . . right square in the
clock! . . . the whole thing flies into smithereens . . . I
stand there frozen like an asshole The racket and the dial
going to pieces like that . . . I'm flabbergasted. People
come running . . . I'm screwed . . . cornered like a rat
. . . They all start tugging at my ears. "Popaul!" I holler
. . . He's melted into thin air . . . He's gone! . . .
They drag me off to my mother. They raise hell with her.
She'd better pay for the breakage . . . or they'll take me
off to jail. She gives her name, her address . . . I try to
explain: "Popaul!". . . The slaps rain down so thick
and fast I can't see straight . . .

At home it starts up all over again, a tempest . . . My
father beats the hell out of me, kicks me in the ribs, steps
on me, takes my pants down. In addition he keeps bellowing that I'm killing him! . . . that I ought to be in jail!
that I should have been there from the start! . . . My
mother pleads, clings to him, falls at his feet, and screams
that in prison "they get even worse." I was the lowest of
the low. I was a gallowsbird. That's what I'd come to!
. . . Popaul had a good deal to do with it, but there was
the fresh air too and the freedom . . . I won't try to
justify myself.

We spent a whole week like that, absolutely frantic. Papa was so mad, he got so red in the face, we were afraid he'd have an attack. Uncle Édouard came in from Romainville just to reason with him. Uncle Arthur didn't have enough influence, he was too frivolous. Rodolphe was far away, touring the provinces with the Capitol Circus.

Our neighbors and relations, everybody in the Passage, thought the best thing would be to give me a good physic and my father too, it would be good for both of us. They racked their brains and finally decided it was worms that made me so wicked . . . They gave me some substance . . . I shat yellow, I shat brown. It sort of calmed me down. It affected my father too . . . he was struck dumb for at least three weeks. All he did was give me a long suspicious look now and then . . . from a distance. I was still his bane, his cross. We took another physic, each of us had his own. He took Rochelle Salts, me castor oil, she took rhubarb. Then they decided that we wouldn't do the markets anymore, that gadding about would be my downfall. I made everything impossible with my criminal instincts.

My mother took me back to school, giving me lots of advice on the way. She was in a terrible state when we got to the rue des Jeûneurs. Everybody had warned her they wouldn't keep me a week . . . But I played it safe, they didn't throw me out. But I have to admit that I didn't learn anything. School made me miserable, the teacher with his goatee, always bleating his problems. It gave me the creeps just to look at him. After all the fun I'd had with Popaul it made me sick to sit still for hours on end listening to a lot of tripe.

The kids tried to have a little fun in the yard, but it was pitiful, the wall in front was so high it crushed you, it killed their desire to play. They went back in to struggle for good conduct tokens . . . Hell!

In the yard there was only one tree with one branch and one bird. The kids got it with a slingshot. The cat spent a whole recreation period eating it. My marks were average. I was afraid of being put back. I was even commended for good behavior. We all had shitty asses. I taught them how to keep their pee in little bottles.

In the shop the jeremiads got worse and worse. My
mother kept mulling over her sorrow. She thought of her
mother on every possible occasion, she remembered the
slightest details . . . If somebody came in at closing time
to sell some knickknack, she'd burst into tears . . . "If
only my mother were here," she'd blubber, "she knew
just what to buy . . ." Those remarks were disastrous . . .
We had an old friend who knew exactly how to take
advantage of Mama's melancholy . . . Her name was
Madame Divonne, she was almost as ancient as Aunt
Armide. After the war of 1870 she and her husband had
made a fortune selling lambskin gloves in the Passage des
Panoramas. The shop was famous and they had another
one in the Passage du Saumon. At one time they had
eighteen people working for them. "All day long there are
customers pouring in and out," Grandma used to say.
Handling so much dough had gone to her husband's head.
One fine day he lost everything and then some in the
Panama Canal. Men have no guts . . . instead of fighting
it out, he ran off with a skirt. They'd sold everything at a
loss. After that she was down and out. Madame Divonne
lived on this one and that one. Her only solace was music.
She had a little something left, but so little that she barely
got enough to eat and not every day at that. She sponged
on her friends. She had married her glove man for love.
She wasn't a tradeswoman by birth, her father had been a
prefect under the Empire. She played the piano beautifully.
She never took off her fingerless gloves because her hands
were so delicate, and in the winter she wore thick mittens,
but of openwork and decorated with pink pompons. She
was always careful about her appearance.

She turned up at the shop . . . she hadn't been to see
us in a long time. Grandma's death had moved her deeply.
She couldn't get over it. "So young!" she'd say at the end
of every sentence. She spoke with delicacy of Caroline,
of their past, their husbands, of the Passage du Saumon
and the Boulevards . . . with fine shadings and exquisite
tact . . . She really had nice manners, I could see that
. . . As she reminisced, everything turned into a fragile
dream. She didn't take off her veil or her hat . . . on
account of her complexion, she said. The real reason was
her wig. We never had much on hand for dinner . . .

We'd invite her all the same . . . But when she'd finished
her soup, she'd take off her veil and her hat and the whole
works . . . she'd pick up her soup plate and drink it
down . . . That seemed the handiest way . . . on account of her false teeth, I guess. You could hear her
wiggling them . . . She distrusted spoons. She was crazy
about leeks but we had to cut them up for her, that was
a bore. When we were through eating, she still didn't want
to go home. She'd get gay. She'd turn to the piano, a
pledge one of our customers had forgotten to redeem. It
was never tuned, but it worked pretty well.

Everything got on my father's nerves and so did the old
lady with her playful ways. But he softened when she
struck up certain arias from *Lucia di Lammermoor,* and especially the Moonlight Aria.

She took to coming all the time. She didn't wait to be
invited . . . She was perfectly aware of the havoc. While
we put the shop in order, she'd race upstairs, she'd settle
herself on the piano stool and toss off two or three waltzes
and then *Lucia* and then *Werther.* She had quite a repertory, the whole *Châlet* and Fortunio's song. We had to go
up sometime. She'd never have stopped if we hadn't sat
down to table. "Peekaboo," she'd call out when she saw
us. During dinner she'd do a good job of crying in unison
with Mama. It didn't spoil her appetite. She didn't mind
noodles. I was always aghast at the way she kept asking
for more. She pulled the same game all over town, sharing
memories with bereaved shopkeepers . . . She had vaguely
known the dear departed of any number of neighborhoods.
That was her way of keeping body and soul together.

She knew the history of every family in the Passages.
And when there was a piano, she couldn't be beat . . .
At past seventy she could still sing *Faust,* but she took
precautions. She stuffed herself full of gumdrops to keep
from going hoarse . . . She sang the choruses all by
herself, making a megaphone with her hands. "Glory and
fame to the men of old!". . . Without taking her hands
off the keys, she managed to pound it out with her feet.

In the end it was so funny we couldn't control ourselves,
we'd die laughing. But once she was started, a little thing
like that couldn't faze Madame Divonne. She was a born

artist. Mama felt ashamed, but she laughed too . . . It did her good.

For all her faults and kittenishness, my mother couldn't do without her. She took her along wherever she went. At night, we'd take her as far as the Porte de Bicêtre. She'd walk the rest of the way, to Kremlin, not far from the Old People's Home.

On Sunday morning she'd call for us and we'd all go to the cemetery together. Ours was Père Lachaise, 43rd Division. My father never went in. He couldn't stand graves. He'd never go any farther than the square outside La Roquette prison. He'd read his paper and wait for us to come back.

Grandma's vault was very well kept. Sometimes we'd empty out lilacs, sometimes it was jasmine. We always brought roses. That was the family's only luxury. We'd change the vases, we'd polish the windows. Inside it was like a Punch and Judy show with colored statues and real lace altar cloths. My mother kept bringing new ones, that was her consolation. She was always putting the house in order.

While we were cleaning up, she sobbed the whole time . . . Caroline was down there, not very far away . . . I always thought of Asnières . . . The way we'd knocked ourselves out for those tenants. I could see her, so to speak . . . The place was spic and span, we washed it out every Sunday, but there was a funny little smell from down below . . . pungent, subtle, kind of sour, insinuating . . . once you'd caught it, you smelled it all over . . . in spite of the flowers . . . mixed in with the scent . . . clinging to you . . . It makes your head spin . . . it comes from the tomb . . . you think you must have been mistaken. And there it is again! . . . It was I who went down to the end of the lane to fill the pitchers for the vases . . . When we'd finished, I didn't say a word . . . And then that little smell came back at me . . . We'd close the door . . . We'd say a prayer . . . And we'd start down the hill to Paris . . .

Madame Divonne never stopped chattering the whole way . . . Getting up so early, working on the flowers, and all that crying whetted her appetite . . . Besides there

was her diabetes . . . In any case she was hungry . . .
The moment we left the cemetery, she wanted to have a
snack. She couldn't stop talking about it, it got to be an
obsession with her. "You know what I feel like, Clémence?
Not meaning to be greedy . . . A little slice of galantine
on a nice fresh roll . . . How does it strike you?"

My mother didn't answer. She was embarrassed. I felt
like throwing up on the spot . . . I couldn't think of
anything else but vomiting . . . I thought of the galantine . . . of what Caroline must be looking like now
down there . . . of all the worms . . . the big ones . . .
the fat ones with feet . . . gnawing, swarming about in
there . . . All that decay . . . millions of them in all
that swollen pus, the stinking wind . . .

Papa was there . . . He had barely time to take me
behind a tree . . . I threw it all up . . . everything
. . . on the grating . . . My father jumped fast . . .
but he didn't dodge it all . . .

"You damn pig!" he yelled. He had it all over his pants
. . . The people were looking at us. He was mortified.
He went off by himself in the other direction, toward the
Bastille. He didn't want to have anything to do with us
after that. We went to a little café for a cup of verbena
to settle my stomach. It was a tiny little café just across
from the prison.

I've often gone by there since. I always look inside.
And I never see a soul.

Uncle Arthur was up to his ears in debt. From the rue
Cambronne to Grenelle he had borrowed so much without
ever returning it that his life was impossible. He was
shiftless. One night he moved on the q.t. A friend helped
him. They tied his stuff on a donkey cart. They were
going out to the suburbs. We were already in bed when
they came to notify us.

Arthur took advantage of the occasion to ditch his
housemaid . . . She'd been talking about vitriol . . .
Anyway, it was time he took a powder.

He and his pal had found a shanty where nobody would
come around, in the hills around Athis-Mons. The very
next day his creditors descended on us. The bastards, they
never budged out of the Passage . . . They even went

after my father at the insurance company. It was disgraceful. My father was in a terrible state . . . We were in for
it again . . .

"What scum! What a family! What a crummy lot they
all are. Never a minute's peace! They even come and
hound me on the job! . . . My brothers act like a bunch
of jailbirds! My sister sells her ass in Russia! My son has
every known vice! It's a fine how-do-you-do! Christ almighty! . . ." My mother couldn't think of anything to
say . . . She'd given up trying to argue with him. He
could go on to his heart's content.

The creditors realized that Papa set store by his honor
. . . They wouldn't give an inch. They never left our
shop . . . As if things weren't rough enough already . . .
If we'd paid his debts, we'd have really starved . . .

"We'll go and see him next Sunday," my father decided.
"I'll give him a piece of my mind . . . as man to man!"

We left at daybreak to make sure of finding him before
he started on his rounds . . . First we got lost . . . Then
we picked up the trail again . . . Finally we located him
. . . I expected to find Uncle Arthur all shriveled up,
repentant, scared out of his wits, hiding in some cave,
hunted by three hundred cops . . . eating stewed rats
. . . That was what happened to escaped convicts in
Illustrated Adventure Stories . . . It was a little different
with Uncle Arthur . . . Early as it was, we found him at
a table outside a bistro—La Belle Adèle. He gave us a
royal welcome in the arbor . . . He was drinking hard on
credit, and no vinegar either . . . A nice little *muscadet
rosé* . . . first class . . . he was in the best of health
. . . He'd never felt better . . . He had the whole neighborhood in stitches . . . they were crazy about him . . .
they ran over to listen to him . . . La Belle Adèle had
never had so many customers . . . Every single seat was
taken, the overflow was sitting on the steps . . . Small
homeowners from as far as Juvisy . . . in phony Panama
hats . . . And all the fishermen from the canal, in wooden
shoes, would come out to La Belle Adèle just to meet
Uncle Arthur. They'd never had so much fun in all their
lives.

He had something up his sleeve for everybody! Every
imaginable game from quoits to pitching pennies . . .

Speeches . . . riddles . . . under the trees . . . for the
ladies. Uncle Arthur was the life of the party, the ladies'
delight . . . He knocked himself out, he spared no effort
. . . But he never took his hat off, his artist's sombrero,
though it was midsummer . . . the sweat ran down his
face in rivers . . . He was always dressed the same . . .
pointed shoes, corduroy pants . . . and that tie, an enormous bow like a lettuce leaf.

With his taste for domestic help he had floored all
three waitresses . . . Happy to wait on him and love him
. . . He didn't want to hear one word about his troubles
in Vaugirard . . . Let bygones be bygones . . . He was
going to start a new life . . . My father was all set to
chew his ear off . . . he wouldn't even let him get started
. . . He kissed us each in turn . . . He was mighty glad
to see us . . .

"Arthur! Will you listen to me for one moment! . . .
Your creditors are blockading our doorway . . . from
morning to night! . . . They're driving us crazy . . . Do
you hear me?" Arthur disposed of all those sordid memories with a sweeping gesture. And the way he looked at
my father! Like he was a poor obstinate crackpot . . .
The truth is he felt sorry for him! "Come along now, the
whole lot of you! . . . Come on, Auguste. You'll talk
later. I'm going to show you the most beautiful view in the
whole region . . . Saint-Germain is nothing . . . Just
another little hill . . . The path on the left and then down
the covered lane . . . My studio's at the end."

That's what he called his shanty. He wasn't lying, the
situation was all right . . . A view of the whole valley
. . . The Seine as far as Villeneuve-Saint-Georges and on
the other side the forest of Sénart. You couldn't conceive
of anything better. He was lucky. He didn't pay rent, not
a sou. Supposedly he was the caretaker, looking after the
landlord's pond . . .

The pond only had water in it in the winter, in the
summer it was dry. He was popular with the fair sex. He
helped the local servant girls to wise up. His place was
full of food . . . *muscadet* like down below, sausage,
artichokes, and mountains of the little cream cheeses my
mother was so fond of. He wasn't badly off . . . He told
us about the orders he was getting . . . signs for every

bar, grocery store, and bakery for miles around . . .
"They do the useful things, I supply the charm!" That was
his philosophy . . . There were sketches all over the
walls: "At the Sign of the Stuffed Pike" with an enormous
fish in blue, red, and vermilion . . . "The Fair Sailor
Lass" for a laundress friend, with luminous nipples, a
mighty ingenious idea . . . His future was assured. We
could all be pleased.

Before we started back for the village, he stashed everything away in three or four big crocks, the food, and the
white wine, as though burying treasure in a furrow . . .
He didn't want to leave a trace. He was suspicious of the
people who came by. On his door he'd written in chalk:
"Never coming back."

We went down to the locks, he knew the bargemen.
It was a long hike on steep paths, my mother limped
along behind us. When we got there, she felt dizzy and
sat down on a stone. We watched the tugboats maneuver-
ing barges through the locks, they looked so frail and delicate against the walls . . . they don't dare to touch the
sides . . .

The pudgy lockkeeper spits tobacco juice three times,
takes off his coat, clears his throat, and curses over his
windlass . . . The gate trembles on its pivot, groans, and
starts moving in little jerks . . . The whirlpools hold it
back . . . a trickle of water and finally she opens . . .
the *Artémise* lets out a long whistle . . . the string of
barges pulls in.

Further on you see Villeneuve-Saint-Georges . . . Little
hills and then the gray bridge over the Yvette . . . Down
below, the country . . . the plain. The wind starts up,
stumbles over the river, whips up water in the floating
washhouse . . . an endless lapping . . . branches beating triplets in the water . . . From the valley . . . from
all sides . . . The modulated song of the breezes . . .
Forgotten the debts . . . we don't even mention them
. . . The air has gone to our heads . . . We bat the breeze
with Uncle Arthur . . . He wants to take us across. My
mother won't let us go . . . He jumps into a scow all by
himself. He wants to show us his talents. He starts rowing
against the stream. My father jumps with excitement and
fires advice at him, exhorts him to be careful. Even my

poor mother's interest is aroused. She fears the worst. Limping, she follows us up the bank . . .

The shore is lined with fishermen casting worms through the air . . . Uncle Arthur gets in their way . . . They give him hell . . . He gets caught in the water lilies, he flounders . . . He starts up again, sweating like a whole football team. He turns, slips into the narrows, he has to row like hell toward the gravel pits, "the big eggbeater" is coming, the *Pride of the Quarries,* you can hear her in the distance, grinding up the river with a terrible clanking of chains . . . She drags at the bottom, bringing everything to the surface . . . every known kind of mud and corpses and pike . . . She kicks up waves that hit both banks at once . . . Wherever she goes, she spreads terror and disaster . . . The boats by the shore toss furiously and crash into the stakes . . . All three basins are rocking at once . . . It's death on the boats. There she is, the *Pride of the Quarries,* coming out from under the bridge. All the hardware, all the catapults and steering gear in hell are rattling inside her carcass and on her balconies. She's dragging at least twenty barges loaded with clinkers . . . This is no time to show off . . . My uncle gets tangled in a rope . . . He hasn't time to reach the shore . . . His boat rises on the swell . . . his beautiful lid falls in the soup . . . He bends forward, this is going to be the great stroke . . . He loses his oar . . . he loses his head . . . He tries again . . . He tips . . . He falls flat on his ass in the drink, exactly like a water fencer. Luckily he knows how to swim! . . . We all come running, we comfort him, we congratulate him . . . the Apocalypse has passed . . . By now she's sowing havoc up by Ris-Orangis.

We all repair to the Lost Minnow, where the lockkeepers hang out, we congratulate each other . . . It's aperitif time . . . Hardly taking the time to dry, Uncle Arthur gathers all his friends around him . . . He has an idea! . . . Wants to start a club called the "Brethren of the Sail." The fishermen are less enthusiastic. He takes up a collection . . . His little girl friends come over and kiss him. We stay on for supper . . . Under the Japanese lanterns, between soup and mosquitoes, he breaks into song: "A poet once told me . . ." Nobody wants Uncle Arthur

to go back to his pond . . . Everybody wants his company . . . He doesn't know whom to please first . . .

We started for the station . . . We slipped away quietly
while he was still warbling . . . But my father wasn't
happy . . . especially when he thought it over . . . He
was burnt up inside. He was furious with himself for not
having spoken up . . . He'd been lacking in firmness.
We went out to see him one more time. Arthur had a new
boat with a real sail . . . and even a little jib up front
. . . He tacked about singing "O Sole Mio." The gravel
pits echoed with his singing. He was as happy as a lark
. . . My father couldn't stand it . . . This couldn't go on
. . . Long before the aperitif we slunk away with our
tails between our legs . . . Nobody saw us leave . . .
We never went back . . . It was impossible to associate
with him anymore . . . He would have debauched us . . .

My father had been working for La Coccinelle exactly
ten years. That entitled him to a vacation, two weeks with
pay . . .

It wasn't very sensible for the three of us to go away
like that . . . it cost a fortune . . . But that was a terrible summer, the heat was killing us in the Passage,
especially me, I looked the greenest, I was growing too
fast. I was so anemic I could hardly stand up. We went
to see a doctor, he was alarmed. "What he needs isn't two
weeks, but three months of fresh air! . . ." That's what
he said.

"Your Passage," he went on, "is a pesthole . . . You
couldn't even get a radish to grow there. It's a urinal without doors or windows . . . You've got to get out of
there."

He was so outspoken about it that my mother came
home in tears . . . We needed more money . . . They
didn't want to dig too deeply into the three thousand francs
we had inherited . . . So they decided to try the markets
again: Mers . . . Onival, and especially Dieppe . . . I
had to promise to watch my behavior . . . to stop bom-
barding clocks . . . to stop going with hoodlums . . .
not to stir from my mother's side. I promised the moon and
the stars . . . I'd be good, I'd even be grateful . . . and

I'd work hard for my school diploma when we got back . . .

That reassured them and they decided we could go. We closed the shop. First my mother and I would spend a month in Dieppe and look around . . . Madame Divonne would come in from time to time to see that nothing went wrong while we were gone . . . Papa would join us later, he'd make the trip on his bicycle . . . He'd spend two weeks with us . . .

Once we were there, the two of us got settled very quickly, we really didn't have too much trouble. We found lodgings in Dieppe over a café, the Tomtit, in an apartment that belonged to a clerk in the post office. We had two mattresses on the floor. The only trouble was the sink. It didn't smell good.

When it came time to unload our stuff on the main square, my mother got jittery. We had brought a complete collection of embroideries, frills, and baubles, all very light and airy. It seemed awfully risky to display all those things out in the open in a strange city . . . After thinking it over, we decided it would be better to go straight to the customers, it was a lot of trouble of course, but there was less chance of being taken . . . We did the whole length of the Esplanade, along the ocean front, from door to door . . . It was hard work. Our stuff was heavy. We'd wait outside the villas, on a bench across the way. The best time to go in was when they'd just filled their bellies . . . You had to hear the piano . . . Now they're moving into the drawing room . . .

My mother would jump up and race to the doorbell . . . The reception could be good or bad . . . Anyway she managed to sell a certain amount . . .

I got plenty of air. There was so much of it and so strong that it made me drunk. It even woke me up at night. I saw nothing but cocks and asses and boats and sails . . . The laundry floating on the clothes lines gave me a terrible hard-on . . . It swells out . . . it drives you crazy . . . all those women's panties . . . .

At first we were afraid of the sea . . . We'd stick to the little sheltered streets as much as we could. The gale makes you delirious. I never stopped playing with myself . . .

A traveling salesman's kid lived in the room next to ours. We did all our homework together. He felt me up a little, he jerked off even more than I did. He came to Dieppe every year, so he knew all the different kinds of boats. He taught me all about their rigging and their sails . . . Three-master barks . . . square-riggers . . . schooners . . . I studied the ships with passion while my mother was doing the villas . . .

She got to be as well known on the beach as the coconut man . . . always hobbling around with her bundle . . . Inside there were embroideries, patterns, needlework sets to keep the ladies busy, and even irons . . . She'd have sold kidneys, rabbit skins, hot air, anything, to help us last out the two months.

In our comings and goings we also had our qualms about the port. We were afraid to go too close to the edge on account of the bollards and ropes that are so easy to trip over. It's a mighty treacherous place. If you fall into the muck, it sucks you down, you sink to the bottom, the crabs eat you, they never find you again . . .

The cliffs are dangerous too. Every year whole families get squashed under them. A moment's carelessness, a false step, a thoughtless remark . . . and the mountain falls down on top of you. We took as few chances as possible, we seldom left the streets. In the evening, right after supper, we'd start ringing bells again. We'd make a grand tour . . . starting first at one end, then at the other . . . We'd do the whole Avenue du Casino . . .

I'd wait on a bench outside the villas . . . I'd hear my mother shouting herself hoarse inside . . . She really knocked herself out . . . I knew all her arguments by heart . . . I knew all the stray dogs . . . They turn up, they sniff, they beat it . . . I knew all the peddlers, that's the time when they come home with their carts . . . They pull, they push, they run themselves ragged . . . Nobody takes any notice of them . . . They're free to curse and swear all they like . . . They grunt and groan and tug at the shafts . . . One more pull . . . just to the next corner . . . The lighthouse blinks its big eye in the night . . . The flash passes over the old man . . . On the beach the surf sucks up pebbles . . . crashes . . . rolls . . . crashes . . . breaks . . .

On the posters we saw there was going to be an automobile race after the fair on August 15. That would be
sure to attract a lot of people, especially the English. My
mother decided we'd stay on a while. We hadn't had much
luck. The weather had been so bad in July that the ladies
stayed home with their embroidery . . . That didn't help
us to sell our bonnets and boleros, or even our needlework
sets . . . If at least they had worked at it! But they never
got through mending their drapes! . . . They yacked even
worse at the seashore than in town . . . like all society
women . . . always about maids and bowel movements . . .

They took it easy, they wallowed in idleness, they'd
dawdle over our merchandise, pick things up a dozen
times . . .

My father had lost hope. His letters were full of worry.
We were done for in his opinion. We'd lost more than a
thousand francs. My mother wrote him to dig into the
inheritance. That was real heroism, all this could end very
badly. I could already see myself getting blamed for the
whole mess. He wrote back that he was coming. We waited
for him in front of the church. He finally hove in sight with
his bike all covered with mud.

I expected him to bawl the hell out of me, blame everything on me. I was all prepared for one of his headlong
corridas . . . but not at all . . . Actually he seemed glad
to be alive and glad to see us. He even congratulated me
on my conduct and my red cheeks. I was really moved.
He himself suggested a little walk in the port . . . He
knew all about boats. He remembered his whole childhood . . . he was an expert on navigation. My mother
went off with her bundles and we made for the docks.
I remember a Russian three-master, all white. She had
made for the harbor mouth on the afternoon tide.

For three days she'd been fighting the storm off Villers,
rolling in the swell . . . her jibs were full of foam . . .
She had an awful cargo of loose lumber, mountains of it,
piled every which way on every deck. In the holds there
was nothing but ice, enormous dazzling blocks, the top of
a river. She'd brought it all the way from Archangel to
sell in the cafés . . . She was listing badly and the crew
weren't happy . . . My father and I and a lot of other

people went over and followed her in from the harbor
light to her berth. She was so drenched with spray that
her mainyard was dragging in the water . . . I can still
see the captain, an enormous roly-poly, shouting into his
funnel, ten times louder than even Papa. His monkeys
climbed up in the shrouds to roll up all the spars and
canvas, all the gaffs and yards up to the big St. Andrew's
cross at the masthead . . . During the night they'd expected her to be smashed against the rocks . . . The
rescue squads had refused to put out, God had taken the
day off . . . Six fishing smacks had been lost. Even the
big buoy off the reef of Trotot had taken too much punishment and broken loose from its chain . . . That gives
you an idea of the weather.

In front of the Saucy Trollop café they maneuvered her
around the mooring buoy . . . The drift wasn't bad. But
the hauling crew were so drunk they couldn't see straight
. . . They hauled in the wrong direction . . . The bow
smashed into the customs wharf . . . The "lady" on the
prow, the beautiful sculptured figurehead, stove her tits in
. . . It was a shambles . . . The sparks flew . . . The
bowsprit went through the window . . . straight into the
café . . . The jib scraped the bar.

Everybody was screaming and yelling . . . People
came running. The curses volleyed and thundered . . .
Finally, as gently as you please, the fine ship pulled alongside . . . Bristling with cables, she tied up at the dock
. . . After a great deal of activity the last sail fell from
the foremast . . . spread out on the deck like a sea-
gull.

The stern hawser gives a last deep groan . . . The land
embraces the ship. The cook comes out of his galley and
empties out an enormous bowl for the squawking birds.
The giants on board stand at the rail shaking their fists,
the drunken longshoremen aren't in the mood to go up the
gangplank. The companion ladders are dangling alongside.

The harbor master's clerk in a frock coat is the first to
go aboard . . . The pulley swings a plank overhead . . .
More insults fly . . . The rumpus goes on . . . the longshoremen swarm over the rigging . . . The hatch covers
are taken off . . . Now we see the iceberg in sections
. . . After the forest . . . Faster, coachman! . . . Here

come the wagons . . . There's nothing more to see, the excitement is elsewhere.

We go back to the semaphore, they're expecting a collier. She comes in past Guignol Rock with her flag at half-mast.

The pilot in his boat dances and splashes from one wave to the next. He's fighting every inch of the way . . . he's thrown back . . . finally he grabs the ladder and climbs up the side. The old tub has been hammering into the storm all the way from Cardiff . . . She's rolling from rail to rail in a mountain of foam and spray . . . She's caught in the current, carried toward the breakwater . . . Finally the tide shifts a bit, sets her right, and drives her into the harbor mouth . . . Her whole hull is trembling as she pulls in, the waves are still chasing her. She grunts and rumbles and blows out steam. Her rigging screeches in the gale. Her smoke falls back on the crests of the waves, the ebb tide beats against the jetties.

Now you can make out the "helmets" in the Emblemeuse narrows . . . the little rocks come up at low tide . . .

Two cutters in trouble are trying to feel their way through . . . There's going to be a tragedy; we mustn't miss a mouthful . . . The fans collect at the end of the breakwater by the bell . . . They study the situation through binoculars . . . A man beside me lends me his . . . The squalls are getting so thick they gag you. You can't breathe . . . The wind blows up the water rougher than ever . . . it splashes in streams high up against the lighthouse . . . way up to the sky.

My father pulls his cap down . . . We wouldn't be going home before nightfall . . . Three dismasted fishing boats come in . . . You can hear the voices from the channel . . . They're calling each other . . . They get tangled up in each other's oars . . .

Mama was beginning to worry, she's waiting for us at the Little Mouse, the fishmongers' hangout . . . She hasn't sold much . . . But the two of us aren't interested in anything but ocean voyages.

Papa was a good swimmer, he was crazy about bathing. It didn't appeal to me. The beach at Dieppe is no good.

But after all, this was vacation. And besides I was even filthier than in the Passage.

At the Tomtit we only had one little basin for the three of us. I got out of washing my feet. I was beginning to smell very bad, almost as bad as the sink.

Sea bathing takes a lot of courage. The crest of the wave seethes and foams, rises high in the air, roars, descends reinforced with thousands of pebbles. It catches me.

Chilled to the bone, bruised, the child totters and falls . . . A universe of pebbles beats my bones amid the flaking foam. First your head wobbles, sways, staggers, and pounds into the gravel . . . Every second is your last . . . My father in a striped bathing suit, between two roaring mountains, is shouting like mad. He bobs up in front of me . . . he belches, thrashes about, makes wisecracks. A roller knocks him over too, turns him upside down, there he is with his feet in the air . . . He's wriggling like a frog . . . He can't straighten himself out, he's done for . . . At this point a terrible volley of pebbles hits me in the chest . . . I'm riddled . . . drowned . . . It's awful . . . I'm crushed under the deluge . . . Then the wave carries me back and lays me down at my mother's feet . . . She tries to grab me, to rescue me . . . The undertow catches me, carries me out . . . She lets out a terrible scream . . . The whole beach comes running . . . But it's no use . . . The bathers crowd around, all hysterical . . . The raging sea pounds me down to the bottom, then lifts me gasping to the surface . . . In a flashing moment I see that they're discussing my agony . . . There they are, every imaginable color: green . . . blue, parasols, lavender ones, lemon-yellow ones . . . I whirl about in pieces . . . And then I don't see a thing . . . A life preserver is strangling me . . . They haul me up on the rocks . . . like a whale . . . Brandy scorches my throat, they cover me all over with arnica . . . and those terrible rubdowns . . . I'm burning under the bandages . . . I'm strangled in three bathrobes . . .

All around me people are saying the sea is too rough for me! OK! That suits me fine. I hadn't expected as much . . . It was a sacrifice . . . on the altar of energetic cleanliness . . .

Already ten days had passed. Next week it would all be over. My father would have to go back to the office. It made us sick to think about it. There wasn't a single minute to waste.

We weren't selling much. All of a sudden business had got so slow that only a real moment of panic could have made us decide to go on that excursion . . . to take the boat to England, all three of us . . . It was the idea of going back so soon that sent us off our rockers, that drove us to extremes . . .

We started off at daybreak, hardly time for a cup of coffee . . . Grandma's nest egg . . . well . . . we'd already gone through half of it . . .

We went on board ahead of time . . . We had the cheapest seats, in the bow . . . they were fine . . . We had a wonderful view of the whole horizon . . . It was agreed that I'd be first to point out the foreign shores . . . The weather wasn't bad, but even so, as soon as we were a little way out and had lost sight of the lighthouses, it began to be kind of wet . . . The ship started to seesaw; this was real seafaring . . . My mother took refuge in the shelter where the life jackets were kept . . . She was the first to vomit across the deck and down into third class . . . For a moment she had the whole area to herself . . .

"Watch out for the child, Auguste," she had barely time to yelp . . . That was the surest way to infuriate him . . .

Some of the others began straining their guts over the side . . . In the rolling and pitching, people were throwing up any old place, without formality . . . There was only one toilet . . . in one corner of the deck . . . It was already occupied by four vomiters in a state of collapse, wedged in tight . . . The sea was getting steadily rougher . . . At every rising wave, oops . . . In the trough a dozen oopses, more copious, more compact . . . The gale blew my mother's veil away . . . it landed wringing wet on the mouth of a lady at the other end . . . who was retching desperately . . . All resistance had been abandoned. The horizon was littered with jam . . . salad . . . chicken . . . coffee . . . the whole slobgullion . . . it all came up . . .

My mother was down on her knees on the deck . . .

she smiled with a sublime effort, she was drooling at the mouth . . .

"You see," she says to me in the middle of the terrible plummeting . . . "You see, Ferdinand, you still have some of that tuna fish on your stomach too . . ." We try again in unison. Bouah! and another bouah! . . . She was mistaken, it was the pancakes . . . With a little more effort I think I could bring up French fries . . . if I emptied all my guts out on deck . . . I try . . . I struggle . . . I push like mad . . . A fierce wave beats down on the rail, smacks against the deck, rises, gushes, rolls back, sweeps the steerage . . . The foam stirs up the garbage and spins it around between us . . . We swallow some of it . . . We spit it up again . . . At every plunge the soul flies away . . . at every rise you recapture it in a wave of mucus and stink . . . It comes dripping from your nose, all salty. This is too much! . . . One passenger begs for mercy . . . He cries out to high heaven that he's empty . . . He strains his guts . . . And a raspberry comes up after all! . . . He examines it, goggle-eyed with horror . . . Now he really has nothing left! . . . He wishes he could vomit out his two eyes . . . He tries, he tries hard . . . He braces himself against the mast . . . he's trying to drive them out of their sockets . . . Mama collapses against the rail . . . She vomits herself up again, all she's got . . . A carrot comes up . . . a piece of fat . . . and the whole tail of a mullet . . .

Up top by the captain, the first and second class passengers were leaning over the side to puke, and it came tumbling down on us . . . At every wave we caught a shower with whole meals in it . . . We were lashed with garbage, with meat fibers . . . The gale blows the stuff upward . . . it clings in the shrouds . . . Around us the sea is roaring . . . the foam of battle . . . Papa in a cap with a chin strap . . . supervises our misery . . . He's in the pink, lucky man, he's a born sailor . . . he gives us good advice, he wants us to lie even flatter . . . to crawl on the floor . . . A woman comes staggering . . . she wedges herself in beside Mama so as to throw up better . . . There's a sick mutt, too, so sick he shits on the ladies' skirts . . . He rolls over and shows us his belly . . . piercing screams are heard from the shithouse . . . Those four are still jammed in, they can't puke anymore, they can't pee, they can't shit . . . They're leaning over the toilet, pushing . . . They bellow, begging someone to shoot them . . . And the tub pitches still higher . . . steeper than ever . . . and plunges into the depths . . . into the dark green . . . And she rises again, the stinker, she picks you up again, you and the hole in your stomach . . .

A stocky little character, a wise guy, is helping his wife to throw up in a little bucket . . . he's trying to encourage her.

"Go on, Léonie . . . Don't hold back . . . I'm right here . . . I'm holding you." All of a sudden she turns her head back into the wind . . . The whole stew that's been gurgling in her mouth catches me full in the face . . . My teeth are full of it, beans, tomatoes . . . I'd thought I had nothing left to vomit . . . well, it looks like I have . . . I can taste it . . . it's coming up again . . . Hey, down there, get moving! . . . It's coming! . . . A whole carload is pushing against my tongue . . . I'll pay her back, I'll spill my guts in her mouth . . . I grope my way over to her . . . The two of us are crawling . . . We clutch each other . . . We embrace . . . we vomit on each other . . . My smart father and her husband try to separate us . . . They tug at us in opposite directions . . . They'll never understand . . .

Why bear grudges? It's nasty. Bouah! . . . That husband is a stupid brute! . . . Come on, sweetie, we'll vomit him up together! . . . I give his fair lady a complete hank of noodles . . . with tomato juice . . . a drink of cider three days old . . . She returns the compliment with Swiss cheese . . . I suck at the strings . . . My mother's snarled up in the ropes . . . she comes crawling after her vomit . . . The little dog is caught in her skirts. We're all tangled up with this brute's wife . . . They tug at me ferociously . . . He starts peppering my ass with his boot to get me away from her . . . He was a regular bruiser . . . My father tried to mollify him . . . he hadn't said two words when the other guy rams him in the breadbasket with his head and sends him sprawling against the winch . . . And that wasn't the end of it! The strong man jumps on him and starts hammering at his face

. . . He bends down to finish him off . . . Papa was bleeding all over . . . The blood poured down into the vomit . . . He was slipping down the mast . . . In the end he collapsed . . . But the husband still wasn't satisfied . . . Taking advantage of a moment when the roll has sent me spinning he charges me . . . I skid . . . He flings me at the shithouse . . . like a battering ram . . . I smash into it . . . I bash the door in . . . I fall on the poor sagging bastards . . . I turn around . . . I'm wedged in the middle of them . . . They've all lost their pants . . . I pull the chain. We're half drowned in the flood. We're squashed into the bowl . . . But they never stop snoring . . . I don't even know if I'm dead or alive.

The siren woke everybody up. We climbed up and stuck our heads out the portholes. The jetties at the entrance to the harbor were like a lacework of wooden piles . . . We looked out on England as though disembarking in the other world . . .

Here too there were cliffs and then green . . . But much darker and rougher than on the other side . . . The sea was perfectly flat now . . . It was easy to vomit . . . but you didn't need to so much anymore.

Talk about shivering . . . it's a wonder our teeth didn't crack . . . My mother was weeping spasmodically from having vomited so much . . . I had bumps all over . . . A big silence fell in our ranks . . . everyone felt bashful, worried about going ashore. Corpses couldn't have been any more bashful.

The steamer tugged at the anchor, gave two, three jerks, and then we really stopped. We fished around for our tickets . . . Once we were through customs we tried to clean ourselves up. My mother had to wring her skirt, rivers of water ran out. My father'd taken such a beating a chunk of his moustache was missing. I pretended not to notice but he had some shiner. He dabbed at it with his handerkerchief . . . Little by little we pulled ourselves together. The streets were still heaving pretty bad. We walked past the shops, little tiny ones the way they are over there, with striped shutters and little whitewashed stoops.

My mother did her best, she didn't want to hold us back, but she was limping way behind . . . We thought of going to a hotel, of taking a room right away so she could rest . . . just a little while . . . we'd never get to London, we were already too wet . . . We were sure to get sick if we tried to go any farther . . . And besides, our shoes wouldn't hold out. They were drinking up the mud, making a noise like a flock of sheep . . .

We identified a hotel . . . The word was written on the front in gold letters . . . At the door we got scared and went past . . . The rain kept coming down harder and harder . . . We tried to figure out how much things would cost, the least little things . . . We were afraid of the currency . . . We went into a tearoom . . . they understood us all right . . . Once seated, we looked at our suitcase . . . It wasn't ours! In the confusion at the customs we'd taken the wrong one . . . We ran back p.d.q. . . . ours was gone . . . we gave the one that didn't belong to us to the stationmaster . . . So then we didn't have anything . . . We were really out of luck . . . Such things only happened to us . . . That was perfectly true in a way . . . My father didn't pass up the opportunity to point it out . . . We had no fresh clothes to put on . . . not even a shirt! Still, we had to see the sights . . . People began to notice us in the village, the three of us shivering in the rain. We definitely looked like gypsies. We thought we'd better take a road out of town . . . We took the first one we saw . . . after the last house . . .

"Brighton" said a signpost. Fourteen miles ahead . . . We were good walkers, that didn't scare us. But we couldn't keep together. My father was always way ahead . . . He wasn't very proud of us . . . Even there, soaked, muddy, half crippled, he kept as far away from us as possible . . . He couldn't stand us clinging to him . . . He kept his distance.

My mother was so fagged out she could hardly drag her leg. She was panting like an old hound.

The road wound along the cliffs. We pushed along in the downpour. Down below the ocean roared at the bottom of the chasm . . . full of clouds and landslides.

My father's yachting cap was oozing into his mouth. His dust coat clung so tight his ass looked like an onion.

Mama hobbles along . . . she abandons her hat, the

one trimmed with swallows and little cherries. We gave it
to a bush . . . The gulls running away from the storm
are screeching all around us. They must have been surprised to see us in the clouds too . . . Under the gusts of
rain we kept our foothold as best we could . . . On the
side of the cliff, on hills like waves, another and still
another . . . endless . . . The clouds had spirited my
father away . . . He seemed to melt away in the downpour . . . Every time we saw him he was farther away,
pressing on doggedly, always smaller, heading down the
far slope.

"We'll just climb to the top of this one, Ferdinand . . .
And then I've got to rest . . . Do you think he can see
Brichetonne? Do you think it's still far? . . ." She was at
the end of her rope. It was impossible to sit down. The
embankments were pure mud . . . Her clothes had
shrunk so that her arms stuck way out . . . Her shoes
were swollen up like saddlebags . . . At that point my
mother's leg buckled . . . It caved in under her weight
. . . She toppled over into the ditch . . . her head was
wedged in, stuck fast . . . She couldn't move . . . All
she could do was make bubbles like a toad . . . The rain
in England is like an ocean suspended in midair . . . little
by little you drown . . .

I shouted: "Papa! . . . help! . . ." at the top of my
lungs . . . Mama had fallen head down. I pulled with all
my might . . . it was like a tug-of-war. It was no good
. . . But finally our explorer turns up after all. He's all
dizzy with the clouds. We go at it together . . . we heave
and we hoist. She moves. We extract her from the muck
. . . She comes up smiling. My, was she happy to see her
Auguste again! Was he all right? He hadn't had too bad a
time? What had he seen from the end of the cliff? He
didn't answer . . . He only said we'd better make it
snappy . . . Get back to the port quick . . . Up and
down, another hundred hills . . . breathless and panting.
The storm had made such a mess of the road we couldn't
recognize it on the way back . . . We caught a glimpse
of lights . . . the port, the lighthouses . . . It was pitch
dark . . . Crawling, staggering, we passed the same hotel
. . . We hadn't spent a nickel . . . We hadn't met anybody . . . We hadn't a stitch of clothing to our name

. . . we were all strips and tatters . . . We looked so worn out they were good to us on the boat . . . they let us move from third to second class . . . they told us to lie down . . . At the station in Dieppe we stretched out on the benches . . . We were going right back . . . In the train there was another big scene on account of Mama's constipation . . .

"You haven't gone in a week! . . . You'll never go again."

"I'll go when we get home . . ."

The irregularity of her bowels was an obsession with him . . . it haunted him. Sea voyages are constipating. From then on he couldn't think of anything but her bowels. In the Passage we were finally able to dry ourselves. All three of us had colds. We got off easy. My father had a beautiful shiner. We said it was a horse, he just happened to be behind it when something exploded . . .

Madame Divonne was bubbling with curiosity, she wanted to hear all about it . . . every detail of our adventure . . . She'd been to England too, on her honeymoon. She was so eager to hear about it she stopped playing the piano . . . Right in the middle of the Moonlight Aria . . .

Monsieur Visios was also crazy about stories and discoveries . . . Édouard came by with Tom to hear the news . . . Mama and I had our little impressions too . . . But Papa wouldn't let us open our mouths . . . He hogged the floor . . . He had certainly seen some amazing, fantastic, stupendous, absolutely unexpected things . . . at the end of the road . . . way out beyond the cliffs . . . When he was in the clouds . . . between Brigetonne and the hurricane . . . Papa all alone, cut off from the world! . . . lost in the tempest . . . between heaven and earth . . .

Now it was over he stopped at nothing, he gave them all the wonders they could ask for . . . He shot off his mouth like a machine gun . . . Mama didn't contradict him . . . She was always happy to see him triumph . . . "Isn't that right, Clémence?" he'd ask her when his story was getting a bit too tall . . . She nodded, she backed up everything he said . . . Of course she knew he was overdoing it, but if it gave him pleasure . . .

"But what about London? You didn't get there?" asked
Monsieur Lérosite, the optician from 37, who was completely senile and imported his lenses from over there . . .

"Oh, yes, but only the outskirts . . . We saw the best
part! . . . The harbor! . . . When you come right down
to it, that's the only thing that's really worth seeing! And
the suburbs . . . We only had a few hours." Mama didn't
bat an eyelash . . . Soon word got around that we'd been
in a big shipwreck . . . that the women had been landed
on the cliffs with a cable . . . He made it up as he went
along . . . And the way we'd gone roaming around
London with the other survivors . . . mostly foreigners
. . . He stopped at nothing . . . He even imitated their
accents.

There was a session every night after dinner . . . fantasies, new ones every time . . . Madame Méhon was
beginning to boil and bubble again . . . in her den, she
didn't come over . . . we were too mortally on the outs
for that . . . She made her phonograph sing so as to
interrupt my father . . . so as to make him stop . . .
Mama closed the shop to give us a little peace and pulled
the shutters all the way down . . . Then Madame Méhon
came over and banged on the windows to needle Papa, to
make him come out and start a riot . . . My mother
wouldn't let him . . . The neighbors were all furious.
They were all on our side . . . They were developing a
taste for explorations . . . One night when we came home
from our errands, we didn't hear Madame Méhon and her
phonograph . . . Our usual visitors came in one by one
. . . We settled ourselves in the back room . . . Papa
started in on his story . . . it was something brand-new
. . . Suddenly from the old battle-ax's place . . . boom!
. . . a tremendous blast! And a whole string of firecrackers! . . . The flash is blinding. It explodes against
the shop! The door crashes in! We see the old bag waving
her arms . . . she's holding a torch and some rockets
. . . She lights the fuses! . . . The rockets whistle and
whirl! She'd dreamed up the whole act just to cramp my
father's style! She flails around like a demon. She sets fire
to her skirts. She's going up in flames. The people rush out.
They smother her in curtains. They put out the blaze! But
her shop's on fire, corsets and all. The firemen come run-

ning. We never saw the old witch again. They took her away to the bughouse in Charenton. She stayed there for good. Nobody wanted her back. They signed a petition from one end of the Passage to the other, saying she was insane and impossible.

Hard times were back again. No more talk of vacation or markets or England . . . The rains pounded down on our glass roof, the Passage was closed up tight with the sour smell of people and little stray dogs.

It was fall . . .

The thrashings were coming thick and fast again because I wanted to play instead of doing my homework. I didn't catch on very well in school. Once again my father made the discovery that I was really feeble-minded. The sea air had made me grow but had made me more listless than ever. I was always daydreaming. He flew into terrible tempers. He accused me of hopeless laziness. Mama was beginning to moan and groan again.

Her business was going from bad to worse. The styles never stopped changing. Batiste came in again. We dragged out our old bonnet tops. The ladies rolled them up like napkins and put them on their tits and in their hair. In the crisis Madame Héronde was always busy making things over. She invented boleros of Irish linen, made to last twenty years. Alas, it was only a passing fancy. After the Grand Prix we mounted them on wire, now they were lampshades . . . Sometimes Madame Héronde was so worn-out she got her orders balled up, she gave us little embroidered bibs when we were expecting comforters . . . The scenes were something . . . The customer would split a gut and threaten to haul us into court. We were in despair, we paid for all the damage, which accounted for two months' worth of noodles . . . The day before my examination a volcano erupted in the shop, Madame Héronde had dyed a "négligé" cuckoo-yellow, when it was actually meant to be a bridal dress. People have been killed for less! A criminal blunder! The customer would skin us alive! . . . And it was all written plain as day in the order book! . . . Madame Héronde collapsed sobbing in my mother's arms. My father was upstairs bellowing.

"Ah, you'll always be the same! You'll always be soft. Haven't I warned you forty-six times? Didn't I tell you they'd ruin us . . . those seamstresses of yours . . . Ah! Suppose I made even half a mistake at La Coccinelle! . . . I can just imagine what they'd say in the front office!" The mere idea was so terrifying that he thought he was dead and buried . . . He blanched . . . We sat him down . . . The crisis passed . . . I went back to my arithmetic . . . He reviewed my lessons with me . . . And I couldn't think of anything to say, he got so balled up in his explanations that I couldn't see straight . . . I attacked the problem ass-backwards . . . I didn't know very much to begin with . . . I gave up . . . He started in on my failings . . . In his opinion I was incorrigible . . . For my money he was as nutty as a fruitcake . . . He started up again about my division . . . He tangled himself up to the square roots . . . He slapped my face . . . he pulled my ears . . . He accused me of grinning . . . of taking him for a fool . . .

My mother came in for a minute . . . That redoubled his fury . . . He bellowed that he wanted to die!

On the morning of my exam my mother closed the shop. She thought it would encourage me if she came along. The exam was held at the grade school next to Saint-Germain-l'Auxerrois, right in the entrance hall. On the way she tried to bolster up my self-confidence. It was a solemn occasion, she thought of Caroline. That made her whimper some more . . .

All the way around the Palais-Royal she made me recite my Fables and the list of departments . . . At eight o'clock sharp we were all outside the gate, waiting to have our names taken. The kids were all cleaned up and neatly dressed, but terribly nervous, the mothers too.

First there was dictation, then problems. It wasn't very hard, I remember, all you had to do was copy. This was a bunch that had flunked the previous fall. For almost all of us it was a matter of life and death . . . if you wanted to be taken on as an apprentice . . . When it came to the oral, I was lucky, I pulled a big fat little guy with warts all over his nose. He had a flowing bow tie, sort of like Uncle Arthur . . . he wasn't an artist, though . . . He'd been a pharmacist on the rue Gomboust. Some of the people there knew him. He asked me two questions about plants . . . I hadn't the faintest idea . . . He answered them himself. I was in a complete muddle . . . Then he asked me the distance between the sun and the moon and then between the earth and the other side . . . I was afraid to stick my neck out too far. He had to come to the rescue. When he asked me about the seasons, I knew a little more. I mumbled something kind of vague . . . He really wasn't hard to please . . . He finished all the answers for me.

Then he asked me what I was planning for the future if I got my diploma.

"I'm going into business," I said without enthusiasm.

"It's a hard life, my boy," he said. "Couldn't you wait a while? Another year perhaps?"

I guess he didn't think I was very strong . . . Right away I thought I'd flunked . . . I thought of the return home, of the tempest I was going to unleash . . . I began to feel dizzy . . . I thought I was going to faint . . . I could feel the blows in advance . . . I clutched the desk . . . The old guy saw me turn pale . . .

"Come, come, boy," he said. "Don't worry. All that doesn't mean a thing. I'll pass you. You'll get your start in life. If you want it as badly as all that."

I went back and sat down on a bench, some distance away, by the wall . . . I was still mighty upset. I wondered if he hadn't been soft-soaping me, just to get rid of me. My mother was outside the church, on the little square. She was waiting for the results . . .

Everybody hadn't finished yet . . . there were still some kids waiting . . . I saw the others now . . . stammering their confessions across the table cover . . . the map of France, the continents . . .

Since hearing those words about starting out in life, I looked at my little friends as if I'd never seen them . . . Their dread of failing made them strain against the desk, wriggling as if they were caught in a trap.

Was that what it meant to start out in life? . . . They were trying to stop being kids that very moment . . . struggling to arrange their faces, to look like men . . .

We all looked pretty much alike, all dressed the same

way, in our school smocks. They were all like me, small
shopkeepers' kids . . . or their parents did tailoring at
home or sold stationery or something . . . They were all
pretty puny . . . They opened their eyes big and round,
they panted like puppies in their effort to answer the old
guy . . .

Lined up along the wall, the parents watched the proceedings . . . The looks they shot at their offspring were
fierce, electric, enough to cramp anybody's style.

The kids were wrong every time . . . They shrank up
even smaller . . . The old man was untiring . . . he
answered for everybody . . . The kids were all dunces
. . . The mothers' faces were getting redder and redder
. . . Thousands of thrashings threatened . . . There was
a smell of impending massacre . . . Finally all the kids
were through . . . It was all over, except for the list of
successful candidates . . . And then miracle of miracles
. . . everybody had passed! The government inspector
made the announcement from the platform . . . He had
a paunch with a chain on it, a great big watch charm that
jiggled between sentences. He sort of bumbled and got
all the names screwed up . . . It didn't matter . . .

He took advantage of the occasion to say a few words
. . . they were really kind words . . . cordial and en-
couraging . . . He told us that if we conducted ourselves
as valiantly in later life we had nothing to fear, we'd be
rewarded.

I'd wet my pants and shat in them something awful too,
I could hardly move. I wasn't the only one. None of the
kids were able to walk right. But my mother caught a
whiff while pressing me to her bosom . . . The stink was
so terrible we had to make it fast. We couldn't stop to say
good-bye to all my little friends . . . My studies were
over . . . to get home even faster we took a cab . . .

We made a draft . . . The cab had funny windows that
rattled all the way. She spoke of Caroline again. "How
glad she'd have been to see you succeed! Ah! I only hope
she has second sight! . . ."

My father was on the second floor with the lights out,
waiting to hear the results. He was so excited he had
taken in the sidewalk display and the lamps all by himself . . .

"Auguste! He passed! . . . Do you hear? . . . He passed . . . He came through with flying colors!"

He received me with open arms . . . He lit the lamp to get a good look at me. He gazed at me affectionately. I'd never seen him so moved . . . His whole moustache was trembling . . .

"That's splendid, my boy! You've given us a lot of trouble . . . But now I congratulate you . . . Now you'll be starting out in life . . . The future lies open before you . . . If only you take the right course . . . the straight and narrow! . . . Work hard! . . . Struggle . . ."

I begged his forgiveness for having always been bad. I hugged and kissed him with all my heart . . . Only I stank so bad he began to sniff . . .

"Ah! What's this?" He pushed me away. "Oh, the stinker . . . the little pig! . . . He's filled the whole place with shit! Ah, Clémence, Clémence! For God's sake take him upstairs before I lose my temper! He's revolting . . ." That was the end of his effusions.

They scrubbed me hard, they drenched me in cologne. The next day we went looking for a really respectable establishment where I could start my business career. A place where they wouldn't be too easy on me, where they wouldn't let me get away with anything.

If you really want to learn, you've got to be on the jump. That was Édouard's opinion. He had twenty years of experience. Everybody agreed with him.

In business it's absolutely essential to look your best. An employee who lets himself go is a disgrace to his firm . . . You're judged by your shoes . . . Never look down-at-the-heel! . . .

The Prince Regent, near Les Halles, had been in business for a century . . . You couldn't hope for better. A lifelong reputation for ferocious pointed dress shoes . . . they were known as "duckbills." Your toenails are driven into your flesh, the man of fashion is a cripple! My mother bought me two pairs, guaranteed to last forever. Then we went across the street to the Deserving Classes clothing store . . . We took advantage of the sales, I needed a complete outfit.

She bought me three pairs of pants, of such good

quality, so long-wearing, that we took them a little bigger, with a ten-year hem. I was still growing fast. The jacket was as somber as possible, besides I kept my arm band, my mourning for Grandma. I had to look thoroughly serious-minded. Collars are important too, you mustn't go wrong . . . a wide collar can atone for a multitude of sins when you're young and scrawny. The only flight of fancy permitted was a frivolous snap-on bow tie. Naturally there had to be a watch chain, but darkened too for mourning. I had the whole works. I looked respectable. I was all set. Papa wore a watch too, but his was gold, a precision instrument . . . He counted every passing second on it to the very end . . . The long hand fascinated him, the one that goes around fast. He'd sit there for hours looking at it . . .

My mother herself took me to introduce me to Monsieur Berlope, Ribbons and Trimmings, on the rue de la Michodière, just across the boulevard.

Being the soul of honesty, she had told him all about me in advance . . . That he'd have his hands full with me, that I'd be a hard row to hoe, that I was pretty lazy, disobedient by nature, and passably scatterbrained. That was her idea. I always did my best. In addition she warned them that I picked my nose incessantly, that it was a passion with me. She suggested that they try to shame me. She said they'd always been trying to better me, but it didn't help much . . . While listening to these details, Monsieur Berlope was slowly paring his nails . . . He looked thoughtful and grave. He was wearing a terrific vest sprinkled with golden bees . . . I remember his fan-shaped beard too, and his round embroidered skullcap that he didn't take off for us.

Finally he answered . . . He'd try to train me . . . He still hadn't looked at me . . . If I showed willingness, intelligence, and zeal . . . Well, he'd see . . . After a few months behind the counter, maybe they'd send me out on the road . . . with a salesman . . . to carry the sample cases . . . I'd get to know the customers . . . But before taking any chances, he'd have to see what I was good for . . . If I had a business head! . . . If I was cut out for the job . . . if I had the competence . . . the loyalty . . .

After what my mother had said, all that seemed mighty doubtful. . .

While speaking, Monsieur Berlope ran a comb through his hair, spruced himself up, took a look at his profile, there were mirrors all over the place . . . He was doing us an honor in seeing us . . . Mama never tired of saying so . . . it was a big favor to be interviewed by the boss in person.

Berlope & Son didn't hire just anybody, not even on trial, not even without pay!

The next morning at seven o'clock sharp I was already on the rue Michodière, outside their iron shutter . . . I jumped to it . . . I helped the errand boy . . . I turned the crank for him . . . I wanted to show my zeal first thing . . .

Of course it wasn't Monsieur Berlope himself that broke me in, it was Monsieur Lavelongue . . . He was a real bastard, you could see that right away. He had his eye on you all day long, always trying to catch you off your guard . . . Wherever you went, he came pussyfooting along behind you . . . He slithered after you like a snake, from corridor to corridor . . . His arms dangling, ready to pounce, to crush you . . . on the lookout for a cigarette . . . for the least bit of a butt . . . for any poor tired bastard that sat down . . .

Before I'd finished taking my coat off, he gave me the lowdown.

"I am your personnel director . . . What's your name?"

"Ferdinand, sir."

"Well, you'd better get this straight . . . No monkey-shines around here . . . If you're not absolutely up to snuff in a month from now . . . I personally will fire you . . . Understand? . . . Have I made myself clear?"

Having made himself clear, he vanished like a ghost between the piles of boxes . . . He was always mumbling something or other . . . When you thought he was miles away, he was right on top of you . . . He was a hunchback. He'd hide behind the customers. The salesmen lived in terror of him from morning to night. He always had a smile on his face, but it was a special kind of a smile . . . Really poisonous . . .

Silk gets into a worse mess than any other kind of material. All the different widths and lengths, the samples and leftovers, get rumpled and twisted and scattered all over the place . . . By the end of the day it's a horrible sight . . . Enormous mounds, all tangled up like bushes.

From morning to night the store is full of dressmakers' errand girls, clucking and griping, never satisfied. They rummage, they complain, they splash around . . . the place is a nuthouse of silks and satins . . . wriggling and writhing with ribbons . . .

After seven o'clock we have to put it all away, what a mess! . . . There are too many of us . . . We suffocate in the stuff . . . An orgy of loose ends. Thousands and thousands of colors . . . moiré, satin, tulle . . . Where-ever those yak-yaks get a hand in, it's worse than a battle-field. There isn't a single box left. The numbers are all mixed up. We get the hell bawled out of us and then some . . . By every louse in the department! Fat salesmen with slicked-down hair or wigs à la Mayol.*

Cleaning up is the apprentices' job . . . Rolling up the spools, pinning up ends, turning the baby ribbon . . . the masses of felt . . . macramé, velvet . . . the riot of changeable silk . . . all the leftovers, the whole sickening avalanche of remnants . . . it's all for the apprentices. You've hardly got it straightened out when some more wreckers start in . . . making more havoc . . . ruining all your work . . .

They put on airs . . . they make idiotic remarks, they're so kittenish you want to puke . . . and always carrying their patterns around, looking for some other shade, the one we haven't got . . .

In addition to this I had my regular job that was pretty exhausting . . . running back and forth to the stockroom. About fifty times a day. It was on the eighth floor. I had to tote all the boxes. Whole carloads of tag ends, of mixed-up snippets or plain rubbish . . . All the returns were my job . . . The marquisettes, big pieces and little pieces, the styles of a whole season—I hauled them up seven flights. It was really a rough job. Enough to kill a mule. With all my hurry and effort my collar with the

* See Glossary.

bow tie on it worked itself up around my ears. And yet it was double-starched.

Monsieur Lavelongue was very hard on me . . . and unfair. As soon as a customer came on the scene, he motioned me to beat it. I wasn't ever allowed to hang around. I wasn't fit to be seen . . . Naturally with all the layers of dust in the stockroom and the way I sweated, my face was one big smudge. But the moment I left he began to give me hell for disappearing. It was impossible to please him.

The other punks were in stitches at the way I was always running, the way I raced up the stairs. Lavelongue wouldn't let me rest a minute:

"A little sport is good for young people! . . ." That was his line. I'd hardly come down when they'd slip me another load! . . . "Get going, kid. You can't fool me."

Smocks were not worn in the garment district in those days, it wasn't considered proper. With the kind of work I was doing my beautiful jacket was soon threadbare.

"You're going to wear out more than you make," my mother complained. That wasn't hard, because I wasn't paid at all. It's true that in some trades the apprentices had to pay to learn. In a way I was lucky . . . I was in no position to complain . . . I raced up to the stockroom with so much vigor that the other kids called me the Squirrel. Even so, Lavelongue always had it in for me. He couldn't forgive me for having been taken on by Monsieur Berlope. The mere sight of me gave him the gollywobbles. He couldn't stand my guts. He did everything he could to discourage me.

He even complained about my shoes, he said I made too much noise on the stairs. It's true I had a tendency to walk on my heels, my toes hurt something terrible, especially toward closing time they felt like hot coals.

"Ferdinand!" he'd yell. "You're insufferable. You make more racket all by yourself than a whole bus line." That was an exaggeration.

My jacket was coming apart in several places. I was a bottomless pit for suits. They had to have another one made out of one of Uncle Édouard's old ones. My father was in a constant temper, he was having the worst kind of trouble at the office. While he was away on vacation, those bastards, the clerks, had taken advantage of his absence to slander him . . .

Monsieur Lempreinte, his boss, believed every word they told him. His trouble was stomach cramps. When he was really in pain, he saw tigers on the ceiling . . . That didn't help.

I didn't know what to do to make a good impression at Berlope's. The harder I raced up the stairs, the more Lavelongue couldn't stand me. I really gave him a pain in the neck.

Along around five o'clock he went out for a cup of coffee, and I took the opportunity to take my shoes off for a minute up in the stockroom. I'd do it in the can too when nobody was there. So one day those cocksuckers go and tell the boss. Lavelongue did a hundred-yard dash, I was his obsession . . . He was there in two seconds flat.

"Will you come out of there, you little skunk? Is that what you call working? . . . Jerking yourself off in every corner you can find . . . Is that your way of learning the trade? . . . Flat on your ass with your dick in the air! . . . That's the younger generation for you!"

I found another place where I could give my dogs a little air. I'd hold them under the faucet. My shoes were always getting me in trouble . . . at home too . . . after making such a sacrifice, my mother would never have admitted that she had bought them too narrow. It was just my laziness again. My unwillingness. I was always in the wrong.

The stockroom where I took the boxes was little André's headquarters . . . His job was repairing the boxes and going over the numbers with a brush and blacking. He'd started in the year before. He lived miles away in the suburbs, he had a long way to travel . . . The hole he lived in was after Vanves, the neighborhood was called "the Coconut Palms."

He had to get up at five o'clock so as not to spend too much on streetcars. He brought a basket. His grub was in it. It was closed with a rod and padlock.

In the winter he didn't budge, he ate in the stockroom, but in summer he'd go out to the Palais-Royal and eat on a bench. He'd leave a couple of minutes ahead of time to be there at twelve sharp when the cannon went off. He liked that.

He never showed himself much, he always had a cold, he was always blowing his nose even in the middle of August.

His clothes were worse than mine, all patches. The other apprentices were always picking fights with him because he stuttered and didn't make sense . . . He preferred to stay upstairs, no one came up to bother him.

His aunt whopped the hell out of him too, especially when he peed in bed, terrible lickings, he described them in detail. Mine were nothing in comparison . . . He wanted me to go to the Palais-Royal with him, he wanted to show me the whores, he spoke to them, so he claimed. He had some sparrows too that would even fly down on his bread. But I couldn't go. I had to go straight home. My father had sworn he'd have me locked up in La Roquette if he caught me bumming around.

On the subject of women, my father was a holy terror . . . if he suspected me of wanting to see what it was like, he flew into a ferocious temper. It was enough that I jerked off. He brought it up every day on the slightest pretext. He was suspicious of little André . . . He had the instincts of the common people . . . He was a hoodlum's kid . . . With me it was entirely different, I had respectable parents and I shouldn't ever forget it, I was reminded every night when I got home from Berlope's, so tired I couldn't see straight. I'd get an old-time thrashing if I dared to talk back! . . . I'd better not keep bad company! I already had too many foul habits that I'd picked up God knows where . . . If I listened to little André, I'd be sure to end up a murderer. My father could swear to it. Actually he regarded my loathsome vices as a part of his misfortunes, of the terrible troubles that fate had heaped on him . . .

I did have terrible vices, it was undeniable, it was awful. That's the truth. He didn't know how to go about saving me . . . And I didn't know how to go about making amends . . . Some children are simply untouchable.

Little André smelled bad, his smell was more acrid than mine, the smell of really poor people. He smelled up the whole stockroom. His aunt cropped his hair short with her own scissors, he looked like a lawn with a single tuft left in front.

With all the dust he breathed in, the snot in his nose turned to putty . . . it was stuck tight . . . His favorite pastime was prying out a chunk and quietly eating it. Since we blew our noses with our fingers in the middle of all the blacking and boogers and numbers, we ended up looking like niggers.

Little André handled about three hundred boxes a day . . . His eyes were always dilated from trying to see in that attic. He kept his pants on with strings and safety pins.

Now that I was doing the dumbwaiter work, he stopped coming in through the salesrooms. That was better for him, it spared him a lot of rough treatment. He came in through the court, slipped past the caretaker's lodge, and went up the outside stairs . . . If there were too many numbers, I'd stay late and help him. After hours I was able to take my shoes off.

When we wanted to shoot the shit, we had it pretty nice. On account of his nose we slipped into a little nook between two beams, sheltered from the drafts.

André was lucky with his feet, he had stopped growing. Two of his brothers were still living with another aunt in Les Lilas. His sisters were with his old man in Aubervilliers . . . His father read all the gas meters in the region . . . He hardly ever saw him, he didn't have time.

Sometimes we showed each other our pricks. Besides, I told him what was going on downstairs in the salesrooms, the guys who were going to be fired, because some were always getting the ax . . . That was how those punks spent their time . . . getting each other fired by spreading stories . . . vicious lies . . . We'd also talk about the different methods of getting a look at a customer's ass when she sat down for a minute.

Some of those errand girls were pretty wicked . . . Sometimes they'd put their feet up on a stool just to give you a view of their ass. Then they'd toddle away with a big grin . . . One of them showed me her garters as I was passing . . . And made sucking noises at me . . . I went upstairs to tell little André about it . . . We speculated . . . What would her crack be like? Was it very

runny and what color? yellow? red? did it burn? And her
legs . . . the top part? We made sounds too with our
tongues and saliva, we imitated the kissing routine . . .
Even so we knocked off twenty-five to thirty pieces an
hour. Little André taught me the trick with the pin, which
is the main thing to know when you're smoothing out the
ends of the pieces . . . on the selvedge . . . the little rim
of the satin. One on each side . . . that's where you stick
them . . . You've got to be careful not to mess up the
smooth side . . . You've got to wash your hands first.
It's a real art.

At home they realized I wasn't going to last long at
Berlope's, that I hadn't started out right . . . Lavelongue
would run into Mama around the neighborhood when
she was out shopping. He'd always make some nasty remark. "Ah, madame, that little boy of yours, he's not a
bad sort, but what a scatterbrain! . . . Ah, how right
you were! . . . His head just isn't screwed on right!
. . . I really don't know what we'll be able to do with
him! . . . Everything he touches, he knocks it over!
. . . Ah la la! . . ."
It was all a pack of lies . . . lousy injustice . . . I
knew it perfectly well. I wasn't so innocent anymore! He
told all those stinking lies so I'd go on working for nothing! . . . He took advantage of my parents . . . Let
them go on feeding me! . . . He ran me down so he
wouldn't have to pay me . . . There was nothing I could
do about it . . . If I'd complained, they wouldn't have
believed me . . . they'd only have yelled louder . . .
Even a poor little punk like André was making thirty-
five francs a month. They couldn't exploit him any worse.
My father tortured his imagination about my future . . .
where could they send me? He was at his wits' end . . .
I was no good for office work . . . Probably even worse
than he was . . . I had no education at all . . . If I
failed in business, it was the end . . . Right away he
was at half-mast . . . He clamored for help . . . And
yet I tried . . . I worked up enthusiasm . . . I got to
work hours ahead of time . . . I was the last to leave
. . . And even so they disapproved of me . . . I was

always fouling things up . . . I was in a panic . . . Everything I did was wrong . . .

If you haven't been through that you'll never know what obsessive hatred really smells like . . . the hatred that goes through your guts, all the way to your heart . . .

Nowadays I'm always meeting characters who complain, who bristle with indignation . . . They're just poor bastards that aren't getting anywhere . . . jerks . . . dinner-table failures . . . that kind of rebellion is for weak sisters . . . they didn't pay for it, they got it for nothing . . . They're drips.

Where did they get it from? . . . no place . . . the *lycée* maybe . . . It's a lot of talk, hot air. Real hatred comes from deep down, from a defenseless childhood crushed with work. That's the hatred that kills you. There'll be more of it, so deep and thick there will always be some left, enough to go around . . . It will ooze out over the earth . . . and poison it, so nothing will grow but viciousness, among the dead, among men.

Every night when I came home, my mother asked me if I hadn't been given notice . . . She was always expecting the worst. At supper we talked about it some more. The subject was inexhaustible. Would I ever earn my living? . . .

With all that kind of talk I couldn't stand looking at the bread on the table. I was afraid to ask for any. I hurried through the meal. That drove my mother crazy, though she was a quick eater too.

"Ferdinand! You're doing it again. You don't even see what you're eating. You gulp it all down without chewing. You bolt your food like a dog. And the way you look! You're transparent! You're green! . . . How do you expect to get any good out of your food! We do all we can for you! But you just waste your food."

Little André had a certain amount of peace in the stockroom. Lavelongue hardly ever went up. As long as he painted his numbers, nobody bothered him much.

André loved flowers, invalids often do. He brought them in from the country and stuck them in bottles . . . He decorated all the rafters with them . . . One morning he even brought in an enormous bunch of hawthorn

. . . The others saw him coming in . . . They couldn't stand it . . . They talked about it so much in front of Lavelongue that he went up in person to have a look . . . He bawled hell out of André and threw the whole bundle out in the court . . .

Downstairs in the big showrooms they were all bastards, especially the shipping clerks; I've never known such stinkers, such a slimy lot of fishwives . . . They had nothing to think about but making packages.

One of these characters was Magadur, a big tall guy in the Paris shipping department . . . he was the worst bastard imaginable. He went to work on André and turned him against me . . . They often came in together from the Porte des Lilas . . . He told him all kinds of crap to poison him against me . . . It was easy, André was very impressionable. All alone in his corner, for hours on end in the stockroom, he was always mulling things over. All you had to do was hand him a line and get him worried . . . Once he was started, nothing could stop him . . . Any cock-and-bull story would do it . . . I come in and find him all in a dither.

"Is it true, Ferdinand?" he asks me. "Is it true? That you want to take my job?"

His attack took me by surprise . . . I was flabbergasted . . . I couldn't understand . . . He went on . . .

"Aw, go on! Save your breath. Everybody in the store knows all about it. I was the only one that didn't suspect . . . I'm a sap, that's all!"

He was always pretty pale, now he turned yellow; he he always looked horrible with his snot and the gaps in his teeth . . . when he got excited you couldn't stand to look at him . . . his face all covered with impetigo, the stubble on his head, the way he smelled . . . I couldn't bring myself to say anything . . . I was too much ashamed for him . . .

I'd a thousand times rather have been fired on the spot than have him suspect me of wanting to take his job . . . But then where would I go? That was a big decision to make . . . Much too big for me . . . All I could do was hang on, do my damnedest, try to clear myself . . . I tried to put him straight. But that bastard Magadur had really rubbed it in.

After that he didn't trust me at all. He never showed me his prick anymore. He was afraid I'd go and tell on him. He went to the crapper by himself to smoke in peace. He never even mentioned the Palais-Royal anymore . . .

Between two trips to the eighth floor, hauling all the bundles, I collapsed under the mansard roof. I took off my shoes and my coat and waited for it to pass . . .

André pretended not to see me, he had a copy of *Illustrated Adventure Stories*. He read it all by himself. He spread it out on the floor . . . If I spoke to him even at the top of my lungs, he pretended not to hear me. He brushed in his numbers. Everything I could say or do made him suspicious. In his opinion I was a traitor. If he were ever to lose his job, he had often told me, his aunt would give him such a licking he'd end up in the hospital . . . That was the story. I'd known it all along . . . But even so I couldn't stand having him take me for a rat.

"Say, André," I said to him at my wits' end. "You ought to know I don't want to get you fired . . ."

He still didn't answer, he went on mumbling over his pictures . . . He read to himself out loud . . . I took a look to see what it said . . . It was the story of King Krogold . . . I knew the story well . . . I'd always known it . . . since Grandma Caroline . . . She'd taught me to read with it . . . All he had was one old number . . .

"Say, André," I said. "I know the whole story by heart. I know how it goes on . . ." He still didn't answer. But I was getting somewhere . . . I'd caught his interest . . . He didn't have the next number . . .

"Here's how it goes," I said, grasping at the opportunity. "All the people of Christiania . . . the whole city . . . have taken refuge in the church . . . in the cathedral, under the vaulting, it's four times as big as Notre-Dame . . . They all go down on their knees . . . in there . . . Are you listening? . . . They're afraid of King Krogold . . . They pray to heaven for forgiveness for having meddled in the war . . . for having protected Prince Gwendor . . . the traitor . . . They don't know where to go . . . There are a hundred thousand of them

in the church . . . Nobody dares to leave . . . They're
so scared they don't even know their prayers . . . They
mumble a lot of gibberish . . . Old people, merchants,
young people, mothers, priests, cowards, little children,
beautiful dames, the archbishops, the constables, they're
all shitting in their pants . . . They all lie flat in a heap
. . . A terrible jumble . . . All grunting and moaning
. . . The situation is so desperate they're even afraid to
breathe . . . They entreat . . . they implore . . . that
King Krogold won't burn the whole place . . . but only
the suburbs a little . . . that he won't burn everything
to punish them . . . they're attached to their market,
the granaries, the weighing house, the presbytery, the
courthouse, the cathedral . . . St. Christiania . . . the
most magnificent in the whole world! Nobody knows
where to put himself . . . they're so cowed . . . how
to disappear . . .

"And then from down below, from beyond the walls,
an enormous din is heard . . . It's King Krogold's advance guard . . . the clatter of heavy armor on the
drawbridge . . . Ah, yes, they're coming all right! And
the horsemen of his escort . . . King Krogold is at the
gates . . . he rises up in his stirrups . . . The jangling
of a thousand suits of armor is heard . . . The knights
crossing the suburb of St. Stanislas . . . The enormous
city seems deserted . . . There's nobody in the king's
path . . . Here comes the train of servants . . . The
gate isn't wide enough . . . The wagons will never get
through . . . They rip down the high walls on both
sides . . . Everything comes tumbling down . . . Wagons, legions, barbarians, rush through, catapults, elephants with upraised trunks pour in through the breach
. . . In the city everything is silent, frozen . . . Belfries
. . . convents . . . houses . . . market stalls . . . Nothing stirs . . .

"King Krogold has stopped on the first steps of the
parvis . . . Around him his twenty-three mastiffs mount
the steps, yelping and leaping . . . His pack is famous
for their prowess in hunting the bear and the aurochs
. . . they've torn whole forests to pieces . . . from the
Elbe to the Carpathians . . . In spite of the tumult Krogold hears the sound of hymns . . . sung by that dense,

hidden, harried crowd beneath the vaulting . . . their
prayer . . . The vast doors swing on their hinges . . .
And Krogold sees them all seething and writhing before
him . . . In the depths of the shadow . . . Can the
whole people be in hiding? . . . He fears treachery . . .
He doesn't go in . . . The organs rumble . . . Their
thunder pours out through the triple porch . . . Defi-
ance! . . . This city is disloyal! . . . And always will
be! . . . He orders the provost to clear the church at
once . . . Three thousand henchmen storm in, bruising
and battering . . . chopping and mauling . . . The
crowd gives way, regroups around them . . . squashes
against the doors . . . gathers in the aisles . . . The
ruffians are sucked in . . . They charge and charge
again . . . they aren't getting anywhere . . . Still in his
saddle, the king waits . . . His charger, a huge, shaggy
beast, paws the ground . . . The king is devouring a
great big hunk of meat, a leg of mutton; he bites into it,
he buries his fangs in it . . . He tears it to pieces, he's
awful mad . . . What's this? No headway? . . . The
king hoists himself up in his stirrups again . . . He's the
biggest bruiser of them all . . . He whistles . . . He
calls . . . He gathers his mastiffs around him . . .
He brandishes his big hunk of meat over his crown . . .
He chucks it way out . . . into the darkness . . . It falls
in the middle of the church . . . in the middle of the
cowering mass . . . The whole pack bounds forward,
howling . . . they spring up everywhere . . . leaping
at throats . . . tearing . . . crunching . . . The panic
is terrible . . . The yapping grows louder . . . The
whole terrified flood pours out the doors . . . pushing
. . . scrambling . . . a torrent, an avalanche . . . all
the way to the drawbridges . . . They're dashed against
the walls . . . Between the lances and the wagons . . .
The king's path is open . . . The whole cathedral is his
. . . He spurs his horse . . . He enters . . . He orders
all to be silent . . . the dogs . . the people . . . the
organ . . . the army . . . He rides another two lengths
. . . He's passed the three porches . . . Slowly he un-
sheathes . . . his enormous sword . . . He makes a
big sign of the cross with it . . . And then he hurls it
away . . . far, far . . . It lands in the middle of the

altar! . . . The war is over . . . His brother the bishop approaches . . . He falls on his knees . . . He sings his Credo . . ."

Say what you like, that makes an impression. Little André would really have liked me to go on . . . to throw in some more details . . . He liked nice stories . . . But he was afraid I'd begin to influence him . . . He fished around in his box . . . He jiggled his little pieces of zinc . . . his brushes . . . he didn't want me to cast a spell on him . . . he didn't want us to be friends like before . . .

The same afternoon I came back up again with another load . . . He still wouldn't speak to me . . . I was good and tired, I sat down . . . I really wanted him to talk to me. "Say, André," I said, "I know the next chapter too, when all the merchants go off to Palestine . . . With Thibaut on the crusade . . . And they leave the troubadour behind to guard the castle . . . and Wanda, the princess . . . You never heard about that? It's marvelous . . . especially Wanda's vengeance, the way she washes away her affront in blood . . . the way she humiliates her father . . ."

Little André pricked up his ears. He didn't want to interrupt me, but I heard faint sounds in the corridor . . . I didn't want to break the spell. Suddenly I saw Lavelongue's phizz in the little window . . . I jumped . . . He must have come up that very second to catch me . . . Of course somebody had tipped him off . . . I shot up . . . I put my shoes on . . . He just gives me a little sign . . .

"Splendid, Ferdinand. Splendid! We'll attend to this later. Stay right where you are, my boy!"

I didn't have to wait long. The next day I come home for lunch and my mother gives it to me . . .

"Ferdinand," she starts right in . . . already resigned, absolutely convinced . . . "Monsieur Lavelongue has just left . . . Yes, in person! . . . Do you know what he said? . . . He doesn't want you on the job anymore. Isn't that a fine how-do-you-do? He was dissatisfied before, but this was the last straw. He tells me you hide in the attic for hours on end! . . . Instead of getting ahead with your work! . . . And giving little André bad ideas . . . He caught you . . . Don't deny it . . . telling stories . . . disgusting stories . . . Don't try to tell me any different! . . . With a common child like that! A guttersnipe! Monsieur Lavelongue has known us for ten years, luckily, thank goodness! He knows we're not to blame. He knows how we work our fingers to the bone. Both of us, your father and I, to give you everything you need. He knows the kind of people we are . . . He respects us. He wants to treat us kindly. He's asked us to take you back. Out of consideration for us he won't dismiss you . . . He'll spare us the shame of it . . . Ah, when I tell your father . . . he's going to be sick! . . ."

Just then he comes home from the office. The moment he opened the door, she starts telling him the story . . . As he listened, he clutched the table . . . He couldn't believe his ears . . . He looked me up and down and shrugged his shoulders . . . The two of them collapsed with dismay . . . A monster like me was past understanding . . . He didn't bellow . . . he didn't even hit me . . . He only wondered how he could bear it . . . He gave up. He rocked his chair . . . "Hm! . . . Hm! . . . Hm!" was all he said . . . back and forth . . . Then finally he spoke . . .

"So you're even more unnatural, more underhanded, more abject than I imagined, Ferdinand?"

Then he looked at my mother and called her to witness that there was nothing more they could do . . . that I was incorrigible . . .

I myself was crushed, I searched the depths of my soul, trying to figure out what enormous vices, what unprecedented depravities I could be guilty of . . . I couldn't get it straight . . . I couldn't make up my mind . . . I found a whole raft of them, but I wasn't sure of anything . . .

My father closed the session. He went up to his room, he wanted to be alone to think . . . I slept in a nightmare . . . The whole time I saw little André telling Monsieur Berlope awful things . . .

The following afternoon my mother and I went to get my reference . . . Monsieur Lavelongue gave it to us in person . . . Besides, he wanted to speak to me . . .

"Ferdinand," he said to me. "Out of consideration for your worthy parents I'm not going to dismiss you . . . They are taking you back . . . of their own free will! You see the difference? Believe me, I'm sorry to see you leaving us. But I've got to face the facts: your misconduct has undermined discipline in every department . . . And I'm responsible, you see . . . I have had to take measures, what's right is right! . . . But let this setback be a lesson to you. What little you've learned will surely be of use to you somewhere else! Experience is never wasted. You'll have other employers, maybe some will be even less indulgent . . . It was a lesson you needed . . . Well, Ferdinand, now you've had it . . . I only hope you benefit by it . . . At your age you can always make up for lost time . . ." He shook my hand with a good deal of conviction. My mother's emotion was indescribable . . . She dabbed at her eyes.

"Apologize, Ferdinand," she ordered me as we were getting up to go. "He's young, monsieur, he's young . . . Thank Monsieur Lavelongue for giving you an excellent reference after all you've done . . . You don't deserve it, you know!"

"Don't mention it, madame, it's nothing, nothing at all, I assure you. It's the least I could do. Ferdinand is not the first young man to start out on the wrong foot. Oh, no, far from it. Ten years from now he himself . . . I can assure you . . . will come to me and say: 'Monsieur Lavelongue, you did the right thing. You are a good man! Thanks to you, I found out what's what!' . . . But today he has it in for me . . . It's only natural." My mother protested. He tapped me on the shoulder. He showed us out.

The very next day they took on another apprentice for the stockroom . . . I heard about it . . . He didn't last three months . . . He flopped down on every landing . . . The work killed him.

But innocent or guilty, a lot of good it did me. I was getting to be a real headache for the whole family. Uncle Édouard began to look for another job for me, as a salesman, I'd have to start all over again. But it wasn't so easy for him this time . . . I'd have to try a different line . . .

I already had a past . . . It would be best not to mention it. And that's what we decided.

Once he'd recovered from the shock, my father started raving again . . . He drew up a complete inventory of all my faults, one by one . . . He searched for the vices hidden deep down in me like a scientist looking for mysterious phenomena . . . He let out diabolical screams . . . He was having his fits again . . . He was being persecuted by a whole carnival of demons . . . He really turned on the gas . . . He dragged everybody into it . . . Jews . . . schemers . . . social climbers . . . And most of all the Freemasons . . . I don't know what they had to do with it . . . He tracked his enemies to the ends of the earth . . . He got so lost in his apocalypse that in the end he forgot all about me . . .

He laced into Lempreinte, the monster with the stomach trouble . . . And Baron Méfaize, his managing director . . . Anybody and anything would do, as long as he could rave and splutter . . . He made a terrible hullabaloo, the neighbors were in stitches.

My mother dragged herself at his feet . . . He wouldn't stop bellowing . . . He remembered me and my future . . . He discovered the worst symptoms in me . . . The most abominable profligacy! . . . Oh well, he washed his hands of me . . . Like Pontius Pilate . . . That's exactly what he said . . . His conscience was clear . . .

My mother looked at me . . . her "cross". . . It was sad, but she resigned herself . . . She'd never abandon me . . . Obviously I was going to end on the gallows and she'd stick by me all the way . . .

We had only one thing in common in our family in the Passage, and that was our terror of going hungry. We all had plenty of that. It was with me from my first breath . . . They passed it right on to me . . . We were all obsessed with it . . . As far as we were concerned, the soul was fear. In every room the walls sweated fear of going without . . . It made us swallow the wrong way, it made us bolt our meals and run around town like mad . . . we zigzagged like fleas all over Paris, from the Place Maubert to the Étoile, for fear of being auctioned

off, for fear of the rent, of the gas man, the tax collector
. . . We were always in such a hurry I never had time
to wipe myself properly.

Since my dismissal from Berlope's, I had in addition,
all to myself, the fear of never getting anywhere in the
world . . . I've known poor unemployed bastards, hundreds of them, here and all over the world, people who
were only half a step from the poorhouse . . . They
hadn't managed right.

To tell the truth, my main pleasure in life is being
quicker than the boss when it comes to getting fired
. . . I can see that kidney punch coming . . . I can
smell it a mile off . . . I can tell when a job is folding
. . . I've got some other little racket sprouting in my
other pocket. Bosses are all stinkers, all they think
about is giving you the gate . . . There's only one kind
of real lowdown fear, the fear of being out on your ass,
flat broke and no job . . . I've always had one on hand,
some lousy meal ticket, it doesn't matter what kind . . .
I nibble at it, kind of like vaccinating yourself . . . I
don't give a shit what it is . . . I lug it through the
streets, the mountains, and the muck . . . I've had such
cockeyed ones they had neither shape, size, nor taste . . .
It's all one to me . . . It's no skin off my ass. The sicker
they make me, the less I worry . . .

I hate all jobs. Why should I make distinctions? . . .
You won't catch me singing any hymns of praise . . .
I'd shit on the whole lot of them if I could . . . That's
what it is to work for hire . . .

Uncle Édouard was doing better and better in his
hardware business. He mostly sold stuff for automobiles
in the provinces, headlights and accessories. Unfortunately I was too young to go on the road with him. I'd
have to wait a while . . . Besides, after what had happened I needed watching.

Uncle Édouard wasn't so pessimistic about me, he
didn't think my case was so hopeless. If I was no good
at a sedentary job, he said, maybe I'd make a first-class
traveling salesman.

It seemed to be worth trying . . . Appearance was
important, you had to have the right clothes . . . To
make me really acceptable they added a couple of years

to my age, they got me an extra-stiff collar, I'd wrecked all the others. They got me spats too, nice and gray over my shoes, so my feet wouldn't look so enormous, so they wouldn't clutter up people's doormats. My father was skeptical, he had given up hope in my future. The neighbors put in their two cents' worth, they all gave advice . . . Not that they expected much of my career . . . Even the Passage caretaker was against me . . . When he went around lighting the lamps, he'd drop in at all the shops and bat the breeze. I'd turn out to be a screwball, that's what he told everybody, sort of like my father in his opinion, good for nothing except pestering people . . . Luckily there was Visios, the sailor, he had a soft spot for me, he realized I was doing my best and contradicted everybody. He said I wàsn't a bad kid. There was a good deal of talk . . . but I was still high and dry . . . They still had to find me a job.

At that point they began to wonder what they should have me sell . . . My mother wanted me to be a jeweler. That was her fondest hope . . . It struck her as eminently respectable. A jeweler's staff had to be more than neat and spruce, they had to look really smart . . . And they handled treasures behind gleaming counters. But jewelers are tough when it comes to trusting anybody. They're always trembling for their jewels. They can't sleep, they're so scared of being burgled, strangled, and set on fire! . . . Christ!

One thing that was indispensable was scrupulous honesty! On that score we had nothing to fear. With parents like mine, so meticulous, so strict about honoring their business obligations, I had a terrific reference! . . . I could apply to any employer . . . the most obsessed . . . the most suspicious . . . With me he could rest easy. Never, as far back as anybody could remember, had there been a thief in our family, not a single one.

Once that was settled, we began to look around. Mama reconnoitered some, she went to see the people we knew . . . They didn't need anybody . . . In spite of my good intentions it was no cinch landing a job, even on trial.

They outfitted me again to make me more attractive. I was getting to be as costly as an invalid. I'd worn

out my suit completely . . . I'd gone through my shoes
. . . In addition to my matching spats they got me a
new pair of shoes, Broomfields, the English brand, with
enormous jutting soles . . . they looked like submarines.
They got them twice too big, so they'd last a couple of
years at least . . . They were awfully narrow, I thought
I'd sprain my ankle, but I bore it with grim determination.
I hobbled along on the Boulevards like a deep-sea diver.

Once I was patched up, my mother and I headed for
the addresses we had. Uncle Édouard gave us the ones
he got from his friends, we found the rest in the directory.
Madame Divonne kept the shop every morning until
noon while we went out job hunting. Believe me, we had
no time for dawdling . . . We combed the whole Marais,
door after door, and then the cross streets, rue Quin-
campois, rue Galante, rue aux Ours, rue Vieille-du-
Temple . . . We did the whole neighborhood, take my
word for it, floor by floor . . .

My mother hobbled along behind . . . Tip-tap-plunk!
Tip-tap-plunk! . . . She'd offer my services to every
family, to little home artisans huddled behind their globes
. . . She offered me ever so kindly . . . as an extra tool
. . . a useful little drudge . . . not at all demanding
. . . clever, eager, energetic . . . and best of all, a fast
runner! All in all a good bargain . . . Well trained,
obedient . . . At our timid ring on the bell, they'd open
the door a crack . . . at first they were suspicious . . .
Cigarette immobilized, expectant . . . they'd peer at me
over their spectacles . . . They'd take a good look . . .
Not very appetizing, they decided . . . In the face of
their blousy wrinkled smocks, my mother would start her
song and dance:

"You wouldn't be needing a young salesman, monsieur? . . . I'm his mother. I thought I'd better come
along . . . all he asks is to give satisfaction . . . He's
a very well-behaved young man . . . You can easily
make inquiries about him . . . We've been in business
for twelve years in the Passage des Bérésinas . . . The
child has been raised in business . . . His father works
for the Coccinelle Fire Insurance Company . . . You
must have heard of it . . . We're not rich, either one
of us, but we don't owe anybody a single penny . . .

We honor our obligations . . . His father in the insurance company . . ."

We'd generally do twelve to fifteen of a morning, all kinds . . . Jewel setters, cutters, and polishers, chain makers, silversmiths, and even trades that have gone out of existence, like silver gilders and agate engravers.

They examine us some more . . . They put down their magnifying glasses to get a better look . . . to make sure we're not bandits . . . murderers . . . escaped convicts . . . Once reassured, they became friendly, even sympathetic . . . Except they don't need anybody . . . not for the moment. They couldn't afford any overhead . . . They made their own calls . . . The whole family was in the business, all together, in their tiny niches . . . The seven stories on the court were honeycombed with their burrows, their workshops were like little caves carved out of the walls of what had once been fashionable houses . . . They'd stopped trying to keep up appearances . . . They lived on top of each other, wife, kids, grandmother, all working together . . . At the most they'd take on an apprentice for the Christmas rush . . .

My mother ran out of arguments and suggested as a last inducement that they take me on without pay . . . that really made them jump. They'd clam up tight and slam the door in our faces. They were suspicious of anybody who'd work for nothing. It looked shady as hell. We'd have to start all over again. My mother concentrated on inspiring confidence, but it didn't seem to get us very far. She couldn't very well represent me as an apprentice in stone setting or machining fine metal . . . It was too late for that . . . I'd never be handy with my fingers . . . The most I could expect to be was a blabbermouth, an outside salesman, a common ordinary "young man" . . . My career had been bungled in every way . . .

When we got home, my father wanted to know what what was what . . . We were always empty-handed and it drove him nuts. All evening he'd thrash around in the most terrible nightmares . . . You could have furnished a dozen loonybins with the contents of his dome . . .

My mother's legs were all twisted from climbing stairs

. . . She felt so funny she couldn't stop . . . She kept
limping around the table making the most terrible faces
. . . She had drawing pains in her legs . . . she was
racked with cramps . . .

We'd race off bright and early to other addresses all
the same . . . rue Réamur, rue Greneta . . . the Bastille, rue des Jeûneurs . . . and especially the Place des
Vosges . . . after several months of begging and stair
climbing, of puffing and pestering for nothing, my mother
began to wonder whether people couldn't tell by the cut
of my jib that I was nothing but an insubordinate little
no-good . . . My father didn't doubt it for a moment
. . . He'd known it for years . . . His certainty was
reinforced every time we came home empty-handed . . .
dazed, panting, dog-tired, wet from running, drenched
inside and out with sweat and rain . . .

"It's harder to get that kid a job than to liquidate our
whole stock . . . and I don't have to tell you, Clémence,
that wouldn't be easy."

He hadn't been educated for nothing, he knew how
to make comparisons, to draw inferences.

My last suit was already sagging in all directions, with
great big bags at the knees, stairs are death on clothes.
Luckily I was able to borrow an old hat from my father.
We wore the same size. It wasn't in very good shape, so I
always held it in my hand. The part I wore out was the
brim . . . People were awfully polite in those days. . . .

It was high time Uncle Édouard found me a decent
address. We were really out of luck. We didn't know what
to do. And then one day the whole thing got straightened
out . . . He came in at lunch time, beaming and burbling . . . He was absolutely positive. He'd gone to
see this man, a master engraver. He was going to take me
on. It was in the bag!

Gorloge was his name, he lived on the rue Elzévir, in
an apartment on the sixth floor. He went in mostly for
rings, brooches, embossed bracelets, and small repair jobs.
He took anything that came his way. He struggled along
from day to day. He didn't expect much. He tried to
give satisfaction regardless.

Édouard infected us with his confidence. We couldn't

wait to see him. We didn't even finish our cheese. In two
seconds flat my mother and I were out in the street . . .
A short bus ride, the Boulevards, the rue Elzévir . . .
Five flights . . . They were still at table when we rang
the bell. They ate bread soup too, big bowls of it, and
then noodles with cheese, and nuts for dessert. They'd
been expecting us. My uncle had sung my praises. We
had come at just the right moment . . . They didn't
gild the pill . . . They didn't try to hide anything . . .
They were having a hell of a time with their engraved
ornaments . . . They made no bones about it . . . for
twelve years there hadn't been anything doing . . . They
were still waiting for things to pick up . . . They were
moving heaven and earth . . . but the resurrection didn't
come . . . The customers had other things in mind. Ruin
was staring them in the face.

Even so, Monsieur Gorloge was holding out, he was
putting up a fight . . . He still had hope . . . He
dressed like Uncle Arthur . . . the happy artist, with a
goatee, a flowing bow tie, long pointed shoes, and a
baggy smock all covered with wine spots . . . He sat
there at his ease. He was smoking, you couldn't even see
him behind the eddies of smoke . . . He fanned it away
with his hand.

Madame Gorloge sat across the table from him on a
low stool. Her tits were squashed against the workbench,
she was round all over, magnificent bulges . . . Her
curves overflowed from her apron . . . she was cracking nuts with her fists . . . a staggering blow from way
up, enough to split the table wide open. The whole workshop shook . . . She was quite a number . . . a former
model . . . I found that out later . . . The type appealed to me.

As for wages, the subject didn't even come up. We
didn't want to be indiscreet. That would come later . . .
I didn't expect him to offer anything. But then he made
up his mind after all, just as we were leaving. He said
I could expect a regular wage . . . thirty-five francs a
month . . . transportation included . . . And besides
I had prospects . . . a sizable bonus if by my efforts I
succeeded in reviving the engraver's craft. He thought
me a little young, but that didn't matter because I had

the sacred fire . . . because I'd grown up in the racket
. . . because I'd been born in a shop! . . . It was a deal
. . . all very heartwarming . . . one cheery remark
after another . . .

We went home to the Passage full of enthusiasm . . .
The rainbow at last. We finished our meal. We emptied
the jam pots. Papa took three helpings of wine. He let
a fine fart . . . like he'd almost stopped doing . . . We
kissed Uncle Édouard . . . There was wind in our sails
again after the awful famine.

The next day I went to the rue Elzévir bright and early
to get my collection.

The way Monsieur Gorloge was lounging around when
I came in, I thought he'd forgotten me . . . He was
sitting at the wide-open window, looking at the rooftops.
Between his knees he had a big bowl of coffee. He wasn't
doing a damn thing, that was plain. The view amused
him . . . the thousands of courtyards in the Petit Marais
. . . He had a dazed dreamy look . . . That can be
mighty fascinating, it can't be denied. The lovely lacework of slate . . . the light playing over it . . . the
intermingled colors . . . the way the gutters twist and
twine. And the sparrows hopping about . . . And
the wisps of smoke coiling over the deep chasms of
shadow . . .

He motioned me to keep my trap shut and listen to
things . . . to take in the scene . . . He didn't like to
be disturbed . . . He must have thought me rather un-
couth. He gave me a sulky look.

All around the court, from top to bottom, at every
window it was like a Punch and Judy show . . . heads
popping out . . . bald ones, bushy ones, pale faces . . .
squealing, griping, whistling . . . And then different
noises . . . A watering can tips, falls, bounces down on
the big cobblestones below . . . A pot of geraniums
slips . . . and flops kerplunk on the concierge's lodge.
It breaks into smithereens. The concierge comes bounding out of her grotto . . . flinging her cries out into
space. Help! . . . Bloody murder! . . . The whole house
is in an uproar . . . Every pest in the place rushes to
the window . . . They spew fire . . . they spit at each

other . . . They challenge each other across the void
. . . They're all yelling at once . . . You can't make
out who's in the right . . .

Monsieur Gorloge hangs out the window . . . He
doesn't want to miss one crumb . . . He's crazy about
these scenes . . . When things quiet down, he's heart-
broken . . . He heaves a sigh . . . and then another
. . . He goes back to his bread and butter . . . He
pours himself another bowl . . . he offers me some
coffee too . . .

"Ferdinand," he finally says, "I'd better tell you again
that it's not going to be any sinecure selling my merchandise . . . I've had ten salesmen already . . . They were
good boys, nothing wrong with them! And plenty of grit!
. . . Actually you're the twelfth, because to tell you the
truth, I've tried my hand at it too . . . Well, there you
have it . . . Anyway, come back tomorrow. I'm not in
form today . . . And . . . well no, hang around awhile
. . . Monsieur Antoine will be coming in . . . Maybe
I ought to introduce you . . . Oh well, you might as
well be leaving at that . . . I'll tell him I've hired you
. . . Won't he be surprised! He doesn't like salesmen!
He's my first assistant . . . my foreman in fact . . .
He's a tough customer . . . no doubt about that. You'll
know that as soon as you lay eyes on him. But he's very
helpful . . . yes, yes, I can't deny it . . . I want you to
meet little Robert too, our apprentice . . . He's a good
kid. You'll get along fine, I'm sure. He'll give you the
collection . . . It's in the bottom of the closet . . . It's
unique, see what I mean? . . . It's pretty heavy though
. . . About thirty pounds . . . Nothing but models
. . . Copper and lead . . . The earliest pieces date back
to my father . . . He had some beautiful things! Unique!
Unique! I remember seeing his Trocadéro! . . . All
handcarved, mounted as a diadem. Can you imagine?
It was worn twice . . . I still have the photograph. I'll
show it to you one of these days . . ."

Gorloge was sick of explaining . . . He was disgusted
again, fed up . . . He made a last effort . . . He put
his feet on the table . . . He let out a deep sigh . . .
He was wearing embroidered slippers, I can still see them
. . . with kittens running around on them . . .

"Well, Ferdinand, better go on home . . . Give your mother my best regards . . . On your way out would you tell the concierge to run over to the café at Number 26 and make a phone call for me . . . Tell her to call the Three Admirals Hotel and see if Antoine is sick . . . he's plumb crazy . . . to find out if anything has happened to him . . . He hasn't been in for two days now . . . She can yell up to me from the court . . . Tell her to look it up in the phone book . . . The Three Admirals . . . Tell her to send up some milk . . . The old lady isn't feeling very well . . . Tell her to send up the paper . . . any old paper . . . Well, maybe the *Sports News* . . ."

It wasn't next day, but the day after that I finally got to see the collection . . . Gorloge had understated . . . Thirty pounds! . . . It weighed at least twice that much . . . He had vaguely suggested certain "sales techniques" . . . but nothing very definite . . . He wasn't really sold on any of them . . . I could do exactly as I pleased . . . He relied on my initiative . . . I expected horrors but I've got to admit I had a sinking feeling when I saw that mess close up . . . It was unbelievable . . . Never had I seen such a lot of such disgusting monstrosities all at once . . . A challenge . . . A pocket inferno . . .

Everything we opened was horrible . . . nothing but gargoyles and bottle imps . . . made out of lead, turned and tortured, fussed and finicked . . . it turned your stomach . . . The whole Symbolist orgy . . . Chunks of nightmare . . . A putty "Samothrace" . . . more "Victories" in the shape of little clocks . . . Necklaces made out of Medusas, coils of snakes . . . More chimeras . . . Hundreds of allegorical rings, one crappier than the next . . . My work was cut out for me . . . All those things were supposed to be put on fingers, on belts, or stuck in ties. Or hung on somebody's ears . . . It was unbelievable! . . . Somebody was expected to buy them! Who? Great God, who? No form of dragon, demon, hobgoblin, or vampire was missing . . . A complete collection of nightmares . . . A whole world of sleepless nights . . . The manias of a whole insane asylum served up as trinkets . . . I was going from punk to horrible

. . . Even in my grandmother's store on the rue Mont-orgueil the most moth-eaten white elephants were things of beauty by comparison . . .

I'd never be able to make a living with such garbage. I was beginning to see the point about the ten saps before me. They must have been floored . . . These nightmares weren't being sold anymore . . . Since the last of the Romantics people had tucked them away in terror . . . Maybe people were still passing them around in families . . . when somebody died . . . but taking plenty of precautions . . . It wouldn't be safe to show such loony stuff to people who hadn't been warned . . . They might feel offended. Even Gorloge was afraid to do it . . . in person, that is. He'd given up buffeting the tide of fashion . . . The heroism was for me! . . . I was the last salesman! . . . Nobody had stuck it out for more than three weeks . . .

He himself did nothing but prospect for small repair jobs . . . to keep the shop going until fashions should change . . . He had kept up a few connections in the trade . . . Friends from better days who wouldn't have wanted to let him starve. They sent jobs his way . . . settings and patchwork . . . disgusting toil . . . but he never touched a finger to it himself . . . He passed it all on to our Antoine. Gorloge was an engraver . . . He wasn't going to ruin his touch doing menial work . . . he wasn't going to lose his standing and reputation for a few sous. No, sir. On that score he was adamant.

At nine o'clock sharp I climbed the stairs on the rue Elzévir, I didn't wait for him to come down . . . I flung myself on Paris right away, armed with my zeal and my "few pounds" of samples . . . Seeing as I was the outside man, they gave me a good outing . . . I was used to it. From the Bastille to the Madeleine . . . Miles and miles . . . All the Boulevards . . . every single jewelry store, one by one . . . Not to mention the little side streets . . . There was no room in my heart for discouragement . . . To revive the customers' taste for engraved articles I'd have cut the moon into little pieces. I'd have eaten my dragons. Pretty soon I myself was executing all their grimaces as I walked . . . Frantically conscientious, I'd wait my turn on the salesmen's bench outside the buyers' room.

I ended up believing in the renaissance of the jewel engraver's art. I had the faith of a crusader. I didn't even see my competitors. They went into gales of laughter whenever they heard my name called. When it came my turn at the window, I'd put on my most winning smile, all sweetness and light. Quietly, from behind my back, I'd produce my little jewel case containing the least loathsome items . . . and put it on the counter . . . The beast didn't even bother to say anything . . . He just made a gesture meaning to clear out . . . that I was a dirty-minded brat . . .

I hurried on . . . farther and farther. A fanatic doesn't calculate. Dripping wet in my shell or consumed with thirst, according to the season, I tried the most insignificant little shops, the grimiest little watchmakers, cowering in their suburbs between lamp and globe . . .

From La Chapelle to Les Moulineaux, I did them all. I found a gleam of interest in a junk dealer in Pierrefitte and a ragpicker in Saint-Maur. I tried the shopkeepers who've been dozing all around the Palais-Royal ever since the days of Camille Desmoulins, under the Arcades Montpensier . . . the stalls in the Galeries des Pas-Perdus . . . shopkeepers who've lost all hope . . . grown stiff and sallow behind the counter . . . They don't want to live and they don't want to die. I galloped over to the Odéon . . . to the last of the Parnassian jewelers in the arcades around the theater. They weren't even starving anymore, they digested dust. They had their models too, all of lead, almost identical with mine, enough for a thousand coffins . . . and a whole raft of mythological necklaces . . . And mounds of amulets, a mass so dense that the counters were sinking into the ground . . . They were shoulder-deep in the rubbish . . . they were disappearing, turning into Egyptians . . . They didn't even answer when I spoke. Those guys really gave me a scare . . .

I went back to the suburbs . . . When I had ventured too far in my hunt for enthusiasm, when I was caught by nightfall and felt kind of lost, I'd hurry up and take a bus so as not to get home too late. My parents left me fifteen francs out of my monthly thirty-five . . . It melted away in fares. Without meaning to, by the sheer force of circumstances, I was getting pretty extravagant . . . Of course I should have walked . . . but then it goes out in shoe-leather.

Monsieur Gorloge even got around to the rue de la Paix looking for repair work. The ladies who ran the fashionable shops might have taken a shine to him, the only thing that prevented him from really making a hit was that he wasn't very clean. On account of his beard. It was always full of scabs . . . his "sycosis," as he called it . . .

I'd often catch sight of him in a doorway, scratching furiously. Then he'd walk away happy as a lark . . . He always had a few rings in his pocket to alter, to change the size. A brooch to weld . . . the one that never stays closed. A watch chain to shorten . . . some trinket or other . . . enough to keep his business running . . . He wasn't very demanding.

It was Antoine, his one assistant, who did all these little jobs. Gorloge never touched them. As I was going down the Boulevards, I'd run into him, I'd recognize him in the distance . . . He didn't walk like other people . . . He took an interest in the crowd . . . He looked in all directions . . . I could see his hat turning on its hinges. He also attracted attention by the polka dots on his vest . . . and his hearty manner . . . he made you think of a musketeer. . . .

"Well, Ferdinand, how you doing? Still going strong? Still in there fighting? Everything all right? Everything OK? . . ."

"I'm fine, Monsieur Gorloge. Really fine."

I'd stand up straight to answer him despite the crushing weight of my saddlebags . . . My enthusiasm was undiminished. Except what with making nothing, selling nothing, and hiking all day with that heavy collection, I was getting thinner and thinner . . . Except for my biceps of course. My feet were still growing. My soul was growing . . . and everything else . . . I was getting to be sublime . . .

When I got back from my selling tour, I'd run a few more errands for the shop. To some artisan's. To the

wholesaler's for jewel cases. All that was in the same
street.

Little Robert, the apprentice, was better off tinkering
with little settings, filing openwork, or even sweeping out
the joint. There was never much harmony in the Gorloge
household. They yelled at each other at the top of their
lungs, even louder than in our house. Especially between
Antoine and the boss, there were terrible brawls. No more
respect, especially on Saturday evening when they settled
accounts. Antoine was never satisfied . . . Whether they
figured by the piece, by the hour, by the week, regardless of
the system, he always complained. And yet he was his own
boss, there were no other helpers . . . "Your lousy joint
. . . you can stick it up your ass! How many times do I
have to tell you? . . ."

That was the tone they took with each other. You should
have seen Gorloge's face . . . He scratched his beard
. . . he was so upset he'd nibble at the scales.

Some days Antoine got so mad about money that he
threatened to smash the glass globe on his head . . .
Every time I expected him to leave . . . But not at all!
. . . It was getting to be a regular habit, like with us at
home . . .

But Madame Gorloge didn't get upset like Mama . . .
The roaring and bellowing didn't interfere with her knit-
ting. Whenever things began to look desperate, little Robert
would crawl under the workbench . . . There he was
safe . . . but he wouldn't miss a second of the corrida.
He'd eat a slice of bread and butter . . .

When there wasn't a sou in the place to pay Antoine on
Saturday, we'd always, at the last minute, find a few coins
in the bottom of a drawer to round out the sum . . .
There was always something . . . We even had our
emergency fund in the big kitchen closet . . . our cargo of
cameos . . . our stock of delirium . . . our mythological treasure . . . that was our last resort . . . It was no
time for hesitation . . .

In the leanest weeks I'd unload them by weight, some
place . . . any place . . . at the Village Suisse, across
the street at the Temple . . . on the sidewalk at the
Porte Kremlin . . . They'd always bring in five francs or
so. . . .

Never since engraving had gone out had a single gram of gold spent more than three days at Gorloge's. What repair work we picked up we'd deliver in hurry, the same week. Nobody was very trusting . . . Three or four times, on Saturdays, I took care of the deliveries, to the Place des Vosges, the rue Royale, as usual on the run. In those days nobody talked about hardship. It wasn't until much later that people began to realize how lousy rotten it was to be a worker. The suspicion was just dawning. About seven in the evening, in the middle of the summer, it wasn't cool on the Boulevard Poissonnière on my way back from my cross-country efforts. I remember that we'd stop at the fountain, under the trees by the Théâtre de l'Ambigu . . . and toss off two or three cups of water, we even had to wait in line . . . We'd sit down on the steps of the theater and rest a minute. There were stragglers from all over, still trying to get their breath . . . It was a perfect place for collectors of cigarette butts, sandwich men, pickpockets, bookmakers on the prowl, small-time pimps, and bums of every description, by the tens and dozens . . . You'd hear talk about hard times, about little bets you could make . . . horses that were sure to place . . . and news of the velodrome . . . We'd pass *La Patrie* from hand to hand for the races and the want ads . . .

The song hit at the time was "Matchiche" . . . Everybody'd whistle it while sauntering around the kiosk . . . waiting to take a leak . . . And then we'd cross the street and start off again . . . The dust was thickest on the rue du Temple, where the street was being ripped up . . . They were digging for the métro . . . Then came the square with the trees on it, a lot of alleys, the rue Greneta, the rue Beaubourg . . . The rue Elzévir is a long way . . . around seven in the evening. It's way at the other end of the district.

Little Robert the apprentice . . . his mother lived in Épernon, he sent her all his pay, twelve francs a week, plus his board . . . he slept under the workbench on a mattress that he rolled up himself in the morning. I watched my step with the kid. I was very careful, I didn't tell any stories, I'd decided to keep my nose clean . . .

Antoine, our skilled assistant, was awfully strict, he'd

smack him for nothing at all. But he liked the job all the same, because after seven nobody bothered him. He could have fun on the stairs. The court was full of cats, he'd bring them scraps. On his way back upstairs he'd look through all the keyholes . . . That was his main amusement.

When we got to know each other better, he told me all about it. He showed me his system of looking into the can to see the women pissing, right on our landing, two holes in the door. He'd put little plugs in them when he was through. He'd seen them all, Madame Gorloge too, she was the biggest slob of the lot, he could tell by the way she picked up her skirts . . .

He was a peeping tom by instinct. It seemed she had thighs like monuments, enormous pillars, and so much hair on her pussy, the fur went up so high it covered her belly button . . . Robert had seen her right in the middle of her monthlies . . . It splattered up the whole shithouse . . . She had the most amazing ass . . . you can't imagine . . . He promised to show me. And something even worse, another hole he had bored . . . something really terrific . . . in the bedroom wall, right next to the bed. And there was still another way . . . If you climbed up on the stove . . . in the corner of the kitchen, you could look down through the transom . . . and see the whole bed.

Little Robert would get up at night just for that. Lots of times he'd watched the Gorloges fucking. The next day he told me all about it, except he could hardly stand up from jerking off so much . . .

Little Robert worked mostly with filigree . . . the rough polishing . . . He had a file no thicker than a hair that he stuck into the tiniest openings . . . He'd also put patina on the finished pieces . . . It was close work, those things were as fine as cobwebs . . . He'd squint at them until his eyes hurt . . . Then he'd stop and sprinkle the floor.

Antoine never let him get away with anything, he always had it in for him . . . He couldn't stand my guts either. We wanted to catch him laying Madame Gorloge. Apparently he did . . . Robert said so, but he wasn't really sure . . . Maybe it was a red herring. At the table during meals Antoine was insufferable, you had to watch your step. At

the slightest word he'd fly off the handle and start packing
up his tools. They'd promise him a raise . . . ten frances
. . . maybe only five . . . "Go shit in your hat!" he'd
say. Right to Gorloge's face. "You give me a good pain in
the ass . . . How can you make promises when you
haven't got a pair of shoes to your name! . . . Bullshit!"

"Don't get excited, Antoine! I assure you that things are
going to pick up . . . One of these days . . . I'm positive . . . Soon . . . Sooner than you think . . ."

"Balls! They'll pick up when I'm an archbishop . . ."

That was the way they spoke to each other. The sky was
the limit . . . The boss would stand for anything . . .
he was so scared Antoine would pick up and leave. He
didn't want to do anything by himself . . . he didn't want
to ruin his hands. While waiting for the renaissance . . .
his main pleasure in life was his cup of coffee and looking
out the window smoking his pipe . . . The neighborhood
panorama . . . He didn't like anybody to talk to him
. . . You could do anything you pleased as long as you
didn't bother him. He told us so perfectly frankly: "Just
pretend I'm not here."

I still wasn't finding any takers, neither wholesale nor
retail. I still had every one of my bats and chimeras on
my hands . . . And yet I hadn't left a stone unturned
. . . From the Madeleine to Belleville . . . I'd been
everywhere, I'd tried everything . . . From the Bastille
to Saint-Cloud there wasn't a single door that I didn't open
sooner or later . . . Every junk dealer, every watch-
maker from the rue de Rivoli to the cemetery of Bagneux
. . . Every little Yid knew me . . . every punk . . .
every goldsmith . . . All I got was the brush-off . . .
They didn't want anything . . . This couldn't go on forever . . . Even bad luck gets tired . . .

Finally one day it happened. A miracle . . . on the
corner of the rue Saint-Lazare . . . I'd been passing the
place every day . . . And I'd never stopped . . . They
sold Chinese bric-a-brac . . . Not a hundred yards from
La Trinité. Funny I hadn't noticed before that they went in
for grimaces too, and not little ones, great big ones! Whole
windows full of them. And they weren't just kidding, they
were real horrors. Pretty much like mine . . . Every bit

as ugly . . . But they went in more for salamanders, flying dragons . . . Buddhas with enormous bellies . . . all gilded . . . furiously rolling their eyes . . . Smoke was coming up from behind the pedestal . . . like an opium dream . . . And rows of arquebuses and halberds all the way up the ceiling . . . with fringes and sparkling glass-beads. Real fun. Lots of snakes too, spitting fire . . . twined around columns . . . wriggling down toward the floor . . . And along the walls a hundred flaming parasols and next to the door a devil, life-size, surrounded by toads with wide-open eyes lit by thousands of lanterns . . .

Since they sold that kind of truck, the idea came to me —a real inspiration . . . that they might like my little things.

I screw up my courage, I push through the door . . . with my saddlebags . . . I unpack . . . of course I stammer a little at first . . . then finally the patter begins to flow.

The guy was a little character with slanting eyes and a voice like an old woman, as sly as they come . . . he was wearing a silk dress with a flower design, and clogs . . . in short he looked like a Chinese goblin except for his soft hat . . . At first he didn't say much . . . But I could see I was making an impression with my large selection of charms . . . my mandrakes . . . my knots of Medusas . . . my Samothrace brooches . . . For a Chink it was hot stuff! . . . You had to have come a long way to appreciate my collection . . .

Finally he thawed . . . In fact he was frankly excited . . . enthusiastic . . . exultant . . . He even stuttered with impatience . . . He came right out with it: "I believe, my dear little young man, that I shall be able to do something for you . . ." And he went on in his singsong . . .

He knew an art lover near the Luxembourg . . . A very respectable gentleman . . . A real scholar . . . who was crazy about high-class artistic ornaments . . . exactly my style . . . This guy was a Manchu, he was here on vacation . . . He filled me in . . . I mustn't talk too loud . . . He couldn't stand noise of any kind . . . He gave me his address . . . It wasn't a very good hotel, it was on the rue Soufflot . . . All the Chink on the rue

Saint-Lazare wanted for himself was a little "present" . . . if I got the order . . . Only five percent . . . It wasn't too much . . . I signed his little paper . . . I didn't waste a second . . . I even jumped into the Odéon bus on the rue des Martyrs.

I tracked down my art lover. I show him my boxes, I introduce myself. I dig out my samples. He's even more slant-eyed than the other guy . . . He's wearing a long dress too. He's delighted with my stuff . . . He makes a whole speech . . . about his pleasure at discovering such beautiful things.

Then he shows me on the map where he came from . . . From the end of the world . . . even a little farther, way off in the left-hand margin . . . This was the mandarin on vacation . . . He wanted something beautiful to take home with him, except he wanted to have it engraved to order . . . He'd even selected his model, he just had to have it. He wanted me to make it up for him . . . A real order! . . . He explained where I could go to copy it . . . It was in the Galliera Museum, on the third floor, in the middle showcase . . . I couldn't go wrong, he made me a little sketch. He wrote the name in big letters: SAKYA-MUNI, it was called . . . the god of happiness . . . He wanted an exact copy of it for a tiepin, because back home, as he told me: "I dress in the European style. I'm the chief justice."

He'd got this idea. He was very trusting. He gave me two hundred francs just like that to buy the gold with . . . It was more convenient . . . that way we wouldn't lose any time. . . .

I can swear I made a face like Buddha myself when I took those two bills . . . This weird way of doing things knocked me for a loop . . . I staggered on my way down the boulevard . . . I was so dizzy I almost got myself run over. . . .

Finally I get to the rue Elzévir . . . I tell the whole story . . . What luck when we'd given up hoping! . . . Engraving was coming back . . . Gorloge had been right . . . We drank on it . . . Everybody hugged and kissed me . . . Everybody made up . . . We went out and changed the two hundred frances . . . There was only a hundred and fifty left . . .

Gorloge and I went to the museum to sketch the little Chink. He was mighty interesting in his little case, all alone, still as a mouse, on a little camp chair, laughing to himself, holding a shepherd's crook . . .

We took our time, we copied our sketch and reduced it one to a hundred . . . We made a little model . . . It all went off fine. Then Robert and I dashed over to the Comptoir Judéo-Suisse on the rue Francoeur for some eighteen-carat gold, a hundred francs' worth at one throw, and fifty francs' worth of solder . . . We put the little ingot away carefully, we double-locked the safe . . . That hadn't happened in four years . . . keeping metal overnight on the rue Elzévir . . . When the model was finished, we sent it to be cast . . . Three times they messed it up . . . they had to start all over again . . . Founders never know what they're doing . . . The time passed . . . We were getting annoyed . . . And then finally they caught on. All in all, it wasn't bad . . . The god was beginning to shape up . . . It only needed to be finished, polished, and engraved . . .

Then we had lousy luck . . . The cops come looking for Gorloge . . . The whole house is in an uproar . . . On account of his four weeks of military service . . . No further postponement was possible . . . He'd already had too many . . . He couldn't miss the big maneuvers . . . No two ways about it, he'd have to leave the "god of happiness" unfinished . . . It wasn't the kind of job you could do in a hurry . . . It needed fine finishing . . .

Since there was no way out, this is what Gorloge decided. Antoine would finish the job . . . he'd take his time . . . and I'd deliver it . . . There was only another hundred francs to collect . . . Gorloge would collect in person . . . he made that very clear . . . when he got back from his hitch . . . He was awfully suspicious.

If our Chinaman liked it, we'd make more, we'd make a whole pile of Sakya-Munis in solid gold! What could stop us? The future, as we saw it, was one glowing sunrise . . . Why wouldn't the renascence of engraved ornaments come to us from the Far East? . . . Why not? Our whole stairway . . . Stairway B . . . was buzzing with our story, all the little tinkers upstairs and downstairs were flabbergasted at our luck, they couldn't get over it! What a windfall! There were rumors that we were getting checks from Peking.

Gorloge hung around to the last minute. He was building up to a mess of trouble. He and Antoine took turns working on the little character. There were crazy details, things so small, so tiny you couldn't see them properly even with the magnifying glass. The little chair . . . the shepherd's crook . . . and especially his little puss . . . it was hard to catch that tiny little smile! They were still scraping away particles with a fine tool, as sharp as a fingernail . . . He was almost done . . . It was a perfect copy. But even so, maybe Antoine had better give it a little more thought . . . go back to it in four or five days . . . Then it would be really first-class . . .

Finally Gorloge made up his mind to get going, it was high time. The cops had been back again . . .

The next day when I got there, I saw him . . . He was dolled up like a soldier from top to toe . . . The enormous floating cape, with the two buttons so you could turn up the corners like a sack of French fries . . . the kepi with the green pompon and the bright-red pants that went with it . . . That's what he was wearing when he went downstairs . . . Little Robert carried his musette bag. It was packed mighty full . . . there were three camemberts, so much alive that everybody made remarks . . . And two quarts of white wine and some smaller bottles, an assortment of socks . . . and his woolen nightgown for sleeping in the open . . .

The neighbors all came trooping down in denims and slippers . . . They were all hawking like mad, spitting all over the doormats . . . They wished him luck. I took Gorloge to the station, I left him outside the Gare de l'Est, on the corner of the Boulevard Magenta. He was worried about having to leave right now, with this job on hand. He kept giving me instructions. It burned him up that he couldn't finish it himself . . . Finally he said good-bye . . . He told me to be good . . . He followed the sign . . . The whole place was full of soldiers . . . Some of

the guys said we were blocking the traffic with our gabfest
. . . I had to beat it . . .

When I got back to the rue Elzévir, I passed by the
lodge. The concierge calls me:

"Hey," she says, "come in here a minute, Ferdinand. So
he's gone? So he finally made up his mind! Well anyway,
he won't be cold out there. They'll make it plenty hot for
him. It's a good thing he took all those bottles. 'Cause
they're going to make it mighty rough for him. Whew! The
bastards! They'll make your cuckold sweat!"

She said all that to get me started, to make me talk. I
didn't answer. I was fed up on gossip. That's God's truth.
I was getting to be very cautious . . . I was right . . .
But I wasn't cautious enough! . . . As I was soon to find
out.

Once the boss was gone, little Robert couldn't contain
himself. He was determined to see Antoine and the
patronne fucking . . . He said it would happen, it was
bound to . . . He was a natural-born peeping tom.

The first week we didn't see much . . . So's to keep the
shop running it was me that went over to the rue de Pro-
vence and down the boulevard looking for repair work
. . . I brought back what I found . . . It was barely
enough . . . I didn't tote my collection around anymore.
That would have made them throw me out.

Antoine went on fussing with the little priest, he was
doing fine. He knew his business. About the second week
the *patronne* suddenly began to change. She'd always been
kind of standoffish . . . when Gorloge was there, she
hardly ever spoke to me. All of a sudden she began to be
friendly, ingratiating, intimate. At first I thought there was
something phony about it. But I kept my suspicions to
myself . . . I decided maybe it was because I was getting
to be more useful . . . Because I was bringing in little
jobs . . . Still, they weren't getting us any dough . . .
not one of our bills had been paid . . .

Gorloge, who was always suspicious . . . had made it
very clear that we weren't to collect a single bill! He'd do
all that when he got back. He'd notified the customers.

One morning I came in early and found Madame Gorloge already up, roaming around the room . . . She pre-

tended to be looking for something by the workbench . . .
She was wearing a swishy dressing gown . . . For my
money she was acting pretty weird . . . She comes close.
She says to me:

"Ferdinand, on your way home from your errands this
evening, be a good boy and bring me a little bunch of
flowers. It'll cheer the place up . . ." She heaves a sigh.
"Since my husband went away, I haven't had the heart
to go out."

She waggled her ass around the room. She was putting
on a seduction act. That was plain. The door to her bedroom was wide open. I could see her bed . . . I didn't bat
an eyelash . . . I didn't make a move . . . Antoine and
Robert came up from the café . . . I didn't breathe a
word . . .

That evening I brought back three peonies. That was all
I could afford. There wasn't any money left in the till. As
far as I was concerned it was plenty. I knew I'd never be
paid back.

And then Antoine gets polite too, almost palsy-walsy
. . . when only a week before he'd done nothing but yell
at us . . . He was perfectly charming . . . He didn't
even want me to go out anymore, to go looking for
work. . . .

"Take it easy," he said. "Stick around the shop . . .
Watch us work, you'll learn something . . . you'll make
your rounds later . . ."

In spite of all our shilly-shallying the pin was finished
. . . it came back from the polishers. It was my job to
deliver it . . . Just then the *patronne* gets a letter from
Gorloge . . . he said we shouldn't hurry . . . we should
keep the pin a while . . . wait for him to get back. He'd
take it to the Chinaman himself . . . Meanwhile if I felt
like it, I could show it to some of our customers, the ones
that would appreciate it . . .

Right away I began to feel worried. Everybody admired
the little character, that's a fact . . . He looked real good
on his little throne, Sakya-Muni in solid gold . . . eighteen
carats after all . . . that meant something in those days.
You couldn't have asked for anything finer . . . All our
neighbors came around and complimented us . . . and

some of them were connoisseurs . . . It was an honor to the house . . . Our customer could have no cause for complaint . . . Gorloge was going to be away for another ten days . . . That left me plenty of time to show it around the shops . . .

"Ferdinand," the *patronne* advised me, "why don't you leave it here at night, in your drawer? Nobody'll touch it, you know. You can pick it up again in the morning."

I preferred to keep it in my pocket and take it home with me. That struck me as much more conscientious . . . I even fastened it with safety pins, a great big diaper pin and two little ones, one on each side . . . Everybody laughed. "He won't lose it," they said.

The way our shop was situated, right under the tiles, it was awfully hot, even at the end of September the heat was so bad we were always drinking.

One afternoon Antoine went off his rocker from guzzling so much. He was singing so loud you could hear him all over the court as far as the concierge's lodge at the other end . . . He'd brought up some absinthe and a lot of little cakes. We all nibbled. Robert and I put all the little bottles out under the faucet on the landing to cool. We bought them on credit, whole baskets full . . . There was trouble though . . . The grocers got mean . . . It was crazy in a way . . . We'd all gone berserk, it was the hot weather and the freedom.

The *patronne* joined us. Antoine sat down right beside her. We laughed to see them necking. He went looking for her garters. He lifted her skirts up. She was giggling like a goat. She was irritating as hell, you wanted to sock her . . . He pulled out one of her tits. She just sat there beaming. He poured out the rest of the bottle. Robert and I finished it. We licked the glass. It was better than Banyuls . . . In the end everybody was crocked . . . the frenzy of the senses . . . Antoine hiked up her skirts completely . . . at one stroke . . . way over her head! . . . He got up too and just as she was, all bundled up in her skirts, he pushed her into the bedroom. She was still laughing . . . She had the giggles . . . They closed the door behind them . . . She went right on cackling . . .

The time had come for Robert and me to climb up on the

kitchen stove and watch the show . . . It was a good
place . . . ringside . . . You could see the whole bed
. . . we couldn't miss a trick. Right away Antoine pushed
the fat mama down on her knees . . . He was awfully
brutal . . . She had her ass up in the air . . . He tickled
and teased her . . . He couldn't find her dingbat . . .
He tore her ruffles . . . he tore everything in sight . . .
And then he attacked . . . He took out his cock . . . He
began to charge her . . . And it was no make-believe
. . . I hadn't expected he could be so wild . . . I couldn't
get over it. He was grunting like a pig . . . She was
making noises too . . . Louder and more piercing every
time he charged. Robert had told me the truth about her
ass . . . We could see it good now . . . All red . . .
enormous, scarlet! Her fine lace panties were all in tatters
. . . and sopping wet . . . Antoine was coming in like
a battering ram . . . You could hear the smack . . .
They wrestled like savages . . . The way he was going at
her I was sure he'd kill her . . . His pants were dragging on the floor . . . His smock was still in his way, he
ripped it off with one tug . . . It fell right next to us . . .
He was naked now . . . Except he still had his slippers
on, the boss's, the ones with the embroidered kittens . . .
He was so excited he skidded on the carpet . . . He
banged his head against the bar of the bed . . . he was
madder than a hornet . . . he felt his head . . . he had
bumps. He slipped out . . . He bounded back in a fury
. . . "You stinking bitch!" he bellows at her. "You lousy
whore!" He drives his knee into her ribs. She tries to get
away, she begins to simper and moan. . . .

"Antoine, oh, Antoine darling, I can't stand it . . .
Stop, I implore you . . . Be careful . . . Don't make me
a kid! I'm wringing wet."

That was for the birds, she was asking for more.

"Go on, you old cow, shut your trap. Open your basket."

He didn't listen to her. He put her back on again with
three enormous clouts in the gizzard . . . Bam! they resounded . . . She gasped for breath, the stinker . . . She
wheezed like a bellows . . . I wondered if he was going to
kill her . . . finish her off on the spot! . . . He gave
her another vicious clout . . . right while he was pump-

ing . . . They were both roaring like wild animals . . .
She was coming . . . Robert was green around the gills.
We climbed down off our diving board . . . We went
back to the workbench . . . We didn't say a word . . .
We'd wanted a show . . . we'd had our money's worth
. . . Except it was dangerous . . . The corrida was still
going on. We went down to the court . . . to get the pail
and brooms, supposedly to clean up . . . We went in to
see the concierge, we thought that was a better place to be
in case he strangled her . . .

There was no tragedy and no corpse . . . They came
out beaming . . . we just had to get used to it . . .
The next few days we ordered provisions from all over,
from three different grocers, on the rue des Écouffes and the
rue Beaubourg, who didn't know us yet . . . We set up a
whole food department and quite a cellar too, beer and
sparkling Malvoisin, all on credit. We were going to the
dogs . . .
I found excuses for not eating with my people at home.
It was getting to be something on the rue Elzévir, we never
stopped pouring it down. We didn't do a lick of work. In
the afternoon, about four o'clock, Robert and I would wait
for the corrida to start . . . We weren't scared anymore
. . . It didn't excite us so much either.
Besides, Antoine was weakening, the fight had gone out
of him, the least little effort was making him winded.
She began to resist . . . to fight him off. Then his fury
came back . . . It was a regular circus . . . She was
braying like a jackass . . . He kept skidding every time
he tried . . . He couldn't get it in anymore . . . So he
jumps out of bed and heads straight for the kitchen . . .
Luckily, being as we were on top of the stove, he didn't
see us, he was too hot and bothered . . . He went right
by and began rummaging around the cupboard, just like
that, mother-naked in his slippers . . . He was looking for
the butter dish . . . his cock kept bumping into things:
"Ow ouch, oh oh ouch!" he kept yelping. We were in
stitches . . . Christ, it was funny . . . we thought we'd
explode. . . .
"The butter, damn it, the butter! . . ."
Finally he found his dish . . . He took a whole ladleful

. . . He went back with a whole mess of it . . . He runs back to the bed quick . . . She was putting on airs again . . . wriggling and writhing . . . He buttered her treasure, the whole thing and all around it, slowly and very carefully, like a specialist . . . She was all shiny . . . He had no trouble . . . He took her by storm . . . It went in easy . . . The excitement was terrific . . . They let out piercing yells . . . They collapsed on their sides. Then flat on their backs . . . They went to sleep . . .

It wasn't any fun anymore . . .

The first ones to make a stink were the grocers on the rue Berce . . . They refused to give us any more food on the cuff . . . They came around with their bills . . . We heard them coming up . . . We didn't answer . . .

They went back down to the concierge . . . They raised hell . . . Things were getting rough. So then Antoine and the *patronne* began going out all the time, they did their drinking on the outside, they ran up terrible bills in every joint in the neighborhood . . . I didn't breathe a word about all this at home . . . They'd have blamed it all on me . . . They'd have thought I was at the bottom of all the monkeyshines.

The main thing was the jewel case . . . That solid gold Sakya-Muni . . . I didn't let him run around, he didn't get out much. I kept him very carefully way down in the bottom of my pocket . . . and fastened with three diaper pins. I had stopped showing it to people, I didn't trust anybody anymore . . . I was waiting for the boss to come back.

In the shop Robert and I took it easy . . . Antoine hardly did a lick of work. After their parties he and the old bitch would come in and kid around with us. We turned the whole place into a shambles. Meanwhile in the afternoon they'd saw wood for hours . . . We were one happy family . . . as thick as thieves and twice as sticky.

But one night the ax fell. We hadn't bolted the door . . . It was dinner time . . . There was a lot of bustle on all the landings . . . So one of our enraged liquor suppliers, the meanest of the lot, comes dashing up the stairs, four at a time . . . We didn't hear him until it was much too late. He opens the door, he comes in . . . He finds the

two of them in bed! Antoine and Her Fatness . . . He
begins to yap like a dozen seals . . . His eyes were all
bloodshot . . . He wanted to murder Antoine on the spot.
He was brandishing his big hammer . . . I thought he was
going to emboss him one . . .

It was true, we owed him plenty . . . for at least
twenty-five bottles . . . white . . . rosé . . . cognac,
and even vinegar . . . It degenerated into a pitched battle
. . . It took eight of us to handle that gorilla. . . . We
called in all our friends . . . Antoine was bleeding like a
stuck pig . . . he had two enormous shiners . . . a blue
one and a yellow one . . .

From downstairs in the court he went on threatening us.
He was delirious. He called us every name in the book:
"Crooks! . . . Scum! . . . Cocksuckers! . . ."

"You just wait, you lousy chiselers. You'll hear from
me . . . Sooner than you think, you crumb-bums . . .
You'll see when the police get here."

Things were getting sticky . . .

The next day, in the afternoon, I say to Robert: "Listen,
kid. I got to go out. They came around again from Tracard's this morning asking for their brooch, it should have
been delivered at least a week ago . . ." "OK," he says,
"I got to go out too. I got a date with a guy on the corner
outside the Matin."

The two of us race down the stairs . . . Neither Antoine nor the *patronne* had been home for lunch . . .

When we get to the third-floor landing, I hear her
coming up . . . All out of breath, red in the face, incan-
descent . . . They must have been eating too much . . .

"Where are you going, Ferdinand?"

"Just a little errand . . . On the boulevard . . . to see
a customer."

"Oh, don't go," she said. She seemed put out. "Come
back upstairs a minute . . . I've got something to tell
you."

OK. I go back upstairs with her. Robert runs off to his
date.

The minute we get in she closes the door, she locks
everything, she pushes both bolts . . . She steps in ahead
of me, she goes into the bedroom . . . She motions me to

come in too . . . I come closer . . . I wonder what's
going to happen . . . She starts feeling me up . . . She
blows up my nose . . . "Ah! Ah!" she goes. That excites
her . . . I pet her a little too . . .

"Oh, what a little pig! I hear you look through keyholes
. . . Is that right? . . . Oh! . . . tell me it isn't true
. . ." With one hand she starts massaging me under-
neath . . .

"I'm going to tell your mama. Oh what a little pig! Oh,
sweet little pig! . . ."

She begins to gnash her teeth . . . She begins to wriggle
. . . She clutches me . . . She sticks in her tongue, a
real lowdown kiss . . . I see stars . . . She makes me
sit down beside her on the bed . . . She flops down backwards . . . Suddenly she hikes up her skirts . . .

"Touch me!" she says. "Touch me down there."

I put my hand on . . .

"Go ahead!" she insists . . . "Go ahead, angel dumpling . . . Go ahead . . . Call me Louison! Your Louison! You slimy little pig! Call me . . . You will, won't
you? . . ."

"Yes, Louison," I say.

She sits up, she kisses me again. She takes everything
off . . . blouse . . . corset . . . shift . . . I see her all
naked . . her thingamajig so voluminous . . . spread
out all over the place . . . It was too much . . . I was
sick to my stomach . . . She grabs me by the ears . . .
She pulls me down to mother nature . . . She bends me
with all her might . . . My nose is in a hell of a state
. . . It's dazzling and all runny . . . It's all over my neck
. . . She makes me kiss it . . at first it tastes like fish,
then like a dog's muzzle . . .

"Go on, little love. Go on, don't be bashful."

She manhandles me, she pesters the life out of me . . .
I'm up to my ears in marmalade . . . I'm afraid to sniff
too hard . . . I'm afraid of hurting her . . . She's shaking like an apple tree . . .

"Bite me, sweet little puppy . . . Bite into it! Go
ahead," she encourages me. She's heaving like mad! She
lets out little squeals . . . I plunge in deep . . . it smells
like eggs and shit . . . My collar is strangling me . . .
the celluloid . . . She pulls me out of the pit . . . I come

up for air . . . My eyes are like covered with varnish, even my eyebrows are all sticky . . .

"Get undressed," she orders me. "Take all that stuff off. I want to see your cunning little body. Quick. Quick. You'll see, you little rascal. You a virgin? Tell me, angel. You'll see how I'm going to love you up . . . Oh, what a nasty little pig! I'll teach you to look through key-holes . . ."

She billowed and writhed while waiting for me . . . The whole bed was zigzagging . . . She was a regular vampire . . .

I didn't dare take off too much. Just the choker that was killing me . . . and my coat and vest . . . She hung them up beside the bed, on the back of the chair . . . I didn't want to take everything off . . . the way Antoine did . . . I knew my ass was shitty and my feet coal-black . . . I could smell myself . . . To keep her from insisting, I started up again as fast as I could . . . I played the ardent lover, I climbed, I squeezed, I grunted . . . I charged like Antoine, but much more gently . . . I felt my thingamajig sailing all around . . . I was lost in the foam . . . I didn't dare use my fingers, though that's what I should have done . . . I scrabbled around in her moustache . . . Finally it slipped right in . . . all by itself . . . She squashed me against her tits! She was having a hell of a good time . . . It was stifling . . . it was like a furnace . . . She wanted me to work harder . . . She didn't beg for pity like with that bastard . . . Oh, no, she wanted me to be more brutal . . .

"Deeper, angel. Deeper, don't be afraid. My, what a big fat one you've got . . . Ah . . . ah . . . you're ripping me apart, you big thug! . . . Oh, rip me . . . Are you coming? . . . Oh, say yes! . . . Oh, oh! You're killing me, you little bastard! My big little skunk! Isn't it good?" And bam, I plowed into her . . . I was done in. I lay down on the job . . . She blew in my face . . . I had a noseful . . . from her licking too . . . garlic . . . Roquefort . . . they'd been eating sausage . . .

"Swoon good, little pet! Oh, swoon . . . We'll die together! . . . Aren't you going to, little treasure! . . . You're killing me . . . There . . . Don't worry about me . . ." She swooned, she began to list . . . She turned over almost on top of me . . . I felt my chip coming . . .

Suddenly I say to myself: "Cheese it, kid." I was out cold, but just the same . . . One two three . . . I wrench myself loose . . . I pull it out . . . It gushes all over my belly . . . I try to squeeze . . . I get a handful . . .

"Oh, what a little beast!" she hollers. "Oh, what a slimy little toad! . . . Come quick and let me clean you up . . ." She goes for my pecker . . . She makes a meal of it . . . She likes the sauce . . . "Oh, what a delicious little dessert!" she squeals. She goes looking for it all over my legs . . . She pokes into the folds . . . She's really thorough . . . She's going to swoon again . . . She's down on her knees, clinging to my legs, she contracts, she relaxes . . . Fat ass and all, she's as nimble as a cat. She forces me down on her again . . . "I'll show you, you little louse," she says roguishly. She sticks two fingers into my opening. She forces me. What a scrimmage! The stinker, the way she's steamed up, she'll be at it all day!

"Oh," it suddenly occurs to her. "I've got to take a douche." With one jump she was out of the room. I hear her pissing in the kitchen . . . She's rummaging under the sink . . . "Wait for me, angel," she sings out . . . I've had enough. I jump into my suit . . . I grab the door, I push it open, I'm on the landing . . . I take the stairs four at a time . . . I take a good deep breath . . . I'm out in the street . . . It's time to think things over . . . I catch my breath . . . I walk slowly toward the boulevards.

When I got to the Ambigu, I finally sat down. I pick up a newspaper from the sidewalk. I'm just beginning to read . . . I don't know why . . . I feel my pocket . . . I did it without thinking . . . A sudden inspiration . . . I feel again . . . I can't find the bump . . . I feel the other . . . Same result. I haven't got it anymore . . . My jewel case is gone. I look for it harder and harder . . . I feel all my linings . . . My pants . . . inside . . . outside . . . nothing doing . . . I go to the can . . . I undress completely . . . I turn everything inside out . . . Nothing . . . I'm not blind . . . The blood boils in my veins . . . I sit down on the steps again . . . I'm cooked . . . and good! . . . I'm really screwed . . .

I pull out my pockets again . . . And again . . . But I've given up hope . . . I remember perfectly . . . I'd pinned it all right . . .Way in the bottom of my inside pocket. I'd felt it before going out with Robert . . . The safety pins were gone . . . They hadn't come out all by themselves . . . All of a sudden I remembered the funny way she'd held me by the head the whole time . . . And on the other side of the chair . . . she'd been work-ing with one hand . . . It all came to me in waves . . . Fright, terror welled up in me . . . straight up from my heart . . . It pounded worse than forty-nine truck horses . . . My whole head shook . . . That didn't do any good . . . I began to look again . . . The case couldn't have fallen . . . it couldn't have slipped out the way I'd pinned it . . . Impossible . . . Diaper pins don't open so easy . . . And there were three of them . . . They don't come open all by themselves! To make sure I wasn't dreaming I ran back toward the Place de la République . . . When I got to the rue Elzévir, there was nobody home . . . They'd all gone out . . . I waited on the stairs . . . until seven o'clock, to see if they'd come in . . . Nobody came . . .

I tried to put things together . . . words . . . snatches of talk . . . incidents. It all came to me little by little . . . Suppose Antoine had engineered it? And what about little Robert? . . . Maybe they were both in on it . . . in cahoots with the bitch . . . When I stood up, I couldn't feel my two legs . . . I went down the street like I was drunk . . . The people noticed me . . . I stayed a while in the little tunnel by the Porte Saint-Denis. I was afraid to come out . . . I saw the buses in the distance, swaying in the heat . . . I felt dizzy . . . I didn't get back to the Passage until late . . . I said I had a bellyache . . . That stopped them from asking questions . . . I had such cramps I didn't sleep all night . . . Next day I was out at the crack of dawn, I was in such a hurry to know . . .

When I got to the shop, I took a good look at all three of them . . . They didn't seem to be thinking anything . . . neither the bitch . . . nor Antoine . . . nor the kid . . . When I told them the pin had been lost, they gaped at me . . . they were flabbergasted . . .

"What's that, Ferdinand? You're sure? Have you taken a good look at home? . . . Turn your pockets inside out . . . We haven't found anything here . . . How about it, Robert? . . . You didn't see anything?" It was the kid who swept . . . "You'd better sweep again . . ."

The way they talked, they seemed so savage, so villainous that I began to bawl . . . I could see them in the mirror, making little signs to each other . . . Antoine avoided looking at me . . . He kept his back turned, he pretended to be cleaning his emery stone . . . She went on blowing hot air . . . trying to trip me up, to make me contradict myself.

"You don't remember at Tracard's . . . Didn't you say you were going there? . . . Maybe you left it there . . . Are you sure? . . ."

I was floundering in the soup . . . What a vicious rotten trick! . . . There wasn't a thing I could do . . . I was cooked . . . Nobody'd believe me if I told the truth . . . What was the use?

"The boss will be back the day after tomorrow . . . Try to find it before then . . . Robert will help you . . ." She was full of ideas. Any way you looked at it I was screwed . . . If I went into details, they'd call me an impostor, a horrible abject monster . . . trying to wriggle out by slandering the boss's wife, so good, so kind . . . Had I no shame? . . . What colossal gall! . . . what a preposterous calumny! . . . what monumental villainy! . . . I didn't even try to defend myself . . . I didn't even feel like it anymore . . . I couldn't eat . . . My head was all stuffed up . . . my mind, my mouth, my whole face . . .

My mother thought I was looking odd, she wondered what ailment I could be coming down with . . . My guts were all tied up with fear . . . I wanted to disappear . . . to get so thin there'd be nothing left . . .

My father made caustic remarks . . . "You wouldn't be in love by any chance? It wouldn't be spring fever? . . . You got pimples on your ass? . . ." He took me off to one side and asked me: "You wouldn't have a dose of clap? . . ." I didn't know which way to squirm.

Gorloge, who was late wherever he went, had come back by a route of his own, he had dawdled from one town to the next . . . He arrived on a Wednesday, we'd been expecting him since Saturday . . . The next morning when I went to work, he was in the kitchen, sharpening his files. I stood behind him for quite a while . . . in the hallway, I was afraid to move . . . I waited for him to speak to me. I had a shitless lump in my throat. I'd forgotten what I meant to say. He must have been told by then. I hold out my hand just the same. He kind of squints at me from the side . . . He doesn't even turn around . . . He goes back to his work. I wasn't even there anymore . . . So I run into the shop. I was so scared I left half my collection in the bottom of the closet so as to get out faster . . . Nobody called me back . . . They were all there in the room, concentrating on their thingamajigs . . . I left without a word . . . I didn't even know where I was going . . . .Luckily I was used to that . . . I walked along in a dream . . . On the rue Réaumur I was in a terrible cold sweat . . . On the big terrace I went from one bench to another . . . In spite of everything I tried to go into a shop . . . But my hand trembled so on the door handle I never made it inside . . . I thought everybody was following me.

I spent hours like that . . . the whole morning. And the afternoon too, the whole time from one bench to another and so on, as far as the Square Louvois . . . always leaning against the house fronts . . . I couldn't walk anymore . . . I didn't want to go back to Gorloge's . . . Even my parents were better than that . . . It was just as awful . . . but at least it was nearer . . . Only a step from the Square Louvois . . . It's funny when you've got no place to breathe in but places that are all equally horrible . . .

I walked around the Bank of France once, twice, very slowly, with my disgusting junk . . . Then suddenly I pulled myself together and went back to the Passage . . . My father was on the doorstep . . . obviously waiting for me . . . The way he told me to go upstairs left no room for doubt . . . The storm was on . . . He began right away to stammer so bad and so loud that steam came out instead of words . . . I couldn't understand a thing . . . Except that he was blowing off rockets . . . His cap was buffeted by the storm . . . It flew in all directions . . . He rained blows on it . . . He jammed it down on his noodle . . . His face swelled up still worse . . . absolutely crimson . . . with livid furrows . . . He changed color. He went violet.

I was fascinated. Was he going to turn blue? . . . and then yellow? I was so drenched in his fury that I couldn't feel anything . . . He picked up some dohicky on the sideboard. He brandished it with a view to breakage . . . I thought he was going to tear the whole place to pieces . . . He bit his tongue so hard, so furiously, it swelled up like a stopper, a big lump of meat, wedged into his mouth and like to burst . . . But it didn't . . . He put down the hot plate . . . He gagged . . . He couldn't go on . . .

Suddenly he dashed out, he headed for the street, he ran through the Passage. I thought he was going to fly away, he was so blown up . . . so irresistible . . . so horrible . . .

My mother stayed with me . . . She trotted out the whole fool story, every detail of the disaster . . . And all her own little ideas . . . her timeworn certainties . . .

Monsieur Gorloge had been there, he had talked to them for two hours . . . He knew all about it . . . He'd told them everything . . . he had prophesied the whole Future. "That child will be your ruin . . . he's corrupt to the marrow . . . A wretch . . . I trusted him . . . He was beginning to get ahead . . ."

Those were his parting words . . . Mama had been scared he'd turn me in . . . that he'd have me arrested right away . . . She hadn't dared to answer . . . As far as she was concerned, there were no two ways about it . . . I'd been taken in . . . Why didn't I own up right away . . . at least that I'd lost it . . . instead of prevaricating . . . and turning my boss against me . . . That was the least revolting possibility . . . They'd pay him back little by little . . . and in any case my parents . . . That was already settled . . .

"Who set you such an example?" she asked me in tears. "What did you do with the pin? . . . Come, tell me, my boy. We won't eat you . . . I won't say a word to your father . . . I swear I won't! . . . There, you do trust me? We'll go see her together . . . If you gave it to a woman! Tell me right away, before he comes home! Maybe she'll give it back in exchange for a little money? . . . Do you know her well? . . . Don't you think so? . . . That way it'll all come out all right in the end! We won't say a word to anybody!"

I waited for her to calm down some, then maybe I'd be able to explain . . . Just then my father comes in . . . He hadn't cooled off at all. He begins to pound the table and bang at the partitions as hard as he can . . . with both fists . . . all the time letting off jets of steam . . . When he stops for a second, it's only to kick at the furniture . . . His anger lifted him up, he was like a horse galloping through the air . . . bashing into the walls . . . The whole place was shaking . . . What an onslaught, the sideboard capsizes . . . From blast to crash the scene went on all night . . . He'd bounce into the air in his fury and fall on all fours . . . He barked like a mastiff . . . Between fits and frenzies they bellowed the pros and cons . . . It was no time for me to try to say anything . . .

When she ran out of arguments, my mother came upstairs to see what she could do with me . . . I didn't answer . . . She wanted me to confess . . . She went down on her knees by my bed and cried as if I were already dead . . . She mumbled prayers . . . She went on imploring me . . . She wanted me to own up right away . . . to tell her if it was a woman! . . . We'd go and see her together . . .

"I tell you it was the boss's wife," I finally vomited up. I couldn't stand it anymore. Hell and damnation!

"Ah, be still, you little wretch . . . You don't realize how you're hurting us!"

It was no use insisting . . . How could you talk to such mugs! . . . They were stopped up worse than all the shithouses in all Asnières! That's my opinion.

It was a terrible blow all right. I stayed in my room a long time, five or six days without going out. They forced me to come down and eat . . . She called me a dozen times. In the end she came up and got me. I didn't want anything at all. Especially I didn't want to talk. My father talked to himself . . . He went off into monologues . . .

Raging and fuming . . . he went on and on . . . about
the forces of evil . . . his whole repertory . . . Destiny
. . . The Jews . . . his rotten luck . . . The Exposition . . . Providence . . . The Freemasons . . .

As soon as he got home from his deliveries, he'd climb
up to the attic . . . He'd started doing watercolors again,
he really had to . . . We had pressing needs, Gorloge had
to be paid back . . . But he couldn't concentrate . . .
His mind wandered . . . The moment he picked up a
brush he was so exasperated the stem would snap in his
hands. He was so jumpy he'd smash his little India-ink
pen to bits . . . and his paint pots too . . . the colors
flowed all over . . . It was hopeless . . . The mere
feeling that I was anywhere near him made him want to
smash everything to pieces . . . And as soon as he was
with my mother, he started up again . . . he redoubled
his alarms and excursions.

"If you let him bum around the street all day on the
pretext of learning the business, we haven't seen the end
of our troubles. Believe you me. This is only the beginning.
He won't content himself with being a thief. He'll be a
murderer, see? . . . A murderer! I wouldn't give him six
months before he murders some old woman for her
money. He's on the downgrade all right. He isn't slipping.
Take it from me. He's hurtling, he's galloping. Headlong.
I can see it plain as day. Can't you? You don't believe me?
You're blind! But not yours truly. Not on your life . . .
not me . . ."

Here he took a deep breath. He was hypnotizing her . . .

"Will you finally listen to me? . . . You want me to
tell you what's going to happen? . . . No? . . . You
don't want to know . . ."

"No, Auguste, I implore you . . ."

"Ha! So you're afraid to listen? . . . So you know?"

He seized her by both wrists, he wouldn't let her get
away . . . she had to listen to the bitter end.

"It's us, see? It's us he's going to rub out . . . one of
these days . . . Yes, my dear, he'll settle our hash . . .
That's the kind of gratitude you'll get from him . . . Don't
say I didn't predict it . . . Don't say I didn't warn you
. . . Christ almighty . . . My conscience is clear . . .
Ah, godammit, godammit to hell! I've warned you in

every key . . . I've shouted it from the rooftops! For years! Oh well! *Alea jacta!* . . ."

He got my mother so scared she began to foam at the mouth and bleat . . . and blow bubbles . . . she was out of her mind . . . He really knocked her for a loop . . .

"I don't mind being strangled . . . OK. But you can't pull the wool over my eyes, godammit . . . Do what you like . . . You'll be responsible!"

In the face of these savage predictions, she didn't know what to say or do. Convulsed with grief, she kept chewing at her lips, she bled profusely. I was damned, there was no doubt about that. He started his Pontius Pilate act again, he splashed up the whole floor, I was dirt, and he washed his hands of me . . . the water flowed in jets . . . at high pressure . . . He said whole sentences in Latin. It came back to him at dramatic moments. Just like that, standing in the little kitchen, he'd hurl the anathema at me, he'd declaim in the ancient manner. He'd break off occasionally, pause to explain . . . because I had no education, no feeling for the "humanities" . . .

He knew everything. All I really knew was one thing, that I was untouchable, not fit to be handled with a ten-foot pole. I was despised on all sides, even by the Roman moralists, by Cicero, by the whole Empire, by all the Ancients . . . My papa knew all that . . . He didn't have a single doubt left . . . His certainty made him bellow like a polecat . . . My mother went right on bawling . . . He played the scene so often it got to be a regular act . . . He'd pick up the laundry soap, the big heavy cake, and brandish it like mad . . . with wild, sweeping gestures . . . Now and then he'd put it down . . . perorating all the while . . . And pick it up again . . . And brandish it some more . . . The soap would slip out of his hand . . . and go bouncing under the piano . . . We'd all dive for it . . . We'd rummage around with the broom . . . we'd fish with the handle . . . Shit, piss, and corruption! . . . We'd bash our heads against the corners . . . There were wild collisions . . . We'd stick the broom handle in our eyes . . . It would end in a battle. They'd call each other every stinking name in the world. He'd make her hop around the table on one foot.

They'd forget me for a minute.

My mother was so terrified she lost all shame. She went all over the Passage retailing my villainies . . . she asked the other parents for advice . . . the ones that had trouble with their brats . . . that had got into messes on their jobs . . . How had they managed? . . .

"I'm perfectly willing to make more sacrifices," she added. "We'll see this thing through to the bitter end . . ."

All very eloquent, but it didn't get me out of the soup. I still had no work.

Even Uncle Édouard, so ingenious, with so many strings to his bow, was beginning to get upset. He found me a bit of a nuisance . . . He'd already pestered just about all his friends with my shenanigans, my hard luck . . . He was getting kind of sick of it . . . I stumbled over every obstacle . . . There was something wrong with me . . . I was beginning to get his goat.

The neighbors were mighty interested in my tragedy . . . Our customers too. As soon as they got to know me a little, my mother told them all about it . . . That didn't help matters . . . Even Monsieur Lempreinte at La Coccinelle finally got mixed up in it . . . It's true that my father didn't sleep anymore, that he was beginning to look like a corpse . . . He came to work so exhausted that he staggered in the hallways as he carried the mail from one floor to another . . . Besides, he'd lost his voice, he'd gone hoarse from bellowing his inanities . . .

"Your private life, my friend, doesn't concern me in the least. That's your business. But I expect you to do your work properly . . . Look at the face on you . . . You're falling apart . . . You've got to take care of yourself! What have you been doing on the outside? Aren't you getting enough rest?" That was the way he peppered him.

Then my father was scared and told him all about it . . . all his family troubles . . .

"Ah, my poor boy! Is that all? Lord, if only I had your stomach! Believe me, I wouldn't give a good godam . . . not much! . . . about all my neighbors and relations

. . . about all my sons and cousins . . . my wife! my
daughters! my eighteen fathers! If I was in your place,
I'd piss on everybody. On the whole world. You hear
what I say! You're soft, monsieur, that's all I can see."

That was how Lempreinte looked at things, on account
of his ulcer, an inch away from the pylorus, eating into
him, excruciating . . . The whole world for him was
nothing but one mass of acid . . . The only thing left for
him to do was to try to turn into bicarbonate . . . He
worked at it all day . . . he took whole carloads of the
stuff . . . He couldn't put out the fire. He had a poker
at the bottom of his esophagus that was burning his guts
. . . Soon there wouldn't be anything left but holes . . .
The stars would shine through every time he belched . . .
He and Papa were always offering to change places . . .

"I'd take your ulcer any day. Anything you please, if
only you'll take my son off my hands! How about it?"

That was my father. He'd always put moral torment
way above physical pain . . . It was more respectable
. . . More essential. That's how it was with the Romans,
and that's how he saw all the trials of existence . . . At
peace with his conscience . . . Through thick and thin,
come what may! Amid the worst calamities! . . . No
compromise! No evasions! That was his law! . . . his
raison d'être! My conscience is my own! My conscience!
He shouted that in every key . . . when I stuck my fingers
in my nose . . . if I upset the salt cellar. He opened the
window on purpose to give the Passage a treat . . .

Seeing me down like that, my ears chewed off in every
direction, Uncle Édouard finally took pity on me, he was
a very good guy . . . I was up to my ears in shit . . . He
got his connections moving again and found a way . . .
A shrewd trick to get me out of there . . . the foreign-
language routine . . .

Just like that he says I ought to know at least one . . .
if I want a job in business . . . that it was being done
nowadays . . . it was a necessity . . . The hardest part
was getting my parents' consent . . . The suggestion
floored them completely . . . Still, Édouard knew what
he was talking about . . . We'd lost the habit in our
shanty of hearing anything sensible . . . It came as a
big surprise . . .

My uncle didn't believe in being strict all the time . . .
He was for conciliation, he didn't believe in force . . . He
didn't think it would get results . . . He told them so
straight from the shoulder.

"If he does everything wrong, I don't think it's on purpose . . . His intentions aren't bad . . . I've been watching him for years . . . He's just dull-witted . . . He
doesn't understand what people want of him . . . It must
be adenoids . . . He ought to be out in the fresh air
and stay quite a long time . . . Isn't that what your
doctor told you? . . . If you ask me, I'd send him to
England . . . We'd find a respectable boardingschool
. . . not too expensive . . . or too far away . . . maybe
we could make an arrangement for him to work for his
board and lodging? . . . How does it strike you? When he
comes back, he'll know the language . . . It'll be easy to
find him a job . . . I could find him something in the
retail trade . . . In a bookstore . . . Or in haberdashery
. . . Some place where he isn't known. Gorloge would be
forgotten . . . We'd never even mention it again . . ."

When my parents heard that, they were flummoxed.
They pondered the pros and cons . . . It took them off
their guard . . . There were so many dangers and what
about the expense . . . There was nothing left of Caroline's legacy, only a few thousand francs . . . And that
was Édouard's share . . . Right away he offered it. He
put the money on the table . . . They'd give it back when
they could . . . He wouldn't listen to any nonsense . . .
He wouldn't even take an IOU. "Think it over," he said.
"I'll be back tomorrow. By then I'll have some information . . ."

The excitement was at its peak! . . . My father
wouldn't have anything to do with it . . . He was absolutely convinced that all that money would be thrown
out the window, that it was sheer waste and madness to
boot . . . That if I escaped from their vigilant supervision for so much as a week I'd turn into the worst of
thugs . . . That was a certainty and you couldn't tell him
any different . . . I'd murder somebody in England just
as quickly as in Paris! No two ways about it. It was in the
bag . . . All they had to do was turn me loose for a
month . . . Were they asking for disaster? . . . Well,

their prayers would be answered and then some. They'd
be cooked . . . Up to their necks in debt! A son in
the pen! . . . Extravagance all along the line! . . . And
the consequences? . . . Unspeakable. Those people over
there would never look sharp enough, they'd never be
smart enough! The poor bastards! He'll put them through
the mill. And what about the women? I'd rape every
last one of them. It was plain as day: "Go on, tell me
I don't know what I'm talking about!"

He had his penitentiary on the brain . . . No one could
argue with him . . . To him that was the only remedy,
the only palliative . . . the only way to hold me in
check . . . Don't you learn anything from experience?
Haven't we been through enough? . . . Berlope? Gorloge? The clock? Hadn't I proved sufficiently that I was
the scum of the earth? A disaster hanging over their
heads! . . . I'd drag them all down with me in my ruin
. . . He'd expected it from the start! *Alea!* . . . God's
will be done! He gave us another load of Caesar . . . All
by himself he defended Gaul! . . . He stopped up the
kitchen door with his gestures and his ranting . . . He
evoked the past and future, he shook the whole place . . .

He ran to the water faucet . . . He stuck his face in
the jet and gulped . . . He was sopping wet and still
yelling . . . He didn't dry himself, he ran around dripping
in his hurry to acquaint us with the thousand pitfalls in
wait for me . . . with every aspect of the situation . . .
It was inconceivable! Frightful! Unheard-of. The unspeakable surprises that such an expedition would involve! It
was diabolical foolishness, and that's that!

Two days later Uncle Édouard came back to the Passage
with some first-class dope. He had located a school. What
more could we want? From every point of view and in
every way . . . just the thing for me, for my nature, my
intractable disposition . . . On a hilltop. With plenty of
fresh air, a garden, a river down below . . . Excellent
food . . . Extremely moderate prices . . . No supple-
ments, no surprises! . . . Last but not least, the strictest
discipline . . . Supervision . . . It wasn't very far from
the coast, in Rochester to be exact . . . Only an hour
from Folkestone . . .

In spite of all these advantages, my father had his
doubts . . . He'd see . . . He clung to his suspicions
. . . He looked for niggers in the woodpile . . . He read
the little ad a hundred times . . . He went right on insisting that we were headed for disaster . . . It was sure
as shooting . . . First of all it was insane to contract
any more debts . . . Even with Uncle Édouard . . .
Even to pay back Gorloge would be a labor of Hercules
. . . What with the rent! taxes! the seamstress! . . .
They'd have to tighten their belts till they croaked! He
had to pinch himself to believe they wanted to spend
more money! . . . He was aghast to see Mama going out
of her mind too . . . It was the height of damn foolishness . . . How's that? Wasn't she going to think it over
a little more? . . . What's that you say? I'm making
difficulties! Does that strike you as so unusual? My goodness! What am I expected to do? Say yes? Every single
time? Just like that? To every crazy idea that comes into
your head? Go on! I know what I'm doing. I'm responsible.
Who's the father around here anyway? Édouard doesn't
give a damn, that's a cinch. When the trouble breaks,
he'll be miles away. He'll wash his hands of it. But
I'll always be here. With a bandit on my neck. That's
right. Yes, every bit of it. I exaggerate? Wah! . . . Go
ahead, say it. Say I'm jealous. Go right ahead. Damn it
all. Go ahead and say it . . .

"Of course not, darling. Come, come . . ."

"Shut up, you simpleton, will you shut up? Let me
finish and I'll prove it. I can't say anything around here
anymore! Somebody else is always talking. What's that?
That good-for-nothing! That little gangster! That pervert,
who hasn't even felt the first glimmerings of remorse for
his repulsive crime! For his infamous sneaky theft. There
he is. Lounging around! . . . Defying us both! It's disgraceful, I tell you! . . . It's enough to make you dash
your ass against the floor! . . . It makes my hair stand
on end! . . . Just because Édouard has deigned to open
his mouth! That clown! That jumping jack! All you can
think about is travel! Extravagance! Sure! Why not? New
ways of spending our money! Pure tommyrot! Insanity!
Madness . . . Has it ever entered your head, you poor
addled thing, that we haven't even begun to pay his ran-

som! . . . You heard me . . . His ransom! . . . Why, it's unthinkable! . . . Abominable! . . . What are we coming to? I'm going out of my mind! Unspeakable! We're up to our necks in absurdity! I can't stand it! It's killing me!"

Uncle Édouard had taken a powder at the beginning of the session. He'd seen the storm coming . . . He'd left his prospectuses . . .

"I'll be back tomorrow afternoon . . . You'll have made up your minds by then . . ."

He was handling things as best he could, but there wasn't much he could do . . . My father was in full eruption. This plan for my departure upset his whole tragedy . . . He tried to save it by fussing over the conditions . . . He saw completely red . . . He paced the room like a wild animal . . . My mother hobbled along behind him . . . She went on about the advantages . . . the reasonable prices . . . the strict supervision . . . the splendid food . . . the fresh air . . . Lots of fresh air!

"You know Édouard is completely dependable . . . I know you don't think much of him . . . But you've got to admit he's no fool . . . He's not impulsive . . . He doesn't rush into things with his eyes closed . . . When he says something, that means it's so . . . You know that as well as I do . . . Admit it . . . Come along now, Auguste, my poor darling . . ."

"I don't want to be beholden to anybody . . ."

"But he isn't just anybody! . . ."

"That's all the more reason. Jumping Jehoshaphat!"

"We'll give him a note, as if he were a stranger!"

"You know what you can do with your notes, godammit to blinking hell!"

"But he's never let us down. . . ."

"He gives me a swift pain in the balls . . . that damn brother of yours . . . do you hear me? . . . He gives me . . . I hope I've made myself clear . . . He's the biggest damn fool of the lot . . . And you two give me an even worse pain, do you hear me? The whole damn lot of you . . ."

He worked himself into such a lather that his whole head swelled up, he let off jets of steam, and in the end his words exploded like firecrackers. She latched onto him, she wouldn't give an inch. She was stubborn . . . She wrestled him into the corners . . . Her leg dragged so bad it got caught in all the chairs. She supported herself against the walls . . .

"Auguste! Oh, you're hurting me! You're so rough. Oh, my ankle! Now you've done it. I've twisted it!"

The screams went on for an hour . . .

He started up again. He kicked the chairs to pieces. He went raving mad. Even so, she pursued him wherever he went . . . even up the stairs . . . That drove him even wilder . . . Tip-tap-plunk, tip-tap-plunk, to hear her clumping on the stairs . . . He'd have gladly thrown her straight over the banister . . . Or crawled into a rathole . . . She'd make me little signs as she passed . . . meaning that he was beginning to weaken . . . He kept on losing his cap . . . He let her catch up with him . . . He couldn't keep up the pace . . . He fled as from a bad smell . . . "Leave me alone, leave me alone, please, Clémence . . . I beg you, leave me alone, godammit! You stinking bitch! Won't the two of you ever get sick of persecuting me! All you do is talk talk talk, I've got it up to here. Godammit to lousy stinking hell! Will you ever listen to me!"

My good mother didn't care what he said, she was worn to a frazzle, but wouldn't relax her grip. She grappled him by the neck, she kissed him on the moustache, she closed his eyes with kisses . . . She treated him to a convulsion. She spat supplications into his ears . . . In the end she had him gagging. His head was sopping wet with storms and caresses . . . He couldn't stand straight. He collapsed on the stairs. Then she began talking about his own health, his alarming condition . . . Everybody had been saying how pale he was . . . Then he was willing to listen . . .

"You're going to make yourself really sick, my poor angel, working yourself up into such a state! If you come down, where will that get us? What will become of us? . . . I assure you it's better he should go away . . . His being here is making you sick . . . Édouard saw that . . . He told me so before he left . . ."

"What did Édouard tell you anyway?"

"Your husband won't last long. If he keeps on working

himself up like that . . . He's wasting away . . . Everybody's noticed it in the Passage . . . Everybody's talking about it . . ."

"Were those his exact words?"

"Yes, angel. I assure you . . . He didn't want me to tell you . . . You see how tactful he is . . . You see, I assure you, you can't go on like this . . . You see? You agree, don't you?"

"To what?"

"To letting the child go . . . it'll give us a breathing spell . . . Just you and me together . . . Wouldn't you like that?"

"No, certainly not! Not so fast! God almighty! No! Not so fast!"

"Come along, Auguste. Just think. If you fret yourself to death, where will it get us? . . ."

"Die? Me? Good Lord! Die! That's all I'm asking for. Die? Hurry hurry. Good grief! You think I give a damn! Why, it's all I want in the world . . . Ah! Christ! Christ!"

He disentangles himself, he shakes himself loose, he knocks my mother over. He begins to bellow again . . . He hadn't thought of that! Death! . . . Christ! His death! . . . He starts up again in a fine lather . . . He puts his whole soul into it! He jumps up . . . He runs for the sink . . . He wants a drink of water. Pum pum crash! . . . He skids . . . He somersaults . . . He sprawls on all fours ; . . . He plunges into the sideboard . . . he ricochets into the buffet . . . He hollers so the whole place echoes . . . He's bumped his nose . . . He tries to pick himself up . . . The whole shooting match comes down on us . . . All the china, the cutlery, the lamp . . . A waterfall, an avalanche . . . We're snowed under . . . We can't even see each other . . . My mother screams in the ruins . . . "Papa, papa, where are you? Papa, answer me!" . . . He was stretched out full length on his back . . . I see his shoes sticking out over the red varnished tiles in the kitchen . . .

"Papa, answer me. Answer me, darling . . ."

"Shit! Can't you leave me alone! . . . Godammit, am I asking you for anything?"

In the end he was worn down . . . He finally con-

sented . . . My mother had her way . . . The fight had
gone out of him . . . He said it was all one to him . . .
He talked about suicide again . . . He went back to his
office . . . He stopped thinking of anything but himself
. . . He threw in the sponge . . . He went out so as
not to have to look at me. He left me alone with my
mother . . . That was when she began to dish it out
again . . . her grievances . . . her whole litany . . . All
sorts of ideas cropped up in her head . . . and they had
to come out, she wanted me to benefit by them, to get
a whole bellyful before going away . . . Just because my
father had given up didn't mean I should think I could
do anything I pleased . . .

"Listen to me just a minute, Ferdinand! It's high
time we had a little talk: I don't want to pester you,
scold you, threaten you with one thing or another. That's
not what a mother's for and it's not my way. But even so
there are certain things a mother can't help noticing . . .
I often seem to be daydreaming, but I see what's going
on . . . I don't say much, but that doesn't keep me from
thinking . . . It's a big risk we're taking . . . Of course
it is. Just imagine! Sending you to England . . . Your
father isn't crazy . . . He's a thoughtful man . . . Yes,
he's nobody's fool . . . For poor folks like us it's sheer
madness . . . sending you abroad . . . We're deep in
debt . . . And the price of that pin to be paid back . . .
And now two thousand francs to your uncle! Your father
was talking about it only this morning, it's insane . . .
And that's God's truth . . . I don't want to rub it in,
but your father knows what's what . . . He's got eyes
in his head! I'd like to know where we're going to find
all that money! Two thousand francs! . . . Even if we
move heaven and earth! . . . It doesn't grow on trees
. . . Your father, you've only got to open yours eyes, is at
the end of his tether . . . As for me, I'm all in, exhausted, I don't mention it to him, but I'm ready to
collapse . . . You see my leg? . . . It's begun to swell
up every night . . . Do you call this a life? . . . What
have we done to deserve it? Are you listening, my boy?
I'm not reproaching you . . . I just want you to realize
. . . to look the situation in the face . . . to know
what we've been through . . . Because you'll be away

for several months now. You've made life very hard for
us, Ferdinand. I've a right to tell you that, to let you
know. I'm always inclined to be lenient with you . . . I'm
your mother, after all . . . It's hard for me to judge
you . . . But strangers, your employers . . . these people who've had you with them day after day . . . They
haven't got the same weakness . . . Gorloge, for instance!
. . . Only yesterday . . . I can still hear him . . . I
told your father what he said . . . As he was leaving . . .
he'd been here a whole hour . . . 'Madame,' he said, 'I
see the kind of woman I'm talking to . . . Your boy . . .
well, if you ask me, it's all perfectly simple . . . You're
like so many mothers . . . You've spoiled him. He's
rotten. That's all there is to it. You think you're being
kind, you work yourselves to the bone! And you're ruining
your children.' I'm telling you exactly what he said, word
for word. With the best of intentions all you'll make of
him is a lazy, pleasure-seeking egotist . . . I was flabbergasted, take it from me . . . I didn't say boo . . . I
didn't bat an eyelash . . . As a mother, I wasn't going
to tell him he was right! . . . But what do you suppose
I was thinking? . . . He was able to see clearly . . .
With us it's not the same, especially with me . . . If
you're not more affectionate, more reasonable, more hardworking, and especially more grateful . . . if you're not
more considerate . . . if you don't try to help us more
. . . in this hard life of ours . . . there's a reason, and
I'm going to tell you what it is . . . I'm your mother, I
understand because I'm a woman . . . It's because you're
heartless . . . That's the whole trouble . . . I often
wonder whom you can take after. I'm wondering right
now where you get it from? Certainly not from your father
or from me . . . Your father is all heart . . . his heart's
too big, poor man . . . And me, I guess you saw the way
I was with my mother . . . My heart's always been in
the right place . . . We've been weak with you . . . We
were too busy, we didn't want to face the facts . . . We
thought things would straighten out all by themselves . . .
And in the end you did a dishonest thing . . . How perfectly abominable! . . . We're all of us a little at fault
. . . I've got to admit it . . . And this is what it's led
to . . . 'He'll be your ruination!' . . . Ah, he made no

bones about it. Lavelongue warned me long ago . . .
He's not the only one who saw it, Ferdinand . . . Everybody who lives with you catches on after a while . . .
Well, I won't rub it in . . . I don't want to paint you
blacker than you are . . . Over there you'll be in entirely
different surroundings . . . Try to forget your evil ways
. . . to keep out of bad company . . . Don't go running
around with little hoodlums . . . And most of all, don't
imitate them . . . Think of us . . . Think of your
parents . . . Try to mend your ways over there . . .
Play in recreation time, but don't play when you're supposed to be working . . . Try to learn the language
quickly and then you'll come back . . . Improve your
manners . . . Try to mold your character . . . Make an
effort . . . The English always seem so correct . . . So
clean! So nicely dressed! I don't know what to say, my
boy, to make you behave a little better . . . It's the last
try . . . Your father has explained it all to you . . . Life
is a serious business at your age . . . You want to be a
decent man . . . I can't tell you anymore . . ." That
was God's truth, I'd heard just about all there was to hear
. . . The whole business left me cold . . . All I wanted
was to get out of there as quickly as possible and not to
hear any more talk. The main thing isn't knowing whether
you're right or wrong. That really doesn't matter . . .
The main thing is to keep people from bothering you . . .
The rest is eyewash . . .

When it came time to go, I felt bad after all, worse than
I'd have expected. It's hard not to. As the three of us
were standing on the platform in the Gare du Nord, we
were a miserable sight . . . We hung on to each other's
clothes, trying to keep together . . . As soon as we were
in a crowd, we grew timid, furtive . . . Even my father,
who hollered so loud in the Passage, was helpless outside
. . . He shriveled up . . . It was only at home that he
could wield thunder and lightning. Outside he blushed
for fear of being noticed. He peered out of the corner of his
eyes . . .
It took a lot of gumption to send me so far . . . all
alone . . . just like that . . . All of a sudden we were
scared . . . My mother, who was the most heroic, tried

to find somebody who was going my way . . . Nobody
had ever heard of Rochester . . . I went in to get a
seat . . . They repeated all the necessary instructions
. . . to be careful, very careful . . . not to get out
before the train stopped . . . never to cross the tracks
. . . To look in all directions . . . Not to play with the
door handle . . . to watch out for drafts . . . not to get
things in my eyes . . . To keep an eye on the baggage
rack . . . because something can fall down and bash
your brains in when the train jolts . . . I had a pack-
jammed suitcase and in addition a blanket, sort of a carpet,
an enormous oriental rug with colored checks, a green
and blue "plaid" . . . We got it from Grandma Caroline.
We'd never been able to sell it . . . I was taking it back
to its home country. It would be fine for the climate, that's
what we thought . . .

In the middle of all the racket I had to recite my lesson
a last time, everything they'd been dinning into me for the
last week . . . "Brush your teeth every morning . . .
Wash your feet every Saturday . . . Ask to take sitz baths
. . . You have a dozen pair of socks . . . Three nightgowns . . . Wipe yourself properly when you go to the
toilet . . . Chew your food and eat slowly . . . You'll
ruin your stomach . . . Take your worm syrup . . . Get
rid of that habit of touching yourself . . ."

I was treated to many more precepts for my moral
resurrection, my rehabilitation . . . They gave me everything before I left . . . I took it all away with me to
England, good principles, excellent principles . . . and
shame on account of my vicious instincts. I'd want for
nothing. The price was all settled. Two months had been
paid for in advance. I promised to be well behaved,
obedient, courageous, attentive, sincere, grateful, scrupulous, never to lie, especially never to steal, not to stick
my fingers up my nose, to come back completely changed,
a model of good behavior, to put on weight, to know
English, not to forget my French, to write every Sunday
at the very least. I promised everything they asked . . .
if only they'd let me leave right away . . . and cut the
tragedy . . . We'd talked so much there was nothing left
to say . . . It was time to get going . . . Nasty thoughts
came to me, sinister feelings . . . There's something

stupefying about all this loathsome confusion . . . the
steam, the crowd, the whistles . . . In the distance I could
see the rails disappearing into the tunnel. Soon I'd be
disappearing too. I had some rotten presentiments, I
wondered if the English weren't going to be meaner and
crummier, a damn sight worse than the people around
here . . .

I looked at my parents, they were trembling all over
. . . They couldn't hold back the tears . . . I began to
bawl too. I was terribly ashamed, I was breaking down
like a girl, I didn't think much of myself. My mother
clutched me in her arms . . . It was time to close the
doors . . . They were shouting "All aboard!" . . . She
hugged me so hard, with such a storm of emotion, that I
reeled . . . On those occasions the tenderness that welled
up from her misshapen carcass had the strength of a horse
. . . The idea of parting drenched her in advance. A howling tornado turned her inside out, as if her soul were coming
out her behind, her eyes, her belly, her bosom . . . it hit
me in all directions, it lit up the whole station . . . She
couldn't help it . . . it was something awful to look at.

"Calm yourself, Mama, please . . . The people are
laughing at us . . ."

I begged her to control herself, I implored her amid
the kisses, the blowing whistles, the racket . . . But it
was too much for her . . . I extricated myself from her
embrace, I jumped on the step, I didn't want her to start in
again . . . I didn't dare to admit it, but in a way I was
curious . . . I'd have liked to know how far she could go
in her effusions . . . From what nauseating depths was
she digging up all this slop?

With my father at least it was perfectly simple, he was
nothing but a slobbering fool, there was nothing left in his
dome but rubbish, pretense, and uproar . . . a clutter
of idiocy . . . My mother was different . . . She kept
her wits about her, her mind was still in one piece . . .
Even in the lousiest situation . . . the slightest caress
would send her into a tizzy . . . li..e some broken
machine, the piano of genuine unhappiness that had
nothing left but a few sour notes . . . Even when I was
up in the car, I was afraid she'd grab me again . . . I went
in and out, pretending to be looking for something . . .

I climbed up on the bench . . . I took down my blanket
. . . I stepped on it . . . I was mighty glad when the
train gave a jolt . . . We pulled out in a roar of thunder
. . . We had passed Asnières before I settled down like
everybody else . . . I was still anxious . . .

When we got to Folkestone, they pointed out the head
conductor, who was supposed to keep an eye on me and
tell me when to get out. He was wearing a red shoulder
strap with a little bag hanging in the middle of his back.
I couldn't very well lose sight of him. In Chatham he
motioned to me. I grabbed my suitcase. The train was
two hours late, the people from my school, Meanwell
College, had gone back home, they'd given me up. In a
way that suited me. I was the only one getting out, the
others were going on to London.

It was already dark, the place wasn't very well lighted.
It was a raised station, propped up on piles . . . like
stilts . . . It was elongated, a big wooden tangle in the
mist, all covered with colored posters . . . When you
walked on the platform, thousands of planks resounded . . .

I didn't want to be helped anymore, I was sick of
it . . . I left by a side door and then a footbridge . . .
Nobody asked me anything . . . I couldn't see my man
anymore, a different one in a red and blue uniform who'd
been pestering the life out of me. I looked around outside
the station, the square was mighty dark. The town began
right away. Little streets tumbling downhill, from one
dim light to the next. The air was thick and sticky, swirling
around the gas jets . . . The effect was spooky . . .
From way down below came gusts of music . . . carried
by the wind, I guess . . . Tunes . . . like a busted
merry-go-round in the night . . .

It was a Saturday when I arrived, the streets were full of
people, flocking past the shops. The streetcar, which looked
like a fat giraffe, towered over the shanties, compressed the
crowd, shook the windowpanes . . . The crowd moved in
dense, brown waves, it smelled like muck and tobacco and
anthracite, and also like toast and a little like sulphur for
the eyes; it got thick and more enveloping, more suffocat-

ing the farther down I went, it closed in after the streetcar had passed, like fish after a dam . . .

In the eddies the people felt oilier, stickier than our people. My suitcase got tangled up in legs, I passed from one paunch to another. I took a gander at the food piled up in the shop windows. Little mountains of hams . . . Valleys of bologna . . . I was mighty hungry, but I was afraid to go in. I had a pound in one pocket and some change in the other.

After a lot of pushing and poking we ended up on the riverfront . . . The fog was pretty thick . . . You get used to stumbling . . . Mustn't fall in the river . . . The whole place was rigged up like a fair, with little booths and some regular stages . . . Thousands of lamps and what a mob! . . . Peddlers fished for suckers in the crowd . . . shouting themselves hoarse in their language . . . There were lots of stands all along the esplanade, to suit every taste . . . Fish and chips . . . mandolins, wrestlers, weight lifters, a sword swallower, a bicycle track, little birds . . . there was a terrific mob around the canary pecking the "future" in a box . . . There was something for everybody . . . nougat . . . whole barrels of currant jelly, dripping all over the place . . . A dense cloud comes down from the sky . . . it falls on the fair . . . for a moment it hides everything . . . blots out space . . . You can still hear all right, but you can't see a thing . . . neither the man nor his acetylene lamp . . . Ah, a gust of wind! There he is again . . . A real gentleman in a frock coat . . . He exhibits the moon for twopence . . . for three he gives you Saturn . . . it's written on his sign . . . There's the mist again, falling on the crowd, spreading out . . . Everything's muffled . . . The guy breaks off his spiel, folds up his telescope, curses, and clears out. The people are all laughing . . . You can't even move anymore . . . People lose each other, then they get together outside the stands where the light is really bright. Music drifts over from all directions . . . You think you're right in the middle of it . . . It's a kind of mirage . . . Like you were bathing in sound . . . That's a banjo . . . A nigger on a carpet right beside me, whimpering on the ground . . . he imitates a locomotive, he's going to run everybody over. We're all having a fine time, we can't see each other.

The fog lifts and blows away . . . I'm not in a hurry anymore . . . I can take my time about getting to Meanwell . . . This place on the riverfront suits me . . . the fair and the strangers in the haze . . . There's something very pleasant about a language you don't understand . . . It's like a fog swirling around in your thoughts . . . It's nice, it's like a dream, there's really nothing better . . . It's fine as long as the words stay in the dream . . . I sit down for a while quietly on my blanket, against a stone post, on the other side of the chains . . . I can lean back, I'm pretty comfortable . . . I watch the whole show passing . . . A whole string of sailors with lanterns on the end of long poles . . . They're funny guys . . . Confusion! Fireworks! . . . They're all dead-drunk and happy . . . They push and shove and squeal like cats . . . They throw the whole crowd into a panic. They can't get ahead . . . Their snake dance gets tangled up in a lamp post . . . It winds and unwinds . . . One of them collapses in the gutter . . . They've knocked the nigger over . . . Shouts . . . challenges . . . insults . . . Suddenly they're roaring mad . . . They want to hang the nigger from the trolley pole . . . What a racket! . . . A mean fight starts up . . . The whole place is steaming and sizzling . . . The blows fall like drumbeats . . . terrible grunts and groans . . . Whistles blow . . . A troupe of extras come running . . . A screaming cloud . . . A whole squad of police, blue with pointed black helmets . . . They're in a terrible hurry . . . They pop out of the streets, out of the shadows, from all over . . . on the double . . . And the soldiers who've been strutting along the stands, dandling their riding whips, start running too . . . They plunge into the fray . . . Catcalls from the sarabande . . . They stagger and fall . . . Every color in the rainbow! A battle of samples . . . Jonquil . . . green . . . violet . . . A free-for-all . . . a scramble . . . The women escape into the corners with their acetylene lamps, the lights blend with the fog . . . all screaming something awful . . . terrified . . . skinned alive . . . Police reinforcements arrive . . . parrot color . . . Majestically they join in the dance . . . They're

toppled over, their clothes are torn off. A battle in a birdhouse . . . A welter of riding whips and plumes . . . A
charabanc with four horses bounds out of an alley . . . It
stops short in the middle of the riot . . . Some more
bruisers pour out . . . They fling themselves on the mob
like a ton of bricks . . . they're giants and they move
fast . . . They nab the most truculent, the drunkest, the
ones that are yelling loudest . . . They toss them into
the van, completely upside down . . . The corpses pile
up inside . . . The battle dies down . . . The ruckus is
swallowed up in darkness . . . The wagon gallops away
. . . And that's the end of the riot . . . The crowd flows
back toward the bars, to the mahogany counters . . . to
guzzle harder than ever . . . The roadway is clear . . .
little carts go by . . . French fries . . . sausages . . .
periwinkles . . . Glasses are clinked . . . Knives cutting
into sausage . . . The swinging doors are in constant motion . . . right and left . . . A drunk stumbles and falls
flat in the gutter . . . The procession circles around him
. . . People dawdle past . . . A bevy of floozies . . .
cackling and guffawing . . . sailors push them into the
doorways . . . They talk . . . they belch . . . the bar
absorbs them . . . The Scotsmen dash in . . .They'd like
to fight some more, but they really can't. . . .
   I follow them in with my suitcase . . . Nobody asks me
anything . . . They serve me first . . . A whole mugful
of syrup, thick and black and frothy . . . it's bitter . . .
it's beer! It tastes like stewed smoke . . . They give me
back two coppers with the queen on them, the one that
just died, with the face like a rear end . . . the fair Vic-
toria . . . I can't finish their brew, it turns my stomach
and I'm mighty ashamed. I go back to the procession. We
pass the little carts again, with the lamps between the
shafts . . . I hear a regular orchestra . . . I look around
and locate it . . . It's right near the landing . . . It's
coming out of a big tent, a blaring uproar . . . They're
singing in chorus, completely out of tune . . . It's amazing the way they manage to torture their mouths, to dilate
them, to blow them up like real trombones . . . And pull
them in again . . . They're on their last legs . . . They're
dying of convulsions . . . They're praying and singing
hymns . . . There's this big tall battle-ax with only one

eye, she's yodeling so hard it's like to pop out of her head
. . . The way she's jigging and heaving, her bun starts
sliding down over her nose, and her bonnet with the ribbons too . . . she thinks she's not making enough noise,
she grabs her man's trombone and blows, she spits a whole
lung into it . . . But it's a polka she's playing, a regular
hornpipe . . . The gloom is over . . . The people begin
to dance, they hug each other, they hop, they shake each
other up . . . The guy in the uniform that's looking at
her must be her brother, he looks just like her except for
the beard, and besides he's got glasses and a nifty cap with
an inscription. He seems to be sulking . . . He's got his
nose in a book . . . All of a sudden he breaks into a fit
too! He grabs the horn from his sister . . . He climbs up
on the stool, spits a good oyster . . . and begins to jabber
. . . The way he's waving his arms and beating his
breast . . . working himself up into an ecstasy . . . I
can see it must be a sermon . . . His words come out
sobbing . . . tortured . . . it's unbearable . . . The
characters around them are laughing fit to kill . . . He
defies them, challenges them, nothing can stop him . . .
not even the whistles of the boats stemming the current
. . . He goes right on thundering . . . Personally, he
gives me a pain . . . He puts me to sleep . . . I sit down
on my blanket . . . I cover myself, nobody can see me,
I'm hidden by the sheds . . . The Salvation Army guy is
still yelling, screeching his lungs out . . . He makes me
tired . . . It's cold, but I wrap up good . . . I feel a
little warmer . . . The mist is white, then blue. I'm right
next to a sentry box . . . It's getting dark, little by
little . . . I'm going to sleep . . . Over there, that's
where the music is coming from . . . It's a merry-go-
round . . . a barrel organ . . . From across the river
. . . that's the wind . . . the lapping of the water . . .

A terrible groan from a boiler woke me with a start
. . . A ship was coming up the river . . . fighting the
current . . . The Salvation Army characters from before
had cleared out . . . Niggers were jumping up and down
on the stage . . . somersaulting in swallowtails . . .
landing in the street . . . Their lavender coattails spun
around behind them in the mud and the acetylene glare.

"The Minstrels," it said on their big drum . . . They went on and on . . . a roll of the drum . . . a happy landing . . . a pirouette . . . A great big enormous siren rips through the echoes . . . The crowd stops in its tracks . . . They all move down to the edge to watch the ship landing . . . I wedge myself into the staircase right next to the waves . . .

A lot of brats in little boats were whirling around in the eddies looking for the hawser . . . The launch, the big fat one with the enormous copper boiler in the middle, was rolling like a top . . . She was bringing the papers. The East Indiaman was having a tough time with the current . . . She was still in midstream, in the middle of the blackness . . . She didn't want to come closer . . . with her green eye and her red one . . . Finally the wise guy came in after all, bashing against an enormous bundle of sticks that was hanging from the dock . . . It cracked like a pile of bones . . . She had her nose into the current, she roared in the rough water . . . She churned against the mooring buoy . . . a tethered monster . . . She let out one little howl . . . She was beaten . . . all alone in the glistening whirling water . . . We turned back to the merry-go-round, the one with the organs and the mountains . . . The party was still going on . . . I felt better after my nap . . . It was like magic . . . an entirely different world . . . fantastic . . . like a crazy picture . . . All of a sudden I felt they'd never catch me again . . . that I'd turned into a memory that no one would ever recognize . . . that I had nothing more to fear, that nobody'd ever find me again . . . I treated myself to a ride on the merry-go-round, I held out my change. I took three whole rides with three crazy floozies and some soldiers . . . They were cute, they had faces like dolls, eyes like blue candies . . . I was dizzy . . . I wanted to take another turn . . . I was afraid to show my dough . . . I went off a little way into the darkness . . . I tore open my lining, I wanted to take out my banknote, the whole pound. And then the smell of something frying steered me to a place right near the locks . . . It was fritters . . . I could smell them a mile away . . . on a cart with little wheels.

This kid that was messing with the batter . . . I can't say she was pretty . . . She had two teeth missing in

front . . . She never stopped laughing . . . She had a
fringed hat with a big pile of flowers on top . . . crushed
under the weight . . . a regular hanging garden . . . and
long muslin veils that hung down into her kettle . . . She
took them out with a sweet smile . . . She seemed very
young to be wearing such a thing even at that time of
night . . . even under those cockeyed circumstances . . .
that lid really sent me . . . I couldn't take my eyes off
it. She was still smiling at me . . . The kid wasn't twenty,
with pert little boobies and a wasp waist . . . and an ass
the way I like them, taut, muscular, with a good split . . .
I walked around her to get a good look. She was still
absorbed in her grease . . . She wasn't proud or standoffish . . . I showed her my change . . . She served me
enough fritters to stuff a whole family. All she took was
one little coin . . . There was sympathy between us . . .
She could see from my suitcase that I'd just got off the
train . . . She tries to make me understand something
. . . She tries to explain . . . She speaks very slowly
. . . She pronounces each word separately . . . Well,
then I begin to feel jumpy . . . I shrivel up . . . The
poison runs through me . . . As soon as anybody starts
talking to me I get mean . . . I didn't want any more
gabfests . . . Save your breath! I've had enough! . . . I
know what it leads to . . . you can't fool me . . . She
gets politer, sweeter, more endearing than ever . . . Anyway that hole in her mouth when she smiles makes me
sick . . . I make motions to show that I'm going for a
walk over by the pubs . . . to have a little fun . . . I
leave her my suitcase in exchange and my blanket . . . I
put them down beside her camp chair . . . I make a sign
for her to watch them . . . I go back to the crowd . . .

   With nothing to weigh me down, I head for the shops
. . . I stroll past the piles of grub . . . But I'm full up,
I can't eat anymore . . . The clock strikes eleven . . .
Drunks come out in waves and stream down the esplanade
. . . this way and that way, crashing against the wall of
the customs house . . . tumbling, roaring, spreading out,
dispersing . . . The ones that are stewed but still swaggering step into the pub stiffly, rhythmically, buttoned
crooked but buttoned, and head straight for the bar . . .
There they stand speechless, transfixed, riveted by the

mechanical din, the *"valse d'amour."* I've got piles of money left . . . I took two more helpings of beer soup, the kind that makes you piss . . .

I went out with a little thug and another burper with a little cat under his arm. He was miaowing between the two of us . . . I didn't get very far . . . I retreated into the next pub . . . I staggered through the swinging doors . . . I sat down on a bench . . . waiting for it to pass . . . with all the boozehounds . . . There was a crowd of dames in short jackets, in feathers and tams and hard-brimmed straw hats . . . They were all talking like animals . . . barking and belching . . . They were dogs, tigers, wolves . . . crabs . . . I was beginning to itch . . .

Outside, through the window, fish were passing now . . . You could see them clear as anything . . . They were moving slowly . . . undulating past the glass . . . coming out into the light . . . They opened their mouths, little puffs of fog came out . . . There were mackerel and carp . . . They smelled like it too, they smelled of muck, honey, acrid smoke . . . everything . . . Another little slug of beer . . . and I'll never be able to get up again . . . That'll be fine . . . They drool, they chortle . . . all those bums . . . They're all fighting, they give each other clouts on the ass that would kill a mule . . . The stinkers!

But then the piano stops, the bartender in the apron throws us all out . . . I'm in the street again. I unbutton my collar . . . I feel lousy . . . I drag myself through the shadows . . . I can still see the two street lamps a little . . . not much . . . I see the water . . . I can see it lapping . . . Ah! I can even see the way down. I take the steps one by one . . . I lean on the rail, I'm very careful . . . I touch the drink . . . on my knees . . . I vomit on it . . . I make a violent effort . . . I feel better . . . An enormous burst comes down on me from above . . . a whole meal . . . I can see the guy leaning over . . . Seconds . . . A slimy mess . . . I try to stand up . . . Hell, I can't make it . . . I sit down again . . . I take the whole business . . . Oh well . . . it runs into my eyes . . . Another retch . . . Wah! . . . I see the water dancing . . . white . . . and black . . . It's really cold. I'm shivering, I tear my pants . . . I can't

throw up anymore . . . I lie down again in a corner . . .
The bowsprit of a sailboat passes over me . . . It just
grazes my head . . . The guys are coming. A whole
squadron of them . . . They're coming out of the fog.
They're pulling at the oars . . . They pull up at the
dock . . . The sails are furled at half-mast . . . I hear
the mob coming, stamping along the dock, that's the fatigue
squad . . .

I stay by the water's edge . . . I'm not quite so cold
. . . My head's fuzzy . . . I'm all right here. Why not?
I'm not bothering anybody . . . They're some kind of
"tartans" . . . I know about boats . . . Still more of
them coming . . . They crowd together . . . They settle
in the waves . . . up to the rail . . . weighed down with
food. Enough vegetables for an army . . . Red cabbage,
onions, black radishes, mountains of turnips, whole cathe-
drals of them, heading into the stream, towed by a sailboat . . . They rise up out of the darkness . . . proud
and graceful in the beam of the searchlights . . . The
longshoremen have put the ladder in place . . . All at the
same time they swallow their plugs. They hang their
hats on their alpaca coats . . . They looked like a bunch
of bookkeepers . . . They were even wearing cuffs . . .
That's what longshoremen were like in those days . . .
They toted baskets, enormous piles of them . . . balancing acts . . . the tops were lost in the darkness . . .
They came back with tomatoes, they dug deep tunnels in
the wall of cauliflowers . . . They vanished in the holds
again . . . They came back out into the lamplight . . .
with big loads of artichokes . . . the boat wasn't listing
anymore, it was sinking under the weight of the gangplanks . . . Another batch of phony longshoremen tote
some more of the cargo away . . .

That's funny, my teeth are chattering . . . I'm dying
of the cold . . . literally. I'm not dizzy anymore . . .
Suddenly I remember . . . Where did I leave my blanket?
It all comes back to me . . . the kid with the fritters
. . . I look from one stand to the next . . . Finally I find
her. She was waiting for me. She'd put everything away,
all the kettles, the big fork, folded up the whole shooting
match . . . She was all ready to leave. She was glad to
see me back . . . She'd sold her whole stock . . . She

even showed me that all the dishes were empty . . . The French fries . . . the potato salad . . . All she had left was a piece of head cheese . . . She smeared it on bread with a knife, a good chunk, and we shared it . . . I was hungry again. She pulled up her veil to get a better look at me. She made scolding gestures, because I'd stayed away too long. She was jealous already! . . . She wouldn't let me help her pulling at the shafts . . . The shed where she kept her cart was in town . . . I carried the lantern . . . I hadn't seen all of her hat . . . There was more to see . . . streamers hanging down to her waist. A great big peacock feather was tied under her chin with a really magnificent scarf with a mauve and gold flower pattern.

In the shed we piled up the pots . . . We locked the door and went out bumming. She came closer to me . . . she wanted to talk to me seriously . . . But again I wouldn't give in . . . I played dumb. I showed her my address . . . "Meanwell College." I stopped under a lamp so she could read it . . . As it happened, she didn't know how to read . . . She went on gabbing the whole time . . . She kept repeating her name. She tapped on her chest . . . Gwendoline! Gwendoline! . . . I heard her all right, I massaged her tits, but I didn't get the words . . . To hell with tenderness . . . sentiment! That stuff is like a family . . . At first you don't catch on, but it stinks, it's putrid, crawling . . . No Greasy Joan is going to drag any words out of me . . . Pleased to meet you, kid! . . . Go· shit in your hat! . . . Let her carry my bag . . . God bless your kind heart! Go right ahead! Anyway, she was stronger than me . . . She took advantage of the dark corners to smother me with caresses. She hugged me like a wrestler . . . There was no point in resisting . . . The streets were almost deserted . . . She wanted me to knead her . . . to press her . . . to squeeze her . . . She was hot stuff . . . demanding and curious . . . We hid behind the fog . . . I had to keep on kissing her, she wouldn't have given my stuff back . . . It was no use wriggling, I'd have looked like a dope . . . We were under a lamp . . . she had a crust on her . . . she took out my dick . . . it wasn't hard anymore . . . she hardens it up . . . I come . . . That really drives her crazy . . . She goes jumping around in

the fog . . . She hikes up her skirt . . . she dances like
a cannibal . . . I couldn't help laughing . . . It didn't
seem like the right time of day . . . She wanted the whole
works . . . Hell . . . She's running after me . . . She's
getting mean . . . She catches me . . . She tries to eat
me alive . . . with big sucking kisses . . . That kid liked
foreigners . . .

The esplanade was empty, at the other end the jugglers
were folding their tents . . . the little carts with candy
and jam crossed the open space, jolting in the holes and
ruts . . . They had trouble pushing . . . We came to a
booth . . . the last woman in the place, a grandmother,
was rolling up her hangings . . . She was dressed like a
houri . . . She blew out her candles . . . She rolled up
her oriental carpets . . . There were signs all around the
entrance . . . showing the lines of the hand . . . She
was yawning tremendously . . . enough to dislocate her
jaw . . . Wah! Wah! she grunted out through the night.
We came closer, me and my floozie. We interrupted her
housecleaning. The two broads knew each other . . .
They stop to chat . . . They must have been friends . . .
They jabber a lot of stuff . . . They were both interested
in me . . . The Fatima motions me to come up, to step
into her shack. I couldn't refuse; the other one minded my
things . . . The old bag takes my hand, she turns it over,
she looks at my palms . . . Close up, under the lamp.
She's going to tell my fortune . . . I catch on . . .
They're curious about my future . . . Women always
want to know everything . . . the minute you refuse to
talk . . . I didn't give a damn, I was nice and comfortable
on a pile of cushions . . . It was a damn sight warmer
than outside . . . I just took it easy . . . They went on
with their hocus-pocus . . . They were interested in my
case . . . The Fatima was getting excited . . . she was
cooking up my horoscope . . . My girl was frowning
. . . My fate must have been sad . . . I let them work
on my hands . . . It wasn't unpleasant. Anyway I had
other things to worry out . . . I looked around me some
. . . Their tent had stripes and stars on it, and on the
ceiling embroidered moons and comets . . . It was too
late to get up much interest . . . I couldn't understand
a word of their gibberish . . . It was at least two o'clock

. . . They kept at it, drawing things out . . . Now they were talking about the little furrow . . . They were conscientious souls . . . My hands were always dirty, that couldn't have helped much. And the nails . . . I could just as well have dropped off to sleep . . . Finally they were done . . . They didn't agree . . . My kid paid the old bag with her own money, two coins, I was looking . . . She had the cards laid out for her . . . And then we were through with the future . . . We went out under the curtains. The old bag climbed up on her counter and went back to her hangings.

From that moment on, my conquest, this Gwendoline, looked at me differently . . . I wasn't the same guy . . . I felt that she had presentiments . . . she thought me transfigured . . . She didn't pet me the same way anymore . . . My destiny must have been pretty sticky . . . I guess the cards showed the same as the furrows: pure grief . . .

I felt so sleepy I could have dropped on the spot, but it was too chilly. We had to keep tramping around on the dock . . . There really wasn't a soul, just a little dog that tagged around after us for a while. He trailed off toward the storehouses. We went into a shelter right by the water, we listened, we saw the tide lapping against the wall . . . chattering like tongues . . . . And then the sound of oars and the deep breathing of the guys . . .

My Greasy Joan dragged me away, I think she wanted me to go home with her . . . I wouldn't have minded sleeping on the sacks, there were big piles of them all the way up to the rafters . . . They cut the wind . . . She made motions to say she had a real room with a real bed . . . That didn't appeal to me . . . It meant intimacies . . . even then, in the depths of my weariness, she gave me the willies. I make a sign meaning no . . . I've got this address I want to get to . . . "Meanwell College" . . . if it comes to laying Gwendoline, I'd rather go back to school. Not that she was so ugly looking . . . she had charm in her way, even a kind of elegance . . . She had an ass on her and muscular thighs and cute little boobies . . . an ugly-looking puss, but it was dark . . . We could have done our business, we'd certainly have had a good time . . . But once we'd had our sleep out, then what?

. . . Anyway I was too tired . . . And besides, it was impossible . . . It stirred up my gall . . . it cramped my cock to think of it . . . of all the treachery of things . . . as soon as you let anybody wrap you up . . . The whole stinking rotten business . . . And of my mother . . . Ah, the poor woman! And of Gorloge and Madame Méhon and the quotations! And the kitchen faucet! And Lavelongue! And little André! The whole lousy mess! Yes, damn it all, I had as much as I could take . . . a big stinking steaming load of shit up to here . . . See what I mean? Nothing doing!

I'd gladly have knocked hell out of this fritter baby, so innocent, so kind . . . an extra-special thrashing till she couldn't see straight . . . if I'd thought I was stronger . . . to teach her what was what . . . But she'd have knocked me for a loop, that was sure. She could take care of herself, she was built like a wrestler, she would have turned me like a pancake if I'd started getting real mean! . . . That's all I had on my mind in the little side streets while my cutie was unbuttoning me . . . She had the grip of a working girl, rough as a grater, and not at all bashful. Everybody was screwing me. O well . . .

Finally I got my address out. We'd have to find the place sooner or later. She couldn't read at all, so we went looking for a *policemanne* . . . Two or three times we went wrong. It was always some funny-looking fountain at a street crossing in the middle of the fog . . . We had a hell of a time finding one . . . We looked from dock to dock . . . We went stumbling over barrels and gangplanks . . . It was fun in spite of being so exhausted . . . She held me up and my suitcase too . . . She really had a good disposition. She was losing her bun . . . I even pulled her hair. That made her laugh too. The stray dog started following us again . . . Finally through the cracks in a shelter we saw real light . . . The watchman was slumped over, he jumped when he saw us. He had on at least three overcoats one on top of the other. He cleared his throat a long time . . . He came out in the fog, he shook himself like a duck . . . He was very obliging. He was able to read my address. He showed us . . . way up there, he pointed his finger, way at the end of the night . . . where Meanwell College was, on the hilltop after a

string of lanterns that climbed up in a zigzag . . . He
went back into his shack. He squeezed in through the door
with all his layers.

Once we knew the way, we weren't in such a hurry . . .
There was still a climb, a big long slope . . . Our adventure wasn't over . . . We climbed very slowly . . .
She didn't want me to knock myself out . . . She was all
kindness. She didn't dare to molest me anymore . . . She
only kissed me a little when we stopped to rest. She made
signs under the lamp that I was just her style . . . that
she liked me fine . . . About halfway up the slope we
sat down on a rock; from there you could see clouds of
fog moving in the distance across the river . . . they
came swooping down, blotting out the little boats on the
smooth water . . . dousing their lights . . . then there
was moonlight, and then clouds took over again . . . The
kid made some more gestures . . . Wasn't I hungry? She
offered to get me something to eat, her heart really seemed
to be in the right place . . . Dazed as I was, I wondered
if I'd have the strength to topple her off the edge with a
good swift kick in the ass. Well, how about it?

Below us the cliff dropped sheer into the drink.

All of a sudden we hear voices, men, a whole gang, I
recognize them with their lanterns, it was the "minstrels,"
phony niggers with blackened faces . . . They were coming up from the harbor too . . . pulling their cart in the
fog. They're having a lot of trouble with it. It's heavy, all
that setup of theirs, they'd taken it all apart . . . Their
poles and instruments jiggle and clatter . . . They see us,
they talk to Greasy Joan . . . They take time out, they
settle down a while, they go into conference, they pile up
all their coins on the end of the bench . . . trying to count
them, but they can't make it . . . They're too tired . . .
One at a time they go wash their faces in the waterfall
nearby. They come back livid in the morning light . . .
you'd think they were dead already . . . They raise their
heads a moment, they sag, they sit down again in the
gravel . . . They crack some more jokes with my cutie . . .
Finally we all pick ourselves up, we leave together . . .
We push the wheels of their contraption, we tug and pull
to get them up the hill somehow. I still had quite a way
to go. They didn't want to leave us . . . Meanwell Col-

lege was over past the trees, then another turn, and then a slope and a garden . . .

By now things were blue. When we got to the gate, we were all pretty palsy-walsy. It was hard to find the right number. We scratched matches in two three different places . . . Finally we had it . . . The kid began to bawl. But we had to leave each other some time . . . I made gestures, signs . . . to tell her she shouldn't stay there, she should go on with the boys . . . I'd be seeing her again for sure . . . down below . . . in the port . . . one day . . . I made affectionate gestures . . . It was true, all in all I really wanted to. I gave her my blanket to make her believe me . . . I'd go and get it . . . She had trouble understanding . . . I didn't know what to do . . . She was kissing me like mad . . . Our pantomime sent the "minstrels" into stitches . . . They imitated our kisses . . .

In the narrow little street an icy wind was blowing . . . We were all so worn out . . . I could hardly stand up . . . But really our effusions were too funny . . . In the end we were all rocking with laughter . . . it was all so dumb . . . at that time of night . . . Finally she made up her mind . . . She didn't want to go on alone so she followed the minstrels . . . They all pushed off together behind the cart, the instruments, the bass drum . . . A nice litle stroll they were having . . . The kid waved some last good-byes from far off with her lantern . . . Finally they disappeared . . . in the trees, around the bend in the street.

Then I looked at the sign in front of me where I was supposed to go in . . . It was written plainly: "Meanwell College" and above that, in much redder letters: Director J. P. Merrywin. That was the place, I hadn't gone wrong. I lifted the little knocker: Tap! Tap! At first nothing happened . . . then I rang at the other door . . . still nobody answered . . . quite a while . . . Finally I heard somebody moving . . . I saw a light coming down the stairs . . . I could see through the curtains . . . It gave me a rotten feeling . . . For two cents I'd have cleared out . . . I'd have run after the kid . . . I'd have caught up with the other guys . . . I'd have never come back to the school . . . I was already turning on my heels . . .

Bing, I bump right into this guy . . . a little man, all
stooped over, in a dressing gown . . . He pulls himself
up. He looks me over . . . He jabbers explanations . . .
That must be the boss . . . He was all upset . . . He
had side-whiskers . . . they were red . . . with a few
white hairs. A little wig over his eyes. He repeated my
name. He'd come out through the garden . . . taken me
by surprise . . . That was a funny way to act . . . He
must have been afraid of thieves . . . He sheltered his
candle . . . He stood there in front of me, mumbling. It
wasn't a very warm place for an interview. He couldn't
find all the words he needed, the wind blew out his candle:

"Ferdinand . . . good . . . morning . . . I . . . am
. . . glad . . . to see you . . . but . . . you are . . .
very late . . . what happened?"

"I don't know," I said.

He didn't press the point . . . He went ahead. He took
tiny little steps . . . Finally he opened the door . . . He
jiggled with the lock. He was shaking so hard he couldn't
get the key out . . . Once we were in the entrance he
motioned me to wait . . . to sit on the chest . . . he was
going to fix things upstairs. Right in the middle of the stairs
he thought of something, he leaned down over the banister and pointed his finger at me:

"Tomorrow, Ferdinand! Tomorrow . . . I'll only talk
English to you. Eh what? . . ." It made him laugh in
advance . . .

"*Attendez-moi un moment!* Wait! Moment! There, you
see! You're catching on, Ferdinand . . . Already . . ."

He was clowning . . .

It took him forever up there, poking around in drawers,
closing doors, moving cupboards. I said to myself: "What
does he think he's doing? . . . I'm going to sleep just like
this . . ." I was still waiting.

At the end of the corridor I saw the gas jet flickering
. . . it was turned low . . .

Little by little my eyes got used to the light and I saw
the clock . . . a great big one . . . really magnificent
. . . the dial was all copper and a tiny little frigate was
dancing out the seconds . . . tic . . . toc . . . tic . . .

toc . . . She went sailing right along . . . In the end I I was so tired it made me fuzzy . . .

The old codger was still fussing around . . . fighting with bric-a-brac . . . running the water . . . talking with a woman . . . Finally he came down . . . He had gone to a lot of trouble . . . Completely washed, shaved, dressed fit to kill . . . and some style! . . . like a lawyer . . . a flowing black cape . . . hanging from his shoulders . . . accordion pleats . . . and on the top of his dome a pretty little skull-cap with a big tassel . . . I figured it was for my benefit. He wants to impress me . . . He makes a little sign . . . I get up . . . I start moving . . . To tell the truth, I could hardly stand up . . . He cast about for some more phrases . . . something appropriate, about my trip . . . If I'd had trouble finding the place . . . I didn't answer . . . I followed him . . . First through the drawing room . . . around a piano . . . then through the laundry room . . . the washroom . . . the kitchen . . . Finally he opens another door . . . And what do I see? . . . A bed! . . . I didn't waste any time . . . I didn't wait to be told . . . I jumped right on it . . . I spread myself flat . . . Right away the little crab gets all excited, he flies into a rage . . . He couldn't stand it. He hollers . . . he jumps up and down . . . he dances around the sack . . . He hadn't been expecting such a thing . . . He grabs me by the shoes . . . He tries to pull me off . . .

"*Chaussures! Chaussures!* Boots! Boots!" He was getting madder and madder. He was in a terrible state. My mud on his lovely bed . . . . on all those big flowers . . . That's what was upsetting him, sending him into an epileptic fit. "Go shit in your hat!" I was thinking. "Go split a gut, you little asshole . . ." He was desperate . . . He ran up and down the hall . . . looking for reinforcements . . . If they'd touched a finger to me, I'd have gone wild . . . I'd have got right off that bed and given that little fart some thrashing . . . On the spot . . . I was exactly in the mood . . . I was all set . . . He was skinny and puny . . . He was getting on my nerves with his damn nonsense . . . I'd have turned him inside out like a glove . . . I was fed up . . . He went right on yapping, but I had no trouble falling asleep.

For fresh air and the view, you couldn't have asked for anything better than Meanwell College. The location was marvelous . . . From the garden and even from the windows of the study you could look out over the whole countryside. When the weather cleared, you could see for miles, the river, the three towns, the port, the docks huddled together by the shore . . . The railroad lines . . . the ships disappearing . . . and coming back into view a little way out . . . behind the hills past the meadows . . . toward the sea, past Chatham . . . The effect was magnificent . . . Only it was awfully cold at the time I got there, the place was so unprotected on top of the cliff it was impossible to keep warm. The wind hammered against the house . . . The squalls and storms came bounding over the hill . . . The wind roared through the rooms, the doors rattled day and night. We were living in the middle of a tornado. When the tempest began to roar, the kids yelled like deaf people, they couldn't hear each other . . . Nothing could stand up against that wind! It was bend or break. The trees were stooped over, they never straightened up, the lawns were in tatters, whole patches were ripped up. You can imagine . . .

In a rough, ravaged climate like that you get a ravenous appetite . . . It turns out husky kids, real bruisers. When there's enough to eat. But at Meanwell College the grub wasn't so hot. It was worse than middling. Their prospectus was a big lie. There were fourteen of us at table, including me. Plus the boss and his wife . . . In my opinion that was at least eight too many, considering what there was to eat . . . Six of us could have handled it . . . On days when the wind was blowing strong . . . the eats were very meager.

I was the biggest and the hungriest of the crew. I was growing like mad . . . it was almost time for me to stop. In a month I doubled in bulk. The violence of the elements created a revolution in my lungs and in my stature. The way I helped myself, the way I scraped all the platters without being asked, I got to be a regular pest at the table . . . The kids eyed my plate, they gave me dirty looks, I was the enemy . . . naturally . . . I didn't give a damn, I didn't say a word to anybody . . . I was still so hungry I'd even have eaten noodles if anybody'd asked me to

. . . A school that gave you enough to eat would go bankrupt . . . They've got to watch their step . . . I made up for it on the porridge, there I was ruthless . . . I took advantage of my strength, and I was even worse with the marmalade . . . There was a little saucerful for four of us, I gobbled it up all by myself, straight out of the dish . . . I did away with it before anybody could see what was happening . . . The others could gripe all they pleased, I never answered . . . why should I have? . . . You could have all the tea you wanted, it warms you, it bloats you, it's perfumed water, not bad, but it makes you even hungrier. When the tempest went on for a long time, when the whole hilltop roared for days on end, I dug into the sugar bowl . . . with a tablespoon or even my bare hands. It was yellow and sticky, it gave me strength . . .

At meals Mr. Merrywin had the big platter right in front of him, he himself dished everything out . . . He tried to make me talk . . . No soap . . . Me, talk! The mere idea made me see red . . . I was a tough customer . . . Only his lovely wife had me kind of bewitched, she might have softened me . . . I sat next to her . . . She was really adorable. Absolutely. Her face, her smile, her arms, all her movements, everything. She was busy the whole time, trying to make little Jongkind eat, he was a freak, a retarded child. After every mouthful or pretty near she had to help him, clean him up and wipe away his slobber. It was rough work.

This idiot's parents were in India, they didn't even come to see him. A little screwball like that was a real nuisance, especially at mealtime, he'd swallow everything on the table, the spoons, the napkin rings, the pepper, the oil and vinegar bottles, even the knives . . . Swallowing things was his passion . . . He always had his mouth all dilated, distended, like a boa constrictor, he'd suck up all sorts of little objects, even off the floor, grunting and slobbering the whole time. Mrs. Merrywin always stopped him, took the things away, always patient and gentle. Never a harsh word . . .

Aside from his swallowing act, the kid wasn't so bad. He was actually rather good-natured. He wasn't bad looking either, only his eyes were weird. He bumped into everything without his glasses, he was disgustingly near-

sighted, he'd have collided with a mole, he needed thick
lenses, like bottle stoppers. They made his eyes pop out,
they were wider than the rest of his face. The least little
thing frightened him, Mrs. Merrywin always comforted
him with the same two words: *"No trouble, Jongkind!
No trouble . . ."*

He himself would repeat those words for days on end,
for no rhyme or reason like a parrot. After several months
at Chatham that was all I remembered: *"No trouble,
Jongkind."*

Two weeks, three weeks passed . . . They left me
alone. They didn't try to force me . . . they'd have liked
me to talk . . . for me to learn a little English. That was
only natural. My father asked in his letters if I was making
an effort . . . if I was applying myself to my studies . . .

I didn't let them rope me in . . . Talk wasn't for me
. . . I'd had enough . . . I only had to bring back my
memories . . . the hullabaloo at home . . . my mother's
blah-blah . . . all the applesauce people can serve you
up in words . . . Hell no! . . . Not for me. I had my
belly full . . . I'd had all the confessions, all the soft soap
I could take . . . No, thank you . . . I had whole carloads . . . If I even thought of trying, the whole mess
stuck in my throat . . . They weren't going to catch me
again. I'd had enough. I had a good excuse for keeping my
mouth shut, a golden opportunity, and I was determined to
take every advantage of it . . . to the bitter end . . . No
appeals to sentiment, no fiddle-faddle . . . They made me
want to throw up with all their talk . . . Maybe even
worse than noodles . . . And believe me it gave me the
creeps even to think of home . . .

Mr. and Mrs. Merrywin were at their wits' end, they
wondered what made me so silent, so sullen and obstinate
. . . It was mostly he that made overtures, the minute we
sat down to table, on any subject he could think of . . .
He really wanted me to learn . . . "Hello, Ferdinand!"
he'd sing out . . . I wasn't greatly tempted . . . "Hello,
hello," I'd answer, and that was all. It stopped right there.
We began to eat. From behind his glasses he gave me a
pained look. He had spells of melancholia, he must have
said to himself: "That boy won't be with us long . . .

He'll leave if he's unhappy." But he didn't dare to say any more . . . He'd blink his little cockhole eyes, his turned-up chin would twitch, and he'd raise his eyebrows, which shot off in different directions and weren't the same color either. He was the old-fashioned type, with side-whiskers and a little cosmetic moustache, very pointed at the ends . . . He looked rather jolly. He was always on the jump, playing games, and even racing around on a tricycle . . .

She, his wife, wasn't the same at all, she hadn't her equal for charm, I have to admit that she was a dream . . . she made a profound impression on me.

That refectory of theirs on the ground floor was a pretty miserable place. The walls were daubed a kind of snuff color all the way up to the ceiling. It looked out on a blind alley. The first time she came into the room with Jongkind . . . you can't imagine how beautiful she seemed to me . . . I had a feeling, something very unusual . . . I kept looking at her . . . I blinked both eyes . . . I felt dizzy . . . I buried my nose in my slobgullion . . . Nora was her name . . . Nora Merrywin . . .

At the beginning and end of the meals, we all went down on our knees while the old man said prayers . . . He commented at length on the Bible. The kids dug into their noses and wriggled in all directions . . .

Jongkind didn't want to wait, he wanted to eat the door-knob that was right in front of him, on a level with his mouth. The oldtimer really threw himself into his prayers, he liked to mumble . . . he'd bumble away for a good fifteen minutes, it rounded out the meal . . . In the end we'd get up, when he said *ever and ever.*

Only the bottom half of the walls was painted brown, the rest was whitewashed. There were engravings of Bible stories . . . There was Job with his staff, all in rags, crossing a desert . . . Then there was Noah's Ark, crushed under the rain that was bouncing on the waves, on the foaming fury . . . Just like in Rochester . . . Our roof was the same way. I can bet the storms we had were much more violent . . . Even the double windows couldn't stand up to it . . . Later it was calm . . . Then everything was enchanted . . . an enormous realm of mist like another world . . . You couldn't see two steps away in the garden . . . There was nothing left but one

big cloud, it crept softly into the rooms, it hid everything,
it seeped in everywhere, into the classroom, in between
the kids . . .

The sounds of the city, of the port, rose up like an echo
. . . especially from the river below . . . It sounded like
a tugboat coming straight into the garden . . . You could
even hear it panting behind the house . . . It came back
. . . And then it was gone again, down into the valley . . . All the railroad whistles coiled and twisted
through the mists in the sky . . . It was a kingdom of
phantoms . . . We even had to hurry back into the house
. . . We would have fallen off the cliff. . . .

While they were saying their prayers, I had dangerous
sensations . . . As we knelt, I almost touched Nora. I
breathed against her neck, into her hair. I had terrible
temptations . . . It was a desperate moment, I had to hold
myself back from doing something dumb . . . I wonder
what she would have said if I had dared . . . I played
with myself thinking of her, at night in the dormitory,
very late, long after all the others, and in the morning
I'd have a little more . . .

Her hands were marvels, tapering, pink and white,
tender, the same gentleness as her face, just to look at them
was like a glimpse of fairyland. What troubled me most,
what moved me deep inside was the special charm she
had, that lit up on her face when she was speaking . . .
her nose would tremble just a little, and her cheeks and
the curve of her lips . . . I was really damned . . . It
was sorcery . . . It intimidated me . . . I saw stars,
I couldn't move . . . At the least smile, waves of magic
ran through me . . . I was afraid to look at her. I stared
at my plate the whole time. Her hair too, when she passed
by the fireplace, was a pure play of light . . . Hell! She
was turning into a fairy. That was plain. The part I
mostly wanted to eat was the corner of her lip.

She was as kind to me as she was to the idiot, she
translated every word for me, everything that went on
at table, everything the little snotnoses said . . . She
explained everything, first in French, she repeated everything very slowly . . . She took on work for two . . .
Her old man went on twinkling behind his glasses . . . He

didn't chirp very much anymore, he just acquiesced . . .
"Yes, Ferdinand. Yes," he said approvingly . . . After
that he entertained himself, he'd pick his teeth very slowly
and then his ears, he'd play with his dental plate, unhook
it, and pop it back into place. He'd wait till the kids
were done, then he'd start up his prayers again.

Once we were back on our feet, Mrs. Merrywin,
before we went back to school, made another stab at
arousing my interest in things . . . "The table, *la table,*
now come along, Ferdinand . . ." I resisted all her
charms. I didn't answer one word. I let her go out ahead
of me . . . Her buttocks fascinated me too. She had
an admirable ass, not just a pretty face. Taut, compact,
not too big, not too little, all in one piece under her skirt,
a muscular banquet . . . A thing like that is divine, that's
the way I feel about it . . . The witch, I'd have eaten
every bit of her, gobbled her up, I swear. . . I kept my
temptations to myself. I distrusted the other kids in the
place like the plague. They were a bunch of little snotnoses,
always looking for a fight, always shooting the shit, crazy
and dumb as hell. I'd lost interest in that kind of foolishness . . . the way those kids made faces all the time,
they made me sick . . . I was too old, I hadn't the
patience. I couldn't stand school anymore . . . The stuff
they do, the truck they recite . . . it's unbearable . . .
when you think of what's waiting for you . . . the way
you'll be treated as soon as you're out . . . If I'd felt
like shooting my mouth off, I'd have mowed all those
phony little bastards down with three words and a
menacing gesture . . . Knocked them flat . . . Just to
see them bouncing around the cricket field made my blood
boil . . . At first they laid for me in corners, to break
me in, as they put it . . . They'd decided they were going
to make me talk, regardless . . . There were about a
dozen of them . . . They swallowed their cigarettes . . .
I pretended not to notice. I waited until I had them good
and close. Then I went all out, I poked them smack in
the eyes, I kicked them square in the shins, I sent them
sprawling . . . It was a massacre, a pudding! They went
over like tenpins . . . Days later they were still feeling
their bones . . . After that they behaved better . . .
They got to be soft-spoken, respectful . . . They came

back for another sniff . . . I laid out two or three of them . . . After that they knew what was what.

I was really the strongest and maybe the meanest . . . French or English, kids are all the same kind of vermin . . . You've got to step on them quick . . . There's no point in using kid gloves, you've got to teach them right away or you never will. Give them a good shellacking. Otherwise you'll be the one to get stepped on . . . You'll be all washed up. Miss your chance and all you'll get is one good bellyache. If I'd started talking to them, naturally I'd have told them what *business* is really like . . . the realities of life . . . apprenticeship . . . I'd soon have wised those little phonies up . . . Those kids didn't know which way is up . . . They didn't know a damn thing . . . All they knew about was football . . . that isn't enough . . . and looking at their cocks . . .

There wasn't too much school, only in the morning.

Mr. Merrywin was in charge of the schoolwork, religion, and the different kinds of sports . . . he managed all by himself, there weren't any other teachers.

At the crack of dawn he came around himself in slippers and dressing gown to wake us up. He was already smoking his pipe, a little clay one. He waved his long cane over the bed, bringing it down once in a while, but never hard. *"Hello, boys, hello, boys!"* he'd cry with his little old woman's voice. We followed him to the washroom . . . There was a row of faucets, we used them as little as possible. It was too cold to soap yourself. And it never stopped raining. From December on we had a regular deluge. You couldn't see the least bit of the town anymore or the port or the river in the distance . . . Nothing but fog the whole time, a big mess of cotton . . . The rains made holes in it, you could see lights, then they disappeared . . . You could hear all the foghorns, the boats calling, from daybreak on there was always a noise . . . the grinding of winches, the little train along the waterfront . . . puffing and squealing . . .

When he came in, Merrywin turned up the gas jet so we could find our socks. After the washroom we ran, still sopping wet, down to the basement for our measly feed. A bit of prayer and then breakfast. That was the only place where they burned a little coal, the greasy, slippery kind that erupts like a volcano, that explodes and smells like asphalt. It's a pleasant smell, but then it gives off a whiff of sulphur that stings pretty bad.

On the table there were sausages on toast, but Lord were they small! They were mighty good, a delicacy, but there was never enough. I could have bolted the whole lot. Through the smoke, the flames threw reflections on the wall, on Job and the Ark . . . fantastic visions.

Not speaking the English language, I had plenty of time to look around . . . The old man chewed slowly. Mrs. Merrywin came in last. She had dressed Jongkind, she settled him in his chair, she moved the cutlery out of his reach, especially the knives, it was really a wonder he hadn't stuck his eye out yet . . . and greedy as he was . . . that he hadn't swallowed a coffeepot and bust . . . I looked furtively at Nora, Mrs. Merrywin, I listened to her like a song . . . Her voice was like the rest of her, enchanting gentleness . . . What interested me in her English was the music, the way it danced in and out of the firelight. I was living in a daze myself, a little like Jongkind. I was soft in the head, I was letting myself be bewitched. I had nothing to do. The stinker, she must have known. Women are scum. She was as lowdown as the rest of them. "What's the matter with you, Buster?" I said to myself. "You swallowed a kite? You sick? You off your rocker? Flying away? Watch yourself, kid. Pinch yourself. Pull yourself together. Before it's too late." So naturally I tightened up . . . I curled up like a hedgehog. The danger was past. I kept my trap shut.

I had to watch myself, my imagination was running away with me, it was a dreamy kind of place, with its opaque storms and its clouds all over. I had to hole up and keep patching my armor. One question kept coming back to me, how had she come to marry that little worm? That little rat with the cane! It seemed impossible. That goblin! That monster! With that mug! Even on a pipe bowl it would scare people out of their wits, it wouldn't sell for a dime! Oh well, it's her business.

She was always keeping after me, trying to make me converse: *"Good morning, Ferdinand! Hello! Good morning!"* I was all hot and bothered. Her expression was so

adorable . . . Plenty of times I almost fell. But I'd pull
myself together quick . . . I reminded myself of all the
stuff I had on my mind . . . I saw Lavelongue's face,
and Gorloge, all mixed up . . . I had plenty to choose
from to make me puke . . . Madame Méhon . . .
Sakya-Muni . . . I only had to sniff, my nose was always
in the shit. I answered inside: "Go on talking, baby doll,
go right ahead . . . you won't get a rise out of me . . .
You can laugh your head off . . . smile like a dozen
frogs . . . You won't catch me . . . I'm hardened, take
it from me, I've had it up to here." I thought of my
father . . . his scenes, the bilge he was always dishing
out . . . all the shit that was waiting for me . . . the lousy
jobs . . . the crummy customers, all the beans, the
noodles, the deliveries . . . the bosses . . . all the thrashings I'd had . . . in the Passage . . . If I had any
desire to kid around, that knocked it right out of me . . .
I was convulsed with memories . . . I scraped my ass
with them . . . I was so mad I tore off whole patches
of skin . . . My bleeding ass! No, this skirt wasn't
going to take me. Maybe she was good, maybe she was
marvelous! Let her be a thousand times more radiant and
beautiful, you wouldn't catch me going soft on her . . .
She wouldn't wring a single sigh out of me . . . She
could cut her face in ribbons to please me, she could roll
them around her neck, she could cut three fingers off her
hand and stick them up my ass, she could buy herself a
pure-gold pussy! I still wouldn't talk to her! Never! . . . I
wouldn't even kiss her! All that was the bunk, more of the
same. And that was that. I preferred to stare at her old
man, to look him up and down . . . that kept me from
having dumb ideas . . . I drew comparisons . . . He
was part turnip . . . green diluted blood . . . part carrot too, on account of the squiggly hairs coming out of
his ears and at the bottom of his cheeks . . . How had
he ever got hold of this beauty? . . . It couldn't have
been money . . . Then it must have been a mistake . . .
Of course, you've got to remember, women are always in
a hurry . . . They'll grow in anything . . . any old
garbage will do . . . They're just like flowers . . . The
more beautiful they are, the worse the manure stinks . . .
The season is short. Bzing! And the way they lie all the

time . . . I'd seen some horrible examples. They never stop. It's their perfume. That's the long and the short of it.

I should have talked to her? Beans! She'd have taken me for a ride. That was sure as shit . . . I'd have understood even less . . . Buttoning up built my character at least.

In school Mr. Merrywin tried to persuade me, he went to a lot of trouble, he put all the kids to work making me talk. He wrote whole sentences on the blackboard in capital letters . . . easy to decipher . . . and the translation underneath . . . The kids repeated them all together, in chorus . . . in cadence . . . over and over. I opened my mouth wide . . . I pretended something was coming . . . I was waiting for it to come out . . . Nothing came out . . . Not a syllable . . . I shut my mouth again . . . The try was over . . . They'd leave me alone for another twenty-four hours . . . *"Hello, Hello! Ferdinand!"* the old ape would sing out, crestfallen, at the end of his wits . . . When he did that, he really gave me a pain . . . I'd have made him swallow his big stick . . . I'd have put him on a spit . . . I'd have hung him up on the window by the ass . . . Ah! He caught on finally . . . He stopped pushing me . . . He suspected the kind of instincts I had. I frowned . . . I grunted when my name was called . . . I kept my overcoat on even in school, I slept in it . . .

I meant a lot to Merrywin, he didn't want to lose me, his school wasn't overcrowded, he didn't want me to go home before my six months were up. He was worried about my impulses. He kept on the defensive . . .

In the dormitory we kids were left to ourselves . . . once the prayers were over . . . We said them in our nightgowns, kneeling on the floor at the foot of the bed . . . Merrywin delivered a kind of sermon, we formed a circle around him . . . and then he went off to his room . . . We didn't see him anymore. After hurrying through our responses, we hit the sack quick, impatient to start playing with ourselves. It warms you up . . . Nora shut the idiot up in a special bed with a grating over it. He was always trying to get out . . . he walked in his sleep so bad that sometimes he upset the bed . . .

I'd made friends with a crazy little kid that jerked me off almost every night, he suggested a lot of other things, he had ideas, I had plenty of juice, more than the others . . . He was greedy, he made all the kids laugh with his clowning . . . He sucked two of the other kids . . . He pretended to be a dog . . . Woof! Woof! he'd bark . . . he'd crawl around like a puppy, he came when we whistled, he liked being ordered around . . . On the nights when the storm was really acting up, when the wind was howling in the alley under our windows, we made bets whether the wind would put out the lamp . . . the one that creaked so bad, that was hanging above the gate . . . I used to hold the bets, the ginger, the chocolate, the pictures, the cigarette butts . . . even a few lumps of sugar . . . and three matches. They trusted me . . . They put it all on my bed . . . The woof-woof dog often won . . . He had an instinct about stormy weather . . . On Christmas Eve there was such a cyclone that the lamp in the alley smashed to bits. I can still remember . . . Kid Woof-Woof and I ate up all the bets.

It was the style and tradition that in the afternoon everybody put on sport clothes, a green-and-yellow-striped uniform and a cap to match, all decorated with the college seals and blazons . . . I wasn't very eager to dress up like a jester and one of those outfits, I felt sure, must be mighty expensive . . . Especially the cleated shoes . . . I wasn't in the mood for toys . . . I didn't see any games in my future . . . It was just some more damn foolishness, made to order for little punks.

Right after lunch old man Merrywin himself took off his half-soutane, put on his Pied Piper coat and bzing! . . . out he went. All of a sudden he was full of beans, you wouldn't have known him . . . He'd go romping up and down the field like a pony . . . Under the squalls and showers he was especially happy . . . His little harlequin suit had a magical effect on him. He was comical, as jumpy as quicksilver.

Englishmen, you've got to admit, are a funny sight . . . A cross between a pastor and a little boy . . . Everything about them is ambiguous. Mostly they bugger each other . . . He was awfully keen on having them buy me a complete set of livery, so I could be rigged out like a champion from Meanwell College. So I wouldn't stick out like a sore thumb when we went for a walk, or on the football field . . . He even showed me a letter he'd written my father on the subject . . . Maybe there was something in it for him. Maybe he'd get a rake-off. There was something suspicious about the way he kept insisting . . . I didn't bat an eyelash when I saw the letter, but I had a little laugh to myself . . . "Go ahead and send it, you old fool, you don't know my parents. They don't give a good godam about sports." Obviously he had no idea . . . Obviously they'd tell him what for . . . They'd stick at the monkeysuit . . . any bets? There'd be hell to pay . . .

Well anyway, after lunch, rain or shine or earthquake, we all had to go out . . . Two by two we had to climb another hill behind ours, absolutely waterlogged, a chaos of bogs and torrents . . . I brought up the rear with Mrs. Merrywin and the idiot in between us . . . We brought his pail and shovel, so he could make mud pies, big mushy ones, that kept him quiet for a while . . . Umbrellas and raincoats were no use at all . . . nothing could resist the tornadoes . . . If it hadn't been for the slush that was thicker than lead, we'd have flown away with the birds . . .

I had the best position in the football game, I kept goal . . . that gave me a chance to meditate . . . I didn't like to be disturbed, I let almost everything through . . . When the whistle blew, the brats flung themselves into the battle, they plowed through the muck till their ankles cracked, they charged at the ball, full steam into the clay, they plastered themselves with it, their eyes were full of it, their whole heads were covered . . . When the game was over, our little angels were nothing but molded garbage, staggering hunks of clay . . . with big wads of pigeon shit sticking to them. The muddier they were, the shittier, the more hermetically sealed, the happier they felt . . . They were wild with joy under their crusts of ice, welded into their clay helmets.

Our only trouble was lack of competition . . . Rival teams were rare, especially nearby. Actually the only ones that played us regularly, every Thursday, were the kids

from Pitwitt Academy, on the other side of the bridge at
Stroud, a gang of miserable pimplefaces, foundlings, a
charitable institution . . . They were mighty skinny, even
lighter than our gang . . . Actually they didn't weigh
anything. At the first violent charge downwind, they flew
away just like the ball . . . The main thing was to hold
them, to flatten then down . . . We used to beat them
12 to 4. Regularly. It was the custom . . . If there
were any complaints, if we heard the slightest murmur,
we didn't hesitate a second, we beat the shit out of them,
we massacred them . . . That was the custom too. If
they kicked so much as a single goal more than usual,
our boys got really vicious . . . They said they'd been
double-crossed . . . they began looking for the guilty
parties . . . murder was in the air . . . When we got
home in the evening, they went over the whole business
again . . . after prayers, when the old man had closed
the door . . . Hell broke loose for five minutes . . .
Jongkind was to blame . . . The fool things he did, he
was always responsible for the penalties we got . . . He
got his punishment . . . It was epic . . . They lifted up
the grating and spilled him out of his crib . . . First they
spread him out on the floor like a crab, ten of them
all together gave him a mean whipping with belts . . .
even with the buckles . . . When he yelled too loud,
they'd pin him under a mattress and everybody stamped
on him . . . Then they went after his pecker . . . to
teach him how to behave . . . till there wasn't any
more . . . not a single drop.

Next day he couldn't stand up . . . Mrs. Merrywin
was puzzled, she couldn't make the kid out . . . He
didn't say *"No trouble"* anymore . . . He crumpled up at
the table and in class . . . for three days he was a wreck
. . . But he was incorrigible, you'd have had to tie him
to make him keep still . . . You had to keep him away
from the goal . . . The minute he saw the ball go in,
he went off his rocker, he dashed in like a madman, jumped
on the ball, wrenched it away from the goalkeeper . . .
Before we could stop him, he'd run away with it . . . At
times like that he was really out of his mind . . . He ran
faster than anybody else . . . "Hurray, hurray, hurray!"
he'd keep shouting all the way down the hill. It wasn't

easy to catch him. He'd run all the way to town. Often
we'd catch him in a shop . . . kicking the ball into
shop windows, smashing signs . . . He was a demon
athlete. He had funny ideas, you never knew what he
was going to do next.

· For three months I didn't say boo; I didn't say hip or
hep or oof . . . I didn't say yes . . . I didn't say no . . .
I didn't say anything at all . . . it took some heroism
. . . I didn't speak to a living soul . . . That suited
me fine . . .

In the dormitory everything went on as usual . . . the
jerking and sucking . . . I wondered about Nora, but I
didn't really know a thing . . .

Around January and February it was terribly cold and
the fog was so thick we could hardly find our way home
from the playing field . . . We groped our way . . .

The old man let me alone in school and on the hill,
he'd stopped trying to argue with me. He caught on to my
character . . . He thought I was thinking things over
. . . that I'd come around after a while, if handled
gently . . . That's not what interested me. What gave me
the creeps was the thought of going back to the Passage.
It gave me the shivers three months in advance. It drove
me crazy just to think about it . . . Christ! Having to
start talking again! . . .

On the physical side I had nothing to complain about,
I was doing all right. I was feeling a good deal stronger
. . . The rough climate, the glacial weather was just what
I needed . . . It built me up more and more, if the eats
had been better I'd have turned into a regular strong
man . . . I'd have laid them all flat . . .

Another couple of weeks went by . . . That made four
months of silence. Then all of a sudden Merrywin got
kind of scared . . . One afternoon when we came in from
sports, I saw him grabbing a sheet of paper. He begins
to write my father, hysterically . . . a lot of bilge . . .
It was a dumb thing to do . . . By return mail I got three
big long letters that I can safely describe as vile . . .
stupid, bristling with threats, bloodcurdling oaths, insults
in Greek and Latin, warnings, prospective punishments,
selected anathemas, infinite grief . . . My conduct was

diabolical! Apocalyptic! . . . That got me down again
. . . He writes me an ultimatum to plunge into the study
of the English language, immediately, in the name of his
terrible principles, of their extreme privations . . . of
their twenty million sacrifices, of the horrible sufferings
they had endured, all for my sake. Merrywin, the stupid
bastard, stuttered and stammered . . . he was all upset,
flummoxed at having brought on such a deluge . . . A lot
of good it had done him! Now the dikes were broken . . .
it was every man for himself . . . I can't begin to say how
rotten sick it made me to see all my old man's damn
foolishness right there on the table, spread out in black
on white . . . It was even crummier in writing.

What an asshole he turned out to be . . . old Swallow-
tail Merrywin! Worse than all the brats lumped together
. . . And ten times stupider and stubborner . . . I was
sure he'd be my downfall with those glass eyes of his.

If he'd kept quiet and minded his business as agreed, I
was good for another six months . . . Now that he'd
put his foot in it, it was only a question of weeks . . . I
locked myself up in my silence . . . I was very angry
with him . . . If I picked up and left, he'd asked for
it . . . It would be a disaster for the school. He'd brought
it on himself. Meanwell College wasn't doing very well
to begin with . . . Without me on the football team,
they were all washed up, the team would never get through
the season.

After Christmas vacation four kids left—that is, they
didn't come back . . . The school would have one hell of
a football team even if they let Jongkind play . . . It
would be nonexistent . . . With only eight snotnoses left
it was no use even lining up . . . They'd wipe the floor
with us. Pitwitt would score whenever they felt like it . . .
even if their kids had been lighter than feathers, even if
they'd been twice as undernourished . . . Our boys would
cut and run . . . They wouldn't wait for the massacre
. . . Meanwell was washed up . . . No more football
meant bankruptcy . . . The old man was scared shitless
. . . He made a last despairing try . . . He questioned
me in French . . . Did I have any complaints, was anything wrong? . . . Did the kids bully me? . . . I'd have

liked to see them try! Did my feet get too wet? . . .
Was there something special I'd like to eat? There was
no sense in talking, I was ashamed to sulk and act like
an ass in front of Nora . . . but self-respect wasn't the
half of it . . . Once you've made up your mind, you got
to go through with it . . . The more pupils they lost,
the more indispensable I was getting . . . They were
always making up to me . . . smiling . . . doing me
favors . . . The kids knocked themselves out . . . Little
Jack, the one that put on the puppy act at night, brought
me candy . . . he even gave me some of his watercress
. . . the little tiny leaves . . . stiff as whiskers . . .
that taste like mustard . . . and grow in special moldy
boxes on the windowsill . . .

The old man had told them all to be nice . . . and try
and keep me until Easter . . . for the sake of our sports,
the honor of the school depended on it . . . If I left any
sooner, the team would be shot . . . they wouldn't be
able to play Pitwitt anymore . . .

To make things even nicer for me they let me off
classes. In class I distracted everybody's attention . . . I
was always banging my desk . . . or I'd go and look out
the window . . . at the fog and the movement in the port
. . . I had projects of my own, I did things with chestnuts and walnuts, I set up naval battles . . . I made big
sailboats with matches . . . I prevented the others from
learning anything . . .

The idiot behaved pretty well, except he kept sticking
his penholder up his nose . . . Sometimes he put two
or even four of them in one nostril . . . He pushed them
way up and yelled . . . He drank the ink out of the
inkwells . . . It was better he should take walks . . .
The more he grew the harder it got to handle him . . .
They took us out together . . . I missed the classroom
a little . . . I didn't learn anything but I felt good, I
didn't mind the sound of English . . . It's pleasant,
elegant, supple . . . It's a kind of music, it comes from
another planet . . . I had no talent for learning . . . It
wasn't hard for me to resist . . . Papa always said I was
stupid and opaque . . . There was nothing to be surprised about . . . My isolation suited me better and
better . . . Obstinacy is my strong point . . . They had

to give in, to stop bothering me . . . They flattered my
instincts, my taste for bumming . . . They walked me all
over the region, up hill and down village, with the idiot,
his wheelbarrow, and all his toys . . .

As soon as school started, we lit out for the country,
Jongkind, Mrs. Merrywin, and I . . . We often came
back by way of Chatham, depending on the errands we
had to do. We held the idiot by a rope fastened to his belt,
so he wouldn't make off through the streets . . . He was
always up to something . . . We'd mosey down to town,
we'd saunter along the shop fronts, we'd have to watch out
for the carriages, he was scared of horses, he'd practically
jump under the wheels . . .

While doing the shopping, Mrs. Merrywin tried to teach
me the signs on the shops . . . That way I'd learn without
even trying, without the slightest effort . . . I let her
talk . . . I just looked at her face, at the particular spot
that fascinated me, her smile . . . that saucy little jigger
. . . I'd have liked to kiss her right there . . . It was
itching me something terrible . . . I went around behind
her . . . I hypnotized myself on her waist, her movements,
her undulations . . . On market day we took the big
basket . . . it was like a cradle . . . Jongkind and I
each held a handle. We brought back all the food for the
whole week . . . Our shopping took all morning.

I saw Gwendoline, my Greasy Joan, in the distance.
She was still cooking her fritters, she was wearing a different hat, it was even bigger, with more flowers . . . I
refused to go in that direction . . . I'd never have extricated myself from all the explanations and gush. When
we stayed home because Jongkind had a cold, Nora lay
on the couch in the drawing room and began to read, there
were books all over the place . . . Our blessed angel
was a sensitive soul, poetic, imaginative . . . She didn't
soil her hands, she never touched a finger to the food
or the beds or the floors. There were two maids when I
first came: Flossie and Gertrude. They seemed to be
pretty hefty . . . How did they manage that? They must
have kept all the grub for themselves, or maybe it was
some disease . . . They were neither of them any spring
chickens . . . You could hear them griping the whole
time, they were always sniffing on the stairs. They'd shake

their brooms at each other . . . But they didn't knock themselves out . . . It was filthy in the corners . . .

Flossie smoked on the sly, I caught her one day in the garden . . . No washing was done in the house, we took it all to town to a special laundry, at the end of the world, way past the barracks. On those days Jongkind and I didn't rest a minute, we went up and down the hill any number of times with enormous bundles . . . We'd have contests to see who could carry more and faster . . . That was a sport I understood . . . it reminded me of the days on the Boulevards . . . Our walks got to be wild adventures when the rain came down so heavy and wet . . . when the sky crashed against the roofs and burst into torrents and waterfalls. The three of us clung together to resist the tempest . . . The storm was so violent that Nora . . . her curves, her buttocks, her thighs . . . looked like solid water, everything was stuck together . . . We weren't making any headway . . . We couldn't take the stairs that went up our cliff . . . We had to go around by the park . . . to make a detour past the church. We stopped outside the chapel, under the portico . . . waiting for the storm to pass.

The rain drove the idiot crazy with excitement . . . He'd run out of his shelter . . . He tilted his head back and took the rain full in the face . . . With his mouth wide open . . . He gulped down the rivers, he was having a hell of a good time . . . He bobbed up and down, he flew into a frenzy . . . He danced a jig in the puddles, he jumped like a woodsprite . . . He wanted us to dance too . . . It was one of his fits . . . I was beginning to understand him, it was hard to calm him down . . . You had to pull his rope and hitch him to the foot of a bench.

I knew my parents. This business with the striped suit wasn't going to suit them one bit, I knew it all in advance . . . They answered after some delay, they still hadn't got over it, they yelled like stuck pigs, they thought I was trying to put one over on them, that the whole thing was a subterfuge to cover up my wild extravagance . . . They took advantage of the occasion to remark that if I wasted my time kicking a ball around, no wonder I wasn't learning two cents' worth of grammar . . . This was their

final notice . . . my last chance . . . I needn't worry
too much about the accent . . . any old accent would do
. . . as long as I could make myself understood . . . I
read the letter over again with Nora and her old man . . .
it lay open on the table . . . There were some passages
they didn't dig. The whole thing struck them as very
strange and mysterious . . . I didn't do any explaining
. . . I'd been there for four months, I wasn't going to let
myself in for a lot of applesauce on account of a jacket
. . . It upset them though. Even Nora seemed unhappy
. . . that I didn't want to wear a sport uniform with the
monkey jacket and the rainbow cap . . . Probably for
roaming around town, it would be good publicity for
Meanwell, especially me, because I was the biggest and
gawkiest . . . the way I looked on the football field was
a disgrace to the school . . . Finally they carried on so
much that I softened a little . . . I accepted a compromise . . . Nora pieced together a rig out of two of
her old man's castoffs . . . and I said I'd try it . . . Some
combination . . . it made me look real cute . . . twice
as grotesque . . . I had no shape or middle . . . But
I didn't have to listen to their lamentations anymore . . .
At the same time I inherited a cap, two tones, with a
crest, a tiny little thing the size of half an orange . . . It
looked weird on my enormous bean . . . But they thought
all that stuff helped the prestige of their establishment . . .
the honor of the school was saved . . . Now they made
a point of taking me out . . . they didn't have to think
of excuses anymore . . .

As long as we could roam around and no one tried to
make me open my heart . . . it was OK with me . . . I
couldn't hope for anything better . . . I'd even have worn a
topper if they'd insisted . . . if it gave them pleasure . . .
They wore them on Sunday when they went to sing hymns
at their Protestant mass . . . That temple of theirs was
like a drillground: Stand up! Sit down! . . . Nobody
asked me how I felt about it . . . they just took me
along . . . they were afraid I'd be unhappy all alone in
the house . . . In church, too . . . between the pews
. . . we had to keep an eye on Jongkind, it was pretty
rough. He kept fairly quiet between the two of us, Nora
and me.

In church Nora seemed even more beautiful than outside, that's what I thought at least. With the sound of the organ and the half-tints of the windows, her profile was dazzling . . . I can still see her . . . It was years ago, but I can bring back her image whenever I please. At the shoulders her silk blouse forms lines, curves, miracles of flesh, agonizing visions, soft and sweet and crushing . . . Yes, I could have fainted away with delight while our kids were bawling the Psalms of Saul . . .

Sunday afternoon there'd be another hymn-singing session at home, I'd be kneeling beside her . . . The old geezer read something interminable, I had to hold my cock down with both hands, way at the bottom of my pockets. In the evening, after all the meditations, I was bursting with desire . . . The kid that came around to lap me up had his money's worth on Sunday night, he had his fill . . . But I wasn't satisfied, it was her I wanted, every last bit of her . . . Beauty comes back at you in the night . . . it attacks you, it carries you away . . . it's unbearable . . . I was soft in the head, from jerking off on visions . . . The less we had for meals, the more I masturbated . . . It was so cold in the house we put all our clothes back on as soon as the old geezer had cleared out . . .

The lamp under our window, the one we made bets about, creaked the whole time . . . To save a little warmth we went to bed two by two . . . We did each other up brown . . . I was ruthless, I couldn't stop, my imagination kept winding me up . . . I devoured Nora in all her beauty, every nook and cranny . . . I ripped up the bolster . . . I'd have ripped out her quiff if I'd really bit into her, her entrails, the juice of her marrow, I'd have drunk it all . . . I'd have sucked up every bit of her . . . left nothing . . . I'd have taken all her blood, every drop . . . Still it suited me better to ravage the bed, to chew up the sheets . . . than to let Nora or any other skirt take me for a ride. I'd caught on, believe me, I knew the score with women. Ass is a rat race, a suckers' caravan! An abyss, a bottomless pit, and that's that . . . My way was to strangle my dick . . . I was oozing like a snail . . . but I didn't let it come out . . . Not me . . . Cock that wets will suck eggs . . .

To hell with all that stinking mush! . . . Yak! yak! I love
you. I adore you! Sure, sure! Let her shit in your face!
Why worry, it's a party. Bottoms up! It's so lovely! It's
so innocent! . . . I'd wised up when I was a kid! Sentiment, hell! Balls! . . . Go jump in the lake . . . Go fly
a kite! . . . I clutched my oil can. My fly was all twisted!
Ding dong dell! You won't catch me dying like a sucker
. . . with a poem on my lips! Ugh!

Aside from the business with the prayers, I had other
tortures to put up with . . . The crafty demon of lechery
walked every path, he was hiding behind every bush . . .
I walked enormous distances with the idiot and my lovely
and got to know every inch of the country around Rochester in every kind of weather . . .

We explored every valley, every path and bypath. I
looked at the sky a good deal to distract my attention. It
changed color with the tides . . . During calm spells pink
clouds came up, on the land side and on the horizon . . .
and then the fields turned blue . . .

The way the town was laid out, the roofs sloped down
toward the river, it looked like an avalanche . . . an
enormous herd of cattle, all black and pressed together in
the mists that blew down from the open country . . . all
steaming in the yellow and violet fog. . . .

She was always making detours and arranging for long
rests at propitious moments. It didn't get her anywhere,
it didn't make me open my heart . . . Even when we
spent hours coming home through little narrow streets . . .
Even one evening when it was already dark on the bridge
that goes to Stroud . . . We looked down at the river . . .
A long time, the eddies swirling around the arches . . .
we heard all the bells . . . from the villages . . . far far
away in the distance . . . Then she took my hand and
kissed it . . . just like that . . . I was all stirred up,
I didn't react . . . I didn't move . . . No one could
see us . . . I didn't say a word, I didn't bat an eyelash
. . . She never suspected . . . It wasn't easy to resist
. . . The harder it was for me, the stronger I became . . .
She wasn't going to soften me, the bloodsucker, even if
she were a hundred times as pretty. Anyway, she was
going to bed with that little ape! When you're young, it
makes you puke to see the old fossils they shack up with

. . . If I'd said anything, I'd have tried to find out why it was him . . . why him when he was so ugly? It was incongruous . . . Maybe I was slightly jealous. I guess I was. But it's true that he was horrible to look at and listen to . . . with his little short arms . . . flapping like stumps . . . all the time, for no reason . . . He waved them around so much he seemed to have ten of them . . . It made you scratch just to look at him . . . He was always snapping his fingers, clapping his hands, twirling his cane, crossing his arms . . . but just for a second . . . Bzing! He was off again . . . like a jumping jack . . . what a guy! . . . twitching and jerking . . . like a loony chicken . . .

She, on the contrary, emanated grace, every movement was lovely . . . She was a mirage of charm . . . When she left the room, you felt a void in your soul, your heart slipped down to the basement in sadness . . . She had every reason to be downcast, she might have shown signs of worry. During the first months I always saw her happy, patient, untiring with the snotnoses and the idiot . . . They weren't always a pleasure to handle . . . Her life was no joke . . . With her beauty, she should have been able to marry a bag of money . . . She must have been bewitched . . . or taken some kind of a vow. And he certainly wasn't rich. It stuck in my craw, in the end I couldn't think of anything else . . .

For Nora the idiot was an awful nuisance, she had every reason to be exhausted at the end of the afternoon . . . Just wiping his nose, taking him to pee, keeping him from getting run over, from swallowing everything in sight . . . it was really a rotten chore . . .

She was never in much of a hurry. As soon as the weather picked up a little, we stayed out even later, we dawdled around the village and by the riverbank . . . Jongkind didn't drool as much when we were out walking as at home, only he swiped things, matches for instance . . . The minute you left him alone for a second, he set fire to the curtains . . . Not to be bad . . . he'd come and tell us right away . . . He'd want us to see how pretty the little flames were . . .

The shopkeepers in town saw us passing so often they all got to know us . . . They were *"grocers"* . . . that's

what they call them . . . something like *épiciers* . . .
That's one word I actually learned . . . In their windows
they piled up regular mountains of apples and beets, and
whole valleys of spinach on their enormous counters . . .
The stuff went all the way up to the ceiling . . . the hills
ran from one shop to the next . . . cauliflower, margarine,
artichokes . . . It made Jongkind happy to see those
things. He'd jump up on a pumpkin, he'd bite into it like
a horse . . .

The shopkeepers thought I was crazy too . . . They
asked her how I was getting along . . . the minute I
turned my back, they made motions to Nora . . . with
their fingers, they'd tap their heads . . . *"Better? Better?"*
they whispered. *"No, no!"* she answered sadly . . . I
wasn't any *"better,"* dammit. I'd never be *"better"* . . .
It gave me the creeps the way they carried on . . . So
worried . . . so sympathetic . . .

When we went shopping, there was one little thing
I'd always noticed . . . it puzzled me quite a lot . . .
Those bottles of whiskey . . . In the course of a week
we always brought back one and often two . . . And
sometimes brandy too . . . And I never saw the stuff on
the table . . . or in the parlor . . . or in the glasses
. . . not a single drop . . . We always drank water,
absolutely straight . . . So where did the booze go?
Was there a tippler in the house? I had strong suspicions
. . . I kept saying to myself . . . Somebody's lapping
it up . . . There's one spoiled brat around here that
doesn't feel the cold . . . The way he's pouring it down,
he doesn't have to worry about rheumatism . . . that's
a cinch.

The weather began to improve, the winter was over
. . . It had passed in walks, games, cross-country races,
storms, and masturbation . . .

To get a little more to eat, I did a little sleight-of-hand
in the shops . . . They thought I was so simple they
never suspected my tricks . . . I put on the innocent
mischief act, I disappeared . . . I played peekaboo with
Jongkind behind the posts and counters. I snitched a
little sausage, an egg here and there, a few crackers, a

banana or two . . . just a few odds and ends . . . Nobody ever bothered me . . .

In March we had another rainy spell, the sky was heavy,
crushing, it gets on your nerves in the end after all those
months . . . It weighs on everything, on the houses, the
trees, it falls right down to the ground. You walk on it,
you're sopping wet, you walk in the clouds, in mists that
melt into slush, in the soup, on broken bottles . . . It's
miserable!

The farthest we went on our walks was past Stroud,
on paths, through woods and over hills, to an enormous
estate where they raise pheasants. They weren't wild at
all, they roamed around by the dozens. They pecked like
chickens on a big lawn with some kind of monument in
the middle, an enormous black block of coal, standing
upright, tremendous, almost as big as a house. It dominated
the landscape . . . We never went any farther . . . After
that there wasn't any path . . .

One place I was sorry I couldn't go in the evening
was the waterfront at the bottom of the town, especially
on Saturday . . . Nora would have been delighted to
please me by going there more often . . . But it was
dangerous on account of Jongkind, he tripped over the
ropes, half a dozen times he almost drowned himself . . .
On the whole it was better for us to stick to the heights,
and best of all, to the open country, where you see the
dangers in the distance, big dogs, bicycles, and so on . . .

One afternoon, just by chance, as we were looking for
something new, we climbed a different hill, the one that
went up toward Bastion 15 . . . on the other side of
the cemetery . . . where Scotsmen, the 18th regiment,
drilled every Thursday . . . we watched them drill, and
they weren't fooling . . . They really gave themselves a
workout, marching up and down behind their bagpipes
and trumpets. They churned up the ground, they sank
in deeper and deeper. They went right on parading,
harder than ever . . . They were up to their shoulders . . .

Our walk wasn't over, we went on through the valley.
Right in the middle of the fields we saw something being
built . . . Lots of workmen . . . They were putting up
a big house . . . We looked through the fence . . .
there was an enormous sign . . . it was easy to decipher

. . . They were building another school . . . A magnificent location between the fort and the villas . . . And
a clearing for sports, at least four times as big as ours . . .
The track had already been laid out and covered with
cinders . . . the little flags were in place at all four
corners . . . the goals were marked . . . Everything was
just about ready . . . The builders didn't seem to be
laying down on the job, they were almost finished . . .
Three stories were done already . . . The place seemed to
be swarming with workmen . . . The name was written
in red letters: "The Hopeful Academy"—for boys of all
ages. It was quite a shock.

Nora Merrywin was flabbergasted . . . She stood there
gaping like a statue . . . Finally we left on the double.
She was in a big hurry to report the news to the little
stinker . . . I didn't give a damn about their business,
but I realized that this was a real tragedy, a catastrophe
. . . We didn't see either of them all day . . . It was I
that fed Jongkind, at the table after the other kids . . .

Next day Nora was still white as a sheet, she was all
upset. She, who was usually so charming, so playful, so
mild-mannered, was making movements almost like him,
snapping her fingers all the time. It looked like she hadn't
slept, she couldn't sit still, she stood up, went upstairs,
came down again to talk to him . . . And then she'd
leave again . . .

The old geezer sat motionless, he'd even stopped
blinking, he was in a daze. He stared into space. He didn't
eat, he only drank his coffee . . . He kept pouring himself whole cups . . . Between gulps he'd smack his right
palm with his left fist, with all his might . . . Smack!
Smack! And that was all . . .

Two days later he went up with us as far as the Scotsmen . . . He wanted to see for himself . . . They were
making great strides in fixing up the "Hopeful." They'd
done the track over and mowed the cricket field . . .
Besides, they had two tennis courts and even a miniature
golf course . . . They were sure to open by Easter . . .

The overgrown kid went jumping up and down by the
fence . . . He wanted to look over . . . He was a runt,
he couldn't see much . . . He looked through the
cracks . . . We found a ladder . . . He motioned us to

keep on going, he'd catch up with us on our grounds . . .
He did actually come back . . . He wasn't so frisky anymore. He sat down beside his wife, this thing had knocked
him cold . . . He'd had an eyeful of the wonders of
Hopeful College.

I could see what this competition meant. Our kids were
taking it on the lam already . . . They thought Meanwell
stank . . . And now? . . . What was to prevent them
from leaving? . . . It was a hopeless catastrophe . . . I
couldn't catch what the old folks were saying, but the tone
was mighty gloomy . . . The three of us went back and
looked at the scaffolding . . . They were building
walls for kicking practice. The place was an orgy
of luxury . . . While gazing at all the splendor, the old
man stuck his fingers up his nose, three at a time in his
confusion, trying to think . . . At the table he was in a
trance. I guess he couldn't see much future ahead . . .
He let the gravy get cold. He chewed so hard on his false
teeth that they popped out . . . He put them on the
table, right beside his plate . . . He didn't know what
was going on . . . He kept mumbling snatches of prayers
. . . and thoughts . . . Then he says Amen! Amen!
Suddenly he gets up . . . He rushes to the door. He takes
the stairs four at a time . . . The kids were in stitches
. . . His teeth were still on the table. Nora didn't know
which way to look . . . Jongkind came right over, he
bent down, he was foaming at the mouth, he sucked up
the false teeth . . . They'd never laughed so hard. We
made him spit them out again.

Discipline was shot. The kids did what they felt like
. . . The old man was afraid to say anything . . . Same
with Nora, in the house or outside . . . To play all
those strenuous games there were only ten of us left . . .
to make up a team on Thursday we'd pick up brats on
the road, anybody we ran into, little hoodlums we didn't
even know . . . We had to hold out till Easter . . .

The days got a little longer . . . To keep my parents
from getting impatient I wrote postcards, I made up fairy
tales, I said I was beginning to talk . . . They all congratulated me . . . It was almost spring . . . Jongkind
caught cold, he coughed for two weeks . . . We were

afraid to take him so far after that. We spent whole
afternoons outside the fortified castle, an old ruin full of
echoes, caves, and dungeons . . . At the slightest shower
we took refuge under the vaulting with the pigeons. That
was their home, there were hundreds of them, very friendly
and tame . . . they'd come and coo right in our hands,
they're comical characters, they strut, they make eyes at
you, they recognize you right away . . . What Jongkind
liked best was the sheep . . . he played with them for
all he was worth. He'd run after the young ones that
stumble and topple over. He'd roll with them in the wet
grass, he'd bleat when they bleated . . . He was in
ecstasy . . . he turned into a regular animal . . . He
went home wet to the skin . . . and coughed for another
week . . .

There was lots of clear weather now . . . new breezes,
sweet, enchanting smells. Daffodils and daisies quivered
in every field . . . The sky went back where it belonged
and kept its clouds to itself like everybody else. No more
of that peasoup that never stops coming down, that pukes
all over the countryside . . . Easter came in May, the
kids were bursting with impatience . . . They were going
home to see their parents . . . It would be time for me to
leave too . . . My stay was coming to an end. I was
quietly steeling myself . . . when we received a registered
envelope, a letter from my uncle with money in it and a
few words . . . He told me to stay on, to have patience
for another three months . . . it would be much wiser
. . . Uncle Édouard was a good guy! It was a marvelous
surprise . . . He'd done it on his own hook . . . From
sheer kindness of heart . . . He knew my father . . .
He could imagine the tragedies that would break out if I
came home like a dope, without any English to my name
. . . It was sure to be pretty lousy . . .

All in all I was thoroughly recalcitrant, ungrateful,
repulsive. I could have made a bit of an effort, it wouldn't
have killed me . . . to give him pleasure . . . But just
as I was about to give in, I felt the gall coming back in
my throat . . . the whole rotten business rose up . . .
the whole stinking mess . . . To hell with it . . . I'd
be damned if I'd learn anything . . . I'd come home
crummier than ever . . . I'd been buttoning up for

months . . . Hah, that's the ticket, don't talk to anybody,
not here and not over there . . . If you're little, you've
got to be tough . . . Open your mouth, and they'll step
on you. That's the stuff, if you ask me . . . You're not
very big? So get hard. I could keep my trap shut for
another few years! Absolutely! I only had to think of the
Gorloges, of little André, of Berlope, and even old lady
Divonne with her piano playing, her eighth notes, and her
Moonlight . . . Balls! Time didn't do a bit of good . . .
They came back at me sharper than ever, and even a
damn sight sourer . . . Bah! . . . My head was still full
of it—the thousands of beatings, the slaps, the swift kicks
. . . Christ! And all their stinking rottenness, and my
buddies and the fags and the floozies and all their lowdown
tricks! . . . What was I supposed to do? Think about a
lot of hooey? *"Ever and ever!"* like the little stinker? . . .
Amen! Amen! Applesauce! I made faces. I imitated them
all by myself. I made a face like Antoine when he was
shitting in the can . . . I shat in his face . . . Language?
Language? Speak? Speak? About what? . . .

I'd never seen Nora dressed in a light color, a tight-
fitting blouse, pink satin . . . It brought her boobies right
out . . . The movement of her hips was terrific too . . .
The way they swayed, the mystery of the ass . . .
It was coming on to the end of April . . . She tried
again to cheer me up, to win me over . . . One afternoon
I see her coming out for our walk with a book . . . A
great big one, some kind of Bible, to judge by the size and
weight . . . We go to the usual place . . . we settle
down . . . She opens the book on her knees . . . I can't
help looking on . . . The effect on kid Jongkind was
magical . . . He plunged his nose into it . . . he didn't
budge . . . The colors fascinated him . . . This book
was full of pictures, marvelous illustrations . . . I didn't
need to know how to read it, I knew all about it . . . I
could see the princes, the upraised lances, the knights . . .
the purple, the greens, the scarlets, all the armor studded
with rubies . . . The whole shooting match . . . It was
a good job . . . Well done . . . I knew good work when
I saw it, it was tops . . . She turned the pages slowly
. . . She began telling the story. She wanted to read it to

us word for word . . . Her fingers were terrific . . .
like beams of light on every page that passed . . . I'd
have liked to lick them . . . to suck them . . . I was
under the spell . . . Just the same I didn't say boo . . .
I looked at the book all by myself . . . I didn't ask a
single question . . . I didn't repeat a word . . . what
most amazed Jongkind was the beautiful gilt edges . . .
they dazzled him, he went to pick daisies, he came back
and strewed them all over us, he filled the margins with
them . . . The two most marvelous pages were in the
middle of the book . . . A whole battle spread all over
. . an amazing turmoil . . . Dromedaries, elephants,
Templars charging . . . A hecatomb of cavalry . . . All
the barbarians routed! . . . It was really marvelous . . .
I couldn't stop looking . . . I was almost going to talk
. . . I was going to ask questions. . . . Bing! . . . I
tighten up, I get sore . . . Rotten luck! . . . Another
second! . . . But I didn't say boo . . . I clutched the
grass . . . To hell with it, no more stories for me! . . .
I was vaccinated . . . What about little André? Wasn't
he the prize cocksucker? . . . Hadn't he screwed me
good? Hadn't he? . . . Some skunk he turned out to be!
. . . Didn't I remember plenty of legends? And my own
damn foolishness? Am I right or am I wrong? Once you
get into the habit, where does it get you? . . . So stop
batting my brains out! Leave me alone! . . . Leave me to
my bread and onions! . . . I'd rather be unhappy than
listen to stories . . . OK, that does it. It's all settled . . .
I even proved I was a man, I cleared out with Jongkind,
I let her read her book by herself . . . completely flummoxed in the grass . . .

The idiot and I ran down to the river . . . We came up
by way of the pigeons . . . When we got back, I looked
at her face . . . She was on her way home with her
pictures . . . She certainly thought I was pigheaded . . .
She was certainly sad . . . She was in no hurry to get
back . . . We started off very slowly . . . We stopped
near the bridge . . . It had already struck six . . . She
looked at the water . . . The Medway has a strong current . . . When the tides are high, it gets really wild . . .
It comes down in big eddies. The bridge shakes in the

whirlpools . . . The water is hoarse, it makes hollow sounds . . . it gasps in big yellow knots . . .

Nora leaned way over, then she quickly raised her head . . . She looked far away into the distance, at the day sinking behind the houses on the coast . . . It threw a light on her face . . . A sadness that made her features tremble . . . It grew stronger . . . she couldn't stand it, it made her all fragile . . . She had to close her eyes . . .

As soon as Hopeful Academy was finished, our kids began to leave. The ones that wanted to clear out didn't even wait until Easter . . . Six day-pupils left at the end of April, and four boarders, their old men came and got them . . . They didn't think Meanwell College was good enough anymore . . . They drew comparisons with that other dazzling place . . .

I've got to admit it, Hopeful Academy made quite a splash in the middle of its grounds . . . The building alone was worth the trip . . . All of red brick, it looked out over Rochester, you couldn't see anything else on the whole hillside . . . They'd put up an enormous flagpole on the lawn, they flew great big banners, every pavilion in the Maritime Register, and yards, shrouds, the whole works, for the kids that wanted to learn about rigging and seafaring and prepare for the naval academy.

That's how I lost little Jack, my little jerker-offer . . . He had to transship, his father wanted him to be a sailor . . . The Hopeful made a lot of fancy publicity about getting you ready for the navy . . .

We lost so many boarders that in the end there were only five of us at Meanwell, including Jongkind . . . The survivors weren't very happy, actually they were burned up . . . They must have been behindhand with their payments, they couldn't settle their bills, that's why they were stuck . . . The football team melted away in a week . . . The Pitwitt Pimplies, the charity palefaces, came around twice more, asking us to crush them. We tried to explain, to tell them it was all over . . . they didn't understand . . . They missed their "twelve to nothing." They couldn't understand . . . They had no rivals left . . . not a one . . . It depressed them something awful . . . They went home deep in gloom . . .

The Hopeful boys were too snooty, they wouldn't play them, they snubbed them like lepers . . . They said they were in a higher category . . . The Pitwitts were sunk . . . They had to match up with themselves . . .

At our table at Meanwell the tragedy was getting serious . . . bitter and grim . . . Nora Merrywin did wonders to keep the meals going. The maids left . . . First Gertrude, the older one, and then four days later, Flossie . . . A cleaning woman came . . . Nora hardly touched her food anymore . . . She left us all the marmalade, she didn't touch it, she didn't put any more sugar in her tea, she took her porridge without milk, that left more for the rest of us . . . But I was awfully ashamed just the same . . . When the pudding was passed on Sunday, there was such a rush we almost bent our spoons . . . We chipped all the platters . . . It was a wild scramble . . . Merrywin lost patience, he didn't say anything, but he wiggled all over, he fidgeted in his chair the whole time, he beat a tattoo on the table, he cut the prayers short so we'd get out quicker . . . Things were getting too ticklish in the dining room. . . .

In class he did the same thing . . . He climbed up on his platform . . . He put on his pleated cape, his lawyer's robes . . . He sat behind his desk, all huddled up in his chair, staring at the class . . . He began to blink and wiggle all his fingers, waiting for the time to be up . . . He didn't talk to the pupils anymore . . . the kids could do as they pleased . . .

Merrywin was getting thin, he'd always had enormous protruding ears, now they looked like the wings of an airplane . . . The four kids that were left made enough rumpus for forty . . . and then they got sick of it and simply walked out . . . anywhere . . . to the garden . . . into the street . . . They left Merrywin all alone, they joined us on our walk. Later we'd meet him on the road . . . we'd pass him in the open country . . . we'd see him coming in the distance . . . he'd race toward us, perched on an enormous tricycle . . .

"*Hello, Nora! Hello, boys!*" he'd shout as he passed . . . He'd slow down a second . . . "*Hello, Peter!*" she answered ever so sweetly . . . They smiled at each other very politely . . . "*Good day, Mr. Merrywin,*" all the kids took up in chorus . . . He'd go racing on. We watched him as he left, pedaling away till he was out of sight. He was home before us . . .

The way things were going, I felt I'd be leaving very soon . . . I stopped writing again . . . I didn't know what to say, what to invent anymore . . . I'd thought up everything I could . . . I was fed up with all that bullshit . . . What was the use? . . . I preferred to enjoy the time that was left, not to be bothered with letters. But now that Jack was gone, it wasn't so much fun in the dormitory . . . the little stinker certainly knew how to suck . . .

I was jerking off for Nora too much, my cock was bone dry . . . in the silence I dreamed up some new ideas . . . much more ingenious, more amusing, more tempting . . . my fatigue was even making me affectionate . . . Before leaving Meanwell, I'd have liked to see the kid doing it with her old man . . . The idea got under my skin . . . suddenly I had a craving to see them together . . . it gave me a hard-on just to think of it. What would he do to her exactly?

I had experience at the racket . . . But it wasn't an easy trick to pull off . . .They had separate rooms . . . His was on the right side of the hall, right after the gas jet . . . That was handy enough . . . But to get a look in at Nora's room I'd have had to go out the other end of the dormitory and go up the stairs . . . it was after the washroom . . . It was difficult . . . complicated . . .

How did they fuck? Did they do it in his room? or hers? I made up my mind . . . This was something I had to see . . . I'd waited too long . . .

Now that there were only five boarders, it was much easier to move around . . . Besides, the old man had stopped coming in at night to say prayers . . . The kids went to sleep very quickly once they'd warmed themselves up good . . . I waited till they were sawing wood . . . once I heard their snores, I slipped into my pants, I pretended I was going to the can . . . and then I tiptoed . . .

When I got to the old man's door, I bent down. I looked through the keyhole . . . I was screwed . . . The key hadn't been taken out . . . I went on . . . like I had to take a leak . . . I come back quick . . . I lie down

again . . . But that wasn't the end . . . It's now or
never, I says to myself . . . There wasn't a sound in the
whole place . . . I pretend I'm asleep . . . I lie there a
couple of minutes, tingling but perfectly still . . . I wasn't
nuts . . . I'd seen the light through the transom . . .
Right over the door . . . It was the same layout as on
the rue Elzévir . . . I says to myself: "If they catch you
there, kid, you'll never hear the last of it." I took extreme
precautions . . . I tote a chair into the hall . . . If they
catch me, I figure I'll make out I've been walking in my
sleep . . . I put my chair down right next to the door. I
wait, I sit down a while . . . I flatten myself against the
wall . . . I hear a kind of thud inside . . . Like two
pieces of wood knocking together . . . Could that be
coming from his bed? . . . I make sure the back of the
chair is balanced all right . . . I climb up, an eighth of an
inch at a time . . . I straighten up . . . even more slowly
. . . I'm on a level with the pane . . . Ah! I've made it!
Jeepers! I can see perfectly. I can see everything! . . . I
see my man . . . He's all sprawled out in an armchair
. . . But he's absolutely alone! No sign of the kid! . . .
Ah! He's mother-naked . . . Say! . . . Stretched out by
the fire, all glowing . . . He's positively scarlet! He's so
hot that he's puffing . . . He's naked to the belly . . .
He's kept on his drawers and cloak, the one with the pleats,
his lawyer's robe . . . it's dragging on the floor behind
him . . .

The fire's blazing hot . . . The whole room is crackling
. . . The big dope is all lit up by the glow . . . He
doesn't seem unhappy . . . he's kept his lid on, the little
one with the tassel . . . Ah! The stinker, it tips, it topples
. . . He catches it, he puts it back on . . . He's sadder
than in the classroom . . . He's playing all by himself
. . . He's got a cup-and-ball . . . A big one! A colossus!
He shakes it, he balances, he tries to catch the ball in the
cup . . . He misses, he giggles . . . he doesn't get angry
. . . His cap falls off again . . . his cloak too . . . He
picks them up as best he can . . . He burps, he sighs
. . . He puts his toy down for a minute . . . He pours
himself a big glass of liquid . . . He sips it very slowly
. . . So that's where the whiskey is! . . . He even has
two bottles beside him on the floor . . . And two siphons

. . . within easy reach . . . and a pot of marmalade
. . . a whole pot! . . . He digs into it with a big spoon
. . . he lifts it up . . . he gets it all over him . . . he's
eating! . . . He goes back to his game . . . he empties
another glass . . . The string gets caught, it winds up
around the caster of the armchair . . . He tugs at it, gets
all muddled . . . he grumbles . . . he lets out a big
laugh . . . He can't find his hands . . . He's tied . . .
It only makes him laugh, the damn fool . . . I've seen
enough. . . I come down off my perch . . . I pick up my
chair very quietly . . . I slip back down the hall . . .
Nobody's stirred . . . I go back to bed . . .

We worried along until Easter vacation . . . We had to
cut down something awful . . . on food . . . on candles
. . . on heat . . . The last few weeks the kids, the ones
that were left, didn't listen to anybody . . . They did what
they pleased . . . The old man didn't even give classes
anymore . . . He stayed in his room the whole time . . .
or else he went out all alone on his tricycle . . . on long
excursions . . .

The new maid came . . . She didn't even last a week
. . . The kids were impossible, insufferable, they turned
the whole kitchen upside down . . . A cleaning woman
took the maid's place, but only in the morning. Nora helped
her to do the rooms and the dishes too . . . She put on
gloves for that . . . She protected her beautiful hair with
an embroidered handkerchief, she made a kind of turban
out of it . . .

In the afternoon I took the idiot for a walk, I did it all
by myself. Nora couldn't come anymore, she had the
cooking to do . . . She didn't tell us where to go . . . I
was the boss . . . We took our time . . . We took all
the same streets and sidewalks, and then down along the
waterfront. I looked all over for the fritter kid, I'd have
liked to run into her. She wasn't anywhere in town with her
cart . . . Neither in the harbor nor in the market . . .
nor around the new barracks . . . No sign of her . . .

We had some good times on our walks . . . Jongkind
behaved pretty well . . . Except you had to be careful
not to get him excited . . . When we passed soldiers, for
instance, brass bands, loud music, you couldn't hold him

. . . There were lots of them around Chatham . . . and
sailors too . . . On their way home from drilling they
played wild tunes, triumphant hornpipes . . . That sent
Jongkind out of his mind . . . He ran right into the band
like a dart . . . It knocked him for a loop . . . It had
the same effect on him as football . . . He'd dive right
into the boom-booms!

A regiment is a lively thing, the color, the rhythm . . .
it stands out against the weather . . . The band was scarlet . . . They made a big splash against the sky and the
dun-colored walls . . . The Scotsmen puff their cheeks
out when they play; they're chesty and husky and strong
when they play; winsome and stalwart, they play their
bagpipes; their music has hair on its legs . . .

We followed them to their "barracks," their tents in the
open fields . . . We discovered other parts of the country,
past the soldiers . . . past Stroud and still further . . .
on the other side of another river. We always came back
by way of the school, the girls' school behind the station,
we waited for them to come out . . . We didn't say anything, we just looked, we sopped up the vision . . . We
came back down by way of the Arsenal, the special cinder
field where the "pros" played, real tough guys, who practiced by the numbers, with narrow goals, for the Nelson
Cup. They kicked so hard they split all their footballs . . .

We came home as late as possible . . . I waited until
it was really dark, until I saw all the streets were lighted,
then I took High Street, the one that ends by our steps
. . . Often it was after eight o'clock . . . The old man
was waiting for us in the hall, he was afraid to say anything,
he was reading his paper . . .

As soon as we came in, we sat down to table . . . Nora
waited on us . . . Merrywin didn't talk anymore . . .
He didn't say anything to anybody . . . it was getting to
be the easy life . . . As soon as Jongkind started his
soup, he began to drool. We left him alone now. We didn't
wipe him off until the meal was over.

None of the brats came back from Easter vacation.
There was nobody left at Meanwell but Jongkind and me.
The joint was a desert.

To save on housework they closed off a whole floor. The

furniture had gone, they sold it piece by piece, first the chairs, then the tables, the two cupboards, and even the beds. There was nothing left but our two beds. They were really liquidating . . . There was more to eat though . . . Quantities of jam . . . all we wanted . . . we could take seconds on pudding . . . The food was plentiful, what a change . . . that was really something new . . . Nora did the heavy work, but she prettied up all the same. At the table she was perfectly charming, almost playful . . .

The old geezer didn't hang around long, he'd fill up in a hurry and start off again on his tricycle. Jongkind kept the conversation going, all by himself. *"No trouble!"* And he'd learned another word: *"No fear!"* He was proud of that, it made him jump with joy. He never stopped saying it. "Ferdinand! *No fear!"* he kept saying to me between mouthfuls.

Outside I didn't like to be noticed . . . I gave him a few kicks in the ass . . . He got the drift, he left me alone . . . As a reward I gave him pickles. I always took a supply with me, my pockets were full of them . . . They were his favorite delicacy, that way I made him behave . . . He'd let himself be torn limb from limb for pickles . . .

There wasn't much left in our living room . . . First the knickknacks went . . . then the upholstered pink couch, then the vases, then the curtains . . . For the last two weeks there was nothing left but the piano, the big black monumental Pleyel, all by itself in the middle of the room . . .

I wasn't very eager to get back, because we weren't very hungry anymore . . . We took precautions, we brought provisions along, we looted the kitchen before leaving. I wasn't in any hurry at all . . . Even when I was tired, I was happier roaming around . . . We took a rest whenever we felt like it . . . We'd treat ourselves to a last stop on the steps or on the rocks right beside our garden gate . . . The top of the big staircase that led up from the harbor was almost under our windows . . . Jongkind and I would sit there as late as possible, saying nothing . . .

From there you could see a lot of ships, coming in or passing each other in the harbor . . . It was like a magic game . . . all the reflections moving on the water . . .

the portholes coming and going, glittering the whole time
. . . The train burning, trembling, setting the little arches
on fire as it passed . . . Nora always played the piano
while she was waiting for us . . . She left the window
ajar . . . You could hear her plainly from our hiding
place . . . She even sang a little . . . in an undertone
. . . She accompanied herself . . . Her singing wasn't
loud at all . . . Actually it was no more than a murmur
. . . a little ballad . . . I still remember the tune . . .
I never knew the words . . . Her voice rose softly and
floated down into the valley . . . It came back to us . . .
The air over the river has a way of echoing and amplifying
. . . Her voice was like a bird, beating its wings, the
whole night was full of little echoes . . .

The people had all passed, the ones that were going home
from work, the stairs were empty . . . *"No fear"* and I
were all alone . . . We'd wait till she stopped, till she
wasn't singing anymore, till she closed the piano . . .
Then we went in.

The grand piano didn't last much longer. The movers
came for it one Monday morning . . . They had to take it
out piece by piece . . . Jongkind and I gave them a hand
. . . First they put up a regular hoist over the window
. . . They had trouble getting the piano through. All
morning they were tinkering with ropes and pulleys in the
living room . . . They lowered the big crate down to the
veranda overlooking the garden . . . I can still see that
big black cupboard rising into the air . . . over the
view . . .

As soon as they started in, Nora went down to town,
she stayed out the whole time . . . Maybe she had a call
to make . . . She'd put on her best dress . . . She didn't
get back until late . . . She was very pale . . .

The old geezer didn't come home until eight o'clock, just
in time for dinner. He'd been doing that for several days.
After dinner he went up to his room . . . He'd stopped
shaving, he didn't even wash, he was filthy . . . He
smelled very sour. He sat down beside me. He began to eat,
but he didn't finish . . . He began to poke around in his
pants, in the folds, in the cuffs . . . He pulled up his
dressing gown . . . He looked all through his pockets

. . . He was trembling all over . . . He belched a few times . . . He yawned . . . He grumbled . . . Finally he found his piece of paper. It was another letter, registered this time . . . This was at least the tenth we'd received from my father since Christmas . . . I never answered . . . Merrywin didn't either . . . What was there to say? . . . He opens it, he shows it to me . . . I read it just to be on the safe side . . . I wade through pages and pages . . . It was copious and thoroughly documented . . . I start all over again. It was a formal order to return home . . . It was nothing new for them to bawl me out . . . Far from it . . . But this time there was a ticket . . . an honest-to-God ticket home via Folkestone!

My father was beside himself. We knew his letters. The others had been almost the same, desperate, complaining, full of hooey and threats . . . After reading them, the old geezer piled them up in a special box . . . He filed them very carefully by date and subject . . . He took them all up to his room . . . He shook his head a little and blinked . . . There was no call for him to comment . . . He kept all the letters on file, that was enough . . . Sufficient unto the day is the evil thereof . . . and all the applesauce . . . Still, this was a new kind of ultimatum . . . This time there was a ticket . . . I had only to pack up and leave . . . Time to be going, son . . . Next week it would be . . . the month was almost up . . . My account was closed!

Nora didn't seem to know what was going on . . . She was completely absorbed . . . absent . . . The old geezer wanted her to know . . . He shouted loud enough to wake her up. She came up from her daydream . . . Jongkind began to bawl . . . Suddenly she jumped up and looked through the box, she wanted to read the letter again. She deciphered it out loud . . .

I have no further illusions about the future you hold in store for us—alas, we have had only too many occasions to experience all the ferocity, all the wickedness of your instincts, your terrifying selfishness . . . We all of us know your taste for idleness and dissipation, your well-nigh monstrous appetite for luxury and pleasure . . . We know what to expect . . . We realize that no amount of gentleness, no amount of affection will ever check or diminish your

*unbridled, implacable impulses . . . It seems to me that
in that respect we have done our utmost, tried everything!
And now we are at the end of our rope, there is nothing
more we can do. We can spend no more of our slender
resources trying to save you from your fate . . . We can
only trust in God . . .*

*In this last letter I wished to warn you, as a father, as
a friend, for the last time, before your homecoming, to put
you on your guard before it is too late, against any useless
bitterness, any surprise, and futile rebellion at the fact that
in the future you must count on yourself alone, Ferdinand.
On yourself alone! Count on us no longer, I implore you,
for your daily keep, your subsistence. Your mother and I
are at the end of our tether. There is nothing more we can
do for you . . .*

*We are literally collapsing under the weight of our liabil-
ities, both old and recent . . . On the brink of old age,
our health, already undermined by continual anguish, backbreaking toil, reverses, perpetual worry, privations of all
kinds, is failing, breaking . . . We are* in extremis, *my
dear boy. Materially speaking, we have nothing left . . .
Of the small sum we received from your grandmother,
nothing remains . . . absolutely nothing . . . not a sou!
On the contrary, we have gone into debt . . . under what
circumstances, you are well aware . . . The two houses
in Asnières are mortgaged to the hilt! . . . In her business, in the Passage, your mother is faced with new difficulties which I presume to be insurmountable . . . A change
in the styles, an absolutely unforeseen caprice of fashion,
has just annihilated our prospects of a relatively successful
season . . . All our hopes have been shattered . . . For
once in our lives we took a chance . . . At great expense,
by scrimping on all our expenses and even on our food
. . . we laid in a large stock of "Irish" boleros last winter.
And then suddenly, without the slightest warning indica-
tion, our customers' taste took a radical swing, they began
literally to shun this item in favor of other styles, other
whims . . . It is beyond understanding! Destiny seems to
have conspired against our frail bark . . . It seems likely
that your mother will be unable to get rid of a single one
of her boleros. Not at any price! She is now trying to con-
vert them into lampshades for the new electrical appliances!*

. . . Futile efforts! . . . How long can this go on? Where are we headed? For my part, at La Coccinelle, I am subjected every day to the subtle, perfidious, treacherous attacks of a cabal of young clerks who have recently been taken on . . . Endowed with high university degrees (some of them have their Master's), taking advantage of their influence with the director, of their family ties and social connections, of their "modern" upbringing (a well-nigh total absence of scruples), these ambitious young men have a crushing advantage over mere rank-and-file employees like myself . . . No doubt they will succeed (and very quickly, it appears) not only in getting ahead of us, but in ousting us altogether from our modest positions . . . Without wishing to take too dark a view, it is only a question of months! On that score it is impossible to harbor any illusions.

For my part, I am trying to hold my own as long as possible . . . without losing all dignity and self-respect . . . I am doing my best to minimize the chances and risks of a scandal whose consequences I dread . . . all the consequences . . . I control myself . . . I restrain myself . . . I contain myself to avoid any possibility of a scene, a skirmish! Unfortunately, I am not always successful . . . In their misguided zeal these young opportunists provoke me deliberately . . . I have become the target, the butt of their malice . . . I feel pursued by their plots, their sarcasms, their incessant jibes . . . They amuse themselves at my expense . . . Why? . . . I am lost in conjectures . . . Is it the mere fact of my existence? As you can imagine, this persistent hostility, their very presence, is bitterly painful to me. Moreover, all things considered, I feel myself defeated in advance in this contest of smoothness, skulduggery, and malice! . . . What weapons have I to defend myself with? Without a fortune or family, with nothing more to my credit than a record of service honestly, scrupulously, rendered La Coccinelle over a period of two and twenty consecutive years, my blameless conscience, my perfect probity, my meticulous and unswerving sense of duty . . . What have I to expect? Obviously the worst . . . This ample inventory of sincere virtues will, I fear, be counted rather against me than to

*my credit on the day when my accounts are settled . . .
Of that, my dear son, I have a clear presentiment! . . .*

If my position proves untenable (as it is rapidly becoming), if I am discharged once and for all (any pretext will do, there is more and more talk of reorganizing the whole office)—what will become of us then? Your mother and I cannot think of this eventuality without a sense of the most terrible and justified anguish, without positive terror!

On an off chance, in a last impulse of self-defense, I have undertaken (a desperate measure) the task of learning to operate a typewriter, outside the office of course, taking advantage of the little time I can spare from deliveries and errands for the shop. We have rented the machine (an American make) for several months (one more expense). But here again I harbor no illusions . . . At my age, as you can well imagine, it is not easy to assimilate so novel a technique, new methods, new habits, new ways of thinking! Especially crushed as we are by continual misadventures . . . mercilessly tormented! . . . All this, my dear son, leads us to take the darkest view of our future. And beyond the slightest doubt or fear of exaggeration, we cannot afford the least mistake . . . not even the most trifling imprudence . . . if we, your mother and I, are not to end our existence in the most utter destitution!

We send you our love, my dear child. Once again your mother and I exhort you, adjure you, implore you, before your return from England (if not in our interest or for love of us, then at least in your own interest) to make a brave decision, to resolve above all to apply yourself body and soul to the success of your undertakings.

> *Your affectionate father,*
> *Auguste.*

P. S.   Your mother asks me to inform you of the death of Madame Divonne last Monday at her haven in Kremlin-Bicêtre.

She had been confined to her bed for several weeks. She was suffering from emphysema and a heart ailment. She suffered little. The last few days she slumbered constantly . . . She was not aware of the approach of death. We had been to see her the day before, in the afternoon.

The next day, it must have been about noon, Jongkind

and I were in the garden waiting for lunchtime . . . The
weather was beautiful . . . Along comes a character on
a bicycle . . . He stops, he rings at our gate . . . It was
another telegram . . . I ran to take it, it was from my
father . . . "Return   immediately,   mother   worried.
Auguste."

I run upstairs, I meet Nora on the landing, I pass her the
wire, she reads it, she comes down, she dishes out our
soup, we begin to eat . . . Bingo! She bursts into tears.
She's bawling, she can't stop, she gets up, she leaves the
room, she runs into the kitchen. I hear her sobbing in the
hall . . . it threw me to see her acting like that. It wasn't
her way . . . she never did that . . . Just the same, I
didn't bat an eyelash . . . I stay where I am with the
idiot, I finish feeding him . . . It was time for our walk
. . . I wasn't in the mood . . . That incident had
cramped my style.

And then I thought of the Passage. All of a sudden the
idea began to haunt me . . . my arrival, all the neighbors
. . . the search for some wonderful job . . . No more
independence . . . no more silence . . . No more roaming around . . . My childhood would be starting in again,
the whole stinking business, I'd have to start in again where
I left off . . . I'd have to show enthusiasm! Oh, the lousy
luck, the slimy horror of it all . . . The misery of working
for people! The deserving young man! . . . Twelve dozen
crappers! I couldn't stand thinking about it . . . The mere
thought of my parents and my mouth was full of birdshit.
My mother, her skinny stilt leg, my father with his bac-
chanalias, his hysterical damn foolishness . . .

Kid Jongkind was tugging at my sleeves. He didn't catch
on. He still wanted us to go out. I looked at him: *"No
trouble."* We'd be leaving each other soon . . . This little
screwball that swallowed everything in sight . . . I
guessed he'd miss me out of his world . . . I wondered
how he actually saw me . . . As an ox? As a lobster? . . .
He'd got really used to having me take him out, with his big
round eyes, his perpetual cheerfulness . . . He was lucky
in a way . . . He was pretty affectionate if you were careful not to get his goat . . . He didn't really like to see me
thinking . . . I went over and looked out the window a
second . . . Before I could turn around the little joker

had jumped up on the table . . . He calms down, he pees!
It splashes in the soup . . . He's done it before, I run
over, I grab him, I make him come down . . . Just then
the door opens . . . Merrywin comes in . . . He moves
mechanically, his features are frozen . . . He walks like
an automaton . . . First he goes around the table . . .
twice, three times . . . He starts in again . . . He's
wearing his fancy rig, the black lawyer's robes . . . but
underneath he has on a whole sport outfit, golf pants, binoculars . . . a nifty nickel-plate flask, and a green smock
belonging to his wife . . . He's still walking the same
way, like a somnambulist . . . he goes down the steps
in jerks and jolts . . . He roams around the garden a
while . . . he even tries to open the gate . . . he hesi-
tates, he comes back, he heads for the house . . . still
completely in a dream . . . He passes in front of Jongkind again . . . He salutes us majestically, with a sweeping gesture . . . His arm rises and falls . . . He bows
a little each time . . . He's addressing a crowd far in the
distance . . . He seems to be responding to a tremendous
ovation . . . And then finally he goes back upstairs . . .
very slowly . . . with perfect dignity . . . I can hear him
closing the door . . .

These weird goings-on . . . this mechanical man . . .
had frightened Jongkind . . . He couldn't keep still. He
had to get out of there, he was in a panic. I clicked my
tongue at him and shouted whoa! whoa! . . . like you talk
to a horse. Usually that quieted him . . . I finally had to
give in . . . We went out across the fields . . .

Near the Scottish barracks, we ran into the Hopeful College kids who were out for a walk. They were on their way
to the cricket field on the other side of the valley. They
were carrying their bats and their wickets . . . we recognized all our old boys, they waved to us, all very friendly
. . . Naturally they had filled out and grown . . . They
were very gay . . . They seemed glad to see us . . .
their new rig was orange and blue . . . their caravan
looked mighty bright against the horizon.

We looked after them . . . We came home very early
. . . Jongkind was still trembling.

We were at the top of Willow Walk, the path leading to

the school, when we passed the truck, the big van with three horses . . . more movers . . .

They avoided the steep hill, they went all the way around by the garden, they took more things away. This time they really cleaned the place out . . . they took the scrapings . . . We looked inside, the flaps were rolled up . . . They had the two maids' beds, one of the kitchen cupboards, the little china closet, and the old geezer's tricycle . . . and a lot of other junk . . . They must have emptied the attic! The whole joint! There wouldn't be anything left! . . . They even took the bottles, you could hear them rolling around in the bottom of the crate . . . There wouldn't be much left the way they were going about it . . .

I began to be worried about my two or three scraps and my shoes. If they kept on looting this way, there was no limit, anything could happen . . . The inside of that van looked like a regular auction room. I took the stairs four at a time, I wanted to see the extent of the damage. And besides it was time to eat . . . The table was laid sumptuously . . . with the best silver . . . and the dishes with the flower patterns, and all the cut glass . . . It stood out beautifully in the naked room . . .

The meal consisted of potato salad, artichokes vinaigrette, cherries in brandy, a luscious cake, a whole ham . . . Real abundance, and in addition there were daffodils strewn over the tablecloth, in between the cups . . . It was really something. It was a real surprise.

I was amazed. Jongkind and I stood looking at the marvels . . . neither he nor she came down . . . We were both famished . . . First we take a little taste of everything . . . And then we make up our minds . . . we dive in, we gobble . . . we dig in with our fingers . . . nothing to it once you're started . . . It's delicious! Jongkind was beside himself with pleasure, he was as happy as a king . . . We didn't leave much . . . Still nobody came down . . .

Once we were full, we went out into the garden . . . It was time for his business . . . I look around a little . . . Nothing but night, not a living soul . . . It was really weird . . . Upstairs I saw only a single light in the whole housefront, in the old geezer's room . . . He must have locked himself in again . . . I says to myself, I'm not

going to waste any time, I'm sick of all this hanky-panky
. . . As long as I've got my ticket, I'll pack up . . . Tomorrow morning I'll skedaddle by the first train at seven-
thirty. Sure! Just like that! I won't wait for the end of the
song. I never could stand good-byes.

Still, I'd have liked to lay my hands on a little dough,
maybe a shilling or two for some ginger beer, it's good on a
trip . . . First I put my idiot to bed, so he'll leave me
alone . . . I jerk him off just a little, that usually kept
him quiet . . . it sent him off to sleep . . . But that
night he was frantic with all his fears of the day, he
wouldn't close his eyes . . . I tried shouting whoa whoa!
. . . He kept thrashing around, he jumped up and down in
his cage, he growled like a wild animal. He may have been
nuts, but he suspected something unusual was up . . . He
suspected I was going to leave him in the middle of the
night . . . He didn't like that. It scared him out of his
wits to be left alone . . . Hell!

It's true the dormitory was a big place . . . For him
that was an awful lot of space . . . There were only two
of us left where there'd been twelve of us before, or even
fourteen . . .

I collected my socks, hunted up my handkerchiefs,
picked up my lousy underwear, it was all holes and tears
. . . They'd have to outfit me again. There'd be another
riot . . . A lovely prospect . . . my troubles weren't
over . . . The future is no joke . . . The thought of the
Passage, so close to me now, sent the grimy shivers through
me . . .

I'd been gone for eight months . . . What would they
be like now down there under the glass roof? . . . That
wasn't hard to figure out . . . They'd be even dumber
. . . worse pains than ever . . . The Rochester characters . . . well, probably I'd never be seeing them again!
I took a last look at the view out the window, the big
one that opens up and down like a guillotine . . . The
weather was clear, marvelous . . . You could see all
the paths on the hillside and the docks all lit up . . .
the crisscrossing lights of the ships . . . all the colors
moving in and out . . . like dots looking for each
other at the end of the darkness . . . I'd seen lots
of ships and passengers leaving . . . sailboats . . .

steamboats . . . God knows where they were now . . .
in Canada . . . and some in Australia . . . all sails
unfurled . . . They were chasing whales . . . I'd never see
all that . . . I'd be going to the Passage . . . to the rue
Richelieu, the rue Méhul . . . I'd see my father cracking
his collar . . . my mother picking up her leg . . . I was
going looking for jobs . . . I'd have to talk, to explain
why and how . . . I'd be cornered like a rat . . . They'd
be waiting for me, lousy with questions . . . I'd have to
take my medicine . . . It gave me the gollywobbles to
think of it . . .

It was pitch-dark in the room, I'd blown out the candle
. . . I stretched out on the bed all dressed, I relaxed . . .
I decided to sleep as I was . . . I said to myself: "Don't
peel, kid, that way you can beat it at the crack of dawn
. . ." There was nothing more for me to do . . . all my
junk was ready. I'd even taken some towels . . . Jongkind finally falls asleep . . . I can hear him snoring . . .
I won't say good-bye to anybody . . . Just beat it on the
q.t. . . . No effusions for me! . . . I'm beginning to doze
. . . I play with myself just a little . . . I hear the door
opening . . . My blood froze . . . I says to myself:
"Watch out, kid. It's ten to one they're coming to say
good-bye . . . You got your nerve with you, baby
doll . . ."

I hear a light step, somebody slipping across the floor
. . . It's her . . . breathing . . . I'm cooked . . . No
time to run . . . she won't wait . . . She's down on me
like a cyclone . . . she's on the bed in one jump . . .
A fine kettle of fish! . . . I take the shock full in the
ribs . . . She clutches me . . . I'm crushed, flattened
under her caresses . . . I'm all ground up, there's nothing
left of me . . . The whole weight of her has come down
on my head . . . it's sticky . . . My face is wedged in,
I'm suffocating . . . I protest . . . I implore . . . I'm
afraid to yell too loud. . . The old geezer might hear!
. . . I struggle . . . I try to wriggle out from under . . .
I contract . . . I strain my muscles . . . I crawl under
my own ruins . . . I'm caught again, flattened out,
crushed again . . . An avalanche of tenderness . . . I
collapse under her wild kisses, her licking, her tugging
. . . My face is a mash . . . I can't find my openings to

breathe by . . . "Ferdinand! Ferdinand!" she implores
me . . . She sobs down my windpipe . . . She's out of
her mind . . . I jam all the tongue I can produce down
her throat to make her stop yelling like that . . . the old
geezer in his room is bound to wake up . . . I'm terrified
of cuckolds . . . some of them are ferocious . . .

I try to soothe her pain, to make her control herself
. . . I caulk wherever I can . . . I knock myself out
. . . I try my best . . . I try the subtlest tricks . . . But
she's too much for me . . . She gives me some wicked
holds . . . The whole bed is shaking . . . She flails
around like crazy . . . I fight like a lion . . . My hands
are all swollen from clutching her ass! I want to anchor her,
to make her stop moving. There. That's it. She's stopped
talking. Christ almighty! I plunge, I slip in like a breeze!
I'm petrified with love . . . I'm one with her beauty . . .
I'm in ecstasy . . . I wriggle . . . I bite right into her
tit . . . She moans, she sighs . . . I suck her all over
. . . On her face I go looking for the exact spot next to
her nose . . . the one that tortures me, the magic of her
smile . . . I'm going to bite her there too . . . especially
. . . I stick one hand up her ass, I massage . . . I dig
in . . . I wallow in light and flesh . . . I come like a
horse . . . I'm full of sauce . . . She gives a wild leap
. . . She breaks loose, she's gone, the bitch! . . . She
jumps backward . . . Hell! She's on her feet . . . She's
in the middle of the room . . . She's making a speech
. . . I can see her in the white of the street lamp . . . in
her nightgown . . . all pulled up . . . her hair flying
loose . . . I'm lying there flummoxed with my cock in
the air . . .

"Come on back," I say. I try to quiet her. All of a sudden she seems to be furious . . . She yells, she waves her
arms . . . She moves back toward the door . . . The
bitch, she hands me a line . . . *"Good-bye, Ferdinand!"*
she yells, *"Good-bye! Live well, Ferdinand! Live well . . ."*
What sense does that make? . . .

Another scene! Holy creepers! I jump off the bed! . . .
I'll flatten her out! She'll be the last! Dammit to stinking
hell! She doesn't wait, the slut! She's gone . . . I hear the
downstairs door opening and slamming hard . . . I run
to the window . . . I open it . . . I'm just in time to see

her running out of the alley . . . under the street lamps . . . I see her movements, her nightgown fluttering in the wind . . . She dashes down the steps . . . She's crazy. Where the hell is she going?

It flashes through my mind that something terrible is going to happen . . . I says to myself: "This is it. You're in for it. This is going to be one sweet mess! And you're going to take the rap! That's sure as shit! Bloody murder! She's going to throw herself in the drink . . ." I knew it. She's off her rocker! . . . Dammit to hell . . . Could I catch her? . . . But it's none of my business . . . There's nothing I can do . . . The whole thing is beyond me . . . I listen . . . I look out through the hall door . . . to see if I can see her on the waterfront . . . She must be down by now . . . There she is again . . . still screaming . . . "Ferdinand! Ferdinand!" And then some more Ferdinands . . . her screams cut through the sky . . . That's her again, the bitch, yelling way from the bottom . . . She's got her nerve . . . Dammit to hell! I can hear her from the other end of the harbor . . . I'm scared . . . I stare . . . They'll say I knew something . . . They'll pinch me for sure . . . I'm in for it. It's the handcuffs for me . . . I'm in one hell of a dither . . . I go and shake the idiot in his crib . . . If I leave him alone for a minute and he gets panicky . . . he'll do some damnfool thing . . . He'll set the place on fire . . . Christ! I wake him up . . . I pull him out of his cage . . . I drag him out in his kimono . . . I pull him helter-skelter down the stairs . . .

When we get out into the alley, I lean over the rocks, I try to look down as far as the bridge, under the lights . . . Where can she be? Ah, there she is, I see her . . . A spot . . . wavering through the shadows, a white spot, whirling . . . That's the kid all right, that's my loony! She flits from one lamp to the next . . . Like a butterfly, the stinker! . . . She's still yelling here and there, the wind brings back the echoes . . . And then for a second there's a terrible scream and then another, an awful scream that fills the whole valley . . . "Hurry up, boy," I tell the kid. "Our lady love has jumped in. We'll never make it. We're in for a dip. You'll see, kid. You'll see."

I run like hell, I race down the steps, through space

. . . Bing! Just like that. All of a sudden . . . Right in
the middle of the stairway . . . My blood froze . . . I'd
had an idea. I stop. I'm trembling all over. That's enough!
I'm not taking another step . . . It's for the birds! I pull
myself together. I look back . . . I lean over the rail
. . . I see . . . The place on the waterfront where the
sound was coming from isn't very far . . . There's a big
crowd now . . . People pouring in from all sides . . .

The esplanade is full of rescuers . . . There's more
coming. They're talking it over . . . They're running
around in all directions with poles, lifebelts, and canoes
. . . All the whistles and sirens begin to blow at once . . .
It's a hullabaloo, a riot . . . But they're working hard,
they re knocking themselves out . . . They don't catch
anything . . . The little white square in the waves . . .
It's being carried out farther and farther . . .

I can still see her from where I am, clearly in the middle
of the water . . . she passes out beyond the piers . . . I
can even hear her choking . . . I can hear her gurgling
. . . I can still hear the sirens . . . I hear her swallowing
water . . . She's caught in the tide . . . She's caught in
the eddies . . . The little white speck is passing the
breakwater! O Christ! O holy shit! She's drunk up the
ocean by now! . . . I got to get the brat home . . . I
give him a poke in the ass . . . They mustn't catch us
out . . . We've got to be out of here before they come
back . . . That's for sure.

He's worn out from running . . . I push him . . . I
throw him . . . He can't see a thing without his glasses
. . . He can't even see the lamp posts. He starts bumping
into everything . . . He whines like a dog . . . I grab
him and pick him up, I carry him up the hill . . . I toss
him into his bed . . . I run to the old man's door . . . I
knock hard. No answer, not a word! Come on! I knock
again, I pound! . . . Then I give a good push, I bash it in
. . . He's there all right . . . Just the way I'd seen him
. . . He's stretched out in front of his grate, all pink . . .
He's stroking his belly, as peaceful as can be . . . He
gives me a look as if I'd interrupted him . . . He blinks
a little, his eyelids flutter . . . He don't know from
nothing . . . "She's drowning! She's drowning!" I yell
at him. I repeat it even louder . . . I shout my lungs out

. . . I make motions . . . I imitate the glug-glug . . . I
point down . . . into the valley . . . out the window!
Down there! Down there! The Medway! *"River! River!
Down there! Water! . . ."* He raises himself just a little
. . . the effort makes him belch . . . He loses his balance, collapses on a stool . . . "Oh, nice Ferdinand," he
says . . . "Nice Ferdinand!" He even holds out his hand
. . . But his cup-and-ball gets all fouled up . . . It's
stuck in the armchair . . . He tugs at it, he's exhausted,
he has to stop . . . He upsets all the bottles . . . All the
whiskey drips down . . . The marmalade, the jar tips
over . . . Everything topples . . . like a waterfall . . .
That hands him a laugh . . . he's convulsed . . . He
tries to pick things up . . . the gravy . . . everything
collapses . . . the plate too . . . he skids on the pieces
. . . He slides under the bench . . . He doesn't move
. . . He's wedged against the fireplace . . . He shows me
how it's done . . . He ruminates . . . he grunts . . .
He massages his belly with round strokes . . . He
bunches up wads of fat and gives them a good going over
. . . He kneads them slowly . . . He rubs and squeezes
. . . he pushes them apart . . . he works into the furrows . . .

I've completely forgotten what I was going to say . . .
What's the use? . . . I close the door, I go back to the
dormitory . . . I says to myself: "You're going to clear
out of here at the crack of dawn . . ." My bag is all
ready . . . I lie down on the bed for a minute . . . but I
get up a second later . . . I'm in a panic again . . . I
don't know exactly why. I start thinking about the kid
again . . . I look out the window . . . I listen . . .
Not a sound . . . Nothing . . . There's not a soul on the
waterfront . . . Had they all left so soon?

Then suddenly this thing begins to plague me, in spite of
my terror, in spite of my tiredness . . . I couldn't resist
. . . I wanted to go down and see if they'd pulled her out
of the drink . . . I put on my coat and pants, my suit
. . . The kid was sound asleep . . . I lock him up in the
dormitory . . . I meant to come back right away . . . I
make it quick . . . I'm down at the bottom of the stairs
. . . I see a cop making his rounds . . . I see a sailor
who calls out to me . . . That cools me off . . . I'm

scared again . . . I stop still in my niche . . . Hell! It's
too complicated for me. I'm not moving . . . I'm too
exhausted anyway. I stay there quite a while . . . There's
nobody around . . . Down below, that's the bridge she
jumped from . . . I see the lights, red ones, a big long
string of them, trembling in the reflections of the water
. . . I say to myself, I'll be getting back now . . . It's
not far . . . Maybe the cops are there by now . . . I
begin   wondering . . . imagining . . . I'm   exhausted
. . . I'm knocked out . . . I'm really not feeling very
good . . . I'm all in . . . So help me, I can't move . . .
I'll never make it back to Meanwell . . . I won't even
try . . . I lean back . . . There's nothing I can do after
all . . . This mess has nothing to do with me . . . not
a thing . . . Just let me beat it out of here, all by myself
. . . Slowly I head for the station . . . I wrap up tight in
my overcoat . . . I don't want anybody to recognize me
. . . I slide along the walls . . . I don't meet a soul . . .
The waiting room is open . . . Good deal . . . I stretch
out for a while on the bench . . . There's a stove right
near . . . I'm doing fine . . . I'm in the dark . . . The
first train for Folkestone is at five . . . I haven't got my
stuff, not one damn thing . . . It was up there on the bed
. . . To hell with it! I'll go home without it . . . I don't
want to go back there . . . It can't be done . . . The one
thing for me is to make myself scarce . . . I sit up so as
to keep awake . . . I'm sure of making that five o'clock
train . . . I'm sitting right under the bulletin board . . .
I lie down right there . . . I stretch out. "*5 o'clock.*
Folkestone via Canterbury."

Coming home that way without any of my stuff, I really
expected to be welcomed with the broom handle. Not a bit
of it . . . My folks seemed pleased, they were kind of
glad to see me . . . They were just surprised that I hadn't
brought back a single shirt, a single sock, but they didn't
press the point . . . they didn't start up a scenario . . .
They were too much absorbed by their own private worries . . .

In the eight months I'd been away they had changed a
good deal . . . their whole appearance and bearing. I
found them all shriveled up, with wizened faces and hesi-

tant movements . . . My father's pants bagged at the
knees, they fell down in big folds on all sides like an
elephant. His face was livid, he'd lost all his hair on top,
he disappeared under his sea captain's cap . . . His eyes
were almost colorless now, they weren't even blue at all,
but gray, all pale like the rest of his face . . . He was all
wrinkles, they were a dark color, furrows running from the
nose down to the mouth . . . He was falling apart . . .
He didn't talk to me about anything much . . . He only
asked me once or twice how come we'd stopped answering
his letters to England . . . Were they dissatisfied with me
at Meanwell College? Had I made progress? . . . Had I
caught the accent? . . . Did I understand English when
they talked fast? . . . I mumbled something vague . . .
He didn't seem to expect any more . . .

He wasn't listening to me anyway . . . He was too
panic-stricken to worry about things that were over and
done with. He'd lost interest in arguing . . . Morose
as his letters had been, they hadn't told me the whole
story . . . Far from it . . . There was plenty more to
come . . . Calamities—brand-new ones! So I heard it
all, in every detail . . . They really had put themselves
through the wringer to send me my keep for the first
six months . . . It had been rough . . . The disaster
with the boleros had sunk them completely . . . without exaggeration . . . My father's watch never left the
pawnshop . . . Nor my mother's ring either . . . They'd
taken out some mortgages in Asnières . . . on those beat-
up houses . . .

Not having his watch drove father crazy . . . not having the time on him . . . that contributed to his collapse.
He so punctual, so exact in everything he did, he was
obliged to look at the clock in the Passage every minute
. . . He'd go out on the doorstep . . . Every time Madame Ussel, the seamstress, would be waiting for him . . .
Tic toc, tic toc . . . she'd say to get his goat . . . she'd
stick out her tongue . . .

New difficulties cropped up . . . end to end like a
string of sausages . . . They were too much for them
. . . They huddled up in their misery, disintegrating,
lacerating themselves with despair, shrinking so as to offer
less surface . . . They tried to wriggle out from under

their calamities . . . It didn't help! They got caught, they
got the same going-over every time.

Madame Héronde, our seamstress, couldn't work anymore, she was in the hospital all the time . . . Madame
Jasmin, who took her place, was completely unreliable
. . . A spendthrift, always in debt! Her tastes ran to
liquor. She lived in Clichy. My mother spent all her time
on the bus, she went out there twice a day, morning and
evening . . . She always found her in some bar . . .
She was married to a colonel, she steeped herself in absinthe . . . The customers that gave us things to mend
had to wait months for their doodads . . . They had terrible fits of rage and impatience . . . It was even worse
than before . . . They were always in a fury about the
delays and postponements . . . And when it came time to
pay up, it was always the same song and dance, the same
mists and monkeyshines . . . Whish! . . . Madame was
gone . . . All of a sudden there was nothing but empty
space . . . Or if they did cough up a little, they hollered
and griped so much, they whittled down the tiny little bills,
with such tirades . . . that in the end my mother didn't
know what to say or do . . . She'd sweated blood, limping after that Jasmin woman and all the rest of them, just
to be yelled at, treated like dirt . . . It wasn't worth it.

Anyway my mother was perfectly well aware, she had
to admit it with tears in her eyes, that the taste for lovely
things was dying out . . . you couldn't buck the stream
. . . it was stupid to even try and fight, you were just
wearing yourself out for nothing . . . Rich people had
lost all their refinement . . . all their delicacy . . . their
appreciation for fine work, for hand-made articles . . .
all they had left was a depraved infatuation with machine-
made junk, embroideries that unravel, that melt and peel
when you wash them . . . Why insist on making beautiful
things? . . . That's what the ladies wanted. Flashy stuff
. . . gingerbread . . . horrors . . . rubbish from the
bargain counter. . . Fine lace was a thing of the past
. . . What was the use of fighting? . . . My mother had
had to give in to the contagion . . . She'd filled the whole
place with this cheap junk . . . real crap . . . in less
than a month . . . That was a safe bet! . . . The window
was full of it . . . To see every curtain rod and shelf in

the place full of this trash, miles of it, didn't just make her
unhappy, it gave her a real bellyache . . . But it was no
use arguing . . . The Jews two steps away from us, on
the corner of the rue des Jeûneurs, piled up enormous
pieces of the same, the whole shop front was thrown open,
and the counters were buried under the stuff like at the
fair, by the bobbin, by the rod, by the pound!

It was a real comedown for anybody who had known
the real stuff . . . my mother was overcome with shame
at having to compete with such garbage . . . But she had
no choice . . . She'd have preferred to abandon this line
altogether and get along as best she could with other
things, with her little pieces of furniture for instance, her
marqueterie, her *poudreuses,* her kidney-shaped tables, her
cabinets, or even the gewgaws people put in glass cases,
the knickknacks, the little pieces of pottery, and even the
Dutch globes that leave next to no profit and are so heavy
to carry . . . But she wasn't strong enough . . . it was
too hard with her bad leg . . . running all over Paris, she
could never have carried a bigger load . . . It couldn't be
done. But that's what you had to do if you wanted to find
bargains. And hang around the auction rooms pointing
like a hound dog for hours on end . . . And what about
the store? . . . The two didn't go together . . . Our
doctor, Dr. Capron from the Marché Saint-Honoré, had
been to see us twice on account of her leg . . . He'd
made himself very clear . . . He'd ordered her to take a
complete rest . . . to stop running up and down stairs,
loaded like three dozen mules . . . to give up the housework . . . even the cooking . . . He hadn't pulled any
punches . . . He'd told her in so many words that if she
kept overdoing it . . . he'd warned her . . . she'd get a
real abscess inside the knee, he even showed her the place
. . . From the continual strain the upper and lower part
of her leg had gone stiff . . . they were riveted together
. . . joint and all, they were frozen into a single bone. It
looked like a stick with ridges running all along . . .
They weren't muscles . . . When she moved her foot,
they pulled on it like ropes . . . You could see them
straining . . . It gave her excruciating pain . . . a terrible cramp. Especially in the evening when she was
through, when she came home from running around . . .

She showed me when we were alone . . . She put on hot compresses . . . She was careful not to let my father see her . . . She'd finally noticed what a temper it put him in to have her limping along behind him . . .

Since we were all alone again . . . and I was in the shop, waiting . . . she took advantage of the opportunity to repeat . . . very gently, very affectionately, but with absolute conviction, that it was really my fault if things were going so badly . . . on top of all their other troubles in the shop and the office . . . My conduct, all my misdeeds at Gorloge's and at Berlope's had hit them so hard they'd never get over it . . . They were still stunned . . . Of course they weren't angry with me . . . they didn't hold it against me . . . Let bygones be bygones . . . But at least I ought to realize what a state I'd put them in . . . My father was so shattered he couldn't control his nerves . . . He started up in the middle of the night . . . He woke up with nightmares . . . He'd pace back and forth for hours . . .

As for her, I had only to look at her leg . . . It was the worst of calamities . . . It was worse than a serious sickness, than typhoid or erysipelas . . . Again she repeated all her recommendations in the most affectionate tone . . . that I should try to be more reasonable with my new bosses . . . more settled in my ways, more courageous, persevering, grateful, scrupulous, obliging . . . to stop being scatterbrained, negligent, lazy . . . to try to have my heart in the right place . . . Yes, that's the main thing, the heart! . . . to remember always, and never forget, that they'd deprived themselves of everything, that they'd both of them worked their fingers to the bone for me ever since I was born . . . and now, only recently, sending me to England! . . . that if, by ill luck, I were to commit any more horrible crimes . . . well, it would be the end . . . my father wouldn't be able to take it . . . poor man, he'd be through. He'd come down with neurasthenia, he'd have to leave his office . . . For her part . . . if she had to go through any more agonies . . . over my conduct . . . it would affect her leg . . . there'd be one abscess after another and in the end they'd have to amputate . . . That's what Capron had said.

In Papa's case it was even more tragic on account of

his temperament, his sensibility . . . He ought to take a
rest, right away and for several months, what he needed
was a long vacation in a quiet place, away from it all, in
the country . . . That's what Capron had recommended
. . . He'd examined his heart very carefully . . . it beat
like a triphammer . . . Sometimes it even missed a beat
. . . The two of them . . . Capron and Papa . . . were
exactly the same age, forty-two years and six months . . .
He'd even added that a man is even more delicate than a
woman when the "menopause" sets in . . . that he
should take a thousand precautions . . . His advice came
at the wrong time . . . Right then my father was knocking himself out more than ever . . . You could hear him
typing up on the fourth floor, the machine was an enormous contraption with a keyboard the size of a factory
. . . When he'd been typing a long time, the clickety
click of the keys buzzed in his ears a good part of the
night . . . It kept him awake. He took mustard footbaths.
That brought some of the blood down from his brain.

I began to realize that my mother would always regard
me as an unfeeling child, a selfish monster, a little brute,
capricious, scatterbrained . . . They had tried everything,
done everything they could . . . it was really no use.
There'd never be any help for my disastrous, innate, incorrigible propensities . . . She could only face the facts,
my father had been perfectly right . . . During my absence their griping had got even worse, it had settled into a
groove . . . They were so busy with their troubles they
couldn't even bear the sound of my footsteps. My father
made horrible faces every time I came upstairs.

The business with the lousy boleros had been the last
straw . . . and the typewriter was driving him crazy, he'd
never be able to work it . . . He spent hours making
copies . . . He banged it like he was deaf . . . he ruined
whole pages . . . Either he'd hit too hard or not hard
enough . . . The little bell was ringing all the time . . .
From my bed . . . I was right near him . . . I saw him
struggling . . . missing the keys . . . getting tangled up
in the connecting rods . . . He wasn't cut out for it . . .
He'd get up all in a sweat . . . He'd reel off the most
terrible blasphemies . . . At the office Monsieur Lem-

preinte was still rubbing it in, persecuting him from morning to night. Obviously he was just looking for a pretext . . . "Those downstrokes . . . those curlicues . . . they take you all day. Ah, my poor friend! Take a look at your colleagues. They were done hours ago. You're a calligrapher, monsieur! You ought to set yourself up in business . . ." They really had it in for him . . . He began to look for another job . . . He saw he was on the skids . . . He went to see former associates . . . He knew an assistant cashier in a rival company . . . The Connivance Fire Insurance Company. They'd as good as promised him a tryout in January . . . But there he'd have to type . . . He went at it every night after his deliveries.

It was an antique contraption, absolutely unbreakable, specially made for rental, the bell rang at every comma. He'd hammer away frantically under the transom from suppertime to midnight.

My mother came up for a moment after she'd done the dishes, she propped up her leg on a chair and put on compresses . . . She couldn't chat, it bothered my father . . . We were dying of the heat . . . The beginning of summer was torrid that year.

It was a bad time to be looking for a job . . . Business was quiet just before the slack season. We put out a few feelers . . . We made inquiries here and there . . . with some agents we knew . . . They had no prospects to offer. There wouldn't be much doing until after summer vacation . . . not even in the foreign shops.

In a way it was lucky I had nothing to do, because I hadn't any clothes . . . they'd definitely have to outfit me before I could start making my rounds . . . But it wasn't going to be easy . . . The main trouble was lack of money . . . I'd simply have to wait till September for the shoes and the overcoat . . . I was mighty glad of the reprieve . . . It gave me time to breathe before trotting out my English . . . There'd be hell to pay when they began to catch on . . . Well, it wouldn't be right away . . . I had only one shirt to my name . . . I wore one of my father's . . . They decided they'd order a jacket and two pair of pants all at once . . . But not until next month . . . At the moment it couldn't be done

. . . There was barely enough for grub and even that was touch and go . . .   The rent came due on the eighth and they were behind with the gas . . . Not to mention taxes and Papa's typewriter . . . We were really in the soup . . . There were writs all over the place . . . all over the furniture, violet ones, red ones, and blue ones . . .

So I had a little respite. I couldn't go calling on prospective bosses in a threadbare suit, patched, frayed, with the sleeves only halfway down my arm . . . It was out of the question! Especially in novelties and haberdashery, where they all dress up like fashion plates.

My father was so preoccupied with his typing exercises and his dread of being fired from Coccinelle that even at supper he was deep in thought. He'd lost interest in me. He'd made up his mind about me once and for all . . . the idea was firmly anchored in his dome that I was villainy incarnate . . . a hopeless blockhead . . . and that was that . . . that I had no part in the worries, the anxieties of noble individuals . . . I wasn't the kind that would carry my suffering around with me in my flesh like a knife . . . And keep turning it as long as I lived . . . Far from it . . . And jerk the handle . . . And stick it in deeper! To heighten the pain . . . And bellow and broadcast every new step forward in my suffering! Of course not. And turn into a fakir in the Passage! Side by side with them! Sure, something miraculous, something people could worship! Something more and more perfect! That's it. A thousand times more anxious, more harassed, more miserable! . . . The saint engendered by hard work and family thrift . . . Sure, why not? More muddleheaded . . . Sure . . . A hundred times thriftier! Glory be! Something that had never been seen in the Passage or anywhere else . . . In the whole world . . . Christ! The child marvel . . . the marvel of all France . . . the wonder of wonders! But nothing like that could be expected of me . . . I had a depraved nature . . . It was inexplicable . . . There wasn't a speck or straw of honor in me . . . I was rotten through and through . . . repulsive, degenerate! I was unfeeling, I had no future . . . I was as dry as a salt herring . . . I was a hard-hearted debauchee . . . a dungheap . . . full of sullen rancor . . . I was life's disillusionment . . . I was grief itself. And I ate my lunch

and supper there, not to mention my morning coffee . . .
They did their Duty! I was their cross on earth! . . . I'd
never have a conscience! . . . I was nothing but a bundle
of debased instincts and a hollow that devoured my family's sorry pittance and all their sacrifices. In a way I was
a vampire . . . It was no use thinking about it . . .

In the Passage des Bérésinas, in all the shopwindows, a
lot of changes had taken place while I was gone . . .
They were going in for the "modern style" with lilac and
orange tints . . . Convolvulus and iris were all the rage
. . . They climbed up the windows . . . done up into
carved molding . . . Two perfume stores and a gramo-
phone shop opened . . . There were still the same pictures outside our theater, the Plush Barn . . . the same
posters in the stage entrance . . . They were still playing
Miss Helyett and still with the same tenor—Pitaluga . . .
He had a heavenly voice; every Sunday he bowled over his
female admirers in the *Elevation* at Notre-Dame-des-Victoires . . . For twelve months every shop in the Passage
was talking about the way this Pitaluga sang "Minuit
Chrétien" at Saint-Eustache on Christmas . . . Every
year he was more swooning, more wonderful, more super-
natural . . .

There was talk of installing electricity in all the shops
in the Passage. Then they'd get rid of the gas that started
whistling at four o'clock in the afternoon from three hundred and twenty jets . . . it stank so bad in that confined
space (added to the urine from the dogs, which were getting to be more and more plentiful) that along about seven
o'clock some of the lady customers began to feel faint.
There was even talk of tearing us down completely, of dis-
mantling the whole gallery! Of removing our big glass roof
and building a street eighty feet wide right where we were
living . . . My oh my! But the rumors weren't very
serious, actually it was poppycock, prison gossip. We were
prisoners in a glass cage and prisoners we'd always be
. . . Forever and regardless . . . No getting around it
. . . The law of the jungle . . .

Once in a while the poor bastards got crazy ideas . . .
fantastic fairy tales passed from mouth to mouth as they
were standing outside their shops, especially in hot weather

. . . Like bubbles oozing out of their brains . . . before the September storms. They'd dreamed up harebrained schemes, monumental rackets, all they could think of was big deals, wild swindles . . . Nightmares . . . they saw themselves expropriated, persecuted by the State! They worked themselves up, they went completely off their rockers, they were absolutely crackers, maddened with hokum. Ordinarily so pale, they went crimson . . .

Before going to bed, they'd pass around fantastic estimates, wild memoranda showing the staggering, but absolutely indispensable sums they'd demand if anybody mentioned moving. My oh my! By God, the authorities were in for a little trouble if they tried to turn them out . . . The Council of State didn't know what resistance meant! Don't you worry! And the chancellery and the whole damn government! . . . They'd shit in their pants. They'd see who they were talking to! Oh ho! And the Hall of Writs and Records . . . The whole rotten gang and then some! By my grandmother's crabs! The sparks would fly . . . It wasn't going to be any pushover, hell, no . . . Over their dead bodies . . . they'd lock themselves up in their rooms! In the end they'd have to disembowel the whole Bank of France to build them new shops . . . exactly the same! to the milligram! to two decimals! That's what we're asking, or the deal is off! We won't budge! Now you know the score! That's our last word! . . . Well, in a pinch they'd accept a settlement . . . A big one . . . They wouldn't say no . . . They might agree . . . But it's got to be on the level . . . An income for life! A nice juicy one, guaranteed to the hilt by the Bank of France, to be spent any way they pleased! They'd go fishing! For ninety years if they felt like it! And nightclubs day and night! And that wouldn't be the end of it! They'd have royalties and claims and country houses and other indemnities besides . . . astronomical . . . incalculable!

Well then? It was all a question of guts! The whole thing was perfectly simple, no use arguing . . . Stand up for your rights, don't weaken . . . That was their point of view . . . It was the heat, the terrible atmosphere, the electricity in the air . . . That way at least they weren't shouting at each other . . . They all got together on their "claims" . . . Everybody was in agreement . . . They were all hypnotized on the future . . . Everybody was hoping to be evicted.

All the neighbors in the Passage were flabbergasted at the dimensions I had assumed . . . I was getting to be a big bruiser. I'd almost doubled in bulk . . . That would cost even more when we went to the Deserving Classes for my outfit . . . I tried on my father's clothes They burst at the shoulders, I couldn't even get into his pants. I needed everything new. I'd just have to wait . . .

On her way home from her errands Madame Béruse, the glovemaker, dropped in just to see how I looked: "His mother can be proud of him," she finally concluded. "His stay abroad has done him good." She repeated that wherever she went. The others came in too to form an opinion of their own. The old caretaker of the Passage, Gaston the hunchback, who picked up all the gossip, found me changed, but in his opinion I was thinner. They couldn't really agree, everybody had his own idea. In addition, they wanted to know all about England. They asked me for details about how the *Engleesh* lived over there . . . I spent all my time in the shop, waiting for them to clothe me. Visios, the sailor, the one with the pipes, Charonne, the gilder, Madame Isard from the dry-cleaning shop, they all wanted to know what we ate at my school in Rochester. Especially about the vegetables. Was it really true they ate them raw, or hardly cooked? And the beer and the water? If I'd had whiskey? If the women had big teeth . . . kind of like horses? And what about their feet? A lot of applesauce. And their tits? Did they have any? All this with a lot of snide remarks and scandalized looks.

But what they really wanted was for me to say something in English. They were just dying to hear me, they didn't care if they understood or not . . . the effect was what they wanted . . . to hear me talk a little . . . My mother didn't make too much of a fuss, but all the same it would have made her mighty proud to have me display my talents . . . put all those busybodies in their place . . .

All I knew was: "*River . . . water . . . no trouble . . . no fear*" and maybe two or three more things . . . It really didn't amount to much. Anyway I didn't feel like it . . . I wasn't in the mood . . . It made my mother miserable to see I was just as stubborn as ever. I wasn't worthy of all their sacrifices. The neighbors were vexed too, they began to make long faces, they thought I was acting like a pigheaded mule . . . "He hasn't changed a bit," said Gaston, the hunchback. "He'll never change . . . he's still the same as when he used to piss on my gates . . . I could never make him stop."

He'd never been able to stomach me . . . "It's lucky his father isn't here," my mother consoled herself. "He'd feel so badly. He'd be beside himself, poor man . . . to see you so ungracious . . . so boorish . . . so antagonistic . . . so unfriendly . . . so horrid to everybody! . . . How do you expect to get ahead? Especially nowadays, the way things are in business . . . with all the competition? You think you're the only one that's looking for a job? Only yesterday he was saying: 'Good Lord, if only he lands on his feet! We're on the brink of disaster . . .' "

Just then Uncle Édouard turned up . . . he saved my life . . . He was in high good humor . . . He gave everybody in general a good hearty greeting . . . He'd just put on his beautiful checked suit for the first time, the new summer style, from England as a matter of fact, with a mauve derby, the latest thing, fastened to his buttonhole with a thin ribbon. He seized both my hands, he shook them heartily, a real knockdown, drag-out *"shake-hands."* He was wild about England . . . He'd always wanted to take a little trip over there . . . He kept putting it off because he wanted to learn the names for the things in his business first . . . pump, and so on. He was counting on me to teach him the language . . . My mother was still sniveling about my attitude, my repulsive, hostile ways . . . Far from siding with her he took my part right away . . . In two words he told all those insignificant cockroaches that they were dense, that they didn't know a thing about foreign influences . . . especially England . . . When you come from over there, it changes you completely! It makes you more laconic, more reserved, it gives you a certain aloofness, in a word, distinction. And it's a good thing . . . Why, of course! In high-class business nowadays . . . especially when you're selling . . . the

main thing is to hold your tongue . . . It's a sign of breed-
ing . . . that's what counts in a salesman today . . .
That's right . . . The old style is dead, through, washed
up . . . your slobbering . . . obsequious . . . voluble
salesman . . . . People are sick of them . . . That's
all right for punks out in the sticks, for small-town
jokers . . . In Paris you can't get away with it . . .
If you try that stuff in the Sentier quarter, they'll throw you
out . . . It makes a crawling, servile impression . . .
Got to keep up with the times . . . According to him I
was dead right . . . That was the line he gave them . . .

His patter was a great comfort to my mother . . . it set
her mind at rest . . . she heaved big sighs . . . she was
really relieved . . . But the rest of them, the lousy stool
pigeons, were still hostile . . . They had their ideas . . .
and nobody could make them change their mind . . .
They griped in accompaniment . . . I'd never get ahead
with those kind of manners. It was out of the question.

Uncle Édouard did his best, he racked his brains and
talked himself blue in the face . . . They stuck to their
guns . . . They were stubborner than mules, they kept
repeating that anywhere in the world . . . if you want to
earn an honest living, you've got to be friendly and courteous . . . that's the first requirement.

Days and days passed and we hardly saw any more
customers. It was midsummer and they'd all gone to the
country. My mother finally decided that in spite of her bad
leg and the doctor's orders, she'd go out to Chatou and try
to sell a little something. I'd keep the shop while she was
gone. We had no other alternative . . . we had to bring
in some money. First to buy me a new suit and two pairs
of shoes, and then to paint our whole shop front in attractive colors before the new season started.

Our windows looked heartbreaking beside the others
. . . They were pearl-gray and greenish, while next door
there was Vertune's dry-cleaning shop, all brand-new, a
fancy yellow and sky-blue, and on the other side the
Gomeuse stationery store, an immaculate white, decorated
with scrolls and jiggers and a sweet little pattern of little
birds on branches . . . All that meant a big outlay . . .
And we'd have to do it.

She didn't say a word to my father, she just took the train with an enormous bundle weighing at least forty-five pounds.

Out in Chatou she got started right away . . . She scrounged a stand from behind the Town Hall and set herself up behind the station, a good location. She handed out all her cards to let people know about the shop. In the afternoon she began traipsing around again, loaded like a mule, all over town, looking for villas where some customers might be hiding . . . When she came home to the Passage in the evening, she was so done in she could hardly stand up, her leg was so tied up with cramps she could have screamed, her knee was swollen, and the worst of all was her dislocated ankle . . . She stretched out in my room while waiting for my father to come home . . . She put on soothing lotion . . . good cold compresses.

On her suburban tours she sold her stuff any old place dirt-cheap, so as to bring in a little cash . . . We needed it so bad . . . "So as not to haul it back home," she explained . . . Only two or three people came to the shop all the time she was gone . . . So it made more sense to close up completely . . . that way I could go with her to the suburbs and tote her biggest bundles. We didn't have Madame Divonne anymore to hold the shop down when we were absent. We hung out a sign saying: "Returning immediately." We took the door handle with us.

Uncle Édouard really loved his sister, no fooling, it got him down to see her so miserable, wasting away, getting more and more run-down from all her work and troubles . . . He was worried about her health and her morale . . . He thought of her all the time. The day after a trip to Chatou she couldn't stand up, her face was ravaged with the pain in her leg. She whined like a dog and lay all twisted on the linoleum . . . She'd flop on the floor as soon as my father went out. She said it was cooler than the bed. If he caught her like that when he came home from the office, wan and disheveled, massaging her leg in the dishpan, her skirts hiked up to her chin, he beat it upstairs, he pretended he hadn't seen her, he raced past, he was gone in a flash. He'd plunge into his typewriting or his watercolors . . . We always sold a few, especially his "Sailboats," we had a whole collection of them, and the "Coun-

cils of Cardinals" . . . They had the liveliest colors . . .
Really striking . . . Those things always look good in a
room. And it was high time he got a wiggle on . . . It
was coming on the end of the month . . . To make up for
closing in the daytime during our wanderings through
Chatou, we stayed open pretty late . . . People would go
for a stroll after dinner . . . Especially if a storm came
up . . . If a customer came in, my mother, quick as
lightning, hid the basin and all her wads of cotton under
the couch in the middle of the room . . . She'd pull herself up with a smile . . . She'd start her spiel . . .
Around her neck, I remember well, she'd tie a big muslin
cabbage-bow . . . They were all the rage at the time
. . . It made her head look very big.

Uncle Édouard worked like a dog too, in his own way,
but he had nothing to be sorry about, he got results . . .
He was doing better and better in his line . . . bicycle
accessories . . . That was getting to be a good business,
very good in fact. Soon he was able to buy a share in a
garage, on the edge of Levallois, with some reliable
friends.

He was enterprising by nature and besides he was crazy
about inventions . . . any kind of mechanical idea . . .
Those things really sent him . . . Right away he'd in-
vested the four thousand francs of his inheritance in a
patent for a bicycle pump, the latest thing, it folded up so
small you could keep it in your pocket . . . He always
had two or three of them on him, ready to demonstrate.
He'd blow them up people's noses . . He pretty near lost
his four thousand francs. The sellers were crooks . . . He
managed to wriggle out of it thanks to his quick wits and a
telephone call . . . a conversation he'd overheard at the
last minute . . . An amazing stroke of luck! . . . In
another minute he'd have been cooked . . .

My mother admired my uncle. She wanted me to be
like him . . . After all I needed a model . . . For want
of my father, my uncle was somebody to look up to . . .
She didn't say it straight out, but she dropped hints . . .
In my father's opinion Édouard was a hell of an example,
he was idiotic, absolutely unbearable, grasping, vulgar,
always getting a kick out of something nonsensical . . .

He got on my father's nerves . . . with his mechanical gadgets, his jalopies, his three-wheelers, his funny-looking pumps! Just hearing him talk irritated the hell out of him.

When my mother took it into her head to sing her brother's praises, to tell everybody about his plans, his success, his bright ideas, he'd always interrupt her . . . He wouldn't stand for it. Certainly not. He'd made up his mind once and for all . . . He put it all down to luck . . . "He's disgustingly lucky and that's all there is to it . . ." That was my father's verdict. He never went any further. He couldn't run him down anymore, we still owed him money and gratitude . . . But he had to hold himself in to keep from giving him a piece of his mind . . . Édouard must have known . . . It was perfectly obvious . . . He put up with my father's dislike, he didn't want to make trouble, he was always thinking of his sister.

He was very tactful, he just dropped in for a minute to see how we were getting along . . . wasn't Mama feeling a little better? He was alarmed about the way she looked and the monumental loads she peddled around . . . Afterwards her joints were so stiff she'd moan for days on end . . . It worried him more and more . . . She was getting worse . . . He finally decided to speak to my father . . . The three of them talked it over, and finally they agreed it was high time she took a rest . . . that this couldn't go on . . . But how could she rest? They hit on a plan . . . we'd take on a cleaning woman, maybe two three hours a day, even that would be a relief . . . She wouldn't have to climb stairs nearly so much . . . She wouldn't have to sweep under the furniture . . . she wouldn't need to go shopping . . . But how in our present circumstances could we spend all that money? . . . The whole thing was a pipe dream, sheer lunacy . . . It would be feasible only if I found work . . . Then, with my earnings, which would go into the till after all, maybe, once we'd paid the rent, we could think about a maid . . . That would make it easier for Mama . . . She wouldn't have to work so hard or run around so much . . . They'd thought this out all by themselves . . . They were delighted with their decision . . . They'd appeal to my better nature . . . they'd put me to the test. I wasn't going to be a perverse, self-centered screwball anymore . . . Now I too would have my role, my aim in life! To make things easier for my mama! . . . On the double, boy . . . Get in there and fight . . . find yourself a job! That's the ticket! As soon as they'd bought me my job-hunting suit . . . pronto, roll up your sleeves . . . do your stuff! No more mistakes! No more shilly-shallying! Down to business and no more questions! Show your mettle! Your perseverance! By God, I would! What a marvelous goal in life! It was already in the bag, I thought . . .

First I needed shoes. We went to the Prince Consort again . . . The Broomfields after all were a little too expensive . . . especially for two pairs with buttons . . . And yet, once you begin moving around, what you really need is three or four pairs.

For the suit and pants I had measurements taken at the Deserving Classes, near Les Halles, that was a gilt-edge firm, with a reputation going back a hundred years, especially for all sorts of cheviots and even for "dressy" goods, stuff that lasted practically forever . . . "Working-man's outfits" they called them . . . Only the price was steep. A terrible sacrifice!

It was still August, I was being outfitted for the winter . . . The warm weather doesn't last long . . . But at that particular moment the heat was stifling . . . Oh well, it wouldn't be long, I'd live through it . . . The cold, the bad weather, goes on and on . . . In the meantime, while I was looking around, suppose I suffocated to death . . . hell, I'd simply carry my coat over my arm. I'd put it on as I was ringing the bell . . . it was simple . . .

My mother hadn't said how much it would take out of our household funds to outfit me . . . from top to toe . . . Considering our resources, it was a staggering sum . . . We scraped the bottom of the drawers . . . She ran herself ragged, she racked her brains, she'd dash out to Le Vésinet and come back by the next train, hightail it to Neuilly, to Chatou on market days, hauling her whole stock, everything that wasn't too repulsive . . . that was more or less negotiable . . . She couldn't sell it . . . She couldn't make up the amount . . . It was a real head-ache . . . we were always twenty or twenty-five or thirty-five francs short . . . On top of the taxes that kept

raining down on us and the seamstress's wages and the
rent that was two months overdue . . . An avalanche, it
was sickening . . . She didn't say a word to Papa . . .
She kept looking for some new dodge . . . She took five
of his best water-colors to the rue d'Aboukir, to old Madame Heurgon Gustave (a real filthy junk shop), for less
than a quarter of the usual price. On consignment, so to
speak . . . In short, she tried dozens of crummy expedi-
ents to scrape up the full amount . . . She wouldn't buy
anything on credit . . . After desperate weeks and all
sorts of plots and stratagems I was finally dressed, absolutely resplendent, good strong material, but very hot . . .
When I saw myself dolled up brand-new, I lost some of my
confidence! Hell! It made me feel funny. I still had the will,
but nasty doubts began to crop up . . . Maybe I'd per-
spire too much in my winter suit? I was like a walking
oven . . .

It was God's truth that I didn't feel the least bit pleased
with myself anymore, or optimistic about the future . . .
The immediate prospect of facing bosses . . . of reeling
off my cock-and-bull stories, of shutting myself up in their
rotten morgues, gave me a pain in the gizzard. Over in
lousy England I'd got out of the habit of being shut in . . .
I'd have to get used to it again. It was no joke . . . It
knocked me for a loop just to look at a possible boss! It
made me gag . . . Just figuring out how to get to places
gave me the creeps . . . It was so hot the nameplates on
the doors were melting . . . It was 102 in the shade.

Of course what my folks were saying was perfectly
reasonable . . . that I was at the critical age, the turning
point . . . this was the time to make a supreme effort
. . . to force the gates of destiny . . . to start a career
. . . it was now or never . . . All that was fine and
dandy . . . But even if I took off my suit, my collar, my
shoes, I couldn't stop sweating . . . The sweat ran down
in streams . . . I took the itineraries I knew. I passed
outside the Gorloge's place . . . It gave me the shivers to
see their house and the big carriage door . . . Just thinking about that incident gave me a twinge in the asshole
. . . Holy shit! Some sweet memory!

Faced with the enormity of my task . . . thinking it
over, I lost heart, I just wanted to sit down . . . I hadn't

much money to spend on bocks . . . even little glasses
for ten centimes . . . I hung around in doorways . . .
There was always plenty of shade and treacherous drafts
. . . I sneezed something terrible . . . It got to be a
habit while I was thinking . . . I kept thinking . . . I
thought so much that in the end I almost agreed with my
father . . . I realized . . . experience proved it . . .
that I was worthless . . . I had disastrous impulses . . .
I was completely thickheaded and lazy . . . I didn't deserve their great kindness . . . their terrible sacrifices
. . . I felt absolutely unworthy, infectious, loathsome
. . . I knew what I had to do and I struggled desperately,
but I wasn't up to it . . . less than ever . . . I wasn't
improving with age . . . And I was getting thirstier and
thirstier . . . The heat in itself is a calamity . . . Looking for a job in August is the most thirsty-making thing in
the world, on account of the stairs and the terror that
parches your throat every time . . . while you're cooling
your heels . . . I thought of my mother . . . of her leg
and the cleaning woman we might be able to take on if I
could get somebody to hire me . . . It didn't revive my
enthusiasm . . . I lashed myself, I screwed up all my
strength to rise to the ideal, I couldn't feel sublime anymore. Since Gorloge I had lost all my enthusiasm about
work. It was pitiful! And in spite of all the sermons I'd
had, I felt that I was more miserable than all the other
bastards, more woebegone than the whole lot of them
together . . . What disgusting egotism! All I cared about
was my own troubles, and there they were, all of them
horrible, they made me stink worse than a senile camembert . . . I was rotting in the heat, collapsing with sweat
and shame, climbing stairs, oozing over the bells, I was
falling apart, I'd lost all dignity, all character.

With nothing on my mind but a slight bellyache, I
drifted through the old streets, rue du Paradis, rue
d'Hauteville, rue des Jeûneurs, the Sentier quarter . . .
in the end I took off not only my heavy jacket but also my
extra-solid celluloid collar, it would have killed a dog, and
besides it gave me pimples. I got dressed again on the
landing. I looked up more addresses, I found them in the
directory. At the post office I drew up lists. I hadn't any
money left for a drink. My mother left her purse, the little

silver one, knocking around on the furniture . . . I eyed
it avidly . . . Such heat is demoralizing . . . Frankly,
I came damn near swiping it . . . At a certain point . . .
two steps from the fountain . . . I'd get mighty thirsty
. . . I think my mother noticed, she gave me two francs
more . . .

When I came back from my long wanderings, always
futile and useless, up and down stairs and neighborhoods,
I had to fix myself up before going back into the Passage,
so I wouldn't look too miserable, too crestfallen at meals.
That wouldn't have gone down at all. That was one thing
my folks couldn't have taken, that they'd never been able
to stomach, that they'd never understand, that I, their son,
should be without hope and heroic fortitude . . . They
wouldn't have stood for it . . . I had no right to my share
of lamentations, certainly not . . . Tragedies and con-
dolences were their private preserve . . . All that was for
my parents . . . Children were thugs, hoodlums, ungrateful, thoughtless scum . . . The minute I dropped the
slightest complaint, even the wee little beginning of a complaint, they both saw red . . . That was anathema! Sacri-
lege! Abomination!

"What's that, you little shitheel? What colossal nerve!"
How, with youth on my side, could I put on such airs?
What a beastly imposture! What diabolical impertinence!
Ah! The effrontery of it! Heavens above! Didn't I have my
best years ahead of me! All the treasures of existence! And
I thought I was entitled to gripe . . . About my piddling
little setbacks? Ah! Jumping Jehoshaphat! What monstrous
insolence! What absolute degeneracy! What inconceivable
rottenness! They'd have beaten me to a pulp to make me
eat my blasphemies. Her bad leg, her abscesses, her horrible
sufferings were forgotten . . . My mother leapt to her
feet! "You little wretch! Right this minute! You heartless
little reprobate! Take back those insults . . ."

I did as I was told. I couldn't exactly make out what the
joys of youth were, but they seemed to know . . . They
would have massacred me without hesitation if I hadn't
recanted . . . If I expressed the slightest doubt or seemed
to be running things down, they went right off the handle
. . . They'd rather have seen me dead than hear me pro-
fane the gifts of heaven. My mother's eyes went white with

fury when I let myself be carried away! She'd have bashed me in the nose with anything that was handy just to make me stop . . . My only right was to rejoice! to sing hymns of praise! I was born under a lucky star! Imagine a miserable worm like me having parents who dedicated themselves exclusively . . . wasn't that enough? . . . to the worries, the troubles, the tragic fatalities of existence . . . I was just a brute and nothing else! Silence! An unconscionable family burden! . . . My business was to do as I was told . . . to fix everything up sweet and nice again! To make amends for my faults and nauseating propensities! . . . The misery was all for them! if there was any complaining to do, that was their department! They were the ones who understood life! They were the ones with sensitive souls! Who was it that suffered atrociously? Under the most excruciating circumstances? From outrageous fortune? . . . It was they. They alone, always and forever. They didn't want me meddling, even going through the motions of helping them . . . taking my small share . . . It was their absolute monopoly! That struck me as very unjust. We just couldn't see eye to eye.

They could talk and curse till they were blue in the face, I stuck to my convictions. I too felt myself to be a victim in every way. On the steps of the Ambigu, right near the Wallace fountain,* all these thoughts came back at me . . . It was all as plain as day! . . .

If I'd finished pounding the sidewalks, another day wasted, I frankly aired my dogs . . . I smoked skinny little butts . . . I'd question the boys a little, the bums that hung around there, they always had plenty of dope and phony tips . . . They were big talkers . . . They'd seen all the ads, they knew about all the odd jobs . . . One of them was a tattooer, he clipped dogs on the side . . . They knew all the crummy rackets . . . the food market, the slaughterhouse, the wine market . . . They were as grimy as a railroad station, down at heel, crawling with dirt, they passed their crabs back and forth . . . That didn't cramp their cock-and-bull stories . . . their bragging and bluffing . . . they'd split a gut telling about their connections . . . their triumphs, their fancy deals . . . One big

* See Glossary.

delirious fantasy! . . . There was no limit to the dog they
put on . . . and they were perfectly capable of pulling a
knife . . . if anybody doubted they had a cousin in the
Cabinet . . . or of chucking him in the Canal Saint-
Martin . . . No claim was too wild . . . Even the cock-
eyedest sandwichmen . . . had certain pet episodes in
their lives that it wasn't healthy to laugh at . . . Fairy
tales drive people to crime even worse than liquor . . .
they were so moth-eaten they had no teeth left to chew
with, they'd sold their glasses . . . That didn't prevent
them from dishing out a line . . . You can't imagine such
hokum . . . I could gradually see myself getting to be
exactly like them . . .

It was about five in the afternoon when I suspended my
efforts . . . called it a day . . . It was a good place to
convalesce in, a regular resort . . . We'd give our feet a
good rest . . . Ambigu Beach, catering to bums and
down-and-outers. Some of them weren't so lazy, but they
figured it was better to drink up their luck than drag around
in the heat. Which is easy enough to understand . . . All
along the theater front, under the chestnut trees, there was
a fence . . . handy to hang your stuff on . . . we took
it nice and easy . . . we exchanged mugs of beer . . .
There was white sausage "à la mode" and garlic and red
wine and Camembert . . . on the ramp and the stairs it
was like an academy . . . All kinds . . . They hadn't
changed much . . . since the days when I went out peddling for Gorloge . . . There were lots of little pimps,
and dicks with plenty of time on their hands . . . stool
pigeons of all ages . . . who made good money tipping off
the cops . . . There'd always be a card game going on
. . . And two or three bookies, trying to drum up trade
. . . There were overage salesmen who'd turned in their
sample cases . . . nobody was willing to hire them anymore . . . There were little fairies still too green for the
Bois . . . One of them came around every day, his
specialty was the urinals and especially the crusts of bread
soaking in the drains . . . He told us his adventures . . .
He knew an old Jew who was nuts about those *babas* . . .
They'd go and eat the stuff together . . . One day they
got caught . . . We didn't see him for a couple of months
. . . He was changed beyond recognition when he got

back . . . The cops had given him such a going-over he was fresh out of the hospital . . . That shellacking had turned him inside out . . . He'd moulted in the meanwhile . . . He had a big bass voice . . . He'd let his beard grow . . . He'd given up eating shit.

Another of the charms of the place was the procuress. She had a kid in long red stockings . . . she'd walk her up and down outside the Folies Dramatiques . . . They said she cost twenty francs . . . She'd have suited me fine . . . That was a fortune at the time . . . They didn't even look in our direction . . . we were too crummy . . . We whooped at them, but it didn't get us anywhere . . .

We exchanged newspapers and the jokes we'd picked up on our rounds . . . The bad part of it was the crabs . . . Naturally I caught them too . . . Those cooties out in front of the Ambigu were a pestilence . . . The worst of all were the butt pickers that hung around the terraces of the cafés . . . A whole bunch of them would drop over to the Saint-Louis hospital for ointment . . . Then they'd go off together and rub it in . . .

I can still see my straw hat, the reinforced boater, I always had it in my hand, it must have weighed a good two pounds . . . It was supposed to last me two years, if possible three . . . I wore it till I was drafted, which was in 1912. I took my collar off one more time, it had left a terrible mark, completely scarlet . . . All men had that red furrow around their necks in those days, they kept it until their dying day. It was like a magic sign.

When we'd finished commenting on the ads, all those crazy come-ons, we'd start on the sports column, the try-outs at the Buffalo Stadium and the forthcoming six-day bicycle race, with Morin and pretty-boy Faber, who was the favorite . . . Those who preferred the horse races set up on the opposite corner . . . The little streetwalkers moseyed back and forth . . . They weren't interested in us, they went on walking . . . We weren't good for anything but talk, a bunch of no-soap artists . . .

The very first motor buses, the marvelous Madeleine-Bastille with the high top-deck, gave it the works at that point . . . set off all their explosives to make it up the hill . . . It was some show, an uproar! They dashed boiling water against the Porte Saint-Martin. The passengers

on the balcony took part in the performance . . . They
were nuts. They could have capsized the whole thing the
way they all leaned over on the same side at once in their
ecstatic excitement . . . They clutched the tassels, the
bars and knobs that ran around the railing . . . They
shouted and cheered . . . Horses were a thing of the past,
it was plain as day . . . It was only on bad roads that
they still had a chance . . . Uncle Édouard had always
said so . . . well, in front of the Ambigu, between five and
seven, I witnessed the coming of Progress . . . but I still
didn't find a job . . . Every night I came home empty-
handed . . . I couldn't seem to find the boss who'd give
me a new start in life . . . They wouldn't take me as an
apprentice, I was too old . . . And to be a·regular employee I was apparently much too young . . . I'd never
get past the ungrateful age . . . And even if I talked
English beautifully, it made no difference . . . They had
no use for it. . . Foreign languages were only for the
big shops . . . And there they didn't take beginners . . .
I was out of luck all along the line . . . any way I went
about it . . . it was always the same old shit . . .

Very gently, in small doses, I let my mother in on the
ideas I'd been piling up . . . I told her my prospects
didn't look too brilliant . . . She wasn't one to be discouraged . . . She'd begun to make other plans, this time
for herself, something new, something more backbreaking
than ever. She'd been thinking about it a long time and
now she made up her mind . . . "You see, my boy, I
won't tell your father, so keep this to yourself . . . The
poor man, it would come as a terrible disappointment . . .
He's suffering enough already to see me miserable . . .
But between you and me, Ferdinand, I don't think our poor
shop . . . sh-h . . . will ever pick up again . . . Hum,
hum, I fear the worst. In our lace business . . . there's
no denying it . . . the competition has become impossible
to meet . . . Your father doesn't understand . . . He's
not right in the thick of it, day in day out . . . luckily,
thank God for that . . . What you need nowadays isn't
a few hundred francs, but thousands and thousands, if you
want to lay in a really up-to-date stock! Where can we find
that kind of money? Who's going to give us credit, I ask
you? It's only the big businesses that can afford it, the

enormous stores . . . Our little shops are doomed . . .
It's only a question of time . . . a few years . . . or
months maybe . . . It's a desperate struggle for nothing
. . . The big stores are crushing us . . . I've seen it
coming for a long time . . . Even in Caroline's day things
were getting harder and harder . . . it's nothing new . . .
The slack season went on forever . . . longer each year
. . . worse and worse . . . Well, my boy, one thing I've
got is energy . . . you know that . . . We've got to get
out of this mess! . . . Now here's what I'm going to try
as soon as my leg is better . . . if I could even go out a
little. I'm going to one of the big firms and ask for a card
. . . I won't have any trouble . . . They've known me
for years . . . They know I'm a go-getter . . . they
know I've got plenty of gumption . . . They know your
father and I are the soul of honesty . . . that they can
trust us with anything . . . no matter what . . Yes, I
don't mind saying it . . . Marescal! . . . Bataille! . . .
Roubique! . . . they've known me for thirty years . . .
as a saleswoman and shopkeeper . . . I won't have any
trouble finding something . . . I don't need any other
references . . . I don't like working for other people . . .
But at present I have no choice . . . Your father won't
suspect . . . not a thing . . . I'll tell him I'm going to
see a customer . . . He won't be any the wiser . . . I'll
go out as usual and I'll always be back on time . . . Poor
man, he'd hang his head for shame to think I was working
for somebody else . . . He'd be humiliated . . . I want
to spare him that . . . at all costs . . . He'd never get
over it! . . . I wouldn't know how to buck him up . . .
His wife working for strangers! . . . Good lord! Even
with Caroline it was almost more than he could bear . . .
Anyway, he won't know a thing! . . . I'll make my rounds
regularly . . . One day one street, the next day another
. . . It'll be a good deal simpler than this eternal balancing act . . . this acrobatics that's killing us . . . Always
batting our brains out . . . figuring out how to stop up
holes . . . It's infernal! It would be the end of us! We
won't have nearly as much worry . . . Pay here! Pay
there! Will we make it? How awful! It's torture . . . We
won't make much, but it'll be regular . . . no more surprises, no more nightmares! That's what we've always

needed . . . A steady income! It'll be a change from the
last twenty years! What a rat race! Heavens above! Always
running after five francs! . . . And the customers that
never pay! You've hardly paid one bill when another one
comes in . . . Oh yes, independence is all very fine! It
was my dream, my mother's too! But I can't go on . . .
We'll make ends meet, you'll see, if we all put our
shoulders to the wheel . . . We'll have our cleaning
woman! since that's what he wants . . . Besides, I need
one. You couldn't call it a luxury."

That was just what my mother wanted . . . some horrible new thing to do . . . something inconceivably difficult . . . Nothing could be too hard, too grueling! If
she'd had her own way she'd have done everybody's work.
Run the shop . . . kept the whole family going all by
herself . . . and the seamstress too . . . She never tried
to draw comparisons, to understand . . . As long as it
was lousy work, as long as there was plenty of sweat and
heartache, she was satisfied . . . That was her nature
. . . Whether I ran myself ragged or not, it wouldn't make
a particle of difference . . . With a maid I was positive
she'd work fifty times harder . . . She was really attached
to her horrible fate . . . It wasn't the same with me
. . . I had a little worm in my conscience. But next to her
I was a parasite . . . Maybe that came from my stay in
Rochester, from doing nothing at the Merrywins . . . I'd
got to be frankly lazy. Instead of chasing after work I'd
just sit and think . . . When you come right down to it,
my job hunting was pretty feeble . . . But when I saw a
doorbell, I'd fold . . . I had no martyr's blood in my
veins . . . Hell no! I didn't have the right attitude for a
poor bastard . . . I kept putting things off till next day
. . . I'd try a different neighborhood, not quite so hot, a
little breezier . . . a little shadier . . . for my little bit
of job hunting. I took a gander at the shops around the
Tuileries . . . under those beautiful arcades . . . on the
broad avenues . . . I thought I'd ask the jewelers if they
could use a young man . . . I was baking in my jacket
. . . They didn't need anybody . . . In the end I stayed
in the Tuileries . . . I'd pass the time of day with the
floozies that were wandering around . . . I spent hours in
the greenery . . . not doing a damn thing, just like in

England, except I'd have a cup of water now and then and work the waffle machines, the little dials on cylinders . . . There was also the fellow with the cocoanut drink and the mechanical band by the hobbyhorses . . .

That was all a long time ago . . . One evening I caught sight of my father . . . He was on the other side of the fence on his way to make his deliveries . . . To play it safe I stayed in the Carrousel . . . I hid between the statues . . . Once I went into the Louvre . . . It was free at the time . . . I didn't dig the pictures, but up on the fourth floor I discovered the Navy Museum. I couldn't drag myself away. I went regularly. I spent whole weeks there . . . I knew all the ship models by heart . . . I stood all alone by the showcases . . . I forgot all my troubles, all about jobs and bosses, the whole mess . . . There was nothing in my head but boats . . . Sailboats, even models of sailboats, send me frankly off my rocker . . . I'd have really liked to be a sailor . . . Papa too in his time . . . Our lives hadn't panned out right . . . I had a pretty fair idea of what was what . . .

When I came home at suppertime, he asked me what I'd been doing . . . why I was so late . . . Job hunting, I said . . . Mama had resigned herself. Papa grunted into his plate . . . He didn't press the subject.

They'd told my mother she could try her luck right away at the market in Le Pecq or even Saint-Germain, that now was just the time because of all the rich people . . . it was the new style . . . who were renting villas all over the hillside . . . They'd be sure to appreciate her lace for their bedroom curtains, their bedspreads, and those pretty little blinds . . . A golden opportunity . . .

She hightailed it out there quick. For a whole week she traipsed up and down all the roads with her whole caboodle . . . From Chatou station almost as far as Meulan . . . always on foot and limping . . . Luckily the weather was marvelous! Rain would have been a disaster. She was delighted, she'd sold a good part of her white elephants, fringed point-lace and heavy Spanish shawls that had been in drydock since the Empire. The people in the villas were developing a taste for our genuine curios. They were in a hurry to furnish their houses . . . They kind of lost their

heads . . . The view of Paris from the hillside made them
optimistic, enthusiastic . . . My mother pushed hard, she
followed up on her luck. Except one fine morning her leg
wouldn't move at all . . . That was the end of her foolishness, of her heroic treks . . . Even the other knee was on
fire . . . It swelled up double . . .

Capron came running . . . All he could do was take
note of her condition . . . He threw up his arms to high
heaven . . . An abscess was forming, there was no room
for doubt . . . The joint was affected, it was swollen . . .
Her fighting spirit was no use at all . . . She couldn't
move her rear end, she couldn't change sides or lift herself, not even an eighth of an inch . . . She let out piercing screams . . . She sighed the whole time, not so much
from the pain, she was as tough as Caroline, but because
her ailment had got her down.

It was a terrible defeat.

Naturally we had to take on a cleaning woman . . .
Our habits changed . . . Everything was at loose ends
. . . Mama lay on her bed, my father and I did most of
the work before we left in the morning, the sweeping, the
carpets, the sidewalk outside our door, the shop . . . All
of a sudden my dawdling, my hesitation, my squirming
were over . . . I had to get a wiggle on, to find some work
in a hurry and p.d.q.

Hortense, the cleaning woman, came in for an hour in
the afternoon and for two hours after supper. She worked
all day in a grocery store on the rue Vivienne next to the
post office. She was a reliable soul . . . She made a little
extra working for us . . . She was down on her luck, she
had to sweat double, her husband had lost all their money
trying to set himself up as a plumber. Besides she had two
kids and an aunt dependent on her . . . She couldn't
ever sit down . . . My mother was riveted to her bed and
had to listen to her whole story. One morning my father
and I carried her down. We put her in a chair. We had to
be very careful not to bump her on the stairs or drop her.
We set her up in a corner of the shop, wedged in with
cushions . . . so she could answer the customers . . . It
was rough . . . And having to attend to her knee . . .
and put on "vulnerary" compresses . . .

As for looks, Hortense, even though she worked like an

ox, was pretty crunchy . . . She herself always said that
she denied herself nothing, especially in the way of food,
her trouble was sleep! She had no time to go to bed . . .
It was eating that kept her going, especially café au lait
. . . She'd take at least ten cups a day . . . In her grocery store she ate enough for an army. Hortense was a
card, her stories even made my mother laugh on her bed
of pain . . . It made my father mad to find me in the
same room with her . . . He was afraid I'd lay her . . .
It's true that I jerked off on account of her . . . who
doesn't? . . . but it really didn't amount to much, nothing
like England . . . I didn't put the same frenzy into it, the
flavor was gone, we were really too miserable for me to do
things right . . . Hell and damnation! . . . I wasn't in
the mood anymore . . . It was awful to be on the rocks
with the whole family . . . My head was pack-jammed
full of worries. . . It was a worse headache ·finding me a
job than before I went away . . . Seeing my mother's
distress, I started out again . . . I went looking for more
addresses . . . I did the Boulevards inside out, the Sentier quarter, the streets around the stock exchange . . .
Around the end of August that's certainly the worst of
neighborhoods . . . There's none stinkier, more stifling
. . . I pounded the stairs again with my collar, my tie, my
butterfly bow, my armored boater . . . I haven't forgotten
a single nameplate . . . coming or going . . . Jimmy
Blackwell and Careston, Exporters . . . Porogoff, Merchants . . . Tokima, Traders with Caracas and the
Congo . . . Herito and Kugelprunn, commission merchants for India and the East Indies . . .

Once more I was knocked out, fed up, resolute. I ran
my comb through my hair on my way into the building. I
attacked the stairs. I rang at the first door and then at
another . . . But all of a sudden everything went wrong
when I had to answer questions . . . If they asked me for
my references . . . or what kind of work I wanted to do
. . . my actual aptitudes . . . my demands . . . That
knocked the stuffings out of me . . . I stammered, I made
bubbles . . . I panicked . . . I mumbled vague apologies
and began to back out . . . The faces on those inquisi-
tors scared me green . . . All of a sudden I had this
queasy feeling . . . All the nerve trickled out of me. I

was drained . . . I took my bellyache out of there . . .
Even so, I started in again . . . I rang at the door across
the way . . . It was always the same monsters . . . I'd
do twenty like that before lunch . . . I even stopped going
home to eat. I just had too much on my mind . . . My
appetite was gone in advance . . . I was too fiendishly
thirsty . . . For two cents I wouldn't have gone home at
all. I knew by heart the scenes that were waiting for me.
My mother and all her suffering. My father all tangled up in
his typewriter, with his rages, his screwball ideas, his
insane bellowing . . . A gloomy prospect . . . I knew
the kind of compliments to expect . . . It caked my shit
to think about it . . . I stayed out by the banks of the
Seine, waiting for it to be two o'clock . . . I watched the
dogs swimming . . . I didn't even have a system anymore
. . . I just looked around at random . . . I searched the
whole Left Bank . . . At the rue du Bac my odyssey
would start in again . . . rue Jacob, rue Tournon . . . I
ran across businesses that were almost shut down . . .
agencies for textile mills that had gone out of existence
. . . in provinces that maybe France would recover some
day . . . dealers in objects so dismal they left you speechless . . . Even so I put on the charm . . . I plugged for
an interview at a shop that sold religious articles . . . I
attempted the impossible . . . I put on a good show in a
wholesale house for chasubles . . . It looked like they
were going to hire me in a chandelier factory . . . I was
out of my mind with joy . . . I was even beginning to
like the stuff . . . And then everything collapsed! In the
end the Saint-Sulpice quarter was a big disappointment to
me . . . They were having their troubles too . . . Everybody turned me out . . .

From pounding all those pavements my tootsies were on
fire . . . I took my shoes off wherever I could . . . I'd
give them a quick dip in the toilet . . . I could slip out of
my shoes in one second flat . . . That way I made the
acquaintance of a waiter in a café whose dogs hurt him
even worse than mine. He worked all day until past midnight on the enormous terrace of the German brasserie in
the Cour de la Croix-Nivert . . . Sometimes his shoes
hurt him so bad he stuck little pieces of ice inside . . . I

tried it . . . It helps for a little while, but then it's even worse.

My mother stayed like that in the back of her shop with her leg stretched out for three weeks. There weren't many customers . . . That gave her one more reason to eat her heart out . . . She couldn't go out at all . . .

There were only the neighbors that came in now and then to bat the breeze and keep her company . . . They brought her all the gossip . . . They worked her up good . . . Especially in connection with me they dreamed up the stinkingest stuff . . . Those bastards couldn't stand to see me doing nothing. Why couldn't I find a job? they kept asking . . . It was inconceivable that I should be getting nowhere so fast after such efforts, such extraordinary sacrifices . . . It surpassed the understanding! It was a mystery! Seeing me on the rocks like that gave them a pain . . . Oh-ho, not on your tintype! They wouldn't be saps like my parents . . . They wouldn't make that mistake . . . They made that perfectly plain . . . You wouldn't catch them working their fingers to the bone . . . for kids that didn't give a shit . . . They wouldn't bleed themselves white for their brats . . . Hell, no! Where did it get you? . . . Especially teaching them languages! Christ almighty Jesus, some joke! It only turned them into tramps, that's all . . . it certainly didn't do any good . . . There's the living proof, one look at me was enough . . . A job? I'd never find one! . . . I didn't inspire confidence . . . I just didn't look right . . . They knew, they'd known me all my life . . . And that's a fact.

That song and dance crushed my mother completely, especially in the state she was in, with her painful abscess that was getting worse and worse . . . The whole side of her leg was swollen now . . . Usually she restrained herself a little from repeating all that rot . . . But with the excruciating pain she was in she couldn't control her reflexes . . . She repeated the whole business to my father, almost word for word . . . He hadn't had a tantrum in a long time . . . He jumped at the opportunity . . . He began to holler that I was skinning him alive and my mother too, that I was his shame and opprobrium, that everything was my fault! The worst disasters, past and future! That I was driving him to suicide . . . that I was an absolutely unprecedented type of murderer! . . . He didn't say why . . . He whistled, he blew out so much steam there was a cloud between us . . . He tore his hair . . . He dug his fingers into his scalp till he drew blood . . . He cracked his nails . . . He gesticulated so wildly that he banged into the furniture . . . He knocked the sideboard over . . . The shop was very small . . . There wasn't room enough for a lunatic . . . He bumped into the umbrella stand . . . He sent two vases crashing. My mother tried to pick them up and gave her leg a terrible twist . . . She let out a yell so piercing . . . so horrible . . . that the neighbors all came running.

She almost fainted . . . We gave her smelling salts . . . Little by little she came to . . . She began to breathe, she settled back on her chairs . . . "Ah!" she says. "It's burst." She meant her abscess . . . She was delighted, Visios came and squeezed the pus out. He was used to it. He'd done it often on shipboard.

I was very nicely dressed with my choker collar, my shoes polished fit to kill, but my mother, thinking it over in the room behind the shop, decided I still wasn't quite right . . . that I still didn't look serious enough in spite of my watch and my darkened chain . . . In spite of all their lectures there was still something of the hoodlum about me . . . The way I carried money, for instance, whole pockets full of change . . . That's what gave me my disreputable look . . . like a tough! A tout! Revolting!

She made up her mind on the spot . . . She sent Hortense to the Bazar Vivienne . . . for the ideal change purse . . . Good and solid, hand-stitched, with plenty of compartments, indestructible . . . In addition she made me a present of four fifty-centime pieces . . . But I wasn't to spend them . . . ever! . . . Those were my savings . . . to give me a taste for thrift! She put in my address too, in case of an accident in the street . . . It gave her pleasure. I raised no objection.

I quickly drank up the little nest egg in ten-centime bocks . . . The summer of 1910 was abominably hot . . . Luckily it was easy to wet your whistle around the

Temple . . . It was cheap on the stands all along the
street . . . whole sidewalks full of drinks . . . and the
little bars in the street fairs . . .

I transferred my efforts to the jewel setters. That's a
real trade after all and I knew something about it . . . I
went back to the Marais . . . It was unbearable on the
Boulevards . . . The people were packed like a parade
in front of the Café du Nègre and the Porte Saint-Denis
. . . Like being crowded into a furnace . . . With the
loafers on the Square des Arts it was even worse . . .
there was no use sitting down, the whole place was a dust
bowl . . . just trying to breathe made you choke . . .
All the peddlers from miles around collected there with
their boxes and bundles . . . and the dumb kid that
pushes their pushcarts . . . They all slumped down by
the railing, waiting for it to be time to go up and face the
boss . . . They were sad sacks . . . Business was so
slow that summer they weren't selling anything at all . . .
Even with ninety days' credit nobody wanted their stuff
anywhere . . . They looked dazed . . . They were suffocating in the clouds of sand . . . They'd never get a
single order before the fifteenth of October . . . That
didn't encourage me very much . . . They could close
their order books . . . Their misery paralyzed me . . .

I'd asked people right and left if they didn't know of a
job, I'd pestered everybody, I'd looked at every nameplate in town, analyzed all the directories and telephone
books. I went back to the rue Vieille-du-Temple . . . For
at least a week I roamed along the Canal Saint-Martin,
looking at the barges . . . the quiet movement of the
locks . . . I went back to the rue Elzévir. I was so worried
I woke up with a start in the middle of the night . . . I
had an obsession that got stronger and stronger . . . It
squeezed my head like a vise . . . I wanted to go back
to Gorloge's . . . All of a sudden I felt a terrible pang of
remorse, an irresistible sense of shame, a curse . . . I was
getting ideas like a poor bastard, absolutely screwy . . .
I wanted to go up to Gorloge's and frankly confess, accuse
myself . . . in front of everybody . . . "It was I that
stole . . ." I'd say . . . "It was I that took the beautiful
pin! The pure-gold Sakya-Muni . . . It was I . . . Absolutely positively!" I worked myself up. Hell! Once I

get it over with, I said to myself, my bad luck will leave
me . . . I was under a spell . . . every fiber in my brain!
The idea gave me such horrors I was always shivering . . .
It got to be irresistible . . . Christ! . . . Well, in the end
I actually went back to the house . . . in spite of the
sizzling heat I had the cold shivers . . . I was in a panic!
I catch sight of the concierge . . . She takes a good look
at me, she recognizes me from far away . . . So I try to
remember, to figure out why I'm guilty . . . I start for
her den . . . First I'll tell her all about it! . . . Shit!
. . . No, I can't do it . . . I've got the jitters . . . I
about-face quick . . . I get out of there fast . . . I run
down toward the Boulevards . . . what in hell's the matter
with me? . . . I was acting like an ass! I was going nuts
. . . all sorts of crazy crummy ideas . . . I stopped going
home for lunch . . . I took bread and cheese with me
. . . I was sleepy in the afternoon from sleeping so badly
at night . . . Always being woken up by dreams . . . I
had to keep walking the whole time or I'd fall asleep on a
bench . . . I kept on batting my brains out . . . trying to
figure out what I was guilty of. There must have been some
reason . . . some damn good reason . . . I wasn't educated enough to puzzle it out . . . I covered so much
ground I found another place to rest in the afternoon. At
Notre-Dame-des-Victoires, by the little chapels on the left
as you go in . . . you couldn't have found a cooler place
. . . I felt cruelly persecuted by my stinking luck . . .
You feel better in the dark . . . The flags are soothing on
the feet . . . Nothing could be more refreshing . . . I'd
stay there a long time . . . The candles are nice . . . like
fragile bushes . . . the way they quiver in the deep velvet
of the vaulting . . . They hypnotized me . . . Little by
little they put me to sleep . . . I woke up to the sound of
little bells. Naturally it never closes . . . It's the best
place.

I kept finding excuses for coming home later and later
. . . Once it was almost nine o'clock . . . I'd applied for
a job way out in Antony . . . in a wallpaper factory. They
were looking for salesmen in midtown . . . It was just
the thing for my aptitudes . . . I went back two or three

times . . . Their factory wasn't ready! . . . They hadn't
finished building it . . . Anyway a lot of hooey!

I was scared shitless when I got back to the Passage.
I'd spent all my carfare money on beer . . . So I walked
more and more . . . It was a really unusual summer . . .
It hadn't rained in two months! . . .

My father was twisting and turning like a tiger in front
of his typewriter . . . In my bed right next door it was
impossible to sleep, he cursed so much at the keyboard
. . . At the beginning of September he developed a whole
raft of boils, first on his arms, then on the back of his neck
a really enormous one that turned into a carbuncle right
away. In his case boils were really serious, they knocked
him out completely . . . He went to the office anyway
. . . But people looked at him in the street, all wound up
in cotton. They turned around . . . He took quantities of
brewer's yeast, but it didn't help . . .

My mother was terribly worried to see him all broken
out like that . . . Her abscess was doing a little better,
what with lying still and putting on compresses. It festered
a good deal, but the swelling had gone down. It drained a
little more . . . And then she got back on her feet, she
wouldn't wait for the wound to heal, right away she got
busy around the place, hobbling around the chairs and
things . . . She tried to keep an eye on Hortense, she
climbed the stairs, she wouldn't let us carry her anymore.
She clutched the banister to climb the steps all by herself,
she hoisted herself from one floor to the next while we were
busy . . . She wanted to clean the house, to straighten out
the shop, put the knickknacks where they belonged . . .

My father was so wrapped up in bandages he couldn't
turn his head, he was suffocating in his boils, but that didn't
prevent him from hearing my mother downstairs, bustling
from room to room with her leg dragging behind her . . .
That made him madder than anything else . . . He
banged on his machine . . . He was in such a dither he
scraped the skin off his fists. He yelled at her to watch what
she was doing . . .

"Jumping Jesus, Clémence! You can hear me all right.
Holy suffering catfish, will you lie down, godammit. You
think we haven't trouble enough? Christ, what a stinking life!"

"Come, come, Auguste. Can't you leave me be . . . Let me attend to my business . . . Don't worry . . . I'm feeling fine."

She'd put on her angelic tone . . .

"It's easy to talk," he yelled. "It's easy to talk! Godammit to lousy stinking hell! Will you finally sit down?"

In the morning I notified my mother . . .

"Say, Mama, I won't be home for lunch today . . . I'm going out to Les Lilas again . . . see about that factory . . ."

"All right, Ferdinand," she says. "In that case, listen to me. I've been thinking . . . This evening I'd like Hortense to do the kitchen thoroughly . . . It's been in a disgusting state for the last two months at least, the pots, the sink, and all the brass . . . Since I've been sick, I haven't been able to attend to it . . . You can smell the grease all the way upstairs . . . If I send her shopping, she'll start dawdling again, she'll be out for hours, she's such a chatterbox . . . She hangs around the vegetable store . . . gabble gabble . . . You'll be near the Place de la République . . . so drop in at Carquois' and bring me seventy centimes' worth of their best ham for your father . . . the very best . . . you know the kind I mean? . . . absolutely fresh and not too fat . . . Take a good look at it before you buy it . . . There are some noodles left over for the two of us, we'll boil them up again . . . And at the same time you can bring me three portions of cream cheese and if you can remember a head of lettuce, not too wide open . . . That way I won't have to cook for dinner . . . You'll remember all that, won't you? We've got beer . . . Hortense will get some yeast . . . With your father and his boils I think salad is the best thing for the blood . . . Before you go, take a five-franc piece out of my purse on the mantelpiece in our room. Don't forget to count the change . . . And be sure to get back before dinner . . . Do you want me to write it all down? With this heat I'm afraid to give your father eggs . . . his digestion hasn't been right . . . or strawberries, for that matter . . . They give me a rash . . . so with his nerves . . . we'd better be careful . . ."

I'd had enough instructions, I was all set to go . . . I

took the five francs . . . I left the Passage . . . I sat for
a while in the Square Louvois, beside the fountain . . .
thinking things over, on a bench . . . Lilas, my ass! But
I had a little tip about a jobber, a fellow that made showcase accessories at home, velvet pads, little wooden
plaques. Somebody had told me about him . . . It was
on the rue Greneta, at Number 8 . . . just to have a clear
conscience . . . It must have been about nine o'clock
. . . It wasn't too hot yet . . . So I go there, very slowly
. . . I come to the door . . . I climb up to the sixth floor
. . . I ring, they open the door a crack . . . The job
was taken . . . OK, no point arguing . . . That was a
load off my chest . . . I went down maybe two flights
. . . There on the fourth floor landing I sit down for a
minute, I take off my collar . . . I do a little more thinking . . . After quite some thought it came to me that I
still had another address, a dealer in de luxe leather goods
way down at the end of the rue Meslay . . . There was no
hurry about that either . . . I look around, I take in the
setting. The place was really sumptuous . . . the floors
were all worn down, it smelled terrible of mold and toilets
. . . but what generous proportions, really magnificent
. . . must have belonged to some gravy riders in the
seventeenth century . . . You could tell that by the deco-
rations, the moldings, the wrought-iron railings, the marble
and porphyry steps . . . Nothing phony about it . . . all
handmade . . . I knew about style . . . Hell! . . . It
was really magnificent. . . Not a single fixture was imitation! . . . It was like an enormous drawing room, where
people would never stop again . . . They dashed straight
through into the hovels, to their lousy jobs. I'd contem-
plated enough . . . I myself was a memory . . . a putrid
smell . . .
  There, right beside the water faucet I could see the whole
landing, I was nice and comfortable . . . That's all I
wanted . . . Even the panes of glass dated from the
period . . . Little tiny ones, different-colored squares,
violet, bottle-green, pink . . . So there I was, perfectly at
peace, the people paid no attention to me . . . They were
going to work . . . I pondered how I was going to spend
the day . . . Hey! Suddenly I see an old friend coming
up . . . a big six-footer with a goatee . . . holding on to

the banister and panting . . . He was a salesman, not a bad guy . . . a real joker. I hadn't seen him since I was at Gorloge's . . . He sold watch chains and such . . . He recognized me on the landing . . . He shouts up to me . . . He tells me all about himself and asks me what I've been doing for the last year. I give him all the details . . . He didn't have time to listen, he was just leaving for his vacation . . . early in the afternoon . . . He was all pepped up with the prospect . . . So he leaves me pretty quick . . . He took the stairs four at a time . . . He ran in to see his boss and drop his sample case . . . He barely had time to dash to the Gare d'Orsay and take the train for Dordogne . . . He was going to be away for a week. He wished me plenty of luck . . . I told him to have a good time . . .

But that big palooka had got me down with his line about the country . . . Just like that, he'd punctured me completely. Hell, I wouldn't do a damn thing all day. That was a safe bet . . . I couldn't think of anything but sky-larking, the open spaces, the country . . . Hell, he'd demoralized me . . . I was suddenly frantic to see greenery, trees, flowerbeds . . . I couldn't control myself . . . I was wild . . . Dammit to hell! . . . I says to myself: "I'll do my shopping for supper right away . . ." That was my idea . . . "Then I'll go out to the Buttes-Chaumont . . . First we'll get that out of the way! I won't go home until seven . . . I'll be free all afternoon!" Not bad! . . .

I run to the nearest place . . . Ramponneau's . . . I make it fast . . . on the corner of the rue Étienne-Marcel . . . a model delicatessen store . . . even better than Carquois' . . . Really luxurious for those days and clean . . . I buy the seventy centimes' worth of ham . . . The kind my father liked best, hardly a speck of fat . . . I bought the head of lettuce at Les Halles across the street . . . The cream cheese too . . . They even lend me a container.

So I start moseying down the Boulevard Sébastopol, then the rue de Rivoli . . . I've kind of lost track. It's so stifling you can hardly move . . . I drag myself through the arcades . . . along the shop fronts . . . "How about the Bois de Boulogne!" I says to myself . . . I kept on walking quite a while . . . But it was getting

to be unbearable . . . unbearable . . . When I see the
gates of the Tuileries, I turn off . . . across the street and
into the gardens . . . There was a hell of a crowd already
. . . It wasn't easy to find a place on the grass . . . Especially in the shade . . . It was full up . . .

I get pushed around some, I slide down an embankment
near the big basin . . . It was nice and cool, really pleasant . . . But just then a red-faced mob appears on the
scene, a compact mass, griping and greasy, pouring out of
all fourteen adjoining quarters . . . Whole buildings dis-
gorging their inhabitants on the spacious lawns, every last
tenant and janitor, driven out by the heat, the bedbugs, the
itch . . . They swept on in a sea of wisecracks, the gags
burst like rockets . . . More hordes were on their way
from the Invalides, you could hear their awful rumbling . . .

They tried to close the gates, to rescue the rhododen-
drons, the bed of daisies . . . The horde broke down the
gates, bending the bars, tearing them up by the roots, they
ruptured the whole wall . . . It was worse than a landslide, a cavalry charge over ruins . . . They howled
bestially to make the storm burst at last over the Concorde
. . . But not a drop of rain fell, so they rushed into the
basins . . . rolling and wallowing, whole battalions of
them, naked, in their underdrawers . . . They made it
overflow, they drank up the last drop . . .

I was flat on my ass on the grassy bank, I really had
nothing to complain about . . . I was safe . . . I had my
provisions to the left of me, within easy reach . . . I could
hear the stampeding herds trampling the flowerbeds . . .
More were coming from all directions . . . The numberless
legions of thirst . . . They were battling to lick the bottom of the pond . . . sucking mud, worms, slime . . .
They'd plowed up the whole place, disemboweled the earth,
dug deep crevices. There wasn't a single blade of grass left
in the whole park . . . Only delirium, a chopped-up
crater for three miles around, rumbling with disaster and
drunks . . .

At the bottom of the crater, in the red-hot oven of hell,
thousands of families were looking around for their pieces
. . . Sides of meat, chunks of rump, kidneys gushing and
spurting as far as the rue Royale and up into the clouds

. . . The stink was merciless, tripe in urine, whiffs of corpse, decomposed liver patty . . . You got a mouthful with every breath . . . You couldn't get away from it . . . The terraces were inaccessible, blocked off by three impregnable bulwarks . . . Baby carriages piled as high as a six-story building . . .

But as the purple dusk fell, strains of song were wafted through the putrid breezes . . . Slumped on top of the martyrs, the monster with a hundred thousand cocks stirs up music in his guts . . . I had a couple of beers, swiped free of charge . . . and two more . . . and two more . . . which makes twelve . . . Why not?. . . I'd spent my five francs . . . I hadn't a red cent left . . . I snagged a quart of white wine . . . Nothing to it! . . . and a whole bottle of *mousseux* . . . Why wouldn't I do a little trading with that family on the bench? . . . Sure . . . I swap my cream cheese for a real live Camembert . . . Better watch out! . . . I change my sliced ham for a quart of red ink . . . There's no other word for it . . . Just then the mounted police attack . . . they're brutal . . . Some nerve! . . . The damn fools . . . They can't get anybody to move . . . In half a second they're toppled off their horses, disgraced . . . jerked off . . . beheaded . . . put to flight before you can count three! . . . They run for it, they scatter behind the statues! . . . The masses are in revolt! . . . A storm . . . that's what they're demanding . . . The crater rumbles, grumbles, thunders . . . Spewing empty bottles as far as the Étoile!

I break my salad in two, we eat it just like that, raw . . . I kid around with the young ladies . . . I sit there, drinking whatever I find on the corner of the bench. No more beer! . . . it doesn't quench your thirst . . . It actually heats up your mouth . . . Everything is scorching, the air, the girls' tits. You'd throw up if you moved, if you tried to get up . . . it's a fact, you can't move at all . . . My eyelids are drooping . . . my eyes are closing . . . Just then a sweet refrain passes through the air . . . "I know you're lovely . . ."

Bing! Rat-tat-tat! That's the street lamp, the big white globe breaking into smithereens. A vicious stone. A slingshot! They give a jump. They screech something awful. It's those toughs over there in the corner on the other side of the ditch, wise guys, bastards . . . They want it to be pitch-dark . . . The lousy little heels . . . I sprawl over on the guy next to me . . . He's a fat son of a bitch . . . He's snoring! It's terrible . . . Cut it out! . . . I'm comfortable, though! . . . His hullabaloo is putting me to sleep . . . A lullaby . . . I thought it was Camembert I had . . . It's cream cheese . . . I can see that . . . I've still got some in my breast pocket . . . I shouldn't have left any in the box . . . in the box . . . Here we are . . . here we stay . . . Seems like a breeze is coming up . . . The cream cheese is sleeping . . . It must be very late . . . Or even later . . . Like the cheese . . . Absolutely.

I was sleeping nicely. I wasn't bothering anybody . . . I'd slipped deep down into the ditch . . . I was wedged against the wall . . .

Then some fool comes stumbling around in the darkness . . . He bumps into my neighbor. He falls back on me, he knocks me over . . . He feels me up. I half open my eyes . . . I give a ferocious grunt . . . I look at the horizon . . . way in the distance . . . I see the dial . . . The one over the Gare d'Orsay, those great big clocks . . . It's one o'clock in the morning. Christ! Hell and damnation! Stinking mess! I start up. I disentangle myself . . . I've got two floozies crushing me, one on each side . . . I roll them over . . . All around me they're sawing wood and wheezing . . . Got to get up . . . Got to beat it home . . . I pick up my good jacket . . . But I can't find my collar . . . To hell with it. I was supposed to be home for dinner. Hell. My lousy luck. It was the heat too. Besides, I was in a daze, I wasn't all there. I was scared and I was drunk . . . I was still completely befuddled . . . Christ, was I drunk! Hell!

I remember the way all the same . . . I take the rue Saint-Honoré . . . then the rue Saint-Roch on the left . . . rue Gomboust . . . then straight ahead. I reach the Passage gate . . . It's not closed yet on account of the heat . . . All the neighbors are there . . . in their shirt-sleeves with their collars open, outside their shops . . . taking the air . . . chewing the fat from chair to chair, astraddle, on their doorsteps . . . I'm still kind of tipsy

. . . It's obvious that I can't walk straight . . . That
throws them. I never got drunk . . . They'd never seen
me that way . . . They're amazed . . . "Hey, Ferdinand!" they holler, "You land a job? The frogs having a
party? . . . You run into a cloud? Been struck by a
cyclone? . . ." A lot of hooey anyway . . . Visios was
rolling up his awning, he called after me: "Say, Ferdinand.
Your mother's been down here at least twenty times since
seven o'clock, asking if we hadn't seen you. So help me.
She's mad as a hornet . . . Where you been keeping
yourself anyway?"

So I stagger over to the shop. It wasn't closed at all . . .
Hortense was standing in the hall . . . She must have been
waiting for me . . .

"Oh, if you could see your mother . . . the state she's
in. Poor woman! It's dreadful. She's been out of her mind
since six o'clock . . . They say there's been a riot in the
Tuileries. She's sure you were in it . . . She went out
this afternoon for the first time when she heard the rumors
. . . She saw a runaway horse on the rue Vivienne . . .
She came home more dead than alive. She was all in a
tizzy. I've never seen her so upset!" Hortense herself was
in a terrible state just telling me about it . . . Her face was
all in a sweat and she was dabbing at it with her big
filthy apron. It left her streaked with green and yellow and
black . . . I took the stairs four at a time . . . I went to
my room . . . My mother was there on the bed, prostrated, completely beside herself, her smock unbuttoned
. . . her petticoats pulled up to her waist . . . She was
still bathing her leg with Turkish towels. She rolled them up
into big wads, the water dripped down on the floor . . .
"Ah!" she starts up . . . "So there you are!" She'd
thought they'd made hash of me . . .

"Your father's in a terrible rage. Oh, the poor man!
He was just going to the police station. Where on earth
have you been?"

Just then I hear my father coming out of the toilet. He
comes slowly up the stairs, adjusting his suspenders . . .
He straightens out the bandage on his boils . . . First he
doesn't say a word . . . He pretends not to see me . . .
He goes back to his typewriter . . . He types with one
finger . . . He puffs like a porpoise, he sponges his fore-

head . . . It's stifling, that's a fact . . . absolutely suffocating . . . He stands up . . . He takes the towel from
the nail . . . He splashes water all over his face . . .
He's done in . . . He comes back . . . He gives me a
cross-eyed look . . . He looks at my mother too,
stretched out on the bed . . . "Good Lord, Clémence,
cover yourself . . ." he bellows at her, furious on account
of her leg . . . Here we go again . . . He motions at
her. He thinks I'm looking at her bare legs . . . She
doesn't see what he's excited about . . . She's innocent,
she has no sense of shame . . . He raises his hands to
high heaven . . . He's scandalized, outraged! She's naked
up to her stomach . . . Finally she pulls her skirt down
. . . She changes her position a little . . . She turns
over on the mattress . . . I want to say something . . .
something to put an end to the embarrassment . . . I'll
say something about the heat . . . You can hear the cats
screwing . . . way over there on the glass roof . . .
chasing each other . . . jumping over chasms between
tall chimneys . . .

A breath of air comes up . . . an honest-to-goodness
breeze . . . Glory be! "It's cooling off," my mother says
right away. "Well, it's none too soon . . . You know,
Auguste, I can feel it in my leg that it's going to rain . . .
I'm positive . . . It's always the same pain . . . A drawing pain in the ass . . . That's the sign all right, it never
fails . . . Do you hear, Auguste, it's going to rain! . . ."

"Ah! Can't you shut up a minute! Let me work! Christ!
Can't you stop gassing the whole time?"

"Why, Auguste, I haven't said a word. It's getting on to
two o'clock. My goodness, child, and we aren't in bed
yet."

"As if I didn't know it, Christ almighty asshole blazes.
I know it's two o'clock. Is it my fault? . . . Pretty soon
it'll be three. Hell fire! And four! And thirty-six! And
twelve! Blast it to stinking hell! Why do I have to be
badgered day and night? Is it right? Is it fair?" He gives
his contraption a terrifying blow, enough to smash all the
type, to flatten out the keyboard . . . He turns around.
He's blue in the face . . . Now he turns on me . . . He
gives it to me straight: "Wah!" he bellows. He roars at the
top of his lungs: "You give me a pain in the ass, the whole

lot of you. D'you hear me? . . . That's right. And you,
you dirty little louse! You no-good bum! Where've you
been again? Since eight o'clock this morning? Well? Are
you going to answer me? Speak up, dammit . . ."

At first I didn't say a thing . . . All of a sudden I remember what I'd done with the stuff I'd bought. It was
true, I hadn't brought home a thing! Jesus Christ! What a
mess!

I'd forgotten all about the ham . . . I'd forgotten
everything . . . Now I begin to catch the tune. Christ!
"What about your mother's money? . . . And the food
you were supposed to be bringing home? . . . Well?
Ahh!" He was exultant. "You see, Clémence? . . . Your
handiwork . . . Now do you see what you've done . . .
with your idiotic leniency . . . your stupid blindness
. . . You trust that little thug with money! Your unpar-
donable trustfulness! Your idiotic credulity! . . . You
give him money . . . you hand him your purse! Why not
give him everything? Give him the whole house. Why not?
. . . Ah! Ah! I predicted it, didn't I! . . . He'll shit in
your hand! Ah! Ah! He's drunk it all up! He's guzzled it
all down! . . . He stinks of liquor. He's drunk! He's
caught the syphilis! And the clap! He'll bring us the
cholera! Then you'll be satisfied! . . . Ah! Well, you'll
reap the fruits. You and nobody else, you hear me? . . .
Whose fault is it if we've a stinker for a son? Yours! You
can have him. All for yourself! Lousy, stinking, cocksucking life!"

He winds himself up again . . . He surpasses himself.
He goes all out . . . He rips his shirt open . . . He
bares his chest . . .

"Thunderation asshole Jesus! Why, he's a scoundrel
through and through! He'll stop at nothing! . . . It's
high time you realized . . . you can't trust him with anything . . . not with a single centime! not with a sou! . . .
You promised me a dozen times! twenty times! a hundred
thousand times! But you had to start right in again! Ah!
Ah! You're incorrigible!"

He bounces up from his stool . . . He comes clear
across the room and shouts at me point-blank. He blows
spit in my face, he puffs himself up like a balloon . . .
two inches from my nose . . . Here comes his hurricane

act! . . . I see his eyes right up against mine . . .
Strangely revulsed . . . Quivering in their sockets . . .
It's a tempest between the two of us . . . He stammers so
furiously that the spit flies thick and fast . . . he's drowning me! He clouds my vision, I'm dazed . . . He flails
around so violently he tears the bandages off his neck.
That only makes him thrash harder . . . He twists
around and bellows at me . . . He grabs hold of me . . .
I push him back and recoil . . . I've got my dander up
too . . . I don't want the dirty bastard to touch me . . .
That stops him for a second . . .

"What?" he goes. "What's this? . . . Ah, if I didn't
control myself! . . ."

"Go right ahead!" I say . . . I can feel the gall rising.

"Ah, you little skunk! You defy me? You little pimp!
You swine! The insolence of it! The shame! Do you want
to kill us? Is that it? . . . Why don't you say so right
away? . . . You little coward! You bum! . . ." He fires
all this in my face . . . And then some more incanta-
tions . . .

"Suffering asshole Christ almighty! My poor dear, what
did we do to produce such vermin? As corrupt as three
dozen jailbirds! . . . Profligate! Scoundrel! Idler! And
then some! He's calamity personified! Good for nothing
except to rob us and clean us out! A pestilence! Gouge us
without mercy! That's all his gratitude! . . . for a whole
life of sacrifice! Two lives of torment! We're nothing but a
couple of old fools . . . We're the ones that get it in the
neck! Every time! . . . Go on, say it again, say it, you
poison toad! Come on, out with it. Admit you want to be
the death of us . . . that you want us to die of grief . . .
and misery! Let me hear you say it at least before you
finish me off! Go on, you stinking scum!"

At this point my mother gets up and limps across the
room, trying to come between us . . .

"Auguste! Auguste! Listen to me, my goodness. Listen
to me, I beg of you. Come, Auguste. You're going to be
laid up again. Think of me, Auguste. Think of all of us!
You're going to make yourself sick. Ferdinand. Go away,
child. Go outside! Don't stay here . . ."

I didn't budge. It was he who sat down again . . .

He mops himself off, he grunts . . . He strikes one or

two keys . . . Then he starts to bellow ag
turns toward me, he points a finger at me . . .
solemn tone . . .

"Ah yes, today I can admit it . . . How I regr
was weak. I'm to blame for not having disciplined you
a vengeance! Christ, yes! Disciplined you! Before it w
too late! When you were twelve, do you hear, at the latest.
That's when I should have collared you and locked you up
good. That's right. No later . . . locked you up in a
reform school . . . That's the ticket! They'd have taught
you a thing or two . . . And things wouldn't have come
to such a pass . . . But now the die is cast . . . Our
doom is sealed . . . Too late! Too late! Do you hear me,
Clémence? Much too late! This blackguard is incorrigible!
It's your mother that prevented me! And now you'll pay for
it, my dear!"

He points at her as she limps around the room, sighing
at every step. "It was your mother. Yes, your mother. If
she'd listened to me, you'd never have sunk so low . . .
Jumping Jesus, no! Ah, Christ almighty! . . ."

He pounds the keyboard again . . . wicked punches
with both fists . . . He's going to demolish it for sure.

"Do you hear me, Clémence? Do you hear me? I've told
you often enough! . . . Didn't I warn you? I knew how it
was going to be!"

He's going to explode again . . . His rage is coming
back . . . He puffs up all over . . . his head and his
eyes are bulging . . . all you can see is the whites . . .
She's stumbling in all directions, she can't stand up anymore. She climbs back on the bed. She collapses . . .
She hikes her petticoats way up . . . She uncovers her
thighs, the bottom of her belly . . . She writhes with
pain . . . She gently massages herself . . . She's bent
double . . .

"Jesus, cover up. Cover up, will you, it's disgusting!"

"Please, please, I beg you, Auguste. You're going to
make us all sick . . ." She was at the end of her rope. She
was besides herself . . .

"Sick? Sick? . . ." That shoots through him like a
rocket. A magic word! . . . "Ho ho! Christ, that's the
last straw!" He bursts out laughing . . . "That's a revelation!" He's off the handle again . . . "But it's him. Can't

PLAN
315
ain . . . He
He takes a
t it! I
with
as

t? . . . It's this little hood-
get it through your noodle
in that's making us all sick!
ur hide. He's always been
is dead and buried! That's
esn't even bother to hide it
onk out . . . It's obvious.
the better. His behavior is
t's our wretched two cents
f bread he's got his eye on!
all right. The little scum
. . . . . . The scoundrel! The bloodsucker!
He knows. He's got eyes in his head. He sees how we're
wasting away! He's rotten through and through! Just take
it from me! I know him if you don't! Even if he is my son!"

He starts trembling again, his whole carcass is quaking,
he's beside himself . . . He clenches his fists . . . His
stool is creaking and dancing . . . He's winding up, he's
going to lunge . . . He comes back blowing up my nose
. . . more insults . . . more and more of them . . . I
feel things coming up in me too . . . And the heat besides . . . I pass my two hands over my face . . . Suddenly everything looks cock-eyed . . . I can't see straight
. . . Just one jump . . . I'm over him. I lift up the big
heavy machine . . . I lift it way up. And wham! . . .
I give it to him full in the face! He hasn't got time to parry
. . . He goes over under the impact, the whole business
topples . . . table, man, chair, the whole shebang in all
directions . . . They fall on the floor and scatter . . . I'm
caught up in the dance . . . I stumble, I fall . . . That
does it, I've got to finish the stinking bastard! Bzing! He's
down again . . . I'm going to smash his kisser! . . . So
he can't talk anymore . . . I'm going to smash his whole
face . . . I punch him on the ground . . . He bellows
. . . He gurgles . . . That'll do. I dig into the fat on his
neck . . . I'm on my knees on top of him . . . I'm
tangled up in his bandages . . . both my hands are caught.
I pull. I squeeze. He's still groaning . . . He's wriggling
. . . I weigh down on him . . . He's disgusting . . . He
squawks . . . I pound him . . . I massacre him . . .
I'm squatting down . . . I dig into the meat . . . It's
soft . . . He's drooling . . . I tug . . . I pull off a big

chunk of moustache. . . He bites me, the stinker! . . .
I gouge into the holes . . . I'm sticky all over . . . my
hands skid . . . he heaves . . . he slips out of my grip.
He grabs me around the neck. He squeezes my windpipe
. . . I squeeze some more. I knock his head against the
tiles . . . He goes limp . . . he's soft under my legs
. . . He sucks my thumb . . . he stops sucking . . .
Phooey! I raise my head for a minute . . . I see my
mother's face on a level with mine . . . She's staring at
me, her eyes twice their size . . . Her eyes are so big I
start wondering where I am . . . I let go . . . Another
head appears from the stairs . . . over the corner of the
banister . . . That one's Hortense. Must be. It's her all
right. She lets out a terrible scream: "Help! Help!" She
almost splits a gut . . . That does something to me. I
let go my old man . . . One jump . . . and I'm on top
of Hortense! . . . I'm going to strangle her! I want to see
how she wriggles! She struggles . . . I daub her face . . .
I close her mouth with the palms of my hands . . . The
pus and blood from the boils squash on her face and drip
down . . . She gurgles louder than Papa . . . I latch on
to her . . . She struggles . . . She's hefty . . . I want
to choke her too . . . It's amazing . . . It's a hidden
world that spasms in your hands . . . It's life . . . Get a
good feel of it . . . I knock her skull stubbornly against
the banister . . . It thuds . . . There's blood in her hair
. . . She yells! It's split. I dig a big finger into her eye . . .
I haven't got the right hold . . . She breaks loose . . .
She's up again . . . She gets away . . . She's a strong
one . . . She clatters down the stairs . . . I can hear her
yelling outside . . . raising hell . . . screaming at the top
of her lungs . . . "Murder, murder! . . ." I hear echoes,
voices. A crowd comes running . . . they gallop into the
shop, they jostle at the bottom of the stairs . . . They
push and shove on every landing . . . An invasion . . .
I hear my name . . . Here they come . . . They go into
a huddle on the third floor . . . I look out . . . Somebody's coming . . . It's Visios! He's the first one to pop
out . . . He plunges in from the landing . . . There he
is, firm, menacing, resolute . . . He points a revolver at
me . . . straight at my chest . . . The other bastards
come around behind me, encircle me, grunting, bawling the

hell out of me . . . Hurling threats at me, insults . . .
The old man is still out cold . . . still on the floor . . .
with a little trickle of blood flowing from his head
. . . I'm not angry anymore . . . I don't give a damn
. . . Visios bends down, touches the bundle, Papa grunts
and moans a little . . .

The bastards push me around, they're stronger . . .
They're pretty brutal . . . They drag me down the stairs
. . . they won't even listen to my mother . . . They push
me into the room downstairs . . . I take the blows as they
come . . . I've stopped resisting . . . I get some from
everybody, especially in the balls . . . I can't fight back
. . . The wickedest of the lot is Visios . . . I get a kick
square in the stomach . . . I stagger . . . I don't double
up . . . I stay put, glued to the wall . . . They leave,
spitting in my face as they go . . . They lock me in.

I'm all alone . . . pretty soon I begin to tremble . . .
My hands . . . my legs . . . my face . . . inside . . .
all over . . . I have a lousy sick feeling, a panic in my
kidneys . . . like everything was falling apart, coming off
in shreds . . . like a hurricane was shaking me . . . My
whole carcass is rattling, my teeth are chattering . . . I'm
dead to the world . . . I've got a spasm in my asshole
. . . I shit in my pants . . . My heart's pounding so hard
I can't hear what's going on . . . I can't make out what
they're doing . . . My knees are knocking together . . .
I stretch out on the floor . . . I don't know what's what
. . . I'm scared . . . I feel like yelling . . . I haven't
knocked him off, have I? Shit! To hell with that . . . But
my asshole is opening and closing . . . A spasm . . .
it's awful.

I think of Papa again . . . The sweat's dripping off me
and what's left is cold . . . I swallow it through my nose
. . . I'm bleeding . . . The cocksucker scratched me
. . . I wasn't very rough . . . I'd never have expected
him to be so weak, so mushy . . . It's amazing . . . It
was easy to squeeze . . . I remember how I was kneeling
there with my fingers locked in front . . . the slobber
. . . and the way he suckled my thumb . . . I can't
stop shaking . . . I'm trembling all over . . . All you've
got to do is squeeze! . . . My face is twitching all over
. . . I groan! Now I can feel every one of those bastards'

blows . . . I'm scared shitless . . . It's my asshole that
hurts worst . . . It keeps on twisting and tightening . . .
It aches like hell.

Shut up in that room, stretched out on the tiles, I kept
on trembling a long while, banging against everything in
sight . . . I bumped into the clothes cupboard . . . it
sounded like castanets . . . I'd never have thought I
could have such a tempest inside me . . . The jolting was
unbelievable . . . I flapped around like a lobster . . .
It came from way inside . . . "I've knocked him off!" I
said to myself . . . I was more and more sure of it, and
then for a moment I heard something like the sound of
steps . . . people talking things over . . . And then they
were pushing the bed upstairs . . .
    "That's it! They're taking him away . . ." But a minute
later I heard his voice . . . That was him all right! . . .
He was only punch-drunk! "I must have bashed his head
in," I began to think. "He'll conk out later. That'll be even
worse . . ." He was still on my bed . . . I could hear
the springs . . . Actually I didn't know a thing. And then
my stomach heaved . . . I began to vomit . . . I even
pushed to make it come up . . . That made me feel a lot
better . . . I vomited up everything . . . The shivers
started in again . . . They shook me so hard I didn't know
who I was anymore . . . I was surprised at myself . . .
I threw up the macaroni . . . I started in again . . . It
did me a whole lot of good. Like I was getting rid of
everything . . . I threw up everything I could all over
the floor . . . I pushed and strained . . . I bent double
to make myself puke still more and then came slime and
then froth . . . It splattered, it spread under the door
. . . I vomited up everything I'd eaten for at least a week
and then diarrhea too . . . I wanted to call them to let me
leave the room . . . I dragged myself to the pitcher that
was standing by the fireplace . . . I shat into it . . .
After that I couldn't keep my balance . . . My head
was spinning . . . I collapsed again and let it all out on
the floor . . . I shat some more . . . A flood of marmalade . . .
    They must have heard me floundering around . . .
They came and opened . . . They took one look at the room

. . . They locked it up again . . . Maybe ten minutes later Uncle Édouard came in . . . He was all alone . . . I hadn't put my pants back on . . . I was covered with shit . . . He wasn't afraid of me . . . "Get dressed now," he says to me . . . "You go down first, I'm taking you away . . ." He had to hold me up. I was trembling so bad all over I couldn't button my pants . . . Finally I did what he said . . . I went down ahead of him . . . There was nobody on the stairs anymore or in the shop either. Everybody had cleared out . . . They must have gone home . . . They had plenty to talk about . . .

By the clock up there under the glass roof it was 4:15 . . . It was dawning already . . .

At the end of the Passage we roused up the caretaker to open the gate. "So you're taking him away?" he asked my uncle . . .

"Yes, he'll sleep at my place."

"Well, I wish you luck. You'll need it, my dear monsieur. That's some number you've got on your hands . . ."

He double-locked the gate behind us. He went back to his shack. You could hear him grumbling in the distance: "Christ! That brat's got himself into a fine mess!"

My uncle and I went down the rue des Pyramides . . . We crossed the Tuileries . . . When we got to the Pont Royal I was still trembling . . . The wind from the river wasn't warm. As we were walking along, Uncle Édouard told me how they'd come for him . . . It seems to have been Hortense . . . He was sound asleep . . . His part of town wasn't exactly around the corner . . . It was beyond the Invalides, behind the École Militaire . . . on the rue de la Convention before you get to the rue de Vaugirard . . . I was afraid to ask for further details . . . We walked fast . . . I couldn't get warm . . . My teeth were still chattering . . .

"Your father's better," he said after a while. . . "But he'll surely be in bed for two or three days . . . He won't be going to the office. Dr. Capron came . . ." That's as much as he told me.

We took the rue du Bac and then turned right as far as the Champ de Mars . . . His place was at the end of the world . . . Finally we get there . . . There it is! . . . He shows me his home, a small house in the back of a

garden . . . His pad was on the third floor . . . I didn't
dare say anything about being tired . . . but I couldn't
stand on my feet . . . I hung on to the banister. It was
broad daylight by now . . . Upstairs a terrible wave of
nausea came over me! . . . He took me to the shithouse
himself . . . I threw up a long time . . . it kept coming . . . He takes a folding bed out of the closet
. . . He takes a mattress off his bed . . . He sets me up
in another room . . . He gives me a blanket too . . . I
collapse . . . He undresses me . . . I spit up another
flood of slime . . . Finally I fall asleep by fits and starts
. . . A nightmare catches hold of me . . . I only slept off
and on . . .

I never really found out how Uncle Édouard managed
to make my father lay off . . . to make him leave me
strictly alone . . . I think he must have given him to
understand that his disciplinary routine, his idea of sending
me to La Roquette, wasn't so very bright . . . That I
wouldn't stay there forever . . . that maybe I'd escape
right away . . . just to come and rub him out . . . and
that this time I'd really finish the job . . . Anyway, he
managed . . . He didn't confide in me . . . I didn't
ask him to.

My uncle's place was nicely situated, it was cheerful,
pleasant . . . It looked out over the gardens of the rue de
Vaugirard and the rue Maublanc . . . There were rows
of little copses and kitchen gardens in front and in back
. . . The honeysuckle climbed all around the front
windows . . . Everybody had his little plot between the
houses, radishes, lettuces, even tomatoes . . . and grape-
vines! All that reminded me of my head of lettuce . . . It
hadn't brought me much luck. I was terribly weak, like
after an illness. But in a way I felt better. I didn't feel
hunted at Uncle Édouard's place.

I began to breathe again . . .

The decoration in his room consisted of whole series of
picture postcards, pinned up fanwise, in frescoes, in garlands . . . The "Kings of the Steering Wheel," the
"Kings of the Handlebars," and the "Heroes of Aviation"
. . . He bought them all, a few at a time . . . His ulti-
mate plan was to have them form a tapestry that would

cover the walls completely . . . It wouldn't be long now
. . . Paulhan and his little fur cap . . . Rougier of the
lopsided schnozzle . . . Petit-Breton with the legs of steel
and the zebra-stripe jersey . . . Farman, the bearded
. . . Santos-Dumont, the fearless fetus . . . Vicomte
Lambert, the Eiffel Tower specialist . . . Latham, the
disillusioned . . . MacNamara, the "black panther" . . .
Sam Langford, all thighs . . . And a hundred other
celebrities . . . Boxing too of course . . .*

It wasn't a bad life . . . We managed pretty well . . .
When my uncle came home from his business and all the
chasing around connected with his pump, he talked to me
about sporting events . . . He figured all the chances
. . . He knew all the weaknesses, the idiosyncrasies, the
tricks of the champions . . . We ate our meals on the
oilcloth, we did the cooking together . . . We talked
things over in every detail, the chances of all the favor-
ites . . .

On Sunday we were full of beans . . . By ten o'clock
in the morning we were in the big Gallery of Machines
. . . it was a fantastic sight . . . We'd get there good
and early . . . We'd take our places way up top, on the
turn . . . We were never bored for a second . . . Uncle
Édouard was always on the run, from one end of the
week to the other . . . He never stopped going . . . His
pump still wasn't exactly the way he wanted it . . . He
was having a lot of trouble with patents . . . He didn't
quite see what the difficulty was . . . It mostly had something to do with America . . . But whether he was in a
good or a bad humor he never made speeches . . . He
never moralized . . . That's what I liked best about him
. . . Meanwhile he put me up. I lived in his second room.
My fate was in suspense. My father never wanted to see me
again . . . He was still gassing as usual . . . He'd have
liked me to start my military service . . . But I wasn't
old enough . . . I only heard about all this bit by bit
. . . My uncle didn't like to talk about it . . . He preferred to talk about sports, his pump, boxing, gadgets . . .
anything . . . Touchy subjects gave him a pain . . . me
too . . .

Even so, he was a little more talkative on the subject

* See Glossary.

of my mother . . . He brought me news . . . She couldn't move around at all anymore . . . I wasn't very eager to see her . . . What was the use? . . . She always said the same thing . . . Anyway, the time passed . . . A week, two weeks, three . . . This couldn't go on forever . . . I couldn't dig in here for good . . . My uncle was OK but that was just the trouble . . . And how was I going to live? . . . At his expense? . . . That was no good . . . I dropped a little suggestion . . . "We'll see about it later on," he said . . . there was no hurry . . . he was attending to it . . .

He taught me how to shave . . . He had a special contraption, tricky and modern . . . you could put it together in all directions and even backwards . . . Except it was so complicated it took an engineer to change the blade . . . This delicate little razor was another nest of patents, he explained to me, about twenty in all.

It was I who set the table and did the shopping . . . I kept on like that, waiting and doing nothing, for almost a month and a half . . . lounging around like a woman . . . That had never happened to me before . . . I did the dishes too. We didn't bother with too much cleaning . . . Then I went roaming around wherever I pleased . . . No kidding! . . . That was something . . . I had no fixed destination . . . I just wandered . . . Every day Uncle Édouard said the same thing before I went out: "Go take a walk. Go ahead, Ferdinand! Just follow your nose . . . Don't worry about a thing . . . Go wherever you like . . . If you've got some special place, that's the place to go. Sure. As far as the Luxembourg if you feel like it . . . Ah! If I only weren't so busy . . . I'd go and watch them playing tennis . . . I'm crazy about tennis . . . Get a little sunshine . . . You never look at anything, you're like your father . . ." He'd stop for a minute, he'd stand still, thinking. Finally he'd add: "And then you'll come home, but don't hurry . . . I'll be a little later than usual tonight . . ." And he'd give me a little extra dough, a franc and a half, two francs . . . "Take in a movie . . . if you're up on the Boulevards . . . You seem to like stories . . ."

Seeing him so generous . . . with me on his hands, I began to feel crummy . . . But I didn't dare to argue. I

was afraid he'd take offense . . . After the latest ruckus
I was always on the lookout for consequences . . . So I
thought I'd wait a while for things to straighten themselves
out . . . To spare expense I washed my own socks while
he was out . . . The rooms in his place weren't strung in
a row, but pretty far apart. The third, next to the stairs,
was weird, it was like a small drawing room . . . But with
hardly anything in it . . . a table in the middle, two chairs,
and a single picture on the wall . . . an enormous repro-
duction of Millet's *Angelus* . . . I never saw such a wide
picture . . . it took up the whole panel . . . "Isn't it
beautiful? What do you say, Ferdinand?" Uncle Édouard
asked every time we passed in front of it on our way to the
kitchen. Sometimes we stopped a moment to contemplate
it in silence . . . We didn't talk in front of the *Angelus*
. . . This wasn't any "Kings of the Handlebars" . . . It
wasn't made to be gassed about!

I think my uncle had an idea it would do me a lot of
good to look at a fine picture like that . . . that it was
a kind of treatment for a rotten character like mine . . .
that maybe it would soften me up . . . But he never made
an issue of it . . . He understood these sensitive things
perfectly . . . He didn't talk about them, that's all . . .
Uncle Édouard wasn't only good at machinery . . . That
would be the wrong idea . . . He was very sensitive,
there's no denying it . . . Actually that was what made me
feel so uncomfortable . . . It made me feel lousy to be
sitting there like a sap, piling his groceries into my belly
. . . I was a skunk and I had my nerve with me . . .
Hell! . . . Enough was enough . . .

I asked him again . . . risked it . . . if there was any
objection to my starting out again. . . having a look at the
want ads . . . "You stay right here," he says to me.
"Aren't you happy? Is anything eating you, kid? Go out for
a walk. It'll be better for you. Don't worry about a thing
. . . You'll only get mixed up with the same dopes . . .
I'll find you a job . . . I'm working on it. Just leave me
alone. Don't stick your nose in. You're still too jittery . . .
You'll only bollix everything up . . . You're too nervous
right now. Anyway I've arranged everything with your
parents . . . Go roaming around some more . . . You
won't always have the chance. Go out to Suresnes along

the river. Or take the boat, come to think of it. Give yourself a change of air. There's nothing like those boats. Get
off at Meudon if you feel like it. That'll clear your mind
. . . I'll tell you in a few days . . . I'll have something
very good for you . . . I can feel it . . . I'm sure of it
. . . But we mustn't try to force things . . . And I hope
you'll be a credit to me . . ."
    "Yes, Uncle."

    You don't meet many men like Roger-Martin Courtial
des Pereires . . . I was a good deal too young at the time,
I've got to admit, to appreciate him properly. My uncle
had the good fortune to meet him one day at the office of
the *Genitron,* the favorite magazine (twenty-five pages)
of the small artisan-inventors of the Paris district . . . in
connection with his scheme for obtaining a patent, the best,
the most airtight, for all kinds of bicycle pumps . . . folding, collapsible, flexible, or reversible.
    Courtial des Pereires, let's get this straight right away,
was absolutely different from the mob of petty inventors
. . . He was miles above all the bungling subscribers to
his magazine . . . that crawling mass of failures . . .
Oh no! Roger-Martin Courtial wasn't in that class . . .
He was a real master! . . . It wasn't just neighbors that
came to consult him . . . but people from all over, from
the departments of the Seine, the Seine-et-Oise, subscribers
from the provinces, the colonies . . . even from foreign
countries . . .
    But the remarkable thing about it was that in private
Courtial expressed nothing but contempt and ill-concealed
disgust for all those small-fry, those weights around the
neck of Science, those misled shopkeepers, those delirious
tailors, those gadget peddlers . . . all those harebrained
delivery boys, always being fired, hunted, cachectic, driving themselves nuts about perpetual motion or the squaring
of the world . . . or the magnetic faucet . . . The whole
miserable swarm of obsessed screwballs . . . of inventors
of the moon! . . .
    He had his bellyful of them right away, just from looking
at them and especially when he had to listen to them . . .
He had to put a good face on it in the interests of the paper
. . . That was his routine, his bread and butter . . . But

it was disgusting and embarrassing . . . It wouldn't have
been so bad if he could have kept quiet . . . But he had
to comfort them! flatter them! get rid of them gently . . .
according to the case and the mania . . . and above all
collect his fee . . . It was a race between all those maniacs, those dreary slobs, to see who could get away a
little quicker . . . only five minutes more! . . . from his
furnished room . . . his workshop, his bus or shed . . .
just time to take a leak . . . and then dash to the *Genitron*
. . . and collapse in front of des Pereires' desk, like a lot
of escaped convicts . . . panting . . . haggard . . . tense
with fright . . . to shake their dunce caps some more
. . . to fire thousands of puzzlers at Courtial . . . about
"solar mills," the junction of the "lesser radiations" . . .
ways of moving the Cordilleras . . . of deflecting the
course of comets . . . as long as they had a gasp of breath
left in their dottering bagpipes . . . to the last twitch of
their stinking carcasses . . . Courtial des Pereires, secretary, precursor, owner, founder of the *Genitron,* always had
an answer to everything, he was never embarrassed or dis-
concerted, never maneuvered to gain time . . . His
aplomb, his perfect competence, his irresistible optimism
made him invulnerable to the worst assaults of the worst
nitwits . . . Besides, he never put up with long conversa-
tions . . . Instantly he parried, he himself took over
. . . Whatever was said, decided, settled . . . was settled
once and for all . . . no use starting up again or he'd
go purple with rage . . . He'd tug at his collar . . . He'd
spray spit in all directions . . . Incidentally he had
some teeth missing, three on one side . . . In every case
his verdicts, the most tenuous, the most dubious, the most
open to argument, became massive, galvanized, irrefutable,
instantaneous truths . . . He had only to open his mouth
. . . He triumphed instantly . . . There was no room
for a comeback.
   At the slightest sign of disagreement he gave free rein
to his temper and the martyred consultant didn't have a
chance . . . Instantly turned inside out, crushed, routed,
massacred, volatilized forever . . . It was a regular fan-
tasia, a trapeze act over a volcano . . . The poor insolent bastard saw stars . . . Courtial was so imperious
when he got mad he would have made the most insatiable

nut drop through the floor, he'd have made him crawl into a mousehole.

Courtial wasn't a big man, he was short and wiry, the small powerful type. He himself told you his age several times a day . . . He was past fifty . . . He kept in good shape thanks to physical culture, dumbbells, Indian clubs, horizontal bars, springboards . . . he did his exercises regularly, especially before lunch, in the back room of the newspaper office. He'd fixed up a regular gymnasium between two partitions. Naturally it was kind of cramped . . . But all the same he swung himself around on his apparatus . . . on the bars . . . with remarkable ease . . . That was the advantage of being little . . . he could pivot like a charm . . . Even so he collided now and then . . . good and hard . . . when he was swinging on the rings . . . He'd shake the walls of his cubbyhole like a bell clapper! Boom! Boom! You could hear him exercising. Never in the worst heat did I ever see him take off his pants or his frock coat or his collar . . . Only his cuffs and his ready-made tie.

Courtial des Pereires had a good reason to keep in perfect form. He had to watch out for his physique and keep limber . . . It was indispensable . . . In addition to being an inventor, an author, and a journalist, he often went up in a balloon . . . He gave exhibitions . . . Especially on Sundays and holidays . . . It usually went off all right, but occasionally there was trouble and plenty of excitement . . . And that wasn't all . . . He led a perilous life, full of unforeseen dangers and a hundred different kinds of surprises . . . That's how he'd always lived . . . It was his nature . . . He told me what he was aiming at . . .

"Muscles without mind, Ferdinand," he'd say, "aren't even horse meat. And intelligence without muscles is electricity without a battery! You don't know where to put it . . . It leaks out all over the place . . . It's a waste . . . It's a mess . . ." That was his opinion. He'd written several conclusive works on the subject: "The Human Battery and its Upkeep." He was gone on physical culture even before the word existed. He wanted a varied life . . . "I don't want to be a pen-pusher." That was the way he talked.

He was crazy about balloons, he'd been an aeronaut almost from birth, ever since his earliest youth . . . with Surcouf and Barbizet . . . highly instructive ascents . . . No records, no long-distance flights, no breathtaking performances. No, nothing showy, colossal, unusual . . . He had no use for the clowns of the atmosphere . . . Nothing but demonstration flights, educational ascents . . . Always scientific . . . That was his motto and he stuck to it. The balloon was good for his magazine, it rounded out his activities . . . Every time he went up it brought in subscribers. He had a uniform for climbing into the basket, he had an uncontested right to it, like a captain with three stripes, he was an "associated, registered, graduate" aeronaut. He couldn't even count his medals. They looked like a breastplate on his Sunday rig . . . He didn't give a damn about them, he wasn't a show-off, but it meant a lot to his audience, you had to keep up appearances.

To the last, Courtial des Pereires was a staunch defender of "lighter-than-air" craft. He was already thinking about helium. He was thirty-five years in advance of his times. And that's something. Between flights he kept the *Enthusiast*, his veteran, his big private balloon, in the cellar of the office, at 18 Galerie Montpensier. As a rule he only took it out on Friday before dinner to straighten out the rigging and fix up the cover with infinite care . . . the folds, the sleeve, the cords, filled the miniature gymnasium, the silk puffed up in the drafts.

Courtial des Pereires himself never stopped producing, imagining, conceiving, resolving, making claims . . . his genius tugged at his brains from morning to night . . . And even at night it didn't rest . . . He had to hold tight to resist the torrent of ideas . . . And be on his guard . . . It was incomparable torture . . . Instead of dozing off like other people, he was pursued by chimeras, new crazes, fresh hobbies . . . Bing! The whole idea of sleeping ran out on him, it was out of the question. He wouldn't have got any sleep at all if he hadn't rebelled against the torrent of inventions, against his own enthusiasm . . . This disciplining of his genius had cost him more trouble, more superhuman efforts, than all the rest of his work . . . He often told me so . . .

When he was overcome in spite of himself, when after no end of resistance he felt swamped by his own enthusiasm and began to see double . . . or triple . . . to hear queer voices . . . there was no other way of stopping the onslaughts, of falling back into his rhythm, of recovering his good humor, than a little trip in the clouds. He'd treat himself to an ascent. If he'd had more free time, he'd have gone up a lot more often, just about every day, but it wasn't compatible with the operation of his rag . . . He could only go up on Sunday . . . And even that wasn't so easy . . . The *Genitron* took up all his time, he had to be there . . . he couldn't fool around . . . Inventors are no joke . . . He always had to be on tap. He stuck to it bravely, nothing diminished his zeal or baffled his ingenuity . . . no problem, however stupendous, however colossal, however microscopic . . . He made faces but he put up with it . . . The "powdered cheese," the "synthetic azure," the "rocker valve," the "nitrogen lung," and the "collapsible steamship," the "compressed café au lait," or the "kilometric spring" that would take the place of fuel. No vital innovation in any of these far-flung fields was ever put into practice before Courtial had found occasion, not once but many times, to demonstrate its mechanisms, to stress its advantages, but also, without mercy, to point out its deplorable weaknesses and defects, its hazards and drawbacks.

All this of course brought him terrible jealousies, hatreds without quarter, long-lasting grudges . . . But he remained impervious to these trifling contingencies.

As long as he wrote for the paper, no technical revolution was recognized as worthwhile or even workable until he had said so and endorsed it in the columns of the *Genitron*. That gives you an idea of the authority he wielded. For every invention of any importance his verdict was decisive . . . The OK had to come from him. Take it or leave it. If Courtial wrote on his front page that an idea was no good . . . heavens above! . . . persnickety, cock-eyed, absolutely unsound, that was the end of it. The contraption was dead and buried . . . The project was sunk . . . But if his opinion was definitely favorable . . . the thing would be all the rage in no time . . . The subscribers came running . . .

In his office looking out over the gardens from under the arcades, Courtial des Pereires, thanks to his two hundred and twenty absolutely original handbooks, read all over the world, and thanks to *Genitron* magazine, exerted a peremptory and incomparable influence on the progress of the applied sciences. He directed, oriented, and multiplied the inventive effort of France, Europe, the universe, the whole vast ferment of the petty "certified" inventors . . .

Naturally all this took some doing, he had to attack people, defend himself, and watch out for underhanded tricks. He could make or break an inventor, you never could tell which, by word of mouth or a stroke of the pen, by a manifesto or a flea in somebody's ear. One day he'd almost started a riot with a series of talks on "the tellurian orientation and memory of swallows." . . . He was a wonder at writing digests, articles, lectures in prose, in verse, and sometimes, to attract attention, in puns . . . "Spare no effort to enlighten the family and educate the masses": that was the motto presiding over all his activities.

Genitron: Discussion, Invention, Aerostatics, that was the range of his interests, and actually those words were written all over the walls of his offices . . . on the title page and on the shop front . . . You couldn't go wrong . . . The most up-to-date muddled, complex controversies, the most daring, most subtly ingenious theories on physics, chemistry, electrothermics, or agricultural hygiene shriveled up like caterpillars at Courtial's command, and there wasn't another wiggle out of them . . . In two seconds flat he punctured them, knocked them cold . . . You could see their skeleton, their fabric . . . He had an X-ray mind . . . It took him only an hour's effort and furious concentration to knock the damnedest damnfoolishness, the most pretentious quadrature into shape for the *Genitron*, to make it accessible to the recalcitrant understanding of the most hopeless dolt, of the most boneheaded of his subscribers. It was magical work and he did it marvelously, turning out definitive, incontrovertible explanations and digests of the most preposterous, hairsplitting, farfetched, and nebulous hypotheses . . . By sheer force of conviction he'd have made a flash of lightning pass through the eye of a needle and light up a cigarette lighter, he'd have put thunder into a tin whistle. That was his des-

tiny, his training, his rhythm . . . to put the universe in
a bottle, to cork it up, and then tell the masses all about
it . . . Why! And how! . . . Later on when I was living
with him, it was frightening to think of all the things I
managed to learn in a twenty-four hour day . . . just by
hints and snatches . . . For Courtial nothing was obscure,
on one side there was matter, lazy and barbaric, and on
the other the mind to understand between the lines . . .
Genitron: invention, discovery, inspiration, light . . .
That was the subtitle of the paper. At Courtial's we worked
under the aegis of the great Flammarion,* his portrait with
a dedication stood in the middle of the shopwindow, he
was invoked like God almighty whenever the slightest argument came up, any pretext would do . . . He was the
highest authority, providence, the shining light . . . we
swore by him alone and maybe a little by Raspail. Courtial
had devoted twelve manuals to summaries of astronomical
discoveries and only four to the brilliant Raspail, to
"nature healing."

One day Uncle Édouard got the brilliant idea of going
up to the *Genitron* office to sound out the possibility of a
little job for me. He had another reason, he wanted to consult him about his bicycle pump . . . He'd known des
Pereires a long time, since the publication of his seventy-
second handbook, the one that people still read more than
any of the others, that was most widely distributed all over
the world and had done the most for his reputation, his
fame: *How to equip a bicycle in all latitudes and climates
for the sum of seventeen francs ninety-five, including all accessories and nickel-plated parts.* At the time of which I
am speaking this little manual published by the specialized
firm of Berdouillon and Mallarmé, on the Quai des Augus-
tins, was in its three-hundredth printing! . . . Today it is
hard to conceive of the enthusiasm, the general craze that
this piddling, insignificant work aroused when it came out
. . . But around 1900 *How to Equip a Bicycle* by
Courtial-Martin des Pereires was a kind of catechism for
the neophtye cyclist, his bedside reading, his Bible . . .
Still, Courtial never ceased to be shrewdly self-critical. A
little thing like that didn't turn his head. Naturally his rising fame brought him bigger and bigger mountains of mail,

* See Glossary.

more visitors, more tenacious pests, extra work, and more
acrimonious controversies . . . Very little pleasure . . .
People came to consult him from Greenwich and Val-
paraiso, from Colombo and Blankenberghe, on the various
problems connected with the "oblique" or "flexible" saddle
. . . how to avoid strain on the ball bearings . . . how
to grease the axles . . . the best hydrous mixture for
rust-proofing the handlebars . . . He was famous all right,
but the fame he got out of bicycles stuck in his craw. In
the last thirty years he had scattered his booklets like seeds
throughout the world, he had written piles of handbooks that were really a good deal more worthwhile,
digests and explanations of real value and stature . . . In
the course of his career he had explained just about everything . . . the fanciest and most complex of theories, the
wildest imaginings of physics and chemistry, the budding
science of radio-polarity . . . sidereal photography . . .
He'd written about them all, some more, some less. It gave
him a profound feeling of disillusionment, real melancholy,
a depressing kind of amazement to see himself honored,
adulated, glorified for the stuff he had written about inner
tubes and freewheeling . . . In the first place he personally detested bicycles . . . He'd never ridden one, he'd
never learned how . . . And on the mechanical side he
was even worse . . . He'd never have been able to take
off a wheel, not to mention the chain . . . He couldn't
do anything with his hands except on the horizontal bar
and the trapeze . . . Actually he was the world's worst
butterfingers, worse than twelve elephants . . . Just trying
to drive a nail in he'd mash at least two of his fingers, he'd
make hash of his thumb, it was a massacre the minute he
touched a hammer. I won't even mention pliers, he'd have
ripped out the wall, the ceiling, wrecked the whole room
. . . There wouldn't have been anything left . . . He
didn't have two cents' worth of patience, his thoughts
moved too fast and too far, they were too intense, too deep
. . . The resistance of matter gave him an epileptic fit
. . . The result was wreckage . . . He could tackle a
problem in theory . . . But when it came to practice, all
he could do on his own was swing dumbbells in the back
room . . . or on Sunday climb into the basket and shout
"Let her go" . . . and roll up in a ball to land when he

was through . . . Whenever he tried to do any tinkering
with his own fingers, it ended in disaster. He couldn't even
move anything without dropping it or upsetting it . . . or
getting it in his eye . . . You can't be an expert at everything . . . You've got to resign yourself . . . But among
his vast panoply of achievements, there was one in particular that he took the greatest pride in . . . It was his soft
spot . . . He'd tremble with emotion if you even mentioned it . . . If you came back to it regularly, you were
his pal. As a digest, it won't be any exaggeration to call it
an incomparable gem . . . a shattering triumph . . .
*The Complete Works of Auguste Comte Reduced to the
Dimensions of a Positivist Prayer in Twenty-two Acrostic
Verses!*

For this unprecedented performance he had been hailed
almost immediately all over America . . . Latin America,
that is . . . as a great renovator. A few months later the
Uruguayan Academy, assembled in plenary session, had
elected him by acclamation *Bolversatore Savantissima*
with the supplementary title of "life member" . . . The
following month the city of Montevideo, not to be outdone,
had proclaimed him *Citadinis Eternitatis Amicissimus*.
With such a title and the triumph he'd been having, Courtial had hoped to achieve new glory, of a somewhat higher
order . . . he'd thought he could really go to town . . .
take over the leadership of a lofty philosophical movement . . . "The Friends of Pure Reason" . . . But not
at all. Absolutely no soap. For the first time in his life he'd
really put his foot in it . . . He'd loused himself up completely . . . The high fame of Auguste Comte was easily
exported to the Antipodes, but couldn't make it back! It
stuck to the River Plate, indelible, undetachable. It refused to come home again. It was "for the Americans,"
and there was nothing to be done about it, though for
months and months he attempted the impossible . . . He
tried everything he could think of, blackened whole columns of the *Genitron,* trying to give his "prayer" a winsome
French flavor . . . he twisted it into a rebus, turned it
inside out like a shirt, sprinkled it with flattery . . . he
made it chauvinistic . . . Corneillian . . . violent, and
in the end contemptible . . . It didn't do him a bit of
good.

Even the bust of Auguste Comte, which had long occupied a place of honor . . . the customers were sick of seeing it there to the left of the great Flammarion, it had to be removed. It was bad for business. The subscribers complained. They didn't care for Auguste Comte. They liked Flammarion fine, Auguste Comte gave them the creeps. He loused up the shop window . . . That's the way it was. It couldn't be helped.

On certain evenings much later when Courtial was in the dumps, he said weird things . . .

"Some day, Ferdinand, I'm going away . . . I'll go far away . . . you'll see . . . to the end of the world . . . All by myself . . . on my own . . . You'll see . . ."

And then he'd stay there in a dream . . . I didn't like to interrupt him. He'd have those spells from time to time . . . It made me very curious . . .

Before des Pereires took me on, my uncle had done everything in his power to find me a job, he'd moved heaven and earth, stopped at nothing, he'd exhausted just about all his leads . . . Wherever he went he spoke of me in glowing colors . . . he got no results . . . He was certainly glad to put me up in his apartment on the rue de la Convention, but after all he wasn't rich . . . This couldn't go on forever. It wasn't right for me to take advantage of him . . . Besides I was in the way . . . His pad wasn't exactly spacious . . . I pretended to be asleep when he brought a tomato home with him on tiptoes . . . but just my being there must have cramped his style.

For one thing he was extremely modest . . . You'd never have expected it, but about some things he was positively bashful . . . Even after he'd known Courtial for months, for instance, he wasn't really at his ease with him. He sincerely admired him and didn't dare to ask anything of him . . . He'd waited too long before telling him about me . . . though it was certainly on his mind . . . He felt responsible in a way . . . for my being left high and dry . . . without the slightest sign of a job . . .

One day he finally screwed up his courage . . . As they were batting the breeze, he slipped in his little question . . . Wouldn't he by some chance need a young secretary, just starting out in life, for his Bureau of Inventors or his

aeronautics? . . . Uncle Édouard had no illusions about
my aptitudes. He realized that I wasn't very hot at the
usual kind of job . . . he had a pretty keen eye . . . that
my type and temperament required something out of the
way, some kind of fly-by-night racket, something on the
screwy side . . . With Courtial's hare-brained schemes,
his long-distance deals, I'd have a chance to make out
. . . That was his idea.

Courtial dyed his hair jet-black and left his moustache
and his goatee gray . . . His hair and his whiskers bristled
like a cat, and his bushy rebellious eyebrows were even
more ferocious, they were distinctly diabolical, especially
the one on the left. He had small restless eyes, his pupils
were always darting about deep in their caverns and then
suddenly stopping dead when he had a bright idea. Then
he'd laugh out loud, his whole belly would shake, he'd slap
his thighs hard and then suddenly subside as though transfixed by thought, lost in admiration of his idea . . .

It was he, Courtial des Pereires, who had obtained the
second driving license for racing cars issued in France.
Over the desk we had his diploma in a gold frame and
his photograph as a young man at the wheel of a monster, with the date and the rubber stamps. The end had
been tragic . . . He often told me about it:

"I was lucky," he admitted. "Take it from me. We were
coming into Bois-le-Duc . . . the carburation was perfect
. . . I didn't even want to slow down . . . I catch sight
of the schoolteacher . . . she had climbed up on the embankment . . . She motioned to me . . . She'd read all
my books . . . She waved her parasol . . . I didn't want
to be rude . . . I threw on my brakes outside the school
. . . In a minute I'm surrounded, fêted . . . I take a
drink . . . I wasn't supposed to stop again before Char-
tres . . . another ten miles . . . The last control station
. . . I invite the young lady to come along . . . 'Climb
in, mademoiselle,' I say . . . 'Climb in beside me. Come
along.' She was cute. She hesitated, she shilly-shallied, she
coquetted some . . . I pressed her . . . So she sits down
beside me and off we go . . . All day long, at every control station, especially all through Brittany, there'd been
cider and more cider . . . My machine was really humming, running fine . . . I didn't dare to make any more

stops . . . But I needed to bad . . . Finally I had to give in . . . So I throw on the brakes . . . I stop the car, I stand up, I jump, I spot a bush . . . I leave the chick at the wheel. 'Wait for me,' I sing out, 'I'll be back in a second . . .' I'd hardly touched a finger to my fly when so help me I'm stunned! Lifted off my feet! Dashed through the air like a straw in a gale! Boom! Stupendous! A shattering explosion! . . . The trees, the bushes all around, ripped up! mowed down! blasted! The air's aflame! I land at the bottom of a crater, almost unconscious . . . I feel myself . . . I pull myself together . . . I crawl to the road . . . A total vacuum! The car? . . . Gone, my boy . . . A vacuum! No more car! Evaporated! Demolished! Literally! The wheels, the chassis . . . oak! pitch-pine! All ashes! . . . The whole frame . . . Oh well! . . . I drag myself around, I scramble from one heap of earth to the next . . . I dig . . . I rummage . . . A few fragments here and there . . . a few splinters . . . A little piece of fan, a belt buckle. One of the caps of the gas tank. . . A hairpin . . . That was all . . . A tooth that I've never been sure about . . . The official investigation proved nothing . . . explained nothing . . . What would you expect? . . . The causes of that terrible conflagration will remain forever a mystery . . . Almost two weeks later in a pond, six hundred yards from the spot, they found . . . after a good deal of dredging . . . one of the young lady's feet, half devoured by the rats.

"For my part, though I can't claim to be absolutely certain, I might in a pinch accept one of the numerous hypotheses advanced at the time to explain that fire, that incredible explosion . . . it's possible that imperceptibly, little by little, one of our 'long fuses' shook loose . . . When you come to think of it, it would suffice for one of those thin minium rods, shaken by thousands of bumps and jolts, to come into contact for only a second . . . for a tenth of a second . . . with the gasoline nipples . . . The whole shebang would explode instantly! Like melinite! Like a shell! Yes, my boy, the mechanism was mighty precarious in those days. I went back to the place a long time after the disaster . . . There was still a charred smell . . . At that critical stage in the development of the automobile, I might add, a number of these fantastic explosions were

reported . . . almost as powerful! Everything pulverized!
Horribly scattered in all directions! Propelled through the
air for miles! . . . If pressed for a comparison, the only
thing I can think of is certain sudden explosions of liquid
air . . . And even there I have my reservations . . .
Those things are commonplace! Perfectly easy to explain
. . . from start to finish . . . beyond the shadow of a
doubt. No mystery at all! Whereas my tragedy remains an
almost complete mystery . . . We may as well admit it
in all modesty. But what importance has that today? None
whatever. Fuses haven't been used in ages. Such specula-
tion only impedes progress . . . Other problems demand
our attention . . . a thousand times more interesting! Ah,
my boy, that was a long time ago . . . Nobody uses
minium anymore . . . Nobody!"

Courtial hadn't, like myself, adopted the celluloid collar
. . . He had his own method of making ordinary cloth
collars wear-proof, dirt-proof, water-proof . . . It was a
kind of varnish that you put on in two or three coats . . .
It lasted at least six months . . . offering protection
against the dirt in the air, fingermarks, and perspiration.
It was a first-class product with a pure cellulose base. He'd
been wearing the same collar for the last two years. Out
of sheer coquetry he'd touch it up once a month . . . just
a stroke of the brush. That gave it the patina, the tone, you
could even say the orient, of old ivory . . . The same
with his shirt front . . . But contrary to what it said in
the prospectus, the fingers left distinct marks on the glazed
collar . . . big spots one on top of the other . . . The
result was a regular Bertillon * collection, the process
wasn't quite perfected. He himself admitted it occasionally.
Besides, he didn't have a name yet for this wonder product.
He said he'd get around to it when the time was ripe.

When it came to height, Courtial wasn't too well fixed
. . . He hadn't a quarter of an inch to spare . . . He
wore very high heels . . . altogether, he was particular
about his shoes . . . tan cloth uppers and little mother-
of-pearl buttons . . . Only he was like me, his feet stank
something awful . . . By Saturday afternoon the smell
was rough . . . He'd wash on Sunday morning, he told
me so. During the week he didn't have time. I knew all

* See Glossary.

those things . . . I'd never seen his wife, he told me all
about her. They lived in Montretout . . . He wasn't the
only one that had smelly feet . . . they were the curse of
the period . . . When the inventors came around all in a
sweat, usually from the other end of town, it was hard to
listen till they were through, even with the door wide open
on the big gardens of the Palais-Royal . . . The smells
that came your way at times were inconceivable . . . They
made me feel disgusted with my own dogs.

The disorder in the offices of the *Genitron* was something monstrous, in a class by itself . . . the place was a
junk shop, absolute chaos . . . From the door of the
shop to the ceiling of the second floor, every step of the
stairs, every ledge, every piece of furniture, the chairs, the
cupboards, were buried under papers, pamphlets, piles of
returns, all topsy-turvy, a desperate hodgepodge, creviced
and lacerated, the complete works of Courtial helter-
skelter, in pyramids, a fallow field. In that loathsome
muddle it was impossible to lay hands on the dictionary,
the historical maps, the oleographed dissertations. You'd
dig in at random, groping your way . . . sinking into
garbage, a leaking bilge . . . a teetering cliff . . . Suddenly it would cave in . . . you were caught in a cataract
. . . a landslide of blueprints and diagrams . . . ten tons
of printed matter would fall on your face . . . That would
start new avalanches, a frothing torrent of paper . . . a
dust storm . . . a volcano of stinking filth . . . Every
time we sold five francs' worth of merchandise the dikes
threatened to burst . . .

But that didn't bother him . . . He didn't even see
anything wrong with it, he felt no desire to change things,
to modify his methods . . . Not at all . . . He felt perfectly at home in the dizzy chaos . . . He never had to
look very long for the book he was after . . . He'd reach
in and there it was . . . He'd dive into any old pile . . .
The tatters would go flying, he'd burrow vigorously into
the heap and drill to the exact spot where the book was
concealed . . . The miracle happened every time . . .
He seldom went wrong . . . He had a feeling for disorder
. . . He was sorry for anybody who didn't . . . Order
is entirely in our ideas! In matter there's no trace of it!
. . . When I ventured to remark that it was absolutely im-

possible for me to find my way in that chaos, that bedlam, he'd get mean . . . he'd blast me. He didn't even give me time to breathe . . . He'd attack instantly . . . "I'm not asking the impossible of you, Ferdinand. You've never had the instinct, the essential curiosity, the desire to learn . . . After all, you can't claim to be deprived of books around here . . . Did you ever wonder, my poor young friend, what the human brain looks like? . . . The mechanism that makes you think? Did you? No. Of course not. That doesn't interest you one bit . . . You'd rather look at girls. So of course you don't know. Because the first honest glance would convince you that disorder, yes, my boy, disorder, is the quintessence of your very life! of your whole physical and metaphysical being! Why, it's your very soul, Ferdinand! millions, trillions of intricate folds . . . plunging deep down into the gray matter, complex, subjacent, evasive . . . limitless! That's Harmony, Ferdinand. All nature! A flight into the imponderable! And nothing else! Put your wretched thoughts in order, Ferdinand! That's where to begin. Not with grotesque, material, negative, obscene substitutions, but with the essential, that's what I'm getting at. Are you going to assault the brain, correct it, scrape it, mutilate it, force it to comply with an assortment of stupid rules? carve it up geometrically? recompose it according to the rules of your excruciating idiocy? . . . Arrange it in slices? like an Epiphany cake? . . . With a prize in the middle. Tell me that. I'm asking you. Frankly? Would that be any good? Would it make sense? Heaven help us! There's no doubt about it, Ferdinand, your soul is overwhelmed by errors. It makes you, like so many others, a unanimous nonentity. Great instinctive disorder is the father of fertile thoughts! It's the beginning of everything . . . Once the propitious moment has passed, there's no hope . . . You, I'm afraid, will spend your whole life in the garbage pail of reason . . . So much the worse for you! You're a numbskull, Ferdinand, a nearsighted, blind, preposterous, deaf, one-armed dolt! . . . befouling my magnificent disorder with your vicious reflections . . . In Harmony, Ferdinand, resides the world's only joy! The only deliverance! The only truth! . . . Harmony! Find Harmony, that's the ticket! . . . This shop is in Harmon-y . . . Do you hear me, Ferdinand? Like a brain,

neither more nor less! Order! Pah! Order! Rid me of that
word, that thing! Accustom yourself to Harmony and Harmony will reward you. You'll find everything you've been
looking for so long on the highways of the world . . . And
far more! Many other things, Ferdinand! A brain, Ferdinand, that's what the whole lot of you will find! Yes! The
Genitron is a brain. Have I made myself clear? That's not
what you're after? You and your kind? An inane ambush
of pigeonholes! A barricade of brochures! A house of the
dead! A Chartist necropolis! No, never! Here everything is
in movement! Swarming with life! You're not satisfied? It
stirs, it quivers! Just touch it! Put out your little finger.
Everything comes to life. Everything trembles instantly.
Asking only to surge up! to blossom! to shine! I don't live
by destroying. I take life as it comes! Do you take me for
a cannibal, Ferdinand? Never! . . . Bent on reducing it to
my chickenshit concepts? Pah! Everything shakes? Everything topples? Splendid! I have no desire to count stars 1!
2! 3! 4! and 5! I'm not the kind that thinks he's entitled to
do anything he pleases. The right to shrink! rectify! corrupt! prune! transplant! . . . No! . . . where would I
get it? . . . From the Infinite? . . . From life itself? It's
not natural, my boy! It's not natural! It's infamous meddling! . . . I prefer to keep on good terms with the
Universe! I take it as I find it! . . . I'll never rectify it!
No! The Universe is master of its own house! I understand
it! It understands me! It gives me a hand when I ask it!
When I'm through with it, I drop it! That's the long and
the short of it . . . It's a cosmogonic question! I have no
orders to give! You have no orders! He has no orders!
. . . Bah! Bah! Bah! . . ."

He got sore as hell, like somebody who's definitely in
the wrong . . .

Courtial's little handbooks were translated into a good
many languages, they were sold even in Africa. One of his
correspondents was a real nigger, the chief of a sultanate
in Upper Ubanghi Shari-Chad. That boy was wild about
elevators of every kind. They were his dream, his mania
. . . We'd sent him all the literature . . . He'd never
actually seen one. About 1893 Courtial had published a
regular treatise, *On Vertical Traction.* He knew all the

details, the many varieties, hydraulic, balistic, "electro-recuperative" . . . It was an excellent work, absolutely irrefutable, but it constituted only a slight and modest fraction of his opus as a whole. His knowledge definitely embraced every possible field.

The official world disapproved of him, looked down its nose at him, but the crustiest pedant couldn't very well do without his handbooks. In a good many schools they were actually a part of the curriculum. You couldn't imagine anything handier, simpler, easier to assimilate, all predigested! You could remember it, you could forget it without the slightest effort. We reckoned by and large that in France alone, at least one family out of four owned a copy of his *Family Astronomy, Economy Without Usury,* and *How to Make Ions* . . . At least one in twelve had his *Color Poetry,* his *Roof Gardening,* his *Poultry Raising at Home.* So far I've been speaking only of his practical works . . . But he had to his credit a whole series of other volumes (in numerous fascicles) that were real classics. *Hindustani Revelation, The Story of Polar Voyages from Maupertuis to Charcot.* Ponderous tomes. Reading matter for several winters, pounds and pounds of stories . . .

Everybody had commented, examined, copied, paraphrased, ridiculed, and looted his famous *Be Your Own Doctor,* his *True Language of Herbs,* and his *Electricity Without a Bulb* . . . All of them brilliant, attractive, definitive popularizations of sciences which in their pure form are exceedingly difficult, complex, and hazardous and which without Courtial would have remained beyond the reach of the general public, in other words, highfalutin', hermetic, and, to sum up without undue flattery, as good as useless . . .

Little by little, what with living in the closest intimacy with Courtial, I really got to know his character . . . Way down deep it wasn't so hot. The fact is he was pretty mean, petty, envious, and sneaky . . . Still, to be fair, I've got to admit that the work he did was a nightmare, struggling desperately, year in year out, to hold his own against that gang of raving maniacs, the *Genitron's* subscribers . . .

He spent ghastly, absolutely devastating hours . . . in a hotbed of asininity . . . And he had to bear up, to

defend himself, to return blow for blow, to sweep away all
resistance, to make a good impression on them, so they'd
all go away happy and want to come back . . .

At first Courtial was reluctant to take me on. He didn't
go for the idea . . . He thought me a little too tall, a little
too broad-shouldered, a little too husky for his shop. Even
without me, you couldn't move in all that mess . . . And
yet I wasn't expensive. I was being offered without pay, just
for board and lodging . . . My parents were perfectly
satisfied. I didn't need money, they kept telling my uncle
. . . I'd only put it to bad use . . . It was much more
important that I shouldn't live with them anymore . . .
That was the unanimous opinion of the whole family, of
the neighbors too, and of all our acquaintances . . . that
I be given something to do, no matter what! that I be kept
busy at any price! no matter where, no matter how! As long
as I wasn't left idle! and kept away! From one day to the
next, to judge by the way I had started out, I might set the
Passage on fire! That was the general sentiment . . .

Of course there was always the army . . . My father
asked nothing better . . . Only I still wasn't old enough
. . . I lacked at least eighteen months . . . So Pereires
and his valiant *Genitron* came in really handy, they were a
gift from heaven . . .

But Courtial hesitated and shilly-shallied a good deal
. . . He asked his wife what she thought about it. She
raised no objection . . . Actually she didn't give a hoot
in hell, she never came to the Galerie, she stayed out in
Montretout in her cottage. Before he made up his mind,
I'd been to see him at least ten times all by myself . . . He
talked abundantly . . . always and incessantly . . . I
was a very good listener . . . My father! England! . . .
Everywhere I'd listened . . . By that time I was in the
habit . . . It didn't bother me in the least. I didn't need
to answer. That was how I won him over . . . By keeping
my trap shut . . . Finally one evening he said:

"Well, my boy. I've kept you waiting quite a while, but
now I've thought things over thoroughly. I'm going to keep
you here with me. I think we'll get along . . . But you
mustn't make any demands on me . . . Oh no! Not a sou!
Not a centime! It can't be done. I should say not. Don't
expect anything. Never expect anything. I'm already having

a hell of a time making ends meet in these unpredictable times! covering the costs of the magazine, keeping the printer quiet! I'm harassed, crippled, exhausted! You understand? They dun me day and night. And surprises with the photographic plates . . . unforeseen expenses . . . It's out of the question. This isn't an industry . . . a business . . . some cushy monopoly . . . Far from it. It's a frail skiff sailing before the wind of the spirit . . . And what storms, my boy, what storms! . . . You want to join us? Good! I take you, I welcome you! Fine! Come aboard! But I'm telling you in advance! You won't find a single doubloon in the hold . . . Empty hands . . . little in your pocket . . . No bitterness . . . No rancor . . . You'll get lunch . . . You'll sleep on the mezzanine, I used to sleep there myself . . . in the Tunisian office . . . you'll make up the couch . . . It's perfectly comfortable . . . you'll be marvelously at peace . . . Lucky boy! . . . Wait and see, in the evening, how pleasant, how peaceful it is! After nine o'clock the Palais-Royal is all yours! You'll be happy, Ferdinand! . . . Just think of me, rain, thunder, or tempest, I still have to traipse out to Montretout! It's abject slavery. I'm expected! Ah, let me tell you, it's awful some days. When I see the locomotive, I'm so exasperated I could fling myself under the wheels! Ah! I restrain myself . . . for my wife's sake. And a little for my experiments. My radio-telluric garden! Well, all in all, I've no business complaining. She's been through a good deal. And she is charming. You'll see Madame des Pereires one of these days. She gets so much pleasure out of her garden . . . It's all hers . . . And she hasn't much in her life . . . That and her house . . . And myself too, a little. I'd forgotten myself. Ha! Ha! That's a good one. Well, we've joked enough. It's settled. Splendid! Shake on it! Then we understand each other? As man to man. Fine. In the daytime you'll run errands. You'll have plenty of them. But don't worry, Ferdinand, I mean to take you in hand too, to guide you, equip you, raise you to the heights of knowledge . . . No salary! Of course not! Not in cash, that is. But spiritual fare! Ah, Ferdinand, you don't realize what you stand to gain. No! no! no! You'll leave me some day, Ferdinand . . . inevitably . . ." Already there was sadness in his voice. "You'll leave me . . . You'll be rich! Yes, rich! I'm telling you!"

He had me flabbergasted, I stood there open-mouthed.

"You understand me, Ferdinand . . . Everything isn't in a pocketbook . . . No! There's nothing in a pocket-book! Nothing!"

I was of the same opinion . . .

"Well, as a starter, here's an idea. How about giving you a title? A *raison d'être!* It's indispensable in our line of business . . . an official label! . . . I'm going to put you on our stationery, on all our paper! 'Secretary in charge of Stock.' What do you think of it? It sounds good to me . . . Is it all right with you? Not too pretentious? Not too vague? . . . OK?"

It was all right with me . . . Everything was all right with me . . . But there wasn't anything honorary about that title . . . the stock was real and it was hard work . . . He set me straight right away . . . My job was to do all the delivering with a pushcart . . . all the hauling to the printer's and back . . . In addition I was responsible for every tear in the big balloon . . . I had to keep tabs on all the hardware he left lying around, the barometers, the ropes, all the little gadgets . . . I had to mend the rips and the big bag . . . patch things up with cord and glue . . . and attend to all the knots in the cables and guy ropes . . . all the tackle that broke in midair . . . The *Enthusiast* was a venerable old balloon, even down there in the cellar sprinkled with moth flakes, it was eminently given to decay . . . thousands of grubs feasted in the folds . . . luckily the rubber repelled the rats . . . there were tiny little mice that nibbled at the silk. I'd locate the tears in the *Enthusiast,* the tiniest holes, and patch them like a pair of pants . . . with oversewing, hems, pleats, depending on the nature of the tear . . . It was in pretty bad shape all over, I mended for hours on end, after a while I got really absorbed . . .

At least in that cubbyhole of a gymnasium there was a little more elbowroom . . . And besides the customers in the shop weren't supposed to see me . . .

Some day, it was stipulated in our solemn agreement, I was to go up in the contraption, to an altitude of a thousand feet . . . Some Sunday . . . I'd be second in command

. . . a different title . . . He told me that, I suppose, to make me mind my mending . . . The old buzzard was pretty sly under those shaggy eyebrows . . . He looked at me out of his mean little eyes . . . I was on to his game . . . As a soft-soap artist he had no equal . . . He was giving me a song and dance . . . But we ate pretty well in the back room . . . I wasn't too unhappy . . . Naturally he had to take me for a ride . . . or he wouldn't have been the boss.

At about four o'clock, when I was knee-deep in my sewing, he'd look in: "Ferdinand," he'd say, "I'm closing up . . . if anybody asks for me, tell them I stepped out five minutes ago. Anyway I'll make it fast. I won't be long."

Putting two and two together, I knew where he was going. He'd run down to the Insurrection, the little bar at the corner of the Passage Villedo and the rue Radziwill, for the racing results . . . That was the time they came out . . . He never told me anything definite . . . But I knew . . . When he had won, he came back whistling a Matchiche * . . . That wasn't very often . . . When he'd lost, he'd chew on his quid and spit in all directions . . . He'd check up in *Turf,* his dope sheet, that he always left lying around . . . He'd mark his ponies with blue pencil . . . This was the first vice I detected in him.

If he wasn't too eager to take me on, it was mostly on account of the horses . . . He was afraid I'd blab . . . go noising it around the neighborhood that he played in Vincennes . . . that the subscribers would get wind of it. He told me so later . . . He lost stupendously . . . he wasn't very lucky. Whether he tried a combination or bet with his eyes closed, he lost his money . . . Maisons, Saint-Cloud, or Chantilly, it was always the same story . . . A bottomless pit . . . All the subscription money went into the "classics"! And the dough he took in with the balloon was swallowed up in Auteuil . . . The Equine Race * was rolling in clover! Longchamp! La Porte! Arcueil-Cachan! Giddyap giddyup, and down the drain. I could see the cash drawer going down. There was no great

* See Glossary.

mystery. Our petty cash was always running with the
ponies . . . trotting! limping! to win! to place! to come in
fourth! . . . simple or fancy, it made no difference . . .
he'd never get back when he went to see about those
proofs . . . We ate beans to try and mollify the printer
. . . My veal stew had to last all week, and we ate on our
knees with a napkin in the back of the shop . . . It didn't
seem so very funny to me . . . When he'd lost heavily,
he didn't explain, he never admitted it . . . But he'd get
vindictive, touchy, aggressive with me . . . He'd abuse
his power . . .

After a trial period of two months, he fully realized that
I'd never be happy anywhere else . . . that the *Genitron*
routine was right down my alley, that it suited me fine, that
anywhere else or in any other racket I'd be impossible
. . . That was my Destiny . . . When he chanced to win,
he'd never put anything back in the till, he got stingier than
ever, like he was trying to get even . . . He'd have curry-
combed a penny . . . Always sly and deceitful, worse
than a dozen false bosoms . . . He told me such whoppers they'd stick in my craw at night . . . They were so
steep, so crummy, so indigestible, I'd mull them over . . .
They woke me up with a start. Sometimes he really over-
did it . . . he'd dream up any damn thing . . . so as not
to pay me . . . But when he came home from the provinces, when he'd put on a good show with his balloon and
made a sensation . . . when they'd bowled him over with
compliments . . . and the *Enthusiast* hadn't split too
many seams . . . there'd be an outburst of generosity
. . . He'd spend like mad . . . He'd bring in piles of
eats through the back door . . . whole baskets full . . .
For a week we shoveled in so much we couldn't chew anymore . . . our suspenders were bursting . . . You had
to make hay while the sun was shining, because soon
there'd be famine . . . the ragouts would begin again
. . . we'd stretch the stew with pickles . . . with sardines
. . . with little onions . . . And around toward rent
time there'd be strictly bread soup, with or without potatoes . . . He at least was lucky, he'd be getting another
meal in the evening with his old lady. He wouldn't lose any
weight . . . I wouldn't get beans.

From going hungry I began to wise up too . . . I op-

erated with the subscriptions . . . The business didn't
have any regular receipts . . . only expenses . . . He
knocked himself out with his bookkeeping. He had to
show his wife the books. Her supervision exasperated him
. . . It put him into a vile temper . . . He'd sweat for
hours . . . Nothing but loops and zeroes . . .

All the same there was one department where he never
cheated me, never disappointed me, never once bluffed me
or let me down. I'm referring to my scientific education
. . . On that score he never weakened, never hesitated a
second . . . He always came through . . . As long as I
listened to him, he was always happy, delighted, overjoyed
. . . He was always ready to give me an hour, two hours,
and more, sometimes he'd spend whole days explaining
something or other . . . Anything that can be understood,
solved, communicated, in connection with the direction of
the winds, the movements of the moon, the functioning of
heating installations, the ripening of cucumbers, the reflections of the rainbow . . . Yes, teaching was really a con-
suming passion with him. He'd have liked to teach me
everything in the world and from time to time play a mean
trick on me! He couldn't help it . . . in either case! I used
to think it all over in the back room, while mending his
contraption . . . That was his nature . . . he was a man
who had to work off his energy . . . He had to throw
himself wholeheartedly in one direction or another, he
never did things by halves. He wasn't boring! No, you
could never accuse him of that. What I'd really have liked
to do was to visit his home some day . . . He often
spoke to me of his old lady, but he never let me see her.
She never came to the office. She didn't care for the *Genitron*. She must have had her reasons.

When my mother was perfectly sure I was all set, that I
wasn't going to pick up and leave, that I had a steady job
with this des Pereires, she came over to the Palais-Royal in
person, to bring me some underwear . . . It was really a
pretext . . . she wanted to look around, to see what the
place was like . . . She was as curious as a titmouse, she
always wanted to see, to find out about everything . . .
What was the *Genitron* like? And my lodgings? Was I getting enough to eat?

It wasn't very far from her shop to our place . . . No more than a fifteen minutes' walk . . . Even so, she was groaning with fatigue when she got there . . . She was completely bushed . . . I saw her in the distance . . . from the end of the Galerie. I was talking with a subscriber. She was leaning on the shopwindows, resting without letting on, every fifty feet she'd stop . . . She looked awfully thin, and besides she'd gone sallow, her eyelids and cheeks had shriveled, she was all wrinkled around the eyes. She really looked sick . . . She gave me my socks, my underdrawers, and my big handkerchiefs, and then right away she started talking about Papa, though I hadn't asked . . . He'd feel the effects of my assault to his dying day, she sobbed. Twice already they'd brought him home from the office in a cab . . . He could hardly stand up . . . He had fainting spells all the time . . . He sent word that he gladly forgave me, but that he didn't want to see me again . . . not for a long time . . . not before my military service . . . until my looks and mentality had changed completely . . . when I got back from the army . . .

Courtial was just coming back from a stroll, probably to the Insurrection. Maybe he hadn't dropped as much as usual . . . in any case he was extremely polite all of a sudden, as charming and friendly as he could be . . . delighted to meet her . . . And about me? Reassuring. Right away he set out to charm my mother, he asked her upstairs for a chat . . . in his private office . . . on the "Tunisian" mezzanine . . . She had difficulty in following him . . . It was a horrible corkscrew staircase and to make matters worse it was littered with piles of garbage and papers that made you skid. He was mighty proud of his "Tunisian office." He wanted to show it to everybody. It was a devastating layout in the hyperpoky style, with "Alcazar" cabinets . . . You couldn't conceive of anything crummier . . . And then the Moorish coffeepot, the Moroccan ottomans, the fringed shaggy carpet that stored up a whole ton of dust all by itself . . . Nothing had ever been done about it . . . not even the slightest attempt at cleaning . . . Anyway the heaps of printed matter, the mountains, the cataracts of proof, of type, of newsprint lying around would have mocked any effort . . . Actually, there's no denying it, it would have been dangerous . . . To come around troubling the equilibrium would be taking a big risk . . . The only way was to leave it perfectly intact, to move things as little as possible . . . Better still, I soon found out, was to toss on new layers of litter as you went along. That gave the surface a certain freshness . . . a kind of gloss.

I heard them talking . . . Courtial told her frankly that he had discerned in me a real aptitude for the kind of journalism that was just what the *Genitron* needed . . . reporting . . . technical investigation . . . scientific research . . . objective criticism . . . that I was sure to get ahead . . . that she could go home with an easy mind and sleep soundly . . . that the future was already smiling on me . . . it would be all mine as soon as I'd acquired all the essential knowledge. It was a matter of simple routine and patience . . . He'd gradually teach me all I needed . . . But all that took time . . . Ah yes, he had no use for haste! Thoughtless precipitation! . . . No use trying to force matters . . . to go too fast . . . That would be idiotic waste! Anyway, according to his song and dance, I displayed a keen desire for education! . . . Moreover, I was learning to be clever with my hands. I did the little jobs that came my way to perfection . . . I was managing very nicely . . . I was getting to be as nimble as a monkey! Eager! Intelligent! Hardworking! Discreet! In short, a dream! He went on and on . . . It was the first time in her life that my poor mama had heard anybody speak of me in such glowing colors . . . She couldn't get over it . . . At the end of the interview, as she was leaving, he insisted on her taking a whole book of subscription blanks to distribute at random among her connections and acquaintances . . . She promised to do anything he pleased. She gaped at him in bewilderment . . . Courtial had no shirt on, only his varnished shirt front over his flannel vest, but the vest always went way up over his collar . . . he took an extra large size, it formed a kind of ruff, and of course it was completely filthy . . . In winter he wore two of them, one on top of the other . . . In the summer, even during hot spells, he wore his long frock coat, his lacquered collar down a little lower, no socks, and he brought out his boater. He took meticulous care of it . . . It was a unique item, a real masterpiece of the sombrero type, a gift from South America, a rare weave! Impossible to match . . . In short, it was priceless! . . . From the first of June to the fifteenth of September he kept it on his head. He hardly ever took it off . . . except for some extra-special reason . . . He was sure somebody'd steal it . . . That was his biggest worry on Sundays, before going up in his balloon . . . But there was no help for it, he had to exchange it for his cap, the tall one with the braid . . . That was part of his uniform . . . He entrusted his treasure to me . . . But the moment he'd touched the ground, the moment he'd rolled like a rabbit into the muck and come bouncing over the furrows, that was his first cry: "Hey, my panama! Ferdinand! My panama, dammit . . ."

My mother noticed the thickness of the flannel vest right off and the fine quality of the prize hat . . . He let her feel the weave, to give her an idea . . . For quite some time she was lost in admiration, exclaiming: "Oh! Ttt! Oh! Ttt! . . . Ah, monsieur, I can see that. It's the kind of straw they don't make anymore!" She was in ecstasy.

All this restored my mother's confidence . . . a good omen . . . She was particularly fond of flannel vests . . . they indicated solidity of character, she'd never gone wrong. After fond farewells, she gradually started on her way . . . For the first time in her life and mine I think she was a little less worried about my future and my fate.

It was perfectly true that I threw myself into my work. From morning to night I had no chance to loaf . . . In addition to my cargoes of printed matter, I had the *Enthusiast* in the cellar, the endless mending, and our pigeons that I had to look after two or three times a day . . . Those critters lived all week in the maid's room on the seventh floor, under the eaves . . . They cooed like mad . . . They never felt gloomy. Their working day was Sunday, they'd be taken out in a basket for a ride in the balloon . . . At six or eight hundred feet Courtial would raise the lid . . . They'd be released . . . with messages . . . They'd all fly straight home . . . to the Palais-Royal! . . . The window'd be left open for them . . . They never dawdled on the way, they didn't care for the

country, they didn't like to bum around . . . They flew
back automatically . . . They loved their attic and their
roo-coo-crooing. That's all they wanted. It never stopped
. . . They were always home before us. I've never known
pigeons less enthusiastic about traveling, so enamored of
peace and quiet . . . And I left their windows wide open
. . . It never occcurred to them to take a turn around the
garden . . . to go calling on the sparrows . . . or the
fat gray cooers gallivanting on the lawns . . . around the
fountains . . . and once in a while on the statues . . .
on Desmoulins * . . . or old Vick * . . . dropping
their beauty marks . . . Not at all . . . they kept to
themselves . . . they were perfectly happy in their attic,
they left it only under duress, when they were tossed into
their basket . . . They were pretty expensive though, on
account of the grain . . . It takes quantities, pigeons eat
a lot . . . They're pigs . . . you wouldn't expect them
to eat so much . . . it's on account of their high body
temperature, normally 107 and a few tenths . . . I swept
up their droppings carefully . . . I made several little
piles along the wall and I let them dry . . . That made up
some for their food . . . It was excellent fertilizer . . .
When I had a whole sack full, about twice a month,
Courtial took it away, he used it in his garden . . . in
Montretout on the hill . . . where he had his tony villa
and his experimental garden . . . there's no better
manure . . .

I got along fine with the pigeons, they reminded me a
little of Jongkind . . . I taught them tricks . . . Naturally after they got to know me, they ate out of my hand
. . . But I did a lot better than that, I got them to perch
on a broomstick, all twelve of them at once . . . I even
managed to carry them down to the shop . . . and back
up again without their moving, without a single one of
them deciding to fly away . . . They were really sedentary. When it came time to throw them in the basket and
push off, they got terribly sad. They didn't coo at all. They
hid their heads in their feathers. They hated it.

Two more months passed . . . Little by little Courtial
gained confidence in me. He was convinced that we were

* See Glossary.

made to get along . . . I had a lot of advantages, I wasn't very particular about food or pay or working hours . . . I never complained . . . As long as I was free in the evening, as long as nobody bothered me after seven o'clock, I felt I was well off . . .

From the moment he lit out for his train, I was the one and only boss of the shop and paper . . . I got rid of the inventors . . . I soft-soaped them . . . then I started out on a cruise, often heading for the shipping office on the rue Rambuteau, pulling the cart loaded with copies of the rag. At the beginning of the week I had to bring back proofs, the typos and plates and engravings. What with the pigeons, the *Enthusiast,* and a million other odds and ends, there was never a letup . . . He dropped everything and pushed off for the sticks . . . He had urgent work out there, so he said. Hm! Neo-agriculture . . . he said it with a straight face . . . but I was convinced it was hokum . . . Sometimes he forgot to come back, he'd stay out for two or three days . . . that didn't worry me . . . I'd take a little rest, I needed it . . . I'd feed the pigeons up in the attic, then I'd paste up a sign in the middle of the shopwindow: "Closed for the day" . . . I'd go take it easy on a bench, under the trees nearby . . . From there I watched the joint, the people coming and going . . . I saw them in the distance, always the same gang of dopes, the same lunatics, the same haggard faces, the old crowd of bellyachers, the disgruntled subscribers . . . They bunked into the sign, they massacred the door handle, they beat it . . . That was fine with me.

When his nibs came back from his spree, he had a screwy look . . . He eyed me curiously to see if I suspected anything . . .

"I was detained," he said. "The experiment wasn't quite perfected . . . I thought I'd never be through."

"That's too bad," I said. "I hope you made out all right in the end . . ."

Little by little he filled me in, he told me a little more each day, he gave me all the details about the beginnings of his racket . . . There were some pretty wild stories, gimmicks that could end you in the cemetery. How it had started, the ups and downs, the risky dodges, the shady little deals . . . He told me the whole story, which was pretty strange when you think of his rotten character, his innumerable suspicions, and all his calamities and hard luck . . . He wasn't the complaining kind . . . But the troubles and messes he'd been through were unbelievable . . . It was no rest cure monkeying around with inventors . . . Don't get the wrong slant . . . Oh no. Some of those boys were real savages, absolutely diabolical . . . they'd go off like dynamite if they felt they'd been taken . . . And naturally you can't hope to please everybody . . . the devil and his brother-in-law! That would be too sweet. I knew something about that myself . . . In that connection he gave me an example of malice that was really hair-raising . . . The lengths people will go to . . .

In 1884 he'd got an order from Beaupoil and Brandon on the Quai des Ursulines, the publishers of *Epoch*, for a textbook intended for the second program of the Preliminary Schools . . . A concise work, of course, but carefully executed, elementary but compact. Specially condensed . . . *The Home Astronomer,* the little book was entitled, with the subtitle: *Gravitation, explained to the whole family.* So he goes to work . . . He dives right in . . . he might have contented himself with delivering a brief work on the specified date, a hurry-up job full of inept borrowings from foreign periodicals . . . slapdash, corrupt, garbled quotations, and in three shakes of a lamb's tail constructed a new cosmogony a thousand times lousier than all the other miniature handbooks, full of mistakes and absolutely senseless! . . . Utterly useless! . . . As everyone knew, that wasn't Courtial's way of doing things. He was conscientious. His chief concern when he sat down to a piece of work was to get tangible results . . . He wanted his reader to form his own ideas in person, by his own observations . . . about the most essential aspects of the work . . . the stars and gravitation . . . to discover the laws for himself . . . He wanted to force the always indolent reader to do real laboratory work and not just cajole him with flattering flimflam . . . He'd appended a little set of instructions: how to build a "family telescope" . . . A few squares of cardboard provided the darkroom . . . a few cheap mirrors . . . an ordinary lens . . . a few lengths of pliable wire . . . a cardboard packing tube . . . By strictly following the instructions you could do it for seventeen francs, seventy-two (reckoned to the centime) . . . for that price (in addition to the exciting and instructive work) you could obtain in your own home, not only a direct view of the principal constellations, but also photographs of most of the large stars of our zenith . . . "All sidereal observations made available to the family" . . . that was his formula . . . As soon as the booklet came out, more than twenty-five thousand readers started without a moment's delay to build the thing, the marvelous miniature photosidereal device. . .

I can still hear des Pereires telling me about all the trouble that ensued . . . The incomprehension of the competent authorities . . . their abject partiality . . . How painful, rotten, sickening it all was . . . All the libels he had received. Threats . . . Challenges . . . A thousand threatening letters . . . Summonses . . . How he'd been obliged to lock himself in, barricade himself in his apartment! . . . He'd been living on the rue Monge at the time . . . Then, more and more harassed, he'd fled to Montretout from the rage of all those insatiable, vicious peeping toms, disappointed by telescopy . . . The mess had gone on for six months . . . and it still wasn't over! Some of those angry stargazers, even pestier than the rest, would take advantage of their Sunday off . . . They'd come out to Montretout, they'd bring the whole family, to kick the boss in the ass . . . He hadn't been able to receive any visitors in almost a year . . . This "photosidereal" business was only a small example among many others of how the masses were capable of reacting the minute you tried to educate them, to uplift them, to wise them up . . .

"I can tell you, Ferdinand, that I've suffered for science . . . Worse than Flammarion, that's certain! worse than Raspail! worse even than Mongolfier! * On a small scale, of course . . . I've done everything! And then some!" He used to repeat that often . . . I didn't answer . . . He gave me a sidelong look . . . suspicious . . . he wanted to see the impression he was making . . . Then he'd dive right into the chaos . . . looking for his file . . . He'd locate it by instinct under the enormous mound . . . He'd

* See Glossary.

pat the dust off it . . . He'd change his mind . . . He'd
cautiously open it up in front of me . . .

"When I think it over, I'm sorry . . . Maybe I too
have become a trifle bitter, carried away by memories . . .
Perhaps I'm a little unjust . . . Good Lord. I've reason
enough . . . I ask you! In the course of time I've forgotten . . . that was very wrong of me . . . not intentionally, to be sure! not intentionally! . . . the most
touching, perhaps the most sincere, the most precious
testimonials . . . Ah! They haven't all failed to appreciate
me! . . . The whole human race isn't so absolutely depraved . . . No! A few noble souls here and there in the
world . . . have been able to recognize my absolute good
faith. Here! Here! And still another!" He pulled out letters
and memoranda at random from his collection . . . "I'll
read you one among many":

> Dear Courtial, honored master and revered pre-
> cursor: It is assuredly thanks to you, to your admir-
> able and so scrupulous telescope (for the family)
> that yesterday at two o'clock on my own balcony I
> was able to view the whole moon, in its *complete*
> totality, with its mountains, its rivers, and even I be-
> lieve, a forest . . . Perhaps even a lake! I hope to
> see Saturn too with my children in the course of the
> coming week, as it is indicated (in italics) on your
> "sidereal calendar" and also Bellegophorus a little
> later, in the last days of the autumn, as you yourself
> have written on page 242 . . . Yours, dear, gra-
> cious, and benevolent master, yours in heart, body,
> and spirit, here below and in the stars.
>
> One who has been transformed.

He kept all these admiring letters in his mauve and
lavender portfolio. As for the others, unfavorable, menacing, draconic, vicious, he burned them on the spot. In this
connection at least, he kept a certain amount of order . . .
"The poison's going up in smoke," he told me every time
he touched a match to one of those monstrosities . . .
How much evil would be eliminated if everybody did the
same. My idea is that he wrote the favorable ones himself
. . . He showed them to visitors . . . He never actually

admitted it to me . . . Now and then I smiled . . .
There was a certain restraint in my approval . . . He
half-suspected that I smelled a rat. Then he'd scowl at me
. . . I'd go up to feed the pigeons or I'd go down to the
Enthusiast . . .

By now I was laying his bets for him at the Insurrection
on the corner of the Passage Radziwill. He preferred for
me to do it on account of the customers, it could have been
bad for business . . . On Cartouche and Lysistrata in the
Vincennes gallops . . . and giddyup and away we go!

"You'll tell them it's your own sugar." . . . He owed
all the bookies money. He had no desire at all to show his
face . . . The character that took most of our bets between the saucers had a funny name, he was called
Formerly . . . He had a way of stuttering, of garbling the
names of the winners . . . He did it on purpose, I think,
to give you a wrong steer . . . Afterwards he'd deny
everything . . . He'd want to skip the number . . . I
always made him write it down . . . we lost anyway.

I'd bring back the *Turf Echo* or *Racing Luck* . . . If
he'd lost heavily, he had the crust to give me hell . . . He
sent all the inventors away . . . He threw them all out
with their models and diagrams . . . "Go wipe your ass,
the whole lot of you. Those blueprints stink . . . You got
a headache? . . . They smell of axle grease, margarine
. . . You call that ideas? Innovations? Hell, I can piss
better ideas than that . . . a whole potful! . . . three
times a day . . . Aren't you ashamed of yourself? Don't
you realize? . . . It's a disaster! You have the gall to
bring that stuff here? To me? When I'm up to my neck in
crap already . . . Get out of here! Christ! You lounge
lizards! You loafers in body and soul! . . ."

The guy would leave all right, he'd run for the door,
he'd fly with his roll of plans. Courtial was fed up with
them. He wanted to think of something else . . . I was
the scapegoat, he started in on me . . . any old baloney
would do . . . "You, naturally, you suspect nothing! You
have time to listen to everything! You've got nothing to do,
is that it? . . . But I'm not exactly in that position . . .
I can't look at things that way . . . I have preoccupations
. . . metaphysical preoccupations! . . . Permanent! In-
eluctable! That's right! They leave me no rest! Never!

Even when I don't show it! When I'm talking to you about one thing and another, I'm haunted . . . harassed . . . tormented by riddles! . . . Well, there you have it! You didn't know! It comes as a surprise to you? You never suspected it?"

He stared at me again as if he hadn't ever really placed me . . . He straightened out his moustaches, he dusted off the dandruff . . . He went for a rag to pass over his shoes . . . All the while telling me what he thought of me . . .

"What can it matter to you? You just drift along. You don't give a good godamm about the universal consequences that can flow from our most trifling acts, our most unforeseen thoughts . . . It's no skin off your ass . . . You're caulked . . . hermetically sealed . . . Nothing means anything to you . . . Am I right? Nothing. Eat! Drink! Sleep! Up there as cozy as you please . . . All warm and comfy on my couch . . . You've got everything you want . . . You wallow in well-being . . . the earth rolls on . . . How? Why? A staggering miracle . . . how it moves . . . the profound mystery of it . . . toward an infinite unforeseeable goal . . . in a sky all scintillating with comets . . . all unknown . . . from one rotation to the next . . . Each second is the culmination and also the prelude of an eternity of other miracles . . . of impenetrable wonders, thousands of them, Ferdinand! Millions! billions of trillions of years! . . . And you? What are you doing in the midst of this cosmologonic whirl? this vast sidereal wonder? Just tell me that! You eat! You fill your belly! You sleep! You don't give a damn . . . That's right! Salad! Swiss cheese! Sapience! Turnips! Everything! You wallow in your own muck! You loll around, befouled! Glutted! Satisfied! You don't ask for anything more! You pass through the stars . . . as if they were raindrops in May! . . . God, you amaze me, Ferdinand! Do you really think this can go on forever? . . ."

I didn't say a word . . . I had no set opinion about the stars or the moon, but I had one about him, the bastard. And the stinker knew it.

"Take a look some time in the little cabinet upstairs. Put them all together. I've received at least a hundred such letters. I wouldn't want them to be stolen . . . There's an

idea, why don't you file them? . . . You like order so
much . . . you'll get a kick out of it . . ." I saw through
him . . . He was handing me a line . . . "You'll find
the key on top of the gas meter . . . I'm going out for a
while . . . you can close up . . ." He changed his mind.
"No, you'd better stick around in case somebody comes in.
Tell them I've gone away . . . far away! far far away! on
an expedition . . . Tell them I've gone to Senegal!
Pernambuco! Mexico! . . . any place you like . . .
Christ, I've had enough for today! . . . It turns my stomach to see them coming in from the gardens . . . I'll puke
if I see one more of them . . . Hell, I don't care . . .
Tell them anything you please . . . Tell them I've gone
to the moon . . . that it's no use waiting . . . And now
open up the cellar . . . Hold the lid properly! Don't let it
fall back on my head the way you did last time . . . I bet
you did it on purpose . . ."

To those words I made no reply . . . He stepped into
the hole. He went down two three rungs . . . He waited
a moment. Then he said . . .

"You're not a bad kid, Ferdinand . . . your father's
mistaken about you. You're not bad . . . You're un-
formed, that's it . . . pro-to-plas-mic! What month are
you, Ferdinand? What month were you born in, I mean!
February? September? March?"

"February, *maître!*"

"I'd have bet five francs on it. February! Saturn! What's
going to become of you! Poor devil! Why, it's insane! Well,
anyway, lower the trap. When I'm all the way down. All
the way, see? Not before! And have me break both my
legs. This ladder's a wreck! it sags in the middle! . . . I
should have repaired it long ago . . . Let her go! . . ."
He went on shouting from deep down in the cellar . . .
"Whatever happens, don't let anybody in! No pests! No
drunks! You hear me, I'm not here for anybody! I want
privacy! Absolute privacy! . . . Maybe I'll be gone two
hours . . . maybe two days . . . But I don't want to be
disturbed. Don't worry about me. Maybe I'll never come
up! If they ask you, you don't know a thing . . . I'm
going into meditation . . . You understand?"

"Yes, *maître!*"

"Total, exhaustive meditation, Ferdinand! Exhaustive retirement! . . ."

"Yes, *maître* . . ."

I let the thing slam full force in a volcano of dust. It thundered like a cannon . . . I pushed the newspapers over the trapdoor, it was completely camouflaged . . . you couldn't see the opening . . . I went up to feed the pigeons . . . I stayed quite a while . . . If he was still in his hole when I came back down, I began to wonder if anything was wrong . . . I waited a while longer . . . half an hour . . . three quarters of an hour . . . then I began to think the monkeyshines had been going on long enough . . . I lifted the trap a little and looked in . . . If I didn't see him, I made a racket . . . I banged the trapdoor . . . He had to answer . . . It brought him out of his nirvana . . . Nearly always he was sawing wood under the transom in the folds of the *Enthusiast,* in the rolling billows of silk . . . It took some doing to get him to move . . . Finally he'd surface . . . He'd reappear . . . rubbing his eyes . . . He'd brush off his frock coat . . . Back in the shop he'd be all befuddled . . .

"I'm dazzled, Ferdinand! How beautiful it is! Beautiful, like fairyland!"

He looked pasty, the talk had gone out of him, he had calmed down . . . He went "bdia, bdia, bdia" with his tongue . . . He went out . . . teetering from his nap . . . He walked slantwise like a crab . . . Port of call: the Pavillon de la Régence! The café that looked like a china birdcage, with pretty piers . . . in those days it was still in the middle of a moldering flowerbed . . . He slumped down the first place he found . . . at the table by the door . . . I had a good view of him from the shop . . . He started off with his usual absinthe . . . It was easy to see him . . . We still had our nifty telescope in the window . . . the one left from the big show . . . Maybe you couldn't see Saturn through it, but you could see des Pereires sugaring his pea soup * . . . Then he had an "anisette" and after that a vermouth . . . The colors were easy to make out . . . and just before taking off for his train a good stiff grog for the road.

* See Glossary.

After his terrible accident Courtial had taken a solemn vow that he'd never again, at any price, take the wheel in a race . . . That was all over . . . finished . . . He'd kept his promise . . . And even now, twenty years later, he had to be begged before he'd drive on some quiet excursion, or in an occasional harmless demonstration. He felt much safer out in the wind in his balloon . . .

His studies of mechanics were all contained in his books . . . Year in year out he published two treatises (with diagrams) on the development of motors and two handbooks with plates.

One of these little works had stirred up bitter controversies and even a certain amount of scandal. Actually it wasn't even his fault . . . It was all on account of some low-down sharpers who travestied his ideas in an idiotic money-making scheme . . . It wasn't at all in his style. Anyway here's the title:

An Automobile Made to Order for 322 Francs 25. Complete instructions for home manufacture. Four permanent seats, two folding seats, wicker body, 12 m.p.h., 7 speeds, 2 reverse gears. Done entirely with spare parts that could be picked up anywhere! assembled to the customer's taste . . . to suit his personality! according to the style and the season of the year! This little book was all the rage . . . from 1902 to 1905 . . . It contained . . . which was a step forward . . . not only diagrams, but actual blueprints on a scale of one to two hundred thousand. Photographs, cross-references, cross sections . . . all flawless and guaranteed.

His idea was to combat the rising peril of mass production . . . There wasn't a moment to be lost . . . Despite his resolute belief in progress, des Pereires had always detested standardization . . . From the very start he was bitterly opposed to it . . . He foresaw that the death of craftsmanship would inevitably shrink the human personality . . .

At the time of this battle for the "made to measure" automobile Courtial was practically famous in the world of innovators for his original and extremely daring studies on the "All-Purpose Cottage," the flexible, extensible dwelling, adaptable to families of every kind in all climates! . . . "Your own house," absolutely detachable,

tippable (that is, transportable), shrinkable, instantly re-
ducible by one or more rooms at will, to fit permanent or
passing needs, children, guests, alterable at a moment's
notice . . . to meet the requirements, the tastes of every
individual . . . "An old house is a house that doesn't
move! . . . Buy young! Be flexible! Don't build. Assem-
ble! To build is death! Only tombs can be built properly.
Buy a living house! Live in a living house! The 'All-Purpose Cottage' keeps pace with life! . . ."

Such was the tone, the style of the manifesto written by
Courtial himself just before the "Future of Architecture"
exhibition held in June, '98, at the Gallery of Machines.
Almost immediately his little book on home building
created an enormous furore among men about to be pen-
sioned, heads of families with insignificant incomes, home-
less young couples, and colonial civil servants . . . He
was bombarded with inquiries from all over France, from
abroad, from the Dominions . . . His cottage, all set up
with movable roof, 2,492 nails, 3 doors, 24 sections, 5
windows, 42 hinges, wood or muslin partitions according
to the season, won a special prize, "hors concours," un-
beatable . . . It could be assembled in the desired
dimensions with the help of two workmen, on any kind of
ground, in seventeen minutes and four seconds! . . . The
wear and tear was minimal . . . it would last forever!
. . . "Only resistance is ruinous. A house in its entirety
must have play, it has to adapt itself like a living organ-
ism! it has to give . . . it has to dodge the whirling winds!
the gales and tempests, the paroxysms of nature! The
moment you oppose . . . what utter folly! . . . the unleashed elements, disaster ensues! . . . Can a building
. . . the most massive . . . the most galvanic . . . the
most firmly cemented . . . be expected to defy the elements? Pure madness! One day or another, inevitably, it
will be overturned, annihilated! If you wish to be convinced, you have only to pass through one of our beautiful,
our fertile countrysides! Isn't our magnificent country inter-
spersed from north to south with melancholy ruins? Once
proud habitations! Haughty manors! Ornaments of our
soil, what has become of you? Dust!"

"The 'All-Purpose Cottage,' on the other hand, is flexible, it adapts itself, it expands, it contracts according to

necessity, according to the laws, the living forces of nature!"

"It bends enormously, but it never breaks . . ."

The day his stand was inaugurated, after President Félix Faure had come through, after all the powwow and congratulations, the crowd broke through the barriers! the guards were swept away! The populace burst in so frantically between the walls of the cottage that the little marvel was instantly torn apart, washed away, swallowed up! The mob was so feverish, so avid, that it combusted all the materials . . . You couldn't say this one and only model was destroyed . . . it was sucked up, absorbed, digested on the spot . . . The evening the exhibition closed there wasn't a trace left of it, not a crumb, not a nail, not a shred of muslin . . . The amazing edifice had been absorbed like a pimple . . . As Courtial told me about all this fifteen years later, he was still in a daze . . .

"Of course I could have started in again . . . In that field, I can say without flattering myself, my ability was remarkable . . . When it came to drawing up a precise, a meticulous estimate for on-the-spot assembly, I had no rival . . . But other, more grandiose projects carried me away, kept me absorbed . . . I've never found the time to resume my calculations of the 'indices of resistance' . . . And after all, in spite of the final disaster, I had proved what I set out to . . . By my boldness I had enabled certain schools, certain young enthusiasts, to step forward . . . to shout their opinions from the rooftops . . . to find their way . . . That and nothing else was my mission! I desired nothing more! My honor was intact! I asked for nothing, Ferdinand! Coveted nothing! Demanded nothing of the authorities! I went back to my studies . . . I didn't scheme or intrigue! . . . And now listen . . . Guess what I get . . . Practically one right after the other? The Nicham, and a week later the Academic Palms! . . . I was really offended! Whom did they take me for all of a sudden? Why not a tobacco counter? I wanted to send all that flimflam back to the minister! I told Flammarion about it: 'Don't do it,' he said, 'don't do anything of the kind. I've got them too!' Well, in that case I was in the clear. But even so they'd swindled me outrageously! . . . Oh, the skunks! My plans had been

plagiarized, pirated, copied, do you hear, in a thousand
revolting ways . . . and incompetently what's more . . .
by so many swelled-headed, unprincipled, shameless official architects that I wrote to Flammarion . . . If they
wanted to make amends, they owed me at least the Legion
of Honor . . . if they'd wanted to butter me up with
honors, I mean . . . He thought I was perfectly right, but
he advised me to keep quiet and not make any more of a
stink . . . it would even get him in trouble . . . to be
patient . . . that the time wasn't quite ripe . . . that
after all I was his disciple and I shouldn't forget it . . .
Oh, I don't feel any bitterness, get me straight! Yes, those
little things still make me feel sad . . . But nothing more!
Absolutely not! . . . A melancholy lesson . . . That's
all . . . I think of it now and then . . ."
    I could tell when the architectural blues came over him
. . . It usually happened in the country . . . and when
he was getting ready to go up in his balloon . . . when he
was climbing into the basket . . . His memories came
back to him . . . Maybe he was a little scared and that
was what made him talk . . . He looked at the country
in the distance . . . Out there in the suburbs, especially
at the housing lots, the shacks and shanties . . . He was
overcome with emotion . . . it brought the tears to his
eyes . . . Those shacks, all lopsided and cross-eyed, all
cracked and rickety, rotting away in the muck, sinking
into the slush, at the edge of the fields . . . beyond the
highway . . . "You see all that," he'd say to me, "you
see that stinking mess?" He'd make a sweeping gesture,
embracing the horizon . . . The whole crawling swarm
of shanties, the church and the chicken coops, the washhouse and the schools . . . The ramshackle tumbledown
huts, gray, mauve, and mignonette . . . all the plaster
thingamajigs . . .
    "It's bad, eh? It's pretty crummy? . . . Well, it's a
good deal my fault . . . I'm responsible! You can put the
blame on me . . . All that is mine, do you hear me? . . .
Mine! . . ."
    "Ah?" I said as though flabbergasted. I knew he was
going into his routine . . . He threw his leg over the
edge . . . He jumped into the wicker basket . . . If the
wind wasn't too strong, he kept his panama on . . . he

was much happier that way . . . but he tied it under his
chin with a broad ribbon . . . I'd wear his cap . . .
"Let her go!" She'd rise inch by inch, very slowly at first
. . . and then a little faster . . . He'd have to get a move
on to clear the roofs . . . He couldn't make up his mind
to throw off ballast . . . But he had to rise somehow . . .
We never inflated her completely . . . The stuff cost
thirteen francs a bottle . . .

Some time after the adventure with the "Homemade
Cottage" that the insane crowd had torn to pieces, Courtial
des Pereires suddenly decided to change his whole tactics
. . . "Capital first!" That's what he said . . . That was
his new motto. "No more risks. Cold cash! . . ." He had
mapped out a program based entirely on these principles
. . . And fundamental reforms . . . all absolutely judi-
cious and pertinent . . .

First of all he decided that come hell or high water the
conditions of inventors had to be improved . . . He
started from the premise that in this racket there'd never
be any shortage of ideas . . . that they were actually too
plentiful! But that capital, on the other hand, is disgustingly evasive! pusillanimous! retiring! . . . That all the
misfortunes of the human race and his own in particular
came from lack of funds . . . the distrustfulness of
money . . . the hideous rarity of credit . . . But all that
could be straightened out . . . All it would take to remedy this state of affairs was action . . . an ingenious
idea . . . So one two three, right there on the Galerie
Montpensier, behind the "Tunisian office," between the
kitchen and the corridor, he founded an "Investors' Corner" . . . a very special little nook, furnished very
simply: a table, a cupboard, a filing cabinet, two chairs,
and to preside over deliberations, a fine bust of de Lesseps
on the top shelf, between folders and more folders . . .

On the strength of the new statutes, any inventor willing
to invest fifty-two francs (total payable in advance) could
run an ad in our paper for three successive issues . . .
saying anything he pleased about all his projects, even the
wildest nonsense, the dizziest phantasmagorias, the most
shameless impostures . . . Not bad! It filled up two full
columns in the *Genitron* and we'd throw in a ten minutes'

private consultation with Courtial, the director . . . And finally, to make the deal even more attractive, an oleographed diploma, certifying him as a "member in good standing of the Eureka Research Center for the financing, study, equilibration, and immediate exploitation of discoveries conducive to the advancement of all the sciences and of industry . . ."

It wasn't so easy to get them to cough up the fifty smackers . . . That was always slow going . . . Even giving them the song and dance . . . talking himself blue in the face . . . when it came to paying up, they nearly always balked . . . even the screwiest of them got to feeling worried . . . even in their delirium, they smelled a rat . . . they realized that this was dough they'd never be seeing again . . . "Registration fees" was the name we dreamed up for our gimmick . . .

The understanding was that from that moment on Courtial would take all the necessary steps, put out feelers, attend to all the calling and contacting, the interviews . . . the documentation . . . the meetings . . . the premonitory discussions, the arguments, in short everything that was needed to attract, propitiate, arouse, and reassure a consortium . . . All this, it went without saying, at the opportune moment . . . On that point we were adamant . . . Haste makes waste . . . easy does it . . . that was our way . . . Impatience can only mess everything up! Precipitation wrecks the best-laid plans! The most fruitful undertakings are those that ripen slowly! . . . We were radically opposed, implacably hostile, to all premature bungling . . . to all hysteria . . . "Your investor escapes on the wings of the swallow, he's a tortoise when it comes to forking up."

To interfere as little as possible with the negotiations, always so delicate, the inventor was advised to leave the field perfectly clear . . . to go straight home . . . to smoke his pipe and wait . . . and not worry about a thing. He'd be duly notified, summoned, acquainted with every detail as soon as things began to shape up . . . But it wasn't often that he'd stay home and mind his business . . . Hardly a week would pass before he came running . . . asking for news . . . bringing us new models . . . complementary projects . . . more blueprints . . . spare parts . . . We could yell ourselves blue in the face, he'd keep coming, he'd come more and more often . . . like shooting pains, worried, dispirited . . . As soon as he began to see the light, he'd start bellowing . . . kicking up a ruckus of varying proportions . . . And after that you'd never see him again. There were some . . . but not very many . . . who weren't so dumb, who threatened to raise hell, legal proceedings, to register a complaint with the police if we didn't return their dough . . . Courtial knew them all. He cleared out when he saw them coming. He recognized them a mile away . . . It's incredible what a piercing eye he had for spotting a rabid customer . . . They seldom caught him . . . He'd disappear into the back room and do a little turn with the dumbbells, but mostly he went down in the cellar . . . There it was even safer . . . He wasn't in . . . The oldtimer who wanted his money back could split a gut, it didn't get him anywhere . . .

"Hold him, Ferdinand. Just hold him," the stinker would say. "Hold him while I think things over . . . I know that gasbag only too well! That drooling ape! Every time he comes here for an interview he stays two hours at least . . . He's made me lose the thread of my deductions a dozen times. It's shameful! It's scandalous! He's a plague! Kill him, I beseech you, Ferdinand! Don't let him contaminate the world anymore! Burn him! . . . Slaughter him! Scatter his ashes! I don't care what you do! But for God's sake, at any price, do you hear me, don't bring him to me. Tell him I'm in Singapore! in Colombo! in the Hesperides! Tell him I'm making elastic banks for the Isthmus of Suez and Panama. That's an idea! . . . Tell him anything! Anything will do, so long as I don't have to see him! . . . I beg you, Ferdinand, I beg you!"

So it was I that had to bear the brunt of the whole tempest sure as shit . . . I had my system, I admit . . . I was like the "Do-it-yourself Cottage," my approach was flexible . . . I put up no resistance . . . I bent in the direction of his fury . . . I went even further . . . I amazed the lunatic by the virulence of my hatred for the loathsome Pereires . . . I took him every time in nothing flat . . . with my hair-raising insults . . . In that province I was supreme . . . I flayed him! I stigmatized him!

I covered him with garbage, with pus! That abject villain!
That mountain of shit! twenty times worse! a hundred
times! a thousand times worse than the customer had ever
thought on his own! . . .
  For his private delectation I turned Courtial . . .
shouting at the top of my lungs . . . into a heap of soft,
slimy, inconceivably sickening turds . . . How unbelievably loathsome he was! . . . He was in a class by himself!
I went at it hammer and tongs! . . . I stamped on the
trapdoor right over the cellar, in chorus with the nut . . .
I outdid them all in violence . . . thanks to the intensity
of my revolt! my sincerity! my destructive enthusiasm! my
implacable tetanism! . . . my frenzy! . . . my anathe-
matic writhing! . . . It was unbelievable what a paroxysm
I could work myself up into in my total fury . . . I got
all that from my dad . . . and the performances I'd been
through . . . For temper tantrums I had no equal . . .
The worst lunatics, the most delirious interpretive screwballs didn't stand a chance if I decided to take a fling, if I
really wanted to bestir myself . . . Young as I was . . .
they all left with their asses dragging . . . absolutely
bewildered by the intensity of my hatred . . . my indomi-
table fury, the eternal thirst for vengeance that I harbored
in my flanks . . . With tears in their eyes they entrusted
me with the task of crushing that turd . . . that execra-
ble Courtial . . . that sink of iniquity . . . of covering
him with new and unpredictable kinds of excrement, slim-
ier than the bottom of the shithouse! . . . a mass of
unconscionable purulence! . . . of making a cake out of
him, the most fetid that could ever be imagined . . . of
cutting him up into balls . . . flattening him out into
sheets, plastering the whole bottom of the crapper with
him, all the way from the bowl to the sump . . . and
wedging him in there once and for all . . . to be shat on
for all eternity . . .
  As soon as our friend was gone . . . as soon as he was
far enough away . . . Courtial would come back to the
trapdoor . . . He'd lift it up a little . . . He'd take a
gander . . . Then he'd surface . . .
  "Ferdinand! You've just saved my life . . . Ah, yes!
My life! It's the truth. I heard it all. Ah! It's just as I
feared! That ape would have torn me apart. Right then and

there! Did you realize that?" Then he'd stop and think. He began to feel worried about what I'd been shouting . . . my little session with the visitor . . .

"But I do hope, Ferdinand, tell me now, that I haven't fallen as low as all that in your esteem? You'd tell me, wouldn't you? You wouldn't hide it from me, would you? I'll explain my position if you want me to. Go ahead . . . I do hope these little acts you put on have no effect on your feeling for me! That would be too dreadful. Your affection for me is unchanged? You can count on me to the hilt, you know that. I'm a man of my word. You do understand me? You're beginning to understand me, aren't you? Tell me you understand me."

"Yes, yes. Of course . . . I think . . . I think I'm beginning . . ."

"Then listen to me, my dear Ferdinand! . . . While that lunatic was raving, I was thinking of thousands of things . . . while he was turning our stomachs . . . mouthing his delirium . . . I was saying to myself: My poor Courtial! All these scenes, this ranting, this infamous uproar is lacerating your existence abominably . . . without furthering your cause any! When I say cause, you understand, I don't mean money. I'm speaking of the great intangible treasure! Immaterial wealth! The great Decision! The eternal theme, the infinite acquisition! The idea that is worthy of our enthusiasm . . . You've got to understand me, Ferdinand . . . Quicker! Quicker! Time is passing! A minute! An hour! At my age, Ferdinand, that's eternity. You'll see . . . It's all one, Ferdinand, all one!" His eyes moistened . . . "Listen to me, Ferdinand. I hope you'll understand me fully one day . . . yes! . . . that you'll really appreciate me . . . When I'm not here to defend myself . . . Then it's you, Ferdinand, who will possess the truth! . . . You who will refute the calumnies . . . It's you, I'm counting on you, Ferdinand. I'm counting on you! If people come to you . . . from all four quarters of the world . . . and say: 'Courtial was nothing but a skunk, the crummiest bastard of them all! A swindler! There was never another like him . . .' What will you say, Ferdinand? . . . Just this . . . You hear me? 'Courtial made only one mistake. But that mistake was fundamental! He thought the world was waiting for the

spirit . . . to help it change . . . The world has changed
. . . That's a fact . . . But the spirit hasn't come to it!
. . .' That's all you'll say . . . Absolutely . . . Not
another word! You will add nothing! . . . The order of
magnitudes, Ferdinand! The order of magnitudes! Maybe
the infinitesimal can be inserted in the immense . . . But
how are we to reduce the immense to the infinitesimal?
Ah? Our misfortunes have no other source, Ferdinand!
No other source! All our misfortunes! . . ."

When he'd had a big scare as he had that afternoon, he
felt a touching solicitude for me. He didn't want to see me
sulking . . .

"Go on out, Ferdinand!" he'd say . . . "Go take a
walk . . . Go to the Louvre. It'll do you a world of
good! Go up to the Boulevards! You like Max Linder.
Our joint still stinks of that mammoth! Let's go, Ferdinand. Let's clear out. Shut up the shop. Hang out the sign.
Join me at the Three Musketoons! It's on me. Take some
money out of the drawer on the left . . . I won't leave
with you . . . I'll sneak out through the hall . . . Take
a look in at the Insurrection . . . You'll see Formerly
. . . Ask him if there's anything new . . . You've placed
a bet on Scheherazade, I hope? And did you put your winnings on Violoncelle? You're still betting for yourself, eh?
You don't even know where I am . . . Understand?"

He began to dish out his Great Decision routine more
and more often . . . He'd disappear into the cellar, supposedly to meditate, for hours on end . . . He'd take a
big fat book with him and his big candle. He must have
owed every bookie in the neighborhood money, and not
just Kid Formerly at the Insurrection, but at the Musketoons, and even the Brasserie Vigogne on the rue des
Blancs-Manteaux . . . That was a real dive . . . He
gave orders that he wasn't to be disturbed . . . I wasn't
always very happy about it . . . his shenanigans made it
my business to deal with all our daily screwballs . . . our
discontented subscribers . . . the harmless little characters with stupid questions . . . the thoroughbred maniacs . . . whole broadsides of them swept over me . . . I
had them all on my neck . . . bellyachers of every description . . . the repulsive mob of deep thinkers . . .

the fanatics of gadgetry . . . They kept pouring in . .
coming and going . . . The bell was having fits . . . It
rang the whole time . . . They were preventing me from
repairing my *Enthusiast* . . . Courtial was cluttering up
the cellar with his clowning . . . And that was my main
job after all . . . I was responsible, I'd be to blame if he
broke his neck . . . which was touch and go every time!
. . . In other words, his act was for the birds . . . In
the end I told him, on this count and several others, that
this couldn't go on . . . that I was fed up . . . that I
washed my hands of it . . . that we were heading for
trouble . . . It was plain as day . . . But he hardly listened. It left him cold . . . He disappeared more and
more. When he was in the cellar, he wouldn't let anybody
disturb him . . . Even his candle bothered him . . .
Sometimes he put it out so it wouldn't interfere with his
meditations.

Finally I gave it to him straight . . . I was so griped
that I couldn't control myself . . . I told him to try the
sewer . . . that was the ideal place to look for his
Decision . . . That did it. He blasts me:

"Ferdinand," he shrieks. "What's that? Is that a way to
talk to me? You, Ferdinand? To me? Stop right there.
Merciful heavens, I beg you! Have pity! Call me whatever
you please! Liar! Boa! Vampire! Skunk! if the words I
utter are not the strict expression of the ineffable truth!
You wanted to do away with your father, didn't you? So
young! Heavens above! That's the truth! Is it a delusion?
A phantasmagoria? No, it's the unbelievable, deplorable
reality! . . . Whole centuries won't wipe out the shame of
it! That's a fact! It's God's own truth! You don't deny it?
I'm not making it up? Well then? And now what? Will
you kindly tell me what you're after? To kill me in my
turn? Why, it's obvious! It's plain as day! Biding your
time! . . . Waiting for the propitious moment! . . .
when I'm relaxed . . . unsuspecting . . . And do me in!
. . . abolish me! . . . annihiliate me! . . . That's your
program! . . . Where have I been keeping my wits? Ah,
Ferdinand, heavens above! Your nature! your destiny! are
darker than the darkest Erebus! . . . Oh, you're sinister,
Ferdinand, though you don't look it! Your waters are
troubled! What monsters there are, Ferdinand, in the

crannies of your soul! Slithering, evasive! I don't know
them all! . . . They pass! . . . They sweep everything
away! . . . Death! To me! To whom you owe a thousand
times more than life! More than bread! More than air! than
the sun itself! The power of Thought! Ah, reptile, is that
what you're up to? Am I right? Relentless! Crawling!
Mercurial! Chameleonlike! Unpredictable! . . . Violence
. . . tenderness . . . passion . . . strength . . . I heard
you the other day . . . You're capable of anything, Ferdinand! Everything! Only the outer coating is human! But I
see the monster within! Do you know where you're
headed? Was I warned? Yes, I had plenty of warning . . .
guile! . . . affection! . . . and then suddenly, every syllable a revelation . . . homicidal frenzy! Yes, frenzy!
. . . A cataract of base instincts! Ah yes, that's the sign,
my friend. The mark of the criminal . . . The lightning
that denounces the murderer, the congenital, innate pervert! . . . That's you, right here in front of me! So be it!
You're not dealing with a coward, the weakling you may
have been expecting to terrorize! You've got another think
coming! I stand up to my destiny! I asked for it! I'll see it
through to the bitter end! All right, kill me if you can! . . .
Go ahead! I'm waiting! Undaunted! What are you afraid
of? . . . I'm right here! I defy you, Ferdinand! You
exasperate me! Do you hear? You're driving me out of my
wits! I'm nobody's fool! I'm wide-awake! Are you afraid
to look a Man in the whites of his eyes? I measured the
risks the day I took you on! Let's call it my last act of
daring! Go ahead! Strike! I defy my assassin! Hurry! . . ."
    I let him drool . . . I looked away . . . at the trees
. . . at the gardens in the distance . . . the lawns . . .
the nursemaids . . . the sparrows hopping around the
benches . . . the fountain bobbing in the breeze . . .
That was better than answering . . . or even turning
around to look at him . . . He'd hit the nail on the head
without knowing it . . . for two cents I'd hit him over the
head with the paperweight . . . the big greaser, Hippocrates . . . my hand was itching . . . it weighed at least
six pounds . . . I had a rough time . . . I controlled
myself . . . It was heroic of me . . . The bastard kept
right on:
    "The younger generation nowadays have murder in

their bones! That kind of thing, take it from me, Ferdinand, will land you in La Santé! With a hood over your eyes! That's right, a hood! Merciful heavens! And I'll have been to blame! . . ."

I had a tongue in my head too . . . I felt the mustard rising . . . Enough was enough! . . . *"Maître,"* I said right then and there. "Go shit in your hat. And make it quick! Get away from me! I'm not going to kill you. I'm going to take your pants down. I'm going to tattoo your ass. Till it looks like thirty-six bunches of peonies . . . I'm going to bust open your asshole, stink and all! That's what's going to happen to you if I hear one more fucking word out of you."

I was going to grab him for real . . . The stinker was quick, though . . . He beat it into the back room . . . He saw I meant business, that I'd put up with as much as I was going to . . . He stayed right there in his hole . . . fiddling with the parallel bars . . . He let me alone for a while . . . He'd gone far enough . . . A little later he came out . . . He passed through the shop . . . He took the corridor on the left . . . he went out . . . He didn't go up to his office . . . At last I could work without being bothered.

It was no rest cure to sew and darn and patch that rotten balloon cover, to fasten together the pieces that were coming apart . . . It was an awful chore . . . Especially because I used the carbide lamp so as to see what I was doing . . . which was pretty risky down there in the cellar . . . with all those adhesives . . . that are always lousy with benzine . . . It was trickling around all over the place . . . I could see myself a living torch! . . . The cover of the *Enthusiast* was a ticklish business, in a good many places it was a regular sieve . . . More rips! More tears! And worse every time he went up, every time he landed . . . from dragging through plowed fields! . . . from catching on the eaves . . . on whole rows of roofs, especially on days when the wind was from the north . . . She left big patches and little shreds in the forests, on the branches, between steeples . . . on the ramparts . . . She picked up tin chimneys! roofs! tiles by the ton! weather vanes on every trip! But the worst punishment, the most terrible rips were when she got impaled on a telegraph

pole! . . . Half the time she'd split in two . . . To give
the devil his due, you've got to admit that des Pereires
took some pretty bad risks on his aerial tours. The ascent
was wild enough . . . it was a wonder he made it with the
thing only half-inflated . . . for reasons of economy . . .
But what was really awful was bringing his moth-eaten
contraption down . . . Luckily he had plenty of experience. He knew his business. All by himself, at the time
when I met him, he had chalked up 1,422 balloon flights!
Not counting captive balloons . . . That was an impres-
sive total! He had all the medals, all the diplomas, all the
licenses . . . He knew all the tricks, but what always
dazzled me was his landings . . . It was marvelous the
way he always landed on his feet. The second the end of
the rope scraped over the ground, the second the thing
slowed down . . . he rolled himself up in a ball at the
bottom of the basket . . . when the wicker touched the
muck . . . and the whole thing was about to bounce up
again . . . he had a feeling for the exact moment . . .
He shot up like a jack-in-the-box . . . he unwound like a
spool . . . he fell like a regular jockey . . . in his tight-
fitting frock coat . . . He seldom hurt himself . . . He
didn't lose a button . . . He didn't waste a second . . .
He ran straight ahead . . . He sped over the furrows
. . . He didn't turn around . . . He chased after the
Enthusiast, at the same time blowing the little bugle he had
slung over his shoulder . . . He made his own music
. . . what a guy! His cross-country race went on a long
time, until the whole balloon settled . . . I can still see
him sprinting . . . It was a beautiful sight, in his frock
coat and panama . . . To tell the honest truth, my auto-
plastic sutures weren't so hot . . . but he wouldn't have
done it himself . . . He hadn't the patience . . . he'd
only have messed things up even worse . . . After all,
that patching was an art! Despite my infinite stratagems
and vast ingenuity, I often despaired of that beastly gasbag
. . . She was thoroughly fed up . . . After being taken
out for sixteen years regardless of conditions . . . in
cloudbursts and tornadoes . . . she only held together by
patches and weird darns . . . Every time we blew her up
was a catastrophe . . . After she'd come down and
dragged along the ground, it was worse . . . When a

whole strip was missing, I'd borrow a piece of the *Archimedes'* old hide . . . She was all in pieces, a lot of rags, piled up every which way in the cellar . . . That was the balloon of his beginnings, a bright red captive, an enormous bag. She'd done the fairs for twenty years . . . I was mighty careful . . . infinitely meticulous . . . about pasting the whole thing together . . . I got some curious effects . . . When at the cry of "Let her go" the *Enthusiast* rose over the crowd, I could recognize my patches in the air . . . I could see them wobbling and shriveling . . . It didn't make me laugh.

But in addition there were the preparations, the preliminaries . . . The balloon racket was no rest cure . . . don't get that idea . . . You had to get ready, make arrangements, palaver for months in advance . . . We had to send out leaflets, photographs . . . saturate the whole of France with prospectuses! . . . get in touch with the local big shots . . . put up with the insults of the festival committees, all terrible tightwads . . . So in addition to the inventors, we had these mountains of mail in connection with the *Enthusiast.*

Courtial had taught me to write letters in the official style. I didn't make out too badly . . . After a while I didn't make too many mistakes . . . We had special stationery for the balloon racket with a natty letterhead: "Paris Section of the Friends of the Dirigible Balloon."

At the end of winter we'd start selling the municipal authorities . . . The programs for the season were drawn up in the spring . . . In principle we expected to have all our Sundays booked up shortly before All Saints. We'd needle committee presidents over the phone. It was my job again, going to the post office. I'd go during rush hours . . . I tried to get away without paying. They'd catch me at the door . . .

We applied for every fair, convention, and carnival in all France . . . No town was too small. Anything was down our alley. But naturally if we had any choice, we tried not to go any farther than Seine-et-Oise . . . or Seine-et-Marne at the worst. It was shipping our equipment that ruined us, the sacks, the bottles of gas, the gear, all our crazy gadgets. For the game to be worth the candle, we had to be back at the Palais-Royal that same night.

Otherwise it would run into money. Courtial cut his prices
as low as possible . . . they were absolutely reasonable:
two hundred and twenty francs . . . plus the cost of the
gas, and pigeons released for two francs a piece . . . We
made no mention of altitude . . . Our most famous rival,
maybe the most immediate threat, was Captain Guy de
Roziers, he asked a good deal more. He performed hazardous feats with his balloon, the *Intrepid* . . . He'd take
his horse up with him and sit in the saddle in midair . . .
at an altitude of 1,200 feet guaranteed! . . . His price
was five hundred and twenty-five francs, return fare payable by the township. But the ones who beat us to the
draw even more often than the equestrian were the Italian
and his daughter, "Calagoni & Petita" . . . We ran into
them wherever we went . . . They were immensely popular, especially in garrison towns! They were very expensive, they did all sorts of tricks up in the sky . . . Besides,
they threw down bouquets, little parachutes, and cockades
from a height of 1,800 feet! They asked eight hundred and
thirty-five francs and a contract for two seasons . . .
They really cornered the market . . .

Courtial didn't go for the showy stuff . . . that wasn't
his style . . . No theatricals! Certainly not. His show
was definitely scientific: an edifying demonstration. He
explained everything in a neat little preparatory chat and
wound up with pigeons, which he released ever so gracefully . . . He himself served notice in his brief introduc-
tory patter: "Ladies and gentlemen . . . if I'm still flying
a balloon at my age, it's not out of vain bravado . . . you
can take my word for that . . . out of any desire to impress the crowd . . . Take a look at my chest! You see
before you all the best known, most highly prized, most
envied medals for merit and courage! If I take to the air,
ladies and gentlemen, it is for purposes of popular education . . . that is my life-long aim! Everything in my power
to enlighten the masses! We are not appealing to any
morbid passion, to sadistic instincts, to emotional perver-
sity! . . . I appeal to your intelligence! Your intelligence
alone!"

He said it again for my benefit, he wanted me to get it
straight: "Ferdinand, never forget that we must preserve
the character of our performances at any price . . . the

mark of the *Genitron* . . . They must never degenerate
into buffoonery! masquerades! aerial tomfoolery! empty-
headed tricks! No, no, and again no! We must preserve the
tone, the spirit of Physics! Of course we have to entertain
. . . and never forget it! That's what we're paid for. It's
only right and proper! But better still, if possible, we must
fire the minds of these rustics with a desire for exact
knowledge, for genuine enlightenment. Of course we have
to go up. But we must also elevate those yokels you see
standing around with their mouths open! Ah! it's not easy,
Ferdinand . . ."

It's perfectly true that he would never have left the
ground without first explaining all the details, the principles of aerostatics, in a cozy little talk. To command his
audience, he balanced himself on the edge of the basket,
resplendently decorated, in frock coat, panama, and cuffs,
with one arm passed through the rigging . . . He explained the working of the valves, the guy rope, the
barometers, the laws of weight and ballast. Then carried
away by his subject, he embarked on other fields, expa-
tiating, ad-libbing without order or plan, about meteor-
ology, mirages, the winds, cyclones . . . He touched on
the planets, the stars . . . Everything was grist for his
mill: the zodiac, Gemini . . . Saturn . . . Jupiter . . .
Arcturus and its contours . . . the moon . . . Bellego-
phorus and its relief . . . He pulled measurements out of
his hat . . . About Mars he could talk at length . . . He
knew it well . . . It was his favorite planet . . . He described all the canals, their shape and itinerary! their flora!
as if he'd gone swimming in them! He was on the friendliest
terms with the heavenly bodies. He was a big success.

While he was perched up there shooting the shit, spell-
binding the masses, I took up a little collection . . . That
was my little private racket. I took advantage of the circumstances, the excitement . . . I slipped into the crowd
. . . I peddled the *Genitron* at two sous a dozen . . . returns . . . little autographed handbooks . . . commem-
orative medallions with a tiny balloon engraved on
them . . . and for the ones I could spot that looked dirty-
minded . . . whose hands went roaming in the crush . . .
I had a little selection of funny, entertaining, spicy pictures,
and transparents you could slide back and forth . . . It

was a bad day when I didn't unload the lot . . . All in all, with a little luck, it brought in twenty-five smackers! That was good money in those days. When my stock was gone and I'd finished collecting, I'd give the master the high sign . . . He'd shut off steam . . . He'd turn off the blarney and climb down into his basket . . . He'd straighten his panama . . . batten down the hatches, unfurl the last sheet . . . and slowly push off. I only had to hold the last rope . . . It was I who sang out "Let her go" . . . He'd answer me with a blast from his bugle . . . With the guy rope dragging, the *Enthusiast* rose into the air . . . I never saw her go straight up . . . She was limp from the start. For a number of reasons we were very careful about blowing her up . . . As a result, she rose crooked . . . She careened over the roofs. With her colored patches she looked like a fat harlequin . . . She bobbed up and down in the air, waiting for a decent breeze . . . She could only puff out in a real wind . . . She was pathetic like an old petticoat on a clothesline . . . even the cowfloppiest yokels caught on . . . The whole crowd laughed to see her teetering over the roofs . . . I was a good deal less cheerful . . . I foresaw the horrible, decisive, disastrous rip! The final smashup . . . I made all kinds of motions to him . . . he should drop the sand right away . . . He was never in much of a hurry . . . He was afraid he'd go up too high . . . There wasn't much to fear . . . Considering the state of the fabric, there wasn't a chance . . . My worry was that he'd flop in the middle of the village . . . that would have been the end . . . It was always a narrow squeak . . . or that he'd collide with the schoolhouse . . . or take the weathercock off the church . . . or get caught in the eaves . . . or settle on the Town Hall . . . or founder in the little clump of woods. He'd be doing all right if he got her up to 150 or 200 feet . . . I figured roughly . . . that was the maximum . . . Courtial's dream, in view of the state of his equipment, was never to go any higher than the second story . . . That was fairly safe . . . Higher was madness . . . In the first place we could never have pumped the bag full . . . With one or two bottles more it would have split for sure, from top to bottom . . . exploded like a bombshell from valve to valve . . . When he'd passed the

last house, cleared the last fences, he'd throw out his
sand . . . He'd make up his mind and unload the lot of
it . . . When the ballast was all gone, he took a little
hop . . . a leap of about thirty feet . . . Then it was
time for the pigeons . . . He quickly opened their basket
. . . They shot out like arrows . . . Then it was time
for me to shake a leg . . . Believe me, I ran like hell
. . . I had to stage a tragedy to get the yokels interested
. . . to make them run after the balloon . . . and help
us to fold up quick . . . the enormous ragbag . . . and
tote the whole mess back to the station . . . to hoist
her up on the derrick . . . We weren't through yet. We
had to do something to prevent our audience from clearing
out, the whole lot of them at once . . . Our best dodge
was the disaster act . . . It worked every time . . .
without it we were sunk . . . We'd have had to pay
them to do any work . . . We'd have lost money . . .
It was that simple . . .

I began to scream and yell! I lit out like a stuck pig! I
ran lickety-split through the muck in the direction of the
catastrophe . . . I heard his bugle . . . "Fire! . . .
Fire!" I yelled. "Look! Look at the flame! . . . He's
going to set the whole place on fire! She's over the trees!
. . . " The mob got moving . . . They came on the
gallop . . . They followed me . . . As soon as Courtial
saw me with the peasantry at my heels, he opened all the
valves . . . He disemboweled the whole contraption from
top to bottom! . . . She collapsed in her rags . . . She
lay down in the muck, crippled, exhausted, bushed . . .
Courtial popped out of the basket . . . He landed on his
feet . . . He blew another blast on the bugle to rally the
pack . . . And he started another speech . . . The hicks
were scared shitless, they expected the whole thing to burst
into flame and set their haystacks on fire . . . They threw
themselves on the bag to keep it from billowing . . . They
folded her up . . . But she was a disgusting wreck . . .
from catching on every branch in sight . . . She'd lost so
much material there was nothing left but heartbreaking
rags . . . She'd brought back whole bushes between the
bag and the net . . . The rescuers were delighted, overjoyed, jumping up and down with excitement; they hoisted
Courtial on their shoulders like a hero and carried him

off in triumph . . . They took him to the taproom to celebrate . . . They drank plenty . . . All the work was left for me, the rottenest lousiest chore . . . Collecting all our junk out of the swamp before nightfall . . . from the fields and furrows . . . Recovering all our tackle, anchors, pulleys, and chains, all the wandering hardware . . . The mile and a half of guy rope . . . the log, the cleats, scattered far and wide in oats and pasture, the barometer, the aneroid pressure gauge . . . a little Morocco leather case . . . the nickel doodads that are so expensive . . . . A picnic, take it from me . . . Keeping those repulsive beggars happy with wisecracks and promises . . . And telling smutty jokes to make them handle those fifteen hundred pounds of exhausting junk all free gratis and for nothing! The gasbag that looked like a massacred shirt, the remains of the hideous catafalque! Getting them to toss the whole junk pile in the last freight car just as the train was pulling out! Hell! Believe me, it took some doing. When I finally squeezed through the corridors and found Courtial, the train was under way. I found my zebra in the third class. Calm as you make them, talking, showing off, handing his audience a brilliant lecture . . . The conclusions to be drawn from his adventure! . . . So attentive to the brunette on the opposite bench . . . considerate of youthful ears . . . watching his language . . . but the life of the party even so . . . drunk as a lord, throwing his chest and his medals around . . . And still drinking, the stinker! Jollity! High spirits! A slug of the red stuff all around! Hold out your glasses, everybody! . . . He was stuffing his face full of bread and butter . . . Why worry . . . He didn't ask about me . . . Take it from me, I was fed up . . . I put a crimp in his merriment.

"Ah, so it's you, Ferdinand? It's you?"

"Yes, my dear Jules Verne! . . ."

"Sit down, boy. Tell me all about it . . . My secretary . . . My secretary."

He introduced me.

"Well then, is everything all right in the freight car? . . . You've attended to everything? . . . You're satisfied?"

I made a very glum face, I wasn't the least bit satisfied
. . . I didn't say a word . . .

"Then it's not all right? . . . Is something wrong? . . ."

"It's the last time," I said. I didn't mince words. I was
very dry and firm . . .

"What's that? Why is it the last time? You're joking?
What do you mean? . . ."

"The thing can't be repaired anymore . . . And I'm
not joking at all . . ."

A real silence fell . . . No more applause and sausage.
You could hear the wheels . . . the creaking of the carriage . . . the glass of the lamp jiggling up top . . . He
tried in the dim light to make out what I was thinking
. . . if I wasn't kidding a little. But I didn't bat an eyelash
. . . I kept my long face . . . I stuck to my guns . . .

"You really think so, Ferdinand? You're not exaggerating?"

"If I say it, I mean it . . . I know what I'm talking
about."

I'd got to be an expert on holes, I refused to be contradicted . . . He sat back gloomily in his corner . . . That
was the end of our conference . . . We didn't say another
word . . .

All the others, on their benches, wondered what was
going on . . . Clankety-clank! Clankety-clank! from one
jolt to the next. And the oil dripping from the top of the
lamp . . . All the heads nodding . . . then drooping.

If there's one thing in the world that needs to be handled
with care, it's perpetual motion . . . Don't touch it or
you'll get your fingers burned . . .

Inventors in general can be classified according to their
bugs . . . There are whole categories that are practically
harmless . . . The ones who go in for mysterious radiations, "tellurism," for instance, or the "centripetals" . . .
They're easy to handle, they'd eat breakfast out of your
hand . . . The little household gadgeteers aren't very
rough either . . . the cheese-graters . . . the Sino-Fin-
nish kettles . . . the two-handled spoons . . . well,
everything that's useful in the kitchen . . . Those boys
like to eat . . . they know how to live . . . The ones
who want to improve the subway? . . . Ah, there you'd

better begin to watch your step. But the real screwballs, the wild men, the vitriol throwers, are mostly all of them in "Perpetual" . . . Those characters will go to any length to demonstrate the value of their discoveries . . . They'll turn your gizzard inside out if you express the slightest doubt . . . They're no good to fool with . . .

One of the boys I met at Courtial's, an attendant at the public baths, was a fanatic . . . He never talked about anything but his "pendulum," and then only in a whisper . . . with murder in his eyes . . . Another one who came to see us was a public prosecutor in the provinces . . . He came all the way from the southwest just to bring us his cylinder . . . an enormous ebonite tube with a centrifugal valve and an electric starter . . . It was easy to spot him in the street, even from far away, he always walked slantwise, like a crab, along the shop fronts . . . That was his way of neutralizing the influence of Mercury and the "ionic" radiations of the sun, that pass through the clouds . . . And he never took off the enormous muffler he wore around his shoulders, day and night, made of braided asbestos, lisle, and silk. That was his ray detector . . . When he walked into "interference" . . . right away he began to shiver . . . bubbles came out of his nose . . .

Courtial had known them for ages . . . he knew what to expect of them . . . He called a number of them by their first names. We were on pretty good terms with them . . . But one day he got the idea of organizing a contest for them . . . That was sheer lunacy . . . Right away I sounded the alarm . . . I let out a howl . . . Anything but that! . . . He wouldn't listen . . . He needed money bad, ready cash . . . It was perfectly true that we were having a hell of a time finishing out the month . . . that we owed at least six issues of the *Genitron* to Taponier, the printer . . . So we had plenty of extenuating circumstances . . . Besides, the balloon flights weren't paying off so well anymore . . . Airplanes were breaking our backs . . . By 1910 the yokels were all hopped up . . . they wanted to see flying machines . . . We were still writing letters like mad . . . incessantly . . . We dedefended every inch of ground . . . We pestered all the hicks . . . the archbishops . . . the prefects . . . the

postmistresses . . . the druggists . . . and the horticul-
ture societies. . . In the spring of 1909 alone we had
more than ten thousand circulars printed . . . we fought
to the last ditch . . . But I also have to admit that Courtial was playing the races again. He'd gone back to the
Insurrection . . . He must have paid his debts to Formerly . . . Anyway, they were on speaking terms again
. . . I'd seen them together . . . At one throw my boss
had won six hundred francs at Enghien on Carrot . . .
and then two hundred and fifty on Célimène at Chantilly
. . . It had gone to his head . . . He began raising his
bets . . .

The next morning he comes into the shop all steamed
up . . . He starts in right off the bat . . .

"Aha, Ferdinand! My luck's turned! This is it! I'm in
luck . . . Do you hear me . . . After ten years . . .
after losing almost uninterruptedly for ten long years . . .
That's all over . . . My luck is running . . . And I'm
holding on! . . . Take a look! . . ." He shows me the
Dingbat, a new racing sheet . . . he had it all marked up
in blue, red, green, and yellow. I said my piece right
away . . .

"Watch out, Monsieur des Pereires! It's the twenty-
fourth already . . . We've got fourteen francs in the till
. . . Taponier has been very nice . . . very patient, I've
got to admit, but even so, he says he won't print the rag
anymore! . . . I might as well tell you right now! He's
been biting my head off for the last three months every
time I show my face on the rue Rambuteau . . . Don't
count on me to go around there anymore! not even with
the pushcart!"

"Don't bother me, Ferdinand. Don't bother me . . .
You're driving me crazy. You depress me with your sordid
gossip . . . I can feel it! I can feel it in my bones! Tomorrow we'll be out of the woods. This is no time to be
quibbling. Go back and tell Taponier . . . Tell him from
me . . . from me, do you understand! That bastard, when
I think of it . . . He's grown fat at my expense . . .
For twenty years I've been feeding him . . . he's piled up
a fortune . . . several fortunes . . . on my paper. I've
decided to do the stinker one last favor. Tell him! Tell
him, do you hear me, to put his whole plant! his machines!

his equipment! his apartment! his daughter's dowry! his
new car! everything! his insurance policy! tell him not to
forget anything! his son's bicycle! Everything! Remember!
Everything! on Bragamance to win! To win, I say! . . .
not to place! not to come in third! At Maisons, on Thursday! . . . That's it! That's the long and the short of it,
son! I can see the finish! And 1,800 francs for five!
Do you hear me, 1,887 to be exact . . . In your pocket
. . . Remember that! With what's left of my winnings
. . . that will be 53,498 francs for the two of us! Net! . . .
Bragamance! . . . Maisons! . . . Bragamance! . . .
Maisons! . . ."

He went on jabbering . . . He didn't hear my answers
. . . He went out through the corridor . . . He was like
a sleepwalker.

The next day I waited for him all afternoon . . . to
show with the fifty-three grand . . . It was after five
o'clock . . . Finally he turns up . . . I can see him
across the garden . . . He doesn't look at anybody in
the shop . . . He comes straight up to me . . . he grabs
me by the shoulders . . . The hot air has all gone out of
him . . . He's sobbing . . . "Ferdinand! Ferdinand! I'm
a viper! A despicable scoundrel! . . . Talk of depravity!
. . . I've lost everything, Ferdinand! Our month's earnings.
Mine! Yours! My debts! Your debts! The gas bill! Everything! I still owe Formerly what I put on that horse! . . .
I owe the binder eighteen hundred francs . . . I borrowed
thirty francs more from the scrubwoman in the theater
. . . I owe another hundred francs to the gatekeeper in
Montretout! . . . I'll be running into him this evening!
. . . You see the morass I'm stuck in . . . Ah, Ferdinand,
you were right! I'm sinking into my own muck! . . ."

He disintegrated completely . . . He flayed himself
. . . He added up the sum . . . He added it up again
. . . How much did he actually owe? . . . It came to
more each time . . . He unearthed so many debts I
think he made some of them up . . . He went for a
pencil . . . He was going to start in all over again. I
stopped him. I was firm.

"See here, Monsieur Courtial," I said. "Calm down.
You're making a spectacle of yourself. Suppose some cus-

tomers came in! What would they think? Better take a
rest . . ."

"Oh, Ferdinand! How right you are! You're wiser than
your master, Ferdinand! The stinking old fool! A wave of
madness, Ferdinand! A wave of madness! . . ."

"It's unbelievable! Unbelievable! . . ." After a moment's prostration he opened the trapdoor . . . He vanished all alone . . . I knew his act! . . . It was always
the same routine . . . When he'd made an ass of himself
. . . first he'd lay on the applesauce, then came meditation . . . But what about eating, friend? I'd have to lay
hands on some dough somehow! . . . Nobody gave me
any credit . . . neither the butcher . . . nor the grocer
. . . The bastard was counting on my having a little nest
egg put by . . . He'd suspected that I'd take my little
precautions . . . that I had some sense . . . I was the
guy with foresight . . . I was the shrewd accountant . . .
With the scrapings from the drawers I held out a whole
month . . . No air bubbles with salt . . . And we didn't
eat so badly . . . We had real meat! . . . plenty of
French fries . . . and jam made out of pure sugar . . .
That was my way of doing things.

He didn't want to put the bite on his wife . . . She
didn't know a thing out there in Montretout.

Uncle Édouard came by one Saturday night . . . He'd
been out of town, we hadn't seen him in a long time . . .
He brought news from home, from my parents . . . Their
luck was still running bad . . . In spite of all his efforts,
my father hadn't been able to leave La Coccinelle . . .
And that was his only hope . . . Even after he knew how
to type, they hadn't wanted him at Connivance Fire Insurance . . . They thought he was too old for an under-
ling's job . . . and that he seemed too bashful to deal
with the public . . . So he'd had to give it up . . . and
stick to the old grind . . . and butter up Lempreinte . . .
It was a terrible blow . . . he wasn't sleeping at all anymore.

Baron Méfaize, the head of "Litigious Life," had got
wind of my father's moves . . . he'd detested him from
way back, he was always torturing him . . . He'd make
him climb five flights of stairs on the other side of the yard

to tell him what an ass he was . . . that he got all the addresses wrong . . . which was absolutely untrue . . .

While talking with me Uncle Édouard began wondering . . . he thought maybe it would give my folks pleasure to see me again for a minute . . . I could make up with my father . . . He'd had trouble enough, he'd suffered enough . . . It came from a good heart . . . But just thinking about it, the gall started coming up . . . I had vomit in my throat . . . I wasn't going to try again . . .

"OK, OK, I'm sorry for them and all that . . . But if I went back to the Passage, I can tell you right now, I wouldn't last ten minutes . . . I'd set the whole place on fire." There was no use trying . . .

"All right, all right," he said. "I can see how you feel."

He dropped the subject . . . He probably told them what I'd said . . . Anyway, his happy-homecoming gambit never came up again . . .

With Courtial, I've got to admit . . . I can't deny it . . . it was one holy mess from morning to night . . . a perpetual rat race . . . He played some rotten tricks on me . . . he was as sneaky as thirty-six bedbugs. It was only at night that I had any peace . . . Once he was gone I did what I felt like . . . I made my own plans . . . Until ten in the morning when he came back from Montretout I was the boss . . . And that's a good deal. Once I'd fed my pigeons, I was absolutely free . . . I always took a little rake-off on the sales of the *Genitron* . . . We had a racket with the returns . . . some of it was for yours truly . . . I put it aside . . . and I got something out of the balloon flights too . . . It was never more than twenty, twenty-five francs . . . but to me, for pocket money, it was a fortune!

The old crocodile would have been glad to know where I stashed my dough away . . . my cute little nest egg . . . He could look till doomsday . . . I was very careful . . . I'd learned a thing or two . . . My little treasure never left my pocket, actually it was a special pocket, carefully pinned, inside my shirt front . . . You couldn't say we trusted each other very much . . . I knew all his hiding places . . . he had three . . . One was under the floor . . . another behind the gas meter (a loose brick) . . . and a third right there in Hippocrates' head! . . . I

dipped into them all . . . He never counted . . . In the
end he began to have his suspicions . . . But he had no
call to complain . . . He never gave me a penny in
wages . . . And what's more, I fed him . . . Supposedly
out of "general" funds . . . The stuff wasn't too bad . . .
and plenty of it . . . He realized that he couldn't say anything . . .

In the evening I didn't cook, I went all by myself to the
Automatic on the corner of the rue de Rivoli . . . I took
a bite standing up . . . I've always liked that best . . .
it only took a minute . . . Then I went roaming around
. . . I had my little circuit . . . rue Montmartre . . .
the post office . . . rue Étienne-Marcel . . . I'd stop by
the statue on the Place des Victoires and smoke a cigarette
. . . It was a majestic square . . . I liked it fine . . . A
quiet place to think things over . . . I've never been so
happy as in those days on the *Genitron* . . . I made no
plans for the future . . . But the present didn't seem too
rotten . . . I'd be back by nine o'clock . . .

I still had plenty of work . . . There was always patching on the *Enthusiast* . . . bundles that were late in getting off . . . and letters for the provinces . . . So then
about eleven o'clock I'd go out under the arcades again
. . . That was the interesting time . . . Our neighborhood was full of whores . . . They did it for five francs
. . . or even less . . . Every three or four columns there
was one with one or two customers . . . They knew me
well from seeing me all the time . . . Sometimes they
were good company . . . I took them up in our office
when there was a raid . . . They hid in between the files,
eating up the dust . . . waiting for the cops to go away
. . . We had some hot brawls in the investor's corner. I
was entitled to all the ass I wanted . . . thanks to my
eagle eye, because I watched all the approaches from my
mezzanine . . . at the critical hour . . . When I saw the
cops coming . . . they all piled in through the little side
door . . . I was the gang's lookout . . . What people
don't know won't hurt them . . . We expected the bulls
a little before midnight . . . Sometimes I had ten or
twelve of these tomatoes in the shambles on the second
floor . . . We doused the candle . . . You couldn't
make a sound . . . We heard their size tens passing on

the flags and doubling back . . . The girls were scared stiff . . . They were like rats skulking in the corner . . . Later on we relaxed . . . The best part of it was the stories . . . They knew all about the Galerie . . . everything that went on . . . under the arches . . . in the attics . . . in the back rooms . . . I found out all about the business people in the neighborhood . . . all the ones who had themselves buggered . . . all the miscarriages . . . all the cuckolds . . . between eleven o'clock and midnight . . . I heard all about des Pereires, how the lowdown swine would get flagellated at the Etruscan Urns at Number 216 in the alley across the way . . . near the exit of the Comédie Française . . . he liked a good shellacking . . . you could hear him bellowing behind the velvet curtains . . . and it cost him twenty-five francs a throw . . . cash on the line, naturally . . . and he seldom went a week without getting himself whipped three times in a row!

It made me good and sore too to hear such stories . . . I was beginning to see why we never had a penny in the till . . . what with the knout and the ponies, no wonder we couldn't make ends meet . . .

The one who told the best stories was Violette. She wasn't young anymore, she came from the North, she never wore a hat, she had a triple bun like a flight of stairs, and long "butterfly" pins. She was a redhead, she must have been forty . . . Always in a tight-fitting black skirt, a tiny pink apron, and high-laced white shoes with "spool" heels . . . She had a weakness for me . . . We all died laughing listening to her . . . she was a wonderful mimic. She had new ones every time . . . She wanted me to bugger her . . . She called me her "ferryboat" because of the way I bucked her . . . She was always talking about "her" Rouen . . . she'd been there for twelve years in the same house, hardly ever going out . . . When we went down in the cellar, I lit the candle for her . . . She sewed on my buttons . . . that was a job I hated . . . I tore off a good many . . . because of my struggles pushing that handcart around . . . I could sew anything at all . . . but not a button . . . never! . . . I couldn't stand them . . . She wanted to buy me socks . . . she wanted me to look nice . . . I hadn't worn any in a long time . . .

Pereires didn't either, to tell the truth . . . When she left the Palais-Royal, she hiked up to La Villette . . . the whole way on foot . . . for the five-o'clock trade . . . She'd do pretty well up there too . . . She didn't want to be shut up in a house anymore . . . From time to time, though, she'd spend a month in the hospital . . . She'd send me a postcard . . . She'd hurry back. I knew her way of tapping on the windowpanes . . . We were good friends for almost two years . . . until we left the Galerie . . . Toward the end she was jealous, she had hot flashes . . . she was hard to get along with.

When vegetables were in season, we piled them in . . . I did them up in mixtures with chopped bacon . . . He brought in salads . . . beans by the basket . . . from Montretout. Bunches of carrots and turnips, and even peas . . .

Courtial went in for sauces. I'd learned all that from his cookbook . . . I could make any kind of stew, I knew all about browning and simmering . . . It's a very convenient method . . . You can dish it out all week. We had a powerful Sulfridor gas heater . . . slightly explosive . . . in the backroom-gymnasium . . . In the winter I made *pot-au-feu* . . . It was me that bought the meat, the margarine, and the cheese . . . We took turns bringing home the liquid refreshments . . .

Violette liked to take a snack around midnight . . . She liked cold veal on bread . . . But all that ran into money . . . On top of our wild expenses.

I argued against it . . . I predicted the most dire disaster . . . it was no use. We had to have a try at his perpetual-motion contest. It was a hurry-up scheme . . . We expected quick results. The situation was desperate! . . . The admission fee was twenty-five francs . . . The first prize was twelve thousand smackers, the winner to be selected by a "grand jury of the world's foremost authorities" and in addition there was a second, consolation prize . . . four thousand three hundred and fifty francs . . . We were no pikers!

We had customers right away . . . a flood . . . a tidal wave . . . an invasion! . . . Blueprints! . . . dissertations! . . . enormous monographs! . . . illustrated

theses! . . . We ate better and better! But we weren't
easy in our minds . . . Far from it! I was dead sure we'd
be sorry . . . that we were in for every kind of headache
and no kidding . . . that we'd pay through the nose for
every cent we took in . . . for our beautiful dreams of
two . . . three . . . maybe five thousand francs . . .
that we were cooking up a mess of indignation that would
come down on our noodles . . . and pretty damn quick.

Models of every description were entered in the contest
. . . every taste, trend, craze was represented . . . There
were pumps, dynamic flywheels, cosmo-terrestrial tubes,
pendulums for dynamos . . . calorimetric clocks . . .
sliding refrigerators, reflectors of Hertzian waves . . .
You only had to reach into the pile, you were sure to
get your money's worth . . . After two weeks the screwball contestants began to come around . . . in person
. . . They wanted news . . . Ever since the contest
started, they'd been on tenterhooks. They besieged the
joint . . . They hammered on our door . . . Courtial
appeared in the doorway . . . he made them a long
speech . . . He put them off for a month . . . He told
them one of our financiers had broken his arm while taking
a walk on the Riviera . . . but he'd be better soon and
would hurry back . . . he wanted to bring his mezuma in
person . . . Everything was all right . . . just this little
hitch . . . It wasn't a bad line . . . They left . . . but
they were disgruntled . . . They moved away from the
window . . . spitting their bile in all directions . . .
some of them in solid lumps . . . something like tadpoles
. . . Courtial had certainly stirred up a mean gang of
maniacs . . . they were really dangerous . . . He himself began to have misgivings, but he wouldn't admit it
. . . instead of admitting his mistake, he took it out on
me . . .

After lunch, while waiting for me to worry the coffee
through the strainer, he'd squeeze the end of his nose . . .
he'd make little drops of grease ooze out. They came out
like worms, then he'd squash them between his filthy,
pointed nails . . . That was some schnozzola he had . . .
a regular cauliflower . . . wrinkled . . . browned . . .
and wormy . . . Besides, it was getting still bigger . . . I
told him so.

We'd drink our mud and wait for the horde of lunatics to come back . . . those feverish Archimedeses . . . for them to begin cussing us out . . . lurching into the joint . . . On these occasions Courtial would light into me and try to humiliate me . . . That seemed to relieve him . . . He'd start in out of a clear sky . . . "One of these days, Ferdinand, I'll have to teach you something about certain major trajectories . . . certain essential ellipses . . . You don't know one thing about Gemini . . . or even the Big Dipper! Not a solitary thing! . . . I noticed it this morning when you were talking to that little louse . . . It was pitiful, shocking . . . Just imagine if some fine day one of our contributors, in the course of an interview, were to ask you a few questions about the Zodiac and its signs? . . . about Sagittarius . . . What would you have to say? Nothing, or just about. Nothing at all would be better . . . We'd be discredited, Ferdinand! And under the sign of Flammarion . . . That's right! It's too much! It's a howling mockery! Your ignorance! What's the sky to you? A hole, Ferdinand! One more hole! There you have it. That's what the sky is to Ferdinand!" He clutched his head in both hands . . . He'd swing it from left to right, he couldn't get over it . . . as if, sitting there with me, such a revelation, such an aberration, had suddenly become just too painful . . . as though he couldn't stand it another minute . . . He sighed so loud I could have knocked his block off.

"But let's get down to more pressing business," he'd snap out . . . "Hand me fifteen or twenty of those files. At random. Just reach in. I'm going over them right away . . . I'll annotate them tomorrow morning. We've got to get started, dammit. And don't let anybody disturb me, that's the main thing. Put a sign over the door: 'Preliminary meeting of the Prize Committee' . . . I'll be up on the second floor, do you hear me? . . . As for you, it's a nice day . . . go drop in on Taponard . . . Ask him how our supplement is coming along . . . First pass by the Insurrection. But don't go in. Don't let them see you. Just look into the back room and see if Formerly's there . . . If he's gone, go ask the waiter, but absolutely on your own hook . . . you understand . . . not a word about me . . . how much Siberia won last Sunday in the

fourth of the Drags. Don't come back the front way. Slip
around through the rue Dalayrac . . . And whatever you
do don't let anybody disturb me . . . I'm not home to a
million . . . I want to work in absolute silence and quiet
. . ." He went up and settled down in his Tunisian office.
He'd eaten too much and I knew damn well he was going
to sleep . . . I still had addresses of small-town notables
to make out . . . and letters to finish . . . I left the shop
and sat down under the trees across the way . . . I hid
behind the kiosk. The idea of going to the printer's didn't
appeal to me . . . I knew in advance what he'd say . . .
I had more urgent things to attend to. I had the two thousand labels and all the wrappers to stick for the next issue
. . . if the printer released it . . . which we couldn't
bank on . . . We'd taken in money in the last two weeks
. . . the money orders for the contest . . . But we owed
a lot more! . . . Three rent bills . . . gas bills for the
last two months . . . and especially the shipping office . . .

    As I was laying low out there, I saw the procession of
contestants coming . . . They stormed the shop . . .
They jumped up and down in front of the showcase . . .
They shook the door in their fury . . . I'd taken the
handle with me . . . They'd have broken the whole place
down . . . They exchanged information . . . and indignation . . . They hung around a long time . . . grumbling outside the door . . . Four, five hundred yards
away, I could hear the hum . . . I gave no sign of life
. . . I didn't show myself . . . They'd have all come
galloping . . . They'd have drawn and quartered me
. . . At seven o'clock new ones were still turning up . . .
That punk up there in his sook must still have been sawing
wood . . . Unless he'd shoved off . . . at the sound of
the pack . . . through the handy little door on the street
side . . .

    Anyway, there was no hurry . . . I had time to think a
while . . . It had been years since I left Berlope's . . .
and little André . . . The little stinker must have grown
. . . He must be working someplace else . . . for other
bosses . . . Maybe he wasn't even in ribbons anymore
. . . The two of us had come around here together quite
a few times . . . right here by the fountain, on the bench

on the left . . . waiting for the cannon to go off at noon
. . . It was a long time since we'd been apprentices together . . . Hell! Doesn't a kid grow up fast! I looked
around to see if little André might be somewhere around
. . . One of the salesmen had told me he was working in
the Sentier quarter . . . as a junior clerk . . . Sometimes I thought I recognized him under the arcades . . .
and then no, it wasn't him . . . Maybe he wasn't close-
cropped anymore . . . his dome, I mean, like in those
days . . . Maybe he'd lost his aunt . . . He was bound
to be someplace, chasing after his pittance . . . and his
fun . . . Maybe I'd never see him again . . . maybe
he'd gone for good . . . swallowed up, body and soul,
in the kind of stories you hear about . . . Ah, it's an
awful thing . . . and being young doesn't help any . . .
when you notice for the first time . . . the way you lose
people as you go along . . . buddies you'll never see
again . . . never again . . . when you notice that
they've disappeared like dreams . . . that it's all over
. . . finished . . . that you too will get lost someday
. . . a long way off but inevitably . . . in the awful torrent of things and people . . . of the days and shapes
. . . that pass . . . that never stop . . . All these ass-
holes, these pests . . . all these bystanders and extras
strolling under the arcades, with their pince-nez, their
umbrellas, and their little mutts on the leash . . . you'll
never see them again . . . Already they're passing . . .
they're in a dream with the others . . . they're in cahoots
. . . soon they'll be gone . . . It's really sad . . . it's
rotten . . . all these harmless people parading along the
shop fronts . . . A wild desire took hold of me . . . I
was trembling with panic . . . I wanted to jump out on
them . . . to plant myself in front of them . . . and
make them stop where they were . . . Grab them by their
coats . . . a dumb idea . . . and make them stop . . .
and not move anymore . . . stay where they were, once
and for all . . . and not see them going away anymore.

Maybe two three days later Courtial was called to the
police station . . . A cop came to notify him . . . That
happened fairly often . . . It was kind of a nuisance . . .
But things always straightened out . . . I'd brush his

clothes with great care for the occasion . . . He'd reverse his cuffs . . . Then he'd go off to clear himself . . .
He'd be gone a long time . . . He always came back
delighted . . . He had confounded them . . . He knew
all the laws by heart . . . he had all the alibis up his
sleeve, all the dodges of the chase . . . But this little joke
wasn't so funny . . . It wasn't in the bag by a long shot
. . . Those low perpetual-motion characters were pestering the *commissaires* . . . The one on the rue des Francs-
Bourgeois was getting a dozen complaints a day . . . and
the one on the rue de Choiseul had lost all patience . . .
he was completely exasperated . . . he was threatening to
raid us . . . He was new, they'd put him on in January
. . . the old one, who'd been so obliging, had been transferred to Lyons . . . The new one was a bastard. He'd
warned Courtial that if we started any more contest rackets, he'd issue a warrant that wouldn't be any joke at all
. . . He wanted to make a name for himself with his
vigilance and zeal . . . He came from some one-horse
town at the end of the world . . . He was full of beans
. . . Hell, he didn't have to pay our printer's bill, our
rent, and the rest of it . . . All he wanted in life was to
terrorize us . . . We didn't even have the phone anymore
. . . They'd stopped it, I kept having to run over to the
post office . . . It had been cut off for the last three
months . . . Inventors with complaints had to come in
person . . . We'd stopped reading our mail . . . There
was too much . . . We'd been getting too nervous with
these legal threats . . . When we opened a letter, we just
took out the banknotes . . . We let the rest ride . . . It
was each man for himself . . . It's easy to panic! . . .

Courtial could say what he pleased . . . The Choiseul
commissaire had spoiled his appetite, this was a real ultimatum . . . He'd come back white as a sheet . . .

"Never, I tell you, never, Ferdinand! Never in all the
thirty-five years I've been laboring in the sciences! . . .
crucifying myself! yes, that's the word . . . to educate
. . . to elevate the masses . . . never have I been
treated like that scum treated me . . . It surpasses all
indignation! That greenhorn! . . . That whippersnapper!
. . . What does that crumb take me for? . . . A crooked
cabdriver? . . . A ticket speculator? The blackguard!

The insolence! He wants to raid us! Like a whorehouse! Raid, raid, that's all he can talk about! All right, let him come, the jackass! What will he find? Ah, it's easy to see that he's new. A greenhorn in the region! A provincial, I tell you! Must be a hayseed! Ambitious, that's what he is, the damn fool! Trying to show imagination! He can't control himself! Imagination! Ah, this will cost him more than it will me . . . That's right, dammit . . . The fellow on the rue d'Aboukir! He thought he'd come around! He had to have his raid! He came! He looked! They turned the whole place inside out! The rotten scum! . . . They wrecked the joint and then they left . . . *Veni, vidi, vici!* The stupid bastards! That was two years ago. I remember all right. And what did that two-bit Vidocq* find . . . papers and plaster . . . My boy, they were covered with rubbish! The despicable bedbug! It was pitiful . . . They'd dug all over! They hadn't understood a word . . . The crawling cockroach! . . . Ah, the cocksuckers! . . . the poor bedraggled nitwits! . . . The legal donkeys . . . Shitass donkeys if you ask me . . ."

He pointed to the piles and piles of junk reaching up to the ceiling . . . the prodigious mounds . . . regular ramparts, menacing promontories! Tottering! . . . He was probably right . . . that Choiseul *commissaire* was bound to be dismayed at the sight of those mountains . . . those suspended avalanches . . .

"A raid! A raid! Will you listen to them talk! Poor boy! Poor infant! Poor larva! . . ."

He put on a front, but just the same those threats got him down . . . He was plenty upset . . . He went back to see the young whippersnapper next day . . . To try to convince him that he'd got him wrong . . . From beginning to end! Completely! . . . That he'd been slandered . . . It was a matter of pride with him . . . That ape's tirade ate him up . . . He didn't even go near his dumbbells . . . It stuck in his craw . . . He sat there mumbling . . . He didn't talk to me about anything but that raid . . . For once he even neglected my scientific education . . . He wouldn't see anybody . . . he said it was no use. I hung up the little sign about the "Committee Meeting" and left it there.

* See Glossary.

It was about this time, when this talk about the place being searched came up, that he started in again about his future . . . About how overworked he was . . . that it was getting him down more and more . . .

"Ah, Ferdinand," he said while looking for files to take up to his little crow's nest . . . "You can see what I need . . . Another day lost! Sullied! spoiled! absolutely corrupted! annihilated by muddles! . . . by idiotic worries . . . If I only had a chance to meditate! . . . Really and truly . . . To get away from all this! . . . do you understand? . . . I'm tied hand and foot by the externals of life . . . corroded! scattered! dispersed! . . . My grandiose plans are clouded over, Ferdinand! I hesitate . . . That's right, clouded over! I hesitate . . . It's terrible! Don't you see? It's the worst of disasters . . . It's like going up in a balloon, Ferdinand . . . I rise . . . I'm crossing a little piece of infinity! I'm going to break through! . . . I pass through some more clouds . . . At last I'm going to see . . . Clouds again! . . . The lightning bewilders me! . . . More clouds! I'm frightened! . . . I don't see a thing! . . . No, Ferdinand! . . . I can't see one thing. I try my best . . . I'm distraught, Ferdinand . . . I'm distraught!" He poked around in his goatee . . . He straightened out his moustache . . . His hand was trembling . . . We'd stopped opening to anybody . . . even to the perpetual-motion maniacs . . . From banging on the door so much they'd given up hope . . . They began to leave us alone . . . There wasn't any search . . . They didn't start any proceedings . . . But we'd had a good scare . . .

By now Courtial des Pereires was suspicious of everything . . . of his Tunisian office . . . of his own shadow! His private mezzanine was still too exposed, too easily accessible . . . They could creep up unexpectedly and jump him . . . He wasn't taking any more chances . . . At the mere sight of a customer, his face would turn to wax . . . he'd almost reel . . . This last Trafalgar had really affected him . . . He was much happier in his cellar . . . He spent more and more of his time down there . . . There he had a little peace . . . He could meditate at his ease . . . He holed up in the cellar for weeks on end . . . I kept the paper going . . . It was

all routine . . . I took pages out of his handbooks . . .
I cut them out carefully . . . I touched them up in spots
. . . I fixed up the titles a little . . . With scissors,
eraser, and paste I did all right. I left plenty of blank space
for "letters from subscribers" . . . reproductions, I mean
. . . I skipped the complaints . . . I stuck to the enthusiastic passages . . . I drew up a list of subscribers
. . . I dressed it up good . . . Four loops after the
zeros! . . I put in photographs. The one of Courtial
in uniform, half-length with medals all over his chest
. . . another of the great Flammarion, picking roses in
his garden . . . That made an amusing contrast . . .
If any inventors came around asking for information
again and disturbing me at my work, I'd found a new
stall . . .

"He's with the minister," I'd say before they could get a
word in. "They sent for him last night . . . It must be for
an expert opinion . . ." They didn't entirely believe it, but
it gave them pause. Time enough for me to beat it to the
gymnasium . . . "I'll go see if he's back."

That was the last they saw of me.

Misfortunes never come singly . . . We had new headaches with the *Enthusiast* . . . she was getting so ripped
and patched, so crippled, leaky and beat-up, she'd just lie
down on her ropes.

The autumn came, it was getting windy. She staggered
in the gale, the poor thing would crumple up right at the
start instead of rising into the air . . . She ruined us in
hydrogen and methane . . . But we kept on pumping and
she'd take a little start after all . . . in two or three jumps
she'd clear the first bushes well enough . . . if she
snagged a fence, she'd plummet in the orchard . . . she'd
start again with a jerk . . . she'd ricochet into the church
. . . she'd carry away the weather vane . . . she'd head
for the country . . . The squalls would bring her back
. . . straight into the poplars . . . That was enough for
des Pereires . . . He'd release the pigeons . . . He'd
blow a big blast on his bugle . . . The whole gasbag was
ripping . . . What little gas he had was evaporating . . .
I had to pick him up in mortal peril all over Seine-et-Oise,
in Champagne, and even in the Yonne department! He

scraped all the beets in northeastern France with his ass. The lovely wicker basket had lost its shape . . . On the Orgemont plateau he spent two good hours completely submerged, stuck in the middle of the pond, a sea of liquid manure . . . frothing and bubbling, fantastic! . . . The farm boys laughed to split a gut . . . When we folded the *Enthusiast,* she stank so bad of hard and liquid substances, and Courtial too for that matter . . . he was completely caked, welded, upholstered with shit . . . that they wouldn't let us into the compartment . . . We had to travel in the freight car with the contraption, the rigging, and all the junk.

When we got back to the Palais-Royal, it wasn't over . . . Our lovely aerostat still stank so bad, even in the depths of the cellar, that all that summer we had to burn at least ten pots full of benzoin, sandalwood, and eucalyptus . . . and reams of Armenian paper . . . we'd have been evicted . . . Petitions were already circulating . . .

All that we could still manage . . . It was part of the risks and hazards of the trade . . . The worst thing, the death blow, was certainly the competition of the airplane . . . That's for sure . . . They took away all our customers . . . Even our most faithful committees . . . the ones that were almost sure to hire us . . . Péronne, Brives-la-Vilaine, for instance . . . Carentan-sur-Loing . . . Mézeaux . . . Reliable committees, absolutely devoted to Courtial . . . who'd known him for thirty-five years . . . Places where they'd always sworn by him . . . All those people suddenly found weird pretexts for putting us off till later . . . subterfuges! . . . cock-and-bull stories! Our business was melting away! Ruin was staring us in the face! . . . It was especially beginning in May and June–July, 1911, that things really went to pot . . . Candemare Julien, to mention only one, did us out of more than twenty customers with his *Dragonfly.*

And yet we'd made almost unbelievable reductions . . . We went further and further . . . We supplied our own hydrogen . . . the pump . . . the condensimeter . . . We went to Nuits-sur-Somme for a hundred and twenty-five francs! gas included! And we paid the shipping costs! . . . It was getting to be too much. The stinkingest holes . . . the most rancid county seats . . . all they cared about was cellules and biplanes . . . flying meets and Wilbur Wright . . .

Courtial knew it was a death struggle . . . He was determined to fight back . . . He attempted the impossible. Within two months he published twelve articles in his rag and four handbooks in quick succession, proving to the hilt that airplanes would never fly . . . that they were a perversion of progress! . . . an unnatural fad! . . . a technological monstrosity! . . . that all this would end in an atrocious shambles! . . . that he, Courtial des Pereires, with his thirty-two years of experience, washed his hands of the whole business! He ran his picture with the article . . . But his readers were way ahead of him . . . He was obsolete . . . submerged by the rising wave. The only answer he got to his diatribes, his virulent philippics, was insults, blistering broadsides, menacing threats . . . The inventor audience wasn't going along with des Pereires anymore . . . That's the plain truth . . . Still he persisted . . . he stuck to his guns . . . He even took the offensive . . . That was when he founded the "Feather-in-the-Wind Society" . . . at the most critical moment . . . "For the Defense of the Spherical, Much Lighter-than-Air Balloon." Exhibitions! Demonstrations! Lectures! Parties! Socials! Headquarters at the *Genitron* office. We never enrolled ten members. There was hunger in the air . . . I went back to my mending . . . I'd taken so much out of the *Archimedes,* our old captive, that there wasn't a decent piece left . . . All moldy rags . . . And the *Enthusiast* wasn't much better . . . There was nothing left but the ropes . . . You could see the warp all over . . . And I'm in a position to know . . .

Our last flight was one Sunday in Pontoise. We'd decided to risk it . . . They hadn't said yes and they hadn't said no . . . we'd drastically overhauled the old carcass, tucked in the frayed edges, turned her inside out . . . We'd reinforced her a little with patches of cellophane . . . rubber, fuse wire, and oakum! But in spite of all our efforts she was condemned, she had her last spasm in front of the Town Hall! We pumped a whole gasometer into her . . . but she was losing more than went in . . . It was a case of endosmosis, as Pereires immediately explained . . . And when we kept trying, the thing split

. . . with a terrible farting noise . . . The foul smell
spread . . . The people fled from the gas . . . It was
a panic, a nightmare! . . . To make matters worse, the
whole enormous cover flops down on the cops . . . it
smothers them, they're stuck in the flounces . . . wriggling under the folds . . . They damn near suffocated
. . . They were caught like rats . . . After struggling
for three hours we got the youngest out . . . the rest had
fainted . . . We weren't popular anymore . . . They
cussed us out something terrible . . . The kids spat at
us.

Even so, we folded up the wreck . . . we found some
charitable souls . . . luckily the fairground wasn't far
from the big lock . . . We hailed a barge . . . They let
us come on board . . . They were going down to Paris
. . . We threw all our crap down in the hold . . .

The trip was fine . . . It took about three days . . .
One night we reached the Port à l'Anglais . . . That was
the end of our balloon flights . . . We hadn't had a bad
time on the barge . . . They were nice friendly people
. . . Flemings from the North . . . we drank coffee the
whole time, so much we couldn't sleep. They played the
accordion fine . . . I can still see the laundry drying all
along the deck . . . The liveliest colors . . . raspberry,
saffron, green, and orange. You could take your pick . . .
I taught their kids to make paper boats . . . They'd
never seen them.

As soon as our old lady, Madame des Pereires, heard
the fatal news, she descended on the office . . . she didn't
let the grass grow under her feet . . . I'd never seen her
in all the eleven months I'd been there . . . It took a real
disaster to move her . . . She was happy in Montretout.
At first glance she looked so weird I thought she must
be an "inventress" . . . that she'd come to talk about
some contraption . . . She was in a terrible state . . .
As she opened the door, she was so upset . . . that was
plain . . . and in such a lather she could hardly get the
words out. Her hat was all crooked, shimmying in all
directions. She wore a thick veil . . . I couldn't see her
face. What I remember mostly is her black velvet skirt

with the big flares, the big embroidered pattern on her
mauve, bolero-style waist sprinkled with beads of the same
color . . . and a changeable-silk umbrella . . . The picture is still with me.

After a certain amount of palavering, I finally got her
to sit down in the big visitor's armchair . . . I ask her to
be patient . . . the master won't be long . . . But right
away she sails into me . . .

"Ah! Why, you must be Ferdinand? Am I right? You
are, aren't you? Then you know all about the tragedy?
. . . Isn't it a disaster? . . . That zebra of mine! . . .
He got what he was after! . . . He doesn't feel like working anymore, is that it? . . ." She kept her fists clenched
on her hips. She sat there anchored in the chair. She
started up again. She was brutal.

"So he wants to sit on his ass all day? . . . So he's sick
of working? . . . He thinks there's no need of it? What
does he expect us to live on? Our investments? Ah, the
bum! the scoundrel! the stinker! . . . the slimy toad!
Where's he keeping himself at this time of day?"

She looked in the back room . . .

"He's not there, madame! He's gone to see the minister . . ."

"Ha, the minister! What's that again? The minister!"
That hands her a laugh. "Oh no, sonny, that won't go down
with me. Not with me! . . . I know him better than you,
the swine! Minister! Oh no. A whorehouse, maybe! In the
clink, you mean . . . in jail, yes. That I'm willing to believe. Anywhere! In Vincennes! In Saint-Cloud! Maybe
. . . but that minister gambit? Oh no!"

She shakes her umbrella in my nose . . .

"You're an accomplice, Ferdinand! That's right, an accomplice! Do you hear? You'll end up in jail, the whole lot
of you . . . That's where your schemes will land you . . .
your slimy tricks . . . your dirty work . . . your rotten
swindles! . . ."

She fell back in the chair, her elbows on her knees, she
made no attempt to control herself . . . her ferocious
harangues gave way to prostration . . . she mumbled and
sobbed . . . She filled up her veil . . . She told me the
whole story.

"Never mind, I know what's what . . . I never wanted

to come . . . I knew how it would hurt me . . . I know
he's incorrigible . . . I've been putting up with him for
thirty years . . ."

Out there in Montretout she had peace and quiet . . .
she could take care of herself. Her health was frail . . . She
didn't like to go out, to leave her house . . . Long ago
. . . Long ago . . . she'd knocked around a lot with des
Pereires . . . in the early days of their marriage . . .
Now she didn't care for change . . . She preferred to
stay home . . . Especially on account of her shoulders
and her back, they were so sensitive . . . If she was
caught in the rain or took a chill, she'd suffer for months
on end . . . excruciating rheumatism and everlasting
bronchitis, a kind of catarrh . . . That's how it had been
all last winter and the year before . . . On the business
end, she told me, they hadn't finished paying for their
house . . . Fourteen years of scrimping and saving . . .
She spoke gently . . . She appealed to my reason . . .

"Dear little Ferdinand! Dear boy! Have pity on an old
woman . . . Why, I could be your grandmother, and
don't forget it. Please tell me . . . tell me, I beg of you
. . . if the *Enthusiast* is really lost. With Courtial I never
know, I can't trust him . . . I can't believe a thing he
tells me . . . How could you expect me to? . . . He's
such a liar! . . . He's gotten to be so lazy . . . But you,
Ferdinand! You can see what a state I'm in! . . . You
can understand how I feel! . . . You won't try to pull the
wool over my eyes! . . . I'm an old woman . . . I've
plenty of experience of life . . . I'm capable of understanding anything . . . I only want someone to explain
. . ."

I had to tell her again . . . I had to swear by my im-
mortal soul that the *Enthusiast* was completely cracked
up, rotten, finished . . . inside and out . . . That there
wasn't one sound stitch in the whole cover . . . in the
carcass or the basket . . . that nothing was left but
stinking rubbish . . . loathsome junk . . . absolutely
impossible to repair . . .

The more I talked, the more miserable it made her. But
now she trusted me, she saw I wasn't lying . . . She
started confiding in me some more . . . She told me all

the details . . . about her life since the early days of her
marriage . . . when she'd still been a certified first-class
midwife . . . How she'd helped Courtial get ready for
his balloon flights . . . how she'd given up her own
career for him and his balloon . . . and never left him
for a second . . . They'd spent their honeymoon in a
balloon . . . from one fair to the next . . . In those
days she'd gone up with her husband . . . They'd gone
as far as Bergamo in Italy . . . even to Ferrara . . . to
Trentino near Vesuvius . . . As she unloaded, I realized
that that woman, in her heart and conviction, expected the
Enthusiast to last forever! . . . And the fairs too! She
expected them to go on and on! . . . She had a good
reason, an absolutely imperative reason . . . Namely, the
balance due on their dump! La Gavotte, at Montretout
. . . They still owed six monthly payments plus arrears
. . . Courtial had stopped bringing money home . . .
They were actually two and a half months overdue and
had been given notice five times . . . Just telling me
about the disgrace of it tied her voice into knots . . .
Which reminded me that our own rent on the shop was
long overdue . . . And what about the gas? . . . And
the telephone bill? . . . There wasn't a chance we'd
ever pay it . . . Maybe the printer would deliver again,
just this once . . . That son of a bitch Taponier knew
what he was doing. He'd put a lien on the joint . . .
He'd snap it up for a song . . . That was a sure thing
. . . He was the crummiest of the lot . . . A fine pickle we
were in! . . . I could feel a whole mountain of headaches
. . . an avalanche of troubles coming down on me . . .
The future and our lovely dreams were all screwed up
. . . I couldn't kid myself . . . The old doll was moaning into her veil . . . She'd sighed so much that she
thought she'd make herself a little more comfortable . . .
She took off her hat . . . I could recognize her by the
portrait and des Pereires' description of her . . . Even so
I was taken aback . . . He'd told me about the moustache that she refused to have removed . . . And it
wasn't any faint shadow . . . It had started growing after
her operation . . . They'd taken everything out in one
throw . . . both ovaries and the womb . . . At first
they'd thought it was her appendix, but when they opened

up the peritoneum, they'd found an enormous fibroma
. . . She'd been operated on by Péan * himself . . .
   Before being mutilated that way, Irène des Pereires had
been a very pretty woman, attractive, affable, charming,
and what have you . . . But since the operation and
especially in the last four or five years, the male charac-
teristics had got the upper hand . . . Regular moustaches
had come out and even a sort of beard . . . They were
bathed in tears, which flew copiously as she talked to me
. . . Colored streams ran down from her makeup. She
had   powdered . . . plastered . . . and   painted   like
mad! She'd made odalisque's eyelashes, she'd given herself a complete overhauling before coming to town . . .
She put her enormous lid back on, with its bed of hy-
drangeas . . . it started wobbling again in the storm . . .
there was nothing to hold it . . . It slid back . . . She
banged it straight . . . She put in long hatpins . . . and
tied her veil again. For a minute I see her rummaging
around in her petticoats . . . She takes out a big briar
pipe . . . He'd told me about that too . . .
   "Is it all right to smoke in here?" she asks.
   "Yes, madame, of course. Only be careful about the
ashes, because of the papers on the floor. They'd catch
fire easily. Hee-hee!" A guy's got to laugh once in a while.
   "You don't smoke, Ferdinand?"
   "No. To tell you the truth, I'm afraid to try. I'm not
careful enough. I wouldn't want to be a living torch. Hee-
hee!"
   She begins to puff . . . She spits on the floor . . . in
all directions . . . She was a little calmer now . . . She
puts her veil back on. She only lifted up one corner with
her little finger. When she'd completely finished her pipe,
she took out her tobacco pouch again . . . I thought she
was going to fill another . . .
   "Say, Ferdinand!" she fires at me . . . An idea had
shot through her head, suddenly she jumps up . . .
"You're sure he's not hiding upstairs? . . ."
   I was afraid to be too definite . . . It was a ticklish
situation . . . I wanted to avoid bloodshed . . .
   "Ha!" She didn't wait. She gave a leap. "Ferdinand!
You've been deceiving me! You're as big a liar as he is."
   * See Glossary.

She wouldn't listen to any explanations . . . She
brushes me aside . . . She dashes into the little winding
staircase . . . She climbs up in a rage . . . He had no
warning . . . She jumps him! . . . I listen . . . Right
away hell breaks loose! . . . She gives him his money's
worth . . . It starts out with a couple of clouts . . . then
screams . . .

"Will you look at the sex fiend . . . the smut hound
. . . the no-good! . . . That's how he spends his time
. . . I suspected his filthy ways . . . It's good I came
. . ." She must have caught him just as he was putting our
postcards away in the album . . . the transparent ones
that I sold on Sunday! . . . He often spent his time that
way after lunch . . .

His troubles weren't over. She didn't listen to what he
said. "Pornographer! False membrane! Anarchist! Dishrag!
Cesspool! . . ." Those were some of the things she called
him . . .

I went up, I risked a glance over the banister . . .
When she couldn't think of anything more to say, she
threw herself on him . . . He flopped on the couch . . .
was she heavy and brutal!

"Down on your knees, you stinker! Ask your victim's
forgiveness!" Finally he put up a bit of struggle . . . She
lashed into his shirt front, but the material was so hard she
cut her hands on it . . . She was bleeding . . . but she
kept on squeezing . . .

"You don't like it, do you? You don't like it!" she
shouted in the thick of the battle. "Ah! You like it, you
infernal windbag . . . What do you say, you swill pail?
Does it give you pleasure to see me angry?" She was square
on top of him. She was bouncing up and down on his belly.
"Wah! Wah! Wah!" he groaned. "You're suffocating me,
you big bitch! You're killing me! You're strangling me!
. . ." Then she let him go, she was bleeding too hard . . .
She ran down the stairs . . . She went to the faucet . . .
"Ferdinand! Ferdinand! Just imagine, it's been a whole
week. All week I've been waiting for him! All week he
hasn't been home once . . . He's eating my heart out!
I'm wasting away! . . . He doesn't care! . . . He only
sent me a postcard: 'Balloon ruined. No lives lost!' Not
another word . . . I ask him what he means to do. Don't

nag, he says . . . Total loss! Since then not a word. His
lordship doesn't show up. Where is he? What's he doing?
The Benoiton Loan Company is dunning me for the payments . . . Complete mystery! Ten times a day they ring
the bell . . . The baker's at my heels . . . The gas has
been shut off . . . Tomorrow they're going to cut off the
water . . . His lordship is doing the town! . . . While
I'm eating my heart out! . . . That rotten failure! . . .
The pervert! . . . The criminal! . . . The infernal, diabolical beast! . . . The baboon! . . . Believe me, Ferdinand, I'd rather live with a real monkey . . . I'd understand him at least! He'd understand me! I'd know where I
was at. But after almost thirty-five years with that lunatic
I don't know what he's going to do from one minute to the
next as soon as I have my back turned! Drunkard! Liar!
Lecher! Thief! He's every one of them . . . You'll never
know how I detest that swine! . . . Where is he? That's
the question I ask myself fifty times a day . . . While I
work my fingers to the bone all alone out there to keep him!
to pay the bills! . . . saving candle ends . . . his highness throws it to the winds . . . on every racetrack . . .
and all those filthy whores! my money! the little I've been
able to put aside! . . . by denying myself everything!
Where does it go? Into the sink of degradation! Don't
worry, I know! He can't hide it from me . . . Vincennes!
. . . Pari-Mutuel! . . . Enghien! . . . rue Blondel . . .
Boulevard Barbès, it's all one to him! He's not hard to
please as long as it's depravity! Any stinkhole will do! . . .
It's all grist for his mill. His highness wallows in vice! He
throws money down the drain! . . . And meanwhile . . .
I'm killing myself trying to save a sou . . . to save an
hour on the cleaning woman's wages . . . I'm the one
that does everything in spite of the condition you see me in!
. . . I wear myself out! I scrub the floor! All of it, in spite
of my hot flashes! even when my rheumatism comes on!
. . . I can hardly stand up, that's the plain truth . . . I'm
killing myself! . . . And that's not the end of it. When
they attach the house! . . . Where are we going to sleep
then? Can you tell me that? You beggar! You rotten nitwit!
Gangster! Bandit!" She was shouting up at him. "Why, in
a flophouse of course! Have you still got the addresses?
You ought to remember, my fine-feathered friend! . . .

That's where he went before we were married . . . And
under the bridges, Ferdinand! . . . I should have left him
there . . . That's right! . . . with his mange and his
vermin . . . Why, he's poisoned my life . . . that's what
he deserved . . . He'd have enjoyed himself! . . . I
should have sent him to the venereal hospital! His highness
likes to indulge his passions! He's a rake, Ferdinand! The
worst kind of ruffian! Nothing holds him back! Neither
dignity! Nor reason! Nor self-respect! Nor kindness! . . .
Nothing! . . . That man has mocked me, made a fool of
me, poisoned my whole existence! . . . Ah, what a daisy
he turned out to be! Ho ho! You can say that again! I've
been a hundred times too good . . . I've been a sap,
Ferdinand! I could die laughing! It's a scream . . . And
now he's fifty-five and then some . . . fifty-six, to be
exact, next April . . . And what does the old clown do?
. . . He ruins us! . . . He sends us to the poorhouse
. . . absolutely . . . He's given up the fight . . . All he
cares about is his vices . . . They've carried him away
. . . He rolls in the gutter . . . And it's up to me to fish
him out . . . to make ends meet, to wear myself to the
bone! . . . His highness couldn't care less . . . he refuses to control himself . . . I've got to mend the pieces
. . . I've got to pay his debts . . . How about it, you
chimpanzee? . . . The balloon? He lets it go . . . He
hasn't two cents' worth of guts . . . Do you want to know
what he does at the Gare du Nord, instead of coming
straight home? . . . Or maybe you've heard? . . .
Where he wastes his vitality? In the toilet, Ferdinand!
That's right! Everybody's seen him. They all recognized
my hubby! . . . Seen him masturbating . . . They
caught him in the waiting room and in the corridors
. . . Exhibiting himself . . . his private parts . . . his
nasty equipment . . . to all the little girls! That's right,
to children! Yes, indeed, there've been complaints, I'm
not making it up . . . Yes, you pervert! . . . They've
had their eye on him for a long time . . . Right in the
middle of the station, Ferdinand! . . . Swarming with
people that know us . . . They come and tell me about
it! . . . Who told me? You're not going to deny it, I
hope . . . You're not going to tell me it was somebody
else . . . The infernal gall of that man! . . . Why, it's

the *commissaire* himself, my friend . . . he came to see
me last night just for that . . . just to tell me about your
slimy ways . . . He had a complete description of you
and even your picture . . . You see they've got your
number . . . Ah, and it's nothing new. He'd taken your
papers! Well, am I telling the truth? . . . You knew all
right . . . You scum, that's why you didn't come home!
. . . You knew what to expect! . . . Anyway, he'd told
you . . . Children is what he needs now . . . Babies!
It's too awful . . . Gambling! Liquor! Lies! . . . Spendthrift! Crook! Women! Every known vice! Minors! . . .
Sink of corruption! . . . Of course I knew all about it
. . . I learned the hard way . . . I've been through hell
. . . But now . . . little girls! . . . It's too much! . . ."
She looked at him, she stared at him from the distance
. . . He was still on the steps, on the winding staircase
. . . He felt safer behind the bars . . . He didn't come
any closer . . . He made me signs not to rile her up
. . . to keep absolutely quiet . . . that it would pass
. . . that I shouldn't say a word . . . And actually she
did calm down slightly . . .

She sank back in the armchair . . . She fanned herself
gently with a wide-open newspaper . . . She puffed . . .
She blew her nose . . . Courtial and I managed to put in
a few words . . . and then a little speech trying to explain
the whys and wherefores of the catastrophe . . . We didn't
say anything about the little girls . . . we stuck to the
balloon . . . If nothing else, that varied the monotony
. . . We went on about the cover . . . that it was really
hopeless . . . He tried flattery . . .

"What you've got to realize, Ferdinand, is that my Irène
is impressionable! . . . She's a model wife . . . the
cream of the cream! I owe her everything, Ferdinand.
Everything! No two ways about it! I can shout it from the
rooftops! . . . Not for a minute would I think of denying
her affection for me! The extent of her devotion! The im-
mensity of her sacrifices! Certainly not! . . . But she's
impetuous, quick-tempered . . . It's only the other side
of her kind heart. Yes, impulsive . . . but not mean. Oh
no! She's the soul of goodness . . . as soft as milk soup!
Aren't you, Irène, my treasure? . . ." He came up to kiss
her . . .

"Go away! Go away, you pig!"
He didn't take offense . . . He only wanted her to
understand. But she persisted in her fury . . . He tried to
tell her that we had attempted the impossible . . . put on
ten thousand patches . . . mended . . . spliced the lining in every shape and color, that in spite of anything we
could say or do, the *Enthusiast* was falling apart . . . that
the moths had eaten the sleeves . . . the rats had gnawed
the valves . . . that it simply wouldn't stick together . . .
neither standing nor lying down! That it wouldn't even be
any good as a strainer! a dishrag! a sponge! or an ass wiper!
. . . that it was no good for anything . . . She still had
her doubts . . . We went into every detail . . . we described every ailment . . . we did our damnedest, we
swore, we perorated, we declaimed, we even exaggerated if
that was possible . . . She shook her head . . . She
didn't believe us . . . We showed her the letters we had,
telling us off in black and white . . . they came from all
over . . . Even without a fee, for what we could make by
passing the hat . . . they turned us down . . . and not
with kid gloves either . . . they couldn't even stand the
sight of us anymore . . . The heavier-than-air craft were
taking all the jobs . . . resorts . . . seaports . . . fairs
. . . That was the honest truth! . . . Spherical balloons
weren't wanted . . . not even at "pardons" in Brittany!
A character in Finistère had given it to us straight when
we kept on pestering him:

Monsieur, you and your contraption belong in a museum
and we haven't got one at Kraloch-sur-Isle. I really wonder
why they still let you out. The curator is neglecting his duties!
Our young people here aren't interested in digging up dead
bodies. They want to be amused. Try to get it through your
head once and for all! . . . A word to the wise! . . .
                              Joël Balavais
                              Local wag and Breton.

She rummaged through the files but she didn't get much
out of it . . . She softened up though . . . She consented
to go out with us . . . We took her into the gardens . . .
We sat her down on a bench between us . . . She began
to talk sensibly . . . But we couldn't shake her conviction
that the *Enthusiast,* in spite of everything, could perfectly

well be repaired . . . that we could still use her . . . for
two or three fairs in the provinces . . . which would give
us enough to placate the architect . . . they'd get another
extension . . . the house would be saved . . . all we
needed was courage and never say die . . . That was
what she thought . . . She couldn't see it any other way
. . . We packed her pipe for her . . . Courtial sat there
chawing. That was mostly always his way of finishing his
cigars . . .

The people, the passersby looked over at our group
. . . they were kind of fascinated, especially by the old
cutie . . . She seemed to listen to me even better than to
her husband . . . I went on with my line . . . my tragic
demonstration . . . I tried to give her an idea of the ob-
stacles we had to contend with . . . how we were wearing
ourselves out with hopeless, more and more futile efforts
. . . She eyed me suspiciously . . . She thought I was
trying to sell her a bill of goods . . . She started bawling
again . . .

"You've no energy, I can see that, neither one of you.
So it's up to me! I'll have to do it all by myself . . . I'll
fly the balloon! You see if I don't get her up! If I don't get
her up to four thousand feet! . . . if monkeyshines at five
thousand feet is what they like! Or six thousand! Anything
they want! I'll do whatever they ask of me!"

"You're talking through your hat, my dear," Pereires
stopped her . . . "You're talking pure blarney . . . With
a bag like ours you won't get up thirty feet . . . That's in
the first place . . . You'll fall into the watering trough
. . . A lot of good that'll do us . . . And they wouldn't
want you anyway . . . Even the captain with his *Friend
of the Clouds* and his horse! The whole bag of tricks! And
Rastoni and his daughter! His trapeze and his bouquets
. . . They're not doing anything either . . . They're
being turned down too . . . We're all in the same boat
. . . It's not our fault, Irène . . . It's the times . . . the
general crack-up . . . It's not just the *Enthusiast* . . ."
He could talk himself blue in the face, he could swear by his
grandmother's ghost . . . she wouldn't give in . . . She
even started up again . . .

"It's you! You let them get you down! That airplane fad
will be all over a year from now . . . You're just looking

for excuses because the both of you are making in your pants . . . Why not face it? instead of telling me fairy tales . . . If you had any guts . . . why not admit it? . . . you'd be in there working instead of dishing out hooey . . . All this stuff you've been telling me is a lot of bunk! What about the house? Who's going to make our payments for us? We're three months behind already . . . Twice we've been given notice . . . You expect your filthy rag to do it? I'll bet you it's knee-deep in debt . . . And summonses up to there! You can't pull the wool over my eyes . . . You think I don't know these things? So you throw it all up, eh? You've made up your mind, haven't you? You shitface! . . . You've written it off! A whole house! Complete! Eighteen years' savings! . . . Purchased stone by stone . . . Centimeter by centimeter . . . You can say that again . . . and land that's going up every day . . . And you leave it all to the mortgage holders . . . You wash your hands of it . . . You don't care . . . That's where the crack-up is . . ." She tapped his head . . . "It's not the balloon, it's in there . . . I'm telling you . . . And now what . . . You want to end up under the bridges? . . . Go ahead! Who's keeping you? Filthy pervert! Swine! You're not even ashamed of yourself! . . . You'll go back with the other bums, you no-good tramp . . . That's where I found you . . . Yes, indeed! . . . I had a family, Ferdinand . . . He's wrecked my whole life! Ruined my career . . . He cut me off from my people . . . The vampire! The scum! . . . And my health . . . He's ravaged me . . . destroyed me completely! And now he wants me to die in dishonor . . . Ho ho! Men have it easy! It's incredible . . . Eighteen years' savings! eighteen years of continuous privation . . . of calamity . . . after all my sacrifices! . . ."

She was awfully violent. Listening to her curse that way, the starch went out of des Pereires . . . he wasn't cracking wise anymore . . . He began to cry . . . He burst into tears . . . He threw himself right into her arms . . . He implored her forgiveness . . . He knocked the pipe out of her mouth . . . They went into a feverish clinch . . . Right there in public . . . And they didn't break . . . But she went on yammering in his arms . . . The same words over and over . . .

"I'm going to mend it, Courtial! I'm going to mend it!
Something tells me I'll be able to! I know she can hold up
. . . I'm positive! . . . I'll bet on it . . . What about
our *Archimedes?* . . . Didn't she hold her own for forty
years? . . . Why, she'd still be in there fighting . . ."
    "But she was only a captive . . . You see, sugarplum
. . . it's not the same wear and tear . . ."
    "I'll go up myself . . . I'm telling you . . . I'll go up!
If you two aren't in the mood . . ."
    She was taking it hard . . . She kept looking for an
out . . . Anything, so long as we didn't give up . . .
    "All I want is to help you. You know that, Courtial,
don't you?"
    "Of course I do, angel . . . That's not the question . . ."
    "That's all I want . . . You know I'm not lazy . . .
I'd even go back to midwifing if that would help . . . I'd
start right in again if I could . . . I wouldn't wait . . .
Even in Montretout . . . Good Lord, even in Colombes,
as assistant to the one who took over my practice . . . I'd
do anything at all . . . Just so they don't come and evict
us . . . You see how I am . . . Actually I've been making inquiries all over . . . But I've lost my hand . . .
And besides there's my face . . . It would hand them a
laugh, I've got to admit . . . I've changed quite a lot . . .
so they say . . . I'd have to fix myself up a little . . .
Hell, I don't know . . . shave, I suppose . . . I refuse to
pluck it out . . ." She lifted her veil. Frankly, she was
quite a sight . . . in broad daylight . . . the caked powder . . . the rouge on her cheeks, her violet eyelids . . .
those thick moustaches, and even a suggestion of side-
whiskers . . . And eyebrows even bushier than Courtial's
. . . Dense enough for an ogre, no kidding! With all that
hair on her face, she'd scare her expectant mothers out of
their wits . . . She'd need quite some fixing . . . she'd
have to change her whole face . . . It gave you pause . . .
    We stayed there a long while side by side in the gardens,
telling each other stories, trying to comfort each other . . .
The night fell very slowly . . . All of a sudden she began
to cry again, so hard it was really the limit . . . A paroxysm of misery . . .
    "Ferdinand," she implored me. "You won't leave us at
least? Look at the condition we're in . . . I haven't known

you long. But already I know that down deep you're a good
boy, aren't you? . . . Besides, everything will come out
all right . . . You can't tell me different . . . It's just
a bad time we're going through . . . Don't worry, I've
seen worse . . . This can't be the end . . . We'll just
have to put our shoulders to the wheel . . . all three of us
together . . . But first I've got to see what's what . . .
I'll see what I can do by myself . . ."

She gets up . . . She goes back to the shop . . . She
lights the two candles . . . We don't stop her . . . She
opens the trapdoor . . . She starts down . . . She stays
down there in the cellar by herself for quite a while . . .
rummaging through the junk . . . unfolding the cover
. . . tugging at the rubbish . . . seeing for herself how
rotten it was . . . how absolutely decrepit and ragged
. . . I was alone in the shop when she finally came up
. . . She couldn't say a word . . . She was suffocating
with real grief. . . She sat in the armchair like paralyzed,
completely bushed . . . pooped . . . finished . . . Her
lid flopping around on the floor . . . Seeing it with her
own eyes had really stunned the old battle-ax . . . I
thought she'd keep her trap shut now . . . that she had
nothing more to say . . . But then she started up again
. . . after maybe fifteen minutes . . . But this time it was
lamentations . . . She spoke very softly . . . like in a
dream . . .

"It's washed up, Ferdinand . . . I admit it . . . Yes
. . . It's true . . . You were right . . . It's done for
. . . It's awfully sweet of you, Ferdinand, not to leave us
now . . . two old folks like us . . . You won't leave us,
will you? . . . Anyway, not right away? . . . Eh, Ferdinand? Not right away . . . not for a few days at least
. . . A few weeks . . . You'll stay on, won't you? What
do you say, Ferdinand?"

"Yes, madame . . . Yes, of course! . . ."

Next morning when Courtial came in from Montretout
around eleven o'clock, he was still pretty embarrassed.

"Well, Ferdinand? Anything new?"

"Oh no," I say. "Nothing unusual . . ." And I start
questioning him in return. "Well? Is it all straightened
out?"

"Straightened out? What?" He plays it stupid. "Ah,

you're referring to yesterday?" And right away he starts
handing me a line. "Listen to me, Ferdinand! I hope you
don't take all that gossip for coin of the realm . . . No,
you couldn't . . . She's my wife, yes, of course . . . I
honor her above everything . . . there's never been a real
quarrel between us . . . So much the better! But we might
as well call a spade a spade . . . She has all the terrible
drawbacks that go with so generous a nature . . . She's
intransigent! Despotic! You see what I mean, Ferdinand?
. . . Impetuous! . . . She's a volcano! She's dynamite!
. . . Whenever anything goes wrong, she blows her top
. . . Sometimes she frightens even me . . . There she
goes . . . And she works herself up . . . she explodes
. . . She splutters and stammers . . . She loses her head
. . . And talks through her hat . . . It's not so bad when
you're used to it . . . It doesn't throw you . . . I forget
it as quickly as a shower at the races . . . But let me
repeat, Ferdinand . . . in thirty-two years of marriage
. . . emotional outbursts, yes. But never a real tempest
. . . All couples have their quarrels . . . I'm even willing to admit that we're going through a nasty moment
right now . . . Unquestionably . . . But it's not the
first time . . . we've seen worse . . . It's not the end of
the world . . . To say we're stone-broke on that account
. . . destitute! evicted! . . . sold out! attached! . . . is
pure imagination . . . I won't stand for it . . . The poor
kitten! Naturally I'd be the last man in the world to hold it
against her! . . . It can all be explained! . . . It's out
there in the cottage that she cooks up these nightmares
. . . alone all day . . . with nothing to do but think
. . . it gets her down . . . in the end it carries her away
. . . She works herself up! . . . She works herself up!
. . . She loses track . . . She sees and hears things that
never happened . . . Yes, since her operation she's been
inclined to . . . imaginings . . . impulses . . . I'd go
even further . . . Sometimes she's a little delirious . . .
Ah yes, several times, I've been really taken aback . . .
Definite hallucinations . . . She's perfectly sincere . . .
Like this thing about the complaint . . . My oh my! You
understood, of course? You caught on right away? . . .
Actually it was very funny . . . It was ludicrous . . .
But she'd done it before . . . That's why it didn't get a

rise out of me . . . I let her go on . . . I didn't seem
surprised, did I? You noticed? . . . I acted as if she were
perfectly normal . . . That's what you've got to do . . .
Mustn't frighten her . . . That's it . . . Mustn't frighten
her . . ."

"Yes, of course. I caught on right away . . ."

"Sure, that's what I thought . . . Ferdinand hasn't
fallen for it . . . he's not that gullible . . . He must have
realized . . . It's not that she drinks, poor thing! No,
never! . . . She's the soul of temperance . . . Except
for tobacco . . . In a way, she's more on the Puritan side
. . . It's the operation that turned her inside out . . . Ah!
She was a very different woman . . . If you'd only known
her before! . . . in the old days . . ." He started looking
under the piles of papers . . . "I wish I could find her
picture when she was young . . . the enlargement from
Turin . . . I ran across it only a few days ago . . . You
wouldn't recognize her . . . It's been a revolution . . .
In the old days, I assure you, before she was operated on
. . . she was a marvel . . . her carriage! the roses in her
cheeks! . . . Beauty personified! . . . And what charm,
my boy! . . . And her voice! . . . A dramatic soprano!
. . . All that was wiped out from one day to the next
. . . with a scalpel . . . It's incredible . . . I can even
tell you without vanity that she was unrecognizable! Sometimes it was almost embarrassing . . . especially while
traveling . . . Especially in Spain and Italy . . . where
they're such ladies' men . . . I remember it all clearly, I
was rather touchy in those days . . . quick on the draw
. . . I'd go off the handle for nothing at all . . . A
hundred times I was on the verge of a duel . . ."

Memories were going through his mind . . . I respected
his silence . . . and then he started off again . . .

"Well anyway, Ferdinand. We've got other worries . . .
Let's get down to serious matters . . . Suppose you
drop over to the printer's . . . And now listen and try
to understand . . . In the villa . . . in the desk . . .
I've found something that may help us out . . . If my
wife comes back . . . if she asks . . . you haven't seen
a thing! . . . you don't know a thing! . . . It's only a
receipt for a charm and a bracelet . . . But they're solid
gold . . . absolutely genuine . . . warranted eighteen

carat . . . Here are the tickets from the Mont-de-Piété
. . . We could give it a try . . . Go see Sorcelleux on the
rue Grange-Batelière . . . Ask him what he'll give for
them . . . Tell him it's for me . . . A favor . . . You
know where it is . . . Fifth floor, staircase A . . . Get
the concierge to show you the way . . . Ask him how
much he'll give me for them . . . That would give us a
little money ahead . . . If he says no, try Rotembourg
. . . on the rue de la Huchette . . . Don't show him the
ticket . . . Just ask him if he's interested . . . And I'll
go around myself . . . He's the worst kind of crook! . . ."

For all his air of not caring one way or another, the
commissaire on the rue des Bons-Enfants was a mean bastard. It was mostly his doing that they took action . . .
And that the public prosecutor got mixed up in it . . . Not
for very long, it's true . . . But long enough to give us a
good pain in the ass . . . The office was full of cops . . .
They went through the motions of searching the joint . . .
What could they expect to find? . . . They were pretty
sore when they left . . . They hadn't found anything to
indict us on . . . There was no clear evidence of fraud
. . . They tried to bluff us . . . But we had our alibis
. . . We had no trouble clearing ourselves . . . Courtial
trotted out some articles of the law that were entirely in
our favor . . . After that they called him up to the Quai
des Orfèvres almost every day. Just listening to his pro-
testations . . . his cock-and-bull stories . . . the examining magistrate laughed for full five minutes. Right off the
bat he said:
"Before presenting your defense, send back those money
orders . . . Reimburse the contestants . . . It's a common confidence racket, out-and-out piracy."
Those words gave the old man a jolt . . . He defended
himself tooth and nail, inch by inch, desperately . . .
"Reimburse what? Destiny is crushing me . . . I'm
being driven to despair! Harried! Hounded! Ruined!
Trampled! Persecuted in a thousand ways! And what does
he want now? That's what I'd like to know? To gouge my
last nickel out of me . . . To hell with them! . . . Imaginary offenses! They're out to get me! A hornets' nest! A
sewer! I can't stand it! . . . The villainy of all those

people! It would drive an angel to drink! . . . But I'm
no angel! I defend myself, but how sickening it is! . . .
I proclaim my innocence . . . I told him off all right,
that jack-in-the-box! that beast! that scoundrel! that little
shyster! . . . A whole life, monsieur, devoted to the
service of Science, of truth . . . my intellect! . . . my
courage! . . . one thousand two hundred and eighty-seven
balloon flights . . . A whole life of peril . . . of relentless struggle . . . against the three elements . . . And
my honeyed friends, where are they now? Ah! The ignorance! The prating! . . . Ah yes . . . for light . . . for
the education of the masses! . . . And have it come to
this! . . . Faugh! . . . to be hunted by a pack of hyenas
. . . Constrained to cavil and quibble! . . . Flammarion
will come and testify! He'll come! And then that no-good
despicable snotnose stops me short . . . why, he was
positively rude . . . 'Hold your tongue,'˙ he says. 'Hold
your tongue, des Pereires, I'm sick of listening to you . . .
Let's get back to the subject. Your perpetual-motion contest . . . I've all the proofs right here . . . is nothing
but a monstrous racket . . . If it were your first . . . but
it's only the most flagrant . . . the most recent . . . the
most barefaced of the lot! . . . An utter imposture! . . .
A cynical shell game! You can't get around Article 222,
Monsieur des Pereires! . . . Your rules don't make sense!
. . . You'd do better to confess . . . Read your own
prospectus over again . . . Look at your ads! . . . What
phenomenal gall! . . . There's not a shred of honesty in
the whole contest! . . . It's completely unjustifiable . . .
Absolutely no way of checking up! . . . You just worm
out of it! . . . It's all eyewash! window dressing! You
carefully frame the rules in such a way as to make the
whole thing impossible! . . . A fine kettle of fish . . .
It's an out-and-out swindle! . . . Pure fraud! . . . Theft
in the most literal sense of the word . . . You're nothing
but a leech, des Pereires, on the grand ideal of Science!
You live by setting traps for enthusiasts . . . high-minded
seekers after truth! . . . You're a despicable poacher on
the preserves of Research . . . You're a jackal, des
Pereires . . . a loathsome beast! . . . Your kind can
only live in the deepest darkness . . . the most inextri-
cable thickets! The least ray of light sends you scurrying!

Light! That's just what I mean to throw on your low activities! Take care, you dangerous specimen . . . You putrid, slimy survivor of the fauna of the estragulums! Every day I send whole litters of crooks that are a lot more pardonable than you out to Rungis! . . .'

"But perpetual motion, I told that brute, is an ideal that runs through all human history . . . Michelangelo! Aristotle! Leonardo da Vinci! Pico della Mirandola! . . .

" 'So you're going to be the judge,' he fires back at me . . . 'You think you're eternal? . . . You'd have to be . . . you're aware of that . . . to judge that contest of yours fairly! Ha! I've caught you there! Am I right! Eternity? . . . You say you're eternal? . . . just like that! There you have it! . . . It's as plain as day! When you started that contest, you had no intention of picking any winners! . . . Am I right? I've caught you red-handed, robbing those poor unfortunates? All right, just sign this, here at the bottom.' He held out his fountain pen! The bastard! The unmitigated gall! I hadn't said boo, and he hands me this paper! . . . I ask you! . . . I was thunderstruck . . . Naturally I turned him down flat . . . It was a trap! . . . A rotten low-down ambush, and I didn't mind telling him so . . . He couldn't get over it! . . . I walked out with my head high!

" 'See you tomorrow, des Pereires,' he said. 'It won't help you any to put it off.'

" 'You think you're eternal?' No, really, I ask you, the crust of him! The unconscionable effrontery! . . . Those savages think they're so clever just because brute force is on their side . . . with their two cents' worth of whiskers and their big mouths. I've got to admit it, though, that was a pretty good crack . . . Absolutely novel and unprecedented! . . . Thundering asshole catacombs! A killer! But he'll need more than that to get me down! A little something more than asinine traps . . . believe you me! . . . His infernal insolence only strengthens my position! That's my impression! Come what may! Let them deprive me of food! drink! bed and board! Let them throw me in prison, torture me in every possible way! I snap my fingers at them! I have my conscience . . . and that's enough for me! . . . Never will I make a move without it! Or in opposition to it! . . . There you have it, Ferdinand! It's my lodestar!"

I knew the music . . . Papa had saturated me with it
. . . You can't imagine how overworked conscience was
in those days! . . . But it was no solution . . . The
prosecutor was seriously thinking of locking him up . . .
The crack about eternity was pretty clever though . . . It
could be interpreted in different ways . . . They gave us
a few adjournments . . . That gave us a chance to sell
some crap . . . Old junk out of the cellar . . . Even
wreckage from the balloon . . . The old bag came in
from Montretout for that very purpose . . . She'd decided to take control, to run things her way, especially
selling the doodads . . . everything that was left of the
balloon . . . We made one trip with the stuff on our
backs and another with the pushcart . . . We unloaded
most of it at the Temple . . . right in the middle of the
floor . . . We had plenty of takers . . . People liked
our little mechanical relics . . . And on Saturday we took
whole job lots of books to the Flea Market . . . we sold
it all wholesale, with little pieces of the *Enthusiast* thrown
in . . . instruments . . . a   barometer . . . and   the
ropes . . . In the end . . . after a good many trips . . .
we got pretty near four hundred francs out of all that junk
. . . It was pretty nice . . . It gave us a chance to soften
up the printer some by giving him a decent slice on account . . . And they gave the Benoiton Loan Company
enough for half an installment on the shack . . .

But after that there was nothing to justify the existence
of our poor carrier pigeons . . . We hadn't been feeding
them much in the last two months . . . Sometimes only
every other day . . . and even so it ran into money . . .
Grain is always expensive, even when you buy it wholesale
. . . If we'd sold them, they'd have certainly come right
back as I knew them . . . They'd never have got used to
other masters . . . They were good little creatures, loyal
and faithful . . . like members of the family . . . They'd
wait for me up in the attic . . . As soon as they heard me
move the ladder, they'd coo double! Courtial was talking
about throwing them in the pot . . . But I wasn't willing
to give them to just anybody . . . If they had to be
bumped off, I preferred to do it myself . . . I tried to
think of a way . . . Supposing like it was me, I said to
myself . . . I wouldn't like it with a knife . . . no! I

wouldn't want to be strangled . . . no! . . . I wouldn't
want to be opened up . . . and have my insides taken
out . . . and be cut in quarters! . . . I have to admit it
made me kind of sad! . . . I knew them awfully well!
. . . But you couldn't get around it . . . I had to do
something . . . There hadn't been any grain in four days
. . . So I went up one afternoon about four o'clock. They
thought I was coming to feed them . . . They didn't suspect at all . . . They were gurgling like mad . . . "Come
along, little glug-glugs," I say. "We're going to the fair. All
aboard for the ride! . . ." They knew the routine . . . I
open the pretty basket wide, the one we took them ballooning in . . . They all come running . . . I batten down
the lid, I run a rope through the handles . . . I tie it in
all directions . . . Finally it was ready . . . First I
leave it in the hall. I pop downstairs a while . . . I don't
say a thing to Courtial . . . I wait until he shoves off
for his train . . . Violette taps on the windowpane . . .
"Come back later, beautiful . . ." I say, "I've got to run
an errand . . ." She hangs around . . . she mutters
something . . .

"Ferdinand," she insists, "I got something to tell
you . . ."

"Scram!"

So I go upstairs for my animals . . . I bring them down.
I balance the basket on my head . . . I go out by the rue
Montpensier . . . I cross the Carrousel . . . When I get
to the Quai Voltaire, I look for a good place . . . I don't
see a soul . . . On the bank at the bottom of the stairs
. . . I pick up a big cobblestone . . . I tie it on . . . I
look around again . . . I pick it up in both hands and
throw it in the drink . . . as far out as I can . . . It
didn't make any noise . . . I did it automatic . . .

Next morning I gave it to Courtial straight . . . I
didn't wait . . . I didn't beat about the bush . . . He had
no comment to make . . . Angelface, who was in the shop
too, didn't either . . . They could see by the way I looked
that this was no time to fool with my ass.

If they'd left us alone, we'd probably have made out all
right . . . We'd have saved our ante without any help
from anybody . . . Our *Genitron* magazine, nobody could

say any different, was getting along fine . . . It was read all over . . . Lots of people remember how interesting it was . . . Lively from cover to cover! From beginning to end! Always perfectly informed about everything connected with inventing and the interests of inventors.

On that end I'm not exaggerating . . . Nothing has ever taken its place . . . What knocked us for a loop was our joker with his racetrack fever . . . I knew he'd start playing again . . . even if he told me different. I saw the money orders coming in . . . fifteen francs for a new subscription . . . and whoopsy daisy! . . . if I wasn't careful to hide them p.d.q., they'd melt into thin air! In a flash! He was a regular prestidigitator! . . . No business can stand up under that kind of drainage . . . not even the Bank of Peru! . . . He must have been spending our dough someplace . . . He wasn't going to the Insurrection anymore . . . He must have got a new bookie . . . I'll find out who it is, I says to myself . . . That's when they started after us some more . . . More proceedings! . . . They call him back to the Préfecture . . . That little bastard on the rue des Bons-Enfants wouldn't let go his bone . . . He started up again . . . He had us in his clutches . . . He was out to get us . . . He found more victims . . . of that damn competition. . . he'd even gone poking around in the furnished rooms on the Avenue des Gobelins . . . He was stirring them up against us . . . getting them sore again. He persuaded them to put in new complaints . . . Our life wasn't worth living . . . It was time to shake the old gray matter and do something about it . . . We thought it over, and this is what we came up with: we'd have to divide and prosper . . . That was the only way . . . All those pests fell into two classes . . . On the one hand and mostly . . . the ones who were griping for the sake of form . . . the melancholics, the hard-luck boys . . . That was easy . . . we wouldn't refund those stinkers anything . . . On the other hand, the characters that were really in a temper and never came out of it . . . That's where the danger lay! . . . We'd have to get to those boys and smooth them down right away . . . talk things over with them . . . a little cash maybe . . . Naturally we weren't going to reimburse them completely . . . It was impossible . . . out of the ques-

tion . . . But slip them a little present . . . say, five
ten francs . . . That way they wouldn't be taking a total
loss . . . They might be made to realize that this was an
act of Fate . . . When it came to carrying out his lovely
plan, Courtial went white as a sheet . . . The stuffing
went out of him . . . Couldn't he do it himself? . . . Inconceivable! . . . How would it look for him to go ringing bells? . . . What about his authority? He'd lose face
with the inventors . . . Better I should go spreading the
good word . . . I had no standing, no dignity to lose
. . . But what a smelly prospect! I could see that in advance! I'd have chickened out too, but then we were sunk
. . . If we let things drift, the rag was through . . . That
would be ruin, we'd be out in the street! . . . Things
really had to be bad for me to take on such a rotten
job . . .

In the end I took a good deep breath, I steeled myself.
I rehearsed the stuff I had to say . . . a whole collection
of bedtime stories . . . Why things had gone wrong . . .
beginning with the preliminary tests . . . because of a
grave disagreement among scientists on a highly contro-
versial technical point . . . We'd try again next year . . .
Well anyway, a ton of baloney . . . So there I go . . .
into the fray! . . . Good luck, kid . . . First of all I was
to give them back all their plans, their models, their blueprints, their cock-eyed knickknacks . . . along with our
apologies . . .

I used the indirect approach . . . I began by asking
them if they'd received my letter . . . announcing my
visit . . . No? . . . That got a rise out of them . . .
They thought they'd won the jackpot . . . If it was dinner
time, they'd invite me to join them. If the whole family
was there, my little mission got kind of delicate with all
those people around . . . I needed plenty of tact . . .
They'd had visions of gold . . . It was an ugly moment
. . . After all, I had to disabuse them . . . That's what
I'd come for . . . I tried to break it gently . . . They'd
start gulping . . . they couldn't eat anymore . . . They'd
stand up hypnotized, their eyes fixed in stupor . . . It was
time for me to keep an eye on the cutlery . . . Stormy
weather in the dishes! . . . I braced my back against
the wall . . . I'd pick up the soup tureen for a sling . . .

ready to block any aggressor! . . . I'd go on with my
spiel. At the first halfway suspicious move, I'd let go! Right
in the guy's face . . . But in most places my resolute
attitude was protection enough . . . it made them think
twice . . . It didn't end so badly . . . with gushing
congratulations . . . and then, after a little wine, a chorus
of sighs and belches . . . especially if I coughed up the
ten francs! . . . But one time, in spite of my caution and
long practice, I got a bad shellacking . . . It was on the
rue de Charonne, I remember, Number 72 to be exact,
the hotel is still there . . . This guy was a locksmith, he
did his inventing in his room . . . believe me, I know
. . . not on the third floor, on the fourth . . . If you ask
me, this character's work was assembling kits of burglar's
tools . . . Well, anyway, his invention for the perpetual-
motion contest was a mill, something like a dynamo, with
a "variable faradic" intake . . . The idea was to store
up the energy of storms . . . After that it kept going
from one equinox to the next . . .

So I go in, I see his porter, I give him the name: "It's
on the fourth floor." I go up, I knock . . . I was worn-
out . . . fed up . . . I spill the beans all at once! The
guy doesn't even answer . . . I'd hardly looked at him
. . . He was a heavyweight champ . . . I hadn't even
finished talking . . . Not a word! Boom! . . . He
charges me . . . He rams me! . . . I take it in the
breadbasket . . . I stagger . . . I topple backward . . .
a wild bull! . . . I fall . . . I cascade down all three
flights . . . They pick me up on the sidewalk . . . I was
all over bumps . . . a bloody mess . . . They took me
home in a cab . . . Seeing as I'd passed out, the boys had
gone through my pockets . . . I didn't even have my
ten francs left . . .

After that little collision, I was even more careful . . .
I didn't go into the rooms right away . . . I'd parley
from outside the door . . . With complaints from the
provinces we had a different method . . . We told them
their dough had been sent by mail . . . that they'd
be sure to get it soon . . . that the address had been
wrong . . . the department . . . the first name . . . any
old thing . . . the contest had brought such a rush of
mail . . . In the end they got sick of corresponding in

all directions . . . They were ruining themselves on
postage . . .

With the wild ones, you know where you're at . . . it's
a bullfight . . . The only problem is jumping the fence
before they gore your insides out . . . But with the
timid, the sensitive souls that lose their grip and want to
commit suicide right away . . . you're in for trouble . . .
The disappointment is too much for them . . . they
can't bear it . . . They hang their heads in their soup and
start mumbling . . . They don't understand . . . They
break out in a sweat, their glasses fall off . . . Their faces
go green, you can't stand to look at them . . . Those are
the sad sacks . . . Some of them want to end it all . . .
They sit down, they get up again . . . They mop themselves off . . . They can't believe their ears when you
tell them their contraption didn't work right . . . You've
got to say it over again slowly, you've got to slip them
their plans . . . They abandon themselves to their misery
. . . They don't want to live . . . they don't want to
breathe anymore . . . They collapse . . .

From laying on words like poultices, I was getting
pretty good at it. I knew the phrases that console . . .
the *De Profundis* of hope . . . Sometimes after my visits
we parted buddies . . . I gained their sympathy . . . Out
by the Plaine Saint-Maur, I had a whole group . . .
really enthusiastic about our studies . . . they appreciated
what I'd done for them . . . From the Porte Villemomble
to Vincennes I knew rafts of them . . . fine hands at
drawing magical plans and not at all vindictive . . . And
in the west suburbs too . . . In a corrugated-iron shack
right after the Porte de Clignancourt . . . there are
Portuguese living there now . . . I met two junk dealers
who with hair, matches, a spiral spring, three violin
strings, and a sleeve-joint had worked up a little com-
pensatory system that really seemed to work . . . Hygro-
metric power! . . . The whole thing fitted inside a
thimble! . . . It was the only perpetual-motion device
I ever saw that worked a little.

It's unusual for women to invent anything . . . But
I met one . . . She was a bookkeeper for the railroad.
In her leisure hours she decomposed water from the Seine
with a diaper pin. She toted around a pile of equipment,

a pneumatic pump, and a Ruhmkorff coil in a fish net.
She had a flashlight too and a picrate battery . . . She
recovered the essences right out of the water . . . and
even the acids . . . She stationed herself for her experiments near the Pont-Marie, not far from the wash
barge * . . . She was nuts about hydrolysis . . . Her
build wasn't bad . . . Only she had a tic and she was
cross-eyed . . . I came around one day, I said I was
from the paper . . . First she thought like all the rest
that she'd won the jackpot . . . She wouldn't let me go
away . . . she went and got me some roses! . . . I talked
myself blue in the face . . . she didn't understand . . .
She wanted to take my picture . . . She had a camera
that worked with infrared rays . . . She had to close
the windows . . . I went back twice . . . She thought
I was some good-looker . . . She wanted me to marry
her right away. She kept on writing me . . . registered
letters! . . . Mademoiselle Lambrisse her name was . . .
Juliette.

I took a hundred francs off her once . . . and fifty
another time . . . But that was very exceptional . . .

Jean Marin Courtial des Pereires wasn't so cocky anymore . . . In fact he was downright morose . . . He
was scared of the oddballs and lunatics from the contest
. . . He got anonymous letters that were no joke . . .
The meanest and crankiest of the lot threatened to come
back some time sure as shooting . . . and knock the shit
out of him . . . flatten him out once and for all . . . so
he'd never be able to swindle anybody again . . . Aveng-
ers! . . . So under his frock coat, over his flannel vest,
he'd taken to wearing a coat-of-mail made out of tempered
aluminum . . . one of the *Genitron's* patents that was
still on our hands, "extra-light and bulletproof." But even
that didn't reassure him completely . . . Any time he
lamped a character that wasn't looking too well . . . that
didn't seem to be entirely happy . . . coming in our
direction with a scowl on his face, he ran straight down
to the cellar . . . He didn't wait for the details . . .

"Open the trap, Ferdinand! Let me through quick. It's
one of them! I can tell! . . . Tell him I'm gone . . . left

* See Glossary.

the day before yesterday! that I'm never coming back!
. . . to Canada! That I'm spending the whole summer
there! Hunting weasels! sables! The great hawk! Tell him
I never want to see him again! Not for all the gold in the
Transvaal! Tell him to go away! . . . evaporate! . . .
scatter! . . . Blow the bastard up! . . . Explode him!
. . . Christ almighty Jesus!" Hermetically sealed in the
cellar, he felt a little easier in his mind. It was empty now
that we'd sold what was left of the balloon, all the
gadgets . . . He could roam around from wall to wall
as he pleased . . . He had plenty of room . . . He could
do his gymnastics again . . . In addition he'd built
himself a "blockhouse" in one corner . . . absolutely
impregnable . . . where he couldn't be seen at all . . .
in case of invasion . . . in among the crates and clothes
racks . . . He'd stay there for hours on end . . . That
way at least he didn't bother me . . . His disappearing
act was all right with me . . . I had my hands full with
the old cutie . . . she was spending all her time in the
shop these days . . . She stuck like granulated glue . . .
She was determined to run everything her way . . . the
paper and the subscribers . . .

At two in the afternoon she'd breeze in from Montretout . . . She'd settle down in the shop in full battle
dress, with her hydrangea hat, her veil, her parasol, and
her pipe. You couldn't fool with her! She was all ready
for the enemy . . . It gave them quite a shock when
they came in and found her staring them in the face . . .

"Sit down," she'd say. "I am Madame des Pereires . . .
I know the whole story . . . I wasn't born yesterday!
Speak up! I'm listening! But be brief! I haven't a moment
to lose! I'm expected at the dressmaker's . . ."

That was her routine . . . It threw them off almost
every time . . . The brutal tone, the powerful voice . . .
a little hoarse maybe, but cavernous and not easy to
shout down . . . They'd stop and think a minute . . .
standing there in front of the old bag . . . She'd lift her
veil a little . . . They'd lamp the moustaches, the paint,
the odalisque's eyes . . . And then she'd frown . . . "Is
that all?" she'd say . . . And they'd pull out trembling
. . . half the time backwards . . . As meek as Moses
. . . "I'll call again, madame . . . I'll call again . . ."

So one afternoon she was giving her audience . . . She was finishing up her dish of compote on the corner of the table . . . it was about four o'clock . . . that was her afternoon snack . . . it was part of her diet . . . I remember the exact day, it was a Thursday . . . the fateful day when I had to go see the printer . . . It was very hot . . . The audience was drawing to a close . . . Madame had already bounced out a whole gang of jokers from the contest . . . the whole crowd of spluttering argumentative bellyachers . . . she'd punctured them in record time . . . nothing to it! . . . when in comes a priest . . . That was nothing so unusual . . . We knew a few . . . Some of them were faithful subscribers . . . and delightful correspondents . . .

"Won't you sit down, Father . . ." Right away she puts on her company manners. He appropriates the big armchair . . . I look him over carefully . . . I'd never seen the guy . . . Definitely a newcomer . . . At first sight he seemed reasonable enough . . . or maybe even reserved would have been the right word . . . Perfectly calm and well behaved . . . He was toting an umbrella in spite of the weather, which was conspicuously sunny . . . He goes and leans it in a corner . . . He comes back, he gives a polite little cough . . . He was on the pudgy side . . . not the least bit emaciated . . . We were used to freaks . . . Nearly all our subscribers had tics, they made terrible faces . . . This one seemed mighty quiet . . . Then suddenly he opens his mouth . . . the words begin pouring out . . . and right away I could see the lay of the land . . . Some tripe! He'd come to talk about a contest . . . He read our *Genitron,* he'd been buying it at the stands . . . for years . . . "I travel a good deal! yes, a good deal!" He spoke in long bursts . . . You had to catch his words in full flight, the sentences came out in tangled bundles . . . full of knots, garlands, and throwbacks . . . and loose ends that went on forever . . . In the end, though, we made out that he didn't care for our perpetual-motion line . . . He didn't even want us to mention it! On no account! It would make him very angry! He had something very different in mind . . . It left him no peace . . . He wanted us to go in with him . . . Take it or leave it! . . . If you weren't with him

you were against him! . . . He gave us fair warning! We
should consider the consequences! Perpetual motion was
out . . . An absurdity! A hoax! . . . Not for him! . . .
His obsession was a horse of a different color . . . We
finally found out . . . little by little . . . after thousands
of circumlocutions . . . what was eating him . . . Sub-
marine treasure! . . . A noble project! . . . The sys-
tematic salvage of all the ships that were ever wrecked . . .
Of all the galleons and armadas lost beneath the waves
since the beginning of time . . . of all the glitter . . .
strewn and scattered over the bottom of the sea . . . Well,
that was his craze in a nutshell . . . That's what he'd
come to see us about . . . He urged us to get started . . .
there wasn't a minute to lose . . . to organize a contest!
a worldwide competition . . . for the best method . . .
the most reliable, most efficient way of raising all those
treasures . . . He offered us everything he had, his own
little fortune, he was prepared to risk it all . . . He'd
give us a thumping advance that would cover all our
initial expenses . . . Naturally Madame and I were kind
of leery . . . But he kept at it . . . This crazy sky pilot
had his own idea, a diving bell that would go way down
deep . . . say 6,000 feet . . . It would be able to crawl
into the hollows . . . grab hold of objects . . . hook on
to metal and disintegrate it . . . it would absorb safes
by "special suction" . . . As far as he was concerned,
the whole thing was perfectly simple . . . Our job would
be to attract competitors through the paper . . . In that
department we were supreme . . . unrivaled . . . He
was trembling with impatience for us to get started . . .
He didn't give us time to raise the slightest objection . . .
or even the shadow of a doubt . . . Plunk! He lays a
wad of bills right smack on the table . . . Six thousand
francs! . . . He didn't even have time to look at them
. . . I had them in my pocket! . . . Grandma Courtial
let out a whistle . . . I decided to strike the iron . . .
No shilly-shallying for me . . .
   "Stay right where you are, Father . . . just a second
. . . Half a second . . . while I go get the director . . .
I won't be a minute . . ."
   I run down to the cellar . . . I yell for the old man
. . . I hear him snoring . . . I head straight for his hide-

out . . . I shake him . . . He lets out a scream . . .
He thinks they've come to arrest him . . . He was scared
shitless . . . he was shaking in his boots . . .

"Come on," I say. "Get up. This is no time to swoon."

In the trickle of light under the transom I show him
the lettuce . . . Hell, this is no time to lose your voice!
. . . In two words I fill him in . . . He takes another
look at the wampum . . . He tolds it up to the light . . .
He looks at the mint leaves one by one . . . He pulls
himself together quick! He yawns and stretches, he sniffs
at the bills . . . I clean him up! I pick the straw off him
. . . He primps up his moustaches . . . He's ready. He
emerges into the daylight . . . he makes a brilliant entrance . . . He had his outline all ready . . . absolutely
eloquent and resounding! . . . On the subject of divers
he had us dazzled in two seconds flat . . . He dished up
the history of every system from Louis XIII to the present
day! Dates and places, the first names of those precursors
and martyrs . . . the bibliographic sources . . . the research that had been done at the School of Arts and
Trades! . . . It was a dream . . . He had the sky pilot
burping, jumping up and down with joy . . . His highest
hopes were fulfilled . . . He was so delighted that just
like that, in addition to his previous offer—we hadn't
asked for anything—he guaranteed us two hundred thousand . . . cash on the line! . . . for the expenses connected with the contest! . . . He didn't want any skimping
on the preliminary studies . . . the drawing up of
estimates . . . No pettifoggery . . . No swindling . . .
We agreed to everything . . . We wrote in our initials
. . . we closed the deal . . . Now that we were all
buddies, he pulled an enormous map of the ocean floor
from under his soutane . . . So we could see right away
where all the treasures were located . . . where all that
staggering wealth had been swallowed up . . . twenty
centuries ago or more . . .

We closed up the shop . . . We spread out the parchment between our two chairs and the table . . . That
treasure map was a marvel . . . It really made you
dizzy just to look at it . . . Especially when you consider
when this cock-eyed Saviour turned up . . . the trouble
we'd been having! And he wasn't kidding! . . . All that

dough hidden in the drink was exactly marked on his map . . . It was a sure thing . . . And right near the coast . . . with the longitude written in . . . It was a cinch that if we found a bell that would go down to even 2,000 feet, we'd be rolling in clover . . . It was in the bag . . . We'd have all the treasures of the Armada right in our laps . . . We'd only have to bend down to pick them up . . . Literally! Only three nautical miles off Lisbon, in the mouth of the Tagus . . . there was an enormous cache! . . . That was an easy job . . . for beginners . . . If we put some gumption into it and perfected the technique a little, the thing would take on entirely different proportions . . . In three shakes of a lamb's tail we could expect to raise the treasure of "Saar Ozimput," swallowed up in the Persian Gulf two thousand years before Jesus Christ . . . Several rivers of unique gems! Necklaces! Emeralds of inconceivable splendor . . . worth a billion at the very least . . . The priest had marked the exact position of that shipwreck on his map . . . It had been established by hundreds of soundings made over the centuries . . . No mistake was possible! . . . Expenses aside, it was only a little question of oxy-hydrogen drills . . . They'd need perfecting . . . Well, yes, we might have a little trouble raising the treasures of the "Saar" . . . We thought about it all one day . . . And certain "imponderables" of Persian legislation had us stymied for a minute . . . But we had other jobs that were perfectly within our reach, accessible, pure velvet . . . in more clement seas, absolutely free of sharks! We had the divers to think of! Gracious! No tragedies, please!

The truth of the matter was that all the ocean bottoms in the world were full of inviolate coffers, of galleons stuffed with diamonds . . . Few were the straits, coves, bays, roadsteads, or river mouths that did not, on the map, harbor some colossal booty . . . only a few hundred feet down and perfectly easy to raise . . . All the treasures of Golconda . . . Galleys! Frigates! Caravels! Luggers! full to bursting with rubies and Koh-i-noors and "triple effigy" doubloons . . . The waters of Mexico in particular appeared to be positively indecent in this respect . . . The conquistadores seem to have literally filled them in and

plugged them up with their ingots and precious stones . . .
If you really put your mind to it and went down 3,000
feet, diamonds were a dime a dozen . . . Off the Azores,
for instance, to mention only a single instance . . . the
Black Stranger, a steamer from last century with a mixed
cargo, a Transvaal courier, had more than a billion
francs' worth of them on board . . . all by itself (according to the most conservative experts) . . . She was
lying overhung on a rocky bottom at a depth of 4,472
feet . . . already split in two amidships . . . All you
had to do was rummage through the hull! . . .

Our padre knew of plenty more, the choice was staggering . . . He knew all the salvageable wrecks . . .
all of them perfectly simple to clean out . . . several
hundreds actually . . . He'd riddled his chart with holes
. . . those were the places to prospect in . . . It showed
the most urgent salvage jobs . . . to the tenth of a
millimeter . . . They were marked in black, green, or
red, according to the size of the treasure . . . with little
crosses . . .

It was only a question of technique, of ingenuity, of
flair . . . It was up to us to demonstrate our talents . . .
Odds bodkins, we didn't dawdle! . . . In a fever, before
he had time to cool off, des Pereires seized his pen, a
ream of paper, a ruler, an eraser, a blotter, and right there
in front of us, accompanying himself in a loud voice, he
wrote a regular proclamation . . . It was vibrant! . . .
It was sincere! . . . And at the same time it was meticulous and honest! . . . That was the way he worked! . . .
In less than five minutes, in a flurry of inspiration, he'd
formulated the whole problem! It was a first-class job! . . .
"Let's not put anything off until tomorrow! . . . This
article has to appear at once . . . we'll make it a special
number!" Those were his orders . . . The padre was
delighted . . . jubilant . . . speechless . . .

I ran off to the rue Rambuteau . . . I took all the
dough in my pocket . . . I left only fifty francs for the
old cutie . . . Hell! . . . I'd had trouble enough! . . .
If I'd left it in the till, I knew I'd never see it again . . .
The old man looked pretty glum . . . He owed Formerly
a pile . . . He'd already dreamed up a bet . . . He
couldn't resist . . . It was better I should be the treasurer

. . . Less risky . . . We'd spend very gradually . . .
and not one cent on the ponies, I'd see to that . . . I'd
pay the bills . . . First Taponier, top priority, and the
special number! . . . That printer was on his last legs
. . . When he saw the cash, he could hardly believe his
eyes . . . He took a good look at the bills though . . .
he held them up to the light . . . Hard cash! He was
absolutely groggy . . . He didn't know what to say . . .
I paid him six hundred francs on our back debts and two
hundred more for the special number and publicity for
the contest . . . He moved fast all right . . . Two days
later we received the papers . . . shipped, banded, pasted,
stamped . . . the works! . . . I took them to the main
post office in the pushcart with Courtial and Madame . . .

As the padre was leaving, we'd asked him to write out
his address, his name, street, and so on . . . but he'd
flatly refused . . . He wanted to be anonymous. That
puzzled us . . . He was an oddball all right! But a lot
less than a good many other people . . . He was a
corpulent man, he looked very healthy, and he was neat
and clean-shaven, about the same age as Courtial . . .
but completely bald . . . In his spells of enthusiasm he
stuttered like a machine gun . . . The way he writhed
and wriggled, he almost fell off his chair! . . . He
struck us as mighty optimistic . . . certainly eccentric
. . . But one thing he'd proved was that he had plenty
of dough . . . He was a real backer . . . The first we'd
ever seen . . . Let him be a little weird . . .

On the way back from the main post office with the
cart, we passed right in front of the police station on the
rue des Bons-Enfants. "Stop a minute!" I say to the old
man. "Dare me to go tell him? . . . I just want to let him
know that everything's OK." I get this fool idea of
pushing some weight around . . . of telling him we had
plenty of cabbage . . . I run over, I open the door . . .
The coppers recognize me:

"Hiya, Butch," says the one at the desk. "Watcha doing
around here? Like to stay a while?"

"Oh, no," I say. "No, sir . . . The clink's not for me.
I was just passing by. I thought I'd drop in and show you
a little currency . . ." And I take out my four bills . . . I
wave them under his nose . . . "Take a look," I say . . .

"And they're not stolen . . . I just wanted to tell you that it's for a new contest . . . The diving bell!"

"Dive, dive!" he says. "I'll dive you! . . . Are you trying to kid me, you little snot-nosed asshole?"

I ran out even faster than I came . . . I didn't want them to jug me . . . We had a good laugh in the street . . . We galloped a ways with the cart . . . We made it fast as far as the rue du Beaujolais . . .

Naturally that kind of a competition, to recover sunken treasure, was going to draw a crowd . . . Our share as the organizers was fixed at sixteen percent of everything that was brought up . . . That wasn't unreasonable! Even so, on the Armada alone, reckoning it close without forcing the figures, that made about three million for us . . . Not bad! . . .

I've got to admit that the old cutie didn't think it was all in the bag . . . She smelled a slight rat . . . She still had her suspicions . . . Even so, she didn't dare to say anything . . . After all it was a miracle . . . She wasn't swept off her feet . . . She just kept her eye on the cash . . .

Courtial threw himself into the thing body and soul . . . head over heels . . . He could already see those sparklers piled up on the beach, emeralds by the fistful . . . mountains of gold dust . . . ingots . . . The whole treasure of the Incas, pumped from the galleys . . . "We are the looters of the deep," he'd roar through the house . . . He skipped and gamboled over the piles of paper . . . And then suddenly he'd stop, he'd tap his head. "Wait a minute, my sugar bun! We haven't divided it up yet . . ." He'd lay out four columns in red ink . . . He was very strict about sharing the spoils . . . Fiercely meticulous . . . he foresaw the worst kind of trouble. This was no laughing matter . . . He took every possible precaution. He drew up an agreement!

"Never mind, angel pudding, you don't know them . . . You don't know what they're capable of . . . I deal with them every day, I know what we're up against . . . I've seen backers . . . and inventors too, I know what I'm talking about . . . I've been handling them for forty years . . . And now I'm caught between two fires . . .

Ah! Exactly! . . . I don't want to be crushed! . . .
fleeced! . . . drawn and quartered! just when things
start popping . . . at that very moment! Oh no, hell no,
not on your tintype . . . Hell's bells! . . . The pen in one
hand, Ferdinand. Quick! And in the other the scales! And
across my knees a carbine! That's it. There's Courtial
for you! To the life! Justice! Respect! Presence! I've seen
my brilliant inventors . . . as sure as I'm here talking to
you . . . create marvels . . . absolutely stupefying wonders . . . throughout my long career! And nearly always
. . . take it from me . . . for beans! For cheese! For
glory! For less than nothing! . . . Genius is left to rot!
That's the exact truth! It doesn't sell! It goes begging! It's
gratis pro Deo. Cheaper than matches . . . But suppose
you try to be nice, with your heart on your sleeve! You
want to do something for them, an unprecedented kindness! Sure! You believe in this bozo's song and dance!
You want to encourage the scientist . . . dress the martyr's wounds . . . you come around in all innocence,
bringing a small sardine . . . The martyr jumps sky-high!
It's an affront . . . Everything's changed . . . revolu-
tionized . . . Everything collapses! A flash of lightning
and hell opens . . . Your genius turns jackal! Vampire!
Leech! The hounds are unleashed . . . carnage! . . .
an atrocious massacre! To get the money out of you they
disembowel you on the spot! . . . crucify you! vaporize
you! No quarter given! The soul is forgotten! Nothing
counts but gold! Gold! So be careful! Take it easy, take
it easy, pal! You want to search the depths? Why, for a
hundred francs divided up wrong, I know those zebras,
they'd blow up the terrestrial globe! That's right . . . so
help me . . . I'm not exaggerating! I'm in a good position to know . . . To our documents! To our documents,
Ferdinand! Keep your powder dry! Letter-perfect documents! notarized! initialed! deposited before noon with
Maître Van Crock on the rue des Blancs-Manteaux . . .
An excellent notary! in triplicate . . . Our share first!
And stipulated in capitals! Airtight! Oleographic! No
dubious arguments! No underhanded finagling! No, never!
Oh providential padre, you'll soon have plenty to dive
with! Ah, the poor innocent! He hasn't the faintest idea!
Diving bells! . . . Why, before the month is out, they'll

be bringing in three or four a day! What am I saying? A dozen. And meeting our specifications! . . . Two thousand feet? . . . Four thousand? . . . Six thousand? . . . I'm not the least bit worried. Oh no, I won't breathe a word . . . No snap judgments . . . I've got to be impartial . . . I don't want to seem prejudiced . . . I'll wait for the day of the trials . . . Very well! . . . But unless my memory deceives me, I've already written some very well-documented articles on that very question . . . Let's see . . . Maybe I'll remember the exact dates . . . It was before we were married . . . Around '84 or '86 . . . Just before the Amsterdam Congress . . . the Submersible Exhibition . . . Maybe I can lay hands on them . . . They must be around somewhere . . . I explained it all . . . It was in the Supplement . . . Say, it all comes back to me! . . . It was in *The World Upside Down* . . . I can see that bell plain as day . . . Reinforced of course . . . with triple bolts . . . and double-guaranteed walls and a ferromagnetic top . . . So far it's perfectly simple . . . Cushions threaded to the thousandth of a centimeter around the ballast . . . That's it! Iridobronze rivets . . . absolutely impervious to the action of the sea water . . . Not a single acid spot after years in the water! . . . Tempered in chlorido-sodium! A galvanoplastic overstress on a centrifugal pin! . . . A simple matter of computation . . . The factors involved are child's play . . . Radio-diffusible lighting with a Valladon projector! . . . My word, all it takes is a little spunk and initiative . . . No need to bat your brains out . . . A big circular prehensible grab will do the trick . . . That may be a little more ticklish . . . I'd attach it to the outer face . . . How about 23–25? . . . That's an excellent caliber . . . Retrobascule valves for still greater security . . . The drop chain is simple . . . A Rotterdam-Durtex with one-inch links . . . And if they want something even stronger . . . to be absolutely on the safe side . . . the guaranteed maximum . . . they can take special cable plaited from copper and rope, a 28–34 while they're about it! See what I mean? . . . Rastrata is tops . . . I haven't any shares in the firm . . . Reinforced pneumatic hood . . . the Lestragone patent . . . And about portholes? . . . Ah!" He was assailed by

doubt. "If I were in their shoes, I'd steer clear of that
packing they turn out in the arsenals . . . that Tromblon-
Parmesan stuff . . . It hasn't worked too well on submarines. It's a flop! . . . They haven't told the whole
story . . . At the ministry of course they defend it tooth
and nail . . . but I'll stick to my guns . . . I foresaw it!
. . . At medium pressures it does all right . . . Up to
twenty kilos to the square centimeter, all right . . . But
starting with 'twenty tenths'? . . . It's tissue paper, my
boy . . . The fish pass right through it . . . That's my
opinion and you won't make me change it . . . Anyway,
they'll think of that . . . I've no right to influence them
. . . I won't even mention my article . . . Certainly not!
. . . Hell! I will too . . . Sure I'll quote it . . . *in
toto* . . . After all it's my duty . . . Don't you agree,
Irène darling? And you, Ferdinand? Don't you think I
ought to speak out? After all it's a critical moment . . .
It's now or never . . . I'm in this thing . . . I'm in
charge . . . I've got to tell them what I think, don't I?
Today, and not in ten years . . . My opinions are worth
something, aren't they? But enough phrasemongering! . . .
It's all very well to give advice, to play the sage, the
academician, the know-it-all . . . But it's not enough
. . . Not by a long shot! . . . I've always done my share!
. . . Here! . . . There! Everywhere! Irène can bear me
out . . . I've never sidestepped a danger! . . . Never
. . . By what right? . . . Why, I'll go down in their contraption myself . . . Maybe not the first try, but certainly
the second! . . . Nobody can stop me! . . . It's my duty!
. . . my right! Obviously! I'd even say it was indispensable . . . My eye, my authority, will be their only real
security! Make no mistake!"

"Oh no!" the old lady screeches as if somebody'd
taken a bite out of her ass. "Nothing doing! I'd sooner
cut the rope! As I live and breathe! This is the payoff!
Never, you hear me! I'll never let you go down! Haven't
you made an ass of yourself long enough! Go down in that
contraption! You're not a fish, are you? . . . Let the
lunatics dive! It's their business, not yours! . . . Certainly not!"

"Lunatics! Lunatics! You haven't a grain of sense!
Where's your logic? . . . Didn't you pester the life out of

me to make me go up in the air? Yes or no? Weren't you
all for the balloon? You were nuts about it, out of your
mind! 'The *Enthusiast!* The *Enthusiast!*' You couldn't think
of anything else! And I'm not a bird! . . ."

"Bird, bird! Now you're insulting me! You're picking
a fight! . . . All right! I see what you're up to, you
dog! . . . I know, you want to clear out! . . . You want
to go gallivanting around again!"

"Where? On the bottom of the sea?"

"Bottom of the sea, my foot! . . ."

"Oh, leave me alone! Leave me alone, Irène! How do
you expect me to think? You're always balling everything
up! . . . with your idiotic outbursts . . . your insane
frenzies! . . . Let me think in peace and quiet! . . . The
circumstances, it seems to me, are solemn enough . . .
Ferdinand! You hold down the shop . . . And whatever
you do, don't say another word to me!"

He was giving orders again . . . He was recovering
his tone, his color . . . and his crust for that matter . . .
He started whistling his charmer's tune, the "Sole Mio"
of happier days . . .

"Yes, I'd better go out! Take a breath of air . . .
You've still got a hundred francs, haven't you, kid? . . .
I'll go pay the telephone bill . . . That'll give me a
chance to stretch my legs . . . It's high time they turned
it on again . . . Wouldn't you say so? We need it . . ."

He hung around the doorstep . . . He was undecided
. . . He looked out toward the arcades . . . He started
off to the left . . . that probably meant the Insurrection.
If he'd gone right, it would have been the Urns and his
cat-o'-nine-tails . . . As soon as things begin to look
up a little, all people can think of is piggishness . . .

The sale of that number was a real orgy, there's no
getting around it . . . They came in a steady stream . . .
They took the joint by storm . . . Even after nine at night
subscribers came around asking for their supplement . . .
All day long it was a riot . . . The shop shook under
the weight of the mobs . . . The doorstep was all worn
down from their trampling . . . Des Pereires harangued
them . . . He'd stand on the counter, handing out papers
by the armful . . . I was running around the whole time

. . . pestering the printer . . . chasing back and forth . . . with the hod . . . The cart was too slow on the Faubourg Montmartre . . . I'd bring them back in batches as they came off the press . . .

The old cutie made up the wrappers for shipment to the provinces . . . That was important too . . . The diving-bell contest was being talked about far and wide . . . It was getting to be an event . . .

Naturally Uncle Édouard heard about it . . . He dropped over to the Galerie . . . He came in through the side door . . . He was mighty glad our rag was picking up . . . He'd been worried . . . He expected me to be out on my ass again . . . looking for another job . . . And just then our popularity skyrocketed . . . We really had the wind in our sails . . . It was terrific . . .

The hope for treasure is real magic. There's nothing like it . . . At night after my errands, when I came back from the Automatic, I'd have more bundles to tie up . . . until eleven o'clock . . . Violette gave it to me straight: "You're working too hard! You're a sap! You think they appreciate it? . . . If you knock yourself out, who's going to take care of you? Not your boss, I bet! Buy me a *menthe,* kid! . . . I'll sing you 'The Girl from Mostaganem' . . . It'll drive you crazy, you'll see . . ." For that little number she'd hike up her skirt front and back . . . She didn't wear any panties, so it was a real belly dance . . . She'd do it right out in the open . . . in the middle of the Galerie . . . The other floozies would come running . . . usually with three or four customers each . . . Bums, jerkoffs, bankrupt peepers . . . "Do your stuff, Suzy! Don't piss crooked!" She sure threw her twot around . . . You could see it bobbing up and down . . . The crowd clapped and cheered, that Tunisian dance of hers was some excitement . . . It always drew a crowd. When it was over, I'd buy her her *menthe* . . . We'd all end up at the Insurrection . . .

Violette's stand was over by the scales, behind the thickest column, in the Galerie d'Orléans . . . It didn't take her two minutes to do a job . . . If she hooked a real sucker, she'd take him up to the Pelican only a few steps away . . . across from the Louvre . . . The room

cost two francs . . . She liked her pernod straight . . .
We'd get her to sing her song:

> The enchanted Orient came
> And sat in my caravansar-ee . . .
> His ass was bare and from his belly
> A great big eye looked out at me.

That didn't do my work for me . . . Sometimes she'd
hang around chewing the fat for hours . . . When I
wanted to get rid of her, there was only one way.

"Let's go in," I'd say. "Come on, kid. You can help me
tie up some bundles."

"Let me suck just one more . . . Wait for me, little
chickadee! . . . I got to finish my night's· work . . ."

I could never count on her . . . Right away she'd
look for the back door . . . She'd chicken out . . .
Except for sewing on buttons, which was her weakness,
I never got any real work out of her . . . She faded
the minute I brought it up . . . It was surefire.

Hardly a week later the plans and solutions began to
pour in at a terrific rate . . . about a hundred a day.
Our rules had specified *ad libitum* . . . They hadn't let
hard reality faze them! . . . They'd given their fancy
free rein . . . All in all, at first glance, their expositions
and plans were as dopey as they come . . . Our geniuses
had really knocked themselves out! . . .

On the balistic side their ideas were wild . . . but
some of the detail was good . . . We'd get something
out of it . . . Generally speaking, when they used small
sheets of paper, the size of the writing paper they give you
in cafés, it was almost always to advertise some colossal
device, a bell bigger than the Opéra . . . and when the
plans were enormous, sprawled over eighteen octavo pages,
you could bet they were selling some little sounding device
about five inches long.

In that hobby parade there was everything you could
ask for . . . every imaginable system, invention, and
subterfuge for treasure hunting . . . Some of the caissons
suggested were shaped like an elephant . . . Others
were more like a hippopotamus . . . The majority, as we

might have expected, looked like fishes . . . Some had
a human aspect . . . regular people with faces . . . One,
the inventor told us, was actually his landlady, a very
faithful likeness, with eyes that would shine when they
got down below two thousand feet . . . revolving in con-
centric circles . . . to attract all the fauna of the deep
seas . . .

In every mail a fresh load of brilliant solutions turned
up . . . they were somersaulting all over his desk . . .
All we had to do now was wait for our sky pilot. He'd
promised to be back the last Thurday of the month . . .
It was all arranged and settled . . . We were right there
at our posts . . . He was supposed to bring us ten
thousand francs . . . an advance on our share . . . That
would give us a chance to pay our most urgent debts in
the neighborhood, to get the telephone turned on, and
to run some beautiful pictures in an "extra-special
number" devoted entirely to the diving bell . . . Already
the big dailies were talking about us in connection with
salvaging submarines, not just recovering the fabulous
treasures of the deep . . . It was the year after the
Farfadet disaster . . . The excitement hadn't died down
. . . We had a sure chance of winning the gratitude of
the nation . . .

But all those prospects didn't turn the old cutie's head
. . . In fact she was looking pretty glum. She wanted to
see that priest again before taking another step . . .
Sometimes she'd ask me a dozen times an hour if I didn't
see him coming . . . at the far end of the Galerie . . .
And what about the boss? Where could he be keeping
himself again? Painting the town? . . . Wasn't he down
in the cellar? . . . No? . . . He'd been out since morning
. . . All sorts of people were asking for him . . . It was
getting worrisome . . . "Wait a minute," I tell the old
lady. "I'll look in at the Insurrection . . ." I'd hardly
stepped out when I see his nibs taking it easy, strolling
through the gardens . . . making eyes at the nursemaids
. . . without a care in the world . . . He's whistling,
the stinker! He's got his arms full of bottles . . . I
hightail it over to him . . .

"Well, well, Ferdinand! You look mighty anxious . . .

Is the house on fire? . . . Is something wrong? . . . Has he turned up?"

"No," I say, "he's not there . . ."

"He won't be long," he says calmly . . . "Anyway, here's some Banyuls . . . and a bottle of Amer Picon . . . some anisette . . . and cookies . . . How do I know what the priest likes? . . . What do priests drink anyway? . . . Everything, I hope . . ." He wanted to celebrate the success of our venture. "I sincerely believe, Ferdinand, that we've hit the royal road . . . Ah yes! Things are shaping up . . . I was looking at the plans this morning . . . my oh my, what a shipment again! A torrent of ideas, my boy . . . Once the avalanche has subsided . . . I'm going to do some big-time sorting . . . On one side everything that looks promising . . . and on the other, the stuff we'd better forget . . . He wouldn't be able to do that . . . I expect him to give me carte blanche. No hit-or-miss methods! . . . It takes knowledge! We'll talk it over this afternoon . . . And that's not all, you know . . . There's the question of surety . . . I can't go into this thing with my eyes closed . . . Oh no! That would be too easy! Not at my age! Certainly not! . . . First of all a bank account . . . That's the main thing! And two hundred thousand on the line! And joint signatures . . . him and me! I send for the builders . . . we place the order . . . Then we can talk . . . We'll know where we're at . . . After all we're not babes in the woods!" Still, a shadow of doubt grazed his mind . . .

"You think he'll be pleased with all this?"

"Ah," I say, "I'm positive." I hadn't the slightest doubt.

And so, chatting away, we get back to the office . . . We wait another little while . . . Still no priest in sight. It was getting kind of sticky . . . Madame des Pereires was all wrought up, she was trying to make a little order . . . so the place wouldn't look too much like a barn . . . It was a terrible shambles even in normal times, and now with this rush there wasn't an inch of space anywhere! . . . An enormous dungheap! A sow wouldn't find her kittens . . . Garbage in full eruption . . . absolutely sickening . . . from floor to roof . . . torn papers, disemboweled books, putrid manuals, manuscripts, memoranda, all reduced to streamers . . . clouds of flying con-

fetti . . . The bindings all ripped, thrown in all directions
. . . Those hoodlums had even made off with our beautiful
statues . . . They'd decapitated Flammarion! They'd
stuck blotting paper on Hippocrates, lovely violet moustaches . . . After an inconceivable lot of trouble we managed to extricate three chairs, the table, and the big
armchair from the mess. We threw out the customers . . .
We cleared a space to receive the holy man in.

On the stroke of half past five, only half an hour late
. . . there he comes . . . I spy him coming down the
Galerie d'Orléans . . . He was carrying a black briefcase,
stuffed to the gills . . . He comes in . . . We greet him.
He puts his load down on the table . . . Everything's OK.
He mops his brow . . . he must have been walking fast
. . . He catches his breath . . . The conversation starts
up . . . Courtial takes over . . . The old lady goes up
to the Alcazar . . . she comes back with a few folders,
the most remarkable . . . quite a neat little assortment
. . . She puts them down beside his briefcase . . . He
seems satisfied . . . He leafs vaguely through them . . .
picks out one or two at random . . . He doesn't seem
terribly interested . . . We wait . . . we're afraid to stir
a muscle . . . for him to say something . . . We breathe
with care . . . He rummages through a few more pages
. . . Then he screws up his whole face . . . A nervous
tic! . . . And then another! A hideous grimace! Lord,
it's an attack! A regular convulsion comes over him . . .
He takes the whole load of papers and throws them into the
showcase . . . Then he clutches his head . . . He rubs
it with both hands . . . He kneads it, he mangles it . . .
He pinches himself, he massages his chin . . . and his fat
cheeks, his nose too, and his ears . . . A satanic convulsion! . . . He gouges his eyes, he scrapes his scalp . . .
And then all of a sudden he leans over . . . He bends
down and there he is on the floor . . . Plunging his head
into the papers . . . He sniffs at the piles . . . He grunts,
he puffs and blows . . . He picks up a whole armful and
. . . whoops! . . . he tosses them up in the air . . . He
flings them at the ceiling . . . It all comes raining down
. . . papers, folders, plans, pamphlets . . . They're all
over . . . We can't see each other . . . Once . . . twice
. . . and then he does it again! All the time howling with

joy . . . jubilant . . . He squirms . . . he digs in again
. . . The people collect outside the door . . . He turns
his briefcase upside down . . . He takes out more newspapers, a lot of clippings, whole armfuls . . . He scatters
them too . . . In among them, I see them all right . . .
there's a lot of bank notes . . . I see them in with the
papers . . . I see them flying away . . . I dive to pick
them up . . . I know how it's done . . . Just then two
plug-uglies come charging up . . . They bang into the
door with their shoulders . . . They push the crowd
aside. They barge in . . . They jump the padre . . .
They collar him from behind, they rough him up, they
knock him over, they pin him to the floor . . . Ah, the
poor bastard's suffocating . . . He crawls under the table,
groaning . . . "Police," they inform us . . . They pull
him out by the dogs . . . They sit on the poor guy . . .

"Have you known him long?" they ask us . . .

They're inspectors . . . The meanest of the two pulls
out his card . . . We tell them quick that we've got nothing to do with it . . . Absolutely nothing! The sky pilot is
still wriggling . . . still struggling . . . He manages to
get up on his knees . . . He starts sniveling . . . "Forgive me! Forgive me!" he begs us . . . "It was for my
poor! My blind! . . . My poor little deaf-mutes . . ."
All he wants in life is to go on collecting funds . . .

"Shut up! Who's asking you! . . . The dirty bastard's
nuts! . . . When are you going to stop horsing around?"
The one who had shown us his card gives the sky pilot
such a clout that he goes "quack" and folds up . . . He
wasn't talking anymore . . . They put the handcuffs on
him right away . . . They wait a minute . . . They catch
their breath . . . They kick him to make him get up. It's
not over yet. Courtial still has to sign a statement and then
some other paper on both sides. One of the bulls, the one
that's not so mean as the other one, tells us a little about
this screwball . . . He really was a priest . . . he was
even an honorary canon! . . . Monsieur le Chanoine
Fleury! . . . That's what he called himself . . . This
wasn't his first fling or his first run-in with the law . . .
He'd already taken every member of his family for thousands and thousands of francs . . . His cousins . . . his
aunts . . . the Little Sisters of Saint-Vincent-de-Paul . . .

He'd touched everybody . . . the churchwardens of the
diocese . . . the beadle . . . and even the chair attend-
ant . . . He owed her at least two thousand francs! . . .
All for screwy schemes without any rhyme or reason . . .
Lately he'd been burglarizing the sacraments chest . . .
They'd caught him at it twice . . . with his hand in
the chest . . . They'd found the whole of Joan-of-Arc's-
Pence in his room, broken open with a chisel . . . He had
treasure on the brain . . . They'd noticed it too late . . .
Now they were going to lock him up . . . His bishop in
Libourne had insisted on having him interned . . .

There was a crowd under our arcades . . . They were
having a hell of a good time, enjoying the show . . . There
were plenty of comments . . . A lot of thinking was going
on . . . They saw the lettuce scattered around the place
. . . But I'd seen it too . . . I'd had presence of mind
. . . I'd already saved four or five bills and a fifty-franc
piece . . . They did a lot of exclaiming . . .Those lugs
outside the window had been watching me . . . The bulls
pushed our priest into the gymnasium . . . He was still
resisting . . . They had to go around in back to load him
into a cab . . . He held on with all his might . . . He
just didn't want to go . . .

"My poor! My poor poor! . . ." he kept yelling. Finally
after a lot of trouble the cab came . . .

They hauled him in . . . They had to tie him down, to
rope him to the seat . . . Even so, he didn't keep still
. . . He threw us kisses . . . It was shameful the way
they tortured him . . . The cab couldn't get going, the
people were standing in front of the horse . . . They
wanted to look inside . . . They wanted to have the canon
brought out . . . Finally with the help of some more
cops they managed to get the carriage clear . . . So then
the whole crowd of pests stream back in front of the shop
. . . They couldn't make head nor tail of it! They kept
cursing at us . . .

All those insults got the old cutie's dander up . . . She
wasn't going to stand for it another minute . . . She didn't
think twice . . . She leapt to the door . . . She opens it,
she goes out, she stands there facing them . . .

"Well?" she says. "What's the matter with you? . . .
You lousy suckers! You creeps! You're a lot of crummy

snotnoses! Go chase yourselves! Louts! Hoodlums! What
have you got to complain about? . . . Was that crook a
friend of yours?" She had guts all right . . . But it didn't
work . . . They cussed her even worse . . . They bellowed harder than ever. They spat all over our window.
They threw gravel . . . It looked like a massacre coming
on . . . We had to beat it out of there quick . . . by the
back way . . .

After that Trafalgar we didn't know what to do . . .
How were we going to quiet those lunatics now? This deep-
sea diving-bell contest was getting as wild as our perpetual-
motion runaround . . . The place was humming all day
long . . . Often they'd wake me up in the middle of the
night with their screeching . . . A procession of screwballs with their eyes popping out half a mile, ripping their
shirts off outside the door, swollen, bloated with certainties, with implacable solutions . . . It wasn't a pleasant
sight . . . More and more of them kept coming . . .They
were blocking the traffic . . . A sarabande of lunatics! . . .

There was such a seething mass of them in the shop . . .
tangled up in the chairs, clinging to the junk piles, submerged in the papers . . . that you couldn't get in when
you needed something . . . All they wanted was to hang
around and argue a little more, to bowl us over with some
new and conclusive detail . . .

If at least we'd owed them something . . . if they'd
all coughed up an advance, a rake-off, or a registration fee,
we could have understood maybe what they had to be unhappy about, why they were peevish and disgruntled . . .
But that wasn't the case . . . For once in our lives we
didn't owe them a nickel! That was the payoff! Couldn't
they give us credit? . . . Couldn't they see we weren't out
for lucre? . . . that all we cared about was honor and
fair play! . . . that we were quits . . . But nothing of
the kind! . . . It was exactly the opposite! They were riot-
ing for the hell of it . . . just to get us down . . . They
were a thousand times angrier . . . a thousand times
crummier, gripier, than on previous occasions when we'd
bled them white . . . They were regular demons . . .
Every single one yelled like at the Stock Exchange in honor

of his gadget . . . And all of them together . . . The
racket was something awful! . . .

None of them could wait . . . Every damn one wanted
us to get his screwball invention under construction this
minute . . . this second! . . . Hurry, hurry . . . get it
working! . . . Christ, were they impatient to dive to the
bottom of the ocean . . . Each for his own private treasure . . . They all wanted to be first! They said it was in
the rules. They brandished our prospectus . . . We
shouted back that we were sick of their stinking shenanigans and listening to their racket . . . we told them it was
all a lot of hooey . . . Courtial climbed up on the winding
staircase to tell them the whole truth . . . He shouted at
the top of his lungs . . . The occasion was so solemn
he'd put his topper on . . . He made a clean breast of it,
I was there . . . He was perfect, a show like that could
only happen once . . . He told them straight from the
shoulder that we'd lost our backer . . . that the whole
contest was dead and buried . . . No more millions than
butter on his ass! . . . He explained that the bulls had
locked him up . . . this fellow we were expecting to . . .
this priest . . . that he'd never get out, they'd put him
into a straightjacket, that the whole business was gone
overboard! . . . "Overboard, overboard!" At these
words they stamped with enthusiasm . . . They took up
the chorus: "Overboard! Courtial! Lower the bell! . . ."
They kept coming back. There were more of them every
time, bringing new projects . . . They laughed in your
face if you tried to reason with them . . . It didn't take
. . . Their minds were made up . . . They all knew that
you've got to suffer if you've got the faith! The faith that
moves mountains, that upsets the seas . . . Theirs was
sensational! When it came to faith, they were in a class by
themselves! Besides they were convinced we wanted to
keep all the mezuma for ourselves instead of sharing it
with them . . . So they camped outside the door . . .
They watched the exits . . . They settled down along the
fence . . . They lay down, they made themselves at home
. . . They weren't in any hurry . . . They had their conviction . . . it was solid rock! . . . No use trying to
shake it . . . They would have massacred us on the spot
at the slightest sign of contradiction . . . They were

getting more and more ferocious . . . The slyest and
sneakiest of the lot came around in back . . . They
slipped in through the gymnasium . . . They'd motion us
to join them . . . Whispering with us in the corner, they'd
suggest terms, an increase in our cut . . . forty percent
instead of ten for us on the first spoils raised . . . if we'd
take care of them right away, ahead of the rest . . . They
thought we were mighty greedy . . . They tried to bribe
us . . . They held out prospects of golden grease . . .

Courtial refused to look at their stuff, he wouldn't say
a word or even listen to them . . . He didn't even feel like
going out anymore . . . He was afraid they'd spot him
. . . The best place as usual was the cellar.

"You'd better take the air" was his advice to me.
"They'll rub you out! Go sit under the trees . . . on the
other side of the fountain . . . They better not see us together . . . Let them wear themselves down . . . Let
them holler till they're blue in the face . . . It's just a
momentary riot . . . It'll die down in a week or ten
days . . ."

He was way off. It went on much longer . . .

Luckily we'd saved a little nest egg . . . what I'd
swiped off the canon . . . almost about two thousand
francs . . . Our idea was that once the storm had subsided we'd take a powder one night with our dough . . .
We'd take our stuff and give ourselves a change of air . . .
move to a different neighborhood . . . Around here it
was getting too hot . . . We'd start another *Genitron*
along entirely new lines . . . with different inventors
. . . We wouldn't even mention the diving bell . . . It
seemed perfectly feasible . . . why not? . . . The hard
part was putting up with their guff for two three weeks.

Meanwhile I had a rough time convincing the old cutie
that she'd better stay home in her cottage in Montretout
. . . and wait for the storm to blow over . . . She
wouldn't listen, she didn't see the danger . . . I knew our
customers . . . She riled them up with her manner, her
pipe, her veil . . . I heard them passing mean remarks
. . . Besides, she stood up to them . . . You couldn't
tell what would happen . . . They were perfectly capable
of skinning her alive . . . Inventors get terrible waves of

fury, they see red . . . They disembowel everything in their path! She wouldn't have chickened out, that was sure . . . She'd have fought like a lioness, but why ask for trouble? . . . We had nothing to gain . . . That wouldn't save their cottage . . . In the end, after a lot of gulping and heartrending sighs, she saw it my way . . .

She hadn't come that day . . . Courtial was sawing wood in the cellar . . . We'd had lunch together at Raoul's Escargot on the corner of the Faubourg Poissonnière . . . not bad, I've got to admit . . . He'd done all right for himself . . . I didn't hang around the shop . . . I came right out and settled down as usual at a healthy distance on a bench across the way, behind the rotunda . . . From there I could watch the approaches . . . I could even step in if the situation got really rough . . . But it was a quiet day . . . Nothing special . . . Just the usual ferment . . . groups talking things over, chewing the fat . . . that's how it had been since the beginning of last week . . . Really nothing out of the way . . . No call to be scared . . . no fireworks . . . They were only simmering . . . Along about four o'clock a kind of calm settled . . . They sat down in a straggle . . . Their talk was no louder than a murmur . . . They must have been all in . . . They were strung out in a line along the shop fronts . . . You could smell how tired they were . . . They'd have to give up pretty soon . . . I was beginning to think of the prospects . . . we'd have to move and dream up another racket . . . find a fresh batch of suckers . . . start up a new line of business . . . We had our little nest egg. But how long could it last? Hell! Two thousand francs melt away easy . . . if we wanted to start the paper up again and make the payments on their cottage . . . Actually it wouldn't be possible to do both at once . . . Anyway, I was off in my daydreams . . . really absorbed . . . when far in the distance . . . in the Impasse du Beaujolais . . . I see a big lug all by himself making a terrible uproar . . . waving his arms in all directions . . . He comes charging up right in front of our joint . . . He grabs the handle . . . He shakes the door like an apple tree . . . He yells for des Pereires . . . Say, that boy is stark raving mad, he's off his rocker . . . He raises hell a while . . . Nobody answers . . . He takes a brush and daubs the whole shop front with green paint . . . Smut, I guess . . . He shoves off, still raving . . . Oh well, that didn't amount to much . . . I'd feared a lot worse . . .

Another hour or two go by . . . The sun was beginning to go down . . . The clock strikes six . . . That was the nastiest time, the time I dreaded most . . . the stinking hour, made to order for riots and disturbances . . . especially with our customers . . . the crummy time of day when all the shops disgorge their little maniacs, their extra-clever employees . . . That's when the lunatics are on the loose . . . the spawn of the offices and factories . . . They come out in droves, bareheaded . . . they run after the bus . . . the artisans stung by the radiations of Progress. They take advantage of the last few minutes of daylight . . . They leap, they bound . . . They're the sober kind, water drinkers . . . They run like zebras . . . This was the battle hour! . . . I could feel them coming . . . it gave me a bellyache . . . This was the time they regularly landed on us . . . we were their aperitif . . .

I pondered a little while longer . . . I began to think about our dinner too . . . I'd go and wake Courtial up . . . he'd asked me for fifty francs. But suddenly I give a start . . . A terrible noise is coming at me! Through the Galerie d'Orléans . . . swelling, coming nearer . . . It was more than a hum . . . It was a rumble! A storm! . . . Thunder under the glass roof! . . . I jump up . . . I run over to the rue Gomboust, where the worst of the ruckus seemed to be coming from . . . I bump into a horde of haggard maniacs, roaring frothing brutes . . . There must be at least two thousand of them bellowing in the chasm . . . And more keep gushing out of the adjoining streets . . . They're compressed, squeezed against a big heavy cart . . . looks like a gun carriage . . . Just as I get there, they're busy demolishing the double garden-fence . . . They uproot it at one blow . . . That flat cart made a terrible battering ram . . . They smash both arcades . . . Blocks of stone are falling like marbles . . . crashing, collapsing, bursting into smithereens right and left . . . It was terrifying . . They come down like thunder, harnessed to their infernal machine . . . The

earth was trembling half a mile away . . . They're
bouncing in the gutters . . . They're all delirious . . .
bobbing and jumping around their catafalque, carried on
by the fury of the charge! . . . I couldn't believe my eyes!
. . . They're berserk! . . . There's at least a hundred
and fifty of them pulling at the shafts . . . galloping under the arches with that enormous load behind
them!

More lunatics roaring, tangling, tearing each other
apart, trying to get a better hold on the shaft . . . the
keel . . . the axles . . . I come closer . . . Christ! It's
our inventors! . . . I see pretty near all of them! . . . I
recognize them one by one. . . There's De la Greuze, the
café waiter . . . he's still got his slippers on . . . And
Carvalet the tailor . . . He's having trouble running . . .
He's losing his pants . . . There's Bidigle and Juchère,
the two who do their inventing together . . . who spend
their nights at Les Halles . . . carrying baskets . . . I
see Bizonde! I see Gratien, the one with the invisible bottle!
There's Cavendou . . . There's Lanémone with his two
pairs of glasses . . . the one who invented the mercury
heating system . . . I see the whole gang of punks . . .
all yelling blue murder! Christ, are they mad! . . . I climb
up on the fence! Above the tumult . . . I get a good look
at the character in the driver's seat, the big guy with the
curly hair that's egging them on, the ringleader . . . I see
the monumental contraption! It's a cast-iron shell . . . a
fantastic mess! It's Verdunat's diving bell! Armored to the
hilt! . . . That's it all right, I've seen the model a hundred
times . . . his famous project . . . I'd know it in the
dark! With the luminous portholes and the diverging
searchlight beams . . . Hell's bells! . . . There's Verdunat himself, half-naked . . . Riding his monster . . .
He's climbed up on top of it! He's shouting! . . . muster-
ing his lousy troops . . . haranguing them! . . . getting
ready for a new charge! . . .

I have to admit that he'd warned us. He'd told us cate-
gorically that he was going to have it built at his own expense, in spite of our opinions . . . He was going to put
all his savings into it . . . We refused to take him seriously . . . He wouldn't have been the first to hand us a
line . . . The Verdunats were dry cleaners in Montrouge,

from father to son . . . He's brought the whole family
along . . . There they are, the whole lot of them, dancing
around the bell . . . holding each other's hands . . .
doing a square dance . . . mama, grandpa, and the small-
fry . . . They've brought us their invention . . . He'd
promised . . . and we wouldn't believe him . . . They'd
hauled the monster all the way from Montrouge! The
whole screwy tribe! The unholy alliance! . . . I patch up
all my courage . . . I foresee the worst . . . They recognize me . . . They howl at me . . . The fury is general
. . . They have it in for my guts . . . They all spit up at
me . . . They vomit at me! . . .

"I beg your pardon!" I say. "Please listen to me just a
minute." Silence. "You don't seem to understand."

"Come on down, you little stinker . . . so we can
knock the shit out of you once and for all . . . Cocksucker! Chameleon! Baboon! Where's the old wise-guy?
We just want to twist his guts a little . . ."

That was the way they listened . . . There wasn't any
point in my going on . . . Luckily I was able to give them
the slip . . . I hid behind the kiosk. I shouted "help" with
all my might . . . But it was too late . . . Nobody could
hear me in the gardens with all the thunder and lightning
. . . Outside our door the carnage was at its height . . .
It was like I'd stirred them up with my words, made them
madder than ever . . . This was the climax . . .They
undo the harness . . . They come out from the shaft
. . . They aim the infernal machine straight across the
sidewalk . . . with the tip against our shop front . . .
The clamor redoubles . . . The lunatics from all the
Galeries and environs rally around the bell . . . The
whole mob brace themselves . . . "One . . . two . . .
And yoop! Heave-ho!" The crowd heaves . . . With one
swing they drive the whole catapult through the window
. . . Everything flies into smithereens . . . The wood-
work gives way, cracks, scatters . . . The whole place is
wrecked! . . . An avalanche of glass! . . . The monster
drives in, forces its way, vacillates, crashes! A torrent of
plaster! The whole *Genitron* caves in! . . . Our winding
staircase, the investors' corner, the Tunisian mezzanine
. . . There's barely time to see it all collapsing in a cataract of papers, followed by an explosion of dust . . . Then

an enormous cloud flies up, the gardens, all four Galeries
are filled with whiteness . . . The hordes are choking,
enveloped in plaster . . . They spit, they cough, they gag!
That doesn't prevent them from propelling their monster
. . . The ironwork . . . the mirrors . . . the ceilings
join the cascade! The bell staggers! The floor gives way,
cracks, gapes open . . . The horrible machine teeters,
dances at the edge of the precipice . . . tips . . . falls
to the bottom . . . Christ! It's the end of the world!
Thunder all the way up to the sky! Suddenly a blast of
awful piercing screams stops the mob in their tracks! . . .
The gardens are veiled in dense dust . . . Finally the
police turn up . . . they grope their way to the scene
. . . They draw a cordon around the wreckage . . .
More bulls come running . . . They charge . . . The
rioters break up . . . scatter . . . Over by the restau-
rant they start galloping again . . . They're all shivering
with the excitement . . .

The cops clear the onlookers away from the disaster site
. . . I knew all the rioters . . . I could turn in the whole
lot of them . . . It would be a cinch . . . I know who
is the meanest of the whole gang . . . the rottenest, the
most violent . . . the biggest stinker of them all . . . I
know some who'd be in for ten years! That's right! But I
don't go for vengeance much! It would only make things
a little lousier than they are . . . that's all . . . Better
attend to urgent business . . . I run into the crowd, I
pass from group to group . . . I make myself known to
the cops . . . "Have you seen the boss? Courtial des
Pereires?" I ask in all directions.

Nobody's seen him. I'd left him at noon . . . Suddenly
I catch sight of the *commissaire* . . . the one from the
rue des Bons-Enfants . . . The exact same little punk that
had been running us ragged . . . I go up to him . . . I
tell him the boss has disappeared . . . He listens . . .
He's skeptical . . . "You think so?" he says . . . He
doesn't believe me. "I'm positive!" So he climbs down one
side of the crevice with me . . . We both of us search
. . . I yell . . . I call . . . "Courtial! Courtial! . . .
Get up!" The cops yell too . . . Once, twice . . . ten
times . . . I go around the edge of every hole . . . I
lean down over the abyss. . . "If you ask me," the jerk

says, "he's at the whorehouse." They were going to give
up . . . when suddenly I hear a voice!

"Ferdinand! Ferdinand! You got a ladder?"

It's him! It's him all right! He surfaces from a deep pile
of rubble . . . He fights his way out . . . His face is
full of flour . . . We throw him a strong rope . . . He
catches hold . . . we hoist! We pull him out of the crater!
. . . Unharmed, he assures us . . . He was only taken
by surprise, wedged, squeezed, absolutely blocked between
the bell and the wall . . . But we can't find his lid. That
vexes him at first . . . He blusters . . . His frock coat
has suffered . . . He doesn't press the point . . . He
refuses any kind of first aid . . . He refuses to go to the
pharmacy . . . Then he gets snotty with the cops . . .
"I shall bring action, gentlemen," he says just like that
. . . Then without waiting for an answer, he climbs over
the rail and the beams and the wreckage . . . We're outside. "Make way! . . . Make way! . . ." He pushes
through the crowd. His frock coat has lost its tails . . .
He's completely defrocked . . . He's all powdery, he
looks like a Pierrot. The stuffing drops out as he runs . . .
he only runs harder . . . He drags me toward the exit on
the Louvre side . . . He clutches my sleeve. He's trembling something awful . . . He's not the old high and
mighty . . .

"Come on, come on, Ferdinand! Make it snappy! Take
a look behind us. Nobody's followed us? . . . You're
sure? Keep on moving, boy! . . . We'll never come back
here . . . Not to this joint . . . It's an infamous trap!
You can take my word for it! It's an obvious conspiracy
. . . I'll write a letter to the landlord."

Now that our office was all smashed up, I had no place
to sleep . . . So we decided I'd move out to Montretout
. . . We looked in at the Insurrection . . . He couldn't
take the train with his coat in rags . . . The owner was
kind enough to lend him an old coat . . . We had a little
chat with two screwballs . . . Courtial's pants were full
of holes . . . They had to be mended . . . Everybody'd
seen the riot, heard the screams and all the commotion
. . . they were all excited . . . Even Formerly joined in
. . . He wanted to do something for us, to take up a col-

lection . . . I told him we didn't need it . . . It would
have given me a pain to accept . . . I said we had some
money left! He'd made a pretty pile out of my old man
. . . He could afford to be generous . . . So he paid for
the drinks, another round, and then still another.

It was getting kind of hot . . . It was the end of June
. . . With all that awful dust and talking so much our
throats were mighty parched . . . we must have drunk at
least ten twelve bottles . . . We were zigzagging as we left
. . . It was very late . . . We were still pretty excited
. . . We just barely caught the last train out of the Gare
du Nord.

In Montretout luckily the sky was full of stars . . . and
even a little moonlight. We could almost see the way . . .
Even so, to keep from going wrong on the pathways of
Montretout, especially up on the hill, you had to be mighty
careful . . . At that time street lamps or road signs were
unheard-of . . . It was only by dead reckoning, by instinct, by the feel of it that you could steer your way in
among the shacks . . . It was mighty dangerous . . .
There were always nearly four or five murders every year
as a result of tragic blunders . . . People that got lost
. . . or wise guys . . . that picked the wrong house . . .
that went up to the gate and rang the bell when they
shouldn't have . . . The poor stupid bastards would get
themselves riddled with bullets . . . from service re-
volvers, from Lebel carbines . . . and in two seconds flat
the neighborhood dogs would finish them off . . . It was
a ruthless collection of the most ferocious carnivorous mongrels . . . horribly aggressive, trained specially for the
purpose . . . They'd bound to the kill . . . There
wouldn't be anything left of the poor devil . . . I'd better
explain, though, that this was just when the Bonnot gang *
were doing their stuff, they'd been terrorizing the whole
northwestern suburbs for the last six months, and they were
still at large . . .

Everybody was in a panic, suspicious as hell . . . Once
the door was shut, those people didn't know father or
mother . . . It was no time to be getting lost . . .

Your worried cottager, your rich miser would spend

* See Glossary.

the night peering out through the blinds, sleeping with one eye, clutching his gun!

At the first sign, the crafty burglar, the shifty tramp could consider himself strung up, rubbed out, extinguished . . . They'd have needed a miracle to get their balls out of there . . . Those people were vigilant all right, and the darkness was murder . . .

Under the station shelter Courtial didn't feel easy in his mind . . . He was thinking about the hike ahead of us . . . the assorted ambushes . . . He stopped to think a minute . . . Then "Let's go! . . ." After the first few steps on the road he began to whistle good and loud . . . kind of like yodeling . . . That was his rallying tune . . . It was supposed to identify us in the danger spots . . . We plunged into the night . . . The road got very soft, full of holes and mush . . . We could vaguely make out shapes in the darkness . . . the outlines of shacks . . . At every fence the dogs barked and bayed and howled at us . . . We walked as fast as possible, but then it began to rain . . . A sea of molasses! The road climbed in zigzags.

"We're heading for the top of Montretout," he informed me. "The summit . . . Wait till you see the view."

Their house, La Gavotte was the highest point in the region. He'd often told me, it looked out over the whole countryside . . . He could see the whole of Paris from his bedroom . . . He began to be out of breath . . . Still, the mud wasn't thick . . . Supposing it was winter! Then a little farther, after the bend, I made out signals, a lamp moving . . . up and down . . . "That's my wife," he cries out . . . She's talking to me in code: S . . . T . . . I . . . N . . . One down! Two up." Anyway, we knew we were on the right road . . . We were still climbing though . . . We went faster and faster. . . Pooped and panting, we come up to the house . . . Our old battle-ax with her lantern comes running down from her platform . . . she jumps on the boss . . . She was good and mad . . . she wouldn't let me get a word in . . . She'd been making signals after every train since eight o'clock and then some . . . She was really in a dither . . . And besides, what was I doing there . . . I wasn't expected . . . What was the big idea? . . . She kept firing questions at us . . . all of a sudden she noticed that he'd

changed his rig . . . We were too dog-tired to break it to
her gently . . . Balls! . . . We go in . . . We sit down
in the first room . . .We give it to her straight . . .
Naturally, when he was so late she'd been expecting some
kind of trouble . . . But now this total disaster, we
couldn't have told her anything worse . . . bang, right
square in the puss . . . It knocked her cold . . . her
whole face began to tremble, even her moustache . . .
She couldn't get out a sound . . . Finally the tears unwound her . . .

"So it's all over, Courtial? . . . Tell me, is it all over?"
She collapsed onto her chair . . . I thought she was going
to conk out . . . The two of us were standing there . . .
we got ready to lay her out on the floor . . . I got up to
open the window . . . But she comes to . . . She's
frantic . . . She jumps up from her chair, quivering all
over . . . She pulls herself together . . . She hadn't been
out for long . . . She's up again . . . She wobbles a bit
on her pins . . . She steadies herself . . . She gives a
hefty clout on the table . . . on the oilcloth . . .

"Christ almighty! It's too much," she yells all of a
sudden.

"Too much! Too much! You said it! . . ." He's off the
handle too. He stands right up to her . . . He's not going
to take it lying down . . . He clucks like a rooster.

"Ah, it's too much! Too much, you say? Well, my dear,
I regret nothing! No, absolutely! Nothing, nothing!"

"Ah, you miserable stinker! You regret nothing? . . .
You're perfectly happy, aren't you? And what about the
house? . . . Have you thought about the payments?
They'll be coming back on Saturday, my friend . . . Saturday, not a day more . . . Have you got those twelve
hundred francs? Have you got them on you? . . . We
promised . . . They're expecting them . . . They're coming at twelve! . . . Have you got them on you? . . . Not
at one o'clock, at twelve!"

"Balls and counterballs! To hell with your cottage . . .
You know what you can do with it . . . The events have
set me free . . . Do you understand that, you blockhead?
. . . No bitterness or rancor! No debts or protests! . . .
To hell with it all! Do you hear? I shit on the whole busi-
ness, I . . . ."

"Shit! Shit! Debts! Debts! All I want to know is whether you've got the money on you, you big jerk . . . Ferdimand, he's got six hundred smackers in all, I know that . . . Have you got the money, Ferdinand? . . . You haven't lost it? It's twelve hundred francs they're coming for, not six . . . Can't you get it through your head?"

"Bah! Foo! Never a step backward! . . . Gangrene! . . . You want to defend gangrene? . . . It's got to be amputated! . . . Don't you know that, you big hunk of baloney! It's got to be amputated high up! Say, have you been drinking up all the white wine? I can smell it from here. High up! Garlic! What do you want to save? Say, your breath stinks! The rotten stump? The maggots? The flies? The bubo? No putrid flesh for me! I won't make another move! Not one, you hear me? . . . Never, you fishwife, as long as I live . . . Defeat! Recantation! Guile! Oh no! My toe! Do you expect me to jerk off my executioners? . . . Me? Never! . . . Do you hear me, Ferdinand? . . . Profit from what you see! Observe! Try to recognize grandeur when you see it, Ferdinand! You won't see much of it in this world!"

"My goodness, it's you that's been drinking . . . Why, you've both been drinking . . . They come here drunk, the rotters! . . . And then they have the gall to cuss me out!"

"Grandeur, detachment, you simpleton! I'm going away! Did you know that? . . . You know nothing! . . . Far away! Even farther! I'm telling you! I despise their provocations, even the foulest . . . the most sickening! What unspeakable vileness germinates in those unclean goatskins? . . . those mangy curs? . . . What is the measure of my essence? Nobility, you old bag . . . Do you hear? You who stink of garliacic acid! Do you get me, you shallot? Nobility! Are you listening? Shit on your Gavotte and double shit! Nobility! Light! Ineffable wisdom! . . . Ah! O delirious bandits! Demons of pillage! . . . O Marignan! O debacle, poor little Ferdinand! I can't believe my eyes! nor my own voice! I'm magical! I'm carried away! O turn of events! . . . Only yesterday at my zenith! Overloaded with favors! Adulated! Plagiarized! Pursued! Feted like a god! What am I saying? Consulted from all over the world! You've seen it, you've read about it! And today?

Crash bang! Nothing! The bolt has struck . . . Nothing
. . . An atom . . . The atom, it is I! . . . But the atom,
Ferdinand, is everything . . . Exile, Ferdinand! . . .
Exile?" His voice was drowned in sadness . . . "Yes!
That's it! I am finding myself! Destiny is opening its gates!
Exile? So be it! You and I . . . I've been praying for it
too long! And now it's come! The blow has fallen, tran-
scendent . . . Hosannah . . . irrevocable! . . . Villainy
has thrown off her mask . . . At last . . . She owed me
that . . . All these years she's been tracking me, under-
mining me, exhausting me! . . . But now, compensation!
. . . She shows herself! I uncover her! And I ravish her
. . . to the full! Ah yes! She is forced to my will, seething!
On the public square! . . . What a vision, Ferdinand!
. . . What a spectacle! . . . O Irène, all my desires are
fulfilled! . . . Frothing, bleeding, howling! Do you hear
me? . . . This very afternoon we saw her attacking our
proud journal! Assaulting the human spirit! Ferdinand here
is my witness! Wounded, bruised, mutilated! . . . And
yet I collect myself, I pull myself together, I wrench myself
away from the nightmare! Oh, what a foul battle! But the
bladder has burst! The gall has gushed in all directions!
. . . hit me square in the eyes! But my spirit is intact. Oh,
the pure, the proud reward! Oh! And above all, no compromise! Get that through your heads, the whole lot of you!
You expect me to cajole my executioners? Give me cold
steel instead! Or fire! . . . Anything, but not that! Bah!
. . . The gods are conspiring! So be it! . . . They honor
me with the bitterest of gifts! Hatred, the hatred of vultures! . . . Exile? . . . Will I refuse it? I? You don't
know me . . . They're putting me to the test! Let them!
. . ." That handed him a laugh. "They choose to put me
to the test? . . . I'm flattered . . . I could roar with
pride! . . . Too cruel? . . . Hum, hum! we'll see! It's
an affair between gods and men! . . . You want to know
how I'll manage, Ferdinand? . . . Don't worry, friend!
Don't worry . . . You won't be bored! See here, Ferdinand, you who like to roam around, you know the Pan-
théon? . . . Tell me, poor muddlehead, haven't you ever
noticed anything? You've never seen the Thinker? He's
there on his pedestal . . . He's there . . . And what's
he doing? Eh, Ferdinand? He's thinking, my boy. That's

right. Nothing else. He's thinking. Well, Ferdinand! He's
alone! . . . There you have it! I'm alone too! . . . He's
naked! I'm naked too . . . What can you do for me, you
poor little creatures? . . ." He was feeling sorry for us,
the old cutie and me . . . "Nothing! You in a pinch! . . .
poor child, benighted by your endocrine glands, tormented
by growing pains, in short invertebrate! Poor gastropod,
destroyed by the slightest dream . . . As for my old
goblin here, what useful or useless thing could she give me?
A touching echo of years long dead . . . Trials! Forgotten hardships! Worm-eaten winters! Carrion! . . ."

"What's that you called me? . . . Say it again . . .
Say it again quick so I can hear you." She hadn't liked
those last words. "Are you trying to make a fool of me?
Just tell me that, you flyspeck!"

She didn't care for allusive language . . . She threatened him with a vase, she demanded further details . . .

"Don't listen to him, Ferdinand! Don't listen to him!
. . . He's just telling more lies! Nothing else comes out of
his mouth . . . What have you been doing in the kitchen?
Tell me this minute! . . . What's become of my marshmallow root? . . . You don't know? . . . He's stolen
that too! . . . And on my washstand . . . The bicarbonate? You don't know that either? . . . You took an
enema with it! . . . Don't try to deny it! And my Vals
water? Where did you put it? . . . He respects nothing!
I'd bought it specially to take on Sunday . . ."

"Leave me alone, can't you? Let me think. You molest
me, you harass me, you exasperate me! . . . How obtuse
you are, my good darling, my sweet little cherub! . . ."

At that she tears her hat off, sniffs up her snot, and toys
with the back of the big heavy chair . . .

"Answer me," she menaces, "what have you done with
my marshmallow root?"

He has no answer . . . she begins to lift the chair . . .
she's clutching the two struts . . . He sees her . . . He
lunges over to the sewing table . . . picks it up under the
drawer . . . They're both nicely armed . . . This is
going to be quite an argument . . . I take refuge in the
chimney corner . . . He parleys . . .

"My sweet angel, please! My sugarplum, I beg you!
Listen to me! Just a word before you get excited . . .

Listen to me! . . . Don't break anything . . . I sold it!
God! I've sold it all!"

"Sold? Sold? What have you sold?"

"Everything! Yes, everything! Only this morning! I've
been standing on my head trying to tell you! To the Lémenthal Bank . . . to Monsieur Rambon! You know him
. . . The lawyer. There was nothing else to do! It's all
over! Liquidated! Washed up! Down the drain! Do you
understand? Do you understand me now, you stupid old
goose! That takes the wind out of your sails, eh? It calms
you down, doesn't it? Tomorrow, see! They're coming
tomorrow morning! . . ."

"Tomorrow? Tomorrow? Tomorrow morning? . . ."
she echoed. She was still in a dream.

"Yes, tomorrow. It's all settled. All you have to do is
sign the papers."

"Oh, the blackguard! The monster! He's tearing out my
entrails! I'd never have thought it possible . . . Oh, what
a numbskull I've been . . ."

She drops the chair, she slumps down on it . . . she
lets her arms dangle, she's out for the count . . . She
sniffles and that's all . . . She really wasn't the stronger
party, he'd got what he wanted . . . She looks across the
table at him . . . that beastly lout over there in the distance . . . the way you'd look at a slimy octopus, a hideous monster in an aquarium . . . an incredible nightmare
from another world . . . She couldn't believe her eyes
. . . There really wasn't a thing she could do. It was no
use trying . . . She gave up, she was completely beaten
. . . She gave in to her grief . . . She sobbed so violently, she beat her head so hard against the sideboard that
the dishes came tumbling out on the floor . . . A little
thing like that couldn't faze him . . . He pressed his advantage . . . He consolidated his position . . .

"Well now, Ferdinand? What do you say? Do you see?
Do you realize . . . Now perhaps you're beginning to
understand what passionate intrepidity is . . . You see
what I mean? Ah, my decision wasn't made yesterday . . .
it matured slowly, by God, and wisely . . . Examples?
Epigones? We have plenty to offer you, madame. How
many? Rafts of them. Illustrious examples! Take Marcus
Aurelius! That's right! What did that old bugger do? In

very similar situations! Harassed! Maligned! Traduced!
On the brink of succumbing under the welter of abject
plots . . . of murderous perfidies . . . What did he do
in such a case? . . . He withdrew, Ferdinand! . . . He
abandoned the steps of the Forum to the jackals! Yes! In
solitude! In exile! That's where he sought his balm! That's
where he found new courage! . . . That's right! . . . He
took counsel of himself! And no one else! . . . He didn't
ask the mad dogs for their opinion! . . . No! Faugh! Ah,
despicable recantation! . . . And what about Vergniaud? *
The pure, ineffable Vergniaud! At the hour of carnage,
when the vultures gathered over the charnel house? When
the sickening smell rose up? What did he do, that man who
was purest of the pure? . . . the very heart of wisdom
. . . in those ravaged minutes where every lie means life?
. . . Did he take back his words? Recant? Eat dirt? . . .
No, he mounted his calvary alone . . . Alone, he rose
above the crowd . . . He withdrew . . . Alone, he ush-
ered in the great silence! He was silent! There you have it,
Ferdinand . . . I too will be silent, dammit all! . . ."

Des Pereires wasn't a very big man. He pulled himself
up to his full height to harangue me better . . . But he
was wedged in between the stove and the big sideboard
. . . He didn't have much room . . . He looks over at
the two of us . . . He keeps on looking . . . An idea was
budding in his brain . . .

"Wouldn't you like to . . . go out?" he says . . . "to
take a little stroll? . . . I want to be alone . . . Just for
a minute . . . There's something I've got to do . . .
Please! I beg of you! Just for a second!"

That was a mighty odd proposition, especially at that
time of night! Standing there in the doorway, all shriveled
in her shawl, the old girl looked pretty mean.

"So now you're throwing us out? . . . Say, you're
completely nuts."

"Give me at least ten minutes. I don't ask more. It's
indispensable! Imperative! Urgent! It's just a little favor
I'm asking of you . . . Leave me in peace for a second!
All alone for just a second . . . You won't? It won't be
any trouble . . . Take a turn around the garden . . . It's

* See Glossary.

much nicer outside than in . . . Go on, go on! I'll call you. Can't you understand?"

He kept at it. He didn't have any big cellar like at the *Genitron* for his meditations . . . He only had three little rooms to pace around in . . . They were so stubborn, so obstinate, so contradictious I could see they were going to tear each other's hair out if I didn't take the old girl away . . . She was the worse hothead of the two . . . So I take her out in the hall . . .

"We'll come back in five minutes," I tell her . . . "Leave it to me . . . Let him stew in his juice . . He's a pain in the neck . . . Anyway, I want to talk to you . . ."

She insisted on taking her lantern . . . It wasn't a very good time for a stroll . . . It was pretty chilly out . . . She was tearing mad, take it from me . . . She was really broken up . . . She kept wailing the whole time.

"Imagine his doing this to me! The swine! The pervert! The scoundrel! To me, Ferdinand! To me! . . ."

Gesticulating, she skirted the fence . . . She stumbled a little with her lantern . . . She kept mumbling insults . . . We came to some garden frames . . . There she stopped . . . Still wailing and sniffling, she wanted to show me . . . she lifted the big pulleys . . . She wanted me to take a good look at the shoots and the little blades that were coming up . . . and the fine soil . . .

"I planted it all myself, Ferdinand . . . All by myself . . . He didn't do it, oh no! rest assured . . ." I had to look again . . . The little turnips . . . and the little slugs . . . and the saucer for the pumpkin. . . She lifted all the lids . . . all the frames . . . There was enough chicory for an army . . . We went around every bed . . . Then she was exhausted . . . She told me, as we went along, about all the trouble she had in times of drought . . . It was she who pumped the water, she who carried the pitchers . . . from over there . . . from the faucet at the end of the walk . . . Her misery took her words away . . . She sat down, she stood up . . . I had to go look at the big rain barrel and see for myself that it wasn't big enough . . .

"Oh yes," she jumps up again. "You haven't seen his system . . . It's mighty cute . . . His precious invention

. . . You really haven't heard about it? . . . Well, believe me it's a nightmare . . . He outdid himself! Of
course I was against it . . . what would you expect?
. . . My oh my! I gave him a good piece of my mind! I
raised hell! But it was hopeless! Absolutely hopeless. He's
as stubborn as thirty-six mules! He slugged me! Well, I
didn't exactly pet him either, believe you me! And what
for? So he could destroy the whole good side of the fence
. . . And eighteen rows of carrots! Yes, eighteen! . . .
And twenty-four artichokes! . . . For what purpose? To
build a shed! . . . You should see the state it's in . . .
A sow wouldn't find her eggs . . . A garbage can, I tell
you . . . a cesspool! That's what he did to my garden . . ."

We started off in that direction, she guided me with her
light . . .

It actually was a little shanty . . . dug into the ground,
almost entirely buried . . . only the roof stuck out . . .
Inside I looked under the tarps . . . nothing but rubbish
. . . a lot of broken-down instruments . . . all in a complete mess . . . and a big dynamo, completely clogged and
rusted . . . a gas tank bottomside up . . . a bent flywheel . . . and a one-cylinder motor . . . That was
Courtial's invention . . . I knew a little something about
it . . . The "Wave Generator"! . . . It was supposed to
make plants grow . . . It was one of his ideas . . .
There'd been a whole special number of the *Genitron* devoted to "The Future of Agriculture Thanks to Radiotellurism" . . . He'd written three manuals and a whole
string of articles (with eighty diagrams) . . . explaining
its use . . . In addition he'd given two lectures in Le
Perreux and one in Juvisy to convince small farmers . . .
It hadn't gone over . . . And yet, according to des Pereires, with the help of a "polarimeter" it was child's play to
radiate the roots of this or that vegetable or plant with
those clusters of telluric rays which are otherwise ridicu-
lously scattered, dispersed, and lost to the world! . . .
"I bring you," he said to them, "my subracinal spray, infinitely more useful than any water! An electric shower!
Providential for beans!" According to him nothing was
easier, with a small amount of equipment, than to make
a salsify swell up to the size of a large turnip . . . The

whole gamut of fructifying infra-terrestrial magnetism was made fully available! . . . Vegetables grown to meet the needs of every individual! In season! Out of season! . . . It was really quite an idea!

Unfortunately, harassed as he was by so many daily cares, by all the snags and setbacks connected with the operation of the *Genitron,* he had been unable to perfect the system . . . Especially the condensers . . . They didn't synchronize properly . . . They needed watching . . . He couldn't run them more than two or three hours on Sunday . . . That didn't provide enough waves . . . On weekdays he had other fish to fry . . . He was busy with the rag and his various contests . . . Madame des Pereires had no faith whatever in this telluric jazz . . . "I told him a million times . . . I was wasting my breath . . . 'That thing of yours will never work! It's impossible! You'll only make one more mess . . . You're going to cave the house in with your trenches . . . That's all the vegetables we'll ever have . . . Electric currents . . . if that's what you want . . . don't stay in the ground . . . they fly through the air, you dope . . . Everybody knows that. What about storms? Or just take a look at the roads . . . Why do they spend all that money on telephone lines? And what about lightning rods? The government isn't nuts, I hope . . . They wouldn't go to all that expense if they could help it! . . .' I'd have said any old thing to keep him from digging up my garden! 'You're talking through your hat!' He always insults me when he knows I'm right . . . He won't give in! He'd rather bust! Oh, I know my little man! Pretentious! Proud! Hell, a peacock is nothing! . . . Having to listen to that tommyrot day in day out! . . . For twenty-eight years I've been putting up with him . . . and this is what I get . . . this is my reward . . . You'll never know how bad I feel . . . But it's no use . . . He's selling us out! . . . Absolutely! That man would sell his shirt! He'd sell yours, Ferdinand! He'd sell anything! . . . When he gets the bug and feels he needs a change, he's not a man anymore, he's a rattle! It's the fairs that ruined him! The older he grows the screwier he gets . . . He's completely cracked . . . I can see it, I'm nobody's fool! He's diabolical, Ferdinand! . . . It's not just a disease with him, it's a disaster . . .

But I can't go along with him anymore . . . Nothing doing . . . I gave him a piece of my mind when he told me about his system . . . 'Courtial,' I said, 'you're always monkeying with things that are none of your business . . . What do you know about agriculture? No more than you do about elevators and piano factories! . . .' But he always thinks he knows it all . . . That's his special vice . . . Knowing it all! Poking his nose into every crack! He's the original busybody! He's too big for his shoes, that's what's wrong with him! One day he comes home and it's chemistry . . . The next day it's sewing machines . . . The day after it's beets . . . Always something new . . . Naturally he doesn't get anywhere . . . The thing for him is balloons. I've thought so all along. I've always told him so . . . 'Courtial, your balloon, Courtial, your balloon! That's the one thing you know how to do! With anything else you'll come to grief. It's stupid to keep trying! Your business is ballooning! It's our only hope. If you keep on with these brainstorms of yours, you'll come to grief. We'll end up in the poorhouse, making paper flowers.' I've told him a thousand times, I've repeated it over and over again. But it's go chase yourself, you old battle-ax! The balloon? He gets so stupid when those pig-headed spells come on he won't even let me mention it! I know what I'm talking about. I've got to bear the brunt. His highness is a 'writer,' I don't understand such things. He's a 'scientist,' an 'apostle'! Hell, I can tell you what he is! He's a loafer . . . a crook! . . . A buffoon! . . . He's a crumb . . . a four-flusher . . . Yes, a bum, that's what he is! He's unscrupulous! He wants to dive, does he? Well, he's heading straight for the bottom . . . a flophouse crawling with lice, that's what he deserves! And that's what he'll get! What a jerk he turned out to be! . . . He's coming apart at the seams! He doesn't know where the next nickel is coming from . . . He thinks I don't know . . . He can gas all day, he won't fool me. I know the score! . . . But he won't get away with it . . . no, sir . . . He'd better not kid himself! He'd better watch his step! I won't stand for it! . . ."

She came back to her obsession . . . She talked about the *Enthusiast* some more . . . about the early days of her married life, expeditions with the balloon . . . Even

then it wasn't easy to pump her up full . . . They never
had enough gas . . . The bag was fragile and not very
airtight . . . But they'd been young and those were the
good old days . . . On Sundays she'd gone up with des
Pereires . . . During the week she'd worked as a midwife . . . She'd applied cups, wet ones and dry ones . . .
little nursing jobs . . . She'd known Pinard well, who'd
delivered the Czarina . . . It got her all excited to talk
about him . . . an obstetrician of worldwide fame . . . I
was beginning to feel chilly in among the vegetables
. . . The sky and the country all around were turning
bluish . . . I was shivering and stamping my feet . . .
We came back up the little path for the hundredth time
. . . We went down again . . . She talked some more
about mortgages . . . Their house was made of millstone
grit . . . It must have been worth quite a lot . . . Did
I think he'd really sold out? . . . I had no way of knowing . . . He was sly and secretive . . . I didn't even
know this Monsieur Rambon! . . . I'd never seen him
. . . And the Lémenthal Bank . . . I'd never heard of it
. . . Actually I didn't know anything . . .

Looking into the distance, I could begin to make out
the shapes of the other shacks . . . And past the big
empty lots there were tall chimneys . . . the factory in
Arcueil . . . that smelled so strong of cinnamon over the
vineyards and the pond . . . By now I could see the
villas all around . . . All sizes . . . Little by little the
colors came out . . . a regular battle . . . all ugly as
hell, fighting in the fields . . . All kinds . . . rocky,
flattened, arrogant, bandy-legged . . . pale, half-finished
ones, skinny, emaciated . . . staggering . . . reeling on
their frames . . . A massacre in yellow, brick-red, and
semi-piss color . . . Not a one that can stand up right
. . . A collection of toys plunked down in the shit!

In the lot next door there was a regular little monument,
a miniature fretwork church something like Notre-Dame, a
cabinet-maker's fancy . . . He kept rabbits in it . . .

The old bag went on talking, drooling, explaining . . .
In the end she ran down . . . she lost the thread of her
thoughts . . . she'd had enough . . . We'd been out
there in the gale for two full hours . . .

"That'll do! Who does he take us for? . . . I'm sick

and tired of his nonsense . . . Hell, why shouldn't he
come out too? . . . I'm going to give that brute a piece of
my mind . . . Come, Ferdinand . . . This way, by the
kitchen door . . . He's going too far . . . What if I
come down with pleurisy? . . ." She hightails it up to the
terrace . . . Just as she opens the door, des Pereires
appears . . . He pops out of the darkness, he was coming
to get us . . . Some cock-eyed rig he had on . . . He
was all wrapped up in the big tablecloth . . . He'd made
a hole for his head and pinned it up with safety pins and
a rope around the waist . . . He comes down the five
steps, he grabs me by the arm . . . He looks completely
absorbed . . . really deep in something . . . He drags
me out to the end of the garden, over by the last frame
. . . He bends down, he pulls up a radish, he shows it to
me, he puts it under my nose . . .

"You see?" he says . . . "Take a good look! . . . You
see? . . . You see how big it is? . . . And this leek?
You see it? And how about this fellow? . . ."

It's some funny-looking vegetable I don't recognize . . .

"Do you see it?"

"Yes," I say, "of course."

"Then come over here! Quick, quick!" He drags me to
the other end of the garden . . . He bends over . . . He
gets down on his knees, he crawls, he puts his whole arm
through the fence . . . He puffs and blows . . . He
pokes around in the neighbor's garden . . . He pulls up
another radish . . . He brings it back . . . He presents
it to me . . . He wants me to compare . . . He's triumphant . . . The other guy's radish is really very little
. . . infinitesimal . . . almost nonexistent . . . And pale!
He thrusts both of them under my nose, his and the
stunted one . . .

"Compare, Ferdinand, compare. I'm not trying to influence you. Decide for yourself . . . I don't know what
Madame des Pereires may have been telling you . . . but
just take a look . . . Scrutinize them . . . Feel their
weight! . . . Don't let anything cloud your judgment
. . . The big one is mine! Thanks to tellurism! Look at it.
His, without tellurism, infinitesimal! Compare! That's all!
I add nothing! Why confuse you? . . . What interests me
is conclusions! Conclusions! . . . What can be done . . .

what must be done . . . *with* tellurism . . . And mark
my words, in this field, so inhospitable in its texture, all I
have to work with is a mere telluric auxiliary! . . . Auxiliary, I repeat! . . . Not the big 'Tornado' model . . .
Of course, I must add, there are certain all-important
requirements . . . The roots have to be bearing roots!
Ah yes, bearing roots! And the soil has to be 'ferro-calcic'
. . . if possible with a certain magnesium content . . .
Otherwise you won't get anywhere . . . So now judge for
yourself . . . You understand? No? . . . You don't understand? . . . You're like her . . . You understand
nothing! . . . Yes, yes, exactly! You're blind, both of
you! But what about that big radish? You see it, don't you?
Right there in the palm of your hand? And the little one?
You see it too, don't you? Stunted! Dwarfed! This miserable puny radish! . . . A radish is a perfectly simple matter, isn't it? No, it's not simple? Ah, you disarm me! . . .
And a giant radish, Ferdinand? Imagine an enormous radish! . . . Say as big as your head! . . . Suppose I take
this ludicrous little radish and blow it up to enormous size
with telluric blasts . . . Well? Like a balloon! Ah? And
suppose I make a hundred thousand of them . . . a hundred thousand radishes! More and more voluminous! . . .
And each year as many as I please . . . Five hundred
thousand . . . enormous radishes! . . . As big as pears!
. . . As big as pumpkins! . . . Radishes such as nobody
has ever seen! . . . Why, it's automatic . . . I eliminate
the small radish . . . I wipe small radishes off the face of
the earth! . . . I corner the market, I erect a monopoly!
All your measly undersized vegetables are finished! Unthinkable! Through! All these baubles! These small-fry! No
more tiny bunches! No more piddling shipments! If they
keep, it's only by miracle . . . It's wasteful, my friend
. . . anachronistic . . . shameful! . . . Enormous radishes, that's what I want to see! And here's our slogan:
The future belongs to the radish . . . my radish . . .
And what's going to stand in my way? . . . My market?
The whole world! . . . Is my radish nutritious? Tremendously! . . . Radish flour is fifty percent richer than the
other kind . . . 'Radicious bread' for the army! . . .
Far superior to all the wheat of Australia! . . . The
analyses bear me out! . . . Well, what do you think of

it? . . . Is it beginning to dawn on you? You're not interested! Neither is she . . . But I am . . . If I devote myself to the radish . . . I'm only taking the radish as an example, I might have chosen the turnip . . . But let's take the radish! The shock value will be greater. So there you are! I'm going into it! To the hilt! . . . to the hilt, do you hear . . . You catch my meaning?"

He's still clutching me, he drags me off toward the view, on the south side . . . From there, it's perfectly true, you could see the whole of Paris . . . The city was like an enormous animal, sprawled across the horizon . . . It's black, it's gray . . . it changes . . . it smokes . . . it makes a sad sound, a soft rumbling . . . it's like a shell . . . notches, holes, spines catching at the sky . . . Des Pereires doesn't give a hoot, he's still talking . . . He harangues the scenery . . . He hoists himself up on the rail . . . He deepens his voice . . . It carries far away . . . It rolls over quarries and landslides . . .

"Look, Ferdinand, look! . . ." I open my eyes as wide as they'll go . . . I make a last effort . . . I'm really awfully tired . . . I wish he wouldn't start in again . . .

"Farther, Ferdinand! Farther . . . Do you see the city now? At the end! Do you see Paris? The capital? . . ."

"Yes . . . yes . . . yes! . . . that's it all right . . ."

"They eat, don't they?"

"Yes, Monsieur Courtial!"

"Every day, don't they?"

"Yes, yes . . . yes!"

"Good! Then listen to me!"

Silence . . . He stirs up the air magnificently . . . He spreads his wings . . . He opens his cape a little . . . His gestures are really something . . . Is he going to fling challenges again? . . . He smiles in anticipation . . . He's sardonic . . . He dispels a vision . . . a phantom . . . he brushes it aside . . . He taps his dome . . . Yes, indeed . . . Good Lord, he'd been mistaken! He'd been deceiving himself all along! Ah! A big mistake! He questions me . . . He calls me to witness:

"So then they eat, Ferdinand? . . . they eat . . . yes indeed, they eat . . . And I, poor fool! Where have I been? . . . Oh futile courage! But I've been punished! Cut to the quick! . . . I bleed! And it serves me right!

Forget? Not I! Oh ho! I'm going to take them as they are!
. . . and where they are! In their bellies! Customers by
and for the belly . . . I will address their bellies, Ferdinand! . . ."

He addresses the city too . . . all of it, rumbling over
yonder in the mist . . .

"Whistle, you bitch! Mutter and roar! Grunt! . . . I
hear you! . . . Gluttons! . . . Bottomless pits . . . All
that's going to change, Ferdinand! . . . Gluttons, I tell
you! . . ."

He calms down. Confidence returns . . . He smiles at
me . . . He smiles to himself . . .

"Ah, that's a thing of the past! I'll lay to that! You can
trust me! You will be my witness! You can tell the old lady!
Ah, the poor darling! Our troubles are over now! I've seen
the light! It's all settled. The spirit is victimized! . . .
They scoff at the spirit! They persecute me! They spit at
me! In the heart of Paris! Good! Very well! So be it! They
can all go shit in their hats! . . . They can rot with
leprosy! They can stew in a million kettles full of snot and
cockroaches . . . I'll stir them myself! Let them pickle!
Let them whirl in gangrene! It's too good for the stinkers!
If they ask for me, I won't be there! . . . I'm through
with the spirit! That's dead and buried! . . . The bowels
are the thing, Ferdinand! . . . The gastric ferments! . . .
Faugh! . . . I'm going to wallow in their bowel movements . . . Phoo! . . . It's going to be an orgy! You
challenge me? Here I stand! I Courtial! Winner of the
Popincourt Prize! The Nicham and all the rest! . . . one
thousand seven hundred and twenty-two balloon flights!
. . . What do I fire my garden with? With radishes! That's
right! I'll show you! You too will see me! O zenith! O my
Irène! O my jealous fury! . . . We haven't a moment to
lose! . . ." He pondered a while.

"In this alluvial gravel? . . . This sandy soil? Never!
Here? Bah! I've proved my point! Small-scale farming! I've
had enough of it! . . . No time to waste on that!" He
started chortling again at the mere thought! . . . It was
just too funny!

"My oh my! Take it away . . ." He swept the poor
cottage off the map.

"To the country! That's the ticket! The country, that's

for me! Open spaces? Forests? . . . Present! . . . Cattle?
Udders? Hay? Poultry? If you will! . . . But above all,
radishes! . . . Take my word for it! And we'll have all the
waves! . . . Every last one, do you hear? . . . Real
waves! You'll see, Ferdinand . . . You'll see it all . . .
The whole works! Orgies of waves! . . ."

The old girl was out on her feet. She had braced herself
against the fence . . . She'd dozed off . . . I shook her
so's she'd come in too . . .

"I'll make you a cup of coffee . . . I think there's some
left . . ." That's what she said . . . but there was no use
looking . . . he'd drunk it all up, the stinker! . . . and
eaten all the leftovers . . . There was nothing left in the
cupboard . . . Not even a crumb of bread! Almost a
whole Camembert . . . While the rest of us were starving
. . . He'd even finished off the beans in the pot . . .
Balls! That really pissed me off . . .

We yelled at him to come in . . . "I've got to send a
wire," he answered from the distance . . . "I've got to
send a wire . . ." He was out on the road already . . .
He wasn't crazy.

We slept all day . . . We were supposed to leave the
day after . . . It was perfectly true that he'd sold the
shack! With a part of the furniture thrown in! . . . The
contractor who'd bought it had even coughed up a small
advance to make us clear out quicker . . . he was scared
shitless we'd wreck the joint before leaving . . .

That same day while we were eating lunch, he started
pacing up and down in front of our gate. We wouldn't let
him in . . . We'd kicked him out several times . . . He
should let us finish, dammit! That bastard couldn't keep
still! He was a horrible sight . . . He was so frantic he'd
rumpled up his hat and was eating the brim . . . tearing
out pieces . . . He started roaming around again, clutching his hands behind his back . . . Humped over and
scowling. He came and went like an animal in a cage . . .
when he had the whole road to himself! And every five
minutes he'd yell in at us: "Don't go smashing up my
crapper! I've seen the bowl! It was in good condition!
Watch out for my sink! A new one costs two hundred
francs! . . ."

Suddenly he couldn't stand it anymore . . . He came into the garden . . . He took three steps up the path . . . We all went charging down . . . We put him out again . . . He had no right! Courtial was outraged at his unspeakable impudence . . .

"You will take possession at six this evening and not a minute sooner . . . At nightfall, my dear sir, at nightfall! . . . That was clearly specified in our deal . . ." It was enough to make you lose control . . .

The guy went back to his rounds . . . He got to grumbling more and more . . . It was so bad we had to close the window so we could discuss our own affairs in private . . . How were we going to get out of there? What would be the best place to go . . . better than someplace else? . . . How much money had we? Between us, Courtial's and mine? . . .

Des Pereires' agricultural plans, his radio-terrestrial contraption were bound to cost us a pretty penny . . . He swore it wouldn't be expensive . . . Anyway, it was a venture . . . We had to take his word for it . . . He'd already picked a place for his experiment . . . On the fringe of the Seine-et-Oise department . . . not too far from Beauvais . . . A splendid bargain. Still according to him . . . a farm they'd let us have for a song . . . Anyway, he'd just about settled with the agency . . . The rotter was wrapping us up! He'd conned us into this thing . . . He'd wired . . . He showed us an ad out of some paper, *The Echo of the Soil.* He got a kick out of watching our faces as we listened to him . . . The old cutie and I weren't looking very good . . . "Lot for several tenants, southern exposure. Market gardening preferred but not required . . . Buildings in perfect repair, etc. . . ."

"Chin up! Chin up, dammit! What did you expect me to find? A chalet in the Bois de Boulogne? . . . In Bagatelle? . . . You should have told me . . . Why, this was a stroke of luck . . . On the Property for Sale page . . ." He was delighted at the prospect . . . He knew how to read between the lines . . . It was now or never . . .

In the course of our lunch the buyer of our cottage got noisier than ever, he clutched the gate . . . We really felt sorry for him with his eyes popping out of his head . . . slithering down over his cheeks. He'd hollered so much he couldn't close his mouth . . . He was coming all over bubbles . . . He'd never hold out till six o'clock . . . His greed was something awful . . . "Have pity! Have pity!" he begged . . .

Courtial had to hurry through his cheese and run over to the telegraph office to confirm his "option." We let our buyer in. The poor bastard was so grateful he licked the terrace steps . . .

Madame des Pereires and I began to pack up . . . to collect all the clothes, the pots and pans, the mattresses . . . all the stuff that hadn't been sold . . . everything we were taking away with us on our venture . . . In addition, under cover of darkness, I was to do a little reconnoitering around the Arcades Montpensier . . . to see if maybe there wasn't something I could salvage . . . to try and rescue our brand-new mimeograph machine . . . our pride and joy . . . and really indispensable . . . And the little Mirmidor oil stove . . . and maybe three or four gross of old pamphlets . . . Especially the cosmogonies on alfa paper that Courtial set so much store by . . . Maybe those brutes hadn't had the time or chance to destroy everything . . . to wreck the whole place . . . Maybe a little something was left under the rubble . . . And the miniature altimeter . . . a gift from South America . . . Courtial would feel very badly if that couldn't be saved . . . Anyway, I'd give it a try . . . It was all right with me . . . The part I didn't like was that she wanted to come along . . . she didn't quite trust me. She wanted to see for herself . . . In case there was something to be saved, she thought I'd better not be alone . . . "I'll go too, Ferdinand! I'll go with you!" She hadn't seen the disaster with her own eyes . . . She still had some hope . . . Maybe she thought we were pulling a fast one . . .

Courtial came back from the post office. Me and Madame des Pereires went to the bedroom to empty the last cupboards . . . Now it was his turn to argue with that drip . . . who kept protesting that we were breaking the contract . . . We almost had to fight to recover our clothes and a few extra towels . . . Taking possession had made him bumptious. We threw him out again to teach him good manners. Then the lug begins shaking the bars so hard that the whole gate fell down . . . He got wedged under it . . . He was caught like a rat . . . I'd never seen a man in such awful convulsions! He was some buyer! . . . He was so fouled up he didn't even notice when the old lady and I shoved off . . . We took a local . . .

It was very late when we got to Paris . . . We made it fast . . . We didn't see a soul in the arcades of the Palais . . . The neighboring shops were all closed up tight . . . Ours was nothing but a hole . . . an enormous yawning chasm . . . a pit with big wobbly beams across it . . . Finally the old lady got it through her head that this was a real disaster . . . that nothing was left of the *Genitron* . . . that we hadn't been kidding . . . All a rotten stinking mess . . . We bent down over the hole and took a good look at the wreckage . . . We even managed to recognize some big chunks of our Alcazar . . . the investors' corner . . . under the huge avalanche of cardboard and garbage . . . That terrible bell was there to! The catapult! It had sunk in sideways . . . between the scaffolding and the cellar . . . Actually it plugged up the whole crevasse . . . When old lady Courtial saw that, she still wanted to go down under and take a look . . . She was sure we'd find something worth saving . . . I warned her of the danger . . . one touch could bring down the whole mountain, she'd be squashed flat . . . She insisted . . . She did a balancing act on a loose joist . . . I held her by the hand from up top . . . Watching her swaying over the void, my cock went limp . . . She'd hiked up her skirts and tied them around her waist. She saw a crack between the wall and the bell . . . She slipped in all by herself . . . She disappeared in the darkness . . . I heard her rummaging around at the bottom of the abyss . . . Then I sang out . . . I was too scared . . . My voice echoed like in a cave . . . She didn't answer . . . Half an hour later she appeared in the opening . . . She called me to come and help her . . . Luckily I managed to grab her by the handles of her smock . . . I hoisted with all my might . . . She came up. She was tangled up in a pile of truck . . . all one enormous bundle . . . I hoisted the whole thing up on the edge . . . It was very hard going . . . There was plenty of resistance . . . I saw she was pulling one more thing

behind her . . . A big chunk of balloon, a whole slice of
the *Archimedes* . . . a big wide flap . . . the red strip
I'd taken patches out of . . . I knew that rag well . . .
I'd hidden it myself between the gas meter and the transom
. . . She had a wonderful memory . . . She was as happy
as a lark . . .

"It'll come in handy, you know," she said briskly. "It's
real rubber, no cheap imitation . . . you can't imagine
how strong it is . . ."

"Sure," I said, "of course . . ." I knew all right. I'd
taken enough hunks out of it to patch up the other one
with . . . In any case it was heavy and bulky . . . Even
folded as small as it would go, it was quite a package . . .
as tall and almost as heavy as a man . . . She refused to
abandon it . . . We had to take it with us . . .

"Well anyway, we'd better hurry," I say . . . She was
mighty strong, she hoisted it up on her back and carried it
. . . I took her as far as the rue Radziwill in a big hurry
. . . When we got there, I said:

"You go ahead, madame, but don't hurry anymore.
Take your time . . . Stop on every corner. Watch out for
the traffic. You've got plenty of time. I'll join you on the
rue Lafayette. I've got to look in at the Insurrection . . .
It's just as well they don't see you . . . I left a key with
the waiter . . . the key to the attic . . . I'd like to take
another look up there . . ."

This was only a pretext for going back awhile . . . I
wanted to look around under the arcades . . . I thought
maybe I'd run across Violette . . . Lately she'd been
hanging out mostly over by the Galerie Coloniale . . .
past the scales . . . She sights me from a distance . . .
"Yoo hoo," she goes and comes running over . . . She'd
seen me with the old lady . . . She'd been afraid to show
herself . . . So then we had a good chance to talk and
she told me all the dirt . . . everything that had been
going on since we left . . . since the disaster . . . What
a mess! . . . Trouble trouble the whole time . . . The
cops had been asking thousands of questions . . . even of
the whores . . . the screwiest stuff about our habits . . .
Did we sell junk? . . . Did we get ourselves buggered?
. . . Were we taking bets? . . . Did we sell dirty pictures? Did foreigners come around? Did we have any re-

volvers? Were we seeing anarchists? . . . The girls were
scared pink . . . They were afraid to hang around near
our wreckage . . . They were doing the other Galeries
now . . . They were scared of having their cards taken
away . . . That's what it meant to them . . . Everybody
was complaining . . . All the shopkeepers in the neighborhood were sore too . . . They really had it in for us
. . . you can't imagine . . . they were in a boiling lather
. . . A petition had been sent to the prefect of the Seine
department . . . to have the Palais-Royal cleaned up
. . . They were sick of living in a hotbed of debauchery
. . . Their business was ruined already . . . They didn't
want to be corrupted by extra-bad eggs like us . . .
Violette liked me fine, she'd have liked me to stay on . . .
But she was convinced that if we came back in the neighborhood there'd be an awful stink and we'd be snagged in
two seconds flat . . . that was definite and no use arguing
. . . The only thing we could do was clear out, make ourselves scarce . . . Why ask for trouble? . . . That's
what I thought too . . . We just had to blow . . . But
what about me, what was I going to do? What kind of
work? She was kind of worried about that . . . I couldn't
tell her much . . . I didn't know myself . . . Except it
would be in the country, that was sure . . . when she
heard that, she said right away that she'd manage to come
and see me . . . especially if she got sick again . . . It
happened now and then . . . Then she always had to go
away for at least two three weeks, not just on account of
her sickness, but for her lungs too . . . She'd been spitting blood . . . In the country she stopped spitting . . .
It was perfect . . . She gained a couple of pounds a day
. . . So that's how we left it . . . that's what we agreed
between us . . . But I was to write her first in care of
General Delivery . . . Circumstances prevented me . . .
We had so much trouble . . . I didn't keep my word
. . . I always kept putting off my letter until the following
week . . . I didn't go back to the Palais until years later
. . . That was during the war . . . I didn't find her with
the other girls . . . I asked them all . . . Even her
name, Violette, didn't register . . . Nobody remembered
. . . They were all new . . .

 So that night I left her on the run . . . I had to make

it fast, that's a sure thing . . . I wanted to drop by the Passage Bérésinas to tell my folks I was leaving town with des Pereires . . . so they wouldn't start acting up and put the bulls on my trail . . .

When I got there, my mother was still in the shop straightening out her junk, she'd come home from peddling her selection around Les Ternes . . . My father came downstairs . . . He'd heard us talking . . . I hadn't seen him in two years . . . Gaslight always makes people look green, but his pallor was something awful . . . On account of the surprise maybe, he began to stammer so bad he had to stop talking . . . He couldn't say a single word more . . . He couldn't understand either . . . what I was trying like mad to explain. That I was going away to the country . . . He wasn't against it . . . Not in the least! . . . They didn't care what happened . . . As long as I didn't go broke on their hands . . . As long as I made some kind of a living, here or somewhere else, it didn't matter how! It was all one to them, in the Île de France or the Congo . . . It was no skin off their ass . . .

My father looked lost in his old clothes . . . Especially his pants had nothing to hold on by . . . He'd got so thin, his head was so shrunk his big cap floated around on his bean . . . it slid down over his eyes . . . He looked at me from underneath . . . He couldn't catch the meaning of what I was saying . . . I kept repeating that I thought there was a future for me in farming . . . "Ah! Ah!" he said . . . He wasn't even surprised . . .

"Say, Clémence . . . I had a bad headache this afternoon . . . That's a funny thing . . . It wasn't hot, was it?"

That still had him puzzled . . . He thought of nothing but his ailments . . . He couldn't take any interest in whether I stayed or went, or where to . . . He had trouble enough . . . especially since his bad setback at Connivance Fire Insurance . . . He couldn't stop mulling it over . . . He was still going through hell at Coccinelle . . . they were always stepping on his feet . . . it was as bad as ever . . . He was so miserable that some weeks he didn't shave at all . . . He was too shaken . . . He refused to change his shirt . . .

They hadn't eaten yet when I got there . . . She told

me about the hard times, the trouble they were having in
the store . . . She set the table . . . She limped kind of
differently, maybe a little less . . . Even so she had a
good deal of pain but mostly in the left leg now . . . She
kept sniffling and making sounds with her mouth . . . the
minute she sat down to ease her pain. He'd just come back
from his errands, from making a few deliveries . . . He
was very weak . . . He was sweating more and more
. . . He sat down with us . . . He didn't talk, he didn't
burp; all he did was eat very slowly . . . There were
leeks . . . From time to time, by fits and starts, he'd
come to life a little . . . Actually it happened only twice
while I was there . . . He'd start muttering hoarse, low
curses into his plate . . . "Christ almighty! Shit, piss, and
corruption! . . ." He'd grumble some more . . . He'd
get up . . . He left the table, he went off teetering . . .
as far as the little partition that separated us from the
kitchen . . . It was as thin as an onion peel . . . He'd
haul off and hit it two three times . . . That was the best
he could do . . . He'd retreat backward . . . He'd flop
on his stool, looking down at the tiles . . . way down
below . . . his arms dangling . . . My mother gently
put his cap straight . . . She motioned me to look away
. . . She was used to it now. Actually it couldn't have
bothered him anymore . . . He didn't really catch on
. . . He was too wrapped up in his troubles at the office
. . . There was no room in his dome for anything else
. . . For the last two months he hadn't been sleeping
more than an hour a night . . . His head was all tied up
with worry like a bundle . . . he wasn't interested in anything else . . . He didn't even care what went on in their
business . . . He didn't want to hear about it . . . That
suited my mother fine . . . I really didn't know what to do
. . . I felt like a sore finger, I was afraid to move! Even so
I tried to tell them a little about myself . . . my little
adventures . . . Not the whole truth . . . just a few
things to entertain them, a little innocent horseplay to break
the embarrassment . . . Christ, what a face they made
. . . just because I was joking . . . The effect was exactly the opposite . . . Hell, that griped me . . . I was
beginning to get sore too . . . I had my troubles too,
dammit all! I was in a jam too, just as bad as they were

. . . I hadn't come to beg . . . either for dough or for food . . . I wasn't asking them for anything . . . Only I didn't want to join in their lousy bellyaching . . I didn't feel like crying into the soup or grazing on their troubles . . . I hadn't come to be comforted . . . Or to complain either . . . I'd simply come to say good-bye . . . Shit and period! . . . They might have been pleased . . .

One time just as a joke I said: "I'll send you some morning-glory seeds from the country . . . They'll grow fine up in the attic . . . they'll climb over the glass roof . . ."

I was saying anything that came into my head . . .

"Ah, it's easy to see that you're not the one that toils and struggles around here . . . that you don't have to work your fingers to the bone trying to meet our obligations. Ah, it's a fine thing to be carefree . . ."

Balls! All the hardship and misery, all the sickening trials were for them. Mine didn't exist by comparison. If I got into a jam it was all my fault . . . according to them, the stinkers . . . oh, the shame of it! They had their nerve with them! Balls and counterballs! Whereas they were innocent victims! Martyrs forever . . . There was no comparison . . . It was all very well to be young, but I'd better watch my step . . . or I'd go wrong for good . . . My business was to listen . . . and to profit by their example! . . . Forever and ever! Hell's bells and never a moment's doubt! . . . Just watching me there at table in front of my beans (there was Swiss cheese afterwards) the whole past came back to Mama . . . She had a hard time holding back the tears, her voice cracked . . . and anyway she preferred not to say anything . . . That was a real sacrifice . . . I'd have gladly asked forgiveness for all my faults, my capricious behavior, my unspeakable debauchery, my disastrous crimes! . . . if that could have cheered her up . . . if that was the only thing that made her start moaning again . . . if that was all that was breaking her heart . . . I'd have begged her forgiveness and shoved off right away . . . I'd have ended up by admitting that I was incredibly lucky, that I was too spoiled for words, that I spent my time having fun . . . Sure! I'd have said anything at all to get it over with . . . I was looking toward the door . . . But she motioned me to

stay . . . He went up to his room . . . He wasn't feeling
at all well . . . He clutched the banister . . . It took
him at least five minutes to climb the three flights . . .
And then, once we were alone, her miseries started up
worse than ever . . . She gave me all the details . . .
What she was doing now to make ends meet . . . Her
new racket . . . She went out every morning for a lace
house . . . in three months she'd made almost two hundred francs in commissions . . . In the afternoon she
doctored herself, she stayed in the store with her leg on a
chair . . . She wouldn't see Capron anymore . . . He
went on telling her to keep still . . . Why, she had to keep
moving . . . It was all she had to live for . . . She preferred to treat herself by the Raspail method . . . She'd
bought his book . . . She knew all the herb teas . . . all
the mixtures and infusions . . . And she had oil of mignonette to massage her leg with at night . . . She got boils
even so, but the pain was bearable and the swelling wasn't
too bad. They burst almost immediately. They didn't keep
her from walking, that was the main thing . . . She
showed me her leg . . . The flesh was all creased, as if it
had been wound around a stick, from the knee down . . .
and yellow . . . with big scabs and places that were running . . . "It's nothing once they begin to drain . . . It's
a relief, it feels better . . . but before that it's terrible,
while they're still all purple . . . while they're closed
. . . Luckily I have my poultice . . . without it I don't
know what I'd do . . . You can't imagine what a help it
is . . . Without it I'd be an invalid . . ." And then she
told me some more about Auguste . . . how he was
making a wreck of himself . . . he'd lost control of his
nerves . . . and his terrors at night . . . The worst was
his fear of being fired . . . it woke him up in a panic
. . . He'd jump out of bed . . . "Help! Help!" he'd
scream . . . the last time so loud that all the people in
the Passage had started up . . . For a moment they'd
thought it was a fight . . . that I'd come back to strangle
him . . . They'd all come running! . . . When Papa had
his fits, he didn't know what was going on . . . They'd
had a time getting him back into bed . . . They'd had to
put cold towels on his head for several hours . . . Ever
since he began having those fits . . . they were getting

more and more exhausting . . . life had been a torment!
. . . He never came out of his nightmare . . . He didn't
know what he was saying . . . He didn't recognize people
anymore . . . He couldn't tell the neighbors apart . . .
He was terribly afraid of cars . . . Often in the morning
when he hadn't slept at night, she'd take him to the door of
the insurance company . . . at 34 rue de Trévise . . .
But her troubles weren't over . . . She'd have to go in
and ask the concierge if there was anything new . . . if
he hadn't heard anything . . . about my father . . . if
he hadn't been dismissed . . . He couldn't distinguish between real and imaginary anymore . . . If not for her it
was perfectly certain . . . he'd never have gone back
. . . But then he'd have gone crazy . . . loony with despair . . . beyond the shadow of a doubt . . . It took
a terrible balancing act to keep him from going under completely . . . And she did all the acrobatics . . . screwing his knob back on again . . . She couldn't let the
grass grow under her feet . . . And what with the meals
in addition . . . they didn't cook themselves . . . And
then she had to go running to the other end of Paris . . .
with her lace . . . finding customers, hurry-hurry . . .
With all that she still managed to open our store . . . for
a few hours in the afternoon . . . She didn't mind if
things were slow in the shop, as long as it didn't go under
completely . . . And at night the whole thing to start
over again . . . So his fears wouldn't get any worse, so
his terror wouldn't increase . . . she put a little lamp on
a table in the middle of the room, turned down low. And
besides, so's he could go to sleep a little faster, she plugged
his ears with little wads of cotton dipped in vaseline . . .
He started up at the slightest sound . . . if anybody
walked through the Passage . . . And it started in again
early in the morning with the milkman . . . It echoed
terribly on account of the glass roof . . . But with the
wads of cotton it was a little better . . . He said so himself . . .

Naturally, it's not hard to see, my mother was more
awfully worn-out than ever from having to keep holding
my father up all the time day and night . . . She was
always at her post . . . bolstering his morale . . . ward-
ing off his obsessions . . . Well, actually she didn't feel

too sorry for herself . . . If I hadn't been cussed . . . if I'd shown some sign of repentance . . . of acknowledging all my vices . . . my stinking ingratitude . . . it would have been balm for her . . . That was plain . . . She'd have been comforted . . . She'd have said to herself: "Ah, my boy, you've still a chance or two left . . . All hope isn't lost . . . His heart isn't all stone! He's not so debased, so absolutely incurable . . . Maybe he'll snap out of it . . ." It would have been a light in her distress . . . a delicious consolation . . . But I wasn't in the mood . . . Even if I'd done my damnedest, I'd never have gotten it out . . . I couldn't have made it . . . Of course I felt sorry . . . Of course I saw how unhappy she was! That was God's truth. If I felt bad, it wasn't to go blabbing it out! And especially not to her . . . And besides . . . after all . . . when I was a kid in their house and didn't know from nothing . . . who always got it in the neck? . . . It wasn't just her . . . It was me too . . . Me the whole time . . . I got the lickings . . . Childhood! Shit! . . . Yes, sure, she was always devoted, she sacrified herself . . . OK, OK . . . it made me sick to be thinking of all that so hard . . . But hell! It was her fault too . . . I never thought about it all by myself . . . That was the worst part of it, worse than all the rest of the crummy business . . . It was no use my trying to say something . . . She turned on me with a look of distress, as though I'd beaten her . . . It was best I clear out . . . We'd start fighting again . . . But I let her pour her heart out . . . I didn't open my mouth . . . Sure, help yourself . . . it's free of charge . . . She took a good slice . . . She gave me plenty of advice . . . All those excellent precepts, I heard them again . . . Everything that was indispensable to uplift my morality . . . To make me stop giving in to my low instincts . . . to make me learn from good examples and imitate them . . . She saw I was holding myself in, that I didn't want to answer . . . So she changed her tune . . . She was afraid of making me mad, she tried cajolery . . . She went to the sideboard and brought out a bottle of syrup . . . It was for me, to take to the country . . . as long as I was going . . . And then a bottle of tonic to build me up . . . She couldn't help harping on my terrible habit of eating too fast . . . I'd

ruin my stomach . . . And finally she asked me if I
didn't need money . . . for the trip or something else
. . . "No, no," I said . . . "We've got all we need . . ."
I even showed her the capital . . . I had it all in hundred-
franc bills . . . See? . . . In conclusion I promised to
write, to let them know . . . how our farming panned out
. . . She didn't understand about such things . . . That
was an unknown world . . . She put her trust in my boss
. . . I was right next to the stairs, I got up, I tied up my
bundle . . .

"Maybe after all it's better not to wake your father up
now . . . What do you think? . . . Maybe he's asleep
. . . Don't you think so? You saw how the slightest excitement upsets him . . . I'm afraid it'll throw him off again
to see you leave . . . Doesn't it seem wiser . . . Suppose
he had another attack like three weeks ago . . . I'd never
get him to sleep again . . . I'd do anything to prevent that
from happening . . ." I was of the same opinion . . . It
struck me as perfectly reasonable . . . to clear out
quietly . . . while the wind was right . . . We whispered
good-bye . . . She gave me a little advice about my
underwear . . . I didn't listen to the end . . . I slipped
into the Passage and then galloped out to the street.

I hightailed it . . . I was late, very late in fact! . . .
It was exactly midnight by the gilded dial of the Crédit
Lyonnais . . . Courtial and his old cutie had been waiting
for me for two solid hours outside the church of Saint-
Vincent-de-Paul . . . with their pushcart . . . I climbed
the whole length of the rue d'Hauteville in high . . . I
could see them in the distance under a gas lamp . . . It
was an honest-to-God moving . . . He'd brought the
whole works. He'd really sweated for once in his life . . .
He must have cleaned out the homestead regardless and
notwithstanding . . . He'd had to murder the old punk
(not for real!) . . . The cart was so loaded full of junk it
was sagging . . . The dynamo and the motor were under
the mattresses and the clothes . . . The double curtains,
the whole kitchen . . . He'd saved as much as possible
. . . You had to hand it to him . . . He was wearing a
new frock coat I'd never seen . . . I wondered where he'd
found it . . . It was pearl-gray . . . I remarked on it
. . . it was from his younger days . . . He'd pinned up

the tails. The old lady wasn't wearing her hydrangea-and-cherry hat . . . It was perched on top of the cart . . . for safekeeping . . . Instead she'd put on a real pretty Andalusian shawl, all embroidered in bright colors . . . It looked good under the street lamp . . . She told me it was really the best thing for long trips . . . it protected the hair.

Well, there we were finally . . . After some discussion about an obsolete timetable we started off very slowly . . . Frankly, I was happy! . . . The rue Lafayette is steep . . . especially between the church and the corner drugstore . . . We couldn't lay down on the job . . . Des Pereires had harnessed himself to the cart . . . The old bag and I pushed from behind . . . And "Come on, kid!" and "I know you got it in you! . . ." And "keep her rolling . . ." And "Never say die!" The only trouble was that we'd lost too much time . . . We missed our train . . . It was my fault . . . We could forget about the twelve-forty . . . now it was the two-twelve . . . the first of the day . . . So now we were ahead of time, pretty near fifty minutes . . . We had plenty of time to take our dolly apart . . . it was the folding reversible type . . . and load all our stuff . . . again! . . . into the freight car at the tail of the train. After that we still had time enough to blow ourselves to some mud, two cups with milk, a *mazagran,* and a "breakfast coffee," all in a row! At the spiffy Terminus . . . We were nuts about coffee all three of us . . . really gone . . . And I had the treasury.

We got out in Persant-la-Rivière . . . It was a sweet little village between two hills and some woods . . . A chateau with turrets provided the finishing touch . . . The dam below the houses made a majestic roar . . . All in all, it was very pretty . . . We could have picked worse, even for a vacation . . . I said as much to the old battle-ax . . . But she was out of sorts . . . We had a hell of a time with our stuff, getting our motor out of the freight car . . . We had to ask for help . . .

The stationmaster looked our paraphernalia over . . . He thought we were itinerants . . . come for the fair . . . to put on movie shows . . . He judged by our rig . . . For the fair we'd have to come back another time . . . It

was over two weeks ago . . . Des Pereires didn't like
leaving him with the wrong idea . . . He put the little jerk
straight right away . . . told him all about our projects
. . . He wanted to speak to the notary! Immediately!
. . . This was no laughing matter, it was an agricultural
revolution . . . A crowd of yokels started poking into our
stuff . . . They clustered around the tarp . . . They
made a lot of remarks about our apparatus. On the road the
three of us by ourselves couldn't make it . . . The cart
was too damn heavy . . . We'd noticed that on the rue
Lafayette . . . And our agricultural hole was too far
away . . . We needed a horse at least . . . Right away
those hicks put up a remarkable show of inertia . . .
Finally we were able to start out . . .

Once settled on the seat, our cutie lit up a good pipe
. . . Our hangers-on laid bets that she was a man dressed
like a woman . . .

To reach our property at Blême-le-Petit it was still seven
miles . . . with plenty of hills . . . They warned us at
Persant . . . Des Pereires had already collected piles of
dope, going around from one group to another . . . It
hadn't taken him long to sign all the papers . . . he'd
hurried the notary . . . Now he was prospecting the green
hills from the top of the cart . . . We'd given one of the
peasants a lift . . . With the map spread out on his knees,
Courtial never stopped talking once the whole time . . .
He commented on every rise, every roll in the ground . . .
He searched for every last brook . . . in the distance with
his hand over his eyes . . . He didn't always find them
. . . He gave us a regular lecture that went on at least
two solid hours, bumpity-bump, on the potentialities, the
lag in development, the agricultural splendors and weaknesses of a region whose "metallo-geodisic infrastructure"
didn't entirely suit him . . . Oh no! . . . He told us right
off and several times over . . . He'd have to make his
analyses before throwing himself into this thing . . . It
was a beautiful day.

At Blême-le-Petit things weren't exactly the way the
notary had said. It took us two whole days to find out . . .

The farm was plenty run-down . . . That much had
been stated in the papers . . . The old man who'd had

it last had died only two months before and nobody in the whole family had wanted to take over . . . It seemed that nobody wanted the land, or the shanty, or even the village . . . We looked over some of the other shacks a little farther on . . . We knocked at all the doors . . . We went into the barns . . . There was no sign of life . . . Finally near the watering trough, in some kind of a shed, we found two old customers so old they couldn't leave the place . . . They were almost blind . . . and completely deaf . . . They kept pissing on each other . . . That seemed to be their only amusement . . . We tried to talk to them . . . They couldn't think of anything to say . . . They made signs that we should go away and leave them alone . . . They'd lost the habit of anybody coming to see them . . . We frightened them.

It didn't look very promising to me . . . That deserted village . . . All those half-open doors . . . Those two old folks who didn't like us . . . And the owls all over the place . . .

Des Pereires, on the contrary, thought it was perfectly splendid . . . He felt invigorated by the country air . . . First thing he wanted to dress the part . . . He'd lost his panama, so he had to borrow a hat from our old sweetie . . . An enormous soft-straw number with a chin strap . . . He kept on his frock coat, the beautiful gray one . . . plus a soft shirt and a pair of wooden shoes (that he never really got used to) . . . When he took a long walk through the fields, he always came home barefoot . . . and so's to look really like a tiller of the soil, he never forgot his spade . . . He carried it jauntily over his right shoulder . . . Spade at the ready, we went out every afternoon to inspect the fallow fields, looking for a suitable place to plant radishes.

Madame des Pereires kept busy on her own hook . . . She did the errands and kept house . . . and most of all she went to the market in Persant twice a week . . . She did the cooking . . . She repaired things and made the place halfway livable . . . Cooking in the hearth was an awful business, we wouldn't have eaten if not for her . . . just to make an omelet you had to light the fire so many

times . . . the logs, the embers . . . you lost your appetite . . .

The two of us, Pereires and me, didn't get up very early,
I've got to admit . . . Even that made her gripe . . . She
always wanted us to be getting a move on . . . to be doing
something really useful . . . But once we'd gone out, we
didn't feel like coming back . . . Then she got mad again,
poor old thing, wondering what we were doing so long outside . . . Des Pereires enjoyed our big excursions . . .
Every day he discovered new aspects of the countryside
. . . and in the afternoon again, thanks to his map, he
could be as instructive as hell . . . Now and then, at the
edge of the woods . . . or on some slope . . . we'd
make ourselves comfortable . . . as soon as a little heat
came on . . . We always had a few bottles of beer . . .
Pereires was free to meditate . . . I didn't bother him
much . . . He talked to himself . . . with his spade in
the ground, dug in right beside us . . . The time passed
pleasantly . . . It was a real change . . . the peace . . .
the quiet of the woods . . . But the dough was going out
fast . . . She was getting worried . . . She went over the
accounts every night . . .

In the matter of dress I wasn't long in adapting myself
. . . Little by little the soil gets you . . . You forget
about the nonessentials . . . In the end I worked out a
rugged little outfit consisting of bicycle pants and a spring
overcoat with the tails cut to half length that I tucked into
my baggy pants . . . kind of warm but comfortable . . .
I could be recognized a mile away . . . The whole thing
decorated with lengths of string . . . with ingenious props.
The old cutie came around to our way of thinking, she
wore pants too like a man . . . She didn't have a skirt to
her name anyway. She thought it was handier . . . She
went to market that way too. The school kids waited for
her on the way into town. They hooted at her, they bombarded her with cowflop and broken bottles and big stones
. . . It ended in a fight . . . She didn't take it lying down
. . . The cops stepped in . . . They asked for her papers
. . . She was very high and mighty: "I'm an honest
woman, messieurs . . . You can follow me home! . . ."
They weren't in the mood.

It was a beautiful summer . . . You really couldn't imagine it would ever end . . . The heat makes for idleness . . . Des Pereires and I, after his pousse-café, we'd head for the fields . . . and all afternoon we'd wander aimlessly over hill and furrow. If we ran into a yokel, we'd give him a polite "good-day" . . . Our life was mighty pleasant . . . It reminded us of the happy days with the balloon . . . But we had to be careful not to talk about our stratospheric setbacks in front of Madame des Pereires . . . or about the *Enthusiast* or the *Archimedes!* . . . Or she'd burst into tears . . . She couldn't contain her grief . . . She treated us like dirt . . . We mostly talked about one thing and another . . . We couldn't stir up the past . . . And we had to watch our step with the future . . . We could only mention it with kid gloves . . . The future was ticklish too . . . Ours was vague . . . it didn't stand out very clearly . . . Courtial was still hesitating . . . He preferred to wait a little longer, he didn't want to dive in until he felt perfectly sure . . . Between meditations, in the course of our afternoon wanderings, he'd prospect around with his spade . . . He'd bend down to examine, weigh, scrutinize the fresh earth he'd stirred up . . . He'd crush it into a powder . . . He'd filter it between his fingers as if looking for gold . . . Finally he'd clap his hands and blow on them hard . . . It would all fly away . . . He'd frown . . . "Tt, tt . . . This soil isn't so hot, Ferdinand. It's not rich. Hm! hm! I'm mighty scared about radishes . . . Hm! Maybe artichokes . . . And even then I wouldn't be too sure . . . My oh my! There's an awful lot of magnesium in it . . ." We'd start off again, undecided.

At table his wife asked us for the hundredth time if we'd picked our vegetable . . . if we'd finally made up our minds . . . if maybe it wasn't high time . . . She suggested beans . . . she didn't put it very tactfully, I've got to admit . . . Hearing a thing like that made Courtial jump sky-high . . .

"Beans? . . . Beans? . . . Here? . . . In these rifts? . . . Did you hear that, Ferdinand? . . . Beans? In a soil without manganese! Why not peas? . . . Or eggplant while you're at it . . . Oh, this is too much!" He was scandalized . . . "Vermicelli! That's the thing! . . . Or truffles! . . . Say, what about truffles?"

He'd thump around the house for hours grumbling like a bear . . . The indignation aroused by an unwarranted suggestion was good for a long session . . . On that score he was uncompromising . . . Free deliberation! Scientific selection! . . . She'd go off to bed all alone in her windowless cubbyhole, a kind of alcove she'd fixed up for herself, far from the murderous drafts, between the threshing machine and the kneading trough . . . You could hear her sobbing through the partition . . . He was pretty rough on her.

You couldn't say she was ever short on courage or perseverance . . . or self-abnegation . . . Not once . . . She did wonders reclaiming that old shack . . . She never stopped fixing . . . Nothing worked . . . neither the pump nor the mill that was supposed to run the water . . . The hearth crumbled into the soup . . . She had to putty all the chinks in the walls, plug up all the holes . . . all the cracks in the fireplace . . . patch up the shutters, put on new tiles . . . She climbed up on the eaves . . . But at the first storm a lot of rain came into the rooms irregardless . . . through the holes in the roof . . . We put glasses underneath . . . one for each stream . . . All those repairs and alterations were a rough job, no petty tinkering . . . She changed the enormous hinges on the big barn door . . . Carpentry . . . locksmithing . . . nothing fazed her . . . She got to be real good at it . . . a regular mechanic . . . And in addition of course all the housekeeping and cooking were her department . . . She said so herself, no line of work bothered her except the laundry . . . There got to be less and less of that . . . Our wardrobe was rock bottom . . . Hardly any shirts . . . and no shoes at all . . .

Plugging the chinks in those thick walls she kind of fouled up . . . her plaster wasn't right . . . Des Pereires was critical, he thought we should do it over . . . but we had other worries . . . Anyway we certainly had her to thank if that mangy den finally began to look like something more or less. It was a ruin even so . . . Whatever you did to patch it up, it kept falling apart . . .

Our old lady was heroic all right, but that operation with her ovaries kept bothering her more and more . . . Maybe the overwork . . . She sweated like a waterfall . . . her moustache dripped . . . she was all flushed and congested . . . By the end of the day she was so het up, exasperated from waiting . . . that at the least misplaced word . . . bam! . . . the storm broke . . . She'd blow her top . . . She'd be waiting there all tensed up . . . She'd explode over nothing . . . The tirades were endless . . .

What we mostly had to avoid was the slightest allusion to the good old days in Montretout . . . She had that on her esophagus . . . It gnawed at her like a tumor . . . If a single word escaped us on the subject, she called us every name in the calendar, she said it was a plot . . . she called us bloodsuckers, homos, vampires . . . We had to put her to bed by force . . .

Des Pereires' problem was still making up his mind about his precious vegetable . . . We had to think of something else . . . We were beginning to have our doubts about radishes . . . What vegetable would we try? . . . Which would be right for radiotellurism? . . . And grow to ten times its normal bulk? . . . And where to plant? . . . That was no small question . . . It would require minute investigation . . . We'd already spaded up samples of every field for ten miles around . . . We weren't going into this thing with our eyes closed . . . We were thinking it over, that's all . . .

One day in the course of our explorations we came across a really sweet little village in the opposite direction from Persant, on the way south . . . Saligons-en-Mesloir . . . It was pretty far on foot . . . at least two good hours from Blême-le-Petit . . . That was one hideout where our old lady wouldn't ever think of tracking us down . . . The soil around Mesloir, Courtial discovered right away, was much richer than ours in "radio-metallic" content and consequently, he figured, infinitely more fertile . . . it would yield quicker results . . . We came back to study it almost every afternoon . . . The remarkable thing about that soil was its "cadmio-potassic" and its special calcium . . . You could tell by the feel and even more by the smell . . . Its composition seems to have been simply amazing . . . des Pereires sniffed it out right away . . .

Thinking it over, he even began to wonder if it mightn't be too rich in telluric catalyst . . . if we mightn't get concentrations so powerful as to make our vegetables burst . . . to make their pulp explode . . . That was the danger, the one questionable point . . . He had a hunch . . . In that case we'd have to give up the idea of growing small early vegetables in this ground that was really too rich . . . choose something coarse, something vulgar and resistant . . . Pumpkins for instance . . . But who'd buy them? . . . A single pumpkin for a whole city? . . . A monumental pumpkin? . . . The market wouldn't absorb them all . . . It was time we put our heads together! New problems to face! It's always like that with action.

In this burg of Saligons they served mostly cider in the cafés . . . and it didn't taste like piss, which, you've got to admit, is very unusual way out in the sticks . . . It went to your head kind of, especially the sparkling kind . . . We got to drinking quite a lot of it on our prospecting tours . . . That was in the Big Ball, the only tavern in the place . . . We got to going there more and more, it was conveniently located right near the cattle market . . . We learned about local customs from listening to the hicks . . .

Des Pereires made a beeline for the *Paris-Sport* . . . He'd been deprived of it for a long time . . . He talked to everybody . . . In exchange for advice about farming . . . little lessons about livestock . . . he was able to give them dope, some really ingenious pointers about placing bets in Vincennes . . . even from miles away . . . He made some fine connections . . . This was a hangout for cattlemen . . . I let him talk . . . The maid suited me fine . . . Her ass was so muscular it was almost square. Her tits too, you can't imagine how hard they were . . . The more you shook them, the harder they got . . . They were solid rock . . . Nobody'd ever licked her crack . . . I showed her the whole business . . . all I knew . . . It was magnetic . . . She wanted to throw up her job, at the bar and come back to the farm with us . . . That wouldn't have gone down with old lady des Pereires . . . especially as she was beginning to smell something fishy . . . It seemed to her that we were spending a lot of time around this Mesloir . . . It didn't look

kosher . . . She asked us some tough questions . . . We
were stumped . . . She set less and less store by our
prospecting for vegetables . . . She was getting persnickety . . . The summer was getting ahead fast . . . it
would be harvest time pretty soon . . . Hell!

At the Big Ball a sudden change came over the peasants,
they got mighty weird . . . Between drinks they read the
Paris Racing News . . . Des Pereires was kept busy . . .
He sent their little bets, never more than five francs each,
to his old pal in an envelope . . . Fifty francs was the
limit . . . he wouldn't take more . . . Tuesday, Friday,
Saturday . . . always through Formerly at the Insurrection . . . We kept twenty-five centimes a bet . . . that
was our little rake-off. I taught the maid, the ironclad
Agathe, how to keep from having babies . . . I showed
her that it's even more terrific from behind . . . After
that she was really crazy about me . . . She wanted to
do everything for me . . . I passed her on some to Courtial to show him how well I'd trained her . . . She was
willing . . . She'd have gone into a house if I'd only said
the word . . . It couldn't have been my clothes that sent
her, we'd have scared sparrows away . . . Nor my
dough . . . We never gave her a cent . . . It was the
prestige of Paris . . . That's the long and the short of it.

But when we got back at night, the hullabaloo was worse
and worse . . . Irène was no joke . . . We got in later
and later . . . We were in for some wild tantrums . . .
horrible sessions . . . She tore out her hair to the blood
. . . by the handful, by the bucket . . . because he
couldn't make up his mind about the "right" vegetable
. . . and his maximum soil . . . The old girl had started
working in the fields all by herself . . . She spaded up the
ground pretty good . . . She still couldn't make a furrow
quite straight . . . but for application she was tops . . .
She'd get there . . . She was mighty good at clearing
brush . . . If she wanted to build up her muscles, there
was plenty of room . . . just about anywhere . . . In
Blême-le-Petit there was nothing to stand in your way
. . . the whole region was fallow . . . to the right, to the
north, south or left . . . There were no neighbors on the
west either . . . The whole place was a desert . . .
parched . . . perfectly arid . . .

"You're wearing yourself out, angel pie," Courtial would sing out in the middle of the night when we'd find her on the job, still spading up the ground . . . "You're wearing yourself out . . . It's no use . . . This soil is hopeless! I keep trying to tell you . . . Even the peasants have gradually given up . . . My feeling is that they'll shift to cattle . . . But even there . . . I don't know . . . Cattle on these plains . . . With the marly subsoil . . . the calcico-potassic seams. . . I can't see them getting anywhere . . . It's a perilous undertaking . . . beset with enormous hazards . . . abominable difficulties . . . I can see it all . . . Irrigate such gook? . . . My oh my . . ."

"What about you, you big lug . . . who's going to irrigate you? Will you tell me that? Go on . . . I'm listening . . ." He refused to say another word . . . He dashed into the house . . . I still had work to do. Every night when we got in I had to classify the day's samples . . . on separate boards . . . strewn around the kitchen in little bags . . . They dried all over the place . . . samples of the whole country for fifteen miles around . . . There'd be plenty to choose from when the time came . . . but our richest selection was certainly from Saligons.

Little by little we'd gotten popular at the Big Ball . . . Our friendly drunks had developed a keen taste for the races . . . We even had to preach moderation . . . They didn't care how they risked their dough . . . They'd put fifteen francs on a single pony . . . Those kind of bets we turned down flat . . . We didn't want to get any more people too down on us . . . We played it safe and cautious . . . Agathe, the maid, was having a fine time . . . She was really enjoying herself . . . turning into a whore right there on the premises . . . What bothered us more was our battle-ax's spells . . . Her fits and ultimatums were more than we could take . . . She was getting on our nerves . . . On one little point, though, des Pereires had changed his tactics . . . He stopped ragging her when he found her toiling . . . He encouraged her to dig . . . he egged her on . . . And actually, patch by patch, week by week, she spaded up enormous areas . . . Sure she was a holy terror . . . but if ever she stopped working, it was a damn sight worse . . . She was fed up with our shilly-shallying, she did the deciding: potatoes . . . We couldn't stop her . . . In the long run, she decided, that was the ideal vegetable . . . She got to work right away. She didn't ask for our opinion . . . Once her tubers were planted, huge fields of them, she went telling everybody in Persant . . . on her way in, on the way back . . . that we were experimenting with "giant potatoes," obtained with electrical waves . . . The news traveled like gunpowder . . .

At the Big Ball in the afternoon they bombarded us with questions . . . up to that point they'd liked us fine, we'd minded our own business at the other end of the county . . . the local hicks had welcomed us and treated us all right . . . they'd even expected us every afternoon . . . And now they began to give us the cold stare . . . This farming of ours looked fishy to them . . . They were jealous right away . . . "Spuds" they started calling us.

We couldn't goof off anymore. The old cutie had gradually turned into a real terror . . . Now that she'd spaded up several acres of land all by herself, she was really leading us a life . . . We were afraid to say a word to her . . . She threatened to follow us if we went out bumming, if we didn't get to work within twenty-four hours . . . Our vacation was over . . . We had to get started, to haul the motor and the dynamo out from under the tarp . . . We cleaned the rust off the big flywheel . . . We started her up a little . . . We drew up a nifty-looking "table of resistances" . . . We let it go at that . . . Anyway we saw we wouldn't have wire enough . . . We needed a hell of a lot of it, spools and spools to zigzag back and forth between the rows of potatoes all over the plantation . . . Fifteen hundred feet wouldn't be enough . . . We needed miles . . . Otherwise it would never work . . . Without wire no radiotellurism . . . no intensive cultivation! no cathode rays . . . Wire was absolutely indispensable . . . Actually it wasn't so bad . . . At first we thought that lousy wire would be the perfect excuse, the airtight alibi, that the price of the stuff would scare our old lady out of this vital purchase . . . that she'd stop to think and leave us alone a while . . . But nothing doing, on the contrary . . . If anything it made her madder . . . She threatened

that if we farted around anymore . . . if we kept letting
things ride, she'd go to Saligons on her own and set up as a
midwife . . . no later than next week . . . love had
flown out the window! She was bluffing . . . But even with
the best of intentions, we hadn't enough money left for
such expensive purchases . . . Great God, they'd ruin
us . . . And who'd give us credit? . . . It was no use
trying . . .

On the other hand, we couldn't very well let the old girl
in on our exact situation . . . Especially we couldn't tell
her we'd just blown our last little reserves, what was left
from the sky pilot, playing the races by mail . . . Well,
anyway we'd lost it . . . It was certainly a terrible blow
. . . the end of our scheme . . . an intolerable cataclysm
. . . We were really in a jam . . . Now that she was
sold on potatoes, she was getting absolutely fanatical and
intolerant . . . It was getting to be exactly the same as
the balloon . . . or her cottage in Montretout . . . She
couldn't be budged . . . Once she threw herself into
something, she latched onto it like a rivet, you had to tear
the whole house down . . . It was very painful . . .

"That's what you said, isn't it? . . . You're not going
to deny it? . . . I heard you, didn't I? . . . You told me
ten times . . . a hundred times . . . that you were going
to run your lousy electrical contraption? I wasn't seeing
things, was I? . . . That's what we all came here for, isn't
it? . . . I'm not making it up? . . . That's why we sold
the house for a song . . . And threw up your paper . . .
That's why you dragged us all here like it or not by force
into this swamp . . . this pigsty . . . this muck! Am I
right?"

"Yes, my love."

"Good! . . . Well, I want to see it, understand? I want
to see it . . . I want to see every bit of it . . . I've sacri-
ficed everything! My whole life! . . . My health . . . My
future! . . . Everything! . . . I haven't anything left!
. . . I want to see them grow! . . . Understand? . . .
Grow!"

She planted herself there defiantly, she handed it to him
full in the face . . . Her hard labor had given her biceps
that were no joke . . . they looked like hams . . . She
chewed tobacco in the fields . . . She only smoked her

pipe in the evening and when she went to market . . .
Eusèbe, the postman, who hadn't delivered in our neck of
the woods for years, had to start in again . . . He came
around two or three times a day . . . The news had spread
around the country like wildfire that certain agriculturists
were doing wonders, performing real miracles raising potatoes with magnetic waves . . .

Our old crowd of inventors had picked up our track
. . . They all seemed mighty happy to hear that the three
of us were safe and sound . . . They besieged us with new
projects . . . They bore us no grudge at all . . . The
postman was good and sick of it . . . Three times a week
he had to tote whole sacks of manuscripts . . . His pouch
was so heavy his frame had caved in . . . He'd been using
a double chain . . . his bike had folded up . . . He'd
put in to the department for a new one . . .

From the very start des Pereires had taken to meditating
again . . . He really took advantage of his solitude and
leisure . . . He finally felt equal to the hazards of fate
. . . all of them . . . He was deep in his meditations!
Absolutely determined! The great Decision! . . . He'd
face up to his Destiny . . . Not overconfident . . . not
overcautious . . . just forewarned! . . .

"Ferdinand! See here and take note! . . . Events are
shaping up pretty much as I predicted . . . But they've
got a little ahead of themselves . . . The rhythm has been
a little hasty . . . which wasn't what I wanted . . .
Nevertheless, you'll see . . . Observe . . . Don't lose a
scrap! Not one luminous atom! . . . Behold, my child,
how Courtial is going to crush, to tame, to chain, to subju-
gate rebellious Fortune! . . . Behold with wonderment!
Open your ears! Try to be fearless, ready at a moment's
notice! The second I catch her, I'll pass her on to you! And
go to it! Clutch her! Strangle her! It will be your turn!
Kiss her! Mangle the bitch! My strictly private needs are
those of an ascetic! I shall soon be replete! Stuffed! Submerged in abundance! Yours to bleed her. Drain her to the
gills! . . . You're at an age for follies! Take advantage!
Overdo it! Gods above! Shine! Do what you please with
her! For me there'll always be too much and to spare . . .
Embrace me . . . Lord, how lucky we are!"

It wasn't easy to do any embracing on account of my

overcoat that was solidly moored with strings inside my
pants . . . It curtailed my movements but kept me good
and warm . . . It was necessary . . . The winter was on
us . . . In spite of the fireplace and the caulking the main
building was lousy with drafts . . . it kept in all the winds
and very little heat . . . It was a strainer for the cold
. . . It was really a very old house.

This inspiration that des Pereires had after all his meditations at the Big Ball and in the woods was really terrific
. . . His ideas were even bolder and more farsighted than
usual . . . He fathomed the needs of the world . . .
"The individual is washed up! . . . You won't get
anything out of individuals . . . It's to the family, Ferdinand, that we'll have to turn! Once and for all, to the
family! Everything for and by the family!"
His grand appeal was addressed to the "Anguished
Fathers of France." To those whose sovereign preoccupa-
tion was the future of their dear little ones . . . To those
who were slowly being crucified by daily life in corrupt,
putrid, unhealthy cities! . . . To those who were ready to
attempt the impossible to save their poor little cherubs from
the atrocious fate of slavery in a shop . . . from bookkeeper's tuberculosis . . . To the mothers who dreamed
of a wholesome spacious existence for their little darlings,
absolutely in the open air . . . far from the city's putrefaction . . . of a future fully secured by the fruits of
wholesome labor . . . in the country . . . of great sunlit
joys, peaceful and complete! . . . Des Pereires solemnly
guaranteed all that and a good deal more . . . He and his
wife would take complete care of those lucky little tikes,
their primary education, their secondary "rationalistic"
education too . . . and finally of their higher learning,
"positivistic, zootechnic, and horticultural . . ."
In two shakes of a lamb's tail our "radio-telluric" farm
was transformed, with the help of our subscribers, into the
"Renovated Familistery for the Creation of a New Race"
. . . That's what we called our farm in our prospectus
. . . In a few days our appeals (all sent out by Taponier)
had covered several Paris neighborhoods . . . the most
populous, the most congested . . . and for the hell of it
a few of the slum districts out by Achères, where it stinks

. . . We had only one worry . . . that the invasion would start too soon! We dreaded overenthusiasm like the plague . . . We knew all about it!

With our radiotellurism plentiful fare would be no problem . . . All in all, there was only one thing to worry about . . . The market would be glutted with our "undigenous" potatoes . . . We'd think about that in due time . . . We'd raise pigs . . . millions of them . . . We'd have plenty of poultry too . . . The pioneers would eat chicken . . . Courtial was all in favor of a mixed diet . . . Meat is good for growth . . . Obviously we'd have no trouble clothing our little charges in the linen we raised on our farm . . . woven in choral cadence on long winter evenings . . . Sounds pretty good . . . All very promising! A beehive of agricultural industry! But under the aegis of Intelligence! not of mere instinct! Ah yes! That distinction meant a good deal to Courtial! He wanted his hive to be rhythmical! . . . flowing! . . . intuitive! That was how he summed up the situation. Playing all the while, learning on every hand, building their lungs, the children of the "New Race" would at the same time joyfully provide a spontaneous labor force . . . quickly trained and stable, absolutely free of charge . . . Without constraint they would harness their youthful vigor to the needs of "neo-pluri-radiant" agriculture . . . This great reform was rooted in the depths, in the very sap of the countryside! It would flourish in the heart of nature! We'd all bask in its perfume! Courtial sniffed in advance . . . We were especially counting on our charges, on their zeal and enthusiasm, to pull out weeds! to uproot them! to clear more ground! . . . A perfect pastime for kids . . . The worst torture for adults . . . Relieved of the petty tasks of common farming by this industrious afflux, des Pereires would be free to devote himself entirely to the delicate regulation, the endless adjustments of his "polarizer complex" . . He'd rule the waves . . . He wouldn't do anything else . . . He'd flood our subsoil, he'd overwhelm it with telluric torrents! . . .

Our pamphlet looked good . . . We had ten thousand of them sent to various neighborhoods . . . It must have responded to a good many secret desires, unspoken longings . . . Anyway, we almost immediately received a deluge of answers . . . with truculent comments . . . almost all of them extremely flattering . . . What seems to have struck most of our subscribers in particular was the extreme modesty of our terms . . . It's true that we'd cut our prices to rock bottom . . . We could hardly have done better . . . To carry a pupil from early childhood (minimum age, seven) to the draft board, to provide him with board and lodging for thirteen consecutive years, to develop his character, his lungs, his mind, and his arms, to inculcate the love of nature, to teach him a magnificent trade, and last but not least to give him, when he left the phalanstery, the magnificent and valid diploma of a "Radio-geometric Engineer," all we asked of the parents, everything included, was the lump, global, and definitive sum of four hundred francs . . . This sum, these immediate receipts were to enable us to buy our wire and set up our circuits . . . our underground currents. We weren't expecting the impossible . . . Four carloads of potatoes a month would do for a starter.

The moment an undertaking begins to shape up, it becomes *ipso facto* the butt of a thousand hostile, treacherous, subtle, and untiring intrigues . . . Nobody can say different . . . A tragic fatality penetrates its very fibers . . . slowly lacerates its warp, so profoundly that, when you come right down to it, the shrewdest captains, the snootiest conquerors can only hope to escape disaster, to keep from cracking up, by some cock-eyed miracle . . . Such is the nature and the burden, the true upshot of the most admirable ventures . . . It's in the cards . . . Human genius is out of luck . . . The Panama disaster . . . it's the same old lesson . . . ought to bring the most outrageous blowhards to their senses . . . make them do some tall thinking about the perfidy of fate . . . the murky harbingers of Hard Luck! Foo! The slings and arrows! . . . Destiny eats prayers like a toad eats flies . . . It jumps on them! crushes them! mangles them! swallows them! It feasts on them and shoots them out in tiny little turds, ex-votive spitballs for the bride to be.

Making due allowances, we in Blême-le-Petit got it liberally in the neck from the very beginning of our operation . . . First the notary in Persant . . . He descended

on us pretty near every afternoon . . . in the most menacing terms . . . to make us pay his balance . . . He'd
read a sensational story in the paper about our magnificent
experiments . . . He thought we had secret funds . . .
He thought we were loaded . . . He demanded immediate
payment for his beat-up farm and his swampy acreage
. . . And our creditors from the Palais-Royal were all
bursting with impatience . . . Taponier too . . . He'd
been so nice at first, now he was getting to be the crummiest
of the lot . . . He read the papers too . . . The jerk
thought we were getting subsidized . . . drawing gravy
from the Ministry of Education . . .

In addition to quantities of manuscripts relating to the
"research" that would surely be required, we were riddled
with court orders . . . of all kinds . . . we were practically attached before we'd even seen the color of our first
potato! The constabulary jumped on the pretext for a little
jaunt out our way, to get an eyeful of our astonishing mugs,
to give us the once-over . . . Our clever prospectus in
behalf of the "Race" had kind of upset the legal authorities
. . . The Inspector of Schools, another envious character,
naturally, had expressed certain doubts about our right to
open an educational institution . . . Doubting was his
business . . . In the end they were only average mean.
They merely took the opportunity, which was to be expected, to give us a not unfriendly warning that all things
considered we'd better content ourselves with something of
the nursery, summer camp . . . or sanatorium type . . .
that if we carried the educational aspect too far we'd inevitably fall foul of the authorities . . . the whole lot of
them . . .

A delicate dilemma if ever there was one! . . . To
perish or to teach? . . . We thought it over . . . We
hadn't really made up our minds . . . when a bunch of
snoopy parents came hiking out one Sunday afternoon
around four o'clock to see for themselves . . . They carefully examined the farm, all the outbuildings, the general
look of the place . . . We never saw them again . . .

Nuts! We were beginning to lose hope . . . So many
adverse winds . . . Such rotten incomprehension! . . .
Such deep-seated malevolence! . . . It was really too
much . . . And then one fine day, the sky finally cleared

. . . Almost all at once we received eighteen enthusiastic registrations! . . . Ah, these were really conscientious parents, who frankly cursed the city and its pestilential air! They frankly agreed with us . . . They subscribed immediately to our "New Race" reform . . . They sent us their kids with an advance on the fee, to be incorporated immediately in the agricultural phalanx . . . A hundred francs here, two hundred there . . . the rest to follow . . . All we got was advances, never the full sum . . . They promised to send the rest later on . . . Plenty of goodwill in any case . . . their enthusiasm was genuine . . . but kind of obscure . . . Economy, foresight . . . and a big helping of suspicion . . .

Anyway the kids came . . . fifteen in all . . . nine boys and six girls . . . Three didn't show up. It seemed best to pay a little attention to the judge's advice . . . a word to the wise . . . We'd play it cagey for a starter . . . A little caution wouldn't hurt us . . . Later on, when the experiment had proved a success, things would take care of themselves . . . They'd come begging . . . We'd unfurl our banner: "The New Race, Flower of the Furrows."

With the dough that first batch of kids brought us, we couldn't buy much . . . not even all the beds we needed! not even mattresses! . . . We all slept in straw . . . in perfect equality! . . . The girls on one side, the boys on the other . . . After all we couldn't send them back to their parents . . . that chickenfeed didn't last a week . . . It was already speculated in all directions . . . It was gone in no time . . . The notary alone claimed three-quarters of it . . . The rest went for wire . . . Maybe about five spools . . . but the large size . . . mounted on a trestle, ready to unroll.

Right at the beginning our old cutie, foreseeing trouble, had planted some kind of super-potato that grew even in the wintertime . . . There's no hardier spud in existence . . . If the worst came to the worst and Courtial's waves didn't yield all we expected . . . we'd still have a crop . . . He couldn't very well prevent them from growing . . . that would be mighty weird, in fact unheard-of. We all got down to work . . . We strung wire wherever he told us . . . With a little extra encouragement, to be on the safe side, we'd have wound three or four copper garlands around the roots of every plant . . . It was a memorable job! . . . Especially the way we were situated on the hillside . . . full in the north wind . . . Even in the most biting gale our kids were happy. All they cared about was being out-of-doors the whole time . . . never a minute in the house. Most all of them came from the suburbs . . . They weren't obedient. Especially a skinny little character, Dudule, who wanted to feel up all the girls . . . We had to sleep him between us . . . They began to cough . . . Luckily our old honeybun knew a little something about medicine, she covered them with poultices from head to toe . . . They didn't even mind having their skin ripped off . . . as long as they weren't shut in . . . They wanted to be outside come hell and high water . . . We ate out of the big kettle . . . enormous quantities of soup . . .

After three weeks of toil the immense potato field was one network of wire, strung just below the surface with a thousand joints in dotted lines . . . It was real needleprick work . . . Turn her on! . . . Des Pereires had only to shoot the juice through the fibers . . . He started his contraption . . . Right away he gave those spuds a series of terrible shocks . . . of powerful, intensely telluric discharges . . . with a few little bursts of "alternating" in between . . . He even got up in the middle of the night to give them a little extra, to stimulate them more completely, to stir them up to the maximum. It worried the old sugarbun to have him going out in the cold like that . . . She woke with a start . . . She yelled at him to put something on.

We'd been worrying along for about a month when all of a sudden our Courtial began casting about for excuses . . . That was a very bad sign . . .

"I'd have preferred," he said "to try leeks . . ." He kept saying that more and more often in front of the old lady . . . He wanted to see her reaction . . . "What would you say to radishes? . . ." His wife gave him a cross-eyed look, she pushed up her dip in front . . . she didn't care for his insinuations . . . Hell, he'd made his bed, he shouldn't try to wriggle out of it . . .

Our pioneers were thriving, they made the most of their freedom . . . We didn't hem them in, they did what they pleased . . . they even attended to their own discipline . . . Terrible thrashings they gave each other . . . The littlest was the worst, the same old Dudule, he was seven and a half . . . The oldest of the flock was practically a young lady: Mésange Rimbot, the blonde with the green eyes, she had a nice billowy ass and her tits stuck out sharp . . . Madame des Pereires wasn't exactly a simple soul, she didn't trust our little wench around the corner, especially when she had her period . . . She'd fixed her up a special bunk in a corner of the barn, so she could sleep all by herself when she fell off the roof . . . That didn't keep her from monkeying around with the brats . . . nature, nature. That ornery postman caught her one night behind the chapel at the end of the village, doing it with Tatave, Jules, and Julien . . . All four of them were together . . .

This Eusèbe, the postman, had it in for us on account of the distances we made him travel . . . The department hadn't given him his bike . . . It would take two years . . . He wasn't entitled to it . . . He couldn't stand our guts . . . He wanted us to supply him with shoes, we didn't have any for ourselves . . . Naturally, moseying along on foot, he saw everything that went on. The day he caught the kids having fun, he doubled back extra, just to tell us what he thought of us . . . after he'd seen it all . . . as if it was our fault. Peeping toms are always like that . . . first they get a good eyeful . . . they don't miss an atom . . . And then when the party's over, they're all indignation . . . We told him off . . . We had more serious things to worry about.

In our beat-up hamlet there hadn't been any traffic for going on twenty years . . . Once this potato jazz got around, it was an invasion . . . a parade of sightseers from morning to night. The whole department was full of false rumors . . . The people from Persant and Saligons took the front row, they wanted all kinds of specimens and explanations. You couldn't put them off . . . They wanted to know if it was dangerous . . . if our system mightn't blow up and "start the earth vibrating" . . . As the ex-

periment went ahead, as time passed, des Pereires was
getting more and more cautious . . . He dropped "ifs"
and "maybes" that sounded really ominous . . . lots of
them . . . more and more . . . It was worrisome . . .
He'd hardly ever said "if" and "maybe" at the Palais-
Royal . . . About a week later he had to stop the dynamo
and the motor . . . It was getting a little risky, he told us
at that point, to pour on more waves and current . . .
we'd better stop a while . . . we could start up again
later . . . after a breathing spell. Waves of the telluric
variety were perfectly capable of engendering certain individual disorders . . . you never could tell . . . absolutely unforeseeable repercussions detrimental to the
physiology . . . Personally des Pereires was feeling the
effects of saturation . . . He was having dizzy spells . . .

Hearing these remarks, the farmers and sightseers began
to get suspicious. They shoved off, plenty worried. New
complaints came in . . . The cops dropped in again . . .
but there wasn't much they could say about our phalanstery
. . . The kids had nothing wrong with them . . . none of
them had taken sick . . . We'd only lost our seven
rabbits . . . A rough case of epizootic! Maybe it was the
climate . . . or the food . . . Finally the cops went away
. . . Not long after that our cunning little pioneers got fed
up on our Spartan fare . . . They griped something awful
. . . They were insubordinate . . . They had to build
up their strength, didn't they? . . . They'd have eaten the
whole county . . . They found a way . . . It was their
idea . . . One day they came home with three bunches of
carrots . . . and the next day a crate of turnips. A ton
of beans! All for the soup. The chow was looking up . . .
Then came a dozen eggs and three pounds of butter and
some bacon . . . It's perfectly true, we were out of all
those things . . . This looting wasn't for the hell for it,
it wasn't from wickedness . . . Madame des Pereires
couldn't hardly go out anymore since we'd started our intensive farming, she was busy all the time with the "circuits," patching them up so the juice would go through
. . . She only got to Persant once a week. At table nobody batted an eyelash . . . We dove right in . . . It
was a case of "compelling circumstances" . . . The next
day they brought home an old hen . . . all plucked . . .

It turned into soup fast . . . As banquets go, we could have used a little wine . . . We didn't exactly suggest it . . . nevertheless and regardless we had wine on the table the following days . . . several different vintages . . . Where the kids found all that we didn't ask . . . We let well enough alone . . . A wood fire is mighty pretty but not very convenient. It's a nuisance to keep up, it burns too fast, you've got to keep stirring it up . . . They found some briquettes . . . They hauled them through the fields in a wheelbarrow . . . We had a beautiful fire . . . But it was getting risky . . . We counted on our potatoes to straighten everything out . . . our honor and all that . . . To dodge the worst reprisals . . .

We went out to look at the spuds, we watched them like gems, we dug one up every hour . . . to see what was going on . . . We started the wave machine up again . . . It was purring almost day and night . . . It used up a lot of gas, we didn't see much results . . . The spuds the kids brought home, their hot vegetables, were always a good deal better looking . . .

Des Pereires had noticed that. He was more puzzled than ever . . . In his opinion our wire wasn't right . . . The conductivity wasn't as good as we'd originally thought . . . or needed . . . That was perfectly possible.

We went back to the Big Ball . . . Only once, just to look in . . . We'd better hadn't . . . Some reception we got! Agathe, the maid, wasn't there anymore, she'd gone off with the town drummer, a married man with children . . . They'd shacked up for the sheer ass of it . . . Moral turpitude, they put the blame on me . . . Everybody was down on me in the village and environs . . . when the whole lot of them had screwed her! . . . So help me! They said I'd debauched her. They wouldn't have anything to do with either of us . . . They refused to gamble with us . . . They wouldn't listen to our Chantilly "starters" . . . They were laying their bets with the barber across from the post office . . . He'd taken over our whole system, envelopes, stamps, and all . . .

Those people at the Big Ball knew plenty more about our smelly ways . . . They knew, in particular, that we were living off the land . . . All those chickens that had

disappeared for fifteen miles around . . . Same with the
butter and carrots . . . We were the gypsies . . . They
didn't say it in so many words, because they were hypo-
crites . . . But they made some mighty pointed remarks
about buckshots in the ass that certain people had coming
to them . . . about a bunch of no-goods that would certainly end up in the pen, amen and so be it! . . . Well
anyway, disagreeable remarks . . . We left without saying good-bye . . . It was a good two-hour hike back to
Blême . . . Time enough to meditate on our cool welcome . . .

Things weren't doing so hot . . . Our affairs weren't
cooking with gas . . . Des Pereires knew it . . . I
thought he was going to talk about it . . . but he talked
about entirely different things on the road . . . About
the stars again and the heavenly bodies . . . about their
distances and satellites . . . about the magical dances
they spin while we're mostly asleep . . . About constellations so dense you'd take them for clouds of stars
. . .

We'd been walking quite a while . . . he was getting
winded . . . He always got too excited when he got talking about the sky and the cosmogonic trajectories . . . It
went to his head . . . We had to slow down . . . We
climbed up on a bank . . . He was panting . . . We
sat down.

"You see, Ferdinand, I can't manage it anymore . . .
I can't do two things at once . . . when I used to be
always doing three or four . . . Ah, it's no joke, Ferdinand . . . it's no joke . . . I don't mean life, Ferdinand, it's Time I mean . . . Life is ourselves, it's nothing
. . . Time is everything . . . Look at the little stars of
Orion . . . You see Sirius? right next to the Snake? . . .
They pass . . . they pass . . . They're heading over
yonder to join the great galaxies of Antiope . . ." He
was done in . . . his arms fell back on his knees . . .
"You see, Ferdinand, on a night like this I could have
located Betelgeuse again . . . a night for vision, a really
crystalline night . . . Maybe with the telescope we still
could . . . It's the telescope I'm not likely to find so
soon . . . Ah, Christ, what a stinking muddle when I

think of it . . . Can you imagine, Ferdinand! Can you imagine! Say, you really went for it, didn't you?"

It made him laugh to think of it . . . I didn't answer . . . I didn't feel like gilding his pill anymore . . . When he got his optimism back, he always did something idiotic . . . He went on talking about one thing and another . . .

"Ferdinand, you see, my boy . . . I wish I were some place else . . . some place completely different . . . Somewhere . . . I don't know . . ." He made some more gestures, he described parabolas . . . He moved his hands through the milky ways . . . high, high up in the atmosphere . . . He discovered another twinkler . . . a little thing to explain . . . He wanted to talk some more . . . but he couldn't . . . His words scraped too hard . . . His chest was bothering him . . . "The fall gives me asthma," he said . . . So then he was quiet . . . He dozed off for a while . . . huddled up in the grass . . . I woke him on account of the cold . . . maybe half an hour later . . . we started off again very slowly.

Nobody has ever seen kids thrive like ours . . . growing so fast, getting so strong and muscular . . . since we'd been eating with no holds barred . . . We had enormous stews, we really put it away . . . and all the brats were on wine . . . They wouldn't take any reprimands or advice . . . They said we shouldn't worry about them, they were doing all right . . .

Our headache was Mésange . . . supposing one of the little thugs knocked her up . . . Sometimes she'd get a dreamy look that boded no good . . . Madame des Pereires had it on her mind . . . She marked crosses on the calendar to show when she was due.

All day long our pioneers sniped and snaffled around in the barns and farmyards . . . They got up again at night when they felt like it . . . It depended on the moon . . . They told us a certain amount . . . Our agricultural labors were mostly in the morning . . . When it came to bringing home the bacon, our little angels had gotten remarkably enterprising and ingenious . . . They were everywhere at once, in everybody's fields . . . But nobody ever saw them . . . They played Indians for real . . . They were crafty . . . After six months of scouting

and fancy trailing in every kind of terrain, they'd learned
to get their bearings by dead reckoning, they could do it in
their sleep . . . they knew the most labyrinthine pathways, the most secret hideouts . . . the position of every
clod of earth . . . better than the native hares . . .
They'd catch them by surprise . . . That'll give you an
idea.

Without them, I don't mind telling you, we'd have
starved . . . We were stone-broke . . . they stoked us
to the gills, it gave them a kick to see us get fat. All they
ever heard from us was compliments . . .

Our old cutie was champing at the bit . . . She'd have
liked to say something . . . It was too late . . . The
food problem comes first . . . With the kids gone we'd
have croaked . . . The country is merciless . . . We
never issued a word of command . . . The initiative was
all theirs . . . Raymond's father, a lampman on the railroad in the Levallois sector, was the only one who came to
see us the first winter . . . It was easier for him because
he had a railroad pass . . . He hardly knew his Raymond
. . . he'd got so big and strong . . . the kid had always
been frail, now he was a champ . . . We didn't tell him
the whole story . . . Raymond was a wonder, for swiping eggs he was in a class by himself . . . He'd snitch
them out from under the hen . . . without making her
squawk . . . the velvet touch . . . The father was the
honest kind, he wanted to settle his debt . . . Now that
his kid was so husky, so perfectly built, he talked of taking
him back to Levallois. He thought he looked well enough
. . . We wouldn't hear of it . . . We put up stiff resistance . . . We made him a present of his dough, he
still owed us three hundred smackers . . . on the sole
condition that he'd leave the kid with us until he'd learned
all there was to know about agriculture . . . That kid
was worth his weight in gold . . . We sure didn't want to
lose him . . . And he was glad to stay with us . . . He
wasn't looking for a change . . . So our life was getting
organized . . . We were detested for fifteen miles around,
they hated us tooth and nail, but tucked away all by ourselves in Blême-le-Petit it was hard for them to catch us
red-handed . . .

The old cutie got fatter than anybody else on the fruits

of the kids' larceny. So she couldn't say a thing . . . Her field didn't feed her! or her hat! or her pants! She heaved some comical sighs after sipping her brandy . . . She couldn't get over it the way little by little she'd got used to this unspeakable piracy . . . She'd taken to drink . . . maybe from repressed sorrow . . . A nip . . . another . . . and pretty soon she couldn't do without her poussecafé . . . "Let fate take its course," she sighed . . . "seeing as you're no good for anything." She was talking to Courtial.

We stored our victuals in our attic, in our basement, and in a corner of the barn . . . The kids had contests to see who could bring back the most in a day . . . We could have held out six months . . . gone through several honest-to-God sieges . . . We were fixed . . . Groceries, beer, margarine! Absolutely everything! . . . But we were eighteen at table, sixteen of whom were growing! A crowd like that can put it away, especially when "stationed" in the country . . .

Two of our pioneer girls, aged eleven and twelve, had brought home pretty near fourteen cans of gasoline for the boss's motor. He was beaming. The next day was his birthday, the other kids came back from Condoir-Ville, five miles away, with a big basket of babas, éclairs, and wafers . . . all kinds of cream buns and an assortment of aperitifs! In addition, to make it even funnier, they brought us stamped receipts . . . That was really sharp . . . They'd paid cash for the whole business . . . our clever little angels! They were swiping money now in the open fields . . . where it doesn't lie around. It was kind of miraculous! This time again we didn't say boo. We'd lost our authority. But those little tricks leave traces . . . Two days later the cops came around asking for big Gustave and little Léone . . . They hauled them off to Beauvais . . . We couldn't protest . . . They'd got themselves pinched picking up a billfold . . . It was a common ordinary trap . . . on a windowsill . . . An ambush if ever there was one . . . A report had been made on the spot . . . There'd been four witnesses . . . The thing couldn't be denied . . . and it couldn't be fixed . . . The best was to make a show of surprise, amazement . . . horror! We made a show.

They arrested our Lucien, the curlyhead, four days later . . . on pure hearsay . . . Something about a chicken coop . . . the farmer had turned him in . . . The following week they came for Glass-eye Philippe . . . But there were no proofs against him, they had to return him to us . . . Even so it was a hecatomb . . . It was getting pretty plain that those hicks, always so slow to make up their minds, had finally sworn to wreck our whole business . . . They hated our guts! . . . Actually they were threatening to burn the whole house down with us in it . . . Eusèbe had tipped us off . . . To be roasted like rats, wouldn't that be nice? . . . They wanted to stop our racket . . .

The old cutie was the first to feel the fury of the insurgent populace . . . They'd run her out of the market in Persant . . . She'd tried to do a little business, to pass off a whole basket of lovely "secondhand" eggs . . . It didn't wash . . . They'd recognized where they came from . . . They got mean, they were delirious with hate and rage . . . She beat it out of there fast! In another minute they'd have beaten the shit out of her . . . She was in a terrible state when she got home . . . Right away she cooked herself up a big coffeepot full of her mixture, a concoction of verbena and mint plus pretty near a third of banyuls . . . She was developing a taste for strong stuff . . . especially distilled wines . . . sometimes she even drank liniment . . . That set her up quickly . . . It was a mixture recommended by a number of midwives at the time . . . they said it was the best thing for night nurses . . .

We were all gathered around her, talking about this assault, examining the consequences . . . The bottles were out on the table . . . In comes the sergeant . . . Right away he starts cussing us out . . . He tells us not to move.

"We'll come and get you at the end of next week. This circus has been going on long enough . . . We're fed up and then some. You've been given plenty of warning . . . Saturday we're taking you up to the county seat . . . we've got a clear case against the whole lot of you . . . If I catch a single one of your little gallows birds on the loose . . . If they set foot outside this village . . .

they'll be picked up immediately! Immediately! Understand? Have I made myself clear?"

It seems the public prosecutor had enough evidence
against us to put us in the pen for twenty years . . .
Courtial, Madame, and myself . . . There were plenty of
charges: Kidnapping . . . moral turpitude . . . obscene
practices . . . illegal gambling . . . fraudulent tax returns
. . . vice . . . burglary . . . abuse of confidence . . .
nocturnal marauding . . . concealment of minors . . .
Anyway a whole waterfall, a complete assortment . . .
That sergeant was giving us a pain in the neck . . . Only
Madame des Pereires, though shaken at first . . . what
would you expect? . . . perked up pretty soon . . . She
didn't bat an eyelash . . . She bounced up like one man
. . . She stood right up to him . . . She leapt to her feet
with an impetus so violent, so bristling with indignation, so
fired with rage, that the sergeant wavered under the charge
. . . He couldn't believe his ears . . . He blinked . . .
She had him hypnotized, there's no other word for it. She
answered in terms that nobody could have refuted. That
dumb farmer couldn't have imagined . . . She came back
at him, she accused him of personally fomenting the whole
yokels' rebellion . . . the whole abominable *jacquerie.*
He was the guilty party. Flummoxed! lashed! flayed, he
was trembling in his boots . . . Contemptuous and sardonic, she called him a "poor bastard" . . . He was on
the defensive . . . He hadn't one word to say for himself
. . . She put her hat on . . . High above him she swayed
from side to side, glaring like a cobra . . . She forced
him backward . . . she threw him out. He skedaddled
like a canary. He climbed on to his bicycle and rode away,
zigzagging all over the road . . . He reeled through the
night with his little red lamp . . . We watched him
disappearing . . . He couldn't keep straight.

One of our campfire girls, Camille, for all she was a
smart little number, got nabbed three days later in the
garden of the presbytery in Landrezon, a stinkhole on the
other side of the forest. She was just slipping out of the
kitchen with a parmesan cheese, a couple of crawfish, and
some sloe gin . . . two bottles . . . She'd taken everything she could lay hands on . . . Plus the altar cruets

. . . That was the most serious, they were solid silver
. . . She'd been caught in the act . . . They'd all chased
her . . . They'd cornered her on the bridge . . . Poor
little kitten, she'd never be back. They'd locked her
up in Versailles! . . . That snake-in-the-grass postman
hurried over with the news . . . He'd gone out of his
way . . . Our situation was getting cock-eyed . . . a
mean balancing act . . . You didn't need to be very
smart to realize at that point that all the kids in our
phalanstery were sunk . . . one by one they'd be caught
foraging . . . even if they were ten times as careful . . .
even if they went out only at night . . .

We tightened our belts, we were more and more
cautious . . . We didn't have much margarine or oil or
sardines . . . we were nuts about sardines . . . It was
the shortage of tuna fish and sardines that really got us
down . . . We couldn't make any more French fries
. . . We holed up behind the blinds . . . We watched
the approaches . . . We were afraid some hayseed would
try to pick us off in the dusk . . . They came around
now and then . . . They passed outside our windows on
bikes with their guns . . . We had a blunderbuss too, an
old double-barreled shotgun . . . and a police pistol
. . . The former tenant had left them . . . They were
still hanging in the kitchen, on a nail over the fireplace.

One night when there was nothing to do and we
couldn't even go out, des Pereires took down the old
blunderbuss . . . He started cleaning it . . . running a
rag dipped in kerosene through the two barrels with a
string . . . working the trigger . . . I could feel the
state of siege coming.

We had only seven left . . . four boys, three girls . . .
We wrote their parents, asking if they wouldn't like to
take them back . . . our agricultural experiment had
been disappointing in certain respects . . . unforeseen
circumstances obliged us to dismiss some of our pupils
. . . temporarily . . .

Those crummy parents didn't even answer . . . Absolutely no conscience . . . Only too glad to leave their
headaches to us . . . So then we asked the kids if they
wouldn't like us to deposit them in some charitable insti-

tution . . . at the county seat maybe . . . Hearing those
few words, they came back at us so aggressive, so absolutely furious, for a minute I expected a massacre . . .
They wanted no part of it . . . We threw in the sponge
right away . . . We'd given those brats too much freedom and initiative . . . it was too late to get them back
in line . . . Hell! . . . They didn't mind running around
in rags and eating once in a blue moon . . . but they
wouldn't stand for interference . . . they got nasty mean
. . . They didn't even try to understand . . . They
didn't give a shit about the circumstances . . . We tried
to explain that life is like that . . . that we all have our
obligations . . . that law and order screw you in the
long run . . . that if you go snaffling right and left you
always get caught sooner or later . . . that one fine day
you come to a very bad end . . . They told us to jerk
off with our rotten bullshit . . . For their money, we
were pisspots . . . miserable drips . . . They wouldn't
do anything we said . . . they wouldn't listen . . . Some
New Race they turned out to be. Dudule, the youngest of
the gang, went out looking for eggs . . . Raymond was
afraid, he was getting too big . . . Little Dudule was our
"Raft of the Medusa" . . . We hoped, we prayed . . .
all the time he was out . . . that he'd come home safe,
sound, and bringing something . . . He brought back a
pigeon, we ate it practically raw with carrots . . . He
knew the country better than any hunting dog . . . You
couldn't see him six feet away . . . He'd lie in wait for
hours to nab his bird . . . Without cord, ball, or string!
With two little fingers . . . Crick! Crick! . . . He showed
me how he did it . . . It was subtle, it was neat . . .
"Betcha a dime I catch her . . . and you won't hear
nothing! . . ." It was true. You didn't hear a thing.

Two of our windows were smashed the same week
. . . Yokels passing lickety-split on their bikes . . .
They stoned us more and more . . . They'd hide, they'd
come back again . . . Christ, were they mean! . . . And
we were on our good behavior . . . We didn't fight back
. . . And we should have . . . they gave us plenty of
provocation . . . A good volley of buckshot in the ass
. . . Our pioneers were keeping out of sight . . . They

only went out before dawn, maybe an hour or two in the gloaming . . . in the first streaks of daylight, so's to have some idea what they were doing . . . The farmers had stationed mutts in every yard in the county . . . wild, vicious, ferocious monsters! . . .

In addition we were sadly lacking in shoes for those awful hikes over rocky paths . . . It was torture . . . With all their practice the kids often cut themselves . . . At daybreak in the rain, especially now it was coming on November, their rags looked like comical patches of bandages . . . They were coughing more and more . . . Sure, they were tough little bandits . . . but they weren't immune to bronchitis . . . They sank in up to their ass in the deep furrows . . . When the dry cold set in, they were through . . . They couldn't make it without shoes . . . Their feet would have fallen off . . . In the winter our plateau came in for plenty of gales . . . it was swept by the north wind . . . We warmed up all right at night, but it was stifling in the room, the smoke came back at us from the fireplace . . . We had nothing but damp wood, there hadn't been any coal for weeks . . . We couldn't stand it . . . we put the whole business out . . . We were afraid it would start up again . . . we threw water on the coals . . . There was nothing for the kids to do but go to bed . . .

Pretty often around midnight Courtial would get up . . . He couldn't sleep . . . He'd take his muffled lamp and head for the barn, he'd fiddle around with his contraption . . . he'd start it up for a few minutes . . . His wife would jump up in her straw and go out too, to see for herself . . . I could hear them cussing each other at the far end of the yard . . .

She'd come running back . . . She woke me up . . . She wanted to show me the spuds . . . They weren't pretty . . . Those spuds growing in the waves . . . They were pimply, repulsive . . . Hell! She called me to witness . . . They weren't getting very fat . . . that was plain as day . . . I didn't dare to say so, to agree with her too much . . . but I couldn't disagree either . . . They were gnawed, shriveled, loathsome, and putrid . . . and in addition they were full of maggots . . . Courtial's potatoes . . . We couldn't even eat them ourselves . . .

not even in our own soup . . . And we weren't hard to
please . . . Madame des Pereires was dead sure the experiment had been a failure . . .

"And that, Ferdinand, is what he thinks he's going to
send to market! What do you think, eh? . . . Who's he
expect to sell them to? . . . It's too much. It's a disaster!
. . . What I'd like to know is . . . where's the sap that's
going to buy such garbage? . . . Just tell me where that
nitwit is keeping himself so I can send him a basket of
flowers . . . My oh my, there's a man I want to see . . .
That dodo of mine is nuts . . . Say, come to think of
it, who does he take me for?"

It's true they were disgusting . . . Yet those spuds
were meticulously cared for . . . choice seeds . . .
coddled day and night . . . They were completely moldy
. . . crawling with vermin, with grubs and centipedes
. . . and the smell was really nasty, infinitely sickening
in spite of the bitter cold . . . That wasn't normal either
. . . an unusual phenomenon . . . It was the smell that
stymied me . . . A stinking potato is something very
rarely seen . . . This was a very strange variety of hard
luck . . .

"Sh-sh," I went . . . "You'll wake up the kids . . ."

She went back to the experimental field . . . She took
her lantern and her spade . . . The temperature was
around fifteen . . . She picked out the wormiest, she dug
them up one by one . . . as many as she could, until
dawn . . .

It was really impossible to keep that invasion of vermin
a secret very long . . . The whole field was alive, even on
the surface . . . The rot was spreading . . . we weeded,
uprooted, hoed more and more, it didn't do a bit of good
. . . In the end the news got around . . . The hicks
came snooping . . . They dug up our potatoes to see for
themselves . . . They sent samples of our produce to the
prefect . . . with a police report on our strange goings-
on . . . They even sent whole basketfuls, completely
chock-full of grubs, to Paris, to the Museum Director . . .
It was getting to be big news . . . Horrible rumors started
up . . . we were the criminal originators of a brand-new

agricultural pestilence . . . an unprecedented garden
blight! . . .

By the effect of intensive waves, of malignant "induc-
tions," by the diabolical instrumentality of a thousand wire
networks, we had corrupted the earth . . . stirred up the
jinni of the grubs . . . in the innocent bosom of nature
. . . There, in Blême-le-Petit, we had given birth to a
special race of absolutely vicious, unbelievably corrosive
maggots, which attacked every kind of seed, every conceivable plant and root . . . trees! harvests! the peasants'
houses! the very structure of the land! even dairy products!
sparing absolutely nothing . . . Corrupting, sucking, dis-
solving . . . encrusting the plowshares! . . . absorbing,
digesting stone, flint as well as beans! demolishing everything in their path! on the surface, under the ground!
Corpses and potatoes alike! Everything without exception!
And thriving, mind you, in midwinter . . . Drawing
strength from the bitter cold . . . propagating in swarms,
in vast myriads! . . . more and more insatiable . . .
crossing mountains! plains! valleys . . . with the speed of
electricity! . . . thanks to the waves generated by our
machines! . . . Soon the whole district around Blême
would be one enormous field of rot . . . a noisome bog!
. . . an immense sewer of maggots! . . . a seism of
swarming grubs! . . . Then it would be the turn of Persant! . . . and then of Saligons! . . . Such was the outlook . . . It was still too soon to predict how and when
it would all end! . . . whether it would ever be possible
to circumscribe the disaster! . . . Only the analyses
would show . . . It might perfectly well spread to all the
roots in France . . . consume the whole countryside . . .
until our national soil in its entirety was nothing but stones
. . . Our maggots might well make the whole of Europe
unfit for cultivation . . . one big desert of rot! . . .
Well, if that happened, believe you me, they'd talk about
the Great Plague of Blême-le-Petit down through the ages
. . . the way we nowadays talk about the ones in the
Bible . . .

It wasn't funny anymore . . . Courtial said so to the
postman when he came . . . It was perfectly natural that
this bikeless Eusèbe should spew a little poison . . . "It's
damn-well fucking possible," was his answer. He added

nothing. Anyway that stinker was getting more and more stinking. We didn't have a drop of anything left . . . we had nothing to offer him . . . He was really pissed off . . . Ten miles without a drink! . . . He was probably putting the evil eye on us . . . He came out from Persant three times a day! Just for our mail! . . . People were writing us from all over, it wasn't our fault . . .

Our mail had multiplied by ten . . . People who wanted to know all about it . . . who wanted to come out for an interview . . . And rafts of anonymous characters who told us off good for the price of a stamp . . . Cart-loads of insults . . .

"OK, OK, the spirit's fermenting . . . Look at all those lovely letters! A hundred thousand times more verminous than all the soil in the planet . . . And God knows it's crawling . . . It's lousy with them. You want to know what putrefaction is? You want me to tell you? It's all the shit we have to put up with . . ."

We thought maybe if we cooked them over a very slow fire . . . putting cheese on them . . . frying them in fat . . . if we cajoled them . . . in some clever way, we'd gradually be able to make them edible after all . . . We tried all the stratagems of cookery . . . Absolutely nothing worked . . . The whole mess turned to jelly at the bottom of the pot . . . At the end of an hour . . . maybe an hour and a half . . . all we had was one enormous grub cake . . . And still that terrifying smell . . . Courtial spent a long time sniffing at the result of our cooking . . .

"It's ferrous hydrate of alumina! Make a note of that name, Ferdinand. Remember it well . . . You see that meconium-like substance? . . . Our land is saturated with it . . . literally! . . . I don't even need an analysis . . . Precipitated by sulphides . . . That's our main trouble . . . undeniably . . . Look at that yellowing crust . . . I'd always suspected as much! . . . Those potatoes . . . that's an idea! . . . they'd make a splendid fertilizer . . . Especially with the potash in them . . . You see the potash? That's our salvation! Potash! Potash! It's remarkably adhesive . . . They're all supercharged with it . . . See how they glisten . . . you observe the

scales? That coating on every radicle? . . . All those infinitesimal crystals? . . . shimmering green? and violet?
. . . Do you see them clearly? . . . Those, Ferdinand,
my dear boy, are the transfers . . . Yes! . . . The transfers of hydrolysis! . . . Yes, yes indeed . . . neither
more nor less . . . conveyed by our currents . . . Yes,
my boy! . . . Absolutely! . . . The telluric signature!
. . . That's it all right . . . Take a good look now . . .
Open your eyes to the maximum! No clearer demonstration
is possible! No need of further proof! What proof? There it
is . . . the best! Exactly as I foresaw! . . . This is a
current that nothing can stop, disseminate, or refract! But
it shows . . . I've got to admit that . . . a slight excess
of alumina . . . And there's another little drawback . . .
but it's temporary . . . very temporary! . . . The question of temperature! The optimum for alumina is 12.05
degrees centigrade . . . Aha! Remember that, O-five
. . . For our purposes! You follow me?"

Another two weeks passed . . . We rationed our bit of
fat so strictly that we only made soup once a day . . .
There was no question of going out . . . It rained enormously . . . The country was having a rough time too
. . . flattened out by winter . . . The trees had the shivers . . . like ghosts rowing in the wind . . . As soon
as we'd emptied our plates, we went back to our straw ticks
to keep warm . . . We lay sprawled for whole days . . .
all bunched up together . . . without opening our mouths
. . . without saying a word . . . Even a wood fire
doesn't help when you're that cold . . . We had terrible
coughing spells . . . And we were getting thin . . . our
legs were like matchsticks . . . and so weak we couldn't
move . . . or chew . . . or anything . . . Starvation is
no joke . . . The postman stopped coming . . . He
must have had orders . . . We wouldn't have been so depressed if we'd had some butter . . . or even a little margarine . . . It's indispensable in the winter . . . About
then Courtial began to have terrible nausea . . . when
the cold got so intense and we were eating less and less
. . . He had some kind of enteritis, really very bad . . .
He had awful bellyaches . . . He writhed in the straw
. . . It wasn't from food . . . He talked it over with the

old girl and they took up the question of enemas . . .
Should he take one? . . . or mightn't it be better if he
didn't? . . . "But you haven't got anything in your bowels," she said . . . "How can you have rumblings? Colic
doesn't start up all by itself."

"I tell you I can feel it going through! Jesus! It was
twisting my bowels all night . . . It's a dry colic . . . It
ties my guts up in knots . . . Oh! Oh! . . ."

"It's the cold, you poor dope!"

"It's not the cold . . ."

"Then it's hunger . . ."

"No, I'm not hungry . . . I feel like throwing up . . ."

"Oh, you don't know what you want . . ."

He didn't answer . . . He burrowed into his straw
. . . He didn't want to be talked to . . .

In the agricultural line there was really nothing more he
could do . . . There was no more gas in the shed, not
even a single can to start the thing up with . . .

Two more days passed . . . in waiting and prostration
. . . Our old ladylove, huddled in a corner, muffled in
curtains, couldn't stand it anymore, her teeth were chattering fit to crack . . . She climbed up to the loft and got
some more sacks . . . She cut herself out a kind of smock
like the kids wore and a good stiff kilt. She put them on
over her pants and padded herself out with cotton waste
. . . It made her look like a Zulu . . . She thought it
was funny-looking herself . . . The cold makes you
laugh something awful . . . She was still cold, so she
started cavorting around . . . clattering her wooden
shoes, hey nonny nonny, around the big heavy table. The
kids split a gut watching her . . . They joined her in a
kind of snake dance . . . They ran after her . . . They
hung on her shirttails . . . She sang a little song:

> See the miller's daughter
> Dancing with the boys—
> The poor thing's lost her garter,
> Her garter, her garter . . .

These kittenish spells didn't come over Ma Courtial
very often . . . It took a special occasion . . . She had
nothing left to chew . . . Courtial had taken all the to-

bacco . . . She started griping a little about her pipe . . .
The kids tore her apart at the seams . . . They pushed
her down in the straw . . .

"Godammit to blazes!" she hollered at them: "Shove
off, the whole lot of you! You swivel-eyed, mangy snotnoses! Leeches . . . floozies! . . ." That made them
laugh still harder . . .

"Courtial, listen . . ." He wouldn't listen . . . He
burrowed his head in his hole . . . He sighed . . . He
groaned . . . it was his belly and the roughhouse . . .
The kids jumped on him, the four boys and the three girls
. . . He still wouldn't answer.

A little later we began wondering what had become of
Dudule . . . He'd been out a good two hours . . . supposedly relieving himself . . . We were all good and worried . . . It was nightfall by the time he got back . . .
He was loaded to the gunwales . . . He'd covered seven
miles . . . to Persant station and back in high . . . He'd
raised a real windfall on the freight platform . . . What
a deal . . . A shipment of groceries . . . He'd brought
us butter, a huge chunk . . . two complete strings of
sausages . . . three baskets of eggs . . . bologna, jam,
and *foie gras* . . . He'd even taken their wheelbarrow . . .
He'd snaffled the whole business outside the baggage room
while the men were over in the switch house trying to get
warm . . . It hadn't taken Dudule two minutes to walk
off with his whole cargo . . . The only thing missing
was bread . . . but that didn't keep us from throwing a
banquet . . . a real spread! . . . We built our fire way
up high . . . We threw on pretty near a whole tree . . .

When he heard what was going on, des Pereires woke up
completely . . . He got up to eat . . . He started guzzling so fast it took his breath away. He was holding his
belly in both hands . . . "Oh my oh my oh my!" he
sighed from time to time . . . The old cutie didn't need
to be asked twice either . . . In a few minutes she was
so stuffed she had to lie down . . . She rolled over on the
ground . . . from her belly to her back . . . very slowly
. . . "Oh, gracious goodness, goodness gracious, Courtial!
It won't go down! Mm, was I hungry! . . ." The kids
kept going off to vomit in the corners . . . Then they
came back and funneled in some more . . . Dudule's

dog was so bloated up he was howling blue murder . . .
"Ah! my children!" des Pereires kept saying, "Ah, the dear
little angels! Ah, my dear darlings! Oh my oh my! It was
high time! Ah, there's nothing like it . . ." He was in
seventh heaven . . . "Ah, it was high time! Oh my oh my!
. . . There's nothing like it! . . ." That was all he could
say. He couldn't get over the miracle . . .

It must have been about five o'clock . . . there was no
sign of daylight . . . when I heard Courtial stirring in the
hay . . . He was getting up . . . I figured the time by
the fireplace . . . the fire was almost out . . . I says to
myself: "There he goes, he's hungry . . . He can't take
the cold . . . He's going to make himself some coffee
. . . We'll all have some . . . *Bueno!* . . ." He actually
did make for the kitchen . . . That was perfectly natural
. . . I hear him fiddling with the coffeepots . . . I felt
like joining him and tossing down a cup . . . But between
my nest and the door the kids were all sleeping . . .
bunched up together, with their heads every which way
. . . I was afraid of stepping on them . . . So I stayed in
my hole . . . After all I wasn't too cold . . . I was sheltered by the wall . . . I was catching less breeze than the
old-timer. I was only frozen stiff. I waited for him to come
back with the coffeepot, I'd stop him on the way . . . But
he was taking his time . . . He was padding around in
the distance . . . For a long time I heard him clattering
pots and pans . . . And then I heard him opening the
door onto the road . . . The thought passed through my
mind: "He's gone out to take a leak . . ." I didn't get it
. . . I kept waiting for him to come back . . . I was
worried for a second . . . I almost got up . . . And
then I fell back asleep . . . I was in a torpor . . .

And then I had a nightmare . . . Deep in the bottom
of my sleep I was fighting with the old bag . . . She was
having things her own way . . . I broke loose . . . She
grabbed me again . . . What a battle! . . . What a
ruckus! . . . I couldn't disentangle myself . . . The
noise was awful . . . She had me in a drowning-man's
grip . . . She was cracking my head with her questions
. . . I tried to shake her off, to cover up with straw . . .

but the bitch was holding me, she latched onto my head
. . . And she yelled! And she bellowed! . . . She twisted
my ears in her fists . . . She wouldn't let go . . . Where
was her Courtial? she yelled in all fifteen keys . . . She'd
just come back from the kitchen . . . she'd wanted some
coffee . . . There wasn't a drop left . . . So she'd started
raising hell . . . Everything was empty . . . He'd
swilled it all up, the swine! . . . every last cup, the three
coffeepots, all by himself . . . before going out . . .
Hadn't he said anything to me? She kept at me . . .

"No, no! Not a word!"

"Which way did he go?" Had I seen him in the yard?

"No! No!" I hadn't seen a thing . . . Mésange jumped
up with a bang and started blubbering . . . She'd had a
crazy dream . . . She'd seen the boss, Courtial, riding on
an elephant . . . This was no time to fall for such hooey
. . . We tried to remember what he'd said that evening
. . . He'd eaten enough for a regiment . . . we remembered that . . . Maybe he'd been sick . . . maybe he'd
passed out . . . It was mighty cold out there . . . We
started listing the possibilities . . . A stroke? . . . We
didn't waste any time, we went looking for him with the
kids . . . We searched all through the straw . . . every
corner of the house . . . the outbuildings, the two barns
. . . and the experiment shed . . . He wasn't anywhere
. . . We went out across the fields . . . the immediate
vicinity . . . and then a little farther . . . Some went up
toward the hillside, searching every gully and clump of
trees . . . The rest combed the plateau like they were
picking berries . . . We sent out Dudule's dog . . . No
hair or hide of Courtial . . . We reassembled . . . We
searched the little woods, bush by bush . . . He often
went roaming around through there . . . Just then one of
the kids noticed something written on the big panel of the
front door . . . "Good luck! Good luck!" . . . in chalk
. . . in big capital letters . . . That was his handwriting
all right . . .

At first the old lady couldn't make head or tail of it . . .
She kept mumbling: "Good luck! Good luck!" She couldn't
stop . . .

"What does it mean? . . . Why, good Lord! Why, he's

blown!" Suddenly it hit her between the eyes. "Say, who does he take me for! . . . Heavens above! . . . Good luck! . . . What's that again? Good luck? He wishes me . . . good luck? . . . He says that to me? . . . Say . . . that's stinking! Oh!" She was outraged . . . absolutely furious . . .

"Why, it's monstrous! . . . His highness blows . . . He steps out . . . He takes a little trip . . . His highness trots off to town for a binge! The skunk! The scoundrel! The no-good! . . . Good luck and that's that! . . . And I'm supposed to shut up and like it! . . . So the eight ball's all for me, is that it? . . . So I'm knee-deep in shit? . . . Well, climb on out, you old bag! . . . Just shake your ass! And good luck! And I'm expected to take it lying down! . . . What do you say, Ferdinand? What do you think? . . . Of all the rotten stinking gall! . . ."

The kids were doubled up listening to her raving . . . I didn't want to stir up the explosion . . . I let her cool off some . . . But I says to myself inside . . . "The poor bastard was sick of us . . . He was fed up on farming too . . . He's cleared out fast and far . . . We won't be seeing him again so soon . . ." That was my hunch . . . I remembered some of the things he said . . . They pinched me hard . . . Sure he talked a lot of hooey . . . But maybe all the same he'd finally gone through with his Great Decision . . . the skunk . . . leaving us to sink . . . up to our necks in shit . . . That was his way . . . He was plenty underhanded, vindictive, deceitful . . . worse than thirty-six bears . . . It was no surprise to me . . . I'd always known it . . . "The details are unimportant . . . They clutter up our lives . . . Decision is what counts . . . The Great Decision, Ferdinand! The Great Decision! You hear me? . . ." I heard him . . . It was all a lot of gas . . . But suppose he'd really cleared out once and for all! . . . Wouldn't that be stinking! Wouldn't that be low-down! . . . How were the rest of us going to get out of this mess? . . . The old lady was dead-right . . . What could we do with this telluric junk? . . . Not a thing! . . . If they all came around accusing us of stinking up the whole earth . . . what would we have to say for ourselves? . . . We'd be out on our ass! . . . He with his glib tongue . . . maybe he could bamboozle the cannibals

. . . maybe he could spellbind them . . . But us? . . .
We didn't have a chance.

We were knocked for a loop . . . We tried to figure it
out . . . Gradually the old lady calmed down . . . The
kids searched the joint again . . . They went up in the
loft . . . They turned over all the hay . . . Will he come
back? Won't he come back? That was the chorus.

In Blême he didn't have his cellar to hide in like at the
Palais-Royal . . . Maybe he hadn't gone far . . .
Maybe it was just some fool idea . . . A little spell of
lunacy . . . Where would we and the kids go if he didn't
come back at all? . . . What with thinking it over, the old
girl began to feel more optimistic . . . She told herself
that it couldn't be . . . he had some heart after all . . .
it was just some idiotic trick . . . he'd be back soon . . .
We began to take hope . . . for no good reason . . .
except there was nothing else to do . . .

The morning was getting along, it must have been about
eleven . . . The lousy postman shows . . . I saw him
first . . . I was looking out the window kind of . . . He
comes up . . . He doesn't come in . . . He just stands
outside the door . . . He motions me to come out . . .
he's got something to tell me . . . I should hurry . . . I
beat it out . . . He's waiting under the arch, he whispers
to me, he's all excited . . .

"Quick, quick . . . Go see your old man . . . He's
down there on the road, after you cross the Druve . . .
on the way up to Saligons . . . You know the little
wooden footbridge? . . . That's where he is, he's killed
himself . . . The farmers at Les Plaquets heard him . . .
Jeanne Arton and the kid . . . It was just after six o'clock
. . . With his gun . . . the big one . . . They said to
tell you . . . So you can take him away if you want to
. . . I haven't seen a thing, understand? . . . They
haven't either . . . They heard the shot, that's all . . ."
Say, here are two letters . . . They're both for him . . ."
He didn't even say good-bye . . . He beat it along the
wall . . . He hadn't taken his bicycle, he cut across the
fields . . . I saw him coming out of the woods by the road
up top, the one that goes to Brion.

I whispered the whole story in her ear . . . so the kids wouldn't hear . . . She made one bound to the door . . . She ran out full tilt . . . She raced over the gravel . . . I didn't even have time to finish . . . I had to quiet the kids down . . . They suspected a disaster . . .

"Don't get excited . . . Don't show your mugs outside . . . I'm going to catch the old bag . . . You keep on looking for Courtial . . . I'll bet he's still here . . . hidden someplace . . . He hasn't gone up in smoke . . . Turn over all the straw . . . bale by bale . . . He's sleeping underneath . . . We're going to see the cops in Mesloirs . . . they've sent for us . . . That's what the postman came about . . . We won't be long . . . Don't shit in your pants! . . . Stay right here and keep quiet . . . We'll be back by two . . . Don't let them hear you from outside . . . Don't go out . . . Search the loft . . . Take a look in the stable . . . We didn't look in the bins . . ."

The kids were scared stiff of the cops . . . That way I knew they wouldn't trail me . . . They smelled a herring all right . . . but where? . . . they had no idea . . .

"Keep the doors closed whatever you do," I told them. I tried to locate the old lady out of the window . . . She was miles away . . . I shook a leg . . . I had a hell of a time catching her . . . She was cutting across field and forest in high . . . Well anyway, I followed her . . . Hell, it took' all I had just to keep her in sight . . . All the same I put my thoughts together . . . I'm running blue blazes . . . And in the fever of the chase a rotten suspicion comes up in me . . . "Hell," I says to myself, "what a business! . . . You're a sucker again, kid . . . it's a frame-up . . . a swindle . . . that stuff about the footbridge! . . . Nuts! . . . It's a big hoax . . . a stinking lie . . . a sinister trap, that's all!" I strongly suspected it . . . A crummy trick of the postman's! . . . It was just like him, the stinker . . . And all those cannibals! . . . I wouldn't put it past them. That's what I was thinking in the middle of running . . . And where was our old man at that exact moment? . . . while we were breaking our necks running after his corpse? . . . Where could he be? Maybe he was only at the Big Ball . . . playing cards and sopping up anisette . . . We were the

suckers again . . . I wouldn't put it past him . . . It
didn't take a suspicious nature to know him for a mean sly
bastard! . . . We were the fall guys . . . That was a
cinch . . .

After a long level stretch through soft fields, there was
a steep climb up the hillside . . . Up top you discovered
the whole countryside so to speak . . . The old lady and
I were puffing like oxen . . . We sat down for a second
on the bank to see better . . . The poor old thing's eyesight wasn't very good . . . But mine was really piercing
. . . You couldn't hide a thing from me ten miles away as
the crow flies . . . From up top there . . . all the way
down the slope . . . the Druve flowing at the bottom
. . . . the little bridge and then the bend of the road
. . . That was the place, I could see it plain as day . . .
right in the middle of the road, kind of a big bundle . . .
I was dead sure . . . Maybe two miles away it stood out
against the gravel . . . And right that minute, the second
I saw it, I knew who it was . . . By the frock coat . . .
the gray one . . . and the rusty yellow pants . . . We
beat it lickety-split . . . We ran down the hill . . .
"Keep on going!" I said . . . "Go straight ahead . . .
I'm going to turn off . . . I'll take the path . . ." It was
a big shortcut . . . I was there in no time . . . Right on
the spot . . . Two steps away . . . He was all shrunk
. . . all shriveled up in his pants . . . It was him all right
. . . But the head was a mess . . . He'd blown it all to
hell . . . He'd hardly any skull left . . . Point-blank
. . . He was still holding his gun . . . He was hugging it
in his arms. . . The double barrel went in through his
mouth and passed straight through his head . . . It was
like hash on a skewer . . . shreds, chunks, and sauce
. . . Big blood clots, patches of hair . . . He had no eyes
at all . . . They'd blown out . . . His nose was wrong-
side out . . . nothing but a hole in his face . . . all
sticky around the edges . . . and plugged up in the middle with a lump of coagulated blood . . . a big mash
. . . and trickles oozing all across the road . . . It was
flowing mostly from the chin, which was like a sponge
. . . Even in the ditch there was blood . . . puddles in
the ice . . . The old lady took a good look . . . She
just stood there . . . She didn't say boo . . . So then I

decided to do something . . . "We'll move him up on the bank," I said . . . The two of us went down on our knees . . . First we tug at the bundle . . . We try to dislodge it . . . We tug a little harder . . . I pull on the head . . . It wouldn't come loose . . . We weren't getting anywhere . . . It was stuck too solid . . . Especially the ears were welded fast . . . The whole thing made a solid block with the ice and gravel . . . We could have unfastened the trunk and the legs by pulling hard enough . . . But not the head . . . the hash . . . It was one solid brick with the stones on the road . . . It couldn't be done . . . The body bent crooked like a Z . . . the head impaled on the gun barrel . . . First you'd have to straighten him and get the gun out . . . His back was all bent, his ass was wedged between his heels . . . He'd spasmed as he fell . . . I looked around . . . I see a farm down below . . . Maybe that was the one the postman had mentioned . . . Les Plaquets . . . I says to myself: "That's it . . . that's the place all right . . ."

"Hey, you stay right here," I tell the old witch. "I'm going to get help . . . I'll be back in a minute . . . They'll give us a hand . . . Don't move . . . That must be Jeanne's farm . . . They're the ones that heard it."

So I come up to the house . . . First I knock on the door, then on the shutters . . . Nobody seems to notice . . . I try again . . . I double back to the stables . . . I go right into the yard . . . I knock . . . I knock some more . . . I yell . . . Still no sign of life . . . But I could feel there was somebody around . . . The chimney was smoking . . . I shake the door with all my might . . . I tap, I clatter on the windowpanes . . . I'll tear the shutters down if they don't come . . . And then a face peeps out after all . . . It's the Arton kid . . . by a first marriage . . . He's not taking any chances . . . He just barely shows himself . . . I tell him what I want . . . Could they give me a hand carrying him? . . . Just those few words send her sky-high . . . She won't allow it . . . she comes to life . . . She wouldn't even think of touching it . . . She won't even let her lousy brat answer me . . . She won't even let him go out . . . He's going to stay right there with his mother . . . If I can't get him off the road, why don't I call the police? . . . "That's

what they're there for . . ." The Artons aren't going to
get mixed up in this . . . not for anything in the world
. . . They haven't seen a thing . . . or heard anything
. . . They don't even know what I'm talking about . . .

Old lady des Pereires up there on the embankment
watched me parleying . . . She let out terrible screams
. . . She was making a disgusting stink . . . That was
the way she was . . . After the first shock you couldn't
hold her . . . I pointed her out to the two savages . . .
the poor woman in despair . . .

"Do you hear that? I suppose you can't hear her? . . .
Her terrible grief! . . . We can't leave her husband out
there in the muck, can we? . . . What are you afraid of?
Good God, it's not a dog . . . he hasn't got rabies . . .
It's not a calf . . . he hasn't got hoof-and-mouth disease
. . . He's killed himself and that's that . . . He was perfectly healthy . . . He hasn't got the glanders . . . The
least we can do is shelter him in the barn for a while . . .
till they can come and take him away . . . Before the
traffic starts up . . . They'll run him over . . ." Those
shitheels were adamant . . . The more I tried, the more
pigheaded they got . . . "No, no!" they yelled. Certainly
not, they wouldn't take him in . . . not on their property
. . . never, never! . . . they wouldn't even open the
door for me . . . they told me to beat it . . . They were
burning me up . . . So I says to this rotten bitch:

"All right, all right! That'll do, madame. I see. You
won't help. That's your last word? You're sure? All right,
It's your ass . . . In that case I'm going to stay right
here . . . That's right . . . I'll stay a week! I'll stay a
month! I'll stay as long as I have to! I'll yell until they
come! . . . I'll yell so everybody can hear me, I'll tell
them it was you . . . that you engineered the whole
thing! . . ." That got them . . . Christ, were they
scared! They were shitless! . . . And I went right on
. . . I wasn't going to stop . . . Those scums made me
so mad I'd have thrown an epileptic fit to show them . . .
They didn't know how to make me shut up . . . The old
lady up on the bank was shouting louder and louder . . .
She told me to hurry . . . "Ferdinand, hey, Ferdinand
. . . Bring hot water . . . Bring a sack . . . a cloth!
. . ." The only thing those two bastards were willing to do

. . . in the end after my song and dance and to make me let go their blind . . . was lend me their wheelbarrow on condition that I'd positively bring it back that same day . . . rinsed, cleaned . . . and scrubbed with Javel water . . . They said it over and over . . . They repeated it twenty times . . . So I toted the thing up the hill . . . I had to come back down to ask for a trowel . . . to pry the ear loose . . . to break up the lumps . . . Little by little we made it . . . But then the blood began to gush again, it flowed profusely . . . His flannel vest was one big jelly, a pudding inside his frock coat . . . the gray was all red . . . But the worst was getting the gun out . . . The barrel stuck so hard to the enormous plug of meat and brains . . . it was so completely wedged into the mouth and skull . . . that it took the two of us . . . She held the head on one end and I pulled at the butt on the other . . . When the brain let loose, it gushed out even harder . . . it dripped down sideways . . . steaming, it was still hot . . . a stream of blood spurted from the neck . . . He'd impaled himself completely . . . He'd fallen on his knees . . . He'd collapsed like that . . . with the barrel deep in his mouth . . . He'd stove his whole head in . . .

Once we got him loose, we turned him over on his back . . . belly and face up . . . but he folded again . . . He was still like a Z . . . Luckily we managed to squeeze him in between the sides of the wheelbarrow . . . We still had trouble though with the neck, the stump of the head . . . It kept dangling against the wheel . . . The old girl took off her petticoat and her heavy kilt . . . to bundle up his head in . . . so it wouldn't drip so hard . . . But the minute we started moving again, with the bumps and jolts, it started gushing thicker than ever . . . They could have followed our tracks . . . It was slow going . . . we took little short steps. I stopped every two minutes . . . Those four miles took us at least three hours . . . I saw the gendarmes way in the distance . . . or rather their horses . . . right outside the farm . . . They were waiting for us . . . There were four of them plus the sergeant . . . And besides there was one in civilian clothes, a big guy I didn't know . . . I'd never seen him before . . . We were crawling . . . I wasn't in

any hurry at all . . . But we finally got there . . .
They'd seen us coming . . . all the way down from the
ridge . . . They must have spotted us even before we
went into the woods . . .

"OK! Leave the wheelbarrow in the doorway, you little
stinker! This way, both of you . . . The inspector'll be
here in a little while . . . Put the handcuffs on him . . .
and her too . . ." They shut us up in the barn. One of the
cops guarded the door.

We waited several hours in the hay . . . I could hear
the mob collecting in front of the farm. The village was
crowding up . . . They were pouring in from all directions . . . Some of the hicks must have been right there
under the arch . . . I could hear them talking . . . The
inspector hadn't come yet . . . The sergeant came and
went, getting madder and madder . . . He was making a
show of activity while waiting for the orders . . . He was
dishing out orders to his men . . .

"Push back the crowd. And bring me the prisoners
. . ." He'd already questioned all the kids . . . He had
us brought in to him and then he sent us back to the barn
. . . After a while he hauled us out for good . . . The
bastard browbeat us . . . He was eager-beavering . . .
He threw his weight around, trying to terrorize us . . .
probably so's to make us talk . . . so we'd confess right
away . . . He had another think coming . . . He said
we had no right to tote the body around . . . That was a
felony in itself . . . We shouldn't have touched it . . .
It was doing fine on the road . . . that now he wouldn't
be able to make his report . . . What do you think of
that? . . . and that twenty-five years in the pen would
teach us a thing or two! Hell! that boy didn't like us . . .
Anyway, the worst kind of bullshit . . . a lot of stupid
cocksucking bellowing . . .

The old lady wasn't acting up much since we'd come
back . . . She just sat there crying, huddled against the
door. Once in a while she let out a hiccup, followed by the
same two three laments . . .

"I'd never have expected it, Ferdinand . . . Oh, it's
too much . . . Too much misery, Ferdinand . . . I
haven't the strength . . . No! . . . I can't go on . . .

I can't believe it . . . I can't believe it's true, Ferdinand
. . . What do you think? . . . Is it really true? Do you
think it's true? . . . Oh no, it can't be . . ." She was
really stunned . . . She was out for the count . . . she
was goofy cross-eyed . . . But when that cop started in
again, calling us criminals in his stupid hayseed accent
. . . that stirred her up . . . Worn-out as she was, she
bridled at the affront . . . Christ! . . . She bounded like
a tiger . . . She was in form again.

"What's that? What's that?" she flung at him . . . "I
don't quite follow you . . . What's that you say? . . ."
She shoved her face into his . . . "What's that you're telling me? . . . That I did him in? . . . Why, you've been
drinking, my good man! . . . You've got your nerve with
you! . . . Or are you crazy, the whole lot of you? . . .
What's that? You're accusing me? . . . Of killing that
scoundrel? That gallows bird? . . . I'll remember that
one . . . Oh, it's rich . . . I'll have to write it down
. . . That stinker who's been my misfortune . . . and
nothing else but . . . He's the murderer . . . He's been
murdering me for years . . . Vampire? He's the vampire!
. . . And not just once! not ten times! not a hundred
times! but a thousand times! Two thousand! . . . Why,
he was murdering me every single day before you were
even born . . . I ran myself ragged for that man! . . .
tore my guts out! . . . I went hungry for weeks on end so
they wouldn't take him away to Rungis . . . All my
life, you hear? Tortured . . . abused . . . that's right
. . . crushed! Yes, all my life for that skunk! . . . I did
everything in my power to save him . . . Everybody
knows that . . . Why don't you keep your questions for
them, for the people who know . . . who know us . . .
who saw what I did? . . . Go to the Palais-Royal . . .
Go to Montretout . . . They know me . . . They know
all I did . . . all I went through . . . Ferdinand can
tell you . . . He's young, but he understands . . . I
performed miracles, monsieur, to keep him from falling
back into the gutter . . . miracles . . . and dishonor
. . . That was his nature . . . He wallowed lower than a
pig if you turned your back for half a minute . . . He
fell into every cesspool . . . He couldn't help it . . .
That's right . . . I'm not afraid to say it . . . He was a

dungheap . . . I've nothing to hide . . . Anyway, everybody knows it . . . He had no shame, heavens above
. . . Every evil instinct . . . every last one . . . the
vilest . . . things you gendarmes are too young to understand . . . You're even too young to hear about them!"

She looked the cops up and down . . . Her hair was
loose, it fell down over her eyes in scraggly gray wisps
. . . She was sweating hard . . . She reeled a little, she
sat down.

"You fellows think it's decent the way he ended up?
. . . Is that all you've got to say? . . . Treat me like a
whore? . . . That's my reward! . . . If you knew about
the debts! . . . Ah? . . . That's news to you? . . . He
didn't give a good godam . . . Bills, bills, bills . . . You
go pay them, you old crab! . . . And always new ones
pouring in . . . Break your back, that's what you're good
for . . . Double-talk! Cock-and-bull stories! Sleighrides!
Hokum! Liquor! . . . That's how he lived! That's all he
knew! Swindling and low living! He hadn't an ounce of
feeling! . . ." She was convulsed with misery, bellowing
between spasms . . .

"It was me! me that saved his house to the bitter end!
If I hadn't fought for it, it would have been sold centuries
ago . . . He couldn't control himself . . . The dirty
bastard took advantage of my being so sick just then that
I didn't know what was going on . . . He unloaded . . .
he drank it all up . . . he sold us out bag and baggage!
Ask if it's not true . . . if I'm a liar . . . He never
spared me anything! Never! He couldn't . . . It was
second nature with him . . . He had to torture me . . .
All for his whores! For his vices! His horses! His races!
His damn foolishness! His drinking, and I don't know what
else . . . Generous? . . . He gave to strangers . . . It
was all the same to him, as long as it went out fast . . .
It slipped through his fingers . . . I could be on my
deathbed, he didn't care . . . That's what he always
wanted . . . Thirty years it went on . . . Thirty years I
put up with it . . . Thirty years isn't five minutes . . .
So now I get accused! . . . After all the vilest affronts
. . . after all I've suffered . . . Oh no, it's too much!
. . ." The enormity of the thing sent her into hysterics
again. "What's that? What's that? It can't be! So now he

disfigures himself . . . He shoves off . . . He makes
hash of himself, and I'm the guilty party? My oh my, that
takes the cake! . . . It's enough to make your hair stand
on end! What a filthy business! To the very end that stinking rotten clown has poisoned my existence . . . you can
say that again! . . . But I'm not going to take it lying
down! . . . I'm still here! . . . It's up to you! . . .
Hold the fort, you old mule! There won't be anything left!
Not a crumb! Nothing but debts! Nothing but debts! He
doesn't give a damn . . . as long as he can spend . . .
He took everything I had . . . Ferdinand knows all about
it . . . He saw how the land lay . . . He saw how I toiled
and struggled and racked my brains to the very last minute
. . . so as not to leave Montretout . . . so as not to
come to this stinking hole . . . and bury myself with his
potatoes . . . All in vain! . . . He was dead set on
disaster . . . Ferdinand knows that too! . . . I've
wasted my life . . . I've lost everything for that jack-in-
the-box . . . that unbelievable scoundrel! My position,
my career! my profession, my friends! . . . Everything!
my parents! . . . Nobody wanted to see us anymore . . .
except a bunch of cutthroats! A gang of crazy hoodlums
. . . escaped from the bughouse . . . I ruined my health
. . . First my operation . . . And I've aged twenty years
in the last six months . . . Before that I never had anything wrong with me . . . I didn't know what a cold was
. . . I could digest anything . . . I had a stomach like an
ostrich . . . But what with one disaster after another
. . . That's all he ever brought home . . . And there was
never an end to it . . . We'd hardly finished one . . .
Whoops! . . . He'd dream up another . . . loonier than
the last . . . It undermined my resistance . . . That's
not hard to understand . . . I was operated, it was bound
to happen . . . They warned me at Péan's: 'Don't keep
on with that kind of life, Madame des Pereires . . . it'll
turn out very badly . . . Take it easy! Take care of yourself! . . . Avoid worry! . . .' Ah, go shit in your hat! It
got worse from year to year! Never a moment's peace . . .
Nothing but lawsuits, summonses . . . Green papers
. . . yellow papers . . . Creditors at every door! . . .
Persecuted! . . . That's the life I've had . . . Persecuted
day and night! Exactly! Hunted like a criminal! For his

sake . . . always for him! . . . Who could bear up
under that? . . . I haven't had a good night's sleep in
twenty years . . . if you want to know . . . That's the
honest truth . . . Everything's been taken away from me
. . . My sleep, my appetite, my savings . . . I've got
such flashes I can't stand up . . . I can't take a bus
anymore . . . I'm sick to my stomach right away . . .
Any time I try to hurry, even on foot, I see stars . . .
And now they tell me I'm the murderer . . . That's the
prize package! . . . My advice to you is to think it over
before you say such things . . ."

She led them out under the arch, the four cops and the
sergeant . . . She went up to the body . . . she lifted
the pants leg . . .

"You see those socks? . . . Take a good look . . .
Well, he's got the only pair . . . There's not another in
the house . . . The rest of us haven't got any . . .
Never did . . . Neither Ferdinand nor the kids . . ."
She hiked up her own pants to show the cops . . ."I'm
barefoot myself . . . Go on, see for yourself . . . We
always went without just for him . . . for him and nobody else . . . He took everything . . . We gave him
everything we had . . He had everything . . . Always
did! . . . Two houses . . . a magazine . . . at the Palais-Royal! . . . motors . . . thousands of gadgets and
infernal majugguses . . . God knows how much they cost
. . . the skin off your ass . . . The whole works . . .
just to satisfy his whims . . . I can't even begin to tell
you . . . I never crossed him . . . Don't worry, that's
not why he bumped himself off . . . He was spoiled!
. . . He was rotten! . . . That's right . . . rotten! . . .
You want electrical jiggers? . . . All right, son, here you
are . . . You think we should go to the country? . . .
OK, we'll go . . . You want some more potatoes? . . .
Sure, go right ahead . . . It never stopped . . . Never
a moment's doubt . . . it was cut-and-dried . . . His
highness couldn't wait . . . Wouldn't you want the moon
by any chance? . . . Splendid, my love, you'll have it
. . . Always more fancy ideas . . . new crazes! . . .
You couldn't be more indulgent with a six-month-old baby
. . . He had everything he wanted . . . before he could
even open his mouth! Ah, that was my weakness . . .

Well, I've got my punishment . . . Ah, if I'd only known
. . . if I'd known what you people were going to say
. . . Believe me, I'd never have brought him back . . .
I don't know how the kid felt about it . . . But as far as
I'm concerned, take it from me, I'd have sooner chucked
him in the ditch! Then you wouldn't come around ma-
ligning me . . . That's where he ought to be . . . The
rotten filthy scum! That's all he deserves! I don't give a
shit about going to prison . . . It's all one to me . . .
I won't be worse off than anywhere else . . . But Christ
almighty Jesus, no! Hell, no! I'm not such a sucker . . ."

"That'll do! Come over here . . . You can tell all that
to the judge! First answer my questions . . . We've heard
enough talk . . . You say you don't know the gun he
killed himself with? . . . But you brought it back . . .
And the kid? Had he seen it? . . . He'd rammed it into
his head, eh? That's how you found it, isn't it? The two of
you pulled it out, eh? . . . How did it happen according
to you?"

"Why, I never said that, I never said I didn't know the
gun . . . It was up there over the fireplace . . . We'd
all seen it the whole time . . . Ask the kids . . ."

"Pipe down! I've had enough of your idiotic remarks
. . . Let's get down to brass tacks . . . name and des-
tination . . . First the victim . . . Date, place of birth
. . . What was his name anyway? . . . Courtial? Cour-
tial what? And where was he born? . . . Reputation?
Occupation?"

"His name wasn't Courtial at all," she answered point-
blank . . . "It wasn't even des Pereires . . . or Jean
. . . or Marin . . . He made that name up . . . It was
like everything else . . . One more invention! . . . A
lie . . . what a liar he was! Always! Everywhere! Still!
. . . His name was Léon . . . Léon Charles Punais! . . .
That's his honest-to-God name . . . It's not quite the
same, is it? . . . Like me, my name is Honorine Beaure-
gard, not Irène! . . . That was just another name he
dug up for me . . . He had to change everything . . .
I can prove it . . . I've got the proof all right! . . . I'm
not trying to pull the wool over your eyes. I never go anywhere without it . . . I've got my family booklet . . .
I'll go get it . . . He was born in Ville-d'Avray in 1852

. . . September 24th . . . That was his birthday . . .
I'll go over and get it for you . . . It's in my reticule
. . . Come with me, Ferdinand . . ."

The sergeant was writing it out . . . "Escort the prisoners!" he ordered the two bulls . . . We passed in front
of the wheelbarrow . . . We came back again. "Can we
take it in now?" one of the cops asked . . . he shouted
from under the arch.

"Take what in?"

"The body, sergeant . . . There's people all around
it."

He had to think it over . . .

"OK, bring it in . . . Put it in the kitchen . . ." So
then they took him out of the wheelbarrow . . . They
lifted him very gingerly . . . They carried him in . . .
They laid him down on the tiles . . . But he was still
all crooked . . . He wouldn't unbend . . . The old lady
went down on her knees to look at him up close . . . She
was sobbing hard . . . Her tears flowed in rivers . . .
she caught hold of me with her handcuffs . . . She was
overcome with grief . . . You'd honestly have thought
she'd just noticed there was nothing left of him but hash
. . .

"Oh! Oh! Look, Ferdinand . . ." She forgot the family
booklet . . . she forgot about getting it . . . she just
slumped there . . .

"Oh God, he hasn't any head! . . . He hasn't any
head, Ferdinand! My darling! My darling! Your head!
. . . It's gone . . ." She implored, she dragged herself at
the gendarmes' feet . . . She crawled between their boots
. . . she rolled on the floor . . .

"A placenta! . . . It's a placenta! . . . I know . . .
His head! . . . His poor head! . . . It's a placenta!
. . . Have you seen it, Ferdinand? . . . Do you see?
. . . Look! . . . Oh! Oh! Oh!" she screamed like her
throat had been cut . . .

"Oh! All my life! . . . Oh! . . . All my life! . . .
Oh! Oh! . . . " More and more piercingly.

"I didn't do it, messieurs . . . It's not me, how could
it be? . . . I swear it! . . . I swear it! . . . I gave him
my whole life! . . . To bring him a little happiness! . . .
to make him comfortable . . . He needed me . . . day

and night . . . believe me . . . I'm not lying . . . Tell
them, Ferdinand . . . Tell them if it isn't true . . . All
my sacrifices! . . . He hasn't any head! . . . Oh, why
are you all against me? . . . There's nothing left for him!
. . . Good luck! . . . Good luck! . . . he says . . .
the poor darling . . . good luck! . . . Oh God! You
saw it? . . It was written . . . It was him, wasn't it?
. . . It's written in his writing! It wasn't me! Good luck!
That's him! All by himself! You can tell his handwriting!
Oh! it wasn't me! . . . It's obvious! . . . Isn't it obvious?"

She'd thrown herself full length on the ground . . .
Her whole body hit the packed earth . . . She pressed
close to Courtial . . . She was shivering . . .

"Courtial, I implore you . . . Courtial, speak to me
. . . Tell me, my angel . . . Why did you do it? . . .
Why did you do such an awful thing? . . . Eh? Tell me,
my dumpling, my treasure! . . ." She turned toward the
cops . . .

"It's him! It's him! It's a placenta! . . ." She threw
another fit . . . She started eating her hair . . . she
was bellowing so loud we couldn't hear each other in the
room . . . The snoopers at the window climbed up on
each other's backs . . . She bit right into her handcuffs.
She flailed around on the floor, possessed. The gendarmes
picked her up by main force, they carried her into the
barn . . . She yelled like a stuck pig . . . She clutched
the door . . . She fell . . . she charged back against it
. . . "I want to see him . . . I want to see him!" she
screamed . . . "Let me see him! . . . They want to
take him away! . . . Murderers! . . . Help, help! My
angel! My angel! . . . Not you, Ferdinand! Not you! . . .
You're not my angel! . . . I want to see him! . . . Have
pity! . . . I want to see him! . . ." This went on for
an hour. They had to go back and take off the handcuffs
. . . Then she calmed down a little . . . They didn't
take mine off . . . though I promised to behave.

In the afternoon another cop came out on a bicycle . . .
He'd been sent specially from Persant . . . He told the
sergeant again that we mustn't touch anything . . . that
the prosecutor was coming . . . and not the inspector

. . . Those were the orders from above . . . He also told us to get the kids' stuff ready, they'd all be leaving next day, first thing in the morning . . . They were expected in Versailles at a juvenile welfare home, the S.P.C.C. . . . Those were the orders . . . By ten A.M. there wasn't to be one kid left on the premises . . . Two special people were coming from Beauvais to get them . . . to take them to the station . . .

We passed the orders on to the brats who were out in the yard . . . after all, we had to let them know that the jig was up . . . dead and buried . . . They didn't exactly get it . . . They tried to figure out what was going on, where they were being taken . . . They wondered if the whole thing wasn't a gag . . . I tried to explain that our show was over . . . the record was busted . . . they didn't get it . . . I told them the judge had sent orders to close up shop . . . and send the "New Race" home . . . that they were closing down our "wave" farm too . . . they were good and sick of it . . . that they were a lot of savages . . . perfectly ruthless . . . that it was finished . . . that they were looking for their parents . . . and this time they'd find them . . .

It was all Greek to them . . . They weren't used to being treated like kids anymore . . . They were too emancipated . . . They'd forgotten about obedience and those kind of things . . . It wasn't much trouble collecting their duds . . . Actually they had nothing but their bones and their pants . . . They had a few "bent" shoes that were never the right size. Half the time they only wore one . . . Mostly they went barefoot . . . All the same they managed to collect a whole pile of junk . . . thousands of nails, hooks, bird traps, slings, ends of string, nooses . . . shears, spiral springs, whole sets of graters, razor blades fastened to long sticks . . . two complete jimmies . . . Only Dudule had nothing . . . He worked with his fingers . . . The kids thought they were being taken someplace where their equipment would come in handy . . . They didn't realize . . . though I'd told them a dozen times . . . They didn't take the whole thing very seriously . . . though they'd seen the old man with his face blown off . . . They could hear the old lady wailing behind the door . . . But that didn't frighten them . . .

"If you ask me," said Dudule, "I betcha we'll be back on Thursday!"

"You don't know them, kid," I said . . . "And for Christ's sake don't pull any rough stuff . . . They'll lock you up for life . . . They got terrible sweatboxes . . . Watch your step, behave . . . Keep your traps shut, the whole lot of you . . ." Even Mésange thought she was smart: "Aw go on, Ferdinand! That's a lot of hooey! They're sending us away so we won't see the funeral . . . It's the bunk . . . We'll be back on Sunday . . . when it's all over . . ." I'd have asked nothing better . . . They packed all their little odds and ends . . . There was an argument about dividing up . . . They all wanted the rubber bands . . . the big thick ones . . . They could peg a sparrow every time . . . They took lots of wire . . . pretty near two rolls . . . It was plenty heavy . . . But hell, there was still a whole trunkful in the shed . . .

The two lady social workers turned up earlier than we expected . . . Kind of like nuns . . . No coifs, but high-necked gray dresses, both exactly the same, and fingerless gloves . . . and funny voices, too soft and very insistent . . . It wasn't dark yet . . .

"So here we are, my dear children . . ." said the skinnier of the two. "We'll have to hurry a little . . . I hope you'll all be very well behaved . . . We'll have a lovely trip together . . ." They lined them up two by two . . . But Dudule was all by himself in front . . . It was certainly the first time they'd ever been put in order . . . They asked them all their names . . .

"And now we mustn't talk any more . . . We're all good little children . . . And what's your name, my dear?"

"Mésange Sweetiepie . . ." It was perfectly true that the others called her that. They were still nine in all . . . five boys, four girls. Dudule left us his mutt . . . They didn't want him in Versailles . . . All of a sudden they all broke ranks . . . They'd forgotten the old lady . . . She was still in her barn . . . They ran over and kissed her good-bye . . . Naturally they cried some . . . It wasn't a very cheerful leave-taking . . . considering the circumstances . . . Mésange cried the most . . .

"Good-bye, Ferdinand . . . Good-bye . . . See you soon," they shouted back from the other end of the yard . . . The ladies rounded them up again . . .

"My goodness, children, goodness me . . . Come along, little girls . . ." Their last cries came to me from way down the road . . . "So long, pal . . . so long . . ."

Balls! Balls! I knew the score . . . Getting older is a crummy trick . . . Kids are like years, you never see them again. We locked up Dudule's dog with the old bag. The two of them cried together. He yammered the hardest. That day, honestly, take it from me, was one of the rottenest in my whole life. Balls!

Once the kids were gone, the sergeant settled down in the kitchen with his men. They saw I was perfectly quiet, they took off my handcuffs . . . The body was next door . . . There wasn't anything to do, because we had to wait for the prosecutor, who was coming next day . . . There'd be a "preliminary investigation," they said. The bulls talked it over . . . Anyway, they'd stopped bawling us out . . . And besides they were hungry . . . They looked through the cupboards . . . for food . . . They felt like gargling too. . . But there wasn't a drop of wine . . . We lit the fire . . . It was raining into the fireplace . . . It was bitter cold again. February is the littlest month but the meanest too . . . The first part of the winter hadn't been so bad . . . but now it was getting even . . . The bulls were talking it all over . . . they were peasants deep down . . . They clumped all over in their boots . . . I looked at their mugs up close . . . They were smoking their pipes . . . they were sitting around our table . . . There was plenty of time to look them over . . . They had a thick layer of blubber from their eyes down. Their cheeks were completely armored . . . and they had rolls of fat all around their necks up to their ears . . . They were all beef and pretty thick in the middle, especially one that was twice the size of the others . . . They wouldn't be easy to fill . . . Their two-pronged hats were piled up in a pyramid in the middle of the table . . . Their boots were the real seven-league

kind . . . steamboats . . . When all five of them stood
up and dragged their sabers around, you can't imagine the
clatter . . . But they were getting thirstier and thirstier
. . . They went and got some cider from the old folks at
the end of the village . . . Later, maybe about eight
o'clock, another bull showed up . . . he'd come from
their barracks . . . He'd brought some wine and a bite
to eat . . . five mess cans . . . We still had some coffee.
I said we could make them some if they'd let us grind it.
They were willing. The old lady came out of her barn.
They opened up for her. Her fit of rage had passed . . .
It was mighty hard on those giants having no more than
that to eat . . . a little mess can apiece . . . and one
bread ration for all five . . . The old girl, I knew, still
had some bacon tucked away . . . And some lentils in
a special hiding place of her own, and some turnips, and
maybe half a pound of margarine . . .

"I could make you some soup," she said . . . "now
the kids are gone . . . Maybe I can feed the lot of you
. . ." They were delighted . . . They slapped their thighs
. . . But she started sniveling again . . . We had a big
kettle . . . it held at least fifteen mess cans . . . Some
more wine arrived . . . all the way from Persant . . .
The sergeant's wife sent a kid out with it with a letter and
a newspaper . . . We sat down with them . . . Naturally we took our share . . . We hadn't had a bite to
eat in twenty-four hours . . . The gendarmes asked for
seconds . . . We emptied the whole kettle . . . First
they only talked among themselves . . . Gradually they
livened up . . . They shoveled it in . . . They unbuttoned without ceremony . . . One of the five . . . not
the sergeant, one that was all bald . . . seemed more
curious than the rest . . . He asked the old lady what
line of business the deceased had been in before taking
up farming . . . He was interested . . . She tried to
answer, but she didn't do very well . . . She gagged on
every word . . . She broke into sobs . . . She blew her
nose in her plate . . . She sneezed into the pepper . . .
In the end they were all laughing . . . Besides, the soup
took the skin off your tongue . . . she'd had a heavy
hand with the seasoning . . . Whew! Hoo! Oof! . . .
The room was hot too . . . The fire was drawing fine

. . . When the wind was right, it was enough to burn the house down . . . but when it changed, it blew back into the room . . . You suffocated in the smoke . . . It's always like that in the country . . .

At the end of the bench the sergeant couldn't take the heat anymore . . . He peeled off his tunic . . . The others followed suit . . . The big shots from the courthouse couldn't get there until morning . . . so there was nothing to worry about . . . They all wondered why the inspector had backed down . . . That question really got them excited . . . And especially why the prosecutor was coming in person! . . . And why in such a hurry? . . . There must have been some tangle between the prosecutor's office and the police . . . That was the conclusion they came to . . . If they were locking horns, we were sure to get it in the neck . . . that's what I was thinking. The sergeant, little by little, started eating again . . . All by himself he wolfed down pretty near a whole Camembert . . . enormous slabs of bread . . . washed down with the red stuff . . . A mouthful . . . a drink . . . A mouthful . . . another drink . . . I watched him . . . he winked at me . . . He was kind of sozzled . . . He got real friendly . . . He asked the old bag, not at all brutally, without the least malice, what her Courtial had done before they came to Blême . . . She heard him all wrong . . . she was all befuddled from crying. "Rheumatism" was her answer . . . she was way off . . . She started bugling again . . . Her tears got the best of her . . . She begged him, implored him, to let her stay in the kitchen . . . next door . . . just a little while . . . to sit with the body . . . until midnight for instance . . . We were all out of oil and kerosene . . . there was nothing but candles, but plenty of those . . . The kids swiped them all over the place, every time they went out . . . whenever they dropped into a farm. They'd brought back every known caliber . . . there were plenty to choose from . . . The old lady wanted to light two . . . The sergeant was sick of her yapping . . .

"Go on, go on . . . But come back quick . . . right away . . . And don't set the place on fire . . . And don't touch the old man, eh? . . . or I'll lock you up in the barn again . . . For good!"

She went out . . . A minute later when she didn't
come back, one of the gendarmes got up to go see . . .
"What in hell's she doing? . . ." they wondered . . . I
went with him . . . She was down on her knees, bent
over the body . . .

"Can't I cover him? . . ." "Nothing doing!" the bull
said. "It's not that he scares me . . . But you're going
to have to wrap him up . . . They can't take him away
like this . . . I won't move him, I promise you . . . I
don't need to touch him . . . I'd only like to put a cloth
around him . . . That's all . . . A cloth under him and
over his head . . ."

I wondered what she was meaning to use . . . Sheets?
. . . We hadn't any . . . We'd never had any in Blême
. . . We had blankets, but they were rags . . . completely rotted away . . . We hadn't been using them in
a long time . . . we slept in our clothes . . . They were
all falling apart . . . The gendarme wanted no part of it
. . . He told her to ask the sergeant for permission herself . . . But the sergeant was asleep . . . He'd collapsed on the table . . . We could see him through the
door . . . The other yokels were playing cards . . .

"Wait, I'll go," he said finally . . . "Don't touch him
before I get back . . ." But she couldn't wait . . .

"Ferdinand, you go. Hurry up, son. Go look in my tick
. . . you know . . . in the slit where I put the straw in
. . . Stick your arm in at the foot end and rummage
around . . . you'll find the big piece . . . you know . . .
out of the *Archimedes* . . . the red one . . . bright red
. . . It's big enough . . . It'll be big enough . . . It'll
go all around him . . . Go get it quick . . . I'll be right
here . . . Hurry up, quick!"

It was perfectly true . . . I found it right away . . .
It stank of rubber . . . It was the piece she'd saved from
under the ruins the night of the disaster . . . She un-
folded it in front of me . . . she spread it out on the
ground . . . It was still good canvas . . . only the color
had changed . . . It wasn't scarlet anymore . . . it had
turned all brown. She wouldn't let me help her to roll
Courtial up in it . . . She did it all by herself . . . She
was careful not to move him . . . She slipped the cloth
all flat under the corpse . . . very gently I've got to admit

. . . She had all the yardage she needed to wrap him up completely . . . And the hash where the head was, was all closed in too . . . The sergeant watched us . . . The other one had woken him up . . . So then he yelled through the door . . . "Say, you hiding him again? . . . Are you off your rocker?"

"Oh, don't scold me, sir . . . don't scold me, I beg of you . . . I've done my best . . ." She turned toward him on her knees. "I haven't done any harm! Come and see! I haven't done any harm! Come and see for yourself! He's still there . . . Believe me . . . believe me . . . I beg of you, Mr. Engineer . . ." she started calling him that all of a sudden, Mr. Engineer . . . She was screaming again . . .

"He went up, Mr. Engineer . . . You people didn't see him . . . Naturally you don't believe me . . . But Ferdinand saw him . . . Didn't you, Ferdinand? . . . How beautifully he went up! . . . You remember, son? . . . Tell him . . . They don't believe me . . . Mercy! Sweet Jesus! I'm going to say a prayer! Ferdinand! Mr. Engineer! Holy Mary! Mary! Lamb of heaven! Pray for us! Ferdinand! I conjure you! Tell the gentlemen! will you? . . . Come and pray! Come quick! Come here! It's the truth, isn't it? . . . In the name of the Father! the Son! and the Holy Ghost! . . . You know that one, don't you, Ferdinand? . . . You know your prayers? . . ."

She was horrified . . . Her eyes gaped white . . . "You don't know it? . . . Sure you know it . . . Forgive us our trespasses . . . Come along! Together! There! As I'll forgive you . . . Come! As I forgive you! . . . Say it after me, dammit . . . you little punk! . . ."

At this she gives me a big clout . . . The cops next door were in stitches.

"Oh, so you do know it . . . after all . . . He went up, Mr. Engineer, he went up . . . it was marvelous . . . He went up to six thousand feet . . . I went up with him wherever he went . . . Yes . . . I went up . . . You can trust me . . . It's the honest truth . . . I swear . . . I swear it . . ." She tried crossing herself . . . She couldn't make it . . . she got tangled up in her rags . . .

"In the hydrogen! In the hydrogen, dear sirs . . . You can ask anybody . . . I'm not lying . . ." She prostrated herself beside the body, she threw herself square on top of it . . . She pleaded . . .

"My poor darling! . . . My poor love! . . . They won't believe you anymore. Oh! . . . It's too awful . . . They won't believe you . . . I don't know how to tell them . . . I don't know what to do . . . I don't know how he went up . . . I don't know how far . . . I'm a hateful woman . . . It's all my fault! . . . It's my fault, Mr. Engineer . . . Oh yes, yes! . . . I did it all! . . . I did nothing but harm! He went up two hundred times . . . a hundred times! . . . I can't remember, my love! . . . Two hundred! . . . Six! . . . Six hundred times . . . I don't know . . . I don't know anything anymore . . . It's terrible . . . Mr. Engineer! . . . Three hundred! . . . More! . . . Much more! . . . I don't know! . . ." She threw her arms around him in the balloon cover . . . she clutched him convulsively . . . "Courtial! Courtial! I've forgotten everything! . . ." She clutched her throat . . . She started in on her head again, tearing out her hair by handfuls, rolling on the ground . . . She ransacked her memory . . .

"Three thousand! . . . Ten thousand! . . . Jesus! . . . Ferdinand! Can't you say anything? . . . It's too much! . . . Holy fucking God! . . ." She lost herself in figures again . . .

"Lieutenants! . . . Ferdinand! . . . Lieutenants!" That's what she was calling them now . . . "In heaven's name! Ah! I've got it! . . ." She raised herself on her elbows . . . "Two hundred and twenty-two times! . . . Yes, that's it . . . Two hundred and twenty-two . . ." She fell back again. "Nuts! I've forgotten everything! . . . My life! My life! . . ." The bulls had to pick her up . . . They took her back to the barn . . . They closed the door on her. All alone like that, she gradually resigned herself . . . she even fell asleep . . . Later on I went in to see her with the gendarmes. She started talking to us perfectly reasonably. She wasn't off her nut at all anymore.

We waited all morning . . . The old lady was still in the straw . . . She was sound asleep . . . Around noon they arrived from the prosecutor's office . . . The examining magistrate, a little fat guy all bundled up in his fur

coat, lisped in the steaming air, he had coughing spells
. . . He got out of his carriage with another character, a
redhead. This one had a cap all pulled down over his eyes.
He was the medical examiner. The gendarmes recognized
him right away.

It was really bitter cold . . . They were chilled to the
bone . . . They'd come from Persant station . . .

"Bring them here!" he ordered the gendarmes the minute
he set foot on the ground . . . "Bring them to me in the
big room! . . . Both of them! The woman and the little
shitass! We'll take a look at the body later! . . . Nobody's moved it? . . . Where'd you put it? . . . And
bring me the exhibits! . . . What was there? . . . A
gun? . . . And the witnesses! . . . Were there any witnesses? . . ."

A few minutes later two more carriages drove up . . .
One was full of cops, plainclothesmen . . . and the other,
a big covered van, was pack-jammed with reporters . . .
Right away they took millions of snapshots . . . every
aspect of the farm . . . the interior . . . the surroundings . . . Those newspapermen were pests, a damn sight
worse than the hicks . . . And so active . . . They absolutely insisted . . . they went into hysterics . . . on
taking a flashlight picture of my mug . . . and then the
old lady from every angle . . . She had no way of hiding
. . . She was forced to stay right between the two bulls
. . . But we couldn't move much, the crowd was too
thick . . . the prosecutor was madder than a hornet! He
was being stepped on . . . He ordered the cops to clear
the room . . . They didn't waste any time . . . They
sent the mob flying . . . The premises were cleared right
away . . . the whole yard too . . .

The character with the lisp was shivering in his furs.
He was in a hurry to get it all over with, that was plain
. . . He was sore at the cops . . . His clerk was looking for a pen, he'd broken his own . . . The Lisp wasn't
comfortable on the bench . . . The room was too big
and damp, the fire was out . . . He beat his hands together . . . He took his gloves off to blow on them. He
sucked his fingers . . . His nose was all amethyst . . .
He put his gloves back on . . . He wriggled his ass . . .
He stamped his feet . . . He couldn't get warm . . .

The papers were all in front of him . . . He blew on them, they flew away . . . The clerk went chasing after them . . . They didn't write anything at all . . . He wanted to see the gun. He said to the newspapermen: "Take my picture with this weapon while you're at it . . ." He said to the sergeant: "Tell me the whole story!" So then the big cocksucker didn't talk big like with us . . . In fact he stammered . . . Actually he didn't know much . . . I saw that right away . . . He went out with the magistrate . . . They paced up and down the whole length of the yard . . . When they were through gassing, they came back inside . . . The Lisp sat down . . . Then it was my turn to talk . . . I told them the whole story right away . . . all I knew, that is . . . He didn't listen much: "What's your name? . . ." I told him "Ferdinand, born in Courbevoie." "Your age? . . ." I told him. "And what do your parents do?" I told him that too . . . "Good," he said . . . "Stay right where you are . . . And you? . . ." It was the old lady's turn . . .

"Tell me your story and make it fast . . ." He'd stood up . . . He couldn't sit still . . . He piddled up and down . . . He couldn't feel his dogs . . . Stamping didn't help . . . An earth floor is cold as hell . . . especially ours, it was so damp . . .

"Oh, Doctor! My feet! . . . Don't they ever make a fire around here? . . ." We were all out of wood . . . The gendarmes had burned every last stick . . . He cut the old lady short . . .

"Hell! I thee you don't know very much . . . Never mind! Never mind! We'll thee about all that later . . . Beauvais will be thoon enough . . . OK, OK leth get out of here! . . . Doctor, you've had a good look at the body? . . . What thay? . . . Well, what do you think? . . . What thay?" The two of them left the room to take another look . . . In the kitchen next door they talked it over . . . They were maybe ten minutes . . . They came back . . .

"Well, then," said the Lisp. . . "You, the wife . . . Madame Courtial . . . No . . . Des Pereires . . . No? . . . Nuts! . . . You're free for the present. But you'll have to come to Beauvais . . . My clerk will let you know . . . I'll send for the body tomorrow . . ." Turning toward the reporters: "You can call it suicide until further notice. After the autopsy we'll see . . . Maybe you'll be perfectly free . . . Anyway, we'll see . . . You, Bozo!" That was me . . . "You can go . . . You can leave . . . Go straight home . . . to your parents . . . Give the clerk your address . . . I'll send for you if I need you . . . OK, let's go! Sergeant, you will leave one of your men here . . . Only one . . . until the ambulance gets here . . . Let's go . . . Make it quick, clerk . . . Let's get going . . . Finished, the fourth estate? All reporters will please leave . . . Nobody can stay but the family and the officer . . . OK men, that'll do it for the night . . . You won't allow anybody to enter . . . to touch anything . . . to leave . . . Have I made myself clear? . . . You've all got it? . . . Good . . . Let's get going! . . . Quick . . . Step on it! All aboard, Doctor . . ."

He was still stamping his feet . . . He was bouncing up and down in front of his carriage . . . He couldn't stand it a minute longer . . . He was frozen stiff in spite of his overcoat and the sheepskin that went all the way up to his eyebrows . . . to his derby . . . As he set foot on the step:

"Driver! Driver! Listen here! You'll make it fast, won't you? And stop at Cerdance, at the little bar on the left . . . after the grade crossing . . . you know the place I mean? . . . Oh, Doctor, I've never had such shivers in all my life . . . I'm going to be laid up for a month . . . again, like all last winter . . . My! What wouldn't I give for a grog! . . . Christ, they've murdered me in this dump . . . Did you ever see such an icebox? . . . It's the limit . . . It's better outside . . . It's unbelievable . . . Ah! Never fear, the stiff will keep! . . ."

As they were starting, he stuck his head out again from under the big top . . . He took in the whole farm . . . The gendarmes at attention . . . "Whip 'em up, driver!" They drove off in a hurricane, heading for Persant . . . The bulls, the clerk, the plainclothesmen didn't let the grass grow . . . They beat it too about five minutes later . . . The reporters came back . . . They took some more pictures . . . They'd been around, they knew the score . . . They were nobody's fools . . . They knew all the dodges . . .

"Hell," they told me, "don't worry . . . Anybody can see you had nothing to do with it . . . It's all a lot of red tape . . . dumb routine . . . window dressing . . . Don't mind them . . . They won't hold you half a minute . . . they've got to go through the motions . . . that's all." The old girl was glum all the same . . .

"We know those characters . . . It's not the first time we've seen this guy on the job . . . If he had any real suspicions, he'd have hung around longer . . . Besides, he'd have arrested you sure as shit . . . Oh, no, he wouldn't have hesitated. We know him. One shred of presumption and hoop-la, he throws you in the clink! That's for sure! . . . Doubt is that boy's middle name . . He's got his feet on the ground . . . He's a shrewd article . . . You can't mess with him!"

"Then, my dear sirs, you're quite sure he won't come back? . . . that it wasn't just the cold drove him away?"

"The cold doesn't scare him! . . . You've got nothing to worry about . . . Hell, no, it's all a lot of moonshine . . . hocus-pocus . . . Baloney . . . If I were you, I'd relax . . . He came out here for beans, that's all . . . So what? So he's sore!" They were all of the same opinion . . .

They got back in their carriage . . . They were talking about women already . . . They had to push off slowly . . . The axles were creaking hard . . . There were too many of them, all in a pile . . . Two of the reporters had made the trip all the way from Paris just on our account . . . They were sorry they'd come . . . The old lady pestered them so bad with questions, in the end they started bellowing in chorus:

> There ain't no crime . . . bingo bing!
> There ain't no crime . . . bingo bing.

Thumping their heels like to crack the floor . . . Actually they were having a fine time. They sang dirty songs . . . As they drove off, they were singing the one about the bishop who went up in a balloon:

High in the sky as he sailed around,
The skin of his balls dragged on the ground . . .

The gendarme who'd stayed there on guard found
another shanty in the village, completely empty, near the
watering trough, where he could put his horse inside. He
liked that better . . . Our stable was a wreck . . . all
the rain came in . . . and the drafts whistled like an
organ . . . His plug wasn't happy in there . . . She
staggered . . . her legs were folding with the cold . . .
So he moved her . . . And then he came back . . .
maybe an hour before suppertime . . . He had something to tell us . . .

"See here, you two jokers, can you keep your shirt on
awhile? I've got to go to Tousne . . ." That was a village pretty far away on the other side of Berlot Forest
. . . "I've got to get some oats . . . There's none left
in my saddlebags . . . My sister-in-law's over there, she's
got the tobacco store . . . Maybe I'll stay for supper . . .
I'll be back a little later . . . But no later than ten . . .
So don't get smart, you two . . . I haven't a grain of
oats . . . While I'm at it, I'll take the nag . . . She's
lost a shoe . . . I'll stop in at the blacksmith's . . . Then
I can ride back . . . that'll be quicker . . . You understand? . . . You won't let anybody in? . . ." We understood perfectly . . . He was bored out there with us
. . . He thought he'd take a little time off . . . We
wished him a fair wind . . . He passed in front of the
farm, leading his plug by the bridle . . . I saw him disappearing in the distance . . . It was getting dark . . .

The old lady and I lay low . . . We waited for it to
be really dark to go out for wood . . . Then I made it
quick . . . I pulled three slats at once off the fence . . .
I broke them up into kindling . . . but naturally they
smoked . . . they were too damp . . . I went back in
with the old lady . . . I was glad we had a chance to
get warm . . . We needed it . . . But we had to keep
our eyes closed . . . it stung too bad . . . She had
calmed down after her session . . . But she was still kind
of worried . . .

"Do you think it's true? . . ." she asked me. "You
think the cops won't bother us anymore? You don't think

they've got some trick up their sleeves? . . . You heard
the way they suspected me? . . . all of them! . . . The
very first thing . . . you saw them . . . Weren't they
disgusting? . . . Oh my oh my!"

"Who? The cops?"

"That's right, the cops."

"Oh, the sergeant's nothing but a big yokel! . . . The
way he lost his tongue, bzing, in front of the persecutors!
. . . in two seconds flat . . . He dropped out . . . He
didn't know what had hit him . . . He hadn't a word to
say for himself . . . The sap, what'd you expect him to
talk about? . . . he hadn't seen a thing . . . The reporters said the same thing . . . you heard them . . .
They'd have noticed . . . they know the ropes . . .
They'd certainly have warned us . . . They don't like
that guy with the lisp . . . All they had was presumptions
. . . hot air . . . They wouldn't have farted out of here
so fast if they'd thought they had anything on us . . .
Hell no . . . Those bulls would still be here, it's perfectly obvious . . . and then some! . . . You heard
him, the Lisp himself, on his way out . . . what he said
to the others: 'It's suicide.' That's all. Don't go looking
for complications . . . The doctor said so too . . . I
heard him telling the little guy: 'It was fired upward, my
friend, upward . . .' That was clear enough . . . he
wasn't spoofing . . . That's all there is to it . . . No use
looking for trouble . . . We got plenty . . ."

"Yes, I guess you're right," she very softly. But she
wasn't convinced . . . She wasn't very confident . . .

"How are they going to bury him? . . . First they do
the autopsy, don't they? And then what? And what for
anyway? . . . Do you know? . . . Are they still looking for something? . . ."

"I couldn't tell you . . ."

"While they're about it, I wish they could take him back
to Montretout . . . But it's too far now . . . if they
take him to Beauvais . . . Is that where the funeral
will be? . . . I'd have liked to have services . . . I'll
ask them . . . Do you think they'll be willing? . . ."
That was something else I didn't know . . .

"I wonder what a little service would cost in Beauvais
. . . only in a chapel . . . the cheapest class for in-

stance . . . It can't cost more than anywhere else . . .
He wasn't religious, you know, but even so . . . They've
tortured him enough. A little respect wouldn't hurt . . .
What are they going to do to him now? . . . Can't they
see well enough as it is? . . . He hasn't anything in his
body, the poor man . . . It's all in his head, isn't it? . . .
Anybody can see that . . . Oh, it's so awful! . . ." She
started wailing again.

"Ah, Ferdinand, my little friend . . . When I think
that they could think such a thing . . . Oh well, while
they were at it, they couldn't use kid gloves, could they?
. . . Oh, it's all the same to me . . . now . . . But
what about you? . . . Do you think it's finished? . . .
With you it's not the same . . . You've got to make your
way . . . you've got your whole life ahead of you . . .
It's not the same . . . You had nothing to do with all this
. . . Goodness, no . . . They ought to leave you alone
. . . Are you coming to Beauvais with me? . . ."

"I'd go . . . if I could . . . But I can't. There's nothing for me to do in Beauvais . . . Remember what the
Lisp said . . . 'You'll go back to your parents.' He said
it twice . . ."

"Well, in that case no monkey business . . . Go, my
boy, go. What'll you do when you get there? . . . Look
around for something? . . ."

"Naturally . . ."

"I'll have to look too . . . that is . . . if they let me
go . . . Ah, Ferdinand . . . while it's on my mind . . ."
She had an inspiration . . . "Come over here . . . I
want to show you something . . ." She takes me to the
kitchen . . . She climbs up on the stepladder . . . the
little one . . . she disappears up the chimney to the waist,
she pokes around in one of the niches . . . She dislodges
the big brick . . . A lot of soot comes down . . . She
shakes another stone, it moves, it jiggles . . . she takes it
out . . . From the hole she takes some bills . . . and
even some change . . . I hadn't known about that hiding
place . . . And Courtial hadn't either, that was a safe
bet . . . There were a hundred and fifty smackers and
a few five-franc pieces . . . Right away she gives me a
fifty-franc bill . . . She kept the rest . . .

"I'll take the hundred francs and the change . . . All

right? . . . That'll cover my trip at least . . . and maybe
my expenses at the church . . . if I'm there five, six days
. . . It can't take any longer than that, can it? . . .
that'll be plenty, don't you think? . . . But what about
you? You've still got your addresses? . . . Do you remember all your bosses? . . ."

"I'll go see the printer right away," I said. "I'd rather
start in that direction . . ."

She rummaged in the hole some more, she took out another twenty-franc piece, she gave it to me . . . Then
she talked some more about Courtial . . . but she wasn't
so excited anymore . . .

"Ah, my little Ferdinand, you know . . . The more I
think of it . . . the more it comes back to me . . . how
fond he was of you . . . He didn't show it, that's a fact
. . . You know that too . . . It wasn't his way . . .
his nature . . . he wasn't demonstrative . . . he wasn't
a flatterer . . . You know that . . . But he was always
thinking of you . . . In the worst situations he often told
me so . . . Only a week ago . . . 'You know, Irène, Ferdinand is somebody I've got faith in . . . He'll never do
us dirt . . . He's young . . . He's scatterbrained . . .
But there's a kid that's as good as his word . . . He'll
keep a promise . . . And that, Irène, that's rare . . .'
I can still hear him saying that . . . Ah, he appreciated
you all right . . . He was sincerer than a friend . . .
Take it from me . . . And the poor man, believe me, he
had plenty to be distrustful about . . . He'd seen a thing
or two . . . and how he'd been deceived . . . In thousands of ways, one more disgraceful than the last . . . He
could have been embittered . . . Never did he say an
unfavorable word about you . . . Never the least un-
pleasantness . . . Nothing but compliments . . . He'd
have liked to spoil you . . . But as he said one time when
we were having a little chat . . . 'Wait just a little while
. . . Patience . . . I'll make that kid's fortune yet . . .'
Ah, how well he understood you . . . You can't imagine
how fond he was of you . . ."

"Me too, madame, me too . . ."

"I know, Ferdinand, I know . . . But with you it's not
the same . . . You're still a kid luckily . . . Nothing is
so sad at your age . . . Now you'll be starting out in

life . . . You're only beginning . . . You can't understand . . ."

"He loved you too," I said . . . "He often told me . . . how terribly fond he was of you . . . that he couldn't do without you . . . without you he didn't exist . . . 'Take my wife,' he'd say . . ." I laid it on pretty thick . . . I was trying to console her . . . I did my best . . . So then she gushes like a fountain . . .

"Don't cry, madame! Don't cry . . . This is no time . . . You've got to harden yourself . . . You're not through yet . . . You'll have to talk . . . when you get to Beauvais . . . maybe you'll have to defend yourself! It gets on their nerves when you cry . . . You've noticed . . . I'll have to look out for myself too. You said so yourself . . ."

"Yes, you're right, Ferdinand . . . Boo hoo! You're right . . . I'm stupid . . . I'm nothing but an old crazy-woman . . ." She tried to control herself . . . she wiped her eyes . . .

"But he was really fond of you . . . Ah, believe me, Ferdinand . . . I'm not saying it to flatter you . . . You knew that, didn't you? . . . He knew what a good heart you had deep down . . . even if he was hard sometimes . . . even if he was a little hard on us . . ."

"Oh yes! I knew, madame . . ."

"And now that he's killed himself . . . It's so awful! Can you imagine? . . . I can't believe it . . . It's incredible . . ." She couldn't tear herself away from the terrible thought . . .

"Ferdinand," she started up again . . . "Ferdinand, listen . . ." She tried to find the exact right words . . . they wouldn't come . . . "Ah, yes . . . He trusted you, Ferdinand . . . and I trust you . . . And you know . . . he didn't believe in anybody anymore . . ."

Our wood wasn't burning at all . . . It smoked up the whole room . . . It popped, it flew up in the air . . . it was going out . . . I tell the old lady . . . "I'm going to get some more that'll burn." I start for the barn . . . maybe I'd find a dry faggot . . . I could rip out a piece of the wall . . . the inside wall . . . I start across the yard . . . I turn to one side to pass around the well, I look across the plain . . . I see something moving . . .

looked like a man! . . . "It can't be the gendarme," I
says to myself . . . "He wouldn't be back so soon . . .
It's some tramp . . . Some guy prowling around . . .
Well," I say, "if he's looking for trouble . . . Hey," I
shouted, "hey there . . . What are you looking for around
here?" He doesn't answer . . . He disappears . . . So
right there I turned back, I didn't even go so far as the
barn . . . I had a feeling something fishy was going on.
"Hell and damnation!" I says to myself. "Beat it, kid
. . ." Quick I tear off a hunk of fence . . . "That'll do,"
I says to myself . . . I run over . . . I go in . . . I
ask the old bag:

"You haven't seen anybody?"

"No," she says . . . "No."

At that very moment, in the windowpane, not two yards
away . . . I see a face staring at me . . . a great big
face . . . I see the hat too . . . through the glass . . .
and the lips moving . . . But I can't hear the words . . .
I move up with the candle, I throw the window wide open
. . . That was brave of me! . . . I recognize him right
away . . . Christ, if it isn't our canon . . . Fleury! . . .
It's him all right . . . the nut! Him and nobody else . . .
Shit! . . . How'd he get here? Where on earth did he
come from? He starts spluttering . . . He sprays me with
spit . . . He gesticulates like mad . . . He seems beside
himself with joy to have found us . . . his friends! . . .
his brothers! . . . He steps through the little window
. . . There he is inside . . . He's jubilant . . . He
prances . . . He wiggle-waggles all around the table . . .
The old lady didn't remember his phizz, or his name, or the
circumstances . . . A little lapse of memory . . .

"It's Fleury . . . Look, it's Fleury! . . . The one
with the diving bell? Don't you remember? Take a good
look . . ."

"Ah, my goodness, it's true! . . . Why, yes, yes, it's
him . . . Oh, Father! . . . oh, forgive me . . . Ah! So
you've heard? Ah, why of course it's you . . . Oh, I'm
going out of my mind! Ah, I didn't recognize you . . .
You haven't heard the awful thing?"

It took more than that to stop him . . . He kept on
prancing . . . hopping . . . skipping . . . He didn't pay attention . . . He did a big leap and then some little jumps

. . . he jerked backward . . . He jumped up on the
table . . . He wiggled around some more . . . He jumped
down, bam! . . . His cassock was all caked and armored
with muck and cowflop . . . up to the armpits . . . up
to the ears . . . Sure, it was him I'd seen out in the field
just now . . . We'd both scared each other . . . My,
was he harnessed! . . . Some load he had on his back
. . . A whole soldier's outfit . . . two musette bags! two
canteens! three mess kits! and on top a hunting horn . . .
an enormous magnificent thing, slung over his shoulder
. . . The whole business clanked every time he moved
. . . and he never stopped moving . . . What bothered
him most was his hat . . . it slid down over his eyes
. . . a big straw affair like a fisherman . . . And the
guy had decorated himself too . . . admirably . . . his
whole soutane was full of orders and medals . . . and
several Legions of Honor . . . They were all caked with
muck, and a big heavy crucifix, an ivory Jesus, dangling
on a long chain . . . He was so wet, this fine canon of
ours, he dripped all over the room . . . He was a walking
watering can . . . His soutane was ripped from top to
bottom in back . . . You could still see the briars . . .

The old lady tried to make him stop moving . . . She
wanted to convince him . . . She just had to! . . . I
motioned her not to work him up . . . maybe he'd leave
of his own accord . . . no use getting him excited . . .
But she didn't want to understand . . . She was glad to
see him again. She crowded him into corners . . . which
made him growl like a wild animal . . . He backed
plunk against the wall with his head down, ready to
charge . . . He didn't listen to her . . . He pressed his
fingers to his mouth . . . "Sh-sh" he went . . . He
darted looks in all directions, and they weren't very
friendly . . . This bozo was on the lam . . .

"Didn't you know, Monsieur le Chanoine? . . . I see
you don't know . . . Oh, if you could only have seen
. . . Oh, if you knew what's happened! . . ."

"Hush, hush! . . . Monsieur des Pereires!" Now he
was asking for him . . . "Where is he? Where's Monsieur des Pereires? . . ." He grabbed her by the shoulders,
he snorted into her face . . . A tic convulsed his whole

mouth . . . It stayed twisted . . . Then in little spasms
he relaxed . . .

"I haven't got him, Father . . . Oh no . . . I haven't
got him! . . . You really don't know? . . . The poor
man's not here . . . He's gone, poor soul . . . Come,
come . . . Didn't they tell you? . . ."

"Hurry! . . . Hurry!" He shook her violently.

"But gracious, he's dead . . . He's passed away . . .
Haven't I told you? . . ." She'd met up with somebody
that was even more pigheaded than she was . . .

"I want to see him . . . I've got to see him . . ." He
had this obsession and he wouldn't let go . . . "It's
urgent! . . . Sh-sh . . . Sh! Hurry, hurry . . ." He tiptoed around the table . . . He looked on top and underneath, he looked up the chimney . . . He opened both
cupboards . . . He tore out the keys . . . He battered
the wood box . . . he broke off the hinges . . . He was
frantic . . . He couldn't stand being crossed . . . His
tic made his whole lip curl . . .

"Father! . . . Father! . . . Don't do that! . . ." She
kept trying to convince him . . .

"Ferdinand! I implore you! Tell Father Fleury. . .
Isn't he dead, boy? . . . Tell him! . . ." She latched
on to his musette bag . . .

"Go look on the door, it's written there . . . Tell him
if it's not true, Ferdinand . . . 'Good luck' . . ." She
grabbed him by the hunting horn . . . He dragged the
whole place after him . . . The old bag, the table, the
chairs, the dishes . . .

"Enough! Enough of your insolence! . . . You're insolent whelps, the whole lot of you! . . . I want the director! . . . *Genitron* Courtial! . . . Can't you hear me?
. . . Him and nobody else! . . . Heavens! He's expecting me! . . . He wants to see me immediately! . . . We
have an appointment! . . . an appointment! . . ." He
threw her off in his rage . . . She went careening into the
wall . . .

"Enough! Enough! I want to talk to him! . . . You
can't stop me . . . Who's going to stop me? . . ." He
hiked up his soutane . . . He rummaged through his
pockets . . . He took out little scraps of paper . . .
crumbs, newspaper clippings . . . He stayed like that on

his knees in feverish confusion for a long time . . . He
spluttered, he counted the papers one by one . . . he
smoothed them out . . . he flattened them . . . He rolled
some of them into little spitballs . . .

"Hush! Hush!" he started in again. He didn't want us
to move. "There it is . . . It's authentic! What? Haven't
you any eyes in your head? . . . It's a genuine Pharaoh
manuscript! . . . This here! . . ." He hands me a pinch
of it . . .

"There you are, my boy . . ." He pressed a spitball
. . . two spitballs . . . into the hollow of my hand . . .
"The director! The director! . . ."

Hell, there he goes again . . . his fury was mounting
. . . He reared up . . . he jumped back on the table
. . . he shouted for Courtial at the top of his lungs . . .
He put the hunting horn to his lips . . . He blew one big
blast and several raucous farts . . . and then a few
squeaks and short hiccups . . .

"He's coming . . . He hears me . . ." Ten times,
twenty times in succession . . . He grabs me by the coat,
he slobbers in my face, he blows in my eyes . . . Christ,
does he stink! . . . In gusts he tells me how he'd got
there . . . He'd got off at Vry-Controvert, the whistle-
stop on the narrow-gauge line, twelve miles from Blême
. . . "They" were after him . . . He pesters the life out
of me, trying to prove it . . .

"Hush, hush," he says again . . . "The Powers! . . .
Yes indeed!" He goes back to the window . . . He looks
out to see if they're coming . . . He hides behind the
shutter, growling . . . He bounces out again . . . He
scans the approaches . . . He pisses in the fireplace . . .
He doesn't button his pants . . . He comes back to the
blind . . . He must have seen the Powers . . . He mulls
. . . He grunts like a wild boar . . .

"Grrr! Grrr!" he goes . . . "Never! . . . Grrr! Grrr!
. . . Never! . . ." He turns on me . . . He shakes his
fists in my face . . . He's certainly changed since the
Palais-Royal! . . . How ferocious he's gotten to be! . . .
They must have given him scorpions to eat . . . in the
nuthouse . . . Hell! He's wild! . . . He's been drinking
vitriol! . . . He never stops! . . . He lunges in all directions . . . He bangs into the walls . . . He threatens

. . . he challenges . . . The old lady and I have given up trying to say anything . . . We're licked . . . That loony padre is beginning to give me a pain . . . I wouldn't mind laying him out with a clout from behind . . . I catch sight of a nifty pole beside the window . . . We use it as a poker . . . with a big long tip and a nice cast-iron handle . . . That would settle his hash . . . We'd have another crime on our hands . . . I motion the old lady to get out of the way . . . just for a second . . . to stand against the wall . . . Shit! . . . If only he'd shut up . . . so I wouldn't have to lay hands on him . . . Christ, what a rotten cocksucker! . . . What an ugly stupid bastard! Why can't the stinker pipe down? . . . Why can't the screwball leave us alone? . . . He won't believe us . . . He thinks we're hiding him . . . Hell, this is infernal . . . I tell the old lady:

"It can't be helped . . . This has gone too far! I'm fed up . . . I'm going to show him . . ."

"Don't, Ferdinand! . . . Don't do it . . . I beg you . . ."

"Oh yes, I will . . . Maybe that'll straighten him out . . . Maybe he'll understand . . . The damn fool has this bee in his bonnet . . . He's screwy . . . he's bats . . . Then we'll throw him out . . ." He was still thrashing around, knocking into everything . . . He lifted up the whole table . . . and take it from me, that table was a monument . . . That Hottentot was strong! . . .

"The director! The director!" he started bellowing again . . . "I've given all I had . . ." He went down on his knees again, he kissed his crucifix . . . He crossed himself a thousand times . . . He stayed there in an ecstasy . . . his arms stretched out on both sides . . . He made a crucifix of himself . . . And then up like a spring . . . And off again on tiptoes . . . his eyes fixed on the ceiling . . . He started up again with the applesauce . . .

She tugged at me, she didn't want me to show him the stiff in the kitchen . . . She made motions . . . "No, no!" This malarky had been going on long enough . . . I had it up to here . . .

"Come this way . . ." I grabbed him by the hunting horn . . . and bam . . . I dragged him to the kitchen

. . . Ah, the stinker . . . he won't believe us . . .
Well, he's going to get an eyeful . . . All nuts are the
same . . . They thrive on opposition . . . "Let's go!
Come on, you lug!" I give him a kick in the ass . . .
That makes him bounce . . . It's his turn to say uncle
. . . I can get mean too . . . He gripes . . . he grum-
bles . . . I push him down the hallway . . .

"Upsy-daisy! . . . Take the candle, madame, take two
. . . Let him have a good look . . . an eyeful . . . We
don't want him coming back for seconds . . ." When we
get to the kitchen, I go down on my knees . . . and a
little lower . . . I show him the body in the balloon cover
right under his nose . . . It's right there in front of him
. . . I put the other candle down beside it . . .

"There you are . . . can you see all right? . . . What
do you say now, you dumb cluck? . . . You going to stop
wasting our time? . . . Is it him all right? . . . You recognize him? . . . You don't? . . ." He comes close . . .
he sniffs . . . he's suspicious . . . He blows all up and
down the legs . . . He lowers his head . . . He says a
prayer . . . He goes on and on . . . Then he turns
around . . . He looks at me some more . . . He starts
praying again . . .

"Well? Did you get a good look? . . . D'you finally
catch on, you jerk? . . . You going to behave? . . .
You going to beat it like a good boy? . . . You going to
shove off and take your train? . . ." But he kept right on
grunting and sniffing at the corpse . . . So I grab him by
the arm . . . I try to take him away . . . I try to make
him get up . . . He goes into one of his tantrums . . .
He gives me a terrible poke with his elbow . . . right
square in the knee . . . Ah, the bum! Say, that hurts
. . . I see stars . . . For two cents I'd have brained him
then and there . . . the crazy bastard . . . I'd have
wiped him out . . . The old lady kept at it though . . .
She appealed to his kind heart . . . to his good intentions
. . . She tried to smooth him down . . .

"You see, Father, you can see he's dead . . . You're
making all of us miserable . . . That's all you're doing
. . . He's gone, poor man . . . The gendarme forbade
us . . . He told us not to let anybody in . . . We promised him! You're going to get us in trouble . . . both of

us, Ferdinand and me . . . What good will that do? . . .
You wouldn't want that, would you? . . ."

At this point I says to myself: "Balls! If he won't believe
us, I'll show him the head . . . If he thinks we're hiding
him . . . And then I'll throw him out quick . . ." So I
lift up a corner of the cover . . . I bring the candle still
closer . . . I show him the whole mulligatawny . . .
"Take a good look! . . ." so he can really see what's
what . . . He kneels down for a close-up . . . I try
again:

"OK, you old souse? You coming? . . ." I tug at him
. . . He doesn't want to move . . . He's adamant . . .
He doesn't want to leave . . . He sniffs full in the meat
. . . "Hm! Hm!" He starts howling! He works himself up
. . . He throws another fit . . . His whole body is shaking . . . I try to cover the head up again . . . "That'll
do! . . ." But he pulls at the canvas . . . He's in a
frenzy . . . stark raving mad! . . . He won't let me
cover him . . . He sticks his fingers into the wound . . .
He plunges both hands into the meat . . . he digs into
all the holes . . . He tears away the soft edges . . . He
pokes around . . . He gets stuck . . . His wrist is
caught in the bones . . . Crack! . . . He tugs . . . He
struggles like in a trap . . . Some kind of pouch bursts
. . . The juice pours out . . . it gushes all over the place
. . . all full of brains and blood . . . splashing . . . He
manages to get his hand out . . . I get the sauce full in
the face . . . I can't see a thing . . . I flail around . . .
The candle's out . . . He's still yelling . . . I've got to
stop him! . . . I can't see him . . . I lose my head . . .
I lunge at him . . . by dead reckoning . . . I hit him
square . . . The stinker goes over . . . he crashes
against the wall . . . smash! boom! . . . I've got my
momentum . . . I'm coming after him . . . but I
straighten out . . . I brake, I get away from him . . .
I'm very careful . . . Hell! . . . I don't want him conking out on account of me . . . I wipe my eyes . . . I
keep my presence of mind . . . I try to get him up . . .
I don't want him lying on the floor . . . I give him a good
kick in the ribs . . . He lifts up a little . . . That's better! . . . I give him a good smack in the puss . . . That
gets him all the way up . . . the old lady empties a whole

basin of water . . . it was plenty cold . . . over his
dome . . . He starts sighing and whimpering again . . .
Isn't that lovely! . . . But then he folds up all in a piece
. . . The rotten stinker! . . . Bam! . . . He collapses
. . . He quivers like a rabbit . . . then he stops moving
completely . . . The louse! . . . He can't take it . . . I
give a look out the door . . . Then the two of us tote him
out to the side of the road . . . We didn't want to have
him around and get blamed for him too . . . Hell no!
. . . Have the cop find him in the house . . . out like a
light . . . completely at our mercy! . . . Wouldn't that
be sweet! . . . We'd be cooked to a crisp! . . . They
mustn't even know we've had him in the house . . . What
people don't know won't hurt 'em . . . We're no suckers
. . . OK . . . out with him . . . hurrah for the fresh
air . . . unconscious or not! . . . He started grunting a
little after all . . . He sniffed around in the muck . . .
The rain was coming down in buckets . . . We ran back
in . . . We bolted the door . . . The wind was coming
in blasts . . . I says to the old lady:

"We're not going to move . . . even if he calls . . .
We don't hear a thing . . . When the cop comes back, we
play it dumb . . . We haven't seen a damn thing . . . If
he bumps into him, that's his business . . ." OK. She
caught on . . . So that was that . . .

Maybe an hour goes by . . . Maybe a little more . . .
I fix up the kitchen . . . The old lady keeps a watch at
the window . . .

"Don't look over here, madame! . . . Don't turn
around . . . Don't worry about the housecleaning . . .
Watch what's going on outside . . ." I stretch out the
corpse . . . I tidy up the straw . . . Rivers of blood
were coming through the canvas . . . I get a little more
hay . . . I scatter it around . . . I mop up the puddles
as best I can . . . I put some fresh straw under the head
. . . a good thickness like a pillow . . . But the hardest
part was the splashes . . . There were spots all the way
up to the ceiling . . . And whole blood clots sticking to
the wall . . . It really looked lousy . . . I tried to rinse
it all off . . . I ran the sponge over it again . . . But the
marks got worse each time . . . Hell, I couldn't stay
there all night . . . I take the candles . . . I leave the

room . . . We wait next door, the old lady and me . . .
Boy, the jitters I had! . . . It was terrible . . . They
kept coming back at me . . . Suppose this cop should
notice? . . . Suppose he got wind of that brawl! . . .
What a mess! . . . How were we going to wriggle out of
that one? . . . Especially if he found the sky pilot out
cold on the road . . . New evidence! . . . Hell! . . .
The lousy cop didn't come and he didn't come . . . He
must have screwed his sister-in-law for dessert . . . Some
nerve! . . . We lay down on the ground . . . We'd
thrown down some hay too . . . I didn't talk . . . I was
thinking . . . The night would never be over . . . I
could never have fallen asleep in the state I was in . . .
I don't think I'd ever been so scared . . . Suddenly I
hear a fanfare . . . Christ almighty Jesus! . . . There
we go! . . . It's the hunting horn! . . . And it came
from the plain . . . from nearby! I says to myself: "It's
him! . . . Oh, the louse!" I recognized every squeak. He
starts up again, an encore! . . . Oh, the stinker! . . .
Oh, the rotten skunk! . . . He drowned out the wind
. . . he drowned out the roar of the gale with his raucous
trumpet . . . Christ! Enough was enough! He blew with
all his heart and soul! . . . Some porpoise he turned out
to be! . . . Imagine a priest being such a whack! . . .
Christ, what a racket! Oh, that bum! That dirty dog! That
pain in the ass! . . . I made up my mind . . . But then
hell's bells, no! Better he should be gargling, horrible as it
was . . . It showed he'd recovered . . . He seemed to be
happy . . . It proved he hadn't conked out . . . Lord,
what a monster! "Bellow away, queen of the cows!" And
there he goes again with his damn trombone! His wind
was doing fine . . . Not a thing wrong with him! . . .
Tally-ho! Tally-ho! Oh, my bleeding ass! Ta-ta-ta, he's
sure giving us our money's worth! . . . It was better than
kicking off though . . . Hell, you got to admit that! But
those belches, that brass bellyache was horrible all the
same . . . The master of the hunt was making some pest
of himself out there with his sewer pipe . . . He never
stopped . . . He'd subside for half a second and right
away he'd start up again . . . Louder and louder . . .
Oh, you couldn't go wrong . . . It was our screwball all
right . . . His concert went on until half past six at least

. . . The day was breaking when somebody tapped on the window . . . It was our cop! . . . He'd just got back . . . in the nick of time . . . He'd slept in Blême, supposedly . . . in with his horse, so he said . . . He couldn't get him shod in Tousnes . . . it had been too late . . . he hadn't found the blacksmith's place . . .

"Say, who was playing the horn around here all night? . . ." he asked us right away . . . "You didn't hear anything? . . ."

"No!" we said. "The horn? . . . Oh no . . . Certainly not, we didn't hear a thing."

"That's funny . . . The old folks told me . . ."

He went and opened the window . . . The priest was right out in front . . . He jumped in like a goat . . . He'd been waiting for the chance . . . He flopped down on his knees in the middle of the room . . . He started in "Our Father which art in heaven . . . Thy Kingdom come! . . ." He said it again . . . He kept repeating it like a phonograph . . . He hammered his ribs with both fists . . . He was trembling all over . . . He bounced around on his shins . . . He took a lot of punishment . . . He didn't stop for a second . . . He grimaced with pain . . . he was playing the martyr . . . "Thy Kingdom come! . . ." he shouted at the top of his lungs . . . "Thy Kingdom come! . . ."

"Say, what is this? . . . Say, what is this?" The gendarme hadn't ever seen such a number, he was flummoxed . . . "Ah, it's a party! . . ." He didn't know what to think . . . It threw him for several loops . . . The old lady was busy in the kitchen, she was heating up coffee for us . . . It didn't seem like the right time . . . Our supplicant St. Anthony broke off his prayers when he saw the mud coming in . . . He made a dive for a cup . . . He tried to drink out of all the bowls . . . He was very active! He sucked the spout of the coffeepot . . . He burned his mouth . . . He puffed like a locomotive . . . The cop was in stitches . . . "My goodness, the man must be crazy . . . Why, he's not normal! . . . that's a sure thing . . . Not that I give a damn . . . It's no skin off my ass . . . Nuts aren't in my line of duty . . . They're no business of mine . . . That's for the Public Welfare department . . . But I don't think he's a priest

. . . He don't look it . . . Where'd he come from? . . .
Escaped from the nuthouse? . . . Or maybe he's been to
a ball? . . . Isn't he drunk? . . . Maybe it's a disguise
. . . Anyway, it's not my line . . . But supposing he's a
deserter! . . . That would be my line . . . I'd have to
look into it . . . But hell, he's overage . . . Say, Pop,
how old are you? . . . You won't tell me? . . ." The
shady character didn't say a word . . . He was draining
the bottoms of the cups . . .

"Say, isn't he clever? He can even drink with his nose!
Hey, Pop . . . Say, ain't that horn pretty? . . . Say,
that's a handsome instrument . . . Say, I wonder where
he came from . . ."

Later that morning a whole army of sightseers descended on our village . . . I wondered where they could
all have come from . . . In that deserted region it was
really a mystery . . . From Persant? There'd never been
so many people there . . . or in Mesloirs either . . . So
they came from much farther . . . from other counties
. . . other districts . . . The crowd was so dense they
overflowed onto our garden . . . They were packed so
tight the road wouldn't hold them all . . . They stamped
through the fields, both embankments caved in under the
weight of the populace . . . They wanted to see everything at once . . . they wanted to know everything and
knock everything over . . . The rain was splashing down
. . . That didn't bother them in the least . . . They hung
around, all plastered with cowflop . . . In the end they
invaded our yard . . . They gave off a raucous rumble . . .

In the front row, right against our windows, there was a
whole slew of grandmothers . . . What a sight! They
fastened on to the shutters, there were maybe at least fifty
of them . . . They croaked louder than anybody else
. . . They fought among themselves with umbrellas . . .

At last the promised ambulance turned up . . . It was
the very first time they'd risked it out of town . . . The
driver tipped us off . . . The big hospital in Beauvais had
just acquired it . . . Some breakdowns he'd had . . .
Three punctures in a row . . . two leaks in the gas line
. . . Now he'd have to hurry to be back before nightfall

. . . We slipped out the stretcher, each of us took a
shaft . . . There wasn't a second to be lost . . . The
driver had another worry too . . . that his motor would
stall . . . He couldn't stop . . . not for a minute! . . .
not for a second! . . . He had to keep it running even
when the car was standing still . . . But that was dangerous too on account of the little flames that shot out when
it backfired . . . We went in for Courtial . . . The mob
rushed the doorways . . . They pushed so hard . . .
they blocked the arch and the little hallway so thoroughly
that even clouting them, even charging them with the cop,
it was like going through a rolling mill . . . We came
back quick with the stretcher, we slipped the shafts into the
grooves made specially for the purpose . . . it went all
the way back . . . it fitted perfectly . . . We drew the
big curtains . . . black oilcloth . . . That was that . . .
The peasants stopped talking . . . They took off their
caps . . . The women . . . young ones, old ones . . .
crossed themselves like mad . . . standing ankle-deep in
the mud . . . The rain came down in buckets . . . They
mumbled all their prayers . . . Lord, was it raining! . . .
The ambulance driver climbed up on his seat . . . He
retarded the spark . . . Pip! Pop! Tap! Pip! Pop! Tap!
Pip! Pip! Terrible hiccups . . . The engine was wet . . .
It snorted from every cylinder . . . Finally it makes up
its mind . . . It gives a jerk . . . another . . . He
throws in the clutch . . . It moves a little way . . .
When Canon Fleury sees the shebang leaving, he lights out
. . . He does a hundred-yard dash . . . He bounds into
the air . . . He jumps on the mudguard . . . We had to
run after him and pull him off by main force! He fought
like a lion . . . We locked him up in the barn. So far so
good . . . But once the motor had stalled, it didn't want
to start again . . . We all had to push it up the hill . . .
to give it momentum . . . Then the new ambulance
clanks down the slope, coughing and jerking and spluttering . . . almost two miles . . . Some sport! . . . We
went back to the farm . . . We sat down in the kitchen
. . . We waited a while for the people to get bored and
clear out . . . There was nothing more to see, that was a
cinch . . . but they didn't budge . . . The ones without
umbrellas settled down in the yard . . . in the middle

shed . . . they'd brought their lunch. We closed our shutters.

We looked through our stuff, the little we had left, to see if there was anything wearable we could take with us . . . frankly there wasn't much . . . The old lady found a shawl . . . Naturally she still had her pants on, she always dressed like the rest of us. She hadn't a skirt to her name . . . As for food, there was still a bit of rind in the pickling jar . . . enough to make a meal for the mutt . . . We were taking him with us to the station . . . We fed him. Luckily I found a little corduroy jacket in the back of the closet . . . a gamekeeper's rig with horn buttons . . . The kids had swiped it . . . They hadn't told anybody . . .

Plus my overcoat it would help to keep me warm . . . I still had my bicycling pants . . . The underwear department was nonexistent . . . not even a shirt! . . . When it came to shoes . . . mine were still holding out, I'd split them open some because they were too narrow . . . and patched them up with sandals underneath . . . that made them flexible but cold . . . The old lady had slippers stuffed into rubbers . . . she'd have trouble lasting out the trip . . . They kept all the water in . . . She bundled them up in old newspapers and string . . . to make them like real boots, so her feet wouldn't rattle around inside . . . Persant was pretty far . . . And Beauvais was still farther . . . There was no hope of getting a ride . . . We ran a little more coffee through the grounds . . . Then we got together with the cop . . . He was going to escort us . . . He was holding his plug by the bridle that still hadn't been shod . . . The priest wanted to come too . . . I'd rather have ditched him . . . locked him in behind us . . . But he made a terrible racket the minute he thought he was alone . . . So that was no solution . . . Suppose we left him locked up in the house . . . and he wrecked the joint . . . Suppose that screwball escaped and climbed up on the roof . . . And suppose he fell off and broke two or three limbs . . . Well, who'd be on the spot? . . . Who'd they accuse? . . . Us again naturally . . . Who'd get thrown in the clink? . . . We would, beyond any shadow of a doubt . . . So I went and opened the door for him . . . He

threw himself into my arms . . . He loved me madly
. . . But we couldn't find the mutt . . . We wasted at
least an hour looking for him . . . in the shed, in the
barn . . . That fleabite wasn't anywhere . . . Finally he
showed . . . We were ready to go . . .

All those hayseeds waiting outside didn't say a thing
when we left . . . They didn't say boo . . . Not a word
. . . We passed right under their noses . . . The ditches
were full of them . . . Hicks and more hicks . . . So we
shot off down the road . . . Shot isn't exactly the word
. . . we walked pretty gingerly . . . Only the lunatic
ran . . . He gamboled about, this way and that way . . .
The padre was curious about our itinerary . . . "Will we
see Charlemagne?" he asked us in a loud voice . . . He
didn't understand a word of our answers, but he didn't
want to leave us . . . Shaking him was hopeless . . .
Hiking set him up . . . He put his hunting horn to his
lips . . . he blew a little tally-ho . . . And just as we
were getting into town, he raced back and joined the main
body . . . He ran like a zebra . . . We came to the first
houses . . . on the way into Persant . . . with the music
going strong . . . The gendarme turned off to the left
. . . that was the end of his assignment . . . We could
shift for ourselves . . . He wasn't keen on our company
. . . he wasn't going our way . . . We headed for the
station . . . Right away we asked about the trains . . .
The old lady's train for Beauvais was leaving in ten minutes . . . an hour before the one to Paris . . . She'd
have to cross over to the other platform . . . It was time
to say good-bye . . . We didn't say anything much . . .
We didn't make any promises . . . We kissed each
other . . .

"My goodness, Ferdinand, you're prickly . . ." She
meant my beard. That was a joke! . . . She was being
brave . . . That was pretty good in such a rotten situation . . . She didn't know where she was going . . .
Neither did I for that matter . . . We'd been sharing the
bad luck for a long time now . . . This time it had really
laid us out . . . That was pretty well to be expected . . .
There wasn't much more to say . . .

In the station the padre was kind of scared right away
. . . He shriveled up in a corner . . . Only he kept his

eyes fastened on me . . . He just stared at me on the
platform . . . The people around us wondered what on
earth we were up to . . . Especially him and his horn
. . . the old bag in her pants . . . me and my coat done
up with strings . . . They were afraid to come too close
. . . Then the dame at the tobacco counter looked out
and recognized us . . . "It's the nuts from Blême," she
sang out . . . They kind of panicked . . . The Beauvais
train pulled in . . . luckily . . . It made for a diversion
. . . The old honeybun hightailed it . . . she climbed in
on the wrong side . . . She stood in the doorway with
Dudule's little mutt . . . She waved me good-bye . . .
I waved back . . . As the train was pulling out, the distress came over her . . . something awful . . . She
made terrible faces in the window . . . She went rrrah!
rrrah! like her throat was being cut . . . like some kind
of animal . . .

"Ferdinand! Ferdinand!" she hollered across the tracks
. . . over all the racket . . . The train beat it into the tunnel . . . We never saw each other again . . . the old
lady and I . . . I found out much later that she'd died
in Salonika, they told me in the Val-de-Grâce military hospital in 1916. She'd gone out there as a nurse on a troop
transport. She died of some kind of epidemic, I think it
was exanthematic typhus. So the two of us, the canon and
I, were on the other platform, the Paris-bound side.
He still had no idea what we were there for . . . But at
least he'd stopped playing his horn . . . He was only
scared I'd leave him in the lurch . . . As soon as the
train pulled in, he jumped in too, right behind me . . .
He stuck to me all the way to Paris . . . I lost him for a
second on the way out of the station . . . The bastard
caught me right away . . . I lost him again on the rue
Lafayette . . . right across from the drugstore . . . I
took advantage of the crush . . . I jumped into a trolley
in between all the traffic . . . I got out again a little later
. . . on the Boulevard Magenta . . . I wanted to be
alone for a while . . . to think and figure out what I was
going to do . . .

My rig was mighty weird . . . hardly presentable in a
city . . . The people stared at me curiously . . . the
shops and offices were just closing . . . It must have been

a little after seven . . . I was quite a sensation with my
abbreviated raglan . . . I hid in a doorway . . . The
hardest to take was my overcoat . . . all bloused out in
my pants . . . it gave me an amazing shape! . . . And I
couldn't change there . . . Besides, I didn't have a hat
either . . . I had Dudule's little one, a patent-leather Jean-
Bart hat.* I'd worn it out there . . . Here it wouldn't do
. . . I chucked it behind the door . . . There were still
too many people for me to venture out on the sidewalk in
my fancy dress . . . I thought I'd wait for the crowd to
thin out . . . I watched the street go by . . . What
struck me first was the new-type buses without an upper
story, and the new motor taxies . . . There were more of
them than hansom cabs . . . They made a terrible
ruckus . . . I wasn't used to heavy traffic anymore . . .
It made my head spin . . . I was kind of sick to my stomach too. I bought a *croissant* and a bar of chocolate . . .
It was time to eat . . . I put them in my pocket . . .
The air always seems muggy when you get back from the
country . . . It's the wind you miss . . . And then I
began to wonder if I'd go home to the Passage . . . And
would I go directly? . . . Supposing the bulls came looking for me? . . . Maybe the Lisp would send them . . .
   Farther up the Boulevard Magenta I ran into the rue
Lafayette . . . If I took it, it wouldn't be very complicated . . . rue Richelieu, the Stock Exchange . . . I
only had to follow the lights . . . Oh, I knew the way all
right . . . But if I turned right, I'd end up at the Châtelet,
the bird vendors . . . the Quai aux Fleurs, the Odéon
. . . That would take me toward my uncle's . . . Finding a bed someplace wasn't the worst part . . . I could
make up my mind at the last moment . . . But what
about landing a job? . . . That would be rough . . .
How was I going to get a new outfit? . . . I could hear
the music already . . . And whom would I go to see?
. . . I came out of my hiding place . . . But instead of
taking the Boulevard, I turned into a little side street . . .
I stop outside a shopwindow . . . I'm looking at a hard-
boiled egg . . . it's all red . . . I says to myself: "I'll
buy it . . ." I count my money in the light . . . I still
had more than thirty-five francs and I'd paid for my rail-

* See Glossary.

road ticket and the padre's too . . . I peel the egg on the counter, I bite into it . . . I spit it out . . . I couldn't swallow anything . . . Hell, it wouldn't go down . . . Christ, I says to myself, I'm sick . . . I was seasick . . . I go out in the street . . . Everything was swaying . . . the sidewalk . . . the gas lamps . . . the shops . . . And I must have been teetering myself . . . A cop's heading my way . . . I speed up some . . . I cross the street . . . I hide in another doorway . . . I didn't feel like moving anymore . . . I sit down on the doormat . . . I'm feeling a little better . . . I says to myself: "What's the matter, kid? . . . You can't be as lazy as all that? . . . Haven't you got the strength to move? . . ." And still sick to my stomach . . . The street put me in a panic . . . seeing it up ahead of me . . . on the sides . . . on the right and left . . . All those housefronts, so closed, so black. Nuts! so uninviting . . . it was even worse than Blême . . . not even a turnip to nibble on . . . I had the heebiejeebies all over . . . especially in my stomach . . . and my head. I wanted to vomit . . . Damn! I couldn't move at all! I was stuck to the housefront . . . With my back to the wall like that . . . no kidding . . . I had a good chance to remember . . . how the poor old lady had knocked herself out keeping us all body and soul together . . . You can hardly imagine . . . Hell, now I was all alone . . . Honorine was gone . . . Balls! . . . She was a good old battle-ax . . . she had guts . . . she'd really struggled for us . . . We were all fucked now . . . I was sure I'd never see her again . . . Positive . . . It hit me all of a sudden . . . it made me feel awful . . . I was sick to my stomach again . . . I found another doormat . . . I threw up in the gutter . . . The passersby were noticing . . . I had to beat it . . . Anyway I had to move on . . .

I stopped again at the end of the rue Saint-Denis . . . I couldn't go any further, I found a niche where I couldn't be seen at all . . . I felt better once I was sitting down . . . it was walking that turned my stomach . . . When I began to feel dizzy, I looked up in the air . . . It relieved my nausea to look up . . . The sky was very clear . . . I think I've never seen it so plainly . . . I was astonished that evening to see it so cloudless . . . I recog-

nized all the stars . . . Well, pretty near all of them . . .
I knew all the names . . . The old clown had pestered me
enough with his trajectory orbits . . . Funny how I'd re-
membered them . . . I hadn't made much of an effort,
I've got to admit. Caniope and Andromeda . . . they
were right there on the rue Saint-Denis . . . right over
the roof across the street . . . A little further right the
Waggoner, that kind of blinks in the direction of Libra
. . . I knew them all right . . . It's a little harder to get
Ophiuchus straight . . . You could easily mistake it for
Mercury except for the asteroid . . . That's a neat trick
. . . But you pretty near always get the Cradle and
Berenice mixed up . . . Pelleas is a hard one to pick out
. . . That night you couldn't miss it . . . That was Pel-
leas to a T . . . north of Bacchus . . . a nearsighted ape
could have found it . . . Even the "great nebula of
Orion" was clear as day . . . between the Triangle and
Ariadne . . . You couldn't go wrong . . . A unique,
exceptional opportunity . . . in Blême we'd only seen
Orion once all year . . . And we'd looked for it every
night . . . Kid Spyglass would have been mighty glad of
the chance to observe it so distinctly . . . he was always
going on about it . . . He'd published a guide about the
"Asteroidal References" . . . there was even a whole
chapter about the nebula of Antiope . . . It was really a
surprise to be seeing it in Paris . . . where the sky is
famous for being so smutty and opaque . . . I could
hear Courtial raving about it . . . I could hear him gassing away beside me on a bench . . .

"You see, my boy, the one that trembles? . . . that's
not even a planet . . . it's a fake . . . It's not even a
point of reference, not even an asteroid . . . It's nothing
but a vagabond . . . see what I mean? . . . So watch
your step . . . A vagabond . . . Wait another two million years, maybe then it will give off a profuse light . . .
Maybe then you'll be able to get a picture . . . Right
now it's a phony and you'll ruin your whole plate . . .
That's all the good it'll do you . . . And those vaporids
are deceptive, my boy . . . It's not even a periodic
comet . . . Don't let them fool you, Antonio . . . The
stars are a lot of floozies . . . Look before you leap!
. . . They're no little white elves . . . Watch your dy-

nameter . . . A quarter of a second's exposure! . . .
A quarter tenth and your film is shot! Oh, they're fierce
. . . they're incorrigible . . . Watch your step, Lolita
. . . They don't give plates away at the Flea Market . . .
Not by a long shot, my dear bishop . . ." I could hear
all the old blarney . . . "Once you've looked at a thing,
you ought to remember it forever . . . Don't force your
intelligence . . . it's reason that gums everything up . . .
Give your instinct a chance . . . Once it gets a good look,
the game is won . . . It'll never deceive you . . ." My
reason had taken a powder . . . all I had left was blotting paper in my legs . . . I kept on walking though . . .
And then I found another bench . . . I crumpled against
the back . . . It wasn't exactly warm anymore . . . it
seemed to me that the old boy was there on the other end,
turning his back to me. I was seeing things . . . I shot the
shit in his place . . . his exact own words . . . I wanted
to hear him talk . . . to remember everything he'd said
. . . He was in front of me on the pavement . . . "Ferdinand! Ferdinand! Ingenuity is man! . . . Don't waste
yourself on low thoughts . . ." He told me all his fairy
tales, and I remembered them all together . . . I was
talking out loud . . . The people stopped to listen . . .
They must have thought I was drunk . . . So then I shut
my trap . . . But it stirred me up just the same . . . my
dome was all full of it . . . Those memories really had a
hold on me . . . I couldn't believe the old clothespin was
dead . . . And yet I could see him with his head all
marmalade . . . the meat still twitching . . . and messing all over the road . . . Hell! And the farm at the bottom of the hill! . . . and that Arton bitch and her kid!
. . . and the trowel! . . . and the wheelbarrow! . . .
and me and the old lady wheeling him down the road . . .
Ah, the bastard! He wouldn't let go! He went bouncing
through my memory . . . I thought of all those things
. . . the Insurrection bar . . . Formerly . . . the *commissaire* on the rue des Bon-Enfants . . . his cock-eyed
rays . . . And all those putrid potatoes . . . Ah, it was
stinking when you think of it . . . the way that bastard
lied to us . . . And now he was starting in again . . .
He was right there in front of me . . . next to the bench
. . . His meat smell was there . . . My nose was full of

it . . . That's the presence of death for you . . . when
you do their talking for them . . . All of a sudden I
stood up . . . I couldn't stand it . . . I was going to let
out one terrible yell . . . and get myself pinched good
and proper . . . I lifted up my eyes . . . so as not to
see the housefronts . . . They made me too sad . . . I
saw his face too much on the walls . . . behind all the
windowpanes . . . in the darkness . . . Up there Orion-
tes had disappeared . . . I'd lost my landmark in the
clouds . . . But I managed to find Andromeda . . . I
kept looking . . . I looked for Caniope . . . the one
that blinks at the Dipper . . . Naturally I got dizzy . . .
I started walking again anyway . . . I went down the
Grands Boulevards . . . I came back to the Porte Saint-
Martin . . . I was dead on my feet . . . I was zigzagging
. . . I knew it myself . . . I was scared pink of the cops
. . . They thought I was tight too . . . In front of the
clock at the Nègre I went "pst, pst" to a cab . . . He
took me in . . .

"To Uncle Édouard's," I said.

"Uncle Édouard? Where's that?"

"Rue de la Convention . . . 14 . . ." I was bound to
get picked up if I kept wandering around like that . . .
feeling so rotten dizzy . . . It was getting awfully risky
. . . If the cops had questioned me . . . I was all mixed
up in the first place . . . I'd never know what to say . . .
The ride in the cab did me good . . . It really picked me
up a little . . . Uncle Édouard was home . . . He didn't
seem very surprised . . . He was glad to see me . . . I
sit down at his table . . . I take off my coat . . . I only
had the little corduroy jacket under it . . .

"That's some rig!" he remarked . . . He asked me if
I'd had dinner.

"No, I'm not hungry," I said.

"So you've lost your appetite?"

He went right on talking . . . He told me all about
himself . . . He had his troubles . . . He'd just come
back from Belgium, he'd been in a terrible mess . . .
He'd finally unloaded his little "extra-collapsible" pump
on a manufacturing combine . . . the terms weren't so
hot . . . He was damn sick of lawsuits and claims . . .
in connection with the "multiple" and "reversible" patents

. . . He was fed up . . . He didn't go for lawyers and headaches . . . With this little spot of cash he was going to buy some simple straightforward business . . . something in the mechanical line . . . a going concern . . . repairing small cars . . . second-hand jalopies . . . That's always a profitable deal . . . In addition he'd take back his customers' lamps and horns . . . that was down his alley . . . He'd modernize them . . . There's always a demand for little nickel and copper accessories . . . All you've got to do is keep up with the styles . . . You fix them up . . . and then you find a customer good for a three hundred percent profit . . . that's business for you! He wasn't worrying . . . He knew all the tricks . . . If he hadn't quite made up his mind, it was on account of the premises . . . He still wanted to think it over . . . The lease wasn't very clear . . . They were asking plenty for the goodwill . . . He smelled a slight rat . . . They weren't giving the equipment away either . . . He was letting the negotiations drag out . . . He'd learned his lesson . . . He'd almost bought into some kind of company that was building a regular factory for body accessories . . . not a hundred yards from the Porte de Vanves . . . Nothing had come of it . . . They'd been screwing him in the contract . . . At the last moment he'd got cold feet . . . He hadn't trusted his partners . . . And he hadn't been wrong . . . He always stopped to think . . . It was too good to be honest . . . Pretty near forty-seven percent . . . Hell, they had to be bandits . . . He didn't regret it much . . . He'd have been taken sure as shit with those kind of gangsters . . . So anyway he spilled his story . . . he told me everything that had happened in his business from the time we'd gone to Blême to the present moment . . . Then it was my turn . . . I started off very slowly . . . He listened all the way . . .

"My Lord! Well, kid . . . say, that's rough . . ." He was flabbergasted . . . "Say, that's unbelievable . . . Say, it's no wonder you're skinny as a rail . . . Say, you've been through the mill . . . Hell . . . That'll teach you . . . You see, kid . . . that's how it is in the country . . . If you come from Paris, you'd better stay there . . . I've often been offered little agencies, garages and stuff in the sticks . . . It sounds good . . . Selling

bicycles, tires, and so on . . . Your own master . . .
free as the air . . . that's the old oil . . . They never
took me in . . . Never, believe you me . . . All those
country rackets, you got to know what you're doing . . .
You've got to be born to their sticky ways . . . You go
out there to the woods . . . as innocent as the day you were
born . . . Imagine! . . . You're raring to go . . . They
take you the minute you get off the train . . . You're a
sitting duck and no two ways about it . . . Everybody
fleeces you . . . They have the time of their lives . . .
You're sunk . . . Profits? . . . Don't make me laugh!
. . . Not a sou . . . They screw you all along the line
. . . How are you going to stop them? . . . You're lost
before you start . . . You've got to learn their ways with
your mother's milk . . . Then you're all right . . .
Otherwise you're a sucker from the word go . . .
How can you expect to succeed? . . . You don't learn
those things overnight . . . Artichokes aren't invented
. . . You haven't a chance in ten thousand . . . And
hell, the way you went about it! . . . With centrifugal
farming . . . That's a hot one . . . You were looking
for trouble . . . Naturally you got screwed . . . What
would you expect? . . . But say, kid, are you skinny! It's
incredible . . . Do you like tapioca soup? . . ." He rummaged around the kitchen . . . It must have been at least
nine o'clock . . . "You've got to build yourself up . . .
Here you're going to eat, I can promise you that . . .
You're going to put it away . . . No two ways about it
. . ." He took another look at me . . . the cut of my
jacket made him smile a little . . . and my combination
pants . . . with the string seat . . .

"You can't run around in rags . . . I'll go get you a
pair of pants . . . Wait a second . . . I'll find something
. . ." He went to the next room and brought me a whole
suit, out of his closet with the sliding door . . . in perfect
condition . . . and a bearskin coat . . . big and shaggy
. . . "You can wear these for the time being . . ." He
also gave me a cap with flaps and a suit of flannel underwear . . . I was all set up . . .

"So you're not hungry? . . . Not at all?" I couldn't
have eaten a thing . . . I felt sick . . . There was some-

thing mean going on inside me . . . My bowels were all gurgling . . . No kidding, I was in bad shape . . .

"What's the matter, kid? . . ." I was beginning to worry him.

"Nothing . . . nothing at all . . ." I was trying to keep hold of myself.

"Have you caught cold? . . . Say, you must have the grippe . . ."

"Oh no . . . I don't think so," I said . . . "But if you feel like it, Uncle, when you're through eating . . . maybe we could take a little walk . . ."

"You think that would make you feel better?"

"Oh yes, Uncle . . . Yes, I think so . . ."

"Do you feel sick to your stomach?"

"Yes, just a little, Uncle."

"Say, that's a good idea . . . Let's go right away . . . I'll eat later . . . I'm a little like your mother, you know . . . subito, presto, don't put things off!" He didn't finish his supper . . . We strolled, very slowly, to the café on the corner . . . He sat us down on the terrace and ordered mint tea for me . . . He talked about one thing and another . . . I asked him for news . . . Had he seen my parents? . . .

"As I was leaving for Belgium . . . that was two months ago yesterday . . . I dropped in at the Passage . . . I haven't seen them since . . . They were really racking their brains over your letters . . . They studied them word for word . . . They couldn't figure out what had become of you . . . Your mother wanted to go see right away . . . I dissuaded her . . . I told her I had news . . . I said you were getting along fine . . . but you didn't have a minute to spare on account of the sowing . . . Anyway a lot of blarney . . . She postponed her trip . . . Your father was still sick . . . He was absent from the office several days in succession this winter . . . They were both afraid that this time would be it . . . that Lempreinte and the other guy wouldn't wait . . . that they'd fire him . . . But in the end they took him back . . . But they docked him in full for the time of his absence! . . . Imagine! . . . For illness! . . . A company with a capital of a hundred million . . . with real estate all over the place! Isn't it disgraceful? . . .

Isn't it disgusting? . . . Well, that's the whole trouble
. . . The bigger they are, the more they want . . .
They're insatiable . . . They've never got enough . . .
All that dough only makes them crummier . . . Com-
panies are horrible . . . I see it in my own little business
. . . They're bloodsuckers the whole lot of them . . .
they're wild beasts, vampires . . . It's hard to imagine
. . . but it's true . . . That's how people get rich . . .
it's the only way!"

"Yes, Uncle . . ."

"Anybody that gets sick on the job can go to hell!"

"Yes, Uncle . . ."

"It's the final shindig,* son, those are the things you've
got to find out . . . and the sooner the better . . .
Watch out for millionaires . . . And say, I forgot to tell
you . . . There's something new . . . about their ailments . . . Your father refuses to see a doctor anymore
. . . Not even Capron, who wasn't bad . . . and really
not dishonest . . . He didn't force his calls on you . . .
Your mother too . . . she won't have him . . . She just
doctors herself . . . And I assure you she limps . . . I
don't know how she manages . . . Plasters and poultices
the whole time . . . with mustard, without mustard . . .
hot, cold, hot, cold! . . . And she never stops working
. . . And she runs herself ragged . . . She's got to go
looking for customers . . . She's found some new ones
for the new Embroidery House . . . Bulgarian lace they
sell . . . Good God! . . . Your father of course doesn't
know anything about it . . . Her territory is the whole
Right Bank . . . That's a lot of mileage . . . If you
could see her face when she comes home from those treks
. . . Ah, you wouldn't believe it! . . . I'd have taken her
for a corpse . . . She really frightened me the other day
. . . I saw her in the street . . . She was coming home
with her boxes . . . At least forty pounds, I'll bet . . .
Forty pounds, do you hear? . . . Holding it all up . . .
That crap is heavy . . . She didn't even see me . . .
Exhaustion will be the death of her . . . You won't last
long either if you're not more careful . . . Take it from
me . . . In the first place you eat too fast . . . Your

* See Glossary.

parents were always telling you that . . . They were right for once . . ."

All that was perfectly possible . . . But it didn't matter . . . anyway not very much . . . I didn't want to contradict him . . . I didn't want to start an argument . . . What troubled me while he was talking . . . was that I wasn't even listening very well . . . That was on account of my bellyache . . . My guts were all twisted . . . He went on talking . . .

"What are you going to do now? . . . Have you got something in mind? . . . After you've put a little flesh on your bones? . . ." He was kind of worried about my future too . . .

"What I'm saying, son, isn't to hurry you . . . Not at all . . . Take your time before you start applying . . . Get your bearings . . . Don't go for any old thing . . . You'll only be making trouble for yourself . . . Naturally you've got to go looking, but easy does it . . . Watch your step . . . A job is like food . . . It's got to be the right kind . . . Think it over . . . use your judgment . . . Ask me . . . Feel around . . . Look in all directions . . . And don't make up your mind until you're sure . . . Then you'll tell me . . . There's no fire . . . Not yet . . . Don't take any damn thing . . . just to please me . . . No little two-week jobs . . . Nothing doing! . . . You're not a kid anymore . . . No more screwball schemes . . . You'll get hurt in the end . . . You'll get a bad reputation."

We started back toward his place . . . We walked around the Luxembourg * . . . He talked some more about jobs . . . It was on his mind, kind of, trying to figure how I was going to make out . . . Maybe in the bottom of his kind heart he was wondering if I'd ever get over my disastrous instincts . . . my jailbird tendencies . . . I let him bubble a while . . . I didn't know what to say . . . I didn't answer right away . . . I was really too tired and I had a rotten ache in the temples . . . I was only listening with half an ear . . . When we got to the Boulevard Raspail, I couldn't even walk straight . . . I was looping all over the sidewalk . . . He noticed . . . We stopped again . . . I was thinking of something en-

* See Glossary.

tirely different . . . I was resting . . . Uncle Édouard
was driving me crazy with his prospects . . . I looked up
in the sky again . . . "Say, Uncle Édouard, do you know
the Veils of Venus . . . and the Hive of Shooting Stars?
. . . " They were just coming out of the clouds . . . all
that stardust . . . "And Amarine . . . and Proliserpe?"
I'd spotted them one right after the other, the white one
and the pink one . . . "Wouldn't you like me to show
you?" Uncle Édouard had known his constellations in the
old days . . . At one time he'd even known the whole
Great Boreal Zenith . . . from the Triangle to Sagittarius, almost by heart . . . He'd known his whole Flammarion . . . and his Pereires too naturally . . . But he'd
forgotten it all . . . He didn't remember a single one
. . . He couldn't even find Libra!

"Ah, my poor boy, I've lost my eyesight . . . I'll take
your word for it . . . You look at them for me . . . I
can't even read my paper anymore . . . I'm getting so
nearsighted these days I wouldn't know a star if it was two
feet away . . . I wouldn't see the sky if I was right in the
middle of it . . . I'd mistake the sun for the moon . . ."
He was kidding.

"Oh, that doesn't matter," he went on . . . "But you're
mighty smart, it seems to me . . . You're sharp as a
razor . . . Say, you're really getting ahead . . . That's
something . . . You didn't eat much out there . . . but
you sucked up knowledge . . . You're as brainy as they
come . . . You really crammed that big noodle of yours,
didn't you, kid? . . . Say, you're full of science, no fooling . . ." I handed him a laugh . . . We talked some
more about Courtial . . . He wanted to hear about the
end . . . He asked me a few questions . . . Christ! I
couldn't stand hearing him talk about it . . . It threw me
into a tizzy . . . I panicked almost like the day before
. . . I couldn't stop bawling . . . Hell! . . . That
looked lousy . . . It shook my bones . . . And I was
pretty tough . . . It must have been the terrible tiredness . . .

"Come, what's the matter, my poor old-timer? . . .
You're all broken up . . . Come now, don't take it so
hard . . . All that stuff about a job was just to be saying
something . . . I wasn't serious . . . why should you

be? . . . You wouldn't let that kind of flumdiddle throw you . . . You know me well enough . . . Don't you trust your uncle? . . . I wasn't saying that to get rid of you . . . Come along, you big sap, don't you understand! . . . Stop that blubbering and make it quick . . . You look like a little girl . . . OK, kid, you going to stop? . . . A man doesn't cry . . . You can stay as long as you please . . . There, that's better . . . First you're going to get your strength back . . . I want to see you stuffed . . . puffed . . . bloated . . . Nobody'd take you like this, I hope you realize . . . You wouldn't get any-where . . . They're not looking for featherweights . . . They want big bruisers . . . You'll give it to them in the kisser . . . Boom! . . . And down they go! Right, left . . . Bam! . . . Waiter! Yes sir? Bring us an order of biceps . . ." He comforted me as best he could, but I couldn't stop the flow. I was gushing like a fountain.

"I want to go away, Uncle . . . I want to go away . . . far away . . ."

"What do you mean go away? . . . Where? . . . China? . . . What do you mean far? . . ."

"I don't know, Uncle . . . I don't know . . ." It was pouring out worse and worse . . . I stood up . . . I was suffocating . . . But when I was up, I started reel-ing . . . He had to prop me up . . . When we got back to his place, he really didn't know what to do or say . . .

"Well, kid . . . my oh my! . . . Let's forget about all that . . . Let's suppose I haven't said a word . . . It's not your fault, poor kid . . . Come now! You had noth-ing to do with it . . . You know what Courtial was like . . . An extraordinary man . . . A magnificent scientist! . . . I wouldn't deny that for a minute . . . I was always the first to say so . . . And I think he had a good heart . . . But he was an adventurer . . . Extremely bright, that's a fact . . . Extremely capable and what have you . . . He suffered a thousand injustices . . . Good, I'll subscribe to that too . . . But that wasn't the first time he went walking on precipices . . . Ah, he was a glutton for risks . . . He was always on the brink of catastrophe . . . People who play the races in the first place . . . it's because they like to get it in the neck . . . They can't change . . . And you can't stop them

. . . They can't help heading for disaster! . . . Well,
there you have it: they like to take chances . . . All the
same I feel very bad about it . . . Believe me, it touches
me a good deal . . . I admired him . . . I even felt
sincere friendship . . . He was a unique mind . . . Ah,
I know all that . . . he was a man of worth . . . I seem
to be dumb, but I understand . . . Only it's no reason
because he's dead that you should forget about everything
else and waste away . . . Christ almighty! It won't do!
. . . Do you think you can make your living in the state
you're in? . . . You don't ruin your health at your age
because you've run into some trouble . . . You're not
going to brood over it the rest of your life . . . It's not
your last calamity . . . you'll see plenty more . . .
Leave the wailing to the dames, it don't stop their bladders . . . They get a kick out of it . . . But you're a
man and you're an up-and-comer . . . Aren't you an
up-and-comer, sonny boy? . . . You wouldn't want to
drown in your waterworks? . . . Ha-ha! . . . Suppose
it fell in your soup . . . Say, wouldn't that be a scream?
. . ." He gave me a couple of gentle pokes . . . He
tried to make me laugh . . .

"Say, will you look at that weeping willow! . . . That's
how he comes back from the country . . . frazzled . . .
washed-out . . . kerflooey . . . Come along, puppy boy
. . . brace up . . . I won't say another word about your
going away . . . You'll stay with me . . . You won't
take a job anywhere . . . It's settled . . . It's a deal
. . . There, do you feel better now? . . . Say, why not?
. . . I'll take you on in my garage . . . Maybe it's not
the best thing in the world to be apprenticed to your uncle
. . . But hell, what can we do? . . . Health comes first
. . . Who cares what people think? . . . The rest will
take care of itself . . . Health, that's the ticket . . . I'll
train you, OK, little pal? . . . First I want you to put on
some weight . . . Oh, I know, it kills you to go looking
for jobs . . . I could see that when you were back home
. . . It doesn't come easy to you, you haven't the temperament . . . If that's what gives you the willies, nobody's
going to force you . . . You'll stay with me the whole
time . . . You won't ring any more doorbells . . . You
wouldn't be a good salesman . . . Hell no! . . . What

more can I say? . . . You don't like applying for jobs?
. . . Fine! . . . That's what gets you down? . . . OK."

"No, Uncle, it's not exactly that . . . I want to go
away . . ."

"Go away! Go away! Where to? . . . That's eating
you, isn't it, little chickadee? . . . I don't get it! . . .
You want to go back to the sticks? . . . You want to
grow carrots?"

"Oh no, Uncle, not that . . . I'd like to enlist."

"Where'd you get that idea all of a sudden? . . . Say,
that's a corker! . . . Enlist? . . . Where? . . . Why?
. . . There's plenty of time for that, son . . . You'll go
with your age group . . . What's the hurry? . . . The
military vocation, is that it? . . . Say, that's a good one!"
He scrutinized me . . . He found me very odd . . . He
examined me carefully . . .

"That's just a bug, bunny boy . . . Like wanting to
take a leak . . . You get over it the same way . . . You
want to turn out like Courtial? . . . You want to be a
flibbertigibbet? . . . What about your parents? . . .
Have you thought of that? . . . The squawk they'll let
out . . . My oh my, some serenade that will be! . . .
I'll never hear the last of it . . . They'll say it's all my
fault . . . Take it easy . . . they'll say I put funny
ideas in your head . . . that you're as screwy as your
boss . . ."

He wasn't one bit happy about it . . . I wanted to
confess everything . . . right then and there . . . anything at all . . . it didn't matter what . . .

"But Uncle, I don't know how to do anything . . .
I'm no good . . . I'm not sensible . . ."

"Who says you're no good, you big dope . . . I know
you in and out . . . You're perfectly sensible . . ."

I couldn't stop bawling . . .

"No, Uncle, I'm a fraud . . ."

"Not at all . . . not at all, angel child . . . You're a
little sap, that's all . . . I tell you you're OK . . . You
haven't a deceitful hair on your head . . . You're just an
all-around sucker . . . The old scoundrel took you in
. . . can't you see that, little bunny? That's what you
can't stomach? . . . He put one over on you . . ."

"No! No! . . ." I was frantic . . . I didn't want to

hear any explanations. I begged him to listen to me . . .
"I only made everybody unhappy!" I told him over and
over again . . . Oof! And then I was sick to my stomach
. . . And then I talked some more . . . I'd always made
everybody unhappy . . . That was my awful certainty
. . .

"You've really thought it over? . . ."

"Yes, Uncle . . . Yes, honest . . . I've thought it
over . . . I want to go away . . . Tomorrow . . . please
. . . tomorrow . . ."

"Come, come! The house isn't on fire . . . I won't have
it . . . Rest up awhile . . . You can't go away just like
that . . . on the spur of the moment . . . You won't
be signing up for one day . . . it's for three years, friend
. . . A thousand and eighty-five days . . . not to mention
the time you have to make up."

"Yes, Uncle . . ."

"Come, you're not a bad boy . . . Nobody's trying to
get rid of you . . . Nobody's accusing you of anything
. . . You're not so badly off here, are you? . . . I've
never mistreated you, have I?"

"No, it's me, Uncle . . . I'm bad . . . I'm no good
. . . You don't realize, Uncle . . . you just don't realize . . ."

"Here we go again! Why, you're nuts working yourself
up like that, you poor little devil! . . . You're going to
make yourself really sick . . ."

"I can't stand it, Uncle . . . I can't stand it . . . I'm
old enough, Uncle . . . I've got to go away . . . I'll
go tomorrow . . . All right?"

"Not tomorrow, pal! Not tomorrow! Right away! Sure
. . . right away! . . ." He was getting excited . . .
"Christ, how stubborn can you be! . . . You're going to
wait two weeks . . . Or a month for that matter . . .
Two weeks to please me . . . We'll see . . . anyway
they wouldn't take you the way you are now . . . I can
guarantee that in advance . . . You'd scare the medics
. . . First you've got to build yourself up . . . that's
the main thing . . . They'd throw you out like a leper
. . . What's the matter with you? . . . You think they
enlist skeletons? . . . You'll have to put on a few pounds
. . . At least twenty, see . . . I know what I'm say-

ing . . . Twenty for a starter . . . Or else . . . vamoose
. . . You want to go to war? . . . Say, you'd blow away!
. . . Who's sent me this soldier who's as skinny as a
rail? . . . Come on, we'll see about it later . . . Come
along, little matchstick, button up those moans . . . Well,
anyway . . . they won't be bored . . . they'll have a good
laugh at the recruiting station when you come in all skin
and bones . . . And on guard duty! . . . They'll split
a gut . . . Hi, Private Crybaby! . . . Wouldn't you
rather be in the Engineers? . . . What branch are you
going to enlist in anyway? . . . You don't know yet?
. . . Well, you'd better make up your mind . . ."

It was all the same to me.

"I don't know, Uncle . . ."

"You don't know? . . . You never know anything
. . ."

"I like you fine, Uncle . . . But I can't stay . . . I
just can't . . . You're mighty good to me . . . I don't
deserve it, Uncle . . . I don't deserve it . . ."

"Why don't you deserve it? . . . Speak up, you little
dope?"

"I don't know, Uncle . . . I make you unhappy too
. . . I want to go away . . . I want to enlist tomorrow
. . ."

"Oh, all right, then it's settled . . . Shake on it . . .
I agree . . . OK . . . But that still doesn't tell us what
regiment you've picked . . . All I can say is you'd better
hurry . . ." He was making fun of me . . .

"You wouldn't want to join the footsloggers? . . . You
don't favor the Queen of Battles? . . . No? . . . Well,
I can understand that . . . you'd rather not carry anything . . . those sixty-five pounds . . . That doesn't appeal to you, does it, daisy boy? . . . You'd rather be
carried . . . Take cover, dammit . . . You're not in
the mood? . . . Under that manure pile over there on
the left . . . And the parades! . . . Hup hoop hip hore!
. . . And don't you care for our lovely maneuvers? . . .
How about it, my bullyboy? . . . Take advantage of the
terrain! . . . You ought to be good at that . . . You've
seen plenty of terrain . . . you know what it's like . . .
The leeks . . . and all the muck around them . . . How
about it? . . . But you preferred the stars . . . Ah, so

you're changing your mind? . . . It didn't take you very
long . . . Maybe you'd like to be an astronomer? . . .
Good! . . . You'll join the First Telescopes . . . Moon
Regiment . . . No? . . . You don't go for anything I
offer . . . Say, you're hard to please . . . I can see
you'd rather be in Infantry after all . . . Are you
a good hiker? . . . Boy, will you have blisters! . . .
"Them boots are heavy in my pack. Them boots . . ." Or
would you rather have boils on your ass? . . . OK,
make it the cavalry . . . Extended order, that's the stuff
. . . Or how about the mountain boys!* . . .

> There's a drop to drink up yonder,
> There's a drop to drink . . .

He made a bugle with his mouth: "Ta ra ta ta ta! Ta ta
ta . . ."
    "Oh, don't do that, Uncle . . . Don't!" It reminded
me of that character.
    "How sensitive you are, you poor lummox . . . What
would you do in one of those nasty battles? . . . Wait
. . . You haven't really thought it over . . . Stay where
you are . . . You can spare another five minutes . . .
Stay with me a little while longer . . . Maybe two three
weeks . . . until you begin to see what's what . . . Say,
why not a month?"
    "No, Uncle . . . I'd rather go right away . . ."
    "Good Lord, you're just like your mother . . . Once
you get a bee in your bonnet . . . Hell, I'm just about
out of ideas . . . How about the Cuirassiers? . . . A big
fatso like you wouldn't look bad on a horse . . . They
won't even be able to see you under your breastplate . . .
You'll be the regimental ghost . . . Say, a lance couldn't
even hit you . . . Good deal! . . . Say, that's a marvelous idea! . . . But even so you'd have to put on
weight . . . there's not even enough of you for a ghost
. . . You poor lug, you're at least twenty pounds short
. . . And I'm not exaggerating . . . it's still the same
twenty pounds . . . You think that's a better idea? . . ."
    "Yes, Uncle."
_____
* See Glossary.

"I can see you charging . . ." I didn't see a damn
thing . . .

"Yes, Uncle . . . Yes, I'll wait . . ."

"The Hefties! Ferdinand the Hefty! . . . The nurse-
maid's dream! The footslogger's friend! The terror of the
artillery! That'll give us a little bit of everything in the
family . . .

"I can't see you in the navy . . . You're seasick already . . . See what I mean? . . . And your father who
was in for five years! . . . What's he going to say? . . .
He was on the heavy guns . . . We'll have a sampling
of everything in the family . . . The whole army . . .
The Fourteenth of July at home, eh? . . . Taratata! Ta
ta ta! . . ."

Still trying to cheer me up, he took his kepi, it was on
the mantelpiece, on the right next to the mirror . . . I
can still see his pompon, a little yellow chick . . . He
slapped it on sideways . . .

"There you are, Ferdinand! The whole army! . . ."
That was a happy ending.

"Nuts!" he reflected. "All that's the bunk . . . You're
not through changing your mind . . . You haven't got
your marching orders yet, son . . . you haven't even got
a serial number . . . You've got plenty of time ahead of
you, soldier boy . . ." He heaved a sigh. "It's never too
late to make an ass of yourself . . . Right now you're
upset . . . That's understandable . . . You've been crying
like a waterfall . . . You must be pretty thirsty . . .
You want some brandy . . . I've got some first-class
calvados . . . I'll give you some sugar with it . . . It
doesn't appeal to you? . . . How about some plain red
wine? . . . I could warm it up for you . . . Or some
camomile? . . . Or a spot of anisette? . . . I guess you'd
rather hit the sack . . . I see how it is . . . A little shut-
eye for a starter . . . That's not a bad idea . . . I guess
I'm the one that's been talking rot . . . What you need
is ten good hours of sleep . . . All right, my dear nephew,
get a wiggle on . . . We've chewed the fat long enough
. . . Let's get out the baby's bed . . . Poor kid . . .
He's had a rough time . . . The country doesn't agree
with you . . . I could have told you that, son . . . You
just stay with me from now on . . ."

"I'd like to, Uncle . . . I'd really like to . . . But honest, I can't . . . Later some time . . . Later . . . is that all right? . . . I wouldn't do anything decent right now . . . I couldn't . . . You'll let me go, won't you, Uncle? . . . You'll ask Papa, won't you? . . . I'm sure he won't mind . . ."

"No! Nothing doing!" I was making him sore . . . "My Lord, are you stubborn! . . . You're as obstinate as Clémence . . . My goodness, it runs in the family . . . You're wearing yourself out for the hell of it . . . The army isn't what you think, son . . . It's even rougher than a job . . . You don't realize . . . Especially at your age . . . The others are twenty-one, that's an advantage in itself . . . You're not strong enough . . . You'll be all worn-out . . ."

"I know, Uncle, but it's best I should try . . ."

"Say, you're plumb crazy . . . Come along now . . . We're going to bed . . . You're talking a lot of hot air now, we'll think about it some more tomorrow . . . In my opinion you're all in . . . This idea of yours is like a fever . . . you're raving, and I've had enough of it . . . Say, they've really cut you down with their pruning hooks . . . It was high time you came home . . . Those farmers have really fixed you . . . It's the payoff! . . . And now you're off your rocker . . . Well, my boy, I'm going to patch you up . . . And you're going to put it away, I'm warning you right now . . . Every day starches, buttter, and meat . . . and the best quality . . . no measly chops . . . And chocolate every morning . . . And cod-liver oil by the glassful . . . Don't worry, I know how it's done . . . No more empty plates and wind dumplings . . . That's right, puppy child . . . No more starvation . . . And now upsy-daisy, to bed with you . . . That's all a lot of rot . . . You're just upset . . . That's my private opinion . . . You're all inside-out . . . At your age it doesn't take long to get over that . . . You just have to stop thinking about it . . . Think of something else . . . And eat enough for four . . . for thirty-six . . . In a week you'll be hunky-dory . . . Guaranteed by the Bank of France and the Higgledy-Piggledy pharmacy!"

We took the bed out of the closet . . . The folding con-

traption that squeaked all over . . . It had shrunk something awful . . . When I tried to stretch out, I got
tangled up in the bars . . . I preferred the mattress on
the floor . . . He gave me another off his own bed . . .
I was still shaking like a leaf . . . He gave me more
blankets . . . My teeth were still chattering . . . He
covered me all up, he buried me under a pile of overcoats
. . . I had all his bearskins on top of me . . . There was
a whole selection in the closet . . . I kept on shivering
all the same . . . I looked at the walls of the room . . .
They'd got smaller too . . . It was the middle room, the
one with the *Angelus* in it . . .

"I can't put on anymore . . . What do you think, you
old crocodile? . . . you wouldn't want me to smother
you . . . Imagine! . . . suppose I couldn't find you
again . . . Wouldn't that be a fine kettle of fish! . . .
My oh my! . . . Some soldier boy you'd be! . . .
Squashed under a pile of blankets . . . I can hear the hue
and cry! . . . Wouldn't I be sitting pretty! . . . Think
what they'd say in the Passage! . . . My goodness! . . .
The dear child! . . . The little treasure! . . . And me
trying to explain . . . Squashed in his own juice, the little
devil! Squish! Absolutely! My oh my! . . . What a mess!
. . . Stop it, emperor, I've had enough . . ." I spasmed,
trying to laugh with him . . . He went to his room . . .
He called out from far away . . .

"Listen, I'm leaving my door open . . . If you need
anything, don't be afraid to sing out . . . It's no disgrace to be sick . . . I'll come right away . . . If you
get the runs, do you know where the can is? . . . The
little hallway on the left . . . Don't take the stairs by mistake . . . The lamp is on the table . . . You needn't
blow it out . . . And in case you need to throw up . . .
wouldn't you like a chamberpot? . . ."

"Oh, no, Uncle . . . I'll go out there . . ."

"Good. But if you get up, put on an overcoat . . . Just
reach into the pile, it doesn't matter which . . . You'd
catch your death out in the hall . . . There's no shortage
of coats . . ."

"No, Uncle."

Glossary

p. 20   "Yid." French *"Zizi."* The translation here is uncertain. The "normal" meanings of the word are the male sex organ and "wise guy." The word recurs on p. 168. In search of a meaning that would make sense in both passages, I came to the conclusion that this may have been a private word with Céline.

p. 20   The Zone (*la Zone* [*militaire de Paris*]). Originally the strip of land between the Paris fortifications and the suburbs, where for military reasons construction was prohibited. In later popular usage, the more depressing suburbs on the periphery of Paris.

p. 35   Federates' Day (*le jour des Fédérés*). Fédérés was the name given to the Paris members of the National Guard at the time of the Commune. Many thousands of them were executed by Mac-Mahon's troops after the fall of the Commune. *Le jour des Fédérés* (May 27) is a day devoted to their memory by left-wing parties and organizations.

p. 49   Lustucru. An old-time clown. The name was manufactured from *"L'eûsses-tu cru?"*—"Would you have believed it?"

p. 55   Raspail method. François-Vincent Raspail (1794–1878) was a chemist and an ardent republican. He wrote books popularizing the principles of medicine and devised a simple, inexpensive method of therapy, intended chiefly for the working class and based principally on camphor and aloes. He was prosecuted (1846) for the illegal practice of medicine.

p. 68   Théâtre Robert Houdin. Theater founded by Robert Houdin, the famous magician, specializing in magic and prestidigitation. Georges Méliès, the film pioneer, was for many years its director.

p. 68   *The Trip to the Moon,* film by Georges Méliès (1902) after Jules Verne's novel *De la Terre à la Lune* (1865). It lasted fifteen minutes and was an enormous success both in France and the United States.

p. 93   Statue of Bordeaux. The east side of the Place de la Concorde is bordered by eight statues symbolizing French cities. Bordeaux and Nantes are the work of Callouet.

p. 138   Wigs à la Mayol. Mayol was a popular cabaret singer (1872–1941), famous in part for the large tuft of hair over his forehead. This feature was imitated in the wigs bearing his name.

p. 290   Wallace fountain. After Sir Richard Wallace (1818–1890), an English philanthropist who in 1872 donated one hundred drinking fountains to the city of Paris.

p. 322   Paulhan. Early aviator. Already famous in 1910. Henri Rougier. Holder of the eleventh airplane pilot's license.
Lucien Petit-Breton. Famous bicycle racer. Winner of the Tour de France in 1907 and 1908.
Henri Farman (1874–1958) and his brother Maurice (1877–1964). Aviators and airplane builders. Also engaged in tandem, motorcycle, and automobile racing, winning numerous prizes. Henri won the Grand Prix de l'Aviation. In 1908, first flight with passengers. Founded one of the

earliest passenger lines in 1919. Maurice was French bicycle champion in 1895.

Alberto Santos-Dumont (1873–1932). Brazilian aviator. Constructed several types of aircraft. In 1906 made the first world record in aviation, a flight of 220 meters, covered in 21 seconds.

Vicomte Lambert. Aviator. Created an enormous sensation by flying over the Eiffel Tower in 1909.

Hubert Latham (1883–1912). French aviator. Established altitude records. Made two unsuccessful attempts to fly across the English channel.

p. 331 Camille Flammarion (1842–1925). Astronomer and author of popular works on astronomy.

p. 337 Alphonse Bertillon (1853–1914). Devised the system of identifying criminals by anthropometric measurements and fingerprints.

p. 345 Matchiche. Popular dance of Spanish origin. Introduced to France from Brazil about 1904, it was all the rage for a few years.

Equine Race. Society for the Improvement of the Equine Race (*Société pour l'amélioration de la race chevaline*): One of several organizations that supervise the French race tracks.

p. 351 Camille Desmoulins (1760–1794). Leader in the French Revolution, executed with Danton on April 5, 1794.

Old Vick = Victor Hugo.

p. 354 Mongolfier. The Mongolfier brothers, paper manufacturers, pioneers in lighter-than-air aircraft.

p. 359 Pea soup = absinthe.

p. 394 François-Eugène Vidocq (1775–1857). Adventurer, convict, spy, and detective, who became chief of the Paris Security Police. He inspired Balzac's character Vautrin.

p. 403   Jules-Emile Péan (1830–1898). Eminent surgeon.

p. 424   Wash barge. The *bateaux lavoirs* were floating laundries, formerly common in France.

p. 453   Bonnot gang (*Bande à Bonnot*). A group of anarchists led by Joseph Bonnot (1876–1912). Specialized in bank robberies for the benefit of the cause. Bonnot and three others were killed at the time of their arrest in 1912.

p. 460   Pierre-Victurnien Vergniaud (1753–1793). Girondist deputy who voted for the death of Louis XVI. Arrested with other leaders of the Gironde party, he was executed in 1793. The basis of Courtial's reflections is obscure.

p. 569   Jean-Bart hat. A hat with a wide turned-up brim, formerly worn by children. In his best-known portraits Jean Bart (1651–1702), the famous privateer, is not wearing anything of the kind. "Hefty" (*Gros-Frère*), slang for cuirassier.

p. 577   The final shindig = "The final conquest" in *l'Internationale,* the Socialist—later Communist— hymn.

p. 578   The Luxembourg. Quite a stroll. The reader is advised to locate the Luxembourg Gardens and the rue de la Convention on a map of Paris.

p. 585   "Mountain boys." The French word *"mataf"* is argot for "sailor." But the following song belongs to the mountain troops. Possibly "mataf" was a misunderstanding for Bat d'Af, Bataillon d'Afrique. Or possibly, as Céline's then-secretary suggests, he chose it for the sound.